THE POOR STATE OF
WAR AND CONFLICT

THE POOR STATE OF
WAR AND CONFLICT

N.B.J.Clayton

The Poor State of War and Conflict
ISBN 978-0-6452540-2-0

BISAC
HIS027090 HISTORY / Military / World War I
HIS027100 HISTORY / Military / World War II
POL061000 POLITICAL SCIENCE / Genocide & War Crimes

Epic poems by this author:

Afghan - Song of the Desert
Orcinus Orca - Song of the Ocean
Hollandia Nova - Song of the Coast
Kibeho - An Epic Poem
Song of the Templar [poetic verse]
Songs of Australia - A Poetic Trilogy
1453 - Constantinople

Other titles by this author:

The Long Road to Rwanda
The Templar: and the City of God [Part 1]
The Templar: and the Temple of Káros [Part 2]
The Templar: and the Cross of Christ [Part 3]
Amazon [Part 4 of The Templar series]
Chivalry [Omnibus]
Underworld
Templar, Assassination, Trial & Torture
Dreamtime - An Aboriginal Odyssey
The Zuytdorp Survivors
Afghan Camel Strings and the Australian Outback
Tom of Twofold Bay
When The Virgin Falls
This Pestilence, Bergen-Belsen
Afghan: The Script
Colonies of Earth: also known as Mildratawa
Fall of the Inca Empire
Kibeho: Original Script
The Kibeho Massacre: As It Happened
Furious George

CONTENT

WHEN THE VIRGIN FALLS

WHEN THE VIRGIN FALLS
- A VERY BRIEF INTRODUCTION -

The term 'British Expeditionary Force' was used to refer to us, the forces present in France prior to the end of the First Battle of Ypres on 22nd November 1914, or Wipers as accepted by us all, for to get your tongue around some of the French names was more than a chore. By the end of 1914 we had almost been wiped out, although we did manage to stop the German advance, and hence, possibly, maybe for morale, custom, or simply courtesy of our sacrifice, BEF continued to remain the official name of the British Army in France and Flanders until the end of the First World War.

The German Emperor, Kaiser Wilhelm, was rather dismissive of our band-of-brothers and although I know today, it being created for propaganda purposes, was reported to have stated: 'Exterminate those treacherous English and walk over General French's contemptible little army'.

Britain declared war on Germany on the fourth day of August in 1914 and within five days the BEF had commenced its deployment, being the best trained and most experienced, for we were volunteers and regulars to a man, whereby a vast majority of the French and German armies were conscripts and had little regular formation to speak of in regard to our percentages. We were initially 80,000 strong; the French and Germans holding over 1 million apiece; but numbers would change drastically over the coming years.

The first British contact with the Germans was on the 21st August, 1914, when a reconnaissance team on bicycles ran into the enemy near a place called Obourg. It was here that the first British casualty was awarded to the Germans. It was the following day that I, as a member of the 2nd Battalion, Royal Dublin Fusiliers, landed upon French soil at a place called Boulogne, where others before us had landed at Le Havre. What happened next was four years of utter devastation and misery, far from the adventure that many sought, and far from being over-by-Christmas, but for those that were home by Christmas… they were in a poor condition in most cases, suffering for the remainder of their pitiful lives, some with two legs and a right arm missing: what a state to be in.

Oh, and one more thing to tell which is hard to admit but very, very true. My wife fell pregnant whilst we were out of wedlock but I suppose in the years to come this became more unimportant with social acceptance and understanding. I shall also tell you something else, unbelievable though it may sound, and that is that my wife was in labour and gave birth to a healthy boy on the 21st August, and here I am on the 22nd, setting foot on foreign soil and not yet having seen the baby's face. All I could hope for was that I would be alive to see them both in the not-so-distant future, but how were we to know the extent of that before us all?

This is my story, and I am Denis Patrick Kelly.

22ⁿᵈ AUGUST, 1914

I say this not to make men look like fools but to allow the world to reflect on just a minute example of patriotism and chivalry, for the old world was far behind us, but there was a place in many hearts where the war did appeal to men of solid idealism. It turned out to be a dangerous thing but also a necessary evil for without the efforts of all those that raced against the bullets of the German machine guns, there would be no victory, and possibly no England to speak of; but for many that joined it was to be their adventure of a lifetime, and was seen as their duty to king and country.

Many a time I sat by a warm and cosy fire to listen upon stories of old men having fought against the Zulu at places like Isandlwana and Rorke's Drift, or the battles of the Boer War, for there was no such thing as television back in the days of glory where one's own fortitude was his good nature and words such as a-trustworthy-Hun were never heard, and cowardice was so seldom seen that I imagined it to be a word made up to aid in the mustering of courage when the shells came tumbling down around you: despite the fact that courage was always in a mustered state.

There were others, too, that joined for oblique reasons; is that the right word? If not then it's a polite one, for some were pressured to join by family, friends, and co-workers, conned and coerced into signing up as beer was poured down their throats: for want of Dutch courage some men need… a sprinkle of bravado: but they were never cowards. For some it was a simple matter of being a family tradition.

My first taste of battle wasn't the fields' of Mons, however, but the ground between it and Paris. It wasn't so much a direct conflict, but being fired upon by heavy guns was part and parcel of battle to me: now that I look upon it as I sit upon my favourite chair wrapped in aging skin some fifty-odd years after those horrid days. It would be a far stride though for one to take without hearing of the battle which was to set us in motion. It was as though my teenage years were knocking at the door for the stories to be voiced; for a voiced, visual representation to be provided.

The Battle of Mons may not be considered by many as a battle but more a withdrawal. I like to look at it as a subsidiary movement of the Battle of the Frontiers, for withdrawal can sound like such a cowardly brand unless employed with the word 'tactical' placed before it.

This is how it came about.

Being a member of the 2nd Royal Dublin Fusiliers we were hard at work getting on with closing the gap upon the front when our brothers sat in position on the left of the French, meaning that the men of the BEF were required to hold the line of the Mons-Condé Canal against a numerically superior enemy trying to encircle them: those evil sods of Europe, the German First Army. It was the spoken word that we were outnumbered six to one and from the stories I heard during our long march westward I can believe it.

The 2nd Dublin was of the 4th Division, 10th Brigade. We had marched through the port and streets to be given a hero's welcome by the citizens of Boulogne, flags flying, children waving, a band playing our favourite tunes as we made our way forward. But the fanfare didn't last long for we were out of there rather quickly and soon could hear the guns firing as we advanced, or when at the halt and awaiting further development. The noise of the crowd behind us simmered and the grinding of our boots on the road momentarily paused. The front was still a long way away but the sound of artillery firing could be heard, and quite ghastly is the sound. But the sound of artillery was nothing compared to what it would be on the morrow.

We hadn't known it at the time but the first action had already taken place at 0600hrs this morning when a patrol made up of men from the 4th Dragoon Guards to the northeast of Mons fell upon a small band of German cavalry at Casteau. Full of vigour and willing to get the job done the guards gave chase and it wasn't until the horses were getting used to the pace of the chase that the Germans turned and fired upon the pursuers.

As the noise of the guns in the distance came upon our ears I considered my position amongst the throng. Here we were, dressed in khaki, webbing pressed around our waists and with packs upon our backs, over sixty-one pounds of equipment weighing us down for not a soul amongst us had yet seen good reason to lessen the load, but the near future would see that change in a hurry. And in my palm I cradled my Lee-Enfield rifle, a most remarkable weapon indeed, so much so that it was incontestably sought after by the Canadians: when they arrived. It was a bolt-action and magazine fed and any soldier of his majesty's BEF was able to fire between twenty and thirty aimed shots per minute. And although the Canadians are not yet here I must advise you accordingly, before I forget, of their Ross rifle. What a shambles it was and many stories surround it, but more on those a little later. As for now I must tell you that those poor bastards, the Canadians, had a hell of a time fighting the war with the Ross, for it was a longer weapon and not so steady in the hand, its weight much heavier than one wished. The bayonet often fell off the weapon and keeping it clean was a chore and a half. We can thank the good lord that we Britons had the Lee Enfield. The Ross was accurate enough but utterly useless at rapid firing where constant jamming was the normal occurrence. It was simply atrocious and had little to no ability when trying to ward off a hoard of sods coming towards you with anger scribed upon their faces and steam pouring from their ears ready to disembowel you with glimmering bayonets of their own. Rapid fire over more than two minutes or more would see it overheat and throw in the towel for the bolt of the weapon could not be unlocked unless hit with the bayonet and kicked back with the heel of your boot: you don't believe me; then you have plenty more to read of this and plenty to learn and maybe then you will accept it all as true.

But back to the story at hand.

And as we made way towards the front the men at Mons welcomed the night with entrenching tools being readied. It was here that Sir John French, commander of the BEF, was to hold the line cast before him: the Mons-Condé Canal. Out with entrenching tools and dig, dig, dig was the order passed around. All along the canal the men put down their positions in order to hold the line, four infantry divisions and five brigades of cavalry, some history books will say a total of almost 80,000 men but I shall tell you different, and although I have no proof of numbers I do have good hearing and sense, and when a man tells me stories of conflict and strategy unfolded I take note, for Sir Horace Lockwood Smith-Dorrien was here, our Corps commander, watching over the 3rd and 5th Divisions with pride, but we were yet to show our face as we made our way to the front to consolidate our 4th Division with the remainder of II Corps under Smith-Dorian, and there were others at our back: should these men yonder, still coming forth, be included in the numbers? But those men on the ground were seemingly in good hands, had good support with fifty-four 18-pounders, four 60-pounders and eighteen 4.5 inch howitzers. But those damn sods, the Hun, had outdone us for the artillery support on their side was far superior in number when compared to our own.

23rd AUGUST, 1914

It was on the morning of the 23rd that the Battle of Mons took place and as usual it was the dawning of the day which welcomed the fall of artillery shells from the sky, a bombardment upon the British lines so fierce that those so new to battle almost soiled their pants through sheer terror, but they held together like all good men do when faced by great adversity.

It wasn't until 0900hrs that the German infantry opened with their initial assaults upon the British line, and it was to be their undoing, a lesson to be learnt for all time, and an ironic beginning to German manufacture that was to see many men killed on the fields of glory; why? Because great emphasis had been placed upon every soldier in the British Army to such a degree that we could kill a man at three hundred yards without so much as one miss in twenty, and were able to pour out such a mass of rapid fire, being twenty and thirty rounds per minute per man, and whether or not you prefer the term, cartridge/bullet, is up to you, the whole German First Army thought they were up against a military organization so well equipped with machine guns that they immediately set about organizing their factories to cough up machine guns of their own. This of course helped create the great massacre known as the Somme two years later: I am sure of this, but there was more than a single factor in the miseries we were all to face during the Somme Offensive.

The sods' assault upon the four bridges spanned the canal, four German battalions alone pressed upon the Nimy Bridge, though later I heard it was six, but despite what you or I may have read or heard, and with all due respect, it is me that's telling the story. Here the ground was defended by the 4th Battalion of the Royal Fusiliers.

The men's great marksmanship skills and solid wall of fire worked wonders this day; possibly too well. It was legendary marksmanship skills now confronting the sod which saw them cower here and there but for the most part they came upon the front line spurred on by men at their rear with orders to shoot any retiring conscript. But the initial assault was not as thick and fast as what it was to become.

It was becoming quite clear; the German sods were attempting a right hook upon the line held by the BEF and the French Fifth Army, to entrap the allies and bring them into ill-repute, looking for a quick victory on this, the Franco-Belgian and Franco-German borders.

Hold the left of the British line, Sir Horse – with all due respect – Smith-Dorrien, for the Germans are about to unleash hell upon II Corps and this would eventuate in what was to become a major British withdrawal. The BEF was about to meet their adversary for the German First Army was made up of 18,000 men, or as one intellectual from Company headquarters had said, ten men for every three feet of ground for each mile of frontage, and our 80,000 [less those on the approach] were not in one place at the same time but spread over a vast, vast area.

I'll be damned. It was well that we were all here of our own choosing and not conscripts, and I don't say this to give a pat-on-the-back to all those involved, for past heroics of services rendered to country cannot be forgotten, but the British Army of 1914 was the finest force that ever departed her soil for war. We also had experience on our side like none other for there were many 'old sweats' amongst us, soldiers who had come under fire in South Africa during the Boer War, and I'm sure I saw a crusty old face the other day which spoke words of Zulu conflict and killings against the marauding impi. There was nothing like a consoling word or two from an old sweat to a young regular; a veteran giving good advice and morale support to a young man who had yet to spill blood.

I could feel the blood spurting through my veins as we made our way towards the war; I could feel the blood causing through my veins as stories unfolded before me during the nights of the withdrawal from Mons. It seemed to me that the valour of those at Rorke's Drift was being witnessed once more at Mons and legendary status was once again being born unto the world. Having heard stories in pubs over the years I reflected upon what would come of this war and its battles yet unborn. Would we be spoken of so fondly; would it be our turn in the future to have stories told of our victories and sunken defeats?

Our men on the front line could not honestly believe their ears and eyes in most cases, and again you might find this hard to believe but the sods were advancing thick as you please, and in some places they had their arms linked and were singing songs. What was it that the Generals had told their men? It seemed as though they were off to a party for dancing, but our blokes took good care to teach them a lesson or two by making them prance around our missed shots, which were few, which improved their ballet upon the field no doubt.

So many young men, conscripts one and all, advancing to their death, or to be maimed, irreparable. It would come to pass that men like General Haig, with or without his promotion to Field Marshal, was branded a warmonger with no regard at all for the safety of his men, nor the lives that they gave so gallantly, but the enemy officers that looked down upon the rank and file of Germany's front line soldier was beyond belief. There was a complete and utter disregard for human life. Compared to this we had hope on our side and with hope there was possible salvation, for we still did not know the full consequences to come of this war in Europe.

Our Generals would come under great scrutiny from historians and ourselves, as men who lead a million lambs to their slaughter, but they were experienced and had been taught great lessons during the two Boer wars of years past. It was here that a landmark change was inducted, in the way in which soldiers advanced their line of attack towards the enemy by conducting a series of rushes within the extended order; known as a ten wave attack. You will be utterly shattered by the stories I will tell you soon enough. It was a method of attack pursued to see to it that large numbers of men would not come under fire at the same time: so why was it not used more often; why in hell's name were we to see so little of this method?

But even though they were conscripts they did have a brain, and the men ordering forward the all-encompassing attack of the private soldier and NCOs, officers dotted here and there, were quick to learn their lesson. Attacking in close order was not to work and so open formation was quickly employed. The initial repulse of the German attack was now to change; their heavy losses would now be given a much sought after reprieve.

The Britons were now to take more care in their delivery of rapid fire and the trigger finger of each master hand was given a little rest, back to fifteen well aimed shots per minute, which was closer to the required standard as given at Aldershot during training. It was now that the Second Division lining up along Sambre Canal took more heed of their instructors.

Firing a high volume of fire into a mass of infantry, so dense that there was hardly room to breathe, allowed for quick and easy kills and wounded to be easily attained, but where the density was more lax, so the numbers in KIA and WIA diminished. Deliberately, well-aimed shots might well have slowed the process of the bullets flying down range but the ability to concentrate all the more on the centre of the seen mass allowed for more KIA rather than WIA. This may or may not have been a better option, even though the situation called for it, for a WIA held up many enemy as they needed to see to the withdrawal of the wounded: hence our orders in the near future, at such places like the Somme, changed for what I would call 'the worse', where we received orders 'not' to attend the wounded and to leave them where they lay in order to continue with the advance. Yes, you hear me right, told to leave our own wounded where they lie upon the earth.

The initial attacks were waved aside as though nothing to be concerned with, for if the sods wanted to die so quickly then the BEF could accommodate, but now they came again at 1100hrs. But here and there the Germans presented themselves as massed infantry, advancing in column almost as before. To wish them a little closer would assure us a quick victory, but some things cannot be granted.

But let me tell you more of the Lee-Enfield rifle. It was rather effective to six hundred yards and a well-trained man was hardly met with a problem in mustering enough skill to drop a target at that range. In the initial phases of war men needed to grapple with the noise of war that surrounded them but it didn't take long for this to be, more or less, ignored, and good marksmanship skills to come of maturity. Although the magazine held ten rounds of .303 ammunition the clips which fed the magazine held five. Fifteen well-aimed shots per minute was the required standard, more than this was often seen and rewarded with a cheery smile and a pat on the back: but fire too fast and miss your shots, receive a well-aimed kicking in the arse.

Although I spoke of numbers in regards to our men against theirs, the situation wasn't rosy. Those at the points of attack were grossly outnumbered and the defence of the crossings at the canal became unbelievably hard going, each man fighting hard to control his fire from hastily dug positions which in most cases was little more than a shallow scrape in the ground.

The Royal Fusiliers did all they could to hold their ground and were tested to the full, and to the right of them was the Middlesex Regiment and the Gordon Highlanders: the Royal West Kent Regiment and the King's Own Scottish Borderers also fell victim to the misgivings of war and suffered horribly. Casualties were so high amongst these units that the divisional reserve, the Royal Irish Regiment, were called upon to bolster the defence along with effective artillery support. With this move the BEF managed to hold the bridges and repulse the sodding advance of the Hun.

The machine gun was tenacious but the remarkable exploits of a German private, swimming across the canal, saw the swing bridge machinery operated and German attack enhanced. By 1500hrs an order to retire, tactically mind you, was received and as the sun said its good night a new line of defence was formed, allowing the sods to build pontoon bridges to aid in the crossing of the canal, for the bridges would not suffice: their number was so great.

Soon after a most unpleasant message had reached the ears of our good men; the French were retreating, which put the British right flank at jeopardy of being overrun and defeated, and I didn't like the sounds of any of this, not then and not now: blast it all!

The situation was remarkably unstable. The forward most positions were abandoned and some close fighting was associated with the movement from one position to another as soldiers fell back. So vicious was it that some of our own were taken as prisoners but not before dismantling the machine guns we had and throwing the parts into the canal to prevent the sod from employing them against the BEF.

24th AUGUST, 1914

The retreat had been ordered at 0200hrs, and such a tactical move saw battalions and regiments of men, horses and artillery, pack their packs, saddle bags and wagons for a move towards the southwest and

Paris, though no one in their right mind considered that the withdrawal would take the BEF that far.

Many rear-guard actions were called for as the rearmost elements undertook a fighting withdrawal, buying the much needed time required for those at the lead to get away relatively unscathed from further damage.

The sod didn't let up for a minute and the follow-up continued without a break until the village streets behind the fighting at the canal were a place of mayhem and immoral activity. The sod were suffering as heavily as us in regards to casualties, be they KIA, WIA, missing or taken prisoner. Many times did the men of the BEF see to it that the Germans paid dearly for the ground they gained by mowing them down with machine gun fire, and in villages all around the Germans continued to advance in the wake of our withdrawal. In places we heard stories of the sod breaking into houses and taking citizens from their property under protest, to use them as human shields against the hostile BEF fire. Such was the way of the conscript and others like them.

The soldiers of the British Army withdrew down streets, taking periodic cover in doorways and behind garden walls, seemingly running further and further as ground was given away to the unstoppable advance.

Cavalry were fast to dismount in places to help slower the advancing Germans, but only due to their great courage in bringing heart-felt relief to those in the greatest need and at places where being outflanked was almost attained by the sod. And all day long it continued without a break; withdraw, withdraw, withdraw.

The French were continuing to retreat and so without a flank to support them the BEF needed to continue as well. The line in which we were to withdraw to was henceforth given up and further withdrawal planned hastily: I'm sure the French were only acting upon orders, and I don't blame them for moving so fast. If only my feet could carry me as though upon a wind.

The withdrawal would last for two weeks and cover over two hundred miles in distance: some say it was one hundred and eighty miles, other say two-fifty; all I can say is that the route wasn't exactly direct and to tell the truth I don't believe my feet gave a damn, for I was a ruined man by the end of it as was everyone else, whether one hundred miles or three, it would have made little difference. It was along this route of movement that we men of the 2nd Royal Dublin Fusiliers were to come under control of our beloved Sir Horse; yes indeed, the man who I like to think of as being a stallion of a leader. The move ever rearward was much the same as the battlefields we were to fight upon in the near future, a flat surface terrain dotted with a copse here and there, in particular around Flanders, and the undulated folds of earth looking like ripples of water upon a reasonably still lake. Yes indeed, the ground on which we trop was very dull and would have remained that way if not for the beatings we endured both physically and mentally, and little chance did I take to actually approve, or otherwise, of the scenery.

And what in God's name were we, the 2nd, doing? We were transported by train in rather a hurry to a quaint enough village called Le Cateau: after an embarrassment with being disembarked at the wrong place and being forced to march as quick-as-you-please; and here we remained, preparing positions for what was to come: the Battle of Le Cateau.

It was a hot day, more so than most of us were used to, but war was hell.

By 1700hrs we were making much progress in regards to scrapes and short fighting trenches, and our minds could not help but wander off slightly to the sky above. Our lads were in aeroplanes high above fighting the Germans in the sky as the German pilots dropped bombs upon us, and bullets were being shot from the guns of the British to try and bring them down. On the ground the scenario was rather different than the spacious above. On the ground there were friendly troops in their thousands moving past us as well as artillery pieces, cavalry, and wagons galore. It seemed to me that the movement away from the firing line was rather… jam-packed – but such thoughts of jam on bread should be cast aside for the minute. It didn't seem to be well organised for there were stragglers all about, and it was very well hurried all along, more like a route than anything else: such a dirty word should not be used; I shall try and refrain from employing it in future, unless referring to the sod and his running-away.

25th AUGUST, 1914

Today was not much different than the day before. There was movement along the road by night but for most of the men busy with the withdrawal there was time to sleep and gather some rest amidst the shelling which could be heard further afield.

We didn't know it at the time but tomorrow would see our baptism of fire come about in great haste, but for the time all we could do was prepare our positions and watch periodically as the men continued past us. I don't mind telling you that I could see us on their tail soon enough, joining the others of the BEF in the withdrawal, our delay action little more than that.

Again it was a terrible day with the heat and dust doing no justice to parched throats as the infantry continued on foot whilst officers sat upon the backs of horses. Sometimes you would see the cavalry come past, leading their horses along by the reins: giving them a rest I suppose; but does a horse get sore feet?

We saw remnants of the French Army cause further congestion, broken down wagons getting in the way of battalions on the go. Limbered artillery rattling past, and on one of them a wheel fell off, and had to be repaired then and there.

I couldn't help considering what it was that these men had gone through at Mons. I took the opportunity during the day to converse with a few but it was not for me to sit idle for too long when hard work was to be carried out. You could see the forlorn look upon their hanging faces; not hanging in shame but hanging through sheer exhaustion. Sure, the 2nd had force-marched from the train station to Le Cateau, but nothing quite like what these men had done before us, having marched on empty stomachs and after a pitched battle. They were so tired looking and seemed so confused by the entire ordeal of the continuing retreat. One man wished to know what we were doing by digging so hard, saying that the positions would be given up soon enough to the advancing Germans, but I needlessly pointed out that we needed to bring the advance to a halt for as long as possible in order for those up ahead to get clean away. There was also a river in front of us, a natural obstacle. That should also afford some time to us all. He moved along soon enough, but as he stood he said something to me, a short story. He asked me if I knew of the Angels of Mons and I naturally enough replied no. He told me that during the withdrawal of the front line at Mons and the subsequent move through the village, a soldier within the ranks bellowed as loud as you please for St George to come to their aid. This chorus of song was then sung by many, all requesting St George to come to their aid. And then from out of nowhere appeared thousands upon thousands of English Long Bowman launching arrows in their tens of thousands into the air. They cut down the German advance and helped the BEF get away as cleanly as they could.

The archers had saved the day for the BEF and it was to become a legend.

I suppose we all have to believe in something.

Later that night I saw a regiment of cavalry; Scottish Greys they were, setting down for a few hours kip in the early hours of the night, as the day turned to dusk. Several hours later and they were off again, and I know not why. I knew that I Corps had been helping to cover the second's retreat from the front; maybe now it was the second's turn to reciprocate and cover them in the withdrawal.

The 2nd RDF was a part of 10th Brigade, 4th Division, under General French: we were commanded, directly or indirectly, depending on how one wishes to see it, by our own Sir Horse, for we were to learn later on of a criticism that existed, but more on that a little later, and I should get myself out of the habit of calling him that, the name being above him. We were at Le Cateau and it was time for us to meet the grinder.

I hear once more men say that they were outnumbered six to one at Mons, possibly even more, and now on the back foot we were outnumbered three to one. These figures alone did not stand well but could have been much worse if not for the bravery of the cavalry, disrupting the enemies progress by putting themselves in harm's way by shielding us as best as possible, so that the infantry could gain further distance from those sods rushing us from behind, providing what respite they could to the poor, underpaid bastards known as the infantry; life and limb for a shilling a day. It was here that I know many good Irish voices were lost of this world. The battalion in which I served was almost down to half, all thanks to this battle called Le Cateau, that which I shall explain shortly, but I don't wish you to tire of my story, of repeated attacks, deaths, bodies, artillery, and so on and so forth. I don't wish you to tire of this story for it must be read or you shall never understand that which should always be purged from existence, and only memory shall provide good reason to steer from such slaughter-houses as world wars.

Four days at war and we were almost wiped out, this BEF of ours. The French Army had itself lost 40,000 men over the past four days, 27,000 on the day in which the order to retreat from Mons was given. We were in a sorry state. Just a few days at war and the suffering expected was already far exceeded; what would the future bring? I had trained at Aldershot, conducted many route marches between Salisbury Plain and our camp on many occasions, but nothing like the past few days, and far more was to come.

As we prepared ourselves for battle at Le Cateau I couldn't help notice the men, who were at Mons, withdrawing past us, we few with entrenching tools and a few sandbags. It was not easy to see because the sun had not fully risen as yet. They marched past wearily and most with their heads down, tired as tired can be. An officer then appeared beside the road and ordered that all greatcoats be left behind for the added burden of weight was so horrific, everyone's feet being so sore; and then the impossible, but obvious, occurred before me. For exchange of greatcoat the men were given a further eighty rounds of .303 ammunition. These poor men, who I was soon to follow in misery, were losing comfort for ammunition. What must be, must be, and so I continued to dig and prepare my position as best I could and the men at the roadside picked themselves up and moved wearily on, no good food in the stomach to think of but something dry and intangible handed to them as they walked on, walk on with the war at their backs, a handful of ammunition, and on only two hours sleep from the night before. It appeared for all intents and purposes that the march to safer quarters had turned horribly sour and the tactical move rearward was now little more than a hobble in most cases.

It was sometime after that, that the sods arrived in number and commenced their assault upon us but our artillery gave them hell. Just several days before our boys of the BEF had gunned them down at the approach with rapid, single shots from the Lee Enfield, but today they were getting good medicine from the heavy guns. It must have been completely unexpected, and the good news was the lack of artillery which they had themselves at hand, for their advance was so quick and seemingly swift that they had a hard time in keeping the supplies up with them as they advanced.

We inflicted many casualties upon the sod but the vast majority were simply blown to bits by the artillery pieces and shrapnel rounds too, bursting here and there, sending scores upon scores of metal through the air and breaking upon the sodding attacks, ripping men apart. Blown apart, ripped apart; either way you look at it the artillery battle of the ages was here and now, only to be outdone in the years ahead by more of the same but in much vaster numbers.

So we hold the ground we have been assigned and do our duty as best we can with the Lee Enfield and entrenching tool. I hope that the bayonet will not have to be used for my stomach for killing other people has not quite grown accustomed to the idea of taking life when face to face, and taking it from a distance is by far preferred than taking it with the cold steel currently residing in the scabbard which knocks upon my buttocks.

By mid-afternoon the casualties are mounting considerably and it looks as though the retreat will be given sooner rather than later, and with the arrival of the French cavalry we are spurred on by orders and officers screaming over the noise of battle.

The cavalry shield works well in our favour, obstructing the advancements of the sod upon the left and right flank. The sod is coming full steam ahead, there seems to be no stopping them in their advance. I have to say this for them; they have nerves of steel: either that or many guards to their rear who threaten to shoot them dead if they should try to withdraw from the fight, for the Kaiser wouldn't give a damn for a conscript.

Later that night, when it is fairly young and with the heat of the day still lingering in the air, though much milder and dissipating fast, we continue with the 'tactical' withdrawal. Of 40,000 men fighting at Le Cateau we have lost 7,812 in all quarters: dead, missing, wounded, and prisoners, a few of the prisoners being left behind on purpose for they had been blinded. We have suffered heavily in casualties ourselves but I later learned that there were entire battalions wiped from the face of the earth. It is hard to believe that the courage of men can be so easily replaced with corpses. And then it starts to rain.

I see many guns to our rear, the artillery men removing their breech blocks and sights, some taking the sights with them and destroying the other. It is a calculated initiative to deny the enemy. But they only leave their guns behind where we must leave our men, those still breathing, good men with air in their lungs, those who I have trained with for so long.

You might now understand how unfortunate it is that men should be left aside to fend for themselves as prisoners of war, to hope that the moral equity of the Germans was enough to secure their lives into the future, for wounded men and those no longer able to walk would have to contend with surrender, so it is here that we part good company and many men, unable to keep up for many and varied reasons, must shake hands, where time is allowed such show of comradeship, and the battalions continue on towards Paris.

You can only feel poorly for those left behind. To surrender to the enemy was a torment of many minds. Never did I wish to hear the words hände hoch [hands up], and would much prefer to hear a wounded German scream out kamerad; lazaretto [comrade; hospital]. It is easy to see why I would prefer to see the fear and desperation painted upon the sods' faces instead of our own, so to express any further the preference would be ignorant of your intelligence, dear reader.

So retreat we do when the time is ripe and we once again make quick time along the hard surface of the road to join with those poor bastards the refugees, walking astride their meagre possessions. There is a vast difference and story to tell upon their faces. Not three days ago and we were greeted with cheers and pats upon the back and today the grim look upon the French is one of sheer misery. Some must leave the old behind; some leave all their possessions, homes, cattle, goats, chickens, clothing, furniture, pianos and other instruments of great luxury and contentment; but photographs are saved where they can be saved, memories of a lifetime where easily ported and taken along for the long journey to safety as the sod wreaks havoc upon their homes and property. I have let them down; we have let them down. I feel ashamed and want to help them all but I can't, for that is an impossible task.

Torrents of rain then assault us throughout the night, joining the sod in the demented abuse upon us all, both soldier, civilian, and even horses alike. This is a journey with no end to misery.

Some men are luckier than others and carry Vaseline with them; where they attained such a prize is beyond me for no one would have left the cliffs of Dover behind with a hasty retreat considered, so I should assume that the treasure itself was one given by a refugee. It then occurs to me that its use would make my feet worse, not better, so I am thankful of not trying it myself, and then I see that some of the men use it between their legs and on their arse, to aid in the long hours of harsh marching, not applying it to their feet at all. And so the march continues towards Paris with a great weight upon our backs and minds. Our water runs very low and stomachs are empty of food but still we do all we must to keep ahead of the sod that snaps at our heels and dispatches groups of cavalry to gather information on our condition, predicament, and weaknesses; but there are few weaknesses found within the bravado held within our hearts as we deny the enemy all satisfaction, and it is from this feeling that we gather much strength.

I see fruit trees here and there, not far off to the side of the road, and several of our men are picking at the fruit. Better for them to eat than the sod, and as my mind drifts from the walk I stagger and trip to find my face buried in the hard road, hardly softened by the rain as it falls upon us. I am helped up immediately by friends who mean more to me than the friends of home for they are of the same heart and mind as me. We come to learn of comradeship, to share in everything that comes our way, the trenches in the years to come helping us bind in a common misery, but at present the misery is the road, the long march, and the little mud upon my face as it drains away in the falling torrents from above.

I never thought it possible to fall asleep whilst walking, but before we are given the order to pull up and rest for a few hours I have seen many men fall down, as I had, during the treacherous walk through the night.

We all halt and fall to the ground as though given mercy and within minutes the entire column for as far as the eye can see is sleeping, all except the cavalry who attend an urgent need to slow the enemy in their approach.

So I close my eyes and then someone yells out that the march is to continue immediately. I have no idea as yet that the blink of the eye was in fact three hours of slumber, for it is impossible to tell the difference: it's as though no sleep has been granted at all.

Men scurry to their feet but some are hard at work opening their haversacks to the world and discarding their equipment, getting rid of all they think they don't need, relinquishing at a throw the weight of their hard drudgery ahead, but I consider the action and give quickly to the temptation, but I am mindful of keeping that which will keep me warm by night for I do not wish to be without a little warmth when the time comes, even at the sake of a few more blisters upon the blisters I already have, and so I place my overcoat back into my haversack. This discarding of equipment is of the greatest temptation to all of us and it is quite against the rules to be doing so, but officers and NCOs seem not to care as they too join in, and any disciplinary action is thrown to the wind and washed away. Some men are seen to give their meagre possessions to those refugees that pass: I saw one little girl give an apple to a man who had handed her his entrenching tool, but we all keep the things that matter the most which include our weapon and all ammunition. It is a beautiful gift that the girl has given, for the refugees are hungrier than us. She will not be forgotten.

I do not know what time it is but I guess it to be after midnight, which in turn would make this particular day the 27th, but it doesn't really matter. And then I hear some artillery, it's very close indeed. I think it's German but not entirely sure. I listen more purposely and yes, it is German, far off to the flank and obviously cutting up others in the retreat; poor, tired infantry like me who even now in the early days of the war are thinking of a nice warm bed to sleep in. Instead I have a sore body, from head to toe, and the soles of my feet are not worth talking of for I feel as though I have none, the soles having been ground down to bare flesh, no skin to think of. But we must continue along and urgently for no one wishes to die like this. We all volunteered for this war but we are not fanatics and did not join in order to die. But if I am to be killed then I can only hope that it is fast, but not too quickly. I would like one last second to contemplate my family so that I may die with a smile upon my face. And what are my chances of living through this war? At the time I considered it to be rather minute, at around twenty per cent; being wounded... four times as heavy, but no matter what happened I did not wish to be blinded or permanently incapacitated with both arms missing. I cared little for my legs and would gladly give them up, but I could not do without my arms, in particular my right.

27 AUGUST, 1914

I have been told that the reason for our little slumber last night was due to the sod not making good use of the situation by following up on their assaults upon us, believing that we had been hit so hard that we resembled little to be concerned about. It was this error which brought the greatest fortune for we could use our time wisely and extend the distance between them and us, gaining what we would all soon learn to be a total of five days of good advantage, allowing the cavalry to conduct their rearguard actions along with selected infantry elements that were relieved of contingency action during the days that followed for all to have a turn. As it turned out we, the second, were praised for what we had done at Le Cateau, for we had done more than was bargained for. We had gained time, we had hit the sod hard with artillery, we had, in effect, turned a ruse upon him without even realising that a ruse had been put into effect. But it had come at a great loss to manpower; but this was war and no one needed reminding of it.

I was to learn later in life that old Sir Horse had been criticized by Field Marshall French for the action at Le Cateau, French having preferred, or so it would seem, for us to have continued with the withdrawal. And where would we all be if that had happened, I ask you all? My wife was very thankful for what she'd heard of the Horse, thankful that I was alive and given five extra days of unmolested marching, in some cases listening to music given by refugees upon the wagons which rattled along the road on which we walked. Mixed in amongst us and along either side of the road are the refugees in their thousands pushing prams, wheelbarrows and carts filled to the brim with their possessions. And so you can see why I said earlier that we were commanded, directly or indirectly, by the Horse and not French: I can only ponder what other disagreements they may have had.

Yes, some of our commanders were not too bad, and neither were the cavalry, whom I shall recall fondly in the years to come. They had allowed the BEF to escape the clutches of the sod. Gratification must also be awarded to the 2nd Royal Munster Fusiliers of I Corps, with whom I would serve directly when transferred in the future to the 16th Irish Division. They were withdrawing upon a different line of approach to ours, and no prouder moment could there be. As I Corps continued to increase their break from the enemy behind them to twelve miles or more the Munsters were hard at it, halting the sod dead in his tracks for fourteen hours around Ètreux, losing almost 80 per cent of all ranks and having been out-numbered six to one. Did they, in some small way, despise us for this? It appears not.

And so the miles fall away far behind us as we continue glumly along, aided by the comradeship of those around us, even in times like this when the energy to continue the march was leaving us for dead, the occasional joke and show of good humour spurring us on.

During the day the dust from the road seemed to swell up around us, turning our khaki into a dirty grey; the dust was everywhere. We could not shave and so our beards turned grey, and I swear to God that the dust was weighing us down without remorse. Irritating it is to have the nose clogged up continuously by that horrid dry snot and crustacean-like layer of dryness, but the dust in the throat made one so dry that it was a wonder we could continue as we did and on the little water made available whilst placing one foot in front of the other with little rest. If it were left to the men themselves then I am sure there would be much more rest and a little slumber, but the sergeants wouldn't allow it and they whipped us on with kind words and harsh, playing good cop, bad cop, giving us reason to continue with the pace and further reason not to halt.

Again there was the poor wretched soul that could continue no more and would collapse out of line upon the ground as we marched. Exhausted beyond belief we would have no choice but to leave the poor men to be taken as a German prisoners of war, but there were sergeants within the BEF that wouldn't stand for it and performed miracle after miracle in driving the men ever onwards, getting them up from the ground and putting them back into gear.

Further on we tread, continuing with the retreat for many days, and rarely do we see any infantry setting up any form of defence to halt the sodding advance, for we have knowledge and with knowledge we shall take advantage, for the Germans are nowhere to be seen: even though several scouting parties of the sod on horseback can be viewed through binoculars from time to time.

I am then reminded of the man that not so long ago accepted an apple from a child as we passed a small orchard: food ever on the mind. There are apples upon the branches of trees, seldom seen now but many earlier on. Not only would the apples fill our stomachs but the delectable juices would give relief to our parched throats, driving the dust away and down into our bowls, until further misery can be drawn into our lungs with the continued march. Several men take the opportunity and grab what they can, sergeants turning a blind eye, officers doing the same, but one has to be careful. I later learn that several men are actually charged with stealing, but we look at it as denying the enemy, who would only come to eat and then destroy the trees in any case. My hand moves subconsciously to my breast pocket. There is a card within it. Upon the card is…. Well; an oath: we all have one.

It reads:

Be invariably courteous, considerate and kind. Never do anything likely to injure or destroy property, and always look upon looting as a disgraceful act. You are sure to meet with a welcome and to be trusted; your conduct must justify that welcome and that trust. Your duty cannot be done unless your health is sound. So keep constantly on your guard against any excesses. In this new experience you may find temptations, both in wine and women. You must entirely resist both temptations, and, while treating all women with perfect courtesy, you should avoid any intimacy.

This is signed by Lord Kitchener and so it is an order, not a reminder of any chivalrous code of conduct.

I removed my hand from my pocket in time enough to aid a man beside me: he fell asleep whilst walking.

We are now covering a good twenty to thirty miles per day in the summer heat that beats down upon us as the dust rises. I am reminded again of the weight we carry, although many have already discarded much. It is sheer agony to continue on with all we have been issued but in all cases I draw witness to seeing not a single man throw away his tin of 100 cigarettes. There are so many cigarettes per man but no one is smoking. There is no time for smoking. Who wants to add dryness to the throat that is caked with dust? But I do see a man gulping down his water as though from a tap when an 'old sweat' pats him upon the back and advises him against it. Ah… you've forgotten… what is an 'old sweat' I hear you ask? A reminder; he is one who has fought before, engaged the enemy in other conflicts. There are many an-old sweat amongst us in the battalion, men who have served in South Africa, fighting against the Boer. These men are full of knowledge, full of patriotism, good ideas, unfathomable courage, and have a fortitude which stands against the hardest times and conditions. Learn from these men and you learn a lifetime's worth of skills.

It is night, it is time for rest. We gather around and fall quickly to the darkness that is sleep, too tired to even dream.

We are suddenly woken. Have we slept? Yes, we have, hoorah; but it's time to get going because the enemy is not far behind and we need to be on our way. It's now past midnight and so we are on another day.

28th AUGUST, 1914

Today is worse than the day before. Our feet feel the pinch of constant agony, in particular after ten minutes rest. We would be better without the rest and to continue forever on for our feet would suffer less for it, but we must allow ourselves time to rest if even for a few minutes, to water ourselves like deprived animals. And the days that follow are all much the same. Falling asleep whilst on the march, thirsty beyond belief, sweltering under a midday sun, drawing the dust into our lungs, crying silently at the pain we suffer underfoot.

I can then hear cheering from behind me and I turn as others do. The Scots Greys are coming our way having delivered blow after blow upon the sod that continues behind us. And there are others too for I see lances held in the air. They rush past us and create a light breeze, the thundering of their hooves upon the ground reaching our ears like music. It is sheer bliss to see them, so proud and high in the saddle. And then the cheering stops. Towards the rear, and following behind, are not stragglers but men towing horses with empty saddles. We can see without a doubt that they have suffered heavy casualties.

31st AUGUST, 1914

Our days of free marching were almost at an end. The time to fight seemed once more to be almost upon us. It would be our turn soon to face the music for the cavalry to date had acted with such exemplary courage and style that the infantry would have no choice but to prove themselves fit for war: though in all truthfulness I may have not said that correctly, for we had no reason to further prove our mettle for what we had already achieved at places such as Mons, Le Cateau and Ètreux, but who am I to give praise to oneself.

I shall now tell you this, all three columns at the withdrawal had come to a halt at some time in the late afternoon to early evening; I Corps was near Villiers and Cotterets, II Corps near Crepy-en-Valois, and III Corps around Verberie. These names may not mean much to you, the reader, but to us they meant everything.

The cavalry had done their duty and it would soon be time for us, even though the cavalry was called upon to fill a large gap which existed between II and III Corps. We would soon continue with the withdrawal on the morrow but maintain good rearguard actions along the entire defensive line now drawn as we continued towards Paris. Our current position to the River Marne was approximately a quarter ways past the River Aisne.

It wouldn't be long now before we started to fall back towards the Marne River along with the French, and the Marne River was placed horizontal to Paris. Imagine Paris; now draw a line out to the east. That is the Marne, and Pairs was literally exposed to a frontal invasion. But our current position was still far from our destination with the cavalry stuck at a place called Néry and employed as gap filler.

To date we'd suffered horrible losses but far more were to come in this war of attrition.

Field Marshall French blamed the losses of the BEF on the French and their inability to hold a line. The French were continually withdrawing, exposing flank after flank, the BEF suffering by such actions, but if it wasn't the BEF that suffered then it was the French. General Lanrezac of the French Fifth Army was equally enraged by what he called our inability to support our ally between Guise and St Quentin through which area the river Oise flowed. It was all finger-pointing to me and all I could hope for was that they would work together instead of apart. In the end it was Kitchener that came to the rescue, insisting that the BEF hold the line as best as possible, which French agreed to so long as the French Fifth Army did not expose another flank as they had done in the past.

We slept soundly this night and were well on the way by morning's first light.

1st SEPTEMBER, 1914

The Action at Néry was upon the BEF and with its disposition upon the ground we were in easy reach of the sound of battle when it opened up, a surprise to all and no doubt those caught in the mayhem that followed.

When battles are fought the news travels fast and in some cases, though fewer than I have been lead to believe, are expressed extravagantly with tall tales of heroism and good deeds, but when you see a list of names of those being awarded the Victoria Cross, and that list is extensive for the action fought, then you know all to be true and passed on without the shred of a lie being spoken, and the Action at Néry was one such memorable episode of great historical worth. The units who fought here were again the cavalry units fighting against cavalry, all being dismounted for the duration of the hostile encounter.

Those units present were as follows: the 1st Cavalry Brigade consisting of three regiments: 2nd Dragoons, 5th Dragoons and the 11th Hussars, each with a supposed strength of 549 men with Vickers machine guns in direct support. They were also in the company of the Royal Horse Artillery of 205 men and six 13-pounder guns.

It all started as dawn commenced to break on the first day of September with a fog enveloping the low lying ground between the buffs of the valley in which they were situated, the fog rather stiff in a windless moment of solitude where not a sound did exist that wasn't part and parcel of the great mystery of nature. It was 0430hrs, or there about, and not a soul was stirring, when sleep-deprived sentries began jostling from their posts and waking all for the day's activities, which included more of the same: withdrawal and rearguard action.

Men saw to their horses as well as themselves but pride and joy was in the beasts of war that were an extension of the weapons that sat slung over shoulders. Some men prepared breakfast for others whilst others attended the horses. It was a fair trade in particular for an animal lover, but fondness for an animal, in particular a horse, was as dangerous as having many comrades upon which to rely and to be friends with. Death was an awful way to part good company and the loss of a well-loved horse was no less excruciating to its rider than losing a man. Better to cook the meals for others than get too acquainted with the horses was my point of view.

The men of the Horse Artillery took the time now to ready theirs by harnessing the guns but ensuring they were lowered so as not to press their great weight upon the horses as they supped and watered, for it would be easy enough to prepare for the move towards the south and then Paris after this breakfast was shovelled down throats.

By 0525hrs the 11th Hussars had been ordered with a patrol that they needed to conduct, to conduct a quick clearance of the area towards the south-east, and although this was towards the general vicinity of II Corps, a strange sound too close for comfort had been heard, hence their interest had been aroused. To their horror they were confronted by cavalry of the enemy twice the size in number to their own currently stationed at Néry, belonging to the sodding 4th Cavalry Division. I'm sure I have no need to tell you that they did scarper out of there as fast as their mounts could carry them and reported their findings, to which they were ordered to dismount immediately and find themselves positions along the eastern edge of the village to prepare for the hasty defence to come.

By 0540hrs the enemy had opened the hostilities by pressing home thunderous fire which disturbed the serenity, a great amount of noise from light artillery and machine guns of the advanced guard, but it wasn't long before the German commander ordered a dismounted attack upon the village of which he no doubt had never heard of until that day.

It was mayhem for the BEF, with riderless horses making a run for it and artillery soldiers endeavouring to get their guns positioned upon a firing line, of which they managed to get three of the six aligned, two of which were unceremoniously taken out of action as quick-as-you-please. From that moment on it was one British gun against twelve enemy field guns that were perched on the ridge to their east from whence the patrol had emerged from the fog within the valley. This single gun managed to continue firing until all of its ammunition had been practically exhausted and reinforcement arrived later in the morning, the German artillery seemingly favouring to conduct counter-battery fire as opposed to directing their massive weapons against dismounted cavalry; this in turn provided our men upon the ground the much desired fire support by drawing the enemy guns away from opportunity targets.

At 0600hrs the Dragoons made a move to outflank the enemy that our-numbered them and by 0800hrs the British reinforcements [the Middlesex Regiment, the 4th Cavalry Brigade and a battery of Horse Artillery] had arrived to conduct a counter-attack upon a demoralised and retreating German division as they were being routed into all directions one could point a stick, leaving their precious commodity behind which entailed eight captured artillery pieces, and due to a lack of horses, all of their food, water and ammunition. The 11th Hussars, still full of adrenaline, pursued their advantage upon the routed mass and gathered 78 prisoners from which to attain much information of great military importance.

Such a grand victory it was in the face of an advancing enemy who were far superior in number. The surprise of the encounter was obviously the point of imbalance for the sod and so happy we were to know this, but with the action over with, so the marching continues, and ever southward we all continue.

4th SEPTEMBER, 1914

It looked at first as though Paris would be taken by the sod and the so-far victorious armies as we were, representing the allies as a whole, were literally forced to fall upon the River Marne for defence, but illustrious, good fortune shined down upon us.

Through poor insight the Germans continued upon our heels and on the 3rd continued with the swerve to the left in a move to crush the French once and for all, a total of 150,000 men in the Sixth Army and 70,000 within the BEF. But the manoeuvre was fraught with danger for the German First and Second Army, for their right flank was to become exposed. This was to turn the tables completely in our favour and about bloody time, too.

Again it was Lord Kitchener whose quiet [or not] words into the ear of French assured that he would assist our French allies as best he could, and the only way to do this was by performing, as all good infantry must, to the highest expectation in the attack. To perform an attack we must hit the enemy hard [or where it hurts], see a strategic move unbalance the threat, and hit home with continued bouts of hostile fire until victory is so thick that is can be plucked from the air, stuck in a cigar tube and smoked for the pleasure it gives.

We were to go from rags to riches overnight. We were about to exit the most terrible march any of us had ever encountered, where men fell upon their faces, where men tripped over small stones, over each other, banging heads into rifle barrels, suffering all manner of deprivation both by day and by night… can I go on, but of course; do I need to, of course not.

Now I know I have promised you more-of-a personal account of action and experience as that which we faced as men of war and combat, and I shall certainly get to it, but some battles need to be painted in order to get to the grindstone of true suffering and conflict. Please bear with me for just a little longer.

5th SEPTEMBER, 1914

Although we had put in a good fight by inflicting what appeared to be many more casualties upon them than they did upon us, the withdrawal was unavoidable. After two weeks and 251 miles, however, the tables would be turned momentarily and we would become the pursuer. The well-ordered and executed tactical withdrawal from the advance of the sods was put to a stop. But miraculous achievements don't just happen, and certainly not over a period of minutes or even hours. Good things take time and so did our coming victory-to-be, which would soon see delivered to us all, four years of trench warfare.

We turned and faced our foe and conducted a counter-attack, hand in hand with the French, still with water canteens as empty as our stomachs. We were now at the Battle of the Marne which constituted seven days and nights of warfare. For all intents and purposes it did appear that we, the BEF, had suffered heavily through the incompetence of the French and at the hand of General Lanrezac, but Sir John French stabbed back, and rather personally I would consider, by refusing to support the French at Guise. I understand the formalities of an eye for an eye and take no pity on poor souls who are dealt what they justly deserve, but to play games with men's lives by not supporting one another was sheer insanity. At the time I could only hope that it would never occur again, but I too suffer from having a naïve personality at times of greatest need.

Yes indeed; autumn was on its way, the morning was fresh and chilly, and men put smiles upon their faces and lips to rifles as the time to strike back fell upon us. Orders were coming down from higher that an attack was to be mounted on the morrow, but something had happened to change all of that, for someone forgot to tell the sod of our intentions and instead of awaiting our assault the German command decided to overextend their general reliance and over exhausted troops. The entire German First Army was wheeling into a position facing the west, their cavalry hitting the advancing French Sixth Army. The Germans pushed very hard against the French and in doing so did expose themselves to an attack upon their right flank.

The next few days passed quickly, with little time to rest and clean our rifles. The next few days seemed to melt into one another like honey into a teacup – ah… the thought of a single cup of tea.

By the 7th of September, and with a besieged French Sixth Army licking their wounds, 10,000 French reserves entered the fighting, 6,000 of which had been delivered to the fight in six hundred Parisian taxi cabs as they streamed out of Paris and towards the unstable front line. It was a deciding factor in the downfall of the German advantage, and with the news that there was now a thirty-miles gap in the German lines, pursuit was almost on with the BEF taking good measure of what the Allied aircraft overhead advised was a sizable and attractive opportunity. The sod tried to blow it out of the sky with percussion shells but their fire, at present and for the remainder of the war, was extremely inaccurate. I would hazard a guess that we might have lost a single aircraft to every three hundred shells fired at one but even with these figures it was best to avoid being fired upon.

By the 8th September the French rallied from their past, poor performances, and carried out an aggressive attack which further saw the divide between the German First and Second Armies grow at an alarming rate.

The sod was done for. And why was this, why a sudden turnaround in French ability? It was rather simple when you considered that General Lanrezac had been replaced by another. It's not the infantry ability to perform a task which merits victory but the officers to enact and give proper orders, and although the skill of the infantry is a driving wedge which sees an army win in conflict it is only by carrying out orders that such is achieved. But let me say here and now that even a lowly private soldier can have the guts to give orders and see them carried out during hard times.

Even now, as we advanced a few miles here and there, the German atrocities could be seen through our own eyes. Previously we had heard that the German sod did this, and he did that, but to see it with your own eyes was to serve lashings of adrenalin during battle, every man wishing to deal blow after vicious blow upon the retreating bastards. They were running scared now. Where we had carried out a tactical withdrawal, they were running with tails between their legs: was I being fair?

Houses with windows smashed, beds and other property thrown out of windows and onto roads, the conscripts had dealt an unfair card. There were victims of crime coming out from hiding, poor women and young girls coming forward to announce that they had been raped, all with tears in their eyes: it hurts the most when the girl is barely into her teens.

The Poor State of War and Conflict

Our feet were less sore now, for what did we have to complain about? We were only fighting a war but these young girls had to carry the disgusting filth of a memory of forced penetration with them for the remainder of their lives.

I feel sick now and consider the safety of my new family at home. I shall not under any circumstances allow the sod to make it to England for fear of what they might do to those I love the most. Maybe it's this fear that will win us the war.

9th SEPTEMBER, 1914

There are not many glorious days in war but when they occur they are so sweet. The sodding retreat of the bastard sons of Kaiser lasted from the 9th to the 13th and not a day during this period went by without a smile to be seen somewhere nearby, and seeing the skies with our planes conducting reconnaissance missions to evaluate the situation regarding the hot pursuit.

Maps in every headquarters… there must have been numerous arrows pointing to the great victory that was the Battle of the Marne, the advancing French Armies and BEF being spurred on by thoughts of the great delivery that fell into our laps, assisted greatly by the seventy-five artillery batteries of French nationality, a decisive key in the turnaround of historical events as they set themselves before us. No longer would the sod be celebrating a quick and easy victory over the allies by plundering Paris, but now they must prepare themselves for four years of war upon two fronts. Pray to God that the Russians don't make peace too early or out of spite, for without their pressure upon the Germans we would be in dire straits.

At one stage it appeared as though the sod was going to be wiped out and that the war would be over, but the hate within the conscripts and their higher authority was bent upon bringing misery to all, and upon a silver platter. Such hatred must be spurred by a venomous breed of man in order for the need for war to be continued. I could not help feeling a great hatred for these men dressed in grey that opposed us, but later in the war I would feel as though I understood them for many proved to be more human than me, myself.

The days and nights continued to pave the way for further misery and twelve miles a day was covered, many with the eyes and ears working overtime in an endeavour to see the sod soldiers killed before I bore the brunt of another's anxieties. But we needn't stress too long for their retreat had ceased at a point just north of the Aisne River, some 40 miles of hot pursuit having been completed.

I shall now give you some hasty figures to chew upon; the Battle of the Marne saw two million men trying to kill one another, almost

500,000 were either killed or wounded. I had had a 25 per cent chance of being killed or wounded and yet I lived. I could come through the other end of this misery unscathed: but far more misery was to come.

If I could survive till now I stood a chance of surviving the war. My spirit was lifted. I was becoming a stranger to that thing called fear; but old enemies have ways of beating back upon the back door as unwelcome guests, and so that stranger would one day come to haunt me again, and that day would not be too far ahead.

Those were feelings that rose from time to time, and happier times were when we saw thousands upon thousands of German prisoners of war being fed through the system and towards our rear, along with much enemy artillery and other supplies. And then I fell upon a poor woman who had a story to tell, one that I still find hard to believe even to this day. She told me of the enemy cavalry and what they had done to her child. They had held him down and used a sword to cut off his legs, but the first attempt missed and cut off his lower limb below the knee and so another attempt was made. Many young girls were also robbed of their virginity. I saw the graves in which they lay, fresh soil heaped upon the face of the earth, forever reminders of war and its horrors.

I could do nothing for her and maybe that was the trick. Was she after sympathy from us soldiers of the BEF or was her story of molestation and rape true? I shall never know. I am torn between truth and lie. I hope the story is untrue so that the idea of so much suffering can be waved aside, but I also hope [and it is not a strong word in this sense] that it is true, for to see someone tell such a lie as that being told, and with such conviction, only achieved a single goal and that was that the hatred within the men that heard the story did rise to greater heights than before, to such a point where they, themselves, might be forced to see greater sin dealt out upon the enemy when the sod surrendered or were captured alive and or brought in wounded.

13th SEPTEMBER, 1914

The Germans were digging in and it would appear for all intents and purposes that the war of mobility had stagnated, but this was so more truthful that it could hardly be believed. The war was to become one of attrition, a system of trenches to soon develop between the Swiss border and the North Sea, a continuous [though with small gaps here and there] system of trenches that scarred the earth for more than 450 miles. Four-fifty miles of twisting trenches, elbow bends along the stretch of protection created so that grenades and artillery rounds falling within caused as little damage to life and limb as possible, the extent of each 'straight' line of trench being limited in purposeful design and nature.

The sod had taken to a defensive strategy upon the northern area of the one hundred foot river, which was said to have been as deep as fifteen feet. There appeared before us a line of fairly steep cliffs which levelled out after sloping ground to meet a plateau covered in thickets and being rather dense in places. The sod had chosen the ground just two miles, give or take, from the crest opposing this river. The Germans had provided themselves a great advantage with marvellous fields of fire in such a position that they were looking in a downward glance upon anything and anyone that made an approach.

It was upon the night that a thick fog fell upon us and an advance over the crest brought us into the fields of fire that the sod had arranged so purposely as though born of the ground around them, having crossed the river with much difficulty upon our manoeuvring being placed. The river crossing itself was swathed with dangers. Crossing hastily prepared pontoon bridges with only flickering light to make our way over turbulent waters, whilst praying that you didn't get hit by one of the many pieces of shrapnel or bullets flying here and there, was not the easiest thing to perform. But the night crossing was the least of our great concerns.

As the mist dissipated on the sun rising above the horizon, glares of sunlight streaming in from the east, a network of gun emplacements commenced to shred us to pieces, the sloping ground serving the trajectory of bullets rather unfairly in favour of the sod.

We had been halted and the command to dig in was given.

We were now, most truly born, to the world of trench warfare, for both armies, those of the allies and axis not considering for a moment any opportunity to back away from upon the ground in which they stood, for retreat was a dirty word as I have already expressed in numerous voices.

14th SEPTEMBER, 1914

The small and shallow scrapes upon the ground were now to become our home for the next four years. Sir John French gave the order for all men under his sway to dig, dig, dig, and when you can dig no more, then do all you can to make war less miserable by preparing trenches for movement between the front line trenches and those behind. And so we did, we dug, dug, dug, and when we couldn't dig any more then we dug anew. Sergeants ordered groups of men to scrounge all they could in regards to pickaxes and spades, for although our entrenching tools did the job of digging that no man wished to do, the tool was rather inadequate and very slow to achieve the goals set before us all, and minor punishments were seen executed upon those willing to discard their tools during the march towards Paris.

Shallow scrapes became trenches seven feet deep. Soon the communication trenches were connected to these. Comforts were seen too, such as sleeping bays within the sides of the trench walls, walls of timber and braces fixed to keep the whole mess from falling in upon it, parapets and even signposts were prepared and erected. And it was good that our defensive position was becoming more stable and better prepared, for the Germans had it over us in so many arenas. Their artillery far outshine ours in number, despite being seemingly inaccurate, their machine guns and grenades were all along the front line, whereby ours were vastly outnumbered, and they had trench mortars and rifle grenades that poured out lashings of misery to fall upon us. Even by night the sod was well endowed with flares and other pyrotechnics. Their resupply was rather easy when compared to ours.

But what we had the sod would never achieve: better training, and we were marksman one and all. But this was also a flaw, for although our combined firing might sound like machine gun fire to the Germans, it certainly did not have the same effects, for cones of fire were a great advantage to machine guns which the rifle simply could not attain.

18th SEPTEMBER, 1914

You have to forgive me, for I forget the date. At some time between now and the 20th some things did occur which are interesting to know, but war is a blur in the mind which recalls only the bloodiest and cruellest of moments. There was much deceit during the war, many heroics performed, many things to be written about, but that is the idea of this text, to enable you to see through my eyes, and so I apologize for not being accurate in all my words but what follows is a strange assortment of actions that occurred at some interval over several days, I think, and I should clarify them but I do not wish to dwell too long on such misfortunes.

There was a fire fight and the trenches were being lashed heavily by German artillery, so much so that the ground vibrated and felt as though I was on a barge within a very rough sea during a hurricane. It was like an earthquake, and many times was this experienced; too many to count. The heavy sodding bombardment was in retaliation and in defence against our progress upon taking some ground to our front. It's not important to know the name of the place, for it is too much for me to recall, but it is what occurred that matters most of all.

The attack was over many miles of ground and in places the fall of artillery was rather sparse, and the opportunity was ripe for a German surrender to take place as we were making great progress.

We had, in places along the line, men in trenches, and upon flanks we had men in the fight. Along the miles of trench there were men under fire of small arms, men under fire from artillery, and several bombs even dropped from planes high above, but the greatest of all illusions were the white flags we saw rising high into the air.

A shout rose here and there and was passed along the entire trench, or so it would seem. Can you imagine what it would be like to be sitting on the steps of the Swiss Alps and receive a message passed on from man to man, that the Germans were surrendering, but the message was for those several hundred miles away to the north, not for those who were positioned to the south. It is ludicrous to believe in such a thing but I tell you now that the message may not have reached the Alps but it was passed a long bloody way down the line of battle.

The word was that the sod was surrendering, that a white flag was seen flying upon a bayonet at the end of a rifle [a handkerchief or some other material]; then the message was of more than one, and I could see them filling the air; what a joyous occasion this was.

We were quickly ordered not to fire and so we became ever watchful as hundreds upon hundreds of the sod departed their trenches and gave themselves up to the men almost upon them, and in places where there was nothing but no-man's land, the sod crossed this to present themselves as prisoners.

It is a strange phenomenon. In the centre of the line the advancing troops of the BEF were moving forward to accept the surrender but towards a flank the Germans were coming to us. Suddenly the advance upon the trenches had seemed to falter as the flags of white pressed home the reward of a victory fulfilled. More Germans then appeared with hands held high.

At my end of the surrender the Germans had crossed the ground and were giving themselves up to us, those men of the BEF who had been passed the order not to fire upon the enemy during this time of transition.

Was this it; was this the end of the war; was it to be over by Christmas?

Those in the line of advance who had been attacking approached the enemy trenches and those men nearer the flanks, such as me, were to be offered surrender in the trenches which were our own. But something was amiss. What was it? It was the terror of men surrendering. There was not a man who looked fearful. Their eyes did not speak of surrender but of mischief. And then it happened all at once. The men of ours who were at the German trenches were suddenly confronted by hundreds more of the enemy behind the first, these suddenly opened fire upon our men who stood in the open; secondly the sod who had crossed no-man's land to our trenches were suddenly jumping in amongst us and ordering us to surrender to them.

Those British troops exposed in the open were cut down rather heinously and those with me had a fight upon their hands which was close quarter battle fighting at its worst.

I struck a man with my fixed bayonet, the bayonet becoming horribly stuck. The bayonet had been driven hard into his chest and was lodged within his ribs. I tugged and tugged as shooting continued around me. The Germans were not surrendering but using it as a ploy to take us, not an ounce of acknowledgement of their abuse against their use of the flag of truce being indicated by a single soul from the grey-clad army.

The sod I had skewered was screaming in pain and I had other matters to concern myself with for there was much action being carried out in our trenches. There was hand to hand fighting going on all around me. And so I kept pulling and pulling, and the sod, now upon the ground, kept weeping in screams of agony, 'no, no, no!' I kept pulling but the bayonet would not give way and the action to my rear seemed to be pressing ever closer. I had to do something quickly, so I fired my weapon and blew his chest apart but at the same time set the bayonet free of the scabbard of flesh and bone encased around it.

Suddenly there was firing from our flank and our boys had regained much initiative by raking the ground before them with machine gun fire from behind their parapets, the Germans falling as though wheat in a field was being harvested.

That is what I remember, that is what I tell you today. War was for heroes and cowards; it was for the deceitful and honest; it was for those that did not know fear and those that sweat at the mere thought of it. War was where normal men turned insane and the insane were woken from their years of sheltered existence.

I still have dreams from time to time of that sod upon my bayonet. I cannot control my dreams.

24th SEPTEMBER, 1914

I have advised you earlier of the way in which trench warfare became a part of our life at war, but how was it that the extent of trenches was so vast? Maybe you should consider it a moment; think for yourself how this might occur.

Well, what do you think? I'll tell you. For three weeks or thereabouts following the stalemate at the Aisne River both the Germans and ourselves did try with the greatest effort to outflank one another, to try and encircle the opposition and bring the war to a quick end. And so the sod would try to outflank us and we would retaliate, and then we would try to outflank them and they would counter this with a counter-attack, we would move against this and so on and so forth. We also had a name for this: no, it wasn't labelled with a profane name, nor did we consider it as 'shit happens', but it was called 'Race to the Sea'. Each side tried with all their effort to outflank the other.

10th OCTOBER, 1914

Almost to a man, apart from a single corps, were we awaiting deployment into our posts. Our staging area prior to this move was between Hazebrouck and Saint Omer – Saint Omer being approximately halfway between Boulogne and Menen, so in effect we were all within thirty miles of the most famous salient in the history of the war where three monstrous battles were waged over many weeks; Ypres. We were currently in France and awaiting a move into Belgium: we were in Flanders.

And so now we have to deal with no-man's land.

And I suppose I should briefly tell you a little about Ypres so that you get a clearer understanding of the situation.

The salient was like half a circle, the convex shape penetrating into what might be considered as enemy territory so that the enemy completely surrounded you and could fire upon the position from any side they wished. The enemy also had the favour of slightly higher ground but more on that much later in the narrative. The amount of ground which the salient stood to take from the Germans was quite considerable for the half-circle of our defensive position penetrated some six miles into enemy territory.

It's a little funny to consider it 'enemy territory' for we were the ones holding the ground, and although there were to be many attempts to dislodge us from the ground on which we stood we were to prove extremely stubborn in our ways.

The salient in effect is the trench system and behind this the town of Ypres sits naked to German artillery fire, for it is near the centre rear that a road enters the system and supplies are made available to those of the defence, which includes replacements for those who have fought for too long at the front. This area of supply transition from storage to stomach and rifle is known as Hellfire Corner [Menin

Gate]. It is also well known to all men that this area is to be passed through on the way to the front and on the way from it. You think that fear will mount out of control on your way through this point towards the trenches but I shall tell you how I felt; I felt the worse for coming from the trenches, thinking how horrible it might be to be killed when being provided a little rest and relaxation, or a ticket home for fourteen days leave: which you will find out soon enough was something that did not happen very often.

It appeared, for all intents and purposes, that two battalions from every brigade in Flanders were occupying the trenches. There was a system in place which was supposed to run like this: spend four days at the front and then be relieved, to be sent back to the billets behind the lines. There was the opportunity for what was 'leave in England', or furlough, which to be granted once a year was experienced maybe once every 18 to 24 months on average.

I am sure as hell that there were people pulling the strings, allowing hardened soldiers to be maintained at the front whilst sending quartermasters and others back to England up to three times in a single year. There was no justice. In the end we all received the same three medals, whether we served four years at the front or 12 months behind the lines as a quartermaster; but this service wasn't about medals and I think I have already stated such, in a roundabout way.

22nd OCTOBER, 1914

Morning routine rarely changed. It was a system which saw each man fed and watered, and weapons cleaned. We would 'stand-to' quite some time before the night was over and wait for the sun to rise. Once wholly in the sky 'stand down' would be given and morning routine conducted. 'Stand-to' lasted for around 30 to 60 minutes. We would also 'stand-to' and 'down' in the evening prior to conducting night routine. Morning Routine: One man might shave whilst another ate, and yet a third would clean his Lee Enfield. To have every man cleaning his weapon at the same time was simply ridiculous for if the enemy chose that moment to attack then there would be no opposing fire to meet them. But there were times when the system was changed in order to meet the strategic needs of the war. Night Routine: Fresh rations would be afforded where absolutely able and even where the front line was on the move – as proved during the final year of the war – the rations would be spared no haste in getting to us with all reasonable measure of consideration and security taken to those work parties in delivering the great sustenance; even if hardtack and corned beef. The field kitchens of the rear seemed to work tirelessly at it, in the billets and the trenches away from the front, and hot food was often taken to the very front: in particular for the benefit of the officers who would be provided all manner of good courtesy at feed time. Quite often the rations to the front came in sandbags with tea, sugar, bacon [cooked or not], bread and the day's mail all combined. It was a poor sap who received the parcel from his mum soaked in stew, for sometimes the containers in which a stew might be afforded would come undone and ruin everything – but we still consumed it all and read our letters as best we could.

The day wore on as any other, pot shots being taken at the enemy, the Race for the Sea at it ends, the attrition phase of war now commencing to take its toll upon us all. Everything we did was to accommodate this theatre of war, the war of attrition. It was a horrid time but by no means the worst.

At the northernmost extremities of the salient at Ypres the Germans were busy laying down an artillery barrage which woke men up quick-smart, their clean weapons ready to see action once more and the wait was a short one. The sod was after our trenches, trying with all their effort to drag us from our prized possession in order to keep it for themselves.

The order was passed around, thunderous voices giving orders to the men on the ground as we watched in eagerness the sod move into position in readiness to attack. "Stand-to! Stand-to! Watch your front for here they come, lads! Mark your targets! Wait! Five hundred yards; four; three hundred. Open fire, ten rounds at the rapid!"

And so the fight was on once more.

Somewhere along the line the sod was successful in his endeavours but our counter-attack saw the trenches back in our hot little hands. It was only a small effort by the enemy. Maybe this was a large-scale, noisy reconnaissance. It was easy to draw a conclusion from this effort of theirs and that was that there was more to come in the morning.

23rd OCTOBER, 1914

As any other day preceding it we were hard at work on improving the trenches for the long haul. A single sodding shell making a direct hit could make for hours of back-breaking work. And this day like all others saw many shells falling in our direction. It seems that my hunches in regards to a 'noisy reconnaissance by force' were to be proven correct. But to tell you the truth, so that you can see the picture in your eye as I see it in my mind, there were many trenches which weren't trench like. It was a fact that a lot of the protection from which we fought was nothing more than hastily dug rifle pits and it was the spoil from these that we packed down to act as parapets. Not everyone had the great convenience of a seven foot deep trench with bearings, walls of planks and floors of pellet. Not everywhere on the front was the same as everywhere else.

Our own artillery did all it could to fire back but the area in which the batteries found themselves was as flat as the ground before us and so it was difficult for them to conduct any good and effective means of countermeasures. This point was also proved during the years that followed for there were many occasions on which gunners were able to target infantry in the open simply by looking over their open sights; a smorgasbord ready for the culling.

It was on the opening of the evening that the Germans commenced their assault, preparatory fire having been conducted to soften us up, but the Kaiser should learn that the BEF could not be softened by the firing of a few thousand shells, for our need to defend our ground was greater than the German need to claim it: therefore I could always see a shadow of doubt within the sods' scheme of things.

The sod was coming forward in such dense ranks that it was impossible to miss a target, and with the rapid fire capability of weapons and men the enemy were in for a lot of trouble. But they kept on coming as though there was no end to them, coming forward at a walk, climbing over the dead bodies of their comrades as they moved ever forward into oblivion. They seemed not to care: was this because they had some form of political officer behind to force them forward with threats hanging over their heads that any coward was to be shot; I don't know but suspected it: I'd heard of this happening earlier during the battle at Mons.

The poor civilians of Ypres were also hit hard for there were many dwellings, homes of generations passed that were now on fire and crumbling down around their ears... for those so silly to remain inside; but what do you do, hide in the shelter of your home or take to the streets and run along between the shells as they plummet to earth.

The first series of waves had been halted, this was pleasing to see, but it wasn't long before another was on its way and as the darkness of the night came to fall about us all another attack in waves had commenced. But it was due to the hard work of men killing men that we lived. So hard they worked their weapons that it wasn't uncommon to see soldiers throw their weapon aside and to grab another for it was too hot to handle from all the firing. This second attempt at taking our trenches lasted for almost two hours but they were repulsed to a man and we saved the day.

It was hard to believe, this audacity that the enemy had to approach us with weapons firing from the hip, coming at us so slow and recklessly. It was to their undoing, what should I care; honestly.

It is now I quickly duck down and prepare some clips for use in my weapon and as I draw my eyes away from the dead that litter the ground before me I see a young face, a man who arrived just a few days before, being a volunteer, a replacement for a fallen comrade: it was easy to be killed; easy to lose a friend and so hard it was to stay alive.

He was a young man and he was crying softly unto himself, clutching his weapon with both arms, the weapon held vertical between his knees. You could see at a glance that his spirit was gone. He was no longer a man but an empty shell. A few days of war had turned him into a shambles. I tried to urge him up, for him to gather his spirit and meet the reality of the day. He needed to fight as we were fighting so that victory would be ours, but he would not move.

It was then that a stretcher bearing party of two came upon the scene and with quick but gentle persuasion took the man away.

I feel guilty now for what that young man had done to me. He gave me courage; he instilled upon me the ambition to forget the fear of death no matter how small because I knew as all men did that you could be brave one day and a mess the next.

So it did seem that the end of battle was upon us this day and the look upon the other men around me was one of great support and merit. Here were men that were suffering as I, and were closer to me than brothers of the same mother. It is wonderful the feeling you get from one another, the idea that you can provide such support in times of need that the fear of being blown to pieces is shrouded by a greater need; to do all you can to aid your comrades in arms. In years to come I would hold in my arms the dying, their blood soaking into my uniform, tears flowing freely from my face. Is it no wonder then that some men prefer, through sheer horror of loss, not to have any friends on the line, for they would be spared the grief that I was to suffer by maintaining good relations with all. Some men were unwilling to make friends with anyone.

It is now time to briefly reflect upon the day, to count our blessings. We had lost many men to the shelling but fewer to the brutality of small arms. And then I see another man standing and watching his front like a good soldier does, but the look upon his face was one of sheer misery. I asked him later what it was that he was thinking and he told me that he didn't want to be killing people, even if they were Germans who had committed atrocities. Killing was not in his blood, but rather than see his friends open to the hostility of the enemy, he had decided to do his bit by killing as many as he could. He would suffer the memory of these killings in years to come but during times with old comrades he would recall the good times spent at war, and yes, there are a few, believe it or not.

The copse before us were starting to look rather… shrivelled. The landscape was starting to look like the surface of the moon. The flatness and greenery that is Flanders was starting to resemble a desert wasteland of churned up earth. One day the earth of Flanders would resemble little more than life-taking mud; cesspools in which men would fall and die and bloat.

We had held our positions proudly and gallantly, if I may be as bold as to say, and to obey an order given me, I provided assistance in getting a wounded man to the rear for some urgent medical attention.

It was a long journey, though not due to distance, but for the sheer effort in supporting another and trying to make gain upon distance through a country marked by killing fields of fire which the sod was happy to sodden with bullets, shrapnel, and our blood.

We eventually came upon the Regimental Aid Post and after a quick drink of water from a canteen, and seeing the line of wounded mounting, I was ordered again to continue on to the dressing station which was reportedly, 'not so far away'. Certainly within the mile it was, but took several more hours to reach from my initial point of departure.

Finally, clambering down into the crowded room with straw upon the floor I saw tables on which to carry out surgery and other medical aid such as bandaging. There were many men upon the floor waiting to be seen, to be attended, and of course the most urgent were seen first. It was also interesting to note the looks upon the faces of the medical officers, orderlies and surgeons. They all seemed stricken with a slight grief though this was certainly not too overbearing. The reason I mention it is because a year later I happened to be in the same dressing station and although most of the people had changed, which was of no surprise, the contrast looks worn by them had changed vastly from those early days. It was as though during the early part of the war I saw medical officers working on human beings and that later in the war, the further you went into the misery of this insanity, there was a transition whereupon it seemed as though they were working upon dead animals or manikins. At present they were men operating on men, later they would become accustomed to the savagery of war and look like robots operating on sacks of potatoes.

So I reported to a busy orderly and was asked to leave. I stepped further back and looked at the one I had helped. I did not know him but now felt the deepest sympathy, his shoulder wound having caused much concern: more concern than pain. I stood momentarily at the door before turning away, turning my back on an orderly holding a candle in the top of an empty wine bottle as the medical officer took the leg off a man screaming in pain because he'd not had enough morphine, or the fear of losing a limb was too much to bear.

I returned to my place upon the front line.

The following days saw further attacks by the sod, much carried out in a similar manner to before, each wave being cut down with great ease as our weapons overheated in the brutal firing of ammunition. I knew the conscripts would be short on training but I didn't think they would be short on brains, which led me even further into my belief that they were being forced to meet their death, that even their officers above them were having their hands tied. And on the 29th day of October I heard a story filtered down that the Kaiser himself was bitter about the great loss and our stubbornness to be moved. It was said that he spoke the following words, or similar to them: 'the men of the BEF are trash and extremely feeble, who will surrender in mass if they are attacked with vigour'. I must say that even a speech like that would not have me wanting to conduct wave upon wave of attack upon such murderous fire that we provided. I was also to hear in future years that what the Kaiser had supposedly said was sheer propaganda and made up by British officers in order to get our spirits up. If my spirits were any higher in conviction then I would be an angel.

11th NOVEMBER, 1914

Ah; Armistice Day, yet we're not to know it for quite some years to come.

It was coming to winter where misery bore many new names such as freezing fog, prolific lice, trench foot, trench nephritis, and hypothermia. But regardless of these, where there was misery to be had during the winter months it could easily be found. And so on this day we saw the last ditch effort of the sod in trying to take the trenches from us at Ypres before we all, on both sides, settled down to the commencement of the war of attrition, living harsh existences in conditions unfit for anything, it would seem, but lice and rats.

Being with General Horace I was a part of the group assigned to occupy a seventeen mile front, Ypres being part of our flank, and so in the following I was not involved.

The Prussian Guard came at us at a faster pace than was normal, seemingly jogging along and actually getting to our trenches in places where hand to hand fighting would be pursued, but their attempt was the same as previous weeks and they were sent back to their own lines with far less than they had started.

The fortification of trenches and elaborate bunker systems was now carried out, none so fine as the Germans, for their bunkers, particularly at the Somme, would prove to be outstanding achievements under such hostile fire that we could manage to send them. But you shall learn of these a little later on.

Further hard work was to be mustered in the direction of field defences, namely barbed wire. Erected at night these were a hazardous task to complete, too much sound and the sod would put up a flare and find you out with machine gun fire. But between the last effort of the sod to take the trenches and the continuing effort to construct field defences and other obstacles came the opportunity to rest a little, in particular during the day.

24th DECEMBER, 1914

The days leading up to Christmas of 1914 were intense to say the least. The war was supposed to have been over by now but here we were, in the cold of the night and day living like morbid creatures trying to keep warm. The scenery was always the same, the trench, for it was almost impossible to look over the parapet and not be shot at by an enemy sniper, or some German with a rifle trying to show off how efficient he was at shooting over iron sights. And then I did a foolish thing, I looked over the top of the trench to see what I would make of no-man's land during the day, for very little could be made out during the night.

I could see one of our men who had received a bullet to the head not so long ago whilst out on a mission – or fools task – to repair a gap in some wire due to an enemy trench mortar. He had a dozen rats or more eating his flesh, they had started from his toes and head, and were working their way both up and down to meet in the middle, as though in systematic operation with one another, refusing to touch certain parts too foul to mention, but I must in order to give you the full picture; they refused to touch any part of the human body that contained faeces. My only wish was to pick up my rifle and shoot the damn things but I couldn't; not only would the firing bring machine gun retaliation but we had orders not to harm the damn things because they helped to keep the battlefield nice and clean. No one enjoyed the smell of death; it was the most disturbing thing to have to experience. But no matter where you looked the rats were at work, literally thousands upon thousands of them nibbling on every carcass there was between the two lines of trenches; and they are absolutely huge in size.

Now, I have heard a story that the rats will never touch a living man, even if asleep, but I tell you now that in the dead of night of my first winter in Flanders I was rudely awoken on at least one occasion by a rodent trying his luck. They had come after the rations [I have no choice in considering this the reason] which, when we have them to spare, are suspended in sandbags from the supporting beams of dugouts where officers are concerned, and so I assume that on their way past me they chose to try for a quick nibble. Imagine his fright to get a punch to the body. Imagine my fright to be woken in such a way. I can still see that rat in my illuminated imagination saying, 'sorry kind sir, but I meant not an ounce of discourtesy towards you, for I thought you were dead'. And sometimes I thought I must have been.

And speaking of courtesy, there were no attacks during the winter months. But on reflection I'm sure this has nothing to do with courtesy at all.

25th DECEMBER, 1914

How could one be so courteous to an enemy? It sounded… foolish… no, no… it sounded simply barbaric to be courteous to someone who had caused so much death and misery, but on reflection I assume the sod must be thinking the same. But then for Christmas Day this year we were all treated to the hospitality, of which I and several others refused to accept, of the enemy in no-man's land: they called it the Christmas truce of 1914.

How could this form of fraternization come about?

The Germans were reportedly the second largest population of all immigrants in England prior to the war and it was often heard that students and young men of English origin went abroad to Germany for a good dollop of education: though I see nothing wrong with the education I received.

And so they met in the middle of no-man's land, between the opposing lines of trenches scarring the earth, to exchange food, cigarettes, good song and commiserations. It is all for nought at the end for on the morrow we shall all be back at the throat of the other, shooting each other with rifle, blowing each other up with bombs and artillery, and generally having a good go at killing the man in the opposing trench.

3rd MARCH, 1915

Winter was over with, at last, and the sun gave increasing amounts of heat for us to be warmed as each day passed into the next. I often forgot what day it was. It didn't seem to matter that much, but when an important day was coming up fast then I would always put extra effort into trying to remember the day.

Our trench system had been improved markedly over the winter months, working by night and sleeping by day; we were also moved around on occasion, back to the billets for a few days, back to the front line again for a few more, and when you returned it was either to a slightly better prepared trench then when you left it or to one that had hardly been touched and needed much work carried out upon it. I didn't mind the idea of working hard to fortify our position and trying to make it more comfortable, but I didn't like working fingers to the bone when others seemed to be sleeping the war away both day and night as opposed to helping his fellow man by digging.

Although the trench system was still not unbroken from one end to the next and gaps did exist here and there [which saw some men, from both sides, getting lost and passing through to the other side of no-man's land] they did resemble the great artefact which was the war of attrition.

Other than the departure of winter there was another reason for us all to wear a smile upon our faces for our good friends from Canada were preparing to move onto the line, and by the 3rd day of this month had been introduced to the trenches. Ah, how marvellous it is to see such a grand example of courage and friendship.

We had the honour of passing over our portion of the trench and managing several newcomers to the new way of life which was to be endured by them. One of them kept going on about having a look over the top so that he could look upon no-man's land but we insisted that he keep his head down because there were many snipers in the area. I recall looking once myself but since that day have stuck with the periscope. I handed it to him. He didn't seem too pleased with having to look upon the enemy through a periscope and so lifted his head then to see the entire area void of any movement, even though in all reality the opposing trench works would have been swarming with the sod.

The newcomer seemed to draw a little confusion on seeing so little action and lifted himself a little more and then we heard the shot and got showered in his blood and brains. I recall having to scrape flesh from my khakis in great distaste. From that moment on they kept their heads down but the length of the line they had moved into was vast and so there were several shots heard ringing out as German snipers targeted their victims.

16th MARCH, 1915

Although winter was over, I could not say the same for the rain. The rain itself could be lived with but what it brought with it was much misery.

The mud was one aspect; you simply could not get it off you. The boots we wore weighed in excess of ten pounds, or so it seemed.

The Poor State of War and Conflict

Walking along in some of the trenches was one way to see a little light at the end of the tunnel for the rain would fill the trenches so that you couldn't see the floorboards you were walking upon, and in some cases you couldn't even see your knees because it was so deep; and yes, it got even worse than that.

Trench foot was ever present, its ugly head appearing at every turn. We were normally forbidden to take our boots off during times of great evil for it was often too hard to get the boots back on again after the foot had swollen. But where the strategic element didn't pose too much difficulty, or the time for a possible enemy attack – or our own upon them – had expired, boots came off. It was very painful.

Lessons were learnt quickly in the trenches and passed along for the comfort of all concerned. During times when supplies were brought up from the rear, usually with meals, clean socks were exchanged for the ones we had been wearing or currently had on our feet. A quick and painful change of socks wasn't something we enjoyed doing so we also put plenty of effort into assuring that we were ready. When push comes to shove and hast was written on the walls, then two men would pair up. They would put themselves opposite one another and take boots off. Quickly remove the other's socks, dry their feet for them, rub whale oil in, where available, on with the clean socks and back on with the boots before they swell. The pain suffered in the exchange was a little better put up with when the feet weren't as swollen.

Even so, when socks were changed we would coat them in whale oil, where available, for this seemed to help us in our combined misery. Our dirty socks would be taken back with any rubbish, letters, and the sick, the socks to be cleaned and then recycled back to us.

It's a funny thing. A man didn't like to shirk his responsibility by going sick on his mates, for we were volunteers as I have already provided your ear, but when it came to honest and well-earned leave then we could not wait to be leaving the trench behind. Of course, leave was very seldom received but it was well earned, a hundred times over, and so anyone going on leave received a good smile and hearty handshake. A comrade never knew if he might see you again and so we always departed on a high note of congratulations and good cheer.

The Canadians were enjoying their new friends the lice and rats. It had only taken a few days for the entire force of Canadians to be well endowed with condominiums in which the lice lived in luxury and warmth, with as much food to chew on as they could ever dream. Many men tried burning the eggs of the lice from the seams of their uniform with candles, seemingly burnt from both ends for it achieved no victory over the uninvited guests. Some men preferred the sod over the lice, but if it wasn't for the sod then none of us would have been here in any case. This and many other incidents within the war, I felt, required recording and so I try to do just that.

I couldn't resist the historical opportunity and took some photographs with the 'Vest Pocket Kodak' which was first manufactured by Kodak in 1912. I couldn't afford one alone but I had other family members who thought it might be interesting and so sent me one – of which I had to take great charge and treated with excessive niceness. It was the size of... about twice the size of a packet of cigarettes and encased in a metal skin with a lens. I was quite distraught on hearing the following news: It would seem that the higher authority didn't like the soldiers, NCO's and officers sending photos back to their loved for it showed the horrors of the war which soiled the news that came from of the war cabinet at large, however, they advised us that the reason for the blanket of security was to deny the enemy any information that they could attain from such photos if the soldier with them was captured. An order had just been received that ensured the use of the VPK would be put to an immediate halt. No cameras were now permitted to be used by any person or any unit travelling into war zones overseas.

So much for fair play. I saw very few photos being taken from that day forward but I also saw an increase in the 'blind eye' being employed by officers for there were a few who believed that the men deserved, and should, secure the history of the war through pictures.

17th MARCH, 1915

I must say for the record that the Canadians proved over the coming months to be an extremely brave bunch of men and they did all they could within their power to ensure that the Germans got back what they dished out, and in oversized proportion, but it was these early days of the introduction of war that saw some tight moments play out between them and us: members of the BEF.

All along the front, but not in all places as we were to learn, there existed an unwritten law of policy between the two forces facing one another that dictated the following, 'live and let live'. The live and let live policy it was, something we had put into place over the winter months and still lived by. I don't know who first thought of the idea but it was sheer brilliance. If only the politicians and other high ranks could see this as a means to bring peace to the table.

The policy meant that we could sleep, and lift our heads out of the muck for a few moments of solace without the fear of being rudely woken or shot at, but the Canadians were somewhat shocked when they first heard of the live and let live policy.

The Poor State of War and Conflict

I recall hearing of one man and his experience. A Canadian was cowering [certainly not normal for them] in his trench, shaking from the violence of the shelling going on all around him, when suddenly it stopped as quick as it had started. He took an opportunity to look over the parapet whereby the light illumination from the moon allowed him to see some enemy at work on their wire. He wanted to pick his weapon up and start blazing away, to shoot all he could, to spill some blood, for his weapon was as virgin as he. He couldn't figure out why he'd been prevented from shooting, a calming hand placing itself upon his shoulder and requesting that he stop what he was about to do; but why? The live and let live policy was then explained to him, explained in full, how we had enjoyed a little peace after almost a year at war. He complied but was not happy.

Not long after the Canadians were moved [and I think it was in early April] into their own position, did they turn the cold shoulder upon the policy and commenced to do as they willed against the enemy to their front.

The sod came to hate the Canadians more than any other. They hated the Canadians for being so brave and forward; they hated the BEF for their proficiency with bayonets and rapid firing; they hated the French for being French, but most of all they hated their Generals: or so I was to learn in the years after the war.

The next four weeks were much the same and nothing of any great importance is worth noting during this period. But it was coming up to April and the Second Battle of Ypres was almost upon us. With many things, however, there must be some form of prologue.

13th April, 1914

The BEF and those heroic Canadians who manned the trenches around Ypres were mostly suppressed by view from the Germans, who, having hold of the higher ground did use their tactical advantage always to our misfortune.

I'm sure as hell that it baffles the mind of the sod as to why we held onto the salient of Ypres, for there was little to be gained, strategically speaking. There was little hope of defending against an enemy breakthrough of any superior model and withdrawal to the opposite side of the canal would be undertaken in a whisper. It is here that I learnt that Sir Horse, my cherished commander of great insight, did wish to move the entire front line: but even in this I cannot be overly sure but I know that withdrawal was on his mind, a withdrawal which others of higher command would learn about in the days to come. So why did we hold the unthinkable line of trenches? Because it was the last semblance of Belgium, the last town of this Flanders land that was not currently under sodding rule. This town of Ypres was a reminder of our great courage and determination. We must hold the line here and now, even if it is too ridiculous for a sane man to consider its overall use and value: but some things hold value of the mind, and that is precisely what Ypres was to us.

When the Canadians, only a third of which were born of that land for most came from Great Britain on the trail of immigration, they inherited trenches which were nothing but potholes on a baby's behind when compared to those in other places. There was enemy aircraft to contend with as they dropped bombs and the enemy trenches were only 150 to 300 yards away. And this is what confuses me. It was said that the French believed in an offensive war, but believed in withdrawing to allow their artillery to hold back the surging Germans when they attacked, and so saw no reason to build extravagant fortifications: but in some places they operated quite differently, and I believe that the slopes of Switzerland told a different tale, completely. We of the BEF on the other hand were taught to act in the defensive, for this is where we had proven to be most effective against the Germans, a strong reliance on counter-attack being more of a tradition than anything else. Either way you look at it, the ground we held in 1914 was pretty much the same as in 1917. Maybe if we'd had more and better artillery during the early stages of the war we could have done something different with the manner in which we conducted the business of this horrid war.

There was also another moment of history to recall of this date and that was the German soldier, August Jäeger. The man deserted his country for some reason or other and at the young age of twenty-four: it appeared at first to have been a ruse of some description for he was extremely adamant that the sod was going to gas the entire line along Ypres and then attack the ground with gusto. He even went as far as describing how it was to be done, the main signal for the release of the gas being three red flares that would be sent skyward as a command to proceed. All they needed was favourable weather conditions. August then showed the allies a respirator made of gauze and cotton, advising that all the assaulting troops had these in their possession to ward off the asphyxiating effect, but first they must be soaked in a chemical in order to work effectively. And do you think the allies, those officers at headquarters listening to the tale, would listen? Of course not; it was too absurd to be true, even if August did have a respirator with him.

17th APRIL, 1915

With the idea of such a gas attack being pushed aside, and no forewarning being given to the soldiers within the trenches, the mammoth task of mining beneath hill 60 continued [little more than sloping ground, really; not a hill at all]. It was from upon this hill that spotters drained away the souls of the men of the BEF, static positions for snipers, and generals drew up plans for attack.

It was in the evening on this day that five tonnes of explosive were detonated and three large craters were added to the landscape. It was so loud that even from where I stood, which was nowhere near the hill, I was stunned by the seemingly immeasurable sound. Wave after wave of man after man rushed the hill and took it. The Germans, knowing the great importance of the hill, and like us British, didn't like to give ground away so easily, and so they conducted a counter-attack, from which we conducted a counter, counter-attack, and the Germans a counter, counter, counter-attack, and for what seemed like eternity to the men fighting the battle, for it seemed like days, it went on and on, and of course there was a lot of killing, but in the end the hill was lost and the sodding bastards stood once more upon the ground of their choosing. But in the midst of this precious fighting was something more sinister which was to occur.

20th APRIL, 1915

The fighting upon the sloping ground known as hill 60 was continued without breath for fresh air when a massive bombardment ensued, all the ground encompassing the Ypres salient seeming to be smeared in hell with debris and dirt flying high into the sky. The carnage was horrific. I had heard that in medieval times they launched cattle at one another from trebuchets and the like, but to see men flying through the air, torn limb from limb, is something that is much worse and could never be celebrated: but some of us might be of different mind when seeing the teenagers of today trying with all their mite to prove how absurdly insolent they can be, laughing at heinous scenes of men being killed on the TV screen or at the cinema. I don't think I need to tell you that it isn't romantic.

The bombardment was considered a measurable response to the three craters made by us. But the sod was stepping precariously too close to the edge, for there was no room in war for the killing of civilians, but that is what they did. They destroyed a most beautiful town and many of its citizens. Until that day there were many that suffered profusely in order to stay in their homes but the German shelling had turned nasty and made up the mind of many men and women in regards to overstaying their welcome in their own homes. But for those that decided to stay, they did not stay long.

The Second Battle of Ypres consisted of four major battles spread over thirty-three days. The Battle of Gravenstafel was from 22nd April to 23rd and I was not there to see what manner of poor judgements – and some would say heinous – that the damn sods were conjuring up and performing for the sake of their generals' sick minds.

I was not yet on the front line at Ypres but I would be soon enough. It was 1700hrs and the French were being assaulted…. The French are from Martinique, an island of the Caribbean Sea of just 436 square miles; even these men of unfathomable courage see to their duty as all good men do and on the grapevine I hear that something is amiss. The ranks are breaking, running from the greenish-yellow mist which fills the air over such a vast area that the retreat forces a seven kilometre gap in the allied defences.

Why are they running from a smoke screen? Is there something others on the adjoining flanks cannot see? Are there waves upon waves of Germans on the attack? No. Nothing can be seen except the smoke that fills the air. And so the trenches are abandoned quickly, left to the Germans if they should take good advantage of the situation, but even they are not moving. There is no German assault. The Kaiser, those dirty sods, are not making good the vacated positions. It then dawned upon me as I heard this story and before being told, just for a moment in time, that the smoke screen is something more than I had first considered and assumed. Why would brave men retreat from trenches, whether good or bad?

But some hearts of steel soon restore faith within the minds of all for it is brought to their attention, colourful NCOs and officers of good character offering words of encouragement, and the 1st Canadian Division, along with remnants of the French, have retaken the trenches left so hastily behind and the land is reclaimed once more, though considerably more sparse in man power than existed before.

The soldiers to a man saw the smoke fill the air, thick and fast, 168 tons delivered in 5,730 cylinders [which I would come to learn in the future, for when something so heinous occurs on your doorstep you are prone to find out about it as surely as you are born, live, and then die]. My stomach turns at hearing the cracked voice of the 'old sweat'. Somehow I wish I was at sea and that the bell would toll 'it's five O'clock and all is well', but all is not well and I am tired, as all are, of this stinking predicament in which we find ourselves. And then I consider, rather stupidly and without good cause, whether or not they would say 'five O'clock', for I am not at sea but a landlubber through and through. Such ridiculous thoughts inhibit the mind, more so to be rid of this insanity called war. But it seems our duty now to live and die for king and country, but the king would not wish death to fall upon us: not such a thought is considered when reflecting upon some of the generals within our courageous army but even they, too, must consider the larger picture, even at the expense of human life. And so we see that chlorine gas has been used for the first time but we know it won't be the last. The first step towards great villainy has been taken and cannot be retrieved.

Oh, my dear God! It was dusk when the gas attack occurred. The men in the trenches and those on the run can smell something similar to pineapple and pepper before coming under the effect of the gas, and it is so thick in many places that it is hard to see the sod as he exits his trenches and comes towards our line. Who can blame our men for running: not I? And although there was no initial German assault, the ranks of the enemy now spilled out of their trenches. The Germans follow the gas cloud some 15 minutes later and have their masks on but don't breathe easily; there are also many who have the masks simply resting upon their heads in order to fight more leisurely. The masks restrict, are a pain to wear, but worse still is the fear that the effects of the gas might just well fall upon them; so why do they advance so?

No matter where one would care to look, the scene is the same. Men are falling all over, severe pains in the chest, burning in their throats. They can hardly breathe, poor bastards. They drop like flies, six thousand dead in ten minutes. The pain; the liver damage; years of misery to come for those that survive, although there are few that can consider themselves lucky, even though they wished themselves dead to alleviate the suffering imposed upon them.

I have heard and seen many atrocities, but what do you call it when a German yanks the weapon you carry in your arms as you crouch dying from gas, and he says to you to lie still and die better? It is understandable in some cases to see why it is not practicable to take prisoners. All the prisoners the Germans might want are before them but they are all dying. Why take a dead man prisoner?

The French on the left flank of the Canadians have also abandoned their positions, along with more than 50 artillery pieces, guns which must be taken back over the coming days if at all possible. If the sod is smart he'll destroy them all, or set booby-traps.

I can imagine the men at the billets now, playing soccer or a game of cards, resting on their behinds and eating a hot meal. I can see them now hearing the news of poison gas and each and every one of them looking at each other and asking what the hell is poison gas. It must be as much of an uproar at the billets as on the front, but at the billets they will be preparing for battle whereby those at the trenches are trying to escape from it.

The gas attack upon our brothers was nothing shy of an incurable shock as wave after wave of insurmountable struts of fear struck each and every one of them in mass and by turn. First a few would come under effect and then the masses would learn. It wasn't a lesson to be taught over a pint at the local, for the learning curve was so acute that it was practically, and for all intents and purposes, non-existent.

How such a thing as this could be allowed to happen. Weren't generals, and other leaders who never dared to take step upon the battlefield, supposed to consider all factors of engagement prior to practical use; but there was no practical way of expressing how such a demon like poison gas could have been allowed to escape the chamber of its existence. Lying dormant and ready to maim and kill, this gas was delivered within projectiles; within shells of the German artillery. Were these sane men that stood opposite us; but no, that couldn't be? I recalled how they had exposed themselves to undue good cause by allowing us to kill them in their thousands during the retreat from Mons. And although I was not present during the early days of Mons I was still to learn from experience for there was no other moment in time that I could recall where men around me would express how similar it was that these bastards took orders from their officers to assault us in waves, to be gunned down like flies, as though a poison of their own to contend with. How could it possibly be that mature men who commanded over a million troops could authorize the use of such a weapon that was lashing out at us in such silence as now?

We would come to learn of many factors in regards to gas exposure during the four years of war in and around France and Flanders. So many names to so many variants existed but all in all it made little difference, for the fear was always the same and could hardly be quelled, and such quelling came in forms of protection which were quick to be granted us, protection which would allow us to kill these bastard Germans who were soldiers just like us: maybe not just like us. Maybe we were a special breed, for we were fighting for different ideas and when your back was against the wall the true colours of the Union Jack came to full fruition. Our blood was not red, but red, white, and blue. We fought for the country we loved, for family which was so dear to us all. To me and many others it didn't matter at all, that after the Battle of Albert [the Somme] there was a piece of paper with signatures upon it declaring that England would abide by its treaty and attack German forces as duty declared in the defence of others. I was here for many reasons, including the men beside me, but most of all I was here to see justice done, to see the innocent protected, to see a bright future cast from our combined miseries in order for unborn children and grandchildren to bear the fruits of our sacrifice. These men beside me, although time spent at training is far different than that spent at war, and which I was to learn solidly over the coming years, that comradeship and general friendship, even towards those that you had little in common with on civilian street, were like twin brothers, men that you cared about more than you cared for yourself. But I also knew from stories told that such feelings of devotion would subside and the experiences of the trenches to come could never be felt again with the power that was currently on the climb at a rapid rate. It is a for a variety of reasons that we find ourselves here, that is true, but for the vast majority, and to answer the question, it is for the man beside you; for those of your platoon, company and division that you suffer as you do, and fight to the death with tooth and nail. Although we would love to feel that it is for king and country, we all know deep down and after long years of fighting that we do not fight for the king, or for devotion to the country we love.

You might well tell me that only a small percentage of those men, like me, exposed to such heathen weapons of war died from such exposure, but what of the wounded.

Towards the end of this war the use of gas was so widespread that it was hard to fathom such; even we, the men of the civilised world, did banter and partake in the dreadful use of poison gas. Our philosophy was an eye for an eye. If they bomb us to hell then we shall bomb them back; if they should gas us then beware, you shall not reap the sweet reward of victory for the stone will be cast right back.

Wasn't it a strange thought, that good always seemed to prosper over evil in the same way that hard work always rewarded those hardest at it and the lazy of the earth dwelled in squalor: but there are always the lucky few but we are referring to statistics and percentages, and the percentage at the moment is that poison gas delivered a three per cent death rate to our ranks, a double-edged weapon which would sometimes, with the unpredictable changing of the wind, wrought havoc upon those so ready to employ the gas in the first place. Statistics didn't stop there however, for two per cent of the total gas fatalities were made permanently invalid, with seventy per cent more than usually able to return to the field within six weeks of contamination; but then again maybe I am wrong. It was a silent killer and seemed to work hand in hand with nature, nature which didn't seem to appear before our eyes on many occasions for the landscape around us was bare of any natural ensemble of woods, grass, flowers or wild animals. How wonderful it would be to see a bird fly by right now.

I had heard, and even now deliberate considerably upon the past, that the French may well have initiated the use of gas by delivering to within the German ranks a tear gas in such small quantities that it was barely noticeable, sent over-the-wall, so to speak, in 26mm grenades. It is to consider whether this was a torment which altered German behaviour or something else rather benign. Surely a tear-inducing agent was fair in war and would allow the enemy to be bayoneted more efficiently, and fell short of going against the Hague Treaty of 29th July 1899 where three main points of interest gained my attention in later years: That the contracting powers agreed to abstain from using projectiles for the delivery of asphyxiating or deleterious gases; that the declaration be binding in the case of war between two or more of the contracting powers, and; the agreement would cease to be a binding agreement where, in the case of war a belligerent should be joined by a non-contracting power.

I see now that the French in August 1914 could well have induced the fear we all now suffer on a day to day basis, outing into the minds of our adversaries this heinous weapon of mental and physical destruction. I could only wish that the Germans had continued with their initial and nonthreatening attacks of October 1914, for their use of gas was as detrimental as the attacks of August and meant very little to anyone. It would be fair to say that only in the darkest crevices of the most insane mind could the thought of a gas possible of killing thousands should be produced and delivered upon the battlefield, yet the Hague Treaty could well see the future to come. What ever happened on the Russian Front I do not know, but hearsay has it that 18,000 shells containing gas were fired at the Russians in January: but I heard nothing more of this – such wicked things were shunned by me for by the end of the war I had truly had enough. My mind had deteriorated to the point of near insanity, on the edge of the abyss, at the point of no return, but I somehow saved myself for the days to come where married bliss would see me with a large and loving family. But back to the war I must tread, for the story has only just begun.

Everyone across the great expanse of the front had soon learnt the truth of the situation however, as news of the situation reached the ears of every man, woman and child, and that was that the smoke was a poisonous gas.

I am lucky and feel that way, but that irritation of guilt fills me like a sieve choking up with filaments that form a thick screen, and I know that it will be my turn soon enough, for the Germans are a sodden lot. They claim that the attacks do not go against the treaty of 1899, that there is no violation of international law, for what they are employing are not chemical shells but gas projectiles. It is a ridiculous way of looking at the situation but all tied up in the German soldier's character for the conscript he is, so wrought with wrong doing that theft, rape and murder are scenarios that replay themselves time and again in countries like Belgium. Yes indeed, the Germans are a sodden lot for what they have done and continue to do. How can they ever be forgiven?

Men drew deeper breaths as they ran and in doing so found death knocking upon their doors all the sooner. Try as they might they could not outrun the gas which was spreading as fast as the wind could carry it, about six miles an hour. Imagine if you will, running along with the cloud of poisonous gas at your back and as it catches you, you try all the more to out-distance it. Death would have been all the easier if the men had stayed in the bottom of their trenches: maybe even survived. Eyes are wide open, the look of shock and terror upon their faces as they cough and cough so heavily, substance like glue pouring out their mouths in many cases. The men were being asphyxiated. Here they are, running for dear life, the town of Ypres in the background burning with fury as flames lick the town clean from the landscape in many places. People were running and screaming, carrying the young and old, buildings collapsing around them and the gas cloud not very far away. But they were too concerned for their welfare and dodging of bombs to be concerned with a damn smoke screen, for behind that screen there would surely be the sod coming upon them at the run. But this wasn't the case, although the gas cloud could be considered a smoke screen, the sod was fifteen minutes behind it.

And so the men continued to retreat in overwhelming panic and the horses of the artillery were absconded and employed to get the hell out of there, the guns left behind, for men were more important than artillery. Others dropped all their gear but the few that were so overwhelmed, they had gone almost insane with terror and pain, had forgotten to get rid of their burden upon their backs.

By 1900hrs the sod had taken much ground and had crossed the Steenbeck, approaching St Julien. It was here that the Germans suffered a vast majority of their casualties for the 10th Field Battery of 18-pounder guns could see the massive column of Germans moving across the ground some three hundred yards away, a moving target in the open, a site for sore eyes, an opportunity of a lifetime. And so with iron sights and quick hands the artillery took to pouring ammunition into the fray. The enemy were obliterated, but many more existed in and around the vast area known as the salient.

It was now becoming quite clear that there existed within the frontline a gap of some 8000 yards, or thereabouts, split into sectors: roughly speaking there was a 2000 yard gap, a 1000, and a 3000 [yes, that's right, adds up to 6000, but its extent is what was of greatest concern, for flanking was a favourite way in which to attack an enemy]. It seemed that the enemy were winning but then they stalled: at around 2000hrs they stalled.

Why did they stall; why did the attack appear to falter? It couldn't have been casualties alone because the Germans cared very little, or so it seemed, about the loss of a few thousand conscripts. Regardless of this I wish that the others in which Smith-Dorrien, the Horse, was sharing his table at dinner, would have seen the light in contrast to rumours of gas and have withdrawn to a position just beyond the canal.

I later learn that the sodding attack has slowed to a crawl, and to a stop in places, because the Germans had advanced into pockets of their own gas, and wearing the masks upon their heads, as most of them do, they had becoming weary: it is true to say that the crude respirators were not so efficient as the higher ranks would have liked. Two miles of ground they have taken and suddenly there is a moment's pause. More and more of them were coming under the effects of the gas and the scene around them didn't provide much comfort, for they could see the dying faces of the French and Canadians as they either died on the ground or thrashed about for air.

The sod had become a victim of his own creation.

But there is something else that I learned to appreciate and that was the unwavering success of the gas which was completely unexpected. The Germans had advanced as far as they had been ordered to advance, and used the gas as a means for which to halt and dig in. The shoe may have been on the other foot had their respirators worked as well as they should have, and the advance may have been undertaken to exploit their current position and route the allies even further afield.

And again, one more note to remember and this being the most important; the sheer courage of the Canadians cannot be expressed enough for even those slightly affected by the passing gas, holding out in the bottom of their holes in the ground, or having the sheer good fortune not to have been hit by the gas at all, stood their ground to repel the sod at every point that they could. So here you have many pockets of resistance standing to fight against the power of the axis as they falter here and there. The Germans knew full well of the BEF and their ability with the Lee Enfield and bayonet as much as they knew the hard core within the Canadians, for many lived in the wilderness, were lumberjacks, and carried more muscle upon their huge frames than they carried in equipment upon their backs.

The sheer terror felt by the Germans, for all manner of reason, was the reason for the garrison of 50,000+ men of the salient to have survived. The sod had come so close to capturing the entire salient and 150 guns: so close but no cigar.

It was now dark, and although the air was filled with the sounds of war the assault had stopped at every point. The wounded were now evacuated. It is here that many disturbing scenes are met. Can you imagine coming upon a man who is sitting there with his back to the wall of the trench with weapon in his hands as though ready to get up and discharge another clip of ammunition, and then on second glance you look upon him further for he hasn't answered your request for aid in helping a wounded mate. You then shake him and realise that he's dead; his head had been pierced with hot shrapnel and he had died instantaneously? It is amazing how men die. It is as though some of them have been frozen in life, a wax model of their true selves performing some duty or another; but dead. It is something that dreams are made of, dreams that haunt you forever.

23rd APRIL, 1915

It wasn't long before we heard filtered words of wisdom from higher, trickling down to us; the men in the trenches. For the moment we were to take preventative measures from the effects of the gas, to avoid the poisonous substance afloat the wind at all costs. I didn't need an officer to tell me that, but I did need them to tell me what to do on breathing it in; after all, it's no use taking a bucket to a horse at feeding time if the bucket is empty.

Instructions soon filtered down that a wet handkerchief or some other form of cloth, held over the mouth as you breathed, would be sufficient enough to protect us from mild saturations of poison gas. If it was a high concentration then we were reminded of our service to the king and country and that we were of the British military. This was well and good and believed by all I knew, but it was a hard pill to swallow when the gas came towards you at six miles an hour, able to outrun most men clad in the equipment of war and ready to fight.

Buckets of water were soon delivered to the trenches to be used against the gas, or we could urinate upon a handkerchief and hold this against our mouths; either would be appropriate until better means could be secured. Even the nuns at the convent at Poperinge started to give good aid by making lint bandages for us to use, and by the time fresh rations were being delivered on the evening of 24th we were most thankful to the brides of Christ, but that was still a day away yet, at present it was only 0100hrs, yes indeed, and the fighting continued with the allies trying to take back ground, fighting for survival.

I cannot tell you too much of what happened this day, for I am a part of the counter-attack. We are moving into position and on the morrow will enter battle once more. I truly feel as though I am an old soldier now, an old sweat, and we have many new faces. I help the new ones as best I can because it is hard to know what to do in trench warfare, for little is taught about it back at Aldershot, but sometimes I feel as though getting too acquainted will bring misery later on. Regardless of these feelings I carry on as best I can for we are all here to help one another and without such help I might very well not survive the war.

24th APRIL, 1915

The Battle of Saint Julien started today and ended on the 4th of May. It is no more difficult to recount than any other part of the beginning of the war because I am getting used to it, and by the time it is over I am like a robot and have accepted that I shall die sooner or later, and so find it harder to recall incidents. Imagine my sheer joy at finding myself still alive at the war's conclusion.

The Royal Dublin Fusiliers, of which you'll be kind enough to recall I belong, are almost at the point of being employed in the thick of battle, but we find that we have a single day's reprieve as we prepare. But the war goes on and so the tale must continue.

What can I tell you of the chlorine gas, very little in fact, in particular at the time of the attacks, but there was a chemist within the Canadian ranks [from Flanders Fields] who did well to work it all out, though one might say he knew from experience of its characteristics. I was also wounded by the gas but not today, so fortunate I was. But having been a sufferer of an attack, in the oh-so near future to come, I have licence, I believe, to understand something of the suffering.

The chlorine was well endowed to cause great pain and death but death only occurred in a very small percentage of cases: but damn it all, the suffering was bad enough. Damage to eyes, nose and lungs were ingredients for an easy fight as the sods from Germany saw it. I heard someone say, just a week after the incident at Ypres, that any prolonged exposure to the high concentration could kill you through asphyxiation. At first he didn't know what asphyxiation meant because he was not a man well tutored in the language of the king, but he was a quick learner. Once he knew the meaning of the word he couldn't stop using it. It was as though he was a fool yesterday and a scholar today. But I tell you this, throw away the damn books and other articles written on the gas because you only need to be scared out of you mind, clawing in the bottom of the trenches to try and hide from the menacing cloud as it approaches, to be killed by it; for exposure over just a few minutes is enough to kill any man: and who wasn't scared of the gas as it crawled its way towards you in a menacing cloud. Oh, sure, when we first saw the cloud we thought little, for old habits die hard and the image initially cast upon the mind is that it is a smoke screen, but I tell you this, if we had known of the dangers then we would have been running up behind the French, who had several days head start, and then overtake them all, just to get away from the affected area.

Pray to God that the wind changes soon.

It is nice to hear the officers and generals give advice as learnt from testing, that to remain at your post was better than to run, for when you ran you breathed hardy and drew the gas into your lungs. Less damage was said to affect those that remained standing in the trench or even sitting upon the edge of the parapet. What was this; it seems that the sod from across no-man's-land has come to join the allies; a spy in officer's clothing. What damn fool would be game enough to sit upon his parapet when the heaviest danger of all was exposure to sniper fire? Or can you convince a man to stand-to in his trench to fight off the damn sods as they come upon you in their thousands with artillery fire as support, which softened up the trenches as the gas came rolling over the flat plains of the Ypres battlefield. Maybe in another place; maybe at another time; but certainly not at a time when one is exposed to immoral weaponry and has no knowledge of it other than the death it causes.

But it is a lesson to be learnt for the future, to sit tight and breathe easily, to stand your ground and allow the gas to flow over you as it continues on with the wind to pass you by. Damn fools; they're all full of advice. Every single man here wants to do his duty but it gets rather hard, sometimes.

That greenish-yellow cloud [and with this the colour seems to change from time to time as though it has something to do with the sky or the sun; I do not know] of death had its moments for the sod, but it probably wasn't as effective as the Germans would have hoped. There were soon many countermeasures one could use against a gas attack, and you could see the damn stuff rolling towards you when an attack was in progress, so it wasn't as though you had no warning. It was easy to detect by smell, which was useful if you ended up in a trench which had been exposed to chlorine gas, for its residue might linger around for some time after it had been employed.

After the war I was always reminded of the gas attacks whenever I saw a bank of fog early in the morning. I could see the dead, recall the horror. But I was not alone.

It didn't take long for counter-measures to be pulled into place although it was more of a command being issued, for orders had to flow from top to bottom, and as any soldier will tell you, that can make the difference between life and death, as the counter-attacks upon the breaches at Ypres had shown.

It is needless for me to say that the sod were all issued with some form of mask, and from what I know, which is usually limited, or has changed so much in its description as it was passed by word-of-mouth, that they had small gauze pads of cotton which were moistened with a bicarbonate solution to either dampen the effects of the gas or null it completely. The German high ranks didn't seem to care about the thousands killed during their wave attacks so why would they care about a few soldiers going through the trauma of inhaling poison gas? This I learnt much later on in the war for our initial counter-measures seemed to be a little cruder but otherwise effective: though in heavy concentrations of the gas it was inevitable that we would suffer in some way.

I hate talking about the gas attacks; it chills me to the bone, so you'll excuse me if I refrain from too much deliberation.

And so the Germans have launched another attack commencing with artillery at 0300hrs, and yes, the gas was amongst the shells delivered. It was directed at the Belgians that existed upon the line. They were exemplary in their will to hold their ground and try to out-manoeuvre the sod by trying to outflank him.

At 0400hrs further gas was released from the ground and the attack fell upon the salient, and although there was fear of the gas, the strength of the men's calibre held strong, for there was little surprise in anything the sod carried out this day.

Ample enough water buckets and handkerchiefs were often enough to ward off the worse of the effects of the gas attack as the Germans, ten minutes later, came pouring out of their trenches, but where the gas came rolling over the ground in its thickest the torture of its effects upon men was most profound. And it is here that bravery cast its beautiful head amongst the ugly caricature of the sod, for many men amongst the Canadians knew that they were going to die but stood their ground to kill as many Germans as they could, to give their deaths good cause, to provide their mates with that support in warfare which matters the most. The Germans were so packed together in mass, so confident of their superiority that it was to become their undoing. Yes, the gas will do its duty, many soldiers will retreat as before, and the French... so pitiful they are. But the Germans failed to count on the true character of good men willing to sacrifice themselves for such a greater cause. With little to no artillery support or the ridiculous Ross rifle, the Canadians put a stop to the German advance upon them.

As I have mentioned before I indicated the poor quality of the

Ross. They continued to jam all along the line and at a time of great need. Here were the Germans in mass and rapid fire was required. Men didn't have time to kick the bolt back with the heel of their boot, or to hit it back with the entrenching tool, so Lee Enfields were taken from corpses here and there. Some men even procured them permanently to replace their Ross, and where officers scrutinized heavily the absconding of the weapon, men were afforded little choice and hence carried both; their Ross in order to keep the officers happy, and the Lee Enfield to keep them safe from harm. There was also a great reliance upon sheer infantry skill at arms and the general use of the machine gun and bayonet. Yes indeed, the bayonet; one of the many pride and joys of the BEF and its supporters; but such a shame that the enemy were too cowardly to come close enough to be skewered by our sheer audacity.

All day long the sod would attack and then retreat; attack and fall back; attack and cower away. When would they learn? It was easier to teach an old dog a new trick.

And when the sun goes down we shall remember them, with their tails between their legs as they scarper away to the reasonable assurance and safety of their trenches: until the morning.

25th APRIL, 1915

And the morning comes soon enough. It is 0330hrs in the morning and there is a huge amount of confusion. I shall tell you what I learnt, not of what I knew, for if I told you simply of what I knew then it would be a very short story.

Zero hour had been planned for 0330hrs, whereupon all those battalions of hardened men beneath the officer Hull were to perform in a counter-attack upon the enemy, to take back from the stinking sod both Kitchener's Wood and St. Julien. And how many battalions did Hull have? Why, ten. How many were to be in the assault? Why, five, of course. I heard that the other five battalions were doing other duties somewhere else either on or behind the line, and/or simply didn't receive orders in time to come to the party: and how lucky they were.

0330hrs and we were still not yet in position, and so Hull delayed the hour of the attack by two hours, but someone had forgotten to give word to all of the artillery. What was supposed to be an attack by night ended up being an attack by day, and the sod was given plenty of warning – as though they needed any – and a gift. The gift was our lives.

The Canadian and British artillery that were so ill-informed that they opened up at 0330hrs as advised, but not only did they commence preparatory, but several units fired upon St. Julien itself. This would normally not have been a great issue but today it brought much regret. It had been reported that 200 men were still amongst the ruins and that we were not to fire upon it, so of course, not only were our artillery firing upon our own men but at the same instant we were signalling to the Germans that the town was empty of allied troops, henceforth the sod entered the town, killed what little resistance might have been left, and set up machine guns to cover the killing ground in which we were to cross in daylight. It was also a great opportunity for enemy snipers to set themselves up for a smorgasbord of human flesh.

As well as bad fortune there was a little good. Canadian artillery, unknowingly but advantageously, cut to pieces a German assault that was preparing itself at Kitchener's wood to attack the allied line. This is the only good news I could see from any which direction I cared to look for zero hour was upon us and we commenced to move forward, the artillery exceedingly good but low on ammunition.

As for the weather; what can I say? It was raining hard and there was a mist that lay thick upon the ground and in the air. If nothing else it should afford a little cover, and also prevent us from easily seeing any landmarks for reference in our movement forward.

Hull had set up his battalions so that the 1st and 2nd Royal Dublin Fusiliers were facing St. Julien on the right of the line, and the 2nd Seaforth Highlanders and 1st Royal Warwickshire facing Kitchener's Wood on the left of the line. The 7th Argyll and Sutherland Highlanders were in support directly behind those on the left of the line.

The whistle blows and we move forward, weapons at the ready, at the hip, or held across the body: each to his own. The rain has stopped but the mist is still around, but there is not enough of it. Snipers open up upon us immediately and men start to fall, the machine guns commence soon after and the misery is heaping up as though dung upon a mound. Bullets whiz and crack-thump from buildings and long grass. Wherever it is that snipers hide, they shoot to kill, and do well at their primary function. They are disciplined individuals that account for many deaths in the first few minutes of the attack across the flat plains of Flanders. Our advance holds strong; for we are as disciplined, if not more so than the stinking snipers hiding like cowards and shooting us down, but I must remember that we too have our own snipers who perform the same task so wonderfully.

Our objectives are one mile to our front and we maintain good direction in the face of murderous fire, but the murderous fire is about to become a lot worse.

We are dealing with the sniper fire, and now dealing with the machine gun fire; but it is hard to also deal with the further, additional machine gun fire which now comes at us from just south of Kitchener's Wood and Juliet Farm. We are seemingly caught in enfilade, crossing fire. There is no way out of it but straight ahead, to literally walk through the wall of fire from all machine guns which cross our path. It is impossible to believe that we can live through this hell fire being poured down upon us; it is beyond horrific; it is beyond insane; it is not human.

We are now rushing forward in groups, taking bounds as best we can, and as I move forward I looked both left and right. I see hundreds and hundreds of my comrades lying down. I think this is good because they must be pouring fire upon the enemy, covering their mates so that we can gain ground upon the objectives, and then the reality of it all sinks in. they are not laying down, putting in covering fire; they are all dead. Dead to a man and in what looks like

straight lines. The walls of machine gun fire have put a stop to many, but the others, including myself, continue on. I cannot believe it. I look again, this time to the right as I take temporary cover. Ten men are rushing forward and then they hit the ground. It seems so uniform; appears so on-purpose; but it isn't; they too are all dead. I get up and move forward some more, I see men coming along with me but the gaps between us has grown. I feel sick in the stomach; I feel like crying; but the adrenalin in my body prevents me from considering the alternatives to doing my duty. We have lost almost half our men and yet we continue forward and the machine gun fire is not abating.

Suddenly I see a signal. A corporal with more guts than garters is telling us all to get down. I see beyond him some men trying to make a break for it by retreating but they have second thoughts. We all lie down then and get out our entrenching tools. We dig for our lives, and if I hadn't an entrenching tool then I'd have used my teeth and nails. A young boy appears beside me. He's crying and shit scared. He has dropped beside me because he didn't want to be alone in death. He sought me out because all those around him had been shredded to pieces by bullets.

I can hear men, just barely, screaming over the noise of battle to comrades. They get together in their small groups and dig, dig, dig. They scrape hollows within the ground to get away from the murderous fire. The boy beside me is looking at me from time to time and so I give him encouragement. I tell him we'll be okay, and that help will come when the reserves are let loose and when the artillery targets the enemy machine guns; but I don't believe it myself. I shall fight to the death but I know I shall die. No man can live through this.

In other places, so I later learnt, they continue on into the fray.

They barely survived.

It was sometime before we got our courage up again and every now and again small groups tried to push forward but the going was too hard. No sooner did you show your untidy little head and the gunners were upon you as fast as the snipers.

The officers were the hardest hit for they were all advancing at the front of their battalions, companies and platoons. So now it is the corporals and sergeants that perform miraculously, with such bravery and great courage that it is hard to believe men can have such steadfast character and will power.

The 7th Argyll and Sutherland Highlanders came in to support those to their front, the Dublin Fusiliers had little aid. Nevertheless, the 7th Argyll and Sutherland Highlanders were decimated as those before them. None of us had come close to encountering the sod with a bullet, let alone our bayonets, and we were only a few hundred yards from our objective.

Later still and two fresh battalions arrived upon the scene. They too were sacrificed for no reason at all, and by 0700hrs we commenced to withdraw and crawl our way back to the rear as best we could. We can praise the artillery for allowing us to live to fight another day but that can't be said for more than half of us. Not including the battalion sent in to give us aid we had lost 73 officers and 2,346 other ranks.

We had been annihilated, but do you know what was to become of us? We were to be put back into the fight, burdened with fighting in the battle of Frezenberg and Bellewaarde over the next four weeks.

And where were the French? I do not know. Maybe they'd been pinned down somewhere because we saw and heard little fighting from them.

But the day was not over yet for at 1830hrs there was to be another effort made against the Germans gains. The French were requested, rather caudally I would presume, to give aid to the Turcos, a unit made up of Africans, along with the Indian Division. The Turcos did not last long and were last seen fleeing to the rear yelling out 'gas, gas' as they ran. There were wild stories floating around after that, that the Turcos had fled back over the canal and were raping nurses and shooting officers trying to prevent them from withdrawing; chasseurs were even called in to help restore order. But I shall refrain from making further comments. It is also at around this time that Smith-Dorrien was ordered to stand down and hand control of all his men to Plumer. I too shall refrain from making any further comment, for I have already advised you how I felt about that good man, full of good, strategic knowledge.

The only good fortune for us was the fact that by the end of this day enough reinforcements had arrived that it appeared impossible for the sod to expel us from the salient. New lines had been drawn but battles would be waged to alter them further, and they would never be the same as before.

28th APRIL, 1915

Today was the day that Smith-Dorrien received the ironic conclusion that he'd not deserved his sacking, for Plumer was given advice on the withdrawal of his troops, a withdrawal which Smith-Dorrien had begged for. Plumer was to be withdraw back to a position that very night as previously suggested by Smith-Dorrien, and so it would seem that we have lost a good commander in Sir Horace, all for the sake of the commander above him [French] to carry out actions which undoubtedly relieved the jealousy he was feeling towards the Horse. It is a pity; no; it is a dying shame that men's lives are treated so poorly because actions such as the relinquishing of commanders for no good reason other than overpowering spite were being carried out. It is however a little rewarding to hear that French was accosted slightly by Foch [his boss] who refused French the option of withdrawal over the option of conducting further counter-attacks over the next few days.

It is true to say however that Plumer was also disgusted by the way in which Smith-Dorrien had been treated. Plumer's orders for the withdrawal were no different than what would have occurred had Smith-Dorrien's appeal fell upon open ears, but French, for all intents and purposes, appeared to be nothing less than a death mute, and no pun of any description is intended here for those poor brethren that are born handicapped, for I fight for them as well as I fight for my own family.

Oh, dear; it does seem that the higher up you climb the ladder in rank the harder it is to find men of great calibre, but maybe we all consider this the way, for we are the ones who live with mud and faeces up to our armpits and with lice in every hem of our clothing.

The main withdrawal, when it finally came, was on the night of the 3rd of May, concluded by sunrise on the 4th, even though some portions of the line were moved rearward on the night previous to this. So here we have Sir Horace, relieved of command for no good reason and French and Foch both finally seeing, one way or another, that he was right in his ideas for the sake of his men and the good of his country. Just how many lives could have been saved from wanton destruction we shall never know?

4th MAY, 1915

The withdrawal is complete but Ypres still stands within the protection of men, a semicircle of defence around the entire town, the salient reduced in size but still very much in allied hands. Being approximately three miles shorter in length meant that fewer men were required to defend it. It was a relief to all of those involved and I shall never forget the decimation of our good units which were flung in front of the murderous fire in an attempt to take back what we had lost; but I also feel as though we have been unjustly deprived the company of our comrades deceased, for we ended up withdrawing in any case.

War… the stupidity of it will boggle our minds for eternity but we shall still be faced with sending men to their deaths, and why is this? Because there will always be mad men in the world that others are too scared to stand up to.

At 1000hrs the Battle of Saint Julien was officially over.

Two further actions in the beginning of May gave that month something to remember it by. Firstly we saw that Smith-Dorrien was sent home and was never to be awarded a command again. Secondly, the Lusitania was sunk on the 7th May 1915 by a German U-boat. This flung the Americans into the war, for the unnecessary and obvious murder of 1,198 civilians could not be accepted and would be retaliated. The only question now is how long will it take for the Americans to send ground troops into the trenches?

8th MAY, 1915

We are at the Battle of Frezenberg which concludes on the 13th of May. There is little to note of our combined efforts to deflect the enemy advance and skew it into oblivion; all I can offer is that the 10th brigade, of which I belonged, proved once more its stubbornness to be moved. Again we fought heroically and conducted counter-attacks as ordered. We seem to be good at what we do, possibly too good, for if we faltered somewhere within the requirements of an infantry soldier then maybe, just maybe, the higher ranks might consider throwing someone else at the line. But we never shirked our responsibility.

On the 10th May the sod released more gas upon the trenches but this had little effect upon us. The cloud was not as thick, it was in smaller pockets as compared to previous attacks, and we had countermeasures to put into place which seemed to help where the gas was not too dense.

I would like to also advise you that at some time during my four

The Poor State of War and Conflict

[plus] years of service in the trenches I was wounded once by the gas which saw me issued with blighty leave, however, the custodian of my word and history [the author of this work] does not know the date of my injury and so he has failed to reflect upon it. This cannot be helped and I know you would love to hear about my withdrawal to the aid station, to hospital, and then home, I cannot tell it to you. Neither can I shed further light on my coming together with my new family. I shall tell you this, and this is all I can manage: before returning to the front I was able to be with my wife and she fell pregnant once more. I was now more determined than ever to come back home in one piece but had to maintain the view that I was dead already in order to accept death and not to lower the morale of the men around me if I should pass into the forever night. The custodian of my memory is making allowances and guessing that I shall be wounded on the 24th May and you shall find out soon enough why; I was on blighty for as few as three weeks.

But back to the reality that is war. The sod had pushed us back 2000 yards and so I must assume that the gas and their artillery were doing the work of their soldiers, for the conscript was no match for our good training.

The idea that the sod seemed to now hold better artillery and more ammunition in which to fire at us was not easy to swallow, but the fault of the issue lies with the English Government's inability to manufacture all we needed. The sheer lack of ammunition was seeing to it that we could not match, round for round, the German onslaught, but this was about to change for the better.

Several points need to be clarified here. The men who were set to work in places such as the munitions factories and coal mines were being swallowed up by the military to replace the fallen within the trenches and to strengthen the front as a whole by increasing the number of battalions, brigades and divisions as a whole. Having factories and mines alone does not help if there is no one to work them.

It is here that we see David Lloyd George being made the Minister of Munitions and a good choice he was. It is thanks to him and the woman of our great nation that we would soon see the new appointment pay hugely in our favour.

The German idea that they had artillery superiority was about to be turned upon its head and it would not be long now before the tables would be turned.

24th MAY, 1915

This was a terrible day for the 2nd Royal Dublin Fusiliers; the Battle of Bellewaarde which lasted but two days. We had been decimated as it was on the lead up to this day, being cut down maliciously on the 25th April, but today was to prove to be even worse.

The Germans were not about to give up on their efforts in taking Ypres, in particular where it appeared to them that they had come so close to completing their task. It must have seemed an extreme amount of bad luck had befallen them and so they tried once more.

The entire line was well prepared for the onslaught and when it came it came as expected. The sod released a heavy gas cloud of chlorine at 0245hrs which extended for approximately four and a half miles. Behind this the sodding infantry followed with their respirators in place here and there and full of confidence but caution. Along with the artillery and gas the Germans did well to take and capture a few key areas upon the ground, namely Mouse Trap Farm and Bellewaarde Ridge on which the attack was named.

The attack lasted all day and although the sod was cut to pieces in many places they appeared to do more damage to us than we did to them. Ypres was also dealt a miserable hand and practically ploughed flat by artillery from the ground on which it stood.

Nearer St. Julien I was doing my duty as others were doing around me. We had been cut to around half our strength but once again, but continued on. We were flanked by another of the 10th and felt comfortable with the support but plainly disheartened by previous losses. It was then that the gas hit us and hit us hard. It seemed to me that the cotton masks we had been issued were cruder than first considered and we succumbed to the terrible uncertainty of what life was like with a lungful of gas. We suffered greatly; too great to honestly fathom.

By last light we were just one officer and 20 other ranks remaining fit for full duty; 645 others were dead, wounded, or missing beneath the great piles of earth which had rained from the sky due to German artillery. It was a most horrid day but the 2nd Royal Dublin Fusiliers would return to continue the fighting. Many of those wounded suffered badly, as bad as any other man drawing in a lungful of gas. It took many men several years to die; others lived in poor health for the remainder of their lives. I would return.

Some good did come of the Second Battle of Ypres, and some bad points are always remembered. A system of gas alert and readiness was devised by alarms, masks, and gas-proof shelters, all of which reduced the impact of the chlorine. Our generals woke up to the fact that the French could not be relied upon for they failed to give aid where aid was required, their lack of support in the attack, defence, and counter-attack taken to heart. And commanders in general continued to put us in harm's way by insisting we do the impossible;

henceforth we were often stunned hard by outrageous losses and little reward. It would be at least two more years before we started to see the light at the end of the tunnel.

6 July, 1915

I received a letter from my wife of ten months. It was actually longer than that but I didn't count the time spent in the trenches. For all I was concerned I had experienced ten months of married life and therefore that was all that mattered.

The letter was dated sometime in June, but the letter had gotten wet and some of it was illegible, but in it she expressed all that a good wife does along with much news on the home-front. It appeared that the Daily Mail had written an article and had placed this in their newspaper. It was to request that every single woman who could possibly give aid by manufacturing cotton pads should do so; these could then be employed by the boys on the front. I tell you, she was none too pleased to hear what the sod was doing to us, and all over the wording of policies so decreed by the Hague Treaty of 1899. I'd never heard of the Hague Treaty until advised by her, something she'd read, somewhere, but much talk on the subject came to air over the news for the immoral way in which Germany went about carrying out its hostile actions against us. The response was staggering; over a million pads were made in a day and shipped along with motorcycle goggles made available to protect our eyes. Don't you just love the heck out of those beautiful British Women; God bless every single one? It broke our hearts to learn that the design was, unfortunately, rather useless, for the design in the newspaper was not the best and actually went as far as causing suffocation when wet and the entire idea behind the cotton pads was for them the be wetted with a solution to help protect us against chlorine gas. Many men died because of this but I refrained from saying anything to her about it. Besides, by July six we were all issued with a supposedly well-designed respirator which consisted of a flannel bag which had a small window in the front, a window made of celluloid. The disappointing truth and reality was that the windows were very small and more often than not fogged over, accommodated for by our breathing: what audacity, for us to breathe. Amongst other things they became very hot, very quickly. The entire thing could be pulled over the head. Wherever I went from that day forth I carried it upon my head, except in winter when more efficient means to keep my head warm required I carry it elsewhere. We even had a standing order which told use where to carry it so that if you died and another guy needed it because his was shot to hell, then he could help himself to yours, and why not, the Canadians did the same with their Ross Rifles, throwing them aside for a Lee Enfield when one could be appropriated.

Many changes were seen from that day however, for with the introduction of means to counteract the gas became more efficient methods along with other poison gases to counteract the defences. It was also no surprise that the allies were quick, not only to condemn the use of poison gas as employed by the sods, but to hit back with a measured response by creating its own gas capabilities. We had every right.

And so I have seen more than 12 months of fighting, and having returned from being wounded the trenches look the same as they always did. I shall now have to get used to the poor conditions of living in the trenches once more, the softness of my bed at home to be forgotten for quite some time to come.

But what did it mean to live in the trenches? I have tried with little effort to give you an idea but I shall now draw further light onto the subject for your benefit.

I have passed a minor word on the sequence of stand-to earlier on, but now I shall discuss it in depth. Everyone in the trenches was required to be up and ready for an impending attack prior to first light. This period of transition was known as stand-to and carried out in total silence with guns and weapons manned, periscopes at the ready and positions maintained. With an uneventful morning and drawing in a brief breath of relief we would breakfast, clean weapons, and carry out menial tasks such as teeth cleaning, toileting and shaving.

Company commanders and RSMs would pass any untoward task onto company captains and CSMs who in turn would pass information onto Sergeants and corporals; LCPLs might then get to flex their muscle and privates would run around carrying out the chores assigned to them. But not all chores [or work parties for a better word] were handed down from so high. Platoon sergeants wore their rank because they were thinkers, able to administer a platoon and the men within it; they rarely required the CSM to go ramming his pace stick in every crevice to gain attention for tasks to be passed.

Much maintenance was carried out during the day but only within the safety on the trench system; any work that required doing which existed on top, our front, or just behind the parapet, trench, or bunker, was normally seen to by night when it was hardest to see our movement, but a single sound would bring machine gun fire to rain down upon us. It was therefore customary for many ruses to be performed in order to drain away the noise of wire being erected or a new trench system to be dug down nearer no-man's land than was preferred.

Sentry duty was also rostered within sections and or platoons, to listen and watch for any sign of enemy assault: anything out of the ordinary reported to the nearest NCO or officer.

Late evening was a time for replenishing supplies, bringing up fresh troops, rations, field equipment, and the forever sought relief, but not before another stand-to, as dusk turned into night. And the idea of bringing hot food up from the rear was because we weren't supposed to cook it in the trenches for signalling the enemy our position, disposition, or mental state. I guess the simple smell of food was harder to pinpoint, but smoke from a small fire drew much attention. A few bombs and machine gun bursts often spoiled a good hearty meal with dirt and crap flying everywhere. Rations were also brought up in either sandbags or hayboxes.

Reliefs were brought forward via the myriad of trenches. You had the 'fire trench' [or fighting/front], the 'support trench', and of course the 'reserve trench'. Each depth trench varied in depth but around six feet will suffice for this explanation, the fighting trench being the deepest at around 12 feet, often the floor of which was covered in duckboards, sandbags, or had firing steps inside – water was forever a problem in the bottom of trenches, in particular where the water table was high, and where there was no water there was mud. I'm sure that from time to time, in particular during the summer months, there was little to no water or mud, but the mind seems to remember the worst of the trench conditions and the more savoury of human souls. If you were to ask me if I remembered Bob I'd say, of course I do, always handy with a joke he was. But if you were to ask me about the trench I occupied on a daily basis I would call it a stinking mud hole in which it would be easy to drown.

Trenches were dug into the ground in a zigzag formation, each length on average being ten yards long, so that is a bomb dropped on your head the blast area was limited by the trenches length: I guess it also prevented your body parts from being blown too far away so your mates could pick up after you, but the job of picking up body litter was not pleasant at all. The lips of the trenches were also built up to help protect against bombs and artillery. The front you should know by now is called the parapet, but the rear was known as the parados. One guy I knew liked to call it paradise instead and said how he'd like to be five miles away from paradise with his feet up. And here's a statistic; it takes six hours for 450 men to dig 275 yards of trench system. You'll notice that I haven't mentioned the casualties within that statistic. Sometimes we were lucky and at others we weren't.

Sleeping conditions, as you can imagine, were not four-star.

Officers and senior NCOs had the best of the conditions with small bunkers in which to sleep, eat and give orders, daily pouring over maps and watches, but the poor old infantry private was doused in the misery of sleeping on two feet; with bottom on firing step in the sitting position; or laid back against the turf of a trench which might have half collapsed during a bombardment of the position. The best positions were those upon the duckboards with groundsheet flung beneath to prevent the damp from rising and issuing you with all manner of medical problems from rashes to chilblains.

Relief in place was something that is considered to have occurred, on average, once every eight days but I tell you this, later in the war some men were lucky to see any relief at all. Around 55 per cent of our time was spent within the three trenches on the front, being the fire, support and reserve. The remainder of our time was considered on leave, rest, or training. I can't agree with this however and must insist that time within the first three trenches amounted to at least 65 per cent, and leave in particular was nowhere near as often as it was supposed to have been: leave to the UK was lucky to come around every 16 months or more but was supposed to have been every eight: but it must have been an administrational nightmare to organize leave for so many men on the front. If you work out the mathematics it is staggering. When casualties are suffered; so do the living. I can also tell you the truth of the matter regarding time on the line. With the passing of time came an increase in the exposure to combat, for all the regular units.

9th SEPTEMBER, 1915

It came to pass that the order banning cameras from the front was given again, but this time with more force in the expression and rather severe punishments for breaking the rule. It just wouldn't do for the civilians at home, who made up mothers, sisters and wives of the convicted; and that's what it was to work in the trenches, hard labour if ever it was experienced. Get caught with a VPK in your possession, in particular taking a photo, and you were arrested on the spot. Needless to say photos from this day on were far scarcer than any previous period known. You will also be well informed to know that further invasion upon our privacy, which seemed non-existent, fell our way. All of our letters home fell under censorship and went under the prying eyes of those in authority, allowing them to read our letters. It was a vile war indeed, both at the front and in the rear.

Our day of days, the day we opened our doors to gas warfare. Our own batches of chlorine gas had been devised and now ready for delivery upon the debacle known as the Battle of Loos.

I had heard that the code name for the gas was Red Star. I could only hope that this was a fundamental method of ruse to deliver us, and keep from the sods, the use of the gas in order for us all to get our masks on if and when required.

You might imagine that the front line was extremely long and to expect the sods to employ gas along every square inch was ludicrous, however, best to be safe than sorry and so we were all prepared for whatever might happen. Unfortunately we were met by a greater calamity than any of us could figure.

The barrage of gas cylinders fired from our artillery occurred on a day when the wind was unfavourable and where it didn't linger upon no-man's land like a heavy mist in the streets of London, it drifted back towards us. This was the worst of luck for the prevailing wind of the Western Front was from the west: it was simply unfortunate. Luck would be more with us in the future but today it did not exist. But this wasn't the only bad luck that we suffered, for upon the firing line there were numerous canisters which could not be armed due to an uncanny reason: the turning keys which had been provided were incorrect and could not be used. It was as though the gas had a mind of its own and on delivery had decided, most purposely, that a withdrawal or retreat was the best form of attack.

The sods soon carried out a counter-barrage and the gas cylinders that sat exposed upon our firing line soon became the target of our greatest despair, the gas erupting in all directions before settling with the wind, lingering around for all to see and breath.

Our own trenches soon became inundated by our own gas and the masks we had sitting upon our heads were brought down over our faces. Some of the men were seen deliberately lifting their masks from place upon them because they could not draw sufficient breath to fight the battle before them and hence they succumbed to one of the worst deaths upon the battlefield.

It was fortunate that the men at home, or even those with the trenches who had been chemists in their former lives, came up with more advanced methods of counteracting the gas. We had what was known as 'hypo', or Hypo helmet. It was a bag that could be placed over the head, or pulled down over it if worn as a hat. Its fabric had been treated with a chemical known as sodium hyposulfite, and the goggles were made of talc and fogged up soon after being fitted. The chemical within the fabric also got into our eyes during foul weather which didn't help matters at all. A mouthpiece was added for good measure which allowed for the build-up of carbon dioxide to diffuse correctly. Later versions such as those employed in January of 1916 were treated with hexamethylenetetramine [the PH Helmet] to ward off the devilish phosgene.

25th DECEMBER, 1915

It is our second Christmas on the front. To think that it was supposed to be over by Christmas. It's a lesson to be learnt, not to accept optimistic views too readily when coming down from higher for it serves morale a short burst but wears off quickly and is hard to restore. We were also becoming so proficient in the trenches that we seemed accustomed to it. How's that; to be accustomed to living in such filthy conditions; to be used to seeing men die and their corpses eaten by over-sized rats. How is it we can be accustomed to lice, disease, and the torment of death on a minute-to-minute time frame? It was as though life itself was sheer misery and I tell you now that the suicide rate amongst the men increased for a while there. I saw it with my own eyes but refuse to speak of it, for it isn't nice to see a young man shoot himself in the head due to the insanity of war turning the tide of your mental clarity of thought. I am also forced to recall the Christmas Truce of the previous year but we would have all been hard-pressed to see or hear of another attempt at fraternization with the enemy.

As for the previous year there was no real fighting on the front, no large scale battles fought, no counter-attacks to be ensued. It was too cold for that. Maybe I can hear you scoffing at the comment but here's the truth of the matter. How can you fire your rifle when your hands are twice their original size due to frostbite and sheer cold? You might know how it is to try to lift something up on a cold and damp morning and find it impossible to feel what you are doing, ah, ha; you see and understand. Now you times that by ten, or maybe a hundred, for in the bitter cold of Europe, when flesh and bone are exposed to the elements hour after hour and day after day, it becomes a sheer impossibility to even lift your cups canteen to your mouth for a drink of lukewarm tea, and our feet are no better, swollen and suffering severe pain every minute of the day. You cannot fight a battle this way, when it's impossible to walk or crawl, when you can't even pick up an item for you cannot feel it, dropping or spilling whatever it is you try to put into your hands.

Some men were more fortunate than others and by sheer good fortune may have found themselves in BHQ for an hour or more with a message requiring a reply, and during this time you get warm and so when you return to the trenches you are good for another hour or more. You become useful to your mates and help them with a cigarette or possibly a shave. There is never a day goes by that one or more men have to file down the line seeking to bring a little life back into comrades too cold to even scratch themselves. Is it no wonder that these men feel closer to me than a brother or twin?

There is much misery suffered in the trenches to date and there is much more to come, all for a shilling a day. It's ludicrous. There are able-bodied men back in England shirking their responsibilities, thieving money from all around them, lying about their inability to fight on the front due to certain illnesses or injuries. It is these same men that seek and steal the medals of others so that they can wear them in later years, pretending to have served overseas. These are the worst kind of men and there are plenty of them in every society.

And before the months of spring are upon us I have the good fortune to come into view of something new. The factories at home are spewing out a new machine gun called the Lewis-gun. It's far easier to carry about, being much lighter and less cumbersome. We are also soon to be introduced to the Stoke Mortar which sounds very reassuring in their funny little way. You feel somewhat… safer, with the sound of such weapons being close at hand.

And so after many weeks of sheer misery in the trenches endured, it is time once more to commence for the many battles to come, but one more thing will bring the temptation to cause havoc amongst us all, but we are too proud to allow it to separate us into factions.

The Easter Rising.

7th MAY, 1916

Letters were coming from England and Ireland, newspaper articles read out to men in the trenches. Padres got involved to try to simmer our dispositions of mind and generals endeavoured to ensure that no wedge was placed between those fighting on the front. But we were strong of mind and conviction and had made our decisions almost two years before. There would be no swaying of mind.

I knew as any other did of the Irish Volunteers, that band of armed men created on the 25th day of November back in 1913, and now of the Easter Rising which lasted for seven days commencing the 30th day of April this year.

Back in Ireland there were seven days of fighting, back here in Flanders we have had our fill with two years of combat and God knows how many more to come.

The Irish Republican Brotherhood [IRB] had created the Irish Volunteers and to tell you the truth it was an insult to what I was trying to achieve; a life for my family which was to be free of fear. Many of us knew, if not all [for we seldom spoke of it], that the IRB was intent upon receiving aid from the sod. In order to do this the IRB must be willing to aid the sod, too. But you won't find a spy of any description in the trenches. Not only is our mail read before being sent home but we don't wish to endanger our own lives of the bitterness felt due to clash of territories or religion by filling them with hate. We had far worse things to bear, such as the frailness of our minds in putting up with the war and our struggle to stay alive. Maybe if the IRB were to experience what we, ourselves, were experiencing, then they would put away their inner ambitions and live in peace, peace as we were fighting for. This stinking IRB was to try and effect a German infiltration from Ireland, to have Irish prisoners of War join together and fight against the English: but they would be fighting against their own as well, for our battalions, regiments and divisions were fighting side by side.

I also heard the rumours of a German boat, disguised as Norwegian, smuggling weapons into Ireland, but this was seized by the Royal Navy.

The Easter Rising is an extensive history in itself, with members and manoeuvres, treachery and sinful reprise, the cause of frustrations and death: frustration being an understatement. It is not for me to here and now go into its detail, but the effect it had upon us good men fighting for a cause was very little. The effect seemed to be slight, if at all. We still fought beside those that opposed the IRB. No matter what the IRB has done in the past, present, or future will distract me, nor those fighting at my side, from our true beliefs in who we were and what we were fighting for.

24th JUNE, 1916

We have suffered annihilation before and we have to face it again. We are now at the Battle of Albert, and many of you will know it as 'Battle of the Somme', and I wish to speak to you about it.

Firstly the Battle of Albert was the opening phase of what was to become the Battle of the Somme. It upsets me sometimes that there is confusion when forgetting about the name Albert, for it is part and parcel of this book's title, in a way. I guess you were wondering where the title came from. But more on this a little later; for the moment I wish to concentrate upon the Battle of Albert, not the Somme as a whole. Let us reflect on the most heinous time of war other than that experienced at the Third Battle of Ypres; or Passchendaele if you so prefer.

This battle to come was a major component of viciousness for those endeavouring to impose a death sentence upon us, and although the idea of making for an historical breakthrough of the enemy lines seemed sound enough, there was a lot that went wrong with the thinking of men in power, whom sat too high upon their horse. I have read in history books that the total length of the front to be fought for by the BEF was fourteen miles, and others offer eighteen. I have wasted little time on the considerations of this for what matters most to me is the bad memories of death and mutilation; the crying out of strong men now broken, calling out for their mothers. It brings a tear to my eye just thinking of it. But for all due purposes in writing this book I have considered the frontage which the BEF be directly responsible for, to be eighteen miles in total.

Zero hour for the operation was not advised to us. It was a secret. But on this day in 1916 a bombardment commenced which could be heard from many places in England along and near the coast, and supposedly up to almost three hundred miles away, 1.7 million shells in all, if not more, in preparatory fire over the duration of the week. This is how the song was sung: it did not stop for eighty minutes and continued for seven days, and it was to be a ruse of which I shall explain. This was the opening stages of the Big Push. After the main bulk of aggressive firing the guns would continue but at a slower rate and by night half of them would cease. The machine guns would then open up during the night until morning, cutting off resupply in the rear. All guns would then open up with another eighty minute barrage followed by a slower rate for the remainder of the day, and so forth.

Consider this if you will, for visual effect only; there was an artillery piece or mortar placed at every seventeen yards apart for eighteen miles firing non-stop for eighty minutes, it is understandable therefore that little ground would go unscathed. We would hit the sod where it hurt; kill them, maim them, shatter their courage and turn them into dribbling idiots. We would smash their shelters and trenches, smash their fortifications, and smash their will to live. But it didn't turn out that way. It was to be the end of the colour of nature, the poppies, yellow tansy and marguerites being obliterated from the scene, and that was about the strength of it all. More artillery ammunition fired in the week as compared to that fired during the first 12 months of war, all for the sake of killing our only current joy; the colour of the flowers around, with one or two bees seen from time to time, placing a smile upon faces.

I hear you ask the obvious and so I shall now reveal the ruse. For seven days the enemy were hit with eighty minutes of fire. On the morning of the attack they would receive sixty-five minutes before we pushed out from our trenches and prepared for our advance upon the presumed, broken line, the enemy expecting a further fifteen minutes of firing. There was one major disappointment in the firing however; one third of all shells were duds.

An important aspect in the lead up to the attack was the question of what damage the bombardment was having on the German defences and the units which opposed us. Information on the different units was rather important for some were gutsier than others, some lending to fear and cowardice more readily than another, and some were willing to fight to the death for their flag, for the keiser, for the officer standing behind them with a pistol held at their heads.

Raiding was always a prompted move and each major unit on the line, being a division, was to conduct at least one raid per night to gather as much information as possible on the subjects of enemy strength, weapons, logistic support, units, possible tactics, equipment, enemy habits, his intentions, and morale. Morale was extremely important and prisoners never went unquestioned, and were very useful.

Raids were many and varied in size from a half-platoon size raid to one being a full company in strength; there were also casualties to be faced for it was rare that a raid was conducted without someone getting a bullet or bayonet in the gut, and not every raid reached its destination, for some raids had been gunned down before reaching the objective and had to crawl back to the line in retreat and vile agony.

Now, having told you that the information was invaluable you would consider it to be taken in and adhered to for all intents and purposes, to aid the assault to come. But no matter how often a returning raid would report that the wire in front of the enemy was not being cut and destroyed as expected by the shelling, it would not be believed. Some may have even considered such a lame report as blasphemous and beyond exaggeration.

26th JUNE, 1916

It would seem like any other day; apart from the barrage taking place; but something different was in the air today.

The RFC had a total of 185 planes in ten squadrons against the sod who held just 129. It gave us air superiority. Air superiority meant that the sod was unable to see from above the battalions, regiments and divisions moving into positions behind the lines in readiness for the main attack to come, and later refused them the information of the huge numbers of cavalry preparing to unleash hell [which never dawned] later on. Try as the sod might to gain information, or even conduct artillery registration from their balloons, of which we had 16 in the air, they could do little against us. It was easy to distinguish the

English balloons from the sodding ones; ours were grey and theirs were black.

And so I looked up into the sky one bright morning to be confronted by no less than six of our aircraft drawing upon some enemy: I think the enemy numbered four. At 8,000 feet it looked spectacular and one can be forgiven to forget the war to their front for a few minutes as one English lad dove down from high above and chased a German towards a fast-approaching ground, turning at the last minute with the English hot on his tail, firing his machine gun with great expertise. Here they flipped and flopped, drawing closer to the crowd of onlookers as we peered up from the trenches, seeing the live show which was mesmerising in every detail. It was hard to believe that a flying machine could manoeuvre in such a way, and the handling of them by the pilots was expertise on a completely new level. Loop the loop, twist and turn, the English plane was joined by another and then the sod had no chance at all and was hit by some fire from their guns, and whether or not the sod was hit directly or not he failed to bail out and the plane screamed down towards the earth with a little smoke coming from behind. He managed to pull his plane up a little and it seemed to skid over the top of a copse of trees before slamming into the earth and bursting into flames. It was a marvellous sight and yells of joy erupted from the men all around, and then a sniper from the enemy trenches shot dead a man exposing too much of himself above the trench. Suddenly a single German plane got through and started shooting his machine gun at a balloon of ours which is registering targets. He passes and then turns to give it another try. Then I can see two dots in the sky as the men jump from the balloon and parachute to safety with the sod trying again and again to see the balloon engulfed in flames but it did not happen, and then he was chased off by several English and I don't know what happened then because they disappeared from sight. It would seem for all intents and purposes that we had the upper hand, but the sod held the higher ground and looked down upon us, seeing far more of us than we could of them. Each German individual could see far more of no-man's land than we could, and that would account for something when the attack started. The Germans also did one other thing of mischief. They realized how ridiculous it was to fire their artillery in retaliation against our counter battery fire, our balloons and aircraft, and so put them to silence. We naturally believed the Germans to be light on guns and breathed a sigh of relief in the thought that the attack would be all the easier when it arrived. It was just another insecurity to be dealt with later. And then something quite ridiculous came into my mind. In watching the show in the air and their race towards the ground, I recall having seen a copse of trees. Such a miracle it was: how on earth had it not been razed?

27th JUNE, 1916

Whilst helping a wounded mate to the rear I came across some men on horseback and enquiring as to whether or not they could help us by providing us a ride; they said that they couldn't as they were going in another direction and were not to delay their orders. They did manage to give slip of some information which my later forages in the pages of history proved to be quite correct; future orders would also reveal much of the plan of attack upon the enemy trenches and towns beyond and I shall now reveal some of this to you.

The first day of the offensive to come was made up solely of the men of Great Britain and Ireland, and Lord Kitchener's New Army, along with small units from Bermuda and Newfoundland. Canadians, ANZACs and South Africans were not present on the first day as many were on leave in England, or at rest behind the lines.

Three cavalry divisions were to be employed to roll up the flanks in the rear once the enemy positions to the front had been breached, but this never eventuated, but this is not to say that an opportunity was not made available, for it was, but the poor reflection of strategy within the eye of our commanders above refused to unleash them of their bonds behind our front line.

There were three lines of enemy trenches that needed to be cleared before sighting the villages and towns beyond, the main road between Amiens and Bapaume [Albert being almost central along this line; approx 16 miles from Amiens and nine from Bapaume], being the centre line for our advance. We had also known for some time of the Russians and their efforts to push upon the Germans in the east, this came on the 4th day of June and hence the sod was forced to endure cutbacks in their strength managing the defences along the Somme. This appeared to give us the upper hand but was an illusion.

I now think it is time to reflect upon Albert and in particular the cathedral there. The town was to change hands during the very early stages of the war and also later on, but seemed to spend most of its time within the hands of the allies [possibly an optimistic point of view]; so close was it to the fighting that all of its citizens had left with everything they could cart or carry, even so, the Germans still held the high ground but the allies held the tower of the cathedral from which to exercise their right in registering artillery targets and their adjustments upon other targets of choice. It was during the early days of the war that Germans tried all they could to see the tower brought down by artillery fire, for the idea of having artillery spotters employ it as the great vantage point it was, was simply too much to ignore. The sodding bastard eventually hit the tower on which stood a marvellous statue of the Virgin Mary but the French engineers took measure to ensure she didn't fall and fixed it into position with lengths of thick and heavy cables.

It boggles the mind to consider why the French went to such great measures to ensure the Virgin stood her ground, even if on an angle, for a legend rose at around that time, in particular amongst French troops, that the war would not finish until the statue fell. I can only presume therefore that the French considered the felling of the statue as a German victory to come. As time went by we English also took up the visualized belief that should she fall the war would end. There seemed to be much confusion in this however for I have heard many versions of the same tale and many of those are that whoever should knock it down would lose the war. So if the Germans knocked it down then we would obviously win. But how did this all come about?

Hundreds of thousands of troops passed through and near, or past, the tower, and the Virgin upon it was quite easy to see and from quite some distance. There was within it a mystique and symbolism; strong belief and understanding. Both sides in this war believed in God. Inside the German prayer book found in the trenches was the picture of Jesus looking down upon a German soldier who had just been killed; an almost identical picture can be found in our [allied] field prayer book: obviously the soldier looks different and wears a different uniform. The words in each mean the same, for in both books can be read the words, With Jesus in the Field. How can this be? It would seem that both sides idolised the statue of the Virgin Mary, and inexplicably for many reasons both sides more or less believed in the same legend.

Let me see if I can find something here. It would seem that the Germans believed that whoever knocked down the Virgin would win the war, but many of the sod, in particular after 1916, seemed to believe that whoever knocked her down would be conquered. I say that fear held all, that religion and belief restrained them all from knocking down the Virgin, and for all the truth there was about it only one thing had become clear; when the Virgin fell the war would be over, and neither side wished to lose.

The attack to come was over ground, not particularly healthy for those that might, in a hail of bullets, seek to take cover. In most places over the length of the ground to be covered was open, and although some rich soil was to be found ahead [great for copse of trees and fields of wheat] most of the ground was chalky. There were no divots in which to seek cover from fire, between villages and copse. Cover was what we made of it.

We were advised in time that it was going to be an easy walk over to the enemy trenches, into which we would find ourselves a defeated enemy with hands up in eagerness to surrender, so in order to make great advantage of our gains we were to carry as much equipment as humanly possible with the waves behind the lead being burdened with additional stores such as duck-boards and rolls of barbed wire. It was no easy feat to carry so much.

So what did we carry? Bayonet and rifle, the two main weapons of the war; as well as these we carried [which changed widely across the entire front] 150-220 rounds of ammunition, grenades, sandbags, entrenching tools and spades, wire cutters, signal flares [seventy pounds-plus of equipment]. One further item which was new to the front was the steel helmet. It came to be that the steel helmets reduced head casualties by around 75%. All of this was on top of everyday field kit such as belt, water bottle, pouches, groundsheet, haversack, mess-tin, iron rations, socks, two gas masks, mortar bombs, and if you were unlucky, a stretcher or telephone cables. The weight seemed to go up and down like a seesaw and with each different attack and season came different needs and requirements.

Our advance into the enemy trenches was to be conducted in waves with two platoons in each wave, each with a four hundred yard frontage, two waves per company, and eight waves per battalion; stretcher bearers and battalion HQ element would bring up the rear. The advance would also be a measured one of around fifty yards per minute: in other words, extremely slow, too slow in fact for many commanders who chose to alter it as they saw fit prior to entering no-man's land. We were not to run even if fired upon, not unless we were twenty yards or less from the enemy, for running across open ground was considered unnecessary. The idea of the slow advance was due to the belief that the artillery would have rendered the enemy barbed wire as 'obliterated' and the trenches as 'empty of opposition': neither was the case. There would be no looking after a wounded comrade, no taking of prisoners, and any man refusing to go over the top would be shot by the Military Police: ah, so now we British are acting as the sod, threatening to shoot any refusing to do his duty.

The Germans were in possession of the best ground, being higher than ours and therefore dryer due to fewer problems with the water table. Not only were their machine gun positions well-endowed and constructed with concrete and steel, and there were 55 machine gun posts for every mile of front to be assaulted, but their trenches were ten foot deep with extremely elaborate dugouts and command posts dug down forty feet or more with tunnels connected to trenches in several directions. The luxury of each, as we were to learn in the near future, were panelled and well furnished, like barracks rooms for officers back in Berlin, with bunk beds and cupboards, dining tables, chairs and a system of ventilation, all wired up to electricity. It put our own dugouts to great shame. Their reserve and depth trenches were as good as those at the front. Trenches and tunnels lead right up to the villages which sat behind them, the buildings and cellars of the crumbling structures being employed well with the ability to defend, and so did this mean that the Germans had no real intention of gaining further ground: it seemed to me they were happy to be where they were. And across the entire frontage of our assault could be found nine major towns so well fortified that you would have to consider them forts of the greatest strength and able to endure great masses of artillery fire with infantry assault supported heavily with tanks, and you'd need engineers in order to help you clear them of all enemy. It is too profound to consider; it appears an almost impossible task when looked back upon. Between the villages where the ground was open and sparse they built other miniature forts to ward off the threat of being flanked.

Haig wanted the attack to take place on the 25th but this was postponed to take place on the 29th at 0730hrs. It was because of the weather; two days of summer storms which made the crossing unfavourable and we needed everything in our favour. And then a bolt of lightning struck several of our men dead because all of us in the trenches carried a rifle with a bayonet on its end. Success could not be won on speculated formulations alone, but we did out-number the sod seven to one and with such outstanding superiority it was seen as impossible for us to be defeated in what was to come. We were just shy of 130,000 men [when considering a full strength division] to take part in the coming attack, made up with what appeared to be 60% of Kitchener's New Army. We were either regular soldiers or volunteers opposing an army made up of mostly conscripts: or so I was led to believe.

28th JUNE, 1916

It was still raining and the time of the attack was scheduled for the morning, and then the news arrived that the attack would be postponed but yet again. We were now set to commence the assault [walkover] at 0750hrs on the 1st of July. The news did not go down well. Tempers were frayed, the weather and conditions were extremely bad, and there were so many men in the trenches that there was hardly room to move. Can you imagine having to stand up all day and all night without sleep for lack of room? We were ready to go, there is no doubt about it. The men were eager to have it over with and the mass graves sat empty behind us ready to be filled. Everything was as well prepared as could possibly be expected, but the poor manufacture of the artillery shells let us down, but maybe the weather had something to do with their poor performance in shredding the wire to our front. Our thoughts were only interrupted here and there with the sound of a single shot being fired far away, a man shooting himself in the leg to get himself away from the war only to find his stretcher being escorted by armed men in readiness for his execution to come.

30th JUNE, 1916

The sun had risen and stand-to was over with. I took the opportunity to grab a periscope and to take a look at the enemy trenches and the ground in which we were to cross in the morning. All I could see were the scars upon the ground indicating the enemy trenches and a mist made of dust laying over the entire area, so thick that it was impossible to see through for any great depth. I was amazed that so much dust could be present after so much rain but it is a sheer indication as to how hot it can get in Flanders during the height of the summer months, and then again I may have been mistaken, for the dust may have been a powder of some description, but I guess I shall never really know. But one thing was most hurtful, most sure; gone were the colours of the wild flowers; gone were most of the trees.

The big guns had been firing now for seven days and I knew that the gunners were tired to the bone, hot and bothered, and stripped to the waist due to the hardship of their forte. And so with these images in my mind I try with all my might to achieve a rest state or even sleep, but the task is not an easy one, not for a single soul in this damn place.

1st JULY, 1916

It was 0400hrs and the big day was upon us, and the men prepared as best they could for what lay ahead. Few concerns seemed to appear on faces for we had had it drummed into us how easy it would be with the enemy trenches empty and the sodding reserve too far away to do anything about reinforcing the front line, and almost every man to the last was so happy to see an end to the waiting, for tonight we might get some decent sleep, but I shall tell you now that only the dead ever gained rest from war.

Our brothers-in-arms, the 1st Royal Dublin Fusiliers, having served in Gallipoli and now serving her on the Somme were to lead the attack in our quarter and I, as a member of the 2nd Royal Dublin Fusiliers were to be their backing, bringing up their rear in what was to be one of our darkest hours. My story of the attack has only just begun but I shall cut to the chase in regards to casualties to put your mind to rest. We went into battle with twenty-three officers and 480 other ranks, and can you imagine how many of us came back [remembering of course that little more than ten per cent of us were now originals]? When the fighting was finished on that first day there were nine officers and 169 other ranks; everyone else was dead, missing, or wounded: wounded in the sense that they could not carry on but needed full treatment in order to recover from injury. What do you say to that, ah? This damn war was cutting us to pieces, literally.

With the thought that the rain was behind us came a reminder that nature would be ever present, for a light rain commenced to fall upon the battlefield. Thankfully it didn't last long and before the whistle blew for us to depart the trenches it had ceased.

The shelling continued at the slow rate which we were now quite used to and it wouldn't pick up for several minutes. It would be then that we could count on sixty-five minutes of heavy barrage prior to our time of departure falling upon us all. And then it came and scared the hell out of us all. We were all expecting it but it jolted us all the same, more so than any previous day. I think this might have been because today we knew we were going over the top and some of us didn't quite believe the words of the generals that the attack was going to be a piece of cake: it's somewhat strange to see men smiling one moment and then see such smiles fade as the guns blazed away. Something rather peculiar happened then. The sodding artillery opened up and rained down upon us. Guns that had been silent for so long were now hitting back at us in retaliation. It was as though they hadn't been scratched at all and that they knew we were coming; but how could that be possible?

I saw the rum going around for the last time and only a few of us refrained; most partook in quenching the dryness within their throats and picked up a little more courage as the warmth of the rum hit the spot. I saw two men get quite drunk and they were laughing away merrily unto themselves for no one could hear them properly over the noise of the barrage. The sergeant then came and saw to it that no further rum was issued to them and the last dregs in the cups canteen was emptied or given to someone else close by; but it was too late. These two men would meet death as drunk as could possibly be, walking aimlessly into the interlocking fire of German machine guns. No one else did much better mind you, being ordered to walk straight ahead into oblivion and of course obeying the order for fear of the Military Police stationed back in the trenches behind us. And so it was time to exit the trenches and line up, or simply step out in line as the whistle blew, and some of those commanders smart enough to order their men to move to the front of the wire, in front of the trenches, before zero hour in some cases, actually made it to the other side of no-man's land in one piece: all that might be left was to try and come back again later: hah, good luck to all.

I saw some men praying to God before shaking out with the formation and thought it a good idea if I might do the same. What could it hurt to ask for some form of protection in what was about to befall us and not a man amongst us really knew what to expect. If we were to believe the generals then we were in for a grand old day of advancing upon empty trenches, but if we believed our gut then we knew we were in for much trouble and misery. I then said two prayers, one for myself and the other for my family. I never prayed again after that day for quite some time. I then looked up and saw we were ready to take the place of the 1st once they had commenced towards the enemy, and then the ground shook violently. It was the artillery along the entire front of 18 miles, rapid fire from every single gun on the line, mortars included. This was to last for ten minutes.

I was sure, as sure as sure could possibly, be that no man could survive such intense fire, and there was more to come. After eight minutes of fury the mines that had been dug beneath no-man's land and towards the enemy were blown sky high. We could see great masses of the earth erupt 4,000 feet into the sky, and I suffered a great calamity then for the man two down from me was shaking with fear. I could see the horror in his eyes and he seemed lost of conscious thought. I could see that he wanted nothing more than to be with his mother but that was not to be. He would go over the top soon enough and meet his end as many others did that day. Clods of earth then swamped the trenches and some men were wounded bad enough not to take part in the crossing of the fields of fire; those lucky bastards who might lose a finger or suffer the remainder of their lives with a permanent scar across the face from such a deep wound that they couldn't carry on with today's fight.

Ten mines in total were fired [one at 0720hrs, eight at 0728hrs, and one being ten minutes late], three of these were detonated by use of more than twenty tonnes of explosive, the remainder consisting of around 5,000lbs apiece. It was sheer ear-blowing, the closer you were to one the worse off you were.

Suddenly the barrage stopped. For a few moments everything appeared to be so at peace. There was not a sound to be heard other than a bird in the distance, for even the sods had stopped firing. New targets were then plotted and the artillery engaged them.

And then the whistle blew and the advance across no-man's land commenced at a crawl. This was it, this was the time we had waited for, and then to our flank a German shell made a direct hit within one of the trenches, almost an entire platoon killed with the blink of an eye, rubbed from existence. The screams just managed to fall upon my ear as the backs of the 1st were moving away from us and towards the enemy. Officers and other NCO's were eager to get on with the job and words of encouragement fell from their mouths, and then the machine guns opened up and the first of many casualties began to fall to the ground as casualties of war.

Bugles were sounding in the German trenches, this could be heard well enough, and I could hazard a guess that the sod would be spilling out of their dugouts in the thousands to man their positions, to join the ranks of the few guns which had opened up, to be joined by many more soon enough.

It wasn't long before the few German guns that had been firing were joined by others and all you could hear from the opposing trench was the noise of the machine guns as they mowed down rank after rank, wave after wave. This chorus of killing was then joined by a few shells from the German artillery which were set upon with counter battery fire. And the machine guns continued without rest to kill and maim; seemingly impossible numbers of men were being hit and when they fell upon the ground they were hit again to make doubly sure that they were dead.

For all intents and purposes it seemed that the 1st had been decimated to the last man when suddenly it was our turn to exit the trenches. Yes, that's correct; there is no calling off an attack when it's in progress. Haig would push on and keep on pushing on until not a man was left to fight this bitter war. And how did I feel to be climbing out of the trenches knowing that death awaited us in no-man's land, for the machine guns of the sod hadn't yet turned upon the parapet of our trenches but were seemingly waiting for us to join our fallen comrades in the middle of the killing ground, and the guns did not cease for a seconds respite.

I let my eyes sway and saw small clusters of men to both left and right, fallen men bleeding badly and tending themselves as best they could with what dressings they had on them. We were not to stop and give aid, I recalled this, but I felt as though I were cheating them by continuing on into the jaws of death, but continue on I did. And as I should look further afield to either flank I could see so few of our men still advancing, for we too had been decimated. It was then that a bullet hit my helmet and knocked me to the ground. It knocked me unconscious but I don't know for how long. When I came too, the waves of men were still moving across no-man's land and being killed so that every foot of ground seemed to carry a dead man. The ground was littered with bodies.

I attempted to move and someone fired at me in anger, but again the bullet hit my helmet but this time knocked it clean off. I scurried forward to shallower ground and a burst of fire from a machine gun almost found me, dirt spraying all over my back as I crawled into safe harbour. I rolled down into the crater and gasped for air before looking around and seeing two badly wounded men and another eight dead.

One of the wounded men, his left arm missing from the elbow down, yelled out for me to keep my head down. He said that so earnestly and loudly for he knew that the slightest move would draw machine gun fire to fall upon them and they didn't need that. He was trying to bandage his own arm. I then glanced at the other man but couldn't see his face because it was a mass of flesh and blood. I would learn soon enough that he had lost his nose, right ear and eye, and his jaw had been so badly shattered that it hung in a poor position. His breathing did not sound at all healthy, as though his throat was filled with blood and guts. He was sitting rather still and obviously in great distress and shock.

German artillery then struck our own trenches and no-man's land with great vigour, and this coupled with the machine gun fire made it impossible for any man to make it across to the enemy trenches in our sector.

I then went against the good advice of the wounded man and glanced back towards our own line and could just manage to see another wave of our lads climb out of the trenches and commence the advance, but it took only a few seconds before there was only a few men left to take on the brunt of the German line. I would learn later that in some places they actually made it to the other side and with very few casualties, but it wasn't to be where I was. It was then that I glanced towards the Germans and saw their infantry getting up onto their parapet and shooting at us along with the machine guns, whose task it now seemed to be, to kill us as we poured out of the trenches, the infantrymen with rifle taking down those that survived the initial onslaught. Another burst of fire made me pull my head down.

Oh; how so clear it was that the enemy dugouts were so superior to our own. It was as though they had gone through the week-long bombardment without a scratch. Here we were outnumbering them seven to one and we were being cut down so easily, but the lads carried out their orders and the waves kept advancing. It was clear that I'd only been concussed for two or three minutes.

I removed my pack and took all the field dressings I could to the wounds of the men in my midst, starting with the one with the missing arm. He was drained of energy and purpose but the bleeding was stopped. He commented on how tired he was and he drifted off to sleep as I then attended the other man. I rummaged through some of the dead and took some dressings from them and gave aid as best

I could. I tried as best I could to clean the hole where his nose was and had trouble stemming the flow of blood, for it was a task and a half for him to breathe through his shattered jaw which I ended up fixing in place with a barrel bandage, and maintained as best I could a gap there for him to breathe through. It seemed like forever but I knew that little time had passed.

A harsh yelling and loud voice then hit my ear. From somewhere outside the crater in which I found myself I heard the order to 'Come on! Get up and rush them, lads!' and then an intense amount of machine gun fire ripped through the air as the scream of men trying to rush the enemy were brought to their end. It was then that another wounded man fell into my crater with blood across the entire front of his chest.

I wasted not a single moment this time and ripped his haversack from his back whilst keeping low so as not to be fired upon. I then ripped off his shirt and found a bullet hole in his chest. His breathing was hard and uncomfortable, his teeth gritted together in agony and he was extremely restless from the pain. I assured him as best I could and a bullet almost found its mark but again the new helmet saved the day but was torn from his head leaving a ghastly red and bleeding gash under his chin where the strap had been.

I looked again at the wound and saw one small hole. I put my right hand behind his back and felt around with my finger tips. I found an exit hole and proceeded immediately to stem the flow from his two holes. I managed as best I could and although he was in horrid pain he seemed to be able to handle being placed upon his right side where his right lung filled with blood but his left remained clear and he was able to breathe with a ghastly sound of gurgling emitting from him. It must have been a horrible time for him, being half drowned in his own blood.

Now it was time to check on my other two patients and I found to my dismay that the man with the shattered jaw was dead. His injuries had been too much for him. The other, with the missing arm, seemed to be in a stable way and so I maintained close visual on the third. It was then that I realised the dilemma we were in. We were stuck three quarters, or thereabouts, of the way across no-man's land and in a crater. There was no getting out of it and therefore my patients would die. What could I do but try and eliminate the threat, and so doing as many were doing along the eighteen miles of frontage I took to taking pot shots at the Germans from the edge of the crater in which I found myself, making sure to lift my eye over the parapet of the crater in a different spot each time to avoid being killed by a sniper. I managed to kill two of the sodding bastards but each time I fired my rifle a machine gun would retaliate by order of someone within their trenches.

I felt like a coward but what good would it do me to try and rush the enemy now. I would be gunned down before I'd gotten six feet, and although I'd managed to get this far into the fight, as the dead and wounded had that were with me, I was no longer flanked by hundreds of men and therefore an easier target. All I could manage to get out of this mess was to try and keep these other two men alive long enough for them to receive proper aid. But I didn't like the chances of the chest wound getting through the day, let alone the night if this failed attempt at taking the German trenches was to continue past dusk.

We had been here for almost two hours when the man with the chest wound motioned for a drink of water. I wasn't sure if I could give it to him because of his wound and couldn't remember what I was to do. If I gave it to him he might choke and die, I was simply lost for any idea of what to do. And then I recalled that only stomach injuries were not to be given water: but I wasn't one hundred per cent sure. His wound was bandaged well enough, as was the one with the missing left arm, but I was not a medical officer nor orderly and couldn't be relied upon to give any assurance that my taking sympathy on him would not kill him. I chanced to say that I had no water to spare and left it at that, but he insisted I search the haversacks and equipment of the dead around us. I therefore had little choice in the matter and did all I could for the man. What little water I did find I gave to him and miraculously enough, after a short choking fit which started his bleeding again, he was brought under control and managed to force a smile upon his face for just a few seconds before remaining still and relatively quiet as he continued with his rasped breathing.

It was well past midday for the sun was high above and the sound of war continued without a break, although the sound had abated quite considerably when compared to earlier on. The worst of the killing had been done and I was to learn in later years that 60,000 men to fight this day were made casualties of war, almost 20,000 of which were dead. It was a dark day indeed.

Darker still was what happened next. A German bomb was thrown into our crater, obviously in retaliation for my firing from it. It landed next to the man with the missing arm. We locked eyes, me and him. I was too far from it to pick it up and throw it out, and he was too damn tired to reach for it with his good arm and toss it out. He smiled then and rolled onto it clumsily with a half-leap and as I covered up my face as the explosion blew him to pieces. I could do nothing now but make sure the living man I had remaining in my care was kept alive as long as possible.

The Poor State of War and Conflict

Suddenly I felt purpose; a man was dragging himself towards the edge of the crater. I saw his face appear as he struggled to draw himself over the lip and into safety. I moved to try and give him aid but a German sniper had other ideas. There was a single shot fired at the wounded man seeking cover and a burst of blood leaped out from the side of his head near his temple. The sods were most certainly killing the wounded, for I learnt as I dragged his body into the crater that he had missing a leg. I shook the image from my mind and sought what I was after; his water and field dressing.

I stripped him of the essentials and then stopped dead. I looked up and there I saw a tiny bird. It had come to perch on the helmet of the man with the shattered jaw, whose helmet was blown onto the lip of the crater. I studied it for a moment and it sang to me. It was so beautiful to hear and then he flew away. Now you might call me crazy but from that moment on I knew I was to survive this day. There was something about that bird and his singing that spoke to me in clear and plain English that I was to live to see another day dawn. And as I looked at the man with the sucking chest wound I could only hope that he would also live, but I wasn't about to pray for him because God didn't seem to be answering too many calls today.

I looked up into the cloudless sky; the heat was building and we were extremely thirsty. It must have been around 1430hrs when I could hear a renewed effort to take the enemy trenches from the enemy. Whistle blasts and the sound of artillery were filling the air. The machine guns added that ghastly nightmare of a picture in my mind and after what seemed to be just minutes the scene around was quieter with the usual battle noise of machine guns, bombs, and mortars being fired; gone was the futile attack which had crumbled from existence. I was later to learn that at 1500hrs our cavalry in the rear were retired and they had been turned around and would not be joining the fighting. It may well have been that they could have saved the day for they would have been faster, breaching the points more vulnerable to attack, but no, the fighting seemed to be coming to an end.

The sun was getting lower; it was 1700hrs. Another artillery barrage had opened up. For thirty minutes they fired and I felt in my bones that generals do not learn from their mistakes. And far, far away I heard more whistle blasts as the artillery was lifted and more machine gun fire killed all of our good men. The insanity of it all is beyond description and I felt dirty.

And then it is night. The sun has gone and the sounds of battle have simmered, but there are still the machine guns of the enemy firing upon every noise they hear, trying to kill the wounded as they crawl about in an effort to get safely back to the lines. It is then that another wounded man crawls to the lip of my crater. I have my weapon ready to kill him because he might well be a sod, but he's not. I speak to him to let him know we are there, and as his dark face appears he answers with a thick Irish accent: I know it's Irish because I understand every damn word he says, and if he'd been from any other country of the BEF I may not have understood it as clearly.

This man is not too badly off. He has a wound to the leg but he'd managed to apply a field dressing of his own, for when he fell he fell into a small hollow in the ground. He was lucky to be alive. He tells me that machine guns have been shooting in his direction as he moved but each time he would stop and wait a few minutes to make the gunner think that he was dead before moving again with more effort to do so quietly.

I had no water to give him but I was able to help him a little with applying a better dressing to his wound by using the fabric of the dead soldiers' uniforms. After this was done we discussed our situation and it was decided that we should try and crawl our way back as best as possible. And so it is here that I find myself crawling back towards our line with the sucking chest wound upon my back and the man with the wounded leg at my side. We do not leave each other for I can feel that these two men with me have a fear of dying alone.

We stop periodically to ensure that the sucking chest wound is still alive, and he is for most of the way back, though in extreme discomfort. When next we stop to check on him he is dead. I consider taking his pay book and ID disc for identification purposes but decide on doing the same as with the others in the crater; I leave the pay book and ID disc with him. If and when the time comes that a burial party can collect his body they will need to identify him for the grave.

There are now only two of us and we don't speak as we continue on our way. We have discarded all of our equipment but I do have my weapon. The wounded man beside me has nothing but his helmet which he fears to lose and I fear to lose the one I picked up from the crater, for although it is only a new item so recently issued it seems to be a part of me and my survival.

We continue one and have to either skirt around all the dead we come into contact with or crawl over them. It is a horrible task. There are so many dead littering the ground that the ground itself can hardly be felt. The ground is also no longer flat; the German artillery saw to that.

After what seems to be an eternity we finally get back to our trenches. There are men here who are quiet and subdued. They listen for the wounded and help get them into the trench before patching them up and getting them back to the dressing stations which are now so grossly overfilled that all the men with severe wounds are left to die in place and those that have wounds that can be managed are seen to. It is all unfair but necessary if lives are to be saved in the long term.

It is a few days later that I can reflect upon what has happened, I also learn that our division [being understrength to start with] have suffered a total of 4,692 casualties, and of all the divisions in the fighting over these past few days we have suffered the fifth highest amount. We have been decimated but once again: I hate to think what has happened to those few units that have lost more.

Five days after the initial attack the medical officers have made a truce with the Germans and bodies are collected for burial. I don't waste time in seeking out the crater in which I lived for twelve hours for I didn't wish to see the faces of the dead again. I simply collected what I could from the ground around and helped give them a burial. The stench of the bodies was immensely horrid and the gases built up within them sometimes escaped their orifices, but it was a task that needed to be done. Occasionally we came upon a wounded man, but an extremely high number were dead.

It was then that it dawned upon me. Why hadn't Haig ensured that a proper reconnaissance had been conducted? He had air superiority; why hadn't it used it to his great advantage? Maybe he had; maybe he'd decided that regardless of the cost we had no choice but to try and break the deadlock. And so, you see, it is a war of attrition. Whoever can continue to furnish the war with fresh bodies the longest will be the winner in the end. The 2nd Royal Dublin Fusiliers is then built back up with numerous fresh men straight from home. I shall refrain from making too many friends of these but shall do all I can to ensure they learn quickly.

13th NOVEMBER, 1916

It was coming on to winter once more. It wouldn't be long now and the fighting would simmer down to allow us to freeze half to death in misery. But as time wears on, new aspects of war are open to us. I have heard of something new, it's called the tank. I have heard it rumbling along some place in September, and then early this month had some hands-on experience with it. But my story is of infantry fighting, not battles with tanks, which for all the good they did in the later stages of the war seemed not to be faring too well at all. I also saw some hand-to-hand fighting which was not something I wish to have to face again. It is one thing to kill a man from a distance whilst looking over iron sights, but something completely different to strike him down with a slash of your rifle before penetrating him with your bayonet. I have done it before now but not on the scale which has just been experienced over the past month. It is something I don't wish to think too much about. Our air superiority has also been cemented in place and does not seem to be able to be budged. I do not believe the Germans will now be able to do so well in the air for the remainder of the war.

The replacements we received after the Battle of Albert are coming along well, though they suffer the heavier casualties when stacked up against the older soldiers, but we are so few and far between that it is hard to come across an old friend.

We are at the end now of what is the Battle of the Somme, the Battle of Albert being the start and now the Battle of the Ancre [River] being the end. I'm sorry I have not reflected upon the fighting in between these two battles but you have grown in your acquaintance of war well enough to understand what it is like: even if not experienced.

We were to attack along either side of the Ancre River. With all we had learnt so far of attacking the enemy in trenches, artillery support, creeping fire, machine gun positions and tanks, we found ourselves in a far more comfortable position than our enemy. We were all starting to believe that we could win the war but it wouldn't be done at a stroke nor so easily awarded, but it was achievable and in sight.

Although not all objectives were taken during the battle, II Corps were rewarded with being able to take and hold all of theirs. Haig was extremely happy and content with what we had achieved but it seemed that Gough wanted more. But Gough's efforts to take more than he could chew gifted him with such little solace, and other than that and all he was rewarded with were excessive casualties. Of the many objectives marked on Gough's map he only managed to take and hold ground at a place called Desire Trench. It all seemed futile to me however for on the 18th we all settled down for the winter and there were no more attacks to be seen until the winter was over with.

I guess that the most important thing for me during November was that on the 16th day of this month we moved from the 10th Division to… to the 48th Brigade, 16th Division [the 16th Irish Division]. Oh, yes. We again had suffered heavy casualties but now reinstated and with men of our own background. I felt as though this was a great reward being bestowed upon me. Don't get me wrong, please; I love the English, but I love the Irish even more.

INTERMISSION

Yes; intermission; what a word, but that's exactly how Christmas felt to me, an intermission between phases of war. War for months with little break and then time to freeze to death; and so, Happy New Year; you bastards. I look forward to shooting you sods down into this bloody mud and stinking filth, and hope the lice are eating you as much as they are eating at me. Take a running jump back to where you belong, that cesspool of shit.

And it would appear that they heard me for in February they withdrew, all through March until April, to what they called the Hindenburg Line. The proof was in the pudding as I've heard spoken on many occasions and the Germans have suffered so badly in this war that they have no decent men left to fight it. They are so thin on the ground that they have to withdraw to a smaller frontage, one which has been fortified using the forced labour of prisoners, both civil and of war. The Hindenburg Line, a defence system like none we have come across before, a new front line some thirty miles shorter than what we had been used to. But not only did this free up thirteen enemy divisions to act as reserve but it also allowed us to reinforce ours. Did this mean that attacks in the future would constitute more waves and hence more dead and dying? Only time would tell.

What was this new line made of; why, concrete bunkers and gun emplacements, dugouts and command posts which put all others to shame; exceptional trenches and tunnels connected the lot. We thought we'd seen everything until we saw the line. The sod is to be congratulated, but then again it was by the forced labour of POWs that this grand structure of defence was possible, but not our POWs, or so I have been informed, but those of Russia. Maybe there is propaganda here, too; the sod advising the Russians that we are a common enemy. And so we find ourselves on the doorstep of the Arras Offensive and the officers in charge seem to be weathering poorly under the pressures of the war.

Winter is over with, and a new year of war has begun, but the tell-tale signs of distress can be seen everywhere, in particular with the officers. Those officers who had served longer than others seemed to be more affected with complaints of poor health: headaches, heart rates, involuntary shaking of the hands. Was it because they felt partly responsible for sending men to their death on a daily basis? One in every forty men on the line were officers, if not more, yet one in every seventeen filled the duties of an officer, so it seemed to me that their life expectancy was a lot less than ours: but I cannot for the life of me consider men like Haig as an officer of men. Officers like Haig don't see war as we do; they simply send us 'to-it' before wiping their hands and reaching for a cup of nice hot tea whilst we attend to our lice and other misgivings in life as it exists on the front. Officers of the peacetime army and territorial; officers of commission and those granted a temporary commission, but all in all the only ones I liked were those fighting to keep me alive, by doing as they knew needed to be done.

9th APRIL, 1917

We are at the Battle of Arras and what a week it has been. There has been a preliminary bombardment of Vimy Ridge as of the 20th March and this was extended to the remainder of the sector on the 4th April prior to our departure over the lines of no return. It is a wonder they call it that. Is it to mean that we shall not return to it alive, or that the attack will be so easily won, just like the Battle of Albert, and a walk-over is expected, in which case there will be no going back? I'm sick to death of the assurances given by the officers sitting in their dugouts and bunkers of luxury when compared to the miserable conditions under which we live, but it is their task I suppose to try with all their effort to keep up morale. Maybe they should stop the MPs from killing deserters and cowards; this would relieve tensions, and probably increase the number of deserters, but shouldn't a proper court of law decide the fate of men so struck by the fear of death? Hard labour and perpetual imprisonment would be a far better tact, but I doubt for a second it's easy for someone who's gone insane to think clearly about their actions before they conduct them. Besides, it is not my position to truly decide the fate of a coward, which is why others get paid a fortune to make these decisions and I get paid a shilling a day to live in shit up to my armpits. What about those blasted cowards at home who refuse to come to war and wear medals they aren't entitled to?

Already the smell of cordite is in the air and so strong that it makes some men physically sick, but it helps hide the smell of death, and the lights of the night sky, flares here and there, give an alternate satisfaction even if for just a few moments of solace during quiet nights. We must take what we can from that on offer, looking for the beauty of the word and not the muck: we deserve to smile from time to time, even if only for a few seconds, and it is these times that I recall most fondly.

There has been another commotion sprung to life. Just three days ago America declared war upon Germany. It came about almost two whole years after the sinking of the RMS Lusitania by a sodding U-boat. It still amazes me today how long it took the Americans to join the fight and as I lived well into my 70s I was also bemused by the Americans late entry into the Second World War. But who am I to judge their reasoning; I'm just happy that they went as far as to provide materials for us to meet the war, head-on, for without that aid we may well have lost everything, including my lovely wife and our children, one of which I have never met and the other I've seen but once. Further news is herald in regards to the Americans joining the war; it will be more than a year before they are ready to fight. Yes indeed; they will come and join us when the war is almost over and take the accolades for a job well done. They come with the conscripts from England but are obviously more ambitious.

Mining and tunnelling prior to the Battle of Arras was extremely excessive, so excessive it would seem that not all of the tunnels built purposely for detonating were left intact for the simple reason that the generals didn't wish to impede the infantry during the opening phases of battle due to the ground being churned up too much, but to get an insight into the actual depth in which mining and tunnelling was conducted I must give you some examples: it's simply mind-boggling, pure and simple.

Facts and figures can be moved around far too much but I shall give them how I understand them. Just in one of the sectors around Arras there were four tunnelling companies who made up a force of 2,000 men in total; these worked around the clock, twenty-four hours a day in eighteen hour shifts for two months. All of this was to aid us in getting men and supplies to the front in the safest environment possible. The tunnels were actually an addition to what already existed for the ground of Arras was chalky and good for digging, there also was to be found many caverns, underground quarries and sewage tunnels; to this was added over twelve miles of what is deemed as 'subways', 'tramways' and' railways' ['foot traffic', 'hand-drawn trolleys' and 'light railway']. It all came with underground electricity, latrines, kitchens, casualty facility and able to hide 24,000 men. And who was responsible for digging it all; Mostly New Zealanders and Bantams [men under the regulation height of five foot, three inches]. Two hundred men were either killed or wounded through the sods efforts to counter-mine ours, and although ten per cent is high it could have been a hell of a lot worse.

But enough talk on this for it is zero hour and a Monday, Easter Sunday having just gone. It's 0530hrs and the earth has been moved with a horrendous bombardment of five minutes' worth of body-and-bunker shattering artillery fire; another five minutes of shelling; further shells to add to that already fired; over 2,689,000 in total.

MY GOD! This is ludicrous! What lengths are we going to in order to kill each other; it's sheer madness!

And that's not all. We added gas shells for the fun of it. The ground on the enemy side of the fence no longer looked like a well-constructed trench but a land of craters with pockets of Germans still prepared to defend the land they sat upon. They also fought well in the air during this period, despite the fact that we had air superiority. On the scene was the Red Baron but I'll refrain from speaking on the matter, for too much on the subject of Manfred von Richtholfen and his infamous squadron will draw your attention away from my story.

I was moments from propelling myself into the air in order to be on my way when a huge fragment of artillery, which exploded not very far away, shot past me and embedded itself in the soil inches from my gut and covered me in dirt. I thank my lucky stars that I was still alive and then saw something hanging there. It was an ancient axe head from centuries past, a relic of the Roman Empire long gone. I wasted not a second and grabbed it up, thrust it away inside my khakis, and was on my way into battle.

Over the next few weeks I took part in two major battles; both the first and second Scarpe. The battles of the offensive are as follows:

First Battle of the Scarpe, 9th – 14th April;
Battle of Vimy Ridge, 9th – 12th April;
First Battle of Bullecourt, 11th April;
Battle of Lagnicourt, 15th April;
Second Battle of the Scarpe, 23rd – 24th April;
Battle of Arleux, 28th – 29th April
Third Battle of the Scarpe, 3rd – 4th April;
Second Battle of Bullecourt, 3rd – 17th May;

My God! How was it that I was still alive!

The offensive officially ended on the 16th day of May and was considered a British victory but I fail to see how a victory can be scored when you suffer more casualties than the opposition. It is fair to say we managed our objectives well but there was no exploitation to be granted us. There was little to be gained strategically and the French offensive at the Aisne did not go at all well: again with the damn French and their inabilities. All in all we suffered 158,660 casualties and the sod received anything up to 130,000; so there lays the truth and the truth is that this was a war of attrition and had little to do with gaining ground and tackling exploitation of objectives in a manner safe enough to save our souls from perpetual hell.

Gains made during the offensive ranged from good, to quite good, with the best gains made in the centre of the line and the less favourable being towards the south at Bullecourt, but the offensive soon reverted back to a stalemate of trench facing trench, and spending time with the rats and the lice.

May I now tell you this? The offensive that has just concluded was a holiday compared to what was to come and I'm sure most of you already know what it is that I speak of.

What are my forethoughts?

Firstly; that there have been so many tunnels dug beneath our feet these past three years that any water upon the surface should surely drain away. Secondly; that I wouldn't wish this experience upon my worst enemy but glad that I suffered it so that my children and children's children won't have to.

I am so naïve.

Once again the softening up of the enemy has commenced. The preliminary bombardment had commenced in some areas on the 21st but others just today. It is a tell-tale sign that something it about to happen; a free signal to the enemy to watch his front; but the enemy might consider it a ruse, but how the hell can you honestly explain the use of so many artillery shells upon an objective which you have no intention of attacking, in particular when resources are so low. And where is this bombardment I speak of taking place, but of course, this is the prelude to the slaughter of Passchendaele, that horrible place which sits in my memory forever and upon the summit of the slopes which draws the salient that is Ypres into its menacing jaws. The prelude I speak of is nothing to what was to occur but a stepping stone is just that and needs to be explained, even if minutely.

It boggles the mind to see the dirt fly into the air during any bombardment around Ypres for if you are nearer the town on a clear day and look towards England you can see and feel a quiet reminiscence, the English Channel. You turn again to look east and see the earth being torn apart, the ground which will turn to mud soon enough, for although there has been extremely little rain these past weeks, the weather was to soon make up for it in the near future, and as we all know, a little rain adds something disastrous to stirred-up dirt, turning it into one gigantic and foul bog. Yes; that is Flanders for you. Be constantly weary of what you wish for, as you may well receive it. Not enough water to drink ah? Wish for more and see what happens. Yes; again it seems here that God is against us all. So little rain, and what water the farmers have in their wells they lock up tight with padlocks so that the soldiers have to revert to vandalism; we have to break the locks to steal the water because there is none to be had. Let's hope that none of us gets caught for it wouldn't go down well to be shot simply because we were thirsty and that the resupply system was not working well in our favour.

The Battle of Messines I took no part but further up the line the 16th Irish, of which you'll recall I was now a member, were assigned Wytschaete [in reality we were further to the south on the line of attack]. These are two villages and the distance between – around nine miles – was symbolic of any strategic objective and constituted a ridge of some importance. I shall speak only briefly upon these attacks for they allowed us to position ourselves for the hell I have referred to, which was the Third Battle of Ypres, or Passchendaele; so let's get on with the story for the memory of it all is burning inside my head and I wish to be rid of the pain it causes.

The sod is retaliating and returning fire but his 630 guns are no match for the 2,266 artillery pieces and 757 heavy guns of ours that continue with their initial task, and we complement this with counter-battery fire: over 3,000,000 shells before the whistle on the 7th. The science of war is sometimes marvellous but the manner of attrition in the lines soon draws your attention away from such progress. It's as though everything that has occurred to me during this horrid war has surpassed everything else I had done before it [and after]. Having lived through it all and approaching old age I can look back upon it and know it is the reason that life has been little more than an anti-climax. Nothing can compare to the suffering and the suffering in turn lingers for a lifetime, draining our souls of all happiness to such a degree that nothing we do can really cheer us up to such heights that war can be forgotten. Yes, looking upon your children and grandchildren do bring a smile upon your face but you are soon reminded by that devil in your head that they smile because of the sacrifices of other men, sacrifices that we are all grateful for: huh; 'all of us are grateful for' indeed; all of us except those bastards in government who made false promises to those that served in the trenches, to come home and find their jobs gone and the cowards rich through the expenses of human flesh and decay.

7th JUNE, 1917

I had learnt, being sometime after the war, that the initial idea of the attacks in which we carried out over the next few months were done so in order to carry out a victory in the seizure of key areas; these areas could be more simply defined as the German U-boat pens which had access to the North Sea and from there caused all manner of war fatality, even civilian as you have learnt, without so much as a shudder of guilt or recognition, the U-boats scouring the Atlantic for easy targets and targets of opportunity, which means the same to me, to deliver their payloads most expectantly in defence against those that stood in their way, in particular vessels of the British Merchant Navy transporting ammunition for the war effort and food for those poor wretches at home half starving to death.

The hope was to do this with some measure of secrecy and surprise, but how much surprise can you obtain when the sod can see you moving copious amounts of men and arms into an area which is being raked bare by vicious artillery fire for days on end? If the Germans were bright then they would lie back a little and build their reserve for what was to come, and whether or not this was done to any worthwhile degree is doubtful for we did manage to gain some ground during the time of Passchendaele.

Once more the operation relied on its old friend the 'mine', and in this case we had twenty-one in total all ready to be exploded beneath the sodding soil of the sods' trenches. It is a wonder that such extensive mining was never discovered but there is always a way in which to deceive the enemy, such as digging a mine long enough towards the enemy and then setting up a hammer upon a pulley which could be operated some distance away, manipulated in such a way that it banged upon a sheet of metal or wood to draw the sods' ears away from our prized possessions. Our teams of miners also had an instrument called a geophone. It was similar to a stethoscope but consisted of a round ball being pushed into the clay surface of the mine wall and connected to this was a tube then fed into both ears. We could now be sure as to whether or not counter-mining had been implemented by the sod upon our hoax and determine whether or not our other mines remained reasonably safe.

At 0310hrs on this day, nineteen of the twenty-one mines were detonated, 1,000,000 pounds of explosive set in motion, a huge portion of the German line and support network utterly obliterated, 10,000 German dead at the drop of a hat, the explosion so loud it was easily heard in London. Can you image that; what it would have been like? Can you imagine furthermore being a mother at home in London being woken by the noise of the explosion, and can you see the tears welling in her eyes for the fear of what must have caused such a horrendous blast?

Parts of Hill 60 were still in the sky when the whistle blew but these finer particles of dirt was nothing compared to the initial scene when the entire surface of the world appeared in the air, large chunks of rock and earth along with the bodies of men as high as could possibly be seen. It was filled with flame and debris, and enemy bunkers made of reinforced concrete were bowled over as though made of paper. The shaking and rumbling of the earth even affected our own trenches but to an obvious lesser degree.

The crescendo of the barrage had not abated but commenced to creep towards the enemy with our good men following behind it. The wounded we suffered from our own demise were fewer than what would have been suffered if the sod was shooting at us with interlocking machine guns or artillery of his own so we cared little for the small sacrifice of a few, for so many had been saved. This in fact was the first time that the attacking force fatalities were lighter than those of the defending team. We had turned around the usual result of war and as an attacking force were coming out on top; but how long would it last?

The taking of Messines Ridge was an important stride towards securing Wytschaete and then the sites further afield, but the pens which housed the U-boats were not to be taken, for Haig on the 23rd September would be forced to cancel his decision due to our progress across Flanders.

By 0500hrs Messines was ours; by 0900hrs we had taken Wytschaete. It was such a smashing victory that we were instilled with great waves of relief and proud stability; but again, how long would it last?

This was a time to celebrate but no time was given. Our tanks were here and worked… as well as can be expected, and the sodding retaliation of counter-attack was repulsed so easily; it was as though a dream was coming true. Could the end of the war truly be in sight?

Can we give praise to the tanks for this momentous success or is it all explosions and guts that provide the reward of victory? Do you know how tanks came to be? Originally cast to be a team of two men: this was the dream of Churchill. The two men were to act so; one man would ride a motorcycle and the other would fire the mounted machine gun upon it from his sidecar, but trench warfare saw that the idea had far too many restraints and that its long leash of operational abilities was stunted by the conditions and scenarios. And what use is it to have highly trained men and nothing to make of them, and so Churchill devised the idea of ships to sail upon the land, huge tubs to plaster the enemy with hot lead, and they looked like water tanks. The Motor Machine Section of the Machine Gun Corps was now operating out of tanks.

In fewer than twelve hours of fighting, not only were Messines and Wytschaete ours but other objectives were in hand as well with more than 7,000 enemy prisoners taken. There is one further thing to tell you which I think is rather important, in particular considering the fighting in Ireland which I spoke of earlier, and that was that we, the 16th Irish, and for the first time ever, were fighting side-by-side with the 36th Ulsters… North and South… Protestant and Catholic… and a mix of atheist here and there but love for country more than making up for it all. A man cannot always choose the company he keeps. Sometimes a man might be born a Protestant but have the heart of a Catholic. Some things remain secret, but the bond that men have as brothers exceeds all else.

And so the night is falling upon us and the rubble of Wytschaete is not far ahead when the first of many grand memories recite their masked beauty, usually unheard for the noise of war is so loud but on this occasion something was unveiled, to be held dear to heart. It was fairly warm because there was no rain and the night had brought out the nightingales. Their singing was a comfort seldom found in war. It was bliss. None of us cares about what the other believes, we only care that they live and breathe, and that we help each other in this time of great need.

We were victorious and the dry weather was killing us through heat and poor water replenishment, and the phase of the operation calling for the capture of the U-boat pens seemed but so close. And so we waited and the generals talked. For two months there was little to nothing occurring worth me telling you about other than a new time table of bombardment commencing on the 16th day of July. With the passing of time the sod improved his fortifications; with the passing of time went the summer months and approaching was a month or more of heavy rain.

It was coming up to the Third Battle of Ypres and the sods had invented another gas to be used against the flesh and bone of our good men and cause. It had various names but the one that sticks in my mind is 'GAS!' and for all apparent reasons. Call it HS [Hun Stuff] if you like, it doesn't matter much, but the word that gets in your ear when most needed to hear is the clear and concise calling of gas. The sods called it Yellow Cross because on their artillery firing line they had stacks of gas shells and needed to differentiate between one and the other, so chlorine gas was marked with a green cross and the mustard gas with a yellow one: maybe the symbol of the cross was to symbolise death.

I soon learnt that mustard gas was far more effective at killing, maiming, and clearing the trenches than chlorine gas, and it certainly did like to linger. Delivered in artillery shells it polluted the ground upon which we lived, soaking into the soil, remaining for anything up to a month or more, which was highly dependent on the atmospheric conditions of the time. It was heavier than air and so didn't act in a similar contrast to its cousin the chlorine, but it could easily be reactivated by a little digging or shelling. One always had to be on their toes and know the history of the ground on which they were on for the more one knew of his surroundings, the better precautions could be taken.

Having said all of this the dangers were sometimes ignored, for although it was a deadly weapon and accounted for 90% of all deaths caused by gas, if a man had to dig then he had to dig, and after several years in the field one trench looked much like the other: although some of the trenches dug by the French were extremely inadequate and I assume it is because of their philosophy of wanting to be on the attack and to keep the momentum moving other than sitting in place and waiting to be attacked: but then again there were so many instances where this could be proved incorrect. It was all well and good, but the French failed to deliver on this philosophy when needed the most, in particular during the counter-attacks at the Second Battle of Ypres and others.

The effects of mustard gas was blistered skin and sore eyes, vomit accompanied with internal bleeding. It was painful at best and excruciating at worst and some of the men who inhaled it sufficiently enough could take up to five weeks to die from the exposure. Worst of all you did not need to breathe it in to feel the effects of it; simply contact with the skin was enough to cause blistering. Many times I saw the flesh of men being eaten away by high concentrations of mustard gas where contact with the skin started what would become an evacuation process, red sores turning into blisters and accompanied by headaches, fluid on the lung and high temperature.

This was a double-edged weapon if ever there was. Any general worth his salt and pepper, as I sometimes like to say, wouldn't allow the use of mustard gas prior to an attack by his troops, not where ground was the main prize over casualties, for the lingering effect of the gas meant it dealt just as much suffering to the axis as the allies. So maybe the sod is telling but once again that they have no intention of taking any more ground. But as experienced in the past the generals of the sods seemed to care little for the conscripts which were forced to party under the banner of the Kaiser, that damn sod, the biggest of them all, that looked at himself in the mirror each day and saw a glorious German Emperor instead of a ghastly monster. What did he care of the innocent, those young men fighting for rights of freedom due every man and woman?

Those poor men that drew large wafts of gas into their lungs obviously suffered the most where others were more fortunate and only suffered a little, but the effects of the gas remained with us for the remainder of our lives in most cases. Respiratory disease was one thing to deal with in old age; failing eyesight another. You might imagine how men felt being returned to the front, to continue with the fight after being given the all clear by medical practitioners, knowing that their lungs were not quite right for scar tissue had formed and would be a permanent reminder of the sodden German attacks of immoral purity, for tuberculosis was common.

It is unlike any other wound for it cannot be bandaged. And the burns are agonizing, far worse than any other wound I fear. You can't help but cry out for the endurance of pain is far more outlasting than a man's conviction to accept it.

Different gas had different effects but all can easily be condemned, in particular by the nurses who treated the poor wounded. The chlorine gas burned heavily in the throat and eyes with that feeling of suffocation. Severe pains in the centre of the chest, coughing, retching, trouble breathing which was often rapid though shallow, vomiting, dryness of the throat, headaches and imbalance experienced when stood up.

There is acute bronchitis, or bronchopneumonia develops; the temperature rises to as high as 104. Delusion sets in, Pleurisy may occur, and gangrene of the lung might follow.

But recovery is sometimes obtained after which the patient remains exhausted and unable to perform any duties for quite some time. The nervous system is affected and headaches, vertigo and dyspepsia may continue for several weeks.

Those that recovered sufficiently to be redeployed into the trenches were due to their exposure being classed as mild but only after the lungs had proved to be clear of the effects of any gas. Others suffer permanent incapacity and may experience Blighty leave, though little joy can be experienced at such a joyous occasion for it would be far better to return with a leg missing than being incapacitated by gas.

And what about the evacuation plan; what can be said about it? It was as good as could be expected under the circumstances, except for at the Somme.

Many stages existed, but some men might miss one or more stages due to their injury. And not all men with injuries could be attended to for those that were seen to be dying were left aside whilst others that could be saved were treated.

The first port of call was our Regimental Aid Post normally situated just behind the front and in the reserve trenches. Have a bandage applied, grab a drink, be sent off further down the line as soon as practically possible. This is what you might term as 'light first aid'. Although the officer was a medical officer, the others would be less endowed and from the ranks of the infantry itself: though each and every one would be accustomed to dressing wounds, and diagnosing sufficiently enough to remedy minor treatment.

Then on to the Advanced Dressing Station 'ADS'. Different means were employed to get men along and if they could walk then they did so under their own presence. There was also a good system of Stretcher Bearer relay established after the first two years of war whereby men were stationed at 1000 yards apart. This didn't only aid in fewer cases of exhaustion through portage of men but also allowed familiarity with the changing landscape of their particular sector.

Further along and there was the Main Dressing Station.

Regimental details were again a formality before the next stop along the line to the rear, again depending on the severity of the wound/s, which was the Field Ambulance. More time was available for treatment here but again the urgency for quick evacuation was always present. Emergency operations were able to be carried out at the Field Ambulance but only where really necessary or time permitted. A Field Ambulance had capacity for around 150 casualties but were often inundated which saw many men lying around upon stretchers awaiting further development or death. Limb amputations would be done at the CCS.

The CCS, or Casualty Clearing Station, was next in line, wounded moved on by any reasonable means such as horse and carriage, ambulance train, canal barge, or other wagon transport. These were usually well equipped facilities set up in a tented camp. From here you would either be treated and returned to the front, remain in place for specialist surgery in readiness for further movement down the line, or keep the wheels turning by sending on the worst but stable cases to other more suited facilities. The CCS could hold 1,000 wounded.

The Base Hospitals were next in the line of evacuation or possibly even good old England for those that had been granted blighty leave.

A Base Hospital can provide a great opportunity for life to be maintained, and can hold between 1,000 and 2,500 patients, providing ample facility for most if not all injuries sustained on the front. Places on the coast such as Boulogne and Le Havre had base hospitals as well as Le Touquet, Rouen and Etaples. But enough of this; to battle we go.

I am not a weatherman but I know that an airstream is approaching towards us and we can feel it in our bones. There is much rain upon the wind of this airstream and we shall feel the full brunt of its unseen power to come.

31st JULY, 1917

The Third Battle of Ypres is said to be between the 31st July and 10th November. The period was more or less the same with the exemption that engineering progress was made in regards to walkways [duckboards] allowing for slightly easier movement from the front to the rear and vice versa. The objective was the village of Passchendaele and the securing of the coast. As well as the usual infantry and artillery there were to be 168 Mark IV tanks [48 in reserve] with five divisions of cavalry to be deployed.

The initial foresight was as grand as the last Allied effort, with a creeping barrage and infantry assault, with tanks securing a 4,000 yards breakthrough, but German counter-attacks took back most of this from our exhausted troops. What happened next was unprecedented for in August the weather turned extremely foul. Much rain was suffered for three days from the 1st August to 4th August; a further deluge was then added to that which could not escape the mud stricken ground on the 8th. On the night of the 11th the sky broke out in horrendous, blistering rain and lightning for a further three days.

Regardless of the weather, however, the Battle of Langemarck must be fought, and at the forefront of it all I find myself once more in a bad place.

16th AUGUST, 1917

We were extremely exhausted and many of the men suffered from some form of illness but stuck it out as best they could. My brigade was at the front, and the 2nd Dublin was just behind the two leading units: the 7th Royal Irish Rifles and the 9th Dublin Fusiliers to our front. I guess I can consider myself extremely lucky but fail to see much luck in the conditions we are made to attack over. There is little semblance of anything at all to our front, such a massive marshland void of any trees, shrubs or grass and behind us were the duckboards that had delivered us this far. It is mud and mud alone which is covered in craters all filled with water. The water has nowhere to go and so these holes in the ground swallow men whole. It's hard to keep on one's feet when the going is rough and you're being shot at. You have to take cover; have to run; and needless to say you slip and fall down time-and-time again. If you should fall into a crater then you can count your blessings having been paid in full if you should survive, for so many die through the sheer exhaustion of holding on to dear life or being drowned in the muck straight away.

We commenced the attack at 0445hrs and so it is rather dark; it is hard to see where you are and where you are going. You can only hope that you aren't heading for the deepest crater there is, for if you are there will be no returning. But before we have even left the line to commence our assault we have lost 65 per cent of our men to the sodding artillery. Can you imagine that, going into battle when two-thirds of you are either dead or dying even before the whistle?

German machine guns then open up and we are decimated once again. How many times must it be like this? So many times my unit is decimated and I come that much closer to dying. But I again must thank my lucky stars, for B Coy have but five soldiers left alive whilst I, under charge of C Coy, move in to give aid to a stricken 9th Dublin Fusiliers who have lost every single solitary man in their battalion except two officers and ten other ranks. Can you see now, dear reader, what it is to be 'decimated'?

And so we continue on with the pain of knowing we are so few and suddenly I find myself up to my armpits in mud. Men are passing me by because it is hard to see and there is a war going on, but I yell as loudly as I possibly can but it is useless because no one will hear me, and so I try to wave my arms about and slip to my chin in mud. A man then stumbles and I have no idea who it is. I think he is dead but he isn't. He has seen my plea for aid and soon there are three men taking the time to get me out of there against their orders and whilst being blindly sprayed by enemy machine guns trying to find their marks with the aid of flares. They use their rifles and with great effort I grasp two of these with my muddy paws and am fortunate enough to be dragged out of my predicament. My saviours then rejoin the attack and instantly two of them are killed but the other continues on. I follow immediately after with the weight of the stinking mud slowing me down.

The sun is trying to come up above the horizon. As it comes I can see the landscape more clearly. I can see the miserable scene about, where bodies decay all around me and there are limbs of men lying here and there: an arm and a leg, then more on top of that; oh, and a head torn from the body with its eyes looking up into the sky searching for the gates into heaven. There are scores of smashed up wagons, tanks, and other articles of war. I can see horses so thin that their skin seems sucked into their bodies with the ribs scoring into the hide, almost worn away from the effects of death and the bad weather. Spouts of mud and water shoot into the air where artillery shells land and machine guns find their targets by using the spouts of water shooting up from craters as points of reference in order to secure a kill. The bodies have been laying around here for anything up to two whole weeks or more and cannot be moved. It is a wasted effort to drag in the dead when so much energy is taken to drag in the wounded, and even then the wounded are lucky to be given aid at all.

This was the mud of Passchendaele and we all knew that the attacks would not be called off.

If I was careful I might survive and then a machine gun burst whizzed past my head. I struck the ground hard but the fall was cushioned by the mud and I was half buried in it as I lay flat upon my stomach in an effort to clear myself from view of the enemy gunner. I crawled further forward and made an effort to get up with the weight of the mud clinging to my body and the machine gun burst upon me again but this time I stayed down and crawled further forward in the hope of getting past the bunker's visual. I came upon a crater lip and was astonished by what I saw.

Below me in a crater about ten feet across were two wounded men and another dead. It was the Somme all over again. Just before plunging in I lifted my head to see what lay before me and what I saw was the bunker once more and further afield yet another. I pulled my head down and slid into the crater where the two living saw me but remained silent through their misery and helplessness.

I could hear the sounds of war as they continued all around me but was hard pressed to ever see anything; everyone was so covered in mud that they blended in with the surroundings and the only hope of seeing anyone was if they moved. I then reflected upon the bunkers and realised how hard it was to actually see them for they too were camouflaged in the mud slung up from artillery fire. There must have been scores of men in small pockets of resistance putting fire down upon the sod as the sod was putting fire down upon us. It was a stalemate once more and no man was going anywhere, and fast. If nothing else this must have been a great scenario for all those snipers wishing to increase their number of kills, to increase their tally for the day.

It was then that one of the wounded men made acquaintance by referring to how hard it was to see the bunker not far to our front and so I chanced another look, and knew I must be pressing my luck, and indeed managed to make out a bunker looking directly down upon us. It must have been them that had been firing at me and then I realised that the bunkers would have been shooting across the front of the bunkers either side of it and not directly to its front, hence a criss-cross effect of fire being formed, an enfilade fire in direct support of the other bunkers which formed an impenetrable wall of fire that could not be crossed by flesh and blood. The only time in fact that the bunkers switched their firing to their front was when in danger of being overrun or bombed by my specialised infantry counterparts. It was easy to see therefore that there was no going forward and no going back. To go forward would be into the face of a machine gun and its crew; to go back would be through the impenetrable wall of fire… to stay put was simply crazy, for we could go hypothermic.

I took to evaluating the wounded and found that both had similar wounds. Both were riddled with bullet holes in their left and right arms, a miraculous coincidence. Both were in sheer agony whenever they moved their limbs and therefore found it difficult to check their wounds and treat them effectively, and so with the mud wallowing up to my waste as I crouched in the centre of the crater I drew myself closer to the side and tried with all my effort to get my feet planted into the mud substantially enough to keep me steady.

I asked if the two wounded were managing okay in preventing themselves from slipping further into the mud and they answered yes, for they were leaning upon the side of the crater with their feet firmly upon the backs of their dead comrades: two dead men below the surface of the mud were allowing these two wounded to remain adrift as it were.

There was no way to clean the wounds and so all I could do was try to fasten them more securely, which I managed to do within ten minutes.

A Lewis-gun was then heard and it sounded quite close; not more than 100 feet away. The enemy retaliated and the Lewis-gun fell silent. I never heard from them again. They could have withdrawn; maybe they were playing dead; or maybe they were killed or wounded. But I had to consider my position as best I could.

I looked at the dead man once my task was complete and felt myself slip into the mud. I knew I had to stay still or drown, but what was to happen if I fell asleep in my exhaustion and drowned? The two wounded were certainly in no way able to give me aid. Another 30 minutes must have passed when one of the wounded said the one thing that was already on my mind. I would have to take the dead man and use his body to keep me afloat. This was the one thing I didn't want to do but did I have a choice in the matter. During the Somme I refrained from taking a wounded man's pay book but this time I reached out and searched his body. I took his pay book and ID discs and then found something more. I found a letter from his wife or girlfriend, for there was also a photo alongside it. I wasn't game to read it: I would leave that to the officers in the rear when they returned his belongings to England. I also found a fob watch which was not working. It seemed to have a dent in it which was put there by a bullet. Maybe it saved his life once and so he maintained it as a good luck charm, as some men do with these things.

I was about to remove his equipment from his body but one of the wounded men said no, it would be better to stand upon him fully dressed. So this soldier was now an 'it'. So I took it and managed to push it before me and then down under my feet. I now had something good to stand on but my conscience would play hell with me in future years.

Some time later, I don't know how long exactly, I fell asleep. I woke up again just before dark when a light rain began to fall. It was very light but still added to our misery. We were caked in mud, unable to move, freezing cold, without much more than half a canteen of water between three men and some iron rations which would parch me further.

What were we to do?

I went into a bit of a trance at that moment. I knew that there were places upon the line which were being relieved now and again, as was the routine in the trenches. After eight days I could possibly count on being relieved. I could only assume that this would be all the sooner due to the poor conditions and the inability to get stores up to the men holding the line, and then I did an amazing thing; I smiled. One of the wounded looked at me as though I was mad and I thought again about our position. Here we were, thin on the ground with pockets of resistance scattered around; some places on the line faring better than ours. We were at what appeared to be a stalemate. The Germans obviously saw no great need to attack us, unless it was a counter-attack to take back valuable ground lost; but that wasn't the case for me, surely. I tried with all my might to listen for Lewis-guns and Lee-Enfields firing, and the darker it became the easier it was to distinguish, but there was always the retaliation of returned fire from the sod to deal with.

No; it was hopeless. To stay here was a death sentence. I had to try and get the two wounded men back but should I take the worst case or the better. I looked at the two wounded and they looked at me. I explained what I intended to do, to try and get back to our line with both of them, but obviously could only manage one at a time. They decided for me. Leave the worst case behind for his pain was not as great, but his wounds were extremely bad. I accepted this decision and loosened my haversack, pulling my arms free from it as it was stuck in the mud. If nothing else it had helped keep my back warm.

With the sun now down and my chances of getting the wounded back all the more sure I made my way as best I could to a position behind the wounded man before trying to pull him up and out, this was brought to a quick close as some flares appeared just above us. I fell to the ground and waited, a mouthful of mud for my trouble. The next opportunity was farer but the wounded man wouldn't budge. He was stuck hard in the mud when I suddenly realised he hadn't undone his haversack. With this now undone I tried again to lift him out; again he wouldn't move. His feet and waist were so well stuck in the mud that it was going to take all of my strength to achieve my goal.

I soon noticed without too much effort that my feet, even outside of the crater, had sunk into the mud up to my knees as I pulled and pulled, but there was still no movement from the wounded and his body from the waist down just would not give an inch. It was then decided against our wishes to try the other soldier but again, no matter how hard we tried he simply wouldn't move. I clambered back into the hole before another flare chanced into the sky above me and chewed upon the dilemma that faced us.

There was no doubt at all that I was unable to move either man and to do this I would need serious aid. I was therefore confronted with two options. Firstly, to stay put and wait for relief, watching over my two companions [but we were out of water and dressings]; secondly, I could go back myself and get a stretcher party to follow me back out to this crater. Neither option sounded great but little choice there was to choose from. If we stayed we would probably die and so back to the line I would have to go.

I commenced to make my way to the far side of the crater and heard whispering in the cold night air between the cracks of rifle fire and artillery; this I ignored and climbed the side with great effort. Once at the lip I heard further whispering. I stopped and turned around covered in mud and looked into the eyes of the wounded as best I could in the light made available by the motions of war. I could just make out the whites of their eyes and see their hands moving around before them as shadows danced around. They knew as well as I that the chances of survival were slim. Wasn't it bad enough that I should have to go back to our own line, let alone come back out to the crater? We all knew from experience that the task was too enormous, far too much to achieve. Their wounds were bad and they'd lost a lot of blood. They would also require two stretcher parties of 6 to 8 men a-piece. The war was lost for them and we all knew it. I then saw a grenade appear in one of the men's hands I thought for a dying moment that they meant to commit suicide, but all I could hear was a simple statement advising me that the grenade was for the enemy if they should chance too close.

I turned and commenced my journey.

I shall not tell you the story of my return to our own lines for the trek was a long one. I should guess that I set out from the crater at around 2000hrs and by the time I'd gotten back to our own line of support it was well past midnight. The reason it took so long is because many of the duckboards that we'd employed the day before to get to the front were actually missing; having either sunk or had been hit directly by artillery; and once your path is lost it is lost, it was also unfortunate and hard to admit that on my way back I only managed to fall upon a duckboard because I was approaching it from an acute angle: in other words, I was going in the wrong direction and instead of towards my lines I was crossing in front of them. There was absolutely no way in which I was going to manage with a wounded man on my back, and then it dawned upon me. How in the hell was I going to find them again?

I could tell you how we made an effort to get to the men but this wasn't until the following night, and we failed miserably to find those we were looking for but managed to get seven wounded men back who were a little closer to the line than they were. The amount of wounded men out there amongst the mud was mind-boggling. When I was returning on my own from the pit of despair, in which I had found myself emotionally and physically drained, I simply couldn't fathom the numbers of bodies I saw laying around. At one stage I heard gurgling noises and wandered aimlessly for a dozen feet to see what I could find, but all there was, was an empty hole from what I could manage to see. Maybe it was another man drowning in the mud, or the gasses of his body escaping the tomb in which the body was set: for the stench was putrid to say the least. And later still I reflected upon this short journey of mine which seemed to last forever and that it never occurred to me that many of the bodies I saw may have been wounded, possibly unconscious or sleeping. But what can a single man do against such over-whelming odds.

And so I never again laid eyes upon the two men that I shared a crater with again, but in the least I returned the letter with the photo of the young woman; her husband – and I wish to think of him as that – had saved my life.

By the 22nd August, some twenty-three days since the commencement of the Third Battle of Ypres, we had suffered 3,420 officer casualties and 64,586 other ranks; many of whom were missing in the mud and would never be found again. May they all rest in peace, in particular after receiving such a restless death.

And so time continues ever on. The Battle of Menin Road was undertaken from 20th to 25th September, 3,500,000 rounds of artillery fired in preparatory, almost four times more than that of 31st July; we gained 1.5 miles of ground.

The Battle of Polygon Wood on 26th September saw another gain of more than one mile, and on the 4th October the Battle of Broodseinde saw the Australians deliver a smashing victory where their heroics shall never be forgotten.

The 9th October saw the Battle of Poelcappelle come and go and the First Battle of Passchendaele arrived in earnest on 12th October.

The Second Battle of Passchendaele commenced on the 26th and ended on the 10th November.

But what is the meaning of all these dates and battles?

4th October – clouds filled the sky and it rained, adding more to that which had fell this past two weeks… 6th October – the bad weather showed not a single sign of slowing up… 11th October – hurricane force winds on the eve of battle… 13th October – it rained non-stop for fifteen solid hours….

Was it not always the same, that rain preceded an attack, which shortly after there might be a little sunshine to dry up the rain and dry out the mud only to be joined again in further flurries and extremely bad weather? What I have stated to you over these last few pages and more is nothing compared to the real horrors of Passchendaele during this sodding war. The misery is simply too much to fathom; too much to sanely bear; it's impossible for you to completely understand unless you wear our boots and slog through the same mud that we have slogged through.

We were so decimated that the 8th and 9th Dublins were amalgamated and the 2nd were provided reinforcements to bring them back up to a reasonable strength. We were now prepared for the Battle of Cambrai and in particular, Tunnel Trench [which meant that we, the men of the 16th Irish Division, were to clear the way for the coming assaults upon the Hindenburg Line and beyond. The fact of the tale is that we were used as a diversionary almost eight miles away to the northwest from the centre of the main action. And let me tell you, we did not disappoint, for along with 3,000 yards of trench system captured we also took over 600 prisoners of war and 300 dead [this was an understatement of course, and derived only from those bodies of the enemy counted within the trenches themselves].

It was a reminder of the Battle of Langemarck with all the machine gun nests harboured in concrete surrounds; the only real difference was the way in which the trench system had been built with an underground tunnel in line with the front trench but forty feet below it, staircases providing access to it every twenty-five yards. It was a marvel. These German engineers needed to be congratulated, and I would have done so under different circumstances.

As a member of the 2nd Royal Dublin Fusiliers I was in the centre of the advance of our small portion of the attack and it smacked of the taste of normal Trench Warfare, but many circumstances placed much favour in our position.

There was some artillery at 0600hrs and we made good use of the stoke mortars in our sector. The stoke and its use of smoke proved to ruse the enemy into believing that they were being gassed and many, if not most, took to hiding below ground with their mask over their faces. At 0620hrs we left our line behind us and made our way forward.

The timing of the artillery was absolutely superb. We had 200 yards of no-man's land to cross and as we crossed this and fell upon the enemy; the artillery had been lifted from the area. It now came to the killing and what we could not see were dealt a savage hand as we cleared the tunnel system with bombs; there would be no counting the dead down there; not by me at least.

Sappers soon joined our victory and put to wiring up explosives to counter any enemy attack whilst the battle continued to rage in other areas around me. Some sectors encountered stiffer resistance than what I had encountered and for that I could only give praise, for I felt that I deserved just a small measure of relief.

With the fight still raging in places the main assault upon Cambrai was well on the way.

The Poor State of War and Conflict

This would see the first real attempt at deploying tanks in large numbers and without the usual aid of a massive pre-planned artillery strike although the small barrage of just 1,003 guns at 0600hrs did well at their task of softening up the enemy positions. The lack of any large scale preliminary must have contributed to pulling the enemy off guard as did our diversionary attack for it all seemed to be met by a huge amount of success, which after the weeks now behind us was a welcome relief.

The amount of ground which we strove to win as an army was also granted in favour of our ambitious tactics and four miles was gained [five on the right flank] upon the newly fought ground known as the Hindenburg Line. It was so satisfying to be a part of something so memorable that I considered for just a moment that maybe I would get to see my loving family once more before I died: they were forever on my mind and helped keep me sane. And is it not wondrous in years post how we remember the great days of war when amongst friends of old and then by night when sleep falls upon us we see the reality of it all as nightmares invade the security of our slumber? Yes; it's a jest.

But back to war I trudge in this short appraisal of my life on the front… yes; the church bells of Old England rang out the great victory for all to hear but it would be a short-lived celebration for the bastard sod had invented a new form of warfare and it involved twenty enemy divisions punching through to the rear of our line, bypassing the strong points, taking out our artillery and cutting off all resupply, creating a huge vacuum of confusion, and taking care of the pockets of resistance once a new front line had been established. Within a week all of our gains had been lost.

It was a dishonour to later learn that generals and the like were pushing and shoving to gain the praise for the initial victory of breaking through the Hindenburg Line where tanks and men fought side by side, but after the demise of the situation and our loss of ground there was not a hand to be seen anywhere. I despised them all for this, their clambering over each other for a good pat on the back but then failing to accept any responsibility for any loss to life and limb, and ground; no, not for the loss of ground; for the loss of life. I was here to fight a war, not for the glory of a few head-strong generals.

But how did we fare; how was the battle waged; with artillery, smoke, 437 tanks and six infantry divisions. So can you do math? How many tanks to each battalion? [Approx 8 per battalion]. Well, I'm no good at math but I can tell you this; I saw bugger-all of any tanks but the occasional appearance of one to my farthest right flank, but then again the effects of war didn't allow me to think of this as a sight-seeing venture, in particular when your visions are marred by the dead and dying, and we were a part of the diversionary. And many mishaps as usual were encountered, like the attempt at capturing a bridge only to have it collapsed under the weight of the tanks as they endeavoured to cross it: when they built these bridges the thought of anything as heavy as a tank crossing over it would have been the furthest thing from the engineers' minds. One eighty tanks were out of action that first day with sixty-five being utterly destroyed; there were in the vicinity of severny-one mechanical failures and around forty-three tanks which had been ditched, and I can only assume that some of these were those lost due to collapsing bridges.

It was said many times and recorded for prosperity that the diversion by the 16th was what provided the edge of victory whereby the first real signs of a true and possible end to the war could be seen; this, regardless of the losses when compared to our gains.

By the end of it all what did we get? We received another transfer on the 3rd December to Gough's Fifth Army. I was a part of the 48th Brigade [1st and 2nd RDF, with the 2nd Munster Fusiliers along for the ride].

DECEMBER, 1917

Christmas Day: it's snowing hard as is to be expected. Maybe if we were pushing south instead of east the temperature would be friendlier towards our vocation and the lice less prone to bite, for the war always simmered during the colder months, but our sufferings quite often all the worse. If there was ever a choice I guess I would have to choose the cold, but even in old age I still haven't made up my mind.

Try as I might I couldn't get comfortable enough to sleep even with my eyelids as heavy as they were, and although all logic told me to stay still and remain warm I was destined to relieve myself before what I carried in my bladder froze within me, and made it impossible to do anything further.

I got up and commenced to make my way to a spot where I could do my duty without making our lives any more miserable by urinating where I stood. I hadn't gone far when I fell upon two men. One seemed to ignore the other for his antics were the strangest and most worrisome I had ever seen.

Give me my baby, he would say. Pass me my baby, I can't reach it. I would look and see that he was talking of a tin cup just out of reach of his extended fingers which bore the horrendous sign of frostbite. Give me my baby, he would say. And so I picked up the tin cup and gave it to him. He pulled it into his chest and hugged it, cradling it in his arms, smiling down upon the thing which if not used for drinking out of might be used for pissing into. There was no doubt in my mind that he was out of his mind and so I did the only thing possible; I ignored it. What should happen if I was to report him but a couple of MPs might appear with a bullet in the chamber? He seemed to have a friend sitting beside him and maybe it was his task to tend to his friend. I can only assume that when next we went over the top that he would still be there cradling his cup and some officer might fall upon him and take pity before the MPs caught sight of him.

Did I do my duty? Did I do what should have been done? I cannot carry the weight of the world upon my shoulders. There are many men around who, no doubt, knew him better than I. I should only hope that I did not come to form the same illusions upon my own mind.

And with the end of winter coming towards us we could feel the robustness of war falling back into place. Our numbers in February, due to many reasons as expressed these past four years, had dwindled at an alarming rate. We now received a… refurbishment. The 8th, 9th, and 10th Dublin's were disbanded and with just under 200 men combined they were amalgamated into the 1st and 2nd Dublin's: we now had new stock but for the most part they were older hands as opposed to new; this literally meant better chances of survival for us all; unless we were to be thrown to the lions once more.

21st MARCH, 1918

By 1918 we were inundated with warnings of gas attacks through the use of a bell system. It was a powerful air horn which had a good range of nine miles, but sometimes hard to hear between bouts of shelling, and most of us older men seemed to be growing rather deaf. We had also learnt to leave signs about warning others coming into the trenches that gas had been employed within the area or might be likely due to an expected up-and-coming sod attack; and the good word was that an attack was imminent.

It was during this month and commencing this day that many factors in the sods' disposition, both military and civilians alike, strove to make their mark upon the declining war effort. It was clear that the citizenry were appalled at the German losses as much as they were starving to death: it would appear that they were growing as tired of the war as we were but they were the bastards that had started it. These face values of the effects of war came tumbling towards us in orders and the occasional newspaper that one man or other might be sent here and there, we were also provided information of the enemy disposition which did not look too grand, and this made me so happy, for awhile.

There was an instance, or should I say, a terrible tragedy; the Russians surrendered and a treaty was signed, called the Treaty of Brest Litovsk; the sod was therefore able to move, as fast as they could possibly muster, 50 divisions towards the BEF and the soon-to-arrive Yanks. But these figures changed rather rapidly. It was said, and I quite believe it [though I'm sure the generalship would rather have these figures understated to prevent panic] that there were around 184, give or take, sodding divisions in France and Flanders, and when you hear that, "the '302nd' Division is such and such", then you know that a lot of men have fought, or are fighting, in this damn war: 110 divisions on the front line and 31 divisions facing the BEF with more than 60 in reserve. Damn it all, numbers here, numbers there; they rarely added up and there was always confusion to put up with. I couldn't make much from it all. All I really cared about was what we had directly to our front, and who was supporting them. With the Americans arriving at our backs sooner rather than later it was time for the Germans to push and push hard before our friends could establish themselves and form upon our flanks, and possibly even amongst us. So what did I care if the Germans had one hundred divisions, two hundred, or even three; what did I truly care that these numbers were what was present now, or what had been over the years to date. We all just wished to see the end of it all.

With all of this upon my mind I could clearly see that they were to either throw everything they had at us in a last-ditch effort to wipe us clean from the face of the earth, for there could be no other explanation for such a well-fitted organisation to be required when the countries populace was so ill-at-ease, or they would stand and fight from where they stood.

There is but one last thing which I think I should mention and that is of the sods' newly invented weapon-of-war. They had invented a form of soldier called the stormtrooper, the cream of all other divisions, the fittest and best taken from here and there to form divisions of fearsome men who would be cut at the leash to advance upon and through us, cutting off and destroying all communication, artillery, headquarters, support, resupply, and so on and so forth. They had used them against the Russians and now it was to be our turn.

The lead up to this days hard duty were masked with gas attacks to keep us from sleep and they did their work well for I was beginning to forget how long it had been since I had received good slumber, but my mind perks up during the opening of the artillery and even more so when I see for the first time the flammenwerfer coming towards me, those evil men with flame-throwers, with jets of flame spurting thirty yards out from the nozzle. The prettiest sight is seeing them flicker and die as they run out of fuel but it's a seldom thing to witness, and it is the last thing you wish to think about as you scramble to kill the men who employ them, or try to seek cover as men burn around you, and you know you have to pray to God once more on conceding that you must now regain his trust after years of neglect and cold-shoulder.

When there is a wall of flame approaching you, you must gather all you can on your side and I apologize to you if you think I am using God to save my life before deciding to shun him again once more, but since those heinous days of morbid horror I have stayed by his side in belief even if not being as attentive in practise.

We had already [the 1st and 2nd Dublins] suffered extremely heavy casualties from the initial bombardment and the sods use of poison gas [1,062 casualties from both combined] and so it was easy, with all that was happening, for the German forces of new to spill over us and keep on moving: do I need to remind you that the normal strength for a battalion was 1,000 men but for some time now many battalions were operating with as few as 500 due to losses; can you see now how so many casualties over a short period of ten hours, even before the whistle blew for the sodding infantry to fall upon us, would see the bastards gain so much ground by penetrating our lines of defence? 1,100,000 artillery shells in five hours they fired over an area of just 150 square miles. That was horrendous, the largest bombardment of the war. And now more of the same slaughter was to come. It was here that those Germans bringing up the rear would take care of those men caught behind by any means they could, to clean our small pockets of resistance up as best they could; I can only thank God that what was left of the 2nd were able to retreat as ordered. Many men along the front were taken prisoner but being taken alive was better than burning to death. As for me and many around us we were lucky to escape with our lives, to live and continue fighting as we evacuated our positions.

The sheer horror of those days is not to be contemplated lightly. In three days we had lost all the gains we'd made since Passchendaele. The enemy were pushing as hard as they could and their new front line left behind them hundreds upon hundreds of pockets of resistance and we continued to fight as best we could. Those men left behind had no food, were low on ammo, and had no communications and little to no support. All any of us could do was to hold out as best we could whether on the move towards the west or holding out in pockets. The worst of the enemy action was by no means over, but for some the main assault had come and gone, and they were now targeting those 'passed-over' with mopping up operations. Many men fought to the last, refusing to surrender and hence giving their life to duty and their country. My only hope during those dark days was that we could hold out long enough for our good men to form up and strike back; my hope was that we could continue our retreat in reasonably good order and not get caught out like so many of those that had been left behind.

22nd MARCH, 1918

It was seen as a gift that those left behind were still fighting and delaying the enemy advance. This was the second day of Operation Michael, the second day of the sodding offensive. It reminded me a little of the retreat from Mons because we were mobile. Trench Warfare seems to have faded away into oblivion.

We retreated; the engineers blew up bridges; the sod did all they could to keep the gap between us closed. But they seemed so disordered and acted erratically. The disorder could not last for long, surely, but then again I guess it was all about who could outlast the disorder the longest for we were not in any great state ourselves. Men from difficult units were fighting with others, here and there it seemed to be the accepted way of today's war to fight with men from units that you didn't know. It was up to the officers and NCOs to take command of what they could and retain some form of discipline, but discipline was never our problem; our issues were always the generals and out-dated policies.

In some places the retreat was holding its own, in others the enemy had penetrated more than ten miles with pockets of resistance being looked to by the enemy reserve. It was not an easy picture to decipher, let alone paint.

25th MARCH, 1918

Some good news; the enemy seems to have advanced as far as they can manage. They were as exhausted as us, if not more; their artillery and resupply could not keep up the pace as was similar to four years previous during Mons: they had not learnt their lessons well. The 16th Irish have also been transferred back to the Third Army.

We were suffering from a lack of food but the enemy were suffering from a lack of artillery. It was a bitter-sweet period of the war, but I guess it is better to be alive and hungry than ducking your head before it gets blown away from shelling.

There was a moment's peace in the air, a little solace to tend our minds, and then the enemy seemed to suddenly pick themselves up and continue on, the pace quickened once more, the hectic war continuing on for God knows how many days to come. Again we were moving alongside civilians with their carts and wagons stacked high with all manner of possessions, moving at best speed away from the stormtroopers, flammenwerfer and death. The cavalry, also, did their bit as before, their actions being the toast of the day.

26th MARCH, 1918

The stage was set for the Doullens conference and the newest tank from England, the Whippet, was to make its debut, a tank that was lighter and faster than the Mark IV. The enemy, in large numbers, fled the advance of twelve of these. A small dominoes effect then saw to it that other German infantry were left without support and consequently taken by force, for the remainder of the day new lines were drawn upon the map and the force from both sides found their footing upon the ground in most sectors.

Disposition? Names like the River Somme, Albert, and Ancre all came back into use; names of places where we'd bled over the years. The ground lost was an enormous blow to morale but we managed to keep our heads above water. Four days later on the 30th we were subjugated to the last real German attack. It was near the Somme. We gave a little ground and they gave a lot of blood; ground for blood; I think we achieved the better deal and so with a smile upon my face I try my best to grasp some sleep, but sleep wouldn't come too easily. The 16th Irish was down to a single infantry battalion and I was still alive. Should I feel some small portion of guilt for being alive when so many were dead? How many had suffered and lost their life? How many Old Sweats were there left remaining? How many of the men that I had joined with were still alive today? I should think that the answer was not worth knowing for it would only demoralise me, and it was hard enough to maintain a reasonably healthy mind as it was.

And what will tomorrow bring?

31st MARCH, 1918

Shall I give it to you in detail or shall I just give it? You have read so much of me and the war and I should hope that you grow tired of hearing about the death and bloody carnage. If you are one that wants to hear more than maybe you are a bloodsucker; I can't help it; that's what you are, reading this miserable piece of crap for your own desire… I'm sorry… forgive me. It is only a few days from today that the 1st and 2nd Royal Dublin Fusiliers were amalgamated. Alongside us are the 5th Royal Irish Fusiliers, 500 Americans and 400 Canadians. What did we do…? We have stopped the German advance near Hamel; we marked the end of the war. We had done it. We had kicked the bastard so hard that he was bleeding from the nose and cowering. The French were on their feet, the Yanks [God bless those bastards] have arrived in number and with much resupply. The Germans had failed to separate the allies by force, and had failed to push us into the sea. It was time for us to commence our hitting and not to let go until we had won the war.

The Germans launch smaller attacks here and there and are largely unsuccessful.

And so the war trudges along and is all more of the same but we feel as though we are on the front foot and mostly eager to get it over with. By June some of our men have gone to the 1st and we are left with a skeleton crew of battle-hardened veterans; we are also so few that we are transferred temporarily to the Lines of Communication [LOC]. So here we are, running here and there, passing along orders, helping with resupply, and giving aid to communications in general.

APRIL, 1918

I think it's time to see the light at the end of the tunnel. The heading of my story has been well explained and it is during the month of April that the Virgin Mary was to fall. The Virgin's demise is also obscured from truth for there is one claim that British Artillery knocked her down from her perch and yet another from a German officer. I tend to think it was the Germans and this is how they went about it.

During their last efforts to hold onto Alfred, having gained her once more during the previous month, it was time to take it back which we did with great honour. The tower once again could be employed to great advantage by using it as a spotting tower for bringing artillery to bear upon the enemy as well as a machine gun being in place and employed to carve up the sod quite nicely. It is here that a German Army Order is received by V Corps Heavy Artillery that no more buildings were to be demolished by fire, an instant later and another officer, Colonel in rank, makes contact with the fifth and requested artillery fire upon the tower due to the allied machine gun being in place.

A young German captain of the times answers the call for aid. Seeing that he is in a position to calculate and give an order he readies himself for an exercise with great initiative. He cannot directly break the original Army Order, but he can place artillery fire to bear upon enemy positions to the rear of the tower. The young captain plots his coordinates to destroy an imagined trench line of enemy and orders a battery to fire upon it. He knows full well that the trajectory itself will fall upon the tower and it isn't long before his calculations bear fruit. The Virgin Mary is no more.

However, there is a small flaw with this for it is also said that what remained of the Virgin Mary when she fell was carried away by the Germans and melted down as scrap. If this is true then it surely must have been the British artillery that had knocked her down, for only if the Germans were in possession of the tower and in place upon the ground, with time up their sleeve, could they have carried the statue away.

This is simply another one of these stories similar to the Angels of Mons which will tear us apart. It's sometimes hard to believe what you read and so I tend to trust my own eyes rather than the stories written by others.

1st JUNE, 1918

We were no longer a part of the LOC but now in the 31st Division as a training cadre. I do believe that these past couple of months have been a reward for our overwhelming losses these past few years; which I accept. But this wasn't to last long.

6th June – we were reconstituted and brought in men from the 7th Battalion.

16th June – we were transferred to the 50th Northumbrian Division.

28th September – we were preparing for our counter-offensive to take back all we had lost and much more. We were the 1st, 2nd, and 7th Dublins.

29th SEPTEMBER, 1918

This was the Battle of St Quentin Canal and a most deciding factor for the sodding bastards to see the defeat of their strengths written upon the wall for all time. British, American, Australian; we were here under the command of… an Australian, and we coherently achieved all of our objectives and smashed through that impenetrable system of bunkers which was the Siegfried and Hindenburg lines.

It wasn't just the mettle of the men that achieved this wonderful success but the metal of the tanks intertwined with us, the Americans taking the lead and the units behind using the leap-frog method of movement to continue an arduous pace towards the enemy positions and machine gun bunkers.

Without the American support I doubt that we would have achieved success so thoroughly and as quickly but success would have been achieved in the long run. It was to be expected, regardless of this support, that the Americans were not quite up to the war for their training was slightly inadequate, but the resources were a glorious thing. As our leap-frog move forward came into effect the Australians found many pockets of Americans sticking hard to the ground without leadership but they soon tagged along with the Australians and fought side-by-side.

Yes indeed, name calling and all jokes aside the men of all calibre and nationality gave aid to one another as though born of the same family, heritage and blood. We strove to make the sod pay for all they had done these past four years and pay dearly they did.

Prisoners were taken much more easily now than ever before. They knew that they had lost the war and were happy to see an easy way to get through it with their lives intact. We were much the same in that contrast, each and every one of us, regardless of which side we fought on, wanted nothing more than to spend the rest of our lives at peace and with loved ones. And I was shocked to hear from the mouth of one prisoner what the officers were telling them, as they fired their weapons through the mouth of bunkers and over the lip of trenches, that it was the civilians back home in Germany that had lost the war, not the soldiers. The slide remarks must have been meant; a true-to-the-heart comment felt by many, for it was no good trying to stoke the morale of soldiers any longer for officers must surely have seen that the fight was falling from them on a daily basis.

You may think that I have left out the Canadians; not by any means. By the 8th October they came together and poured all they had into the Battle of Cambrai, a super-fast storming and bombardment of infantry supported by 324 tanks, the defenders overwhelmed so quickly and so decisively. The Canadian casualties were light.

And now I must speak of something that I did experience and that is the Battle of Courtrai, also known as the Second Battle of Belgium.

OCTOBER, 1918

The Battle of Courtrai was carried out in late September to early October and with the ease of things occurring over the past weeks it was an understatement to realise that morale was peaking at its highest since the beginning of the war. The pictures were being painted for us all to see, the glory of the days ahead where we were the victors, the upholders of good against evil, for we were not the ones to have started this mess but surely here to clean it up.

The Germans were retiring once more and so it was relatively easy to move into the town of Courtrai. As an army we were to hit and hit hard, to keep the sods running until winter was truly upon us so that it was too cold for the sod to do anything to us in return but gain shelter in pits of mud; but with the many villages and such around us, having now been secured, it was hard to see how some little comfort could not be attained by us from time to time. Our position was hence a lot healthier than ever before.

The people of the town were so overjoyed by our arrival that it was as though we were stepping off a train in the heart of London itself to be delivered into the arms of the thankful. There before us all are 40,000 men, women, and children all clambering to get a clear view of us, to clasp our hands on this victorious day. They had been liberated and they knew it. The Germans had been the torturers and rulers for four long years and now they were free. None of them seemed to even consider that the sod might be back to lash out more of the same in the near future for it was more than adamantly clear that the war was near its end and that the allies were the victor. So happy they were that they flew their flags freely from atop churches, public buildings, and every window possible. Wherever you cared to look you could see the picture of their beloved Belgium King and Queen. They were beyond joyous rebellion, they were ecstatic for the freedom being handed to them, a free gift for all they had suffered and had done. If this was how the war was to end then I did not mind as much for all the suffering endured. The joy seen in the eyes of the young and old was so… I was almost on the verge of crying.

I can see past the crowd to a place where there are horses standing amongst a mass of people. The horses suddenly fall, having been slaughtered then and there. The people move in and cut away the flesh of one, for it to be cooked and eaten. So hungry they were; only then did I realize how truly, poorly these people had been treated, but worse was to come, naturally, for where there had been German soldiers then there had been misery and shocking displays of torture and rape, such as a small boy with no fingers for they had been shot off one by one so that his mother would get on her back for the joy of half a dozen German men.

There was no other livestock in this town of 40,000, for every cow, hen and other form of life has been taken by the sod. Oh; it is also Sunday.

And when it is time to move on from the town we do so with the thousands waving us goodbye and into unknown territory we continue on, into a country which we have never seen before, and it is wonderful. There are trees and grass like I have never seen in my entire life. It is like a scene from heaven. I cannot believe that there could be so many colours in life. It is so beautiful that the memories I have of home come suddenly flooding back and I can recall the fields and valleys of home. I am truly ready to get away from here and see my family once more.

16th OCTOBER, 1918

You have heard me say 'the last offensive', or 'the last major battle' or words to this effect. Well, there was one more that stood before us, for those men of the 2nd.

It was as though we could not be rewarded with a victory, nor a ticket home, until our unit had been culled once more and so we met this day with trepid anxiety.

I am not going to go into details for it is much the same. There is more killing and bloodshed than ever I saw, but not nearly as bad as the Somme and the few other battles that stacked the mounting dead beside it. But what I shall tell you will make you think like I: how the hell did I survive the war? We suffered another 44 per cent worth of casualties within just two days; this was the end of the war for me and the others of our unit, a unit which had been present from the very beginning, having arrived on the soil at the commencement of hostilities. And although it was the last time I should see conflict, other than the rare glimpse or odd shot now and again, the same can't be said for the 1st Royal Dublin Fusiliers who fought heroically as ever at the Battle of the Sambre on the 4th day of November, 1918.

We were now advancing a good five miles a day and this continued until the following week.

11th NOVEMBER, 1918

The war has ended.

It is cold and there is a heavy frost. I can still hear firing but only a trickle compared to the past.

The Armistice was signed early on the morning of this day but wasn't to come into effect until 1100hrs. Further to this the soldiers on both sides of the fence, so to speak, weren't told of this until the actual day. I have no real understanding why this might have been other than to consider that the generals in command of us might have seen a tendency for soldiers to act too peacefully and hence place the front line in jeopardy should things go astray. As it were they had nothing to worry about for the fighting continued here and there right up until the eleventh hour.

As for my dear wife at home she wasn't to hear the news until 1020hrs, when David George made the announcement over the radio for all to hear.

Shelling continued on the line and around 11,000 casualties were suffered, more than 2,700 dying of their wounds, either instant- aneously or in great pain. It is a terrible waste of life, to die on the last day when you know the war to be over is sheer agony.

The Poor State of War and Conflict

I have heard in recent years that the last man to die of the allies was an American named Henry Gunther, being stupid and beyond compare by charging a small group of Germans and being shot. What manner of thought goes through a man's head at such a time? As for the Germans it was after 1100hrs that a death was recorded; being an officer of lower rank he decided to approach a small group of Americans to advise them that he was handing over the houses that his men had been using, so that they themselves could harbour there. The Americans shot him and their excuse was that they did not know the war was over.

We celebrated as would be expected, smiles all around being shared, for it was almost time to go home. We were soon quietened down and advised that we had a hefty walk ahead of us to get to the nearest point of departure, but before that we needed to gather some supplies and have ourselves a smoke.

Our officers also did a tour of the ranks to try and get us to sign on for another 12 months. They needed soldiers to stay behind, to clean up the battlefield, to put the dead to rest and help bring a little order back to the country so devastated by war. I for one was to refuse. I had been here more than four years and had earned my ticket home. Surely the men who'd recently arrived should volunteer, those men who had only been here a month or more, maybe a year or two; get them to stay behind. And so I stood in line and waited for my demobilisation papers on reaching a bivouac of necessity. Again I was asked, most formally, to sign on for an extended stay but all I could manage was a smile and a no thank you. I was looking forward to being home with family and friends but didn't know how many friends had survived the war, but on return I found it hard to return to civilian life and harder to accept that there were able-bodied men here that had refused to fight and instead remained behind making ten, no, a hundred times more than I was making as I fought both tooth and nail to stay alive. I was utterly disgusted by these men.

And shall I tell you of my first embrace with my family, of how happy I was and they were? Do I really need to? I think not.

HISTORICAL NOTE

As the writer of this text, which I consider to be historical-fiction more so than a true event, for the simple reason that I cannot guarantee in any way that dates, formations, or locations, are precise, I must apologise if I have got-it-wrong. And so my first dilemma is whether or not to illustrate this book as fiction or nonfiction. I hope I made the correct decision.

For all intents and purposes the research I have conducted points to a narrative that is true in every word apart from the fact that the 2nd Royal Dublin Fusiliers may not have been at Ypres on 22nd October 1914 [as an example] but to otherwise give you, the reader, a more precise understanding of the war it has been required of me to see that my Great Grandfather was 'here' or 'there' in order to give clarity and light to 'this' and 'that' situation.

You might ask yourself what right do I have to play with his thoughts as I have done; what experience have I had which might allow me to say what I have said. I was in Rwanda, 1995; in country at the time of the Kibeho Massacre which saw 10,000 killed for no good reason other than racial vilification; I was here during the build-up of hostilities between the 18th to 21st of April, the general massacre occurring on 22nd April; I further experienced what many others in UNAMIR II did experience during the day afterwards, endeavouring to see the survivors given aid and moved on to their home communes from the 23rd of that month to the 9th May, 1995.

I would also like to state that my Grandfather was one of the first to enter Bergen Belsen during WWII and he saw the atrocities of that camp for himself. He was initially in the infantry, the Royal West Kent, but later transferred to MPs.

And so with such a family-orientated, military background, and much research conducted on Kibeho, Bergen-Belsen, and WWI, I see this text as written history, regardless of whether the man I have placed on the ground, and spoken for him on his behalf, may or may not have been at a particular post at a particular time.

I have done all I could to ensure he was in certain areas during particular battles and hope that you don't remember this book for what he has done and where, but to remember this story in the memory of all those that fought during it and then have to face further troubles when arriving home, to find themselves without work and practically forgotten.

My Great, Grandfather's first two children were born in Ireland and I believe they came to England during the Easter Sunday Massacre but I'm not 100% on this. Blighty for him would have been a headache, for travel time, to and fro, is part-n-parcel of the leave itself. Someone living in Kent would see their son, father, husband, for a good 10 days out of 14; for someone living in Ireland it would reduce his leave significantly, to the point of being pointless. Whether or not my Great Grandfather's wife and first son would have made an effort to get to England would have been doubtful, in particular during the time when he was injured. As to whether or not he received any other injury I do not know, but it would be hard to believe that he escaped with nothing else but the agony of being gassed. I cannot say whether or not he was promoted but given the circumstances of his being alive for the entirety of the war it is hard to believe that he wouldn't have at least made the rank of sergeant.

Thank you for reading thus far.

THIS PESTILENCE,
BERGEN-BELSEN

IN MEMORY

For my grandfather, James Edward Kelly, he died on the 13th day of June, 2008, never having forgotten those thousands that died before him.

He served during World War II, with the Royal West Kent and the Military Police. He served in Europe and was one of the first to step foot into Bergen-Belsen on its liberation. He never spoke of the concentration camp, until lying upon his death bed, and he was more than adamant about one thing, and that was of the atrocities that Germany's Third Reich had committed.

The holocaust was real, and he was angered by all of those that claimed it to be nothing more than a lie, saying that it never happened: it did, and his last message for us all, before he died, was for us not to forget the holocaust or camps similar to Bergen-Belsen.

PROLOGUE

Bergen-Belsen was initially a Prisoner of War and concentration camp of specific need, that need being to provide a place in which to house allied Prisoners of War and to fill an exchange quota designed to release German Prisoners of War of their shackles. This was to be organised and carried out by exchanging imprisoned Jews for German Prisoners of War held by the allies. It came to pass, however, that in the few months before the end of the war – due to an overwhelming allied advance, in particular from the East – an injection of prisoners completely inundated the camp to such a degree that it would become the pestilence of humanity, a thorn in the side of the Nazi Regime, a sickening episode in our history that cannot be explained in simple words or terms. It was a disease, an epidemic, a plague; all of this and much, much more; the Third Reich was responsible; it had single-handedly created this disaster through the habits of its cruelty.

By April, 1945, there were 60,000 prisoners housed in a camp built for no more than 10,000 and the camp as a whole was divided into sections, comprising camps for women, Hungarians, and Prisoners of War; there were also sections labelled 'star' (which comprised mostly of Dutch Jews), 'special', 'neutral', and a tent camp, which comprised mostly of Polish women from Auschwitz. It was testament to Hitler's viciousness.

The camp was liberated by the British on 15th April, 1945, and over the next 30 days the death rate dropped from 500 a day to less than 100 a day. More and more people continued to meet with death in the face of their liberation for many reasons, some of which have been needlessly blamed on the British for their heroic efforts. Of all the care and assistance given to those poor wretches, the shining light from heaven above continued to call out to those too poorly to make it through those trying times, and the Golden gates remained open to them all.

The fight to preserve life was a constant battle but one that was often lost. In total around 14,000 of those imprisoned died in the four weeks after their liberation [Which doesn't spell accurately for that would mean 500 deaths per day and via one source - see previous paragraph - I have found advice that the death rate dropped to around 100 per day - I'm sure you can do the math].

On 21st May, a ceremony was held where the last of the memories was purged by flame, symbols of the Nazi Regime, and the last of the huts was torched and burnt to the ground in one huge emotional wave of relief.

The world's Jewish population in 1939 was around 9,242,500 and by the end of the war only 5,447,000 remained. The death toll was staggering to say the least.

The following story is but one of many, which commences in the latter part of 1944, and concludes in May of 1945.

This is a work of historical-fiction, as names and some actions I speak about are not valid and/or may not have happened precisely as written; nevertheless, Bergen-Belsen and the atrocities carried out there are not fictitious and therefore I have labelled this book as being historical: label me as you will.

CHAPTER 1

The female prisoners were from Auschwitz; all Polish, and all Jews; walking ghosts and with nothing more than strips of blanket wrapped around them: which was the best that they could scrounge. This was all they had, all that stood between them and the weather, the vicious cold of December falling upon them without remorse.

The fingers of all in the column were freezing, fingertips almost turning black – regardless, some discolouration was evident – in this, the cold of the winter which had arrived several weeks before; thin and weary to the bone they were, mere skeletons of their former selves, and so miserable; so miserable that the feeling couldn't even be expressed in simple words, couldn't be classed as an emotion or condition, a state or frame of mind. Their misery was too powerful to be expressed in any way. If you couldn't have experienced the suffering then you had no way of understanding it.

They were like animals being herded to slaughter; animals being abused by every single physical and emotional means possible. In fact, these very means of control, so heinously, sadistic and sitting dormant in the minds of men, which had not been seen for so very long, were reinvented in quick-time by the SS. Each and every guard present had his mind cast hard upon his ideas for control of the Jews that fell under his ever watchful eye.

Yes, indeed; say the SS; the Führer must be right.

And the guards watched on, spitting upon those close enough to be spat upon, those stinking Jews, so wretched they were. What did they deserve other than a good, hard and swift, kicking in the arse?

Their heads were shaved, here and there the tell-tale signs of truncheon blows having been delivered, beaten down hard against the skull of these women, enemies of the Third Reich, the pests of Hitler's demented mind, and highly sadistic he was. He was the savour of Germany in all its glory, and with that went all reality from mind, for he was nothing less than an insane leech of blood-sucking temperament, even too low to be considered a cockroach or other vile insect of contemptible worth.

None of the prisoners were adequately clothed, not a whole blanket seen anywhere amongst the column of women as they marched from one pestilence to another, making their way towards Bergen-Belsen and into the arms of the devil, where women guards were as atrocious as their male counterparts.

One of the poor women, Ruth; her mind was so numb from the abuse and mistreatment, so frozen from the cold and the misery of death that followed her every step, that she couldn't distinguish reality from hallucination. She caught a glimpse of the body of a baby in the snow during one of the few rest stops provided the column. She stooped over from her place amongst the masses and looked the baby in the face, its eyes closed and body frozen. It couldn't have been more than a few months old. It looked so peaceful, so fast asleep. As the freezing wind swept past her view she saw a little love in it's face, frozen for all time, a child which should have been cared for and nurtured until fully grown, not discarded like a piece of common garbage, a piece of filth.

The baby reminded her of her own, a young child she had been unfortunately torn from during the early days of Germany's intervention upon her happy days and the blessed glory of her freedom. It reminded her so much of the one that she had lost that she couldn't help but to smile and stretch out her arms in order to pick up the prize that she had found. She would rescue it, if none other would. She'd care for it, give it a home, and take care of it as it grew into a young child, a child that she'd mould into likeness of herself.

She brought the bundle of frozen flesh to her breast and smiled ever-more, cradling it in her arms as though her own, and then the order to 'move along' was given once more. So she stood up and continued with the walking, the cold now abated, for her mind was awash with the gift she had been given by the war that surrounded her. And she continued to smile as she walked along, unable to register the reality of the situation for she was insanely mad.

Other women, too, felt the emotions of the war around them, its prodding hatred coming from every angle, the hatred for the Jews present on every wisp of wind, and Judith, being no different than the others, couldn't forgive the Nazis for what they had done to her and her family. Would she ever see them again; she had no idea? The question was impossible to answer.

A few of Judith's friends had gone missing; missing since morning, killed by the hands of the guards that marched them to death, insisting that the Jews continue to march in accordance with the army regulations of so many paces per minute and with arms swinging as though with gusto; but these ridiculous demands did not last long – just long enough for the guards to have their little laugh.

Yes, her friends were few and far between now, many having strolled from the path of the march, blanketed by their clouded minds; their forgetfulness; the delusion of their wandering dreams. And here they would fall from their way and into death's arms, and others would be provided a bullet to the head for their inability to keep up with the others. It was nothing to a soldier of the infamous SS to shoot first and ask questions later, holding a pistol to a young woman's head, shooting her dead, and then asking with a stupid look upon his face, 'don't you wish you'd kept up, ah; you pile of filth; you piece of stinking shit.'

The Russians were coming and nothing could stop them. The Red Army was advancing at great speed towards Berlin and before them the citizens of Germany were running with their tails between their legs, like the true maggots they were, upon horse and cart, or simply walking beside their collection of worldly possessions. Their furniture was atop carts and carried in hand, food in all its glory within reach of those walking the road from one hell camp and into another. These men, women and children of Germany, were looking down with such great spite upon the thousands of Jews making their way into the arms of death; but not a single one, not even the innocent; such as young children; none at all ever attempted to throw even the most meagre of food portions down to them; not an apple or its core, not a potato, not even a slice of bread. 'Look, mummy,' would be heard from atop a cart. 'That one has a little hair on her head,' and a guard would lash out with the butt of his rifle on seeing the Jew look up at the little girl. 'She's bad, mummy; I don't like that one.'

The SS were exchanged at rest stops where much food [Ha!], water and rest, would be accompanied by another unkind word directed at a Polish Jew as they watched on, the line of women passing the guards by in a continuous move forward... ever forward, on and on and on. 'Get your arms swinging, you stupid, lazy whore. It's no wonder you look like shit. I'll kick you in the arse before I put up with your insolent stare. Now look to your front, you ugly bitch.' It was always the same; always the curses of the SS that could be heard over the wind as it blew across the face of Europe.

And then it was their time to eat, a rest stop for the guilty; for a prisoner could not be innocent, not by any means. In the minds of the SS these women were all guilty, even without a verdict being read, even without prosecution. These bitches were the scum of the earth and Hitler was right to have them dealt with immediately and viciously.

Yes, at last, a rest stop for the ravenous crowd of women forced to march forever on, forced to march until they dropped, and march until they died. And what of their rations: black bread and soup, but the soup was nothing more than meer water.

The pangs of hunger were throttled aside but only for a few minutes, for what they ate was quickly consumed by their bodies, not an ounce put into energy reserves for the walking that lay ahead; so many miles to go that to think too hard upon the distance would be a death sentence.

The SS pulled their aluminium dishes from within their kit, brushing away invisible germs, giving them a polish with their thumbs in order that they may receive the goodness of the Third Reich. And their dishes were piled high with pea soup and chunks of white bread, chunks of meat and the promise of something with taste, and the steam carried with it the smell of something which would not pass the prisoners' lips for some time to come. So thick was the soup with peas of the SS that it was hard to see the water; what a contrast, the soup of the Jews when compared to that of the guards; there simply was no comparison; there was no relationship between the two. The two soups were as different as were the SS and the Jews.

The snow was also getting much worse, piled high now along the way, falling upon the shaved heads of those that marched along to the beat of the SS curses. The wind was blowing hard and the chill cut into its victims without mercy. But the column pushed on, and then out from the rear came another signal that a SS guard had dealt out his measure of hatred upon one of them, a single shot from a pistol echoing throughout the area, a Jewish woman of forty being kicked from where she lay and into the ditch beyond, her body to fester and decay in the frozen gutter which seemed to follow the road as it disappeared into the distance ahead. But others felt the mercy of the killing, could see how it was an easy way into heaven, to be handed reprieve from the hard walk that lay ahead.

All around them was white with snow, so thick in places that it could devour a man without a trace, but there were no men here, only the Germans of a male persuasion being carried on the backs of carts and the SS with hands on pistols which they used as easily as they used the words, 'your shit', 'you arse', 'you filthy, lazy Jew'.

And the walking continued until they fell upon a train station on the far outskirts of a city unknown.

A SS guard came out from a doorway of the station in front and his voice could be heard congratulating them, the prisoners, in all their glory, showering them with the kindest words they'd heard this day. "You lazy bitches will be taken the remainder of the way by train," said the officer. A few other soldiers could then be seen falling into earshot and orders were passed around, smiles being shared amongst a few, others wearing stern looks as they perused the column of scum, this was followed by the clubbing of the women for they moved too slowly for the likes of Heinrich Himmler, Hitler, and the whole German race.

"Come on, move it," said a soldier of the SS. "We don't have all day," and he struck hard the woman, Ruth, on the back of the head, the little baby of several months in her arms still as dead and frozen as when she'd first picked it up – how did she ever manage to carry the child so far? She fell upon the ground and was hit several times more before the soldier pulled his pistol from his holster. He was the same as most of the other SS, standing there that minute in time in his heavy boots and with a signet ring flashing here and there for everyone to see that he was a real soldier as seen through the eyes of other soldiers, but a monster to those that walked the road under the threats that erupted from within him and the others. They were like worms, grovelling to appease Himmler's and Hitler's every wish; so foul they were that they would be remembered for all time, but for all of the wrong reasons: or should that be 'for all the right reasons', for isn't it right that we remember these savage brutes?

He aimed the weapon and then reconsidered his action: to waste a bullet on one so nearly dead was foolhardy. He locked eyes with another Jew. A snarling grimace then appeared upon the guard's face and he pointed his weapon at the side of the other's head and pulled the trigger. "Look at me like that, you pile of crap." Another prisoner walked on by, past the fallen victim, wiping the blood from her face. "You and you, move that body aside. Quickly now or you'll get the same."

The woman so brutally clubbed to the ground stirred a little and the guard ignored her: let the cold take care of the fallen. As for the prisoner shot in the head: "You should be thankful," said the guard to the others, "for I've just made more room for you on the train," and laughed his heinous laugh.

The SS officer that had given the short speech had managed to push his way through to the point of the commotion, where a few disgruntled voices had been heard to rise, where prisoners were commencing to push from different directions: some towards the empty carriages and others, away.

"What's going on here?" asked the officer.

The soldier stood to attention and reported the incident as was his duty.

"This woman was moving too slowly, sir," said the SS maggot. "It was causing a commotion and so I gave remedy to the situation."

The officer looked down and saw the woman who had been hit several times in the side and back of the head, blood now sporting her skull. He then saw the other, blood already congealed at the wound site where she had been shot.

"No more bullets, private," said the officer. "No more shooting." He raised his voice for all to hear. "Get on board as quickly and quietly as possible or you shall be left to the wilderness, to be delivered your punishment by the hand of the weather. This snow will not stop, so get on board, quickly."

The private could see and feel that this officer was different in some small way. He seemed to care for this sodden lot, just a little, but seemed afraid to announce his feelings to the world in case the Führer should hear of his poor showing.

"Get them on board, private, as quickly as possible. Any problems... drag them to the rear and I'll take care of them personally."

"Yes sir," said the man in SS uniform and commenced with his instructions, kicking the arses of the slow; the old and the frail.

Herded now the women continued to clamber aboard the open carriages at the station, being hit over the back of the head by soldiers too scared to touch them, for they smelt bad and had sores all over their bodies; bruises accompanied with cuts and abrasions. The SS also wished to keep a distance between themselves and the lice which infested some of the women.

The Jews were skinny and all very sick, nothing more than bone in most cases, and where women were once proud owners of breast well shaped and luscious, now lay nothing more than flabby skin against ribcage, perused by others looking through sunken eyes sockets and insane minds, for no one could remain sane in such appalling conditions.

There was silence amongst them as they were forced onto the train, a journey of some five hundred kilometres to be endured. The SS guards were shovelling food into their mouths once more, drinking what water they had and wiping their faces with the rags that they carried as part of their kit, grunting noises coming from them all, like pigs at a trough – but pigs didn't deserve to be affiliated with krauts.

The journey was long and hard, no food or water to be had anywhere. When people died they did so standing up, freezing in place. Bodies of the dead could not be moved until the cramped conditions of the carriages in which they were transported could be vacated; so keep still, and share what warmth can be shared. Not long now, not long until the doors would open for an opportunity to breath and receive fresh water and nourishment, for what lay ahead when the doors did finally open would be Bergen-Belsen, and all knew that Bergen-Belsen was a Shangrila when compared to Auschwitz.

And then the reality of it all hit them hard. Life for them had been a sheer misery, from Auschwitz to Bergen-Belsen, but those of Bergen-Belsen were a dilapidated sight, by far worse off than those currently standing on the train. The prisoners didn't know what to do; stay on the train or get off; which was worse? Never was there a time in history where the unfortunate would cast their eyes upon such a scene as horrific as this 'hell camp' and come to realise that they had had it easy whilst in Auschwitz, but it was only recently that the camp had become as bad as it was and superseded the other camps by becoming the worst in all of known history.

The so-called 'death march' across Germany, train from Dresden, and countless deaths along the way; none of it compared to what was about to unfold. There were twelve tents, seemingly hastily erected, and straw thrown upon the ground to act as a mattress; which would not last long. And so the horrors of being a prisoner, a slave, a dog for which to kick and beat, continues on from one day to the next.

Dishes from which to eat food, if edible food was seen at all, were so few and far between these new inhabitants that to see one was like a vision from heaven. No; tin cans were the way... if they could be secured; and so theft was always present as it was hard to prove ownership of one tin can from another.

These Polish women felt the shame of it all, felt the shame of being a Jew, but why should that be shameful; because it had been instilled within their minds, brainwashed into them every single day of their miserable existence? They looked up and through the barbed wire fence, to see the other Jews of the camp. They, too, were thin and unhealthy, diseased and unsteady upon their feet, but at least they had a barracks which provided better warmth than the thin skin of a useless tent, and a thin layer of straw for a bed.

CHAPTER 2

The camp was in an obvious dilapidated state and it could only get worse before it got any better. The Poles knew very little about the camp itself but it seemed quite obvious, even now, that those at the Russian front were being evacuated to the rear, to this camp, Bergen-Belsen, it taking an influx of disease and wretchedness from the others camps right across Germany, from all quarters in the face of the Third Reich, in this, its downfall.

From high upon its post flew the flag of Germany, a true sign of cruelty within the world, and nothing could be more cruel than this sign, nothing more cruel was there in the entire world than the one that was proudly displayed by the Nazis and their regime.

Row upon row of wooden buildings covered the ground, hastily built refuges where the unfortunate were forced to live out their lives as prisoners. The wooden huts were where the weak stayed and died, where the able bodied were cast upon hard labour, and guards inflicted what they called justice as they saw fit.

Some of the huts had no bunks to speak of and comprised little less than a floor covered in bodies, some dead, but all diseased in some way. The dead would be removed in the morning; always in the morning. Blankets were strewn all over, were hard to come by, but a godsend. To lice it was like heaven, and to disease a haven for spreading its malignity as best it could, going unchecked and free to cast its evil spell upon everyone within the wire cordon known as Bergen-Belsen.

And more and more people arrived each day. Where did they all come from? As already stated, from all over Europe it would seem, those closest to the front line being evacuated to Bergen-Belsen. It was too impossible to believe, but worse was to come. It was hard to believe that there were around 10,000 people sharing a single toilet.

CHAPTER 3

Everyone was woken at 4:45am and the gears for the day's work were shifted ever so slowly into neutral and then engaged.

Different parts of the camp were treated differently and standards of work and living varied from one to the other, but in general terms it was all the same to most of them: so little sleep, and so little food; life in general was such a misery. Hungarian Jews had it the best; being any other nationality of 'exchange' Jew was also fortunate – someone would have to one day have it explained what it meant to be 'fortunate'. No one had the energy to continue as they did, but not to do so would reap the truncheon blow of a guard, or even worse; a bullet to the head - but was a bullet to the head so awful?

It was 6:00am and all prisoners, from all sectors of the camp, were called to assembly in the open, many parades assembled around the camp; which occurred regardless of weather conditions, rain, sleet or snow. The worst thing of all wasn't as simple as the weather though, but the sheer stupidity of the SS and their inability to count. If the roll call was accurate and the numbers added up then the prisoners could continue on to work; in the fields, the kitchen, or elsewhere where shelter might be attained; even if only limited. It was a matter of being damned no matter what the result. If they go to work, they might be warmed, but the sheer agony of sitting upon a stall for eleven hours or more in a single day could be torture upon the back. And what of those poor bastards, the men, who had to surrender themselves to hard labour attached to the 'tree commando', where even the very stumps of the trees had to be dug from the ground in order to be fed to the furnaces within the kitchens. They cut and saw all day, every day; fir and pine; hail, rain or sunshine. The wood was needed in order to prepare the food for the entire camp, but what did they get but a bowl of watery soup; it was sheer stupidity. But to stand for hours on end at roll call when inclement weather was inbound was a recipe for disaster, prisoners literally falling to the ground dead. It was here that prisoners were ordered to carry the dead aside to be cremated later. One might pity the poor mother of a teenager when she saw her child fall upon the ground, her soul giving up the fight to survive, but another would think of the extra ration that might be available to eat at the end of the day. It was all a matter of survival, and the strongest had a better chance than most.

The body of the deceased would be carried away by the prisoners at the convenience of the master doing the count, carried to the crematorium for burning. The crematorium was a lonely station, big enough to burn one body at a time. Two boys were stationed here, two Jews whose sole task it was to cremate the dead. The furnace was kept alive, all day; the bodies kept coming, all day; the work was endured, all day. This was their life; this was what they endured. They talk to no one. The crematorium was a small building built of red brick and surrounded by a seven-foot fence. This was the loneliest station of the camp.

Work was from 6:30am to 11:30am and if the prisoners were lucky – ah; such a silly choice of words, but such words are the only ones available to represent the good fortune called food – then they were marched back to parade outside the huts for another roll call and lunch. The watery soup that the men had worked so hard to help provide, by digging away at roots, was now fed them all, but the hunger still existed, hadn't even waivered the slightest. What had gone down their throats seemed like nothing at all, but not having this ridiculous portion of nourishment would soon see the death of them all through the pain of starvation.

There was plenty of work to be had which was hard on the back, though allowed for much conversation. The work was in the large horse stable which was made of stone, and provided were the tools of the prisoner's trade: tables, hard stools, and plenty of shoes. They mustered around as though they were bees to a honey pot, drawn by the scent of their conviction, to seek a little freedom from that which encased them all. But the freedom was hard fought, even for the hours of the day in which they toiled over the pile of shoes, thousands upon thousands of second hand shoes that were piled high in front of them all.

This was the Shoe Commando where mostly the young girls worked, fourteen year-olds that were looked over as though meat in a market: the SS always had a keen eye for what might bring them pleasure at a later date, but as the months rolled on, and the task became too much for the women, men were employed, a total of six hundred souls conducting what was rather meaningless slave labour with the pain searing up and down their legs and backs.

Quite often, in the hustle and bustle of roll call, it was the accidental allocation of an older woman to the task which was an oversight for the SS guard but a relief – in most cases – for the woman of age and maturity. But the older, more intelligent, were harder to be swayed by the SS guards, and those that were married were seldom seen flirting with the enemy... although there were some that did the unthinkable by sleeping with a guard, or the blockführer, in order to bring an extra ration of bread and turnip to their husband's table, to provide additional nutrition where it was needed the most, for the work amongst the trees was very hard indeed.

After being appointed to the 'shoe commando' by the blockführer, it was time to go and acquaint themselves with the shoes and put up with the unpleasantness of undesired conversation, where roasts, steaks, sandwiches, cakes and food of all description was spoken of, and did nothing to help them through the days of hunger that were pressed upon them all. The labour was quite intensive and it was ordered that each woman was to rip apart 40 pairs of dusty shoes in a single day, where the leather was to be split into three piles upon the tables, each being allocated as either 'good leather', 'cloth', or 'waste'.

It was a form of retribution... no; it was outright justified that when the prisoners saw that a guard had turned his attention away from the table, literally turned his ugly head in another direction, that they did damage to a good piece of leather hence removing it from the service of the Führer, a commodity that could otherwise service his crumbling war machine, for the good of no purpose than to satisfy his desires of demented disposition in ruling the world.

The cloth was something the inmates took care to ensure went to good use and was gathered as something more pleasant on which to wipe their arses when sitting on a toilet, or over a cold iron bar of one of the makeshift toilets, sucking in the disgusting fumes of faeces from the pit below where they sat or crouched, holding their guts in their palms for pain was often present when relieving the bowels. With this said it was not surprising to note that the SS guards did not attend to their flock as well as they should and the number of pairs of shoes attended to by each prisoner was usually well below the required number, some seeing to it that they did as few as fifteen pairs in a single week when more than two hundred pairs was due – due for whom; that damned crazy bastard, Hitler?

The Poor State of War and Conflict

Work for no pay! Work as slaves! The damn Nazis were such lowly scum that the prisoners would prefer to step in dog shit wearing expensive shoes... damn shoes; the thought of shoes; more, and more, and more damn shoes. Shoes during the day, shoes in their nightmares, but not many pairs of shoes on very many feet... so few could walk around with the knowledge that what they stepped on would not quiche between their toes.

Work for the women was scarce but in particular the kitchen duty was sought, especially towards the latter part of their unjustified sentences just prior to their rescue by the allies. Although they dared ro be caught, it was sheer bliss to cram as much peel into one's mouth as possible, or to hide something of a potato in the boots... those poor men; their work could be devastating. Easy was the work with the shoes but hell was the felling of trees, digging of roots, carting of wood, and the stirring of the huge kettles in which water was boiled within the kitchens; it simply sapped the energy from within when energy wasn't to spare; it was sheer torment to work when not an ounce of energy was available to even talk, cough or sneeze.

The mess kettles were huge and varied in size from around twenty to fifty litres, a mammoth task in itself to portage when full, let alone empty. Those whose duty it was to carry the kettles empty had the task cut out for them, but to pull off the same miracle when full of watery soup was sheer agony.

Then back to work, from 12:30pm to 6:30pm, another roll call and then back to the barracks to be drowned in a combined misery and soiled existence; one shared by all.

One old woman had fallen whilst being beaten on parade. She stayed there upon the ground in the mud. No one helped her, for to do so would mean death or bunker, and bunker usually meant death, so you couldn't win. She died where she lay, to be carted away in the morning.

As for now; now they spend time together, male and female, where husbands and wives could provide those encouraging words that there was light beyond the tunnel entrance. A wife would present a slice of bread for the husband and he would shake his head, saying 'No, I've managed to have something before returning to the hut'. So the wife eats some of the bread on insisting that they share it. The husband feels awkward that he should take from his wife but the wife knows that the husband didn't really have any brea earlier on, that he was simply offering all for her to eat. And throughout the barracks, wives and husbands tried their hardest to pull the blanket over the eyes of the other, lying as best they could in order for their companion in life to have something more than watery soup served from large kettles along with a portion of stinking bread.

And so each fights to find a different way in which to provide the other with that added nourishment, but each, in their own way, knew that the other was tricking them into eating what sits before them. The wife would give everything for the husband and the husband for the wife. The hard labour of the men saw to it that they needed twice as much more to eat than the women, where working long hours in the 'tree commando' and fields saps them of all energy, making them more skinny and susceptible to disease as each day passes them by.

At 7:45pm the men and women would separate into their own quarters. They had special treatment and the empowering of a partnership between a man and woman provides them with greater incentive and opportunity for survival. But now the work was done and they no longer had to wait their turn to go to the latrines, but stagger off as they pleased, to be inundated by the fail stench of human shame orchestrated by the blocked pipes, and the SS guards watched over the camp to ensure that all remained peaceful and that no one tried to escape.

CHAPTER 4

A severe storm hit the camp and several tents were ripped apart. The Polish women stood in the pouring rain and cold wind. It was a shocking surprise when half a dozen guards turned up out of the darkness, to press upon them their commands.

"You, Jews," shouted one of the guards, a tall man that seemed to overshadow the other by his side. "Move; quickly, I don't have all day. This rain is pouring down my neck as you fart around. Leave your possessions; move it!"

Judith looked around at the bustling crowd and saw that everyone was moving in a panic. The hail fell upon them, small stones of ice which bounced off of their bald heads.

"Come on, slut; I haven't all day," came the command of a guard as he lashed out with his truncheon, knocking a woman to the ground. Many others continued on, stepping over her, pushing her into the mud. "Move it!"

A bolt of lightning then struck somewhere outside the wire and for a brief moment the lights of the guards' towers flickered off and then on again.

"Leave everything, hurry up."

Judith heard the words but couldn't believe them. She had no possessions, knew of very few that had. Tin cans were all and if clothing was possessed then they would have been worn, no protection from the cold of the night when sleeping in a tent.

"Oh, Judith... help me," came a lonesome voice and Judith looked around as she was shoved alone.

"Hurry up," and a guard kicked her in the arse: better a foot than a bullet.

Judith thought she'd recognised the voice of the woman. It was an elderly lady she'd met just the other day, one that had shared with her a half-slice of bread as she was too sick to even eat.

"Help me, Judith."

Judith looked upon the face of the fallen woman and tried to fight the crowd, but the crowd was too strong; and just then a guard came up behind the woman on the ground and stepped upon her head, driving it into the mud. The sadistic look upon his face was etched, forever more, upon Judith's mind.

There was nothing that Judith could do but give praise that she, herself, was alive.

They were quickly shuffled off to the shed, the horse stable, where shoes were normally being ripped apart, but it was swamped with almost a foot of water and so the misery of their existence continued.

"In here, quickly," yelled a guard. "Find yourselves somewhere dry and out of the rain."

Was he serious, or simply stupid beyond all contemplation?

It was amazing that the guards had acted so quickly by providing shelter but then they turned their cheeks and started to laugh when the leaking roof deposited more water onto the deepening pool that currently splashes against the prisoners' ankles.

It was a joke beyond all jokes, moving from a station in the open, to another which was full of water and leaked like a sieve.

"Be quiet, all of you," shouted another guard as the six of them gathered around briefly to discuss the situation.

"Let's leave them to their misery," said one. "It's damn cold and I'm wet through. Why should we suffer for these... scum of the earth they are?"

"You follow orders, just like me," came the answer. "Come on; let's get out of here."

A pair of eyes was then cast upon the prisoners. "You will stay here until you're moved," ordered a guard. "If you leave this stable without the authority of the SS, you will be taken to the bunker."

Judith stood as did the others, nowhere to sit but in the water that surrounded them like a lake. There they stayed for the duration of the night until they were removed the next day, removed to another part of the camp in order for the shoe commando to recommence with its work upon the shoes.

CHAPTER 5

It's during times of stormy weather that the greatest of entertainment could be attained, although it was true to say that such entertainment could be had at almost any time.

The dark loneliness of the night, where rain, wind or hail might shield the happenings in a particular washroom, a corporal sat upon a stall and had a grin upon his face a mile wide. It's a dirty grin, one filled with the dirt of a sadistic mind, perpetrating to commit, always to commit, some act of attrition against the weak.

Corporal 'Red' Mueller would love to watch two girls taking a bath together, but then again, he would love to watch more than this. It was proposed, once, that he liked to seek the attention of boys, but so young the children would be that it was hard to tell the difference between male and female, where his advances, although less warranted, were just as enjoyable to him: but even children craved food.

It was to his great joy and entertainment that what followed a romp in the shower, by the light of a small globe or even a lantern at times that the power might be out, would satisfy his sexual desires to the very depths of his fantasies. He knew what he wanted, and he too often received it.

His mind was corrupted by years of hatred for the Jews, and years of condemning them as he felt they deserved to be condemned. What was it for him to care what they felt; they were nothing more than pests? Society didn't want them and if society didn't want them then they were turned over to the likes of him, in camps which robbed people of their right to live in freedom. It was nothing to him at all and as he sipped on the small glass of sherry he'd watch with full delight as two girls washed each other down with soapy water.

The girls would be looked after, of course, adequately fed and watered, just like cattle, for they were favourites now and forever. They were pleasing to him and acted out the play that harassed his mind. All day long he would be thinking of these nights of luxury: damned if he cared what others thought, and so as he quickly glanced around to ensure all was quiet and that he was alone as the play to his front continued to unfold.

It might be lights on at 5:00am and lights out at 9:00pm, but when you had rank and position the entertainment of the night could keep you as warm as a good glass of spirit. His sherry he could go without, but go without his luxuries such as this and he was just another man in the system that thought of different ways to ridicule, beat, and hamper.

It was a courtesy of the Third Reich that was little known

elsewhere in the world where blockführers felt it their prime duty to watch the women undress and shower, be they alone, in twos and threes, or en masse.

Mueller would continue to satisfy himself as he watched and after he could take it no more he would have his way with both of them, and at the end of his excitement he would reward both with extra slices of bread, and maybe something more appetising, a slice of cheese or a sliver of fatty bacon.

Oh, how grand it was to be Mueller, so grand that he loved to hear his name called out from within a crowd of women. He could only congratulate himself on his good work and good fortune. He loved himself like he loved no other. He would do all he could to ensure he didn't jeopardise his position.

CHAPTER 6

Being sent to work was either good or bad, and sometimes both. It consisted of the evil doings of the SS more than anything else; but food was all important.

It seemed ludicrous and a sheer waste of time to be standing there on parade for well over an hour in order for the guards to do their count, to add the numbers together, to see how they stacked up in semblance to what should be the correct number; but it was carried out several times in a single day, if not more.

The total number of dead, for the time being, was being recorded, as too, were the numbers reporting sick each day, along with those being given the permission from the medical officer to take the day off, and to have 'so-and-so' many days of rest.

The numbers were tallied and the barracks checked. It appeared that the doctor had awarded several with bed rest, which only came when a temperature of over 39 degrees Celsius was registered on his – no doubt – faulty equipment, for the doctor cared as little for the Jews as did the SS guards.

"You are lucky today," said a guard who was familiar with one of the women on the bunk. "There is much work to be done." He looked around the barrack hut and turned one last time to the woman lying there with horrible pain searing through her. "No soup for you today. Only those that work will be given good food."

She wondered where the 'good' food came from, because she never saw any of it.

"I'll let the other women know when they return. If I see anyone feeding you then you'll be shot, thrown in the bunker, and then shot again. You stupid Jews; you're so lazy that it makes me puke."

He continued outside and reported to the sergeant that his numbers on the sick, as earlier reported, were correct, and so the adding up of numbers continued.

Shortly after this exercise of stupidity came the call for a small group to make its way to the 'peel kitchen' where many hours of labour was to be suffered by the hand of their puppet masters. They, a small group of the poor souls that made up the prisoner formation, were segregated from the others and formed up shortly after roll call to ensure that they were ready for the work that was to be allocated to them all, to be shuffled away under the heavy threat of beatings to a kitchen in readiness to peel… ah, turnips.

They reached the building in which they were to work and all were quick to enter, for it was best to be seated in one area as opposed to another, enabling more turnip peel to be eaten; whether or not it was digested was another matter, for diarrhoea and throwing up were complaints often heard about.

It was here in the kitchen that what could have been classified as 'young and strapping lads' simply stood around in their clean uniform of the SS and watched the prisoners, with nothing better to do, it would seem, than to cuss and curse.

"Can you believe this, Judith?" came the question in a whisper, Sonja careful not to be the victim of a guard's malice.

"What is that?" asked Judith, sadly, continuing along with her work as did the others. She wasn't feeling well today for the 'death march' had taken much out of her, in spirit and emotionally.

"That it takes so many young SS guards to watch over a heap of turnips."

"I heard that the turnips, too, are scared," said Franzi.

"Shut your stinking mouths!" yelled a guard from the rear. "If I hear another word I'll come over there and shit on your head and put the rest of you against the fence."

Here they sat within the confines of a small room, upon benches of rotting wood which sat upon tin drums, canisters which were at one time full to the brim with nourishment but now served other purposes, at a time when the war had confiscated much material and from many quarters.

It was the season for turnips: it always seemed to be the season for turnips, in particular at Bergen-Belsen. Turnips was the staple, a commodity suffered day in and day out, breakfast and dinner, sometimes in the form of a soup comprising little more than a splash of vegetable matter amongst a portion of ladled water. But these turnips before them were practically rotten, full of larvae and too foul to be eaten by a human, let alone a pig. And then it came, the answer for them all.

"You swine will work until the bags are empty," said the corporal in charge, Otto Calesson. "And if a single piece should pass your lips then you'll feel the wrath of the SS as never felt before. Now peel."

The sacks delivered to them were huge and the smell of dust filled the air as each was opened to reveal its contents, and with a blunt knife the women went to work peeling the vegetables in preparation for them to be eaten in one way or another.

Franzi picked up a turnip and her thumb fell into it. It was rotten right through to the core. She wanted to see it thrown out but knew better than that. To be seen throwing food away would result in severe punishment. She took her knife and did what she could, careful not to damage it further, but by the time she'd finished with her task the turnip flesh was all over her hand.

A truncheon blow was quickly felt upon the back of her head from which she winced.

"Take care, shit-bag," said the punishing guard, Karl. "Now clean your fingers."

Franzi fidget to get up when another blow was felt upon the back of her head, a little harder than the first. She'd do well not to provoke him further.

"No, you stay there. Lick your hands clean; come on," ordered Karl. "I want to see them cleaned."

Another guard close by, laughed out loud.

"Come on, hurry up; I'm serious," said Karl as Franzi began to lick her fingers clean.

"No, not like that, you stupid whore. Flick your tongue out, like you mean it. Come on; pretend you're a snake."

The other guard laughed again.

And Franzi entertained the guard until her fingers were clean and the guard had had enough. He moved on and she took another turnip from the pile.

The shame of the exercise didn't stop there, however, for there was some good peel that was going to waste, pushed aside and out of reach, pushed from prying eyes, hungry mouths, and stomachs that grumbled away with expectation that never came.

There seemed to be so much peel that it was impossible.

One of the women, so overcome by hunger, could help herself no longer; it was Judith. The sheer agony of seeing a piece of peel hanging from the blade of her knife was too much to bear. There were several guards present but seemed to be talking amongst themselves at the moment, and so many women in the kitchen that the situation merited the offering which sat before her upon the edge of the knife.

Sonja saw the look in Judith's eyes and warned her not to try the impossible, a whisper so low that it was hardly heard, a warning through partially open lips.

Judith looked out of the corner of her eye to Sonja and then quickly flashed the peel into her mouth, swallowing it whole, the soreness of her throat almost bringing her to convulsion, and then came the stabbing in the arm as a guard from behind her lashed at her with a bayonet positioned upon his rifle, the blade of his instrument of death penetrating her flesh and quickly bringing blood to the surface of her worn rags, infection to come about if given the chance, but from the mouth of the guard came insults and slander, a clear indication that she would soon see death.

"You filthy whore-thief!" yelled Karl. "What manner of prisoner are you to take that which is not permitted?"

She didn't cry or scream out when stabbed but simply put her hand where the wound was, and the guards gathered around to commence their mockery.

"You're a thief," said Otto. "Nothing more than a common thief, you Jewish whore."

Karl spat down upon her as she looked up into his eyes, a thick dollop of spit ending up on her face. She wiped it away with her hand, blood replacing the wet, a clean spot then emerging from beneath the hours of airborne dirt and labour.

"She's washing herself," said the same guard that had laughed before and now laughed out loud once again.

"The slut likes to be clean," said the third. "They say a whore will groom herself before a night with many men."

"How many guards did you sleep with in Auschwitz, slut?" asked Otto.

The other soldiers found the insubordinate nature of the piece of filth before them nothing more than a simple insult to their position as held by the SS; she was blatantly disobeying the order to give an answer.

"Take her, I'll be along shortly," said Otto and two guards picked the woman up, one either side, and commenced to drag her away in silence. "Make her walk," said Otto. "Use your bayonet."

The private, Hans, nodded and felt a little out of place, accepting orders for what should have been common sense, and in front of a group of hapless Jews. He was new to the establishment and needed to be seen as a good man amongst his peers, not to be seen as useless or intimidated. Without warning he lifted his arm across his body and lashed out with his elbow.

Judith fell to the floor almost unconscious, blood spurting from her nose and her mouth, several teeth having been knocked out of place, loosened over the weeks of travelling from the gas chambers of Auschwitz to this place in the middle of the forest, this camp of hell that was sitting on cleared ground in the middle of nowhere, little semblance of humanity anywhere to be seen, human life seen for what it was: very, very sad.

"Get up, you lazy bitch," ordered the young SS soldier, Hans, the new boy on the block. "Get up before I strangle your scrawny neck." He grabbed at a small tuft of hair that she had upon her head and as he pulled her to her feet the hair fell out into his hand. He brushed it away in disgust against his trouser leg.

Otto laughed. "Be careful, Hans. This piece of crap might not have lice, but she might have something else to pass onto you, some deadly disease that can't be cured."

The fidgeting young private showed his unsettled feelings and he pushed the woman along. He'd heard of the diseases carried by these lowlife scum and couldn't shake it from his mind. He was young and immature and would no doubt receive a visit in the night from some of the men, to remind him of his training and to deliver a speech on how to treat the prisoners like the dogs they were, and even though he did give the prisoner, Judith, a good hiding with his elbow, it simply wasn't enough.

CHAPTER 7

Judith felt alone now, even if escorted by two guards, and she was forced into a small room of which she had little knowledge.

"Get in there," said Hans as he pushed from behind with an open palm.

Judith fell forward and hit her head against the floor before she stood once more, half dazed from the hit to the head.

"Corporal Otto will be along shortly," said Hans, "and he will not be kind. You should have heeded the warnings you were given, but now; you will receive punishment."

Hans turned himself outside as did the other with him.

"What will Otto do?" asked Hans.

"Something special," said Karl. "It's always something special with Otto. You're in for a real treat. I know exactly the type of man he is."

"Tell me," urged Hans.

"No, you can wait," said Karl. "You will see soon enough with your own eyes, and when you do you'll be happy that you waited for an answer. It is always better to see rather than hear. Remember that, Hans, always remember. There is nothing like true experience."

"Have you experienced much? Have you been here long?" asked Hans.

"I have been here for more than a year and have seen things grow worse by the month, now they grow worse by the day, but I don't care. I hate the stink in this camp, all thanks to those stupid, shit-eating, Jews. They should have all remained in Auschwitz."

"Is it true then, what they say about Auschwitz?" asked Hans.

"I believe so. I have spoken with some that have come from there. They gas them by the thousands," said Karl as he looked into Hans' eyes, seeing a little disbelief and a little horror. "Imagine that, ah, Hans; thousands of them killed, just like that. That's one way to get rid of them I suppose. It's got to be better than looking after the swine."

"I knew a Jew," said Hans, "a long time again... we weren't friends but... he was of good position and had plenty of money."

"Those scum," snarled Karl as he kicked at the closed door of the bunker. "They steal turnip peels like they stole jobs from us before the war. They don't deserve to live, not a stinking one of them."

A dog bark was then heard and Hans turned with Karl to see Otto coming down the passageway with Juana Bormann beside him, a wolfhound at her heels. She was one of the most hated SS guards in the establishment.

"Otto has brought Juana and her pet. Now you will see," said Karl.

Juana Bormann was a vicious looking sort, her face screwed up like a bull terrier snarling. She was known throughout as 'the woman with the dogs' and was renowned for setting her wolfhounds upon the prisoners, to tear them apart, to rip them to pieces, but she wasn't fond of seeing the dogs put to any danger: only the weak were mauled by her dogs. This wretched woman had no feelings, less than a man of the SS in fact. If she was put into a cage with a male SS guard, and each was to fight to the death, the bets would be even.

CHAPTER 8

Judith was locked in the cell by herself. She looked around as the two guards shut the cell door.

It looked like an interrogation room except there was no office furniture and had but a few small cracks in the masonry of the walls. The floor was made of stone, cold and uninviting, covered in stains, and from an adjoining room she could hear the mumbles of a female having been tormented half to death, seemingly half crazed beyond belief. This was the bunker and had but a solitary item of worth in it, that being a hard wooden bed.

This entire prison was a cesspool and with the thought came the feelings of a cramp within her gut, and she was forced onto all fours. What soup she had received the night before, and this morning before being called upon to work, now spilled from her bowels and ran over her thigh before she could manage to stand properly. She had no energy at all, hardly enough to peel those sodden turnips, let alone to have enough energy within her to stand quickly.

The smell of the shit hit her nostrils almost immediately, the rankness of it slapping her in the face, but it was less than what an outsider would suffer for she was used to the foul stench of the barracks already, used to the treatment suffered at the hands of these German bastards. The Germans; whipping was too good for them, so too was a bullet in the head. She only wished that one day they would get the justice that they all deserved.

She felt so poorly, so bad, so meaninglessly, depressed and scared. She was alone, had blood caked over her face and shit all down the inside of her leg as well as out. She longed for life but also wished for death. She couldn't have both. What she really wanted was for something she could not have: freedom.

She didn't wish to sit just yet, for the bed might actually be clean. The last thing she wished to do was soil it, but she felt so tired.

She could hear the men talking outside and was rather concerned by the path the conversation took and then she could hear a dog bark.

She had no idea of knowing what was install for her for she was relatively new to Bergen-Belsen, but she hoped to learn quickly of this place in order to outwit the system and to survive to see the day when freedom was dealt all that waited within the huts and the kitchens, and the forest; all of those in the 'shoe commando', the 'tree commando', and every other work party that had been invented by the SS; all should be allowed to go free, every person here in this camp except the stinking SS guards. It was her dream.

Further talking then took place outside the door of her cell and it opened to reveal the two guards, the corporal, and one she'd not seen before, a woman with a dog.

The dog appeared well behaved for the moment, for it was awaiting a command from the woman.

"Karl," said Otto. "You help our new friend here, Hans, to experience what it is to issue true punishment. And don't forget to leave something for the dog."

Judith was horrified by the words which she understood. She seldom spoke in German, but she understood enough to get her through her days.

Hans didn't let the corporal down, he went in beside Karl and together they beat Judith from head to toe, beating her with their truncheons, upon the arms, legs and head. They kept beating her until she was almost dead, laying on the ground in pools of her own diarrhoea. She was so badly beaten that all she could do was lay there in a heap and hope for the best, but also wishing that she was dead.

"Okay Hans, that's enough," ordered Otto. "Juana; if you please."

"Thank you, Corporal," said the dog-faced woman. She then antagonized the dog, pulled on his chain and got him angered. The dog's teeth showed in all their glory as the lips around them curled away with its show of strength. A few orders were then given to the dog, short, clear and concise orders which were issued as the dog's leash was unclipped. The dog fell upon its victim and ripped poor Judith apart, sinking its teeth into her and ripped flesh from flesh. Her face was the first thing the dog went for, sinking its teeth into her nose, mouth and cheeks, and within just a few short seconds the face became so disfigured that it could not be recognised as human.

Judith was simply another victim of the guards' cruelty.

CHAPTER 9

The duties performed by the two boys at the crematorium were ceaseless. No sooner did they seem to be on top of the situation and then more bodies arrived for them to incinerate.

The boys had not mingled with others of the camp for a very long time. They were locked in at their post and would do their job as ordered by the authority. They were fed better than most, for the work was usually quite hard and always lonely.

Samuel and Maurice had been together for so long now that they felt as though they were brothers, maybe not of kin, but true brothers all the same. They thought alike, ate the same, and shared the same miserable task. They knew each other inside out and conversation between them was sometimes scarce because they knew everything there was to know about one another.

A body was delivered and they loaded it into the oven, placed the wood beneath the oven and then torched it. It was easy, so easy that a trained monkey could do the task with its eyes sewn shut.

A guard approached the crematorium and the two boys looked up. It wasn't meal time and there was nobody in sight, so what was it that this bastard of a guard wanted?

"Shit-lips," yelled the guard, Oskar. "And you, there, Arse-face."

The boy's knew their names. They were christened some time ago now. The guards' humour was sometimes deplorable to say the least.

"There's to be no burning today," ordered Oskar.

The boys knew that an order couldn't be ignored, but the boys were safe. They were at their post, following the orders of the camp commandant.

"Yes, but these bodies," pointed out Samuel.

"You shut your mouth, or I'll have you both whipped," said Oskar. "You do as you're told," and although an explanation was never required the guard felt that it was a small price to pay, and so gave one. "The wind is blowing very strongly today and the smell will fall towards the Panzer barracks. We have had complaints before. Now do as you are told or I'll see to it that your rations are halved."

The guard turned around and departed the vicinity of the boys' responsibility.

"What are we to do with these ten bodies?" asked Maurice. "Isn't it enough that we have to burn these poor bastards, and now we have to spend the whole day and night looking at them?"

"The wind might change direction later," said Samuel.

"The guard won't return, and even if he does it won't be till late, and I don't want to have to burn bodies all night long. I don't think I can take it much more."

"You don't talk like that, Maurice. We do the job we have to do. It's a way to stay alive. There are many dying from starvation... we are lucky."

"I don't think it's lucky," said Maurice. "This is torture. Every day I spend in this shithole I keep thinking about seeing my mother turn up. What am I to do if my mother turns up dead and I have to burn her? What if she's naked and I have to shove her into the furnace like common garbage?"

"I will do the work," answered Samuel, supportively. "I will see to it that she is given a proper send off, not a quick shove into the fire. Trust me, Maurice. I will handle it if the time arrives, but I feel confident that she'll live."

"So what shall we do now?" asked Maurice.

"We'll prepare the furnace and load a body in place. If we hear nothing by morning then we'll start work again."

"I hate this stinking job. I feel dirty eating food which is payment for doing this... unkind thing. There's no sermon, not of any description. We shove and light and burn. That is all we do, all day long, and sometimes into the night when there is not enough time by day."

"It will be okay, Maurice," insisted Samuel. "We'll rest as much as we can today and hopefully clear this lot away later."

Maurice smiled and went to get into his cot and Samuel did the same. They would continue with their work later.

CHAPTER 10

By late afternoon the wind had changed direction but the guard didn't turn up. The burning would have to wait until morning if orders weren't received along with the main meal of the day.

Samuel awoke first and got to his feet. He helped himself to some water and then looked over to his friend.

There was a sudden felt shock and insurmountable fear penetrated every single pore of his body, for Maurice had masterfully hung himself from the ceiling of the crematorium, having used a piece of rope that was his belt.

Maurice had killed himself and without warning.

Samuel immediately flung himself to his friend, to lift him up and relieve the strain of the rope against his neck, but it was no good for Maurice was stone cold; lifeless.

Samuel let go of the body and let it dangle as he cried for his friend that hung there. A little wind was blowing into the furnace room and so the body swayed a little from side to side.

What was the meaning of it all? Why was death so prevalent in this horrible place? Day after day he and Maurice had cremated bodies and now Maurice was dead. Samuel didn't know what to think, what to do, how to feel. His only friend in the world was gone.

Samuel decided right then and there that Maurice would be cremated, but he would serve a ceremony that his friend so deserved. Maurice was concerned for his mother, concerned for the others that came this way, concerned that little favour was done to anyone that died for there wasn't any service to speak of.

Samuel knew that he wasn't well endowed with the ability to give proper sermon but he did all that he could for his friend, and although he didn't yet have clearance to commence with lighting the furnace he went ahead and did so anyway. If a guard came running down to sling insults or threats then Samuel would tell the guard where he could shove his orders.

And so a brief ceremony was undertaken and Maurice was given the send-off that he so deserved... as all men and women deserved; and as expected a guard was seen walking briskly down the road and even from such a distance Samuel could hear the abuse quite clearly.

It was for him alone, Samuel, to decide his own fate, but to live without the companionship of his friend would simply not do.

Committing Maurice to the flames, therefore, was the last duty that Samuel performed and as he looked over towards the guard he knew immediately what he had to do, for he could take it no more. He would not surrender himself to the whims of the men that held him in captivity like a caged animal.

Samuel was mad to the bone, mad beyond all contemplation from the job he had done these past seven months or more; he was mad with the task he had been provided with. He was no different than his friend, Maurice. He no longer had a clear picture of what it meant to be human and so he stuffed his mouth with twigs, shoving them deep down his throat until he suffocated, until he died by his own hands.

And the month of December was not good for the camp

commandant, Josef Kramer, it being the same for the month before when Kramer was not yet posted, where there were between one and two hundred deaths a month: and the number was growing at an alarming rate.

For Kramer there was no choice, the burning of the dead would continue and so two new men were appointed to the task, two new men with fresh minds and the ability to perform their duty well. The fire would be kept burning; the burning of the corpses must continue.

CHAPTER 11

On the 22nd of December, Kramer had instigated a new system where men were promoted to what would become known as 'kapo'; but now it was January and as he saw his plans being hatched, and his orders put into place, he rubbed his hands together in glee. He did this due to the overcrowding of the camp and the ease by which control could be maintained. It was far easier for a SS guard to look after a half dozen, lowlife scum called kapo, than it was to look after thousands of hapless Jews. The thought disgusted him, gave him pains in the stomach. He hated the Jews, despised them like nothing he despised before.

Kapos would be willing to go amongst the death and decay, weeding out the lazy from the sick, organising the prisoners for work parties which needed to be filled by those deserving such horrendous positions, such as the duties performed by the 'tree commando'.

A kapo would have little choice but to see to it that work was performed and that the prisoners were maintained control of. The last thing a kapo needed was to be cuffed behind the ear by a SS guard or thrown amongst the prisoners of whom he had treated so poorly. It was a win-win situation for the guards and the kapos were their puppets, there to have their strings pulled.

For such duties and position a blind eye was often turned so that the dreaded kapo could have his way with the prisoners as he saw fit, taking from them what he wanted, be it their jewellery for a slice of bread, or the virginity of a young girl for a small chunk of cheese.

Yes indeed, Kapo, such a dirty word, and in a majority of the cases, too, a position of rank which was a reward to those of filthy and dilapidated mind, where want for sexual pleasure and handing out severe beatings went hand in hand. You couldn't have one without the other. To be promoted a kapo, or to be an assistant to a kapo, was so unexpectedly received and received well, for only those prisoners of political or criminal prestige would be granted such a position of favour within the camp, and with favour came many kickbacks.

A kapo was a prisoner in charge of prisoners, and many were more vicious than the average SS guard that roamed the grounds with whip in one hand and pistol in the other.

Kasimir Cegielski was but one such depraved kapo who had rotting teeth in his mouth and he stunk horribly, but he was a man nevertheless and able to get things done. He was a good manipulator and sucked up well to the guards in uniform and played them for the poor eyesight they sometimes suffered when watching over the barracks.

Kasimir saw an opportunity one day that simply couldn't be passed up, for the woman involved looked so beautiful. If he could only get some food into her then she might go unspoiled and last him well, to serve him as he so desired.

He was in the barracks which was being cleared for roll call when he noticed her reaching down for something on the floor. He quickly stepped over to her side and leaned down, touching her on the arm rather gently, squeezing it with great affection before she pulled away and looked in the other direction, to move over to where a shawl hung upon a nail near a crud-filled window.

"Hello," said Kasimir. "Do you know who I am?"

"Yes, I do," said the young woman. She was rather fit and healthy when she'd first arrived, but now the wear and tear of camp life was commencing to take its toll upon her. He must save her. She didn't feel herself, in this horrible place, and felt the hollowness within her grow by the day, a great void that seemed to swallow her whole.

"What's your name?"

"It's Henny."

"Well, Henny," started Kasimir, "is there anything I can do for you?"

"No; no, I don't think so," and she pulled the shawl down and placed it around her shoulders, happy to have something warm to throw around her during the cold winter months.

"Are you warm?"

"Yes, thank you," said Henny and then tried to push past him. "I must be on parade for roll call, or punishment will be expected," and the last of the occupants of the barracks exit to leave them alone.

"Oh, no; that's quite alright, Henny,' said Kasimir as he put his hand into a small pouch he carried and pulled out a hunk of cheese.

Henny's eyes lit up as though seeing the wonder of fire for the very first time, a flame flickering in the breeze. She could even smell the cheese for what it was... a life saver.

"Would you like a taste?"

"It looks so... I'm starving," said Henny. "And so is my husband, but I can't pay you much. Here, take my shawl."

"I don't want to deprive you of your shawl," said Kasimir with a faint smile, ignoring the fact that she had a husband; in fact it helped his cause, greatly. "Can't we just be friends?"

"Friends?"

"Yes, that's all."

Henny looked at the cheese. It was a large piece in her eyes, the largest she'd seen in a long time, big enough for her and her husband. They hadn't been married long and he had been taken away to work in the 'tree commando'.

The 'tree commando', work designed for strong young men, where cutting down trees, cutting up wood, and ripping stumps from the hard ground which encased them, was all a part of a hard day's work.

"It does look lovely," said Henny.

"Look, why don't you take it? Look at it as a favour," said Kasimir.

"Are you sure... that's all; just a savour; from a friend?"

"Of course, my dear Henny. Please, take it, and keep your shawl, too."

"Thank you, Kasimir," said Henny as she took the cheese and brushed past the kapo to head for the parade where roll call was about to commence. "My husband also thanks you. He will be pleased to hear of your hospitality when he returns from the forest."

Kasimir watched as the young woman disappeared from view with his cheese.

"Yes, dear, and I thank you very much, too," he said out loud, though no one could hear, for he was alone at that minute. "You will serve me well."

Kasimir didn't wish to be robbed of the advantage he had found for himself. He wasted no time at all in seeing one of his friends, a guard in charge of the 'tree commando'. His only wish now was for the young man, Henny's husband, to be looked after, not to be beaten; he would take control of the rest. As far as Kasimir was concerned, the husband of Henny's was nothing more than a pawn to him, to be employed as best could be. The husband was his ticket to sexual pleasure, but he must first have a name, and so he goes about his duty and gets the information he needs before confronting his friend, the guard.

CHAPTER 12

Kasimir didn't take long in finding out that Henny's husband's name was Phillipjé, and he was even faster to request special favour for him whilst he was attached to the 'tree commando'.

For two days the work in the forest went well for Phillipje and he was oblivious to the fact that he seemed to be left alone most of the time, and so long as he worked hard he seemed to fit in well with the work. He was cursed from time to time but generally speaking was treated with much favour when compared to the other workers.

The work was hard but he seldom got beaten. Beatings for him were rarely seen for he was young and could get the work done, or so he thought; but a guard secretly received cigarettes from Kasimir, for the kapo had eyes for Henny.

The young man toiled away at his hard labour and was oblivious to the good treatment that he received, and failed to see how it was that his wife, so pretty, could provide him with what appeared to be an extra ration of soup each day that he returned to the barracks.

But favours must be rewarded and to this note, the kapo known of Kasimir stirs his caldron well, bringing great joy to the surface.

Kasimir approached Henny in the barracks, pulling the door closed behind him. It was time for roll call and no one else was in the hut.

"I must go, Kasimir," said Henny with fear in her throat. "I have to go outside."

"Not today, Henny," said Kasimir. "I need to talk to you for a minute... just a minute of your time."

"What is it? Is something wrong, perhaps?"

"No, not at all," assured Kasimir. "But I have been a good friend to you and your husband of late."

"Yes, thank you so much," said Henny, still very fearful.

"In fact, the reason your husband comes home to you each day, unbeaten and well fed, to eat more that you can provide him, is for the favours I have been doing you, and now... it is time to collect on those favours."

"What do you mean to say?" asked Henny, knowing full well what was about to occur.

"I like you, Henny; I find you pretty," said Kasimir with a smile, his rotten teeth showing through the grin. "I think you know what I want, and I'll get it, too."

"But I don't want it," said Henny. "I don't want to be friends any more. I can't take your food or hospitality any longer."

"I'm sorry to hear that, Henny. But look at it this way. If I don't get what I want then the extra food will stop, your rations will be less than the others, and your husband will receive beatings and have his rations stopped."

"You can't do that," said Henny.

"Oh, but I can. I was the one that gave you and your husband the fair treatment that you've received so far and I can stop it with a simple whisper in the guards' ears."

"I'm sorry, Kasimir. I don't wish for any more food," and Henny stormed out of the barracks to the roll call.

Kasimir smiled to himself once more. Of course he could have beaten her and had his way, but to have her permission whilst he assaulted her; that's what he craved.

CHAPTER 13

Phillipje was working with the other men of the 'tree commando', doing as they did and not an ounce more. It was a cunning trick that he'd learnt to pull, for he was growing accustomed to the fair treatment, a dangerous trick where he grew lazy and did no more than he felt he should do, a manoeuvre that could see him in big trouble if he was caught. He was fitter and stronger than all the others of the work party and it was because of the extra ration that he received that he fended so well amongst the growing disease of the camp. But the guards had been given the whisper, a message from another guard who had a friend. And so, Phillipje's days were numbered.

"That one, there," said Erik to the corporal in charge. "He's the one."

"Very well," replied the corporal, looking over his back to the sergeant who was out of good visual range; not that it mattered, for the sergeant would take the corporal's word for whatever he said. "We'll punish him and two others; just pick two, it doesn't matter which."

"That one, the one with the scar on his cheek, and the one that limps... he's a lazy bastard, always using his leg as an excuse to slow his work. It's good he gets beatings, but I think it's time he got more – I hunger for a good cigarette."

"Yes, me too," agreed the corporal. "Okay, let's not waste any more time."

Erik strode up to where Phillipje was standing with a smile upon his face, unaware of what was about to happen to him, and the corporal followed close behind. The SS guard saw a dumb reflection in the Jew's eye, but it wasn't that at all, it was the strength of character and the innocence of man that the guard really saw: for it was the guard that was too stupid to know that his sadistic mind was thwart with hidden agendas.

Erik allowed nothing to slip and then without warning he swung his truncheon to strike the prisoner above the knee, careful not to break it, for to do so would see the stream of cigarettes dry up completely; the cigarettes, always the cigarettes; and the cigarettes were his payment for holding his temper. The corporal quickly deposited several portions of a slice of bread upon the ground at Phillipje's feet.

"You damn Jew, I'll kick your useless arse all the way back to camp if you do that again!" yelled Erik.

The sergeant looked over to see what the matter was, seeing Erik with the corporal just behind him.

Phillipje fell to the ground and Erik gave him a swift kick before the corporal rushed in and throttled the two men beside him.

"What is the matter here?" asked the sergeant as he made his way over to the scene in a slow and uncaring manner, not concerned over the beatings that the men were being subjected to but concerned over the unscheduled stop to the work being carried out.

"These men were seen eating bread, sergeant," said the corporal.

The sergeant looked down upon the three men now lying on the ground in pain, each holding their thighs, their faces screwed up.

"Then they deserve more than to have their arses kicked," said the sergeant.

"Permission to string them up, sergeant?" requested the corporal; formerly, knowing full well that permission would be granted.

"Yes; immediately. I won't stand for such ignorance of the system by a pathetic, stinking Jew, in particular one that looks up into my face from there upon the ground. See to it, corporal."

"I didn't do anything," protested Phillipje. This was followed immediately by a flurry of blows from three separate truncheons.

"If you stinking bastards so much as utter a single word of complaint," said the corporal, "then I swear to God, I'll see you shot and strung from the tallest tree, so that the crows can have their way with you."

One of the Jews, too tired to think straight, too tired to shut his mouth, opened up and voiced his opinion of the guard. "What would you know of God?"

Erik pulled his luger from its holster and waved it in signal for the man to be taken aside.

"It's okay, corporal," said the sergeant. "I'll attend to this one; see the others are strung up."

"Yes, sergeant," and the corporal clicked his heels together in a way of passing a compliment.

A single guard aided the sergeant by following close behind, and with the offender in hand, his arm pushed high from behind, almost tearing it from its socket, the pain written heavily upon the prisoner's face, he was pushed this way and then shoved that.

"God will have his vengeance," said the prisoner between clenched teeth before receiving a swift kick in the guts.

"You get that for free," said the sergeant.

The threesome had gone about three hundred yards into the forest when the sergeant ordered the corporal to stop. The prisoner was pushed to his knees and held in place there for a few moments before being let go.

The sergeant moved to the prisoner's front and placed his boot on the ground. "Lick it clean, Jew."

The prisoner looked up and into the sergeant's eyes, a sparkle within. The sergeant smiled.

"Come on, lick it clean," said the sergeant in a quiet manner. "Your friends aren't here to see you; come on."

The man on his knees commenced licking the entire boot, from sole, to toe, and all the way up to where it finished just below the knee. With the task complete the prisoner withdrew his mouth.

"Now put away your tongue," said the sergeant as he took his luger from its holster and moved behind the man on the ground. "Do you know what is to happen to you; do you know the price for insubordination?"

The prisoner didn't answer and kept looking to his front, knowing full well that he was about to die.

The sergeant pushed the prisoner over, forcing him to the ground with a push with his leg. The prisoner rolled over onto his back and looked up once more and saw the guard's eyes cloud over and his smile evaporate.

"It's good that you can see this coming," said the sergeant, and he pointed his weapon and pulled the trigger.

The shot rang out loud and clear and the Jews all around stopped for a brief second, looking up to see what was going on.

"Get back to work, you scum," yelled a guard. "Or you'll be next."

The corporal looked up at his small quarry, the two men he had rounded up for torture. They were both hanging from a tree, by the hands, hands tied together behind their backs. The pain was excruciating.

"You can both wait there," said the corporal with a laugh. "You'll be let down when it's time to go back to the barracks, in an hour."

The man beside Phillipje could take the insult no more and did the unsavoury thing by speaking out.

"Please, I can't take this. I'll do whatever you want. Please let me down... I'll make it worth your while."

The corporal looked at the limp body as it hung from the tree, arms pulled back and held above his head.

"You," said the corporal. "You will stay here all night. I'll cut you down if you're still alive when we get back tomorrow morning," but all knew very well that the man would not survive to see the sun fall beyond the horizon. The agony which he was about to suffer was beyond his wildest imagination.

CHAPTER 14

When Phillipje returned to the barracks, Henny couldn't believe the state he was in. Four prisoners deposited him upon the entrance to the hut. The man who had felt as though he was emancipated, by his luck and good fortune, was now nothing more than a pile of sad refuse upon the floor for all to see. He'd been well and truly tortured, hung from a tree for a full hour, and when it was time to bring him down he was beaten solidly for three or four minutes, every inch of his body being hammered by the guards.

Henny rushed to him and fell in place beside the mass of flesh, hugging and kissing the poor man as he winced in pain from her delicate caresses. The look in his swollen eyes said that he had no idea why this thing was done to him, but she knew why... she knew exactly.

A call then came for each and every one to line up for their meal and Henny fought hard to pull herself from her man, to take her position in the line. She moved forward slowly as each and everyone received their ladle of watery soup and she continued to look over her shoulder, towards where her husband was curled up in pain. She now stood before the kapo.

"You have done a cruel thing, Kasimir," said Henny.

"Maybe you would like some soup," was Kasimir's reply as he scraped the bottom for a good ladle-full of vegetable flesh. He poured it into her bowl. "Some for your husband, perhaps?" Kasimir looked her in the eyes. "It can always be like this, Henny; always plenty to eat... and good treatment for your husband, too."

Henny held out a second bowl, looking from side to side, seeing a few cold stares come her way from the other prisoners.

"You know the price, do you not?" questioned Kasimir quietly.

"I do," replied Henny.

"Good. I shall speak with my friends in the morning. You will be content. Your husband won't be beaten anymore."

And Kasimir saw to it that his promise was carried out for his feelings of lust were deep, and each night, as the ladle was dipped into the watery soup, he managed to retrieve Henny a good portion that was reward for her devotion to him. His ladle now scraped against the bottom in order to get the vegetable flesh into the scoop, and always there was plenty for her, but others in the barrack were annoyed that she was pretty, for they just got the water which was little flavoured and provided no nourishment at all. Phillipje was also treated with great care and so long as he did his job he came back to the hut each night without a mark upon him.

Kasimir appeared at the barracks which stood empty at midday, for roll call had been called. It was time for him to collect his pleasure. He saw the young girl and approached with a smile and she immediately undressed and climbed upon the bunk in order to get the dirty job done. She wanted for her husband to live, for him to go without the beatings, for them both to have a life together in the unforeseen future to come. The only way she could secure this was to surrender to the whims of the kapo. But when the kapo's lust for her died, so too would the favours, and so she would have to give the best performance she could muster, keeping the kapo as happy as he could be kept.

CHAPTER 15

Whilst at duty with the 'shoe commando', Miriam accidentally cut herself upon the wrist with a knife as she carried out her work on a pair of shoes, doing all she could to stay awake, just managing to keep her eyes open by talking freely with those around her, all in the hope that her work would continue as the guards looked around at those under their command. She was now paying for her lapse in concentration, and although the cut didn't penetrate deep it was enough to bring much blood to the cold air, covering her hand and lower arm in seconds; all over her knife and the table top: the blood got everywhere, but the guard was either too ignorant to attend or too stupid to notice that something had happened.

She let out several muffled cries for help and the lady beside her, Hetty, grabbed at a helmet full of cloth and commenced to bandage the wound which was initially seen as quite the threat to life. All of those around continued to work but did so silently, looking upon the unfortunate woman as she tried to help the one that bandaged her.

One of the SS guards in view was finally drawn to the commotion and quickly strutted over with his curiosity entwined with frustration and anger, searching for an explanation for the disturbance. There was work to be done and the last thing the guard wished was for something to go wrong during the course of his duty.

"What is this," he demanded, the intrusion upon his daily choir too much to handle. "What's going on here?"

"Miriam has cut herself," said Hetty, concerned for her friend. Friends were hard to come by, hard to trust, and needed to be held on to for the duration of their unlawful incarceration in Bergen-Belsen.

"Cut herself," stated the guard. "Let me see."

"Here," said Hetty as she pushed Miriam's arm out for the guard to see. "The blood is everywhere. She'll have to see the doctor."

The guard looked at the cut. "You should have your arse kicked all the way back to the barracks for being so careless. I'm tired of you stinking people; it's always something with you. You should be given a good whipping; that's what."

"What's going on?" said another guard as he approached. "What's going on here?"

"This stupid slut, Miriam—," started the guard.

"I don't care what her name is," interrupted the other guard. "What's her number," and laughed out loud at his own joke. "Roll up her sleeve and take a look."

"She's cut herself," repeated the first.

"This miserable piece of shit has tried to commit suicide and failed to achieve a result," came the answer to the concern. "Don't bother yourself with this lazy scum. She's after a day off," the guard looked down upon Miriam as Hetty finished the task of applying a bandage as best she could. "If you wanted to commit suicide then you should have told me. I can help you out; free of charge," and spat upon the woman where she sat. "She'll stay and work like the others," said the guard as he looked his companion in the eye. "Ensure she does her share," and he walked off, shaking his head.

The first guard remained in place. "You stupid slut; what are you about? Do you want me to look like a fool? I'm tired of being nice to you. You will get your work done, like the others, and if I find that your quota has been neglected then I shall see you all standing at the fence for the entire night."

Hetty continued to tie the bandage in place for Miriam as the work around them continued and the guard moved away.

"You will have to take care of your injury," said Hetty. "You aren't going to get any favours here. Get some rest tonight, Miriam."

Miriam looked after the guard as he continued to assess the work further down the table. "Who is he, so high and mighty; what favour has he done us? I've had nothing to eat except dry cabbage in water for two days running, treated like a slave, spoke to like an animal, and he says he's tired of being nice."

"Don't let him trouble you, Miriam. He'll hear you," said Hetty.

"And when he does we'll all be punished for your stupidity," said one of the women from across the table, angered that Miriam should jeopardise her safety.

CHAPTER 16

Even now, the introduction of three-tiered bunks was prominent in most parts of the camp, in particular where the former stables had been arranged in quarters for one faction of prisoner, mattresses so thin that they couldn't be accounted for anything, nothing more than bedding enough for the bugs of the night which would choose to come out by dark for their chance of something to eat.

Ashamed the prisoners all were in such dilapidated conditions that it never even entered their minds that conditions could get much worse.

The stables consisted of four quarters with three toilets and a washing shed; it was a sheer pity that the toilets often became clogged with faeces that, given time, the inmates en mass would simply shrug their shoulders and await as patiently as possible in line for their turn at the one which was in good working order, or simply employ the hollowed out space of a jug or vase which could be emptied at its earliest convenience. Such were the rudiments of life here that little decorum of any description was seen, and shitting was a daily choir.

There was no respectability in standing within line and awaiting your turn to use the toilet when, with the expulsion of gas from within, the remnants of the meagre meals consumed during the day, came gushing out and quite often down the legs.

"Olga; where are you going?" asked Sarah as she gently grabbed hold of her friend's arm. "There are only a few people in front of you now."

Olga looked to the front of the line and towards the toilet; she then looked down upon the ground.

Sarah followed her glance and saw the shit as it pooled around her friend's feet, the smell going unnoticed for the stench in the barracks was much the same no matter where you went.

"Don't let it get you down, Olga," encouraged Sarah. "It has happened to all of us."

"Yes, I know," said Olga with a tempted smile. "I need my rest. I'm going to try and clean myself and then go to sleep."

"Won't you stay up until the soup arrives?"

"That's why I shit so much," replied Olga. "I'm too tired. I have to sleep."

"You take care, Olga," insisted Sarah. "You're my good friend. I don't want to see you too depressed. I'll wake you when the soup arrives."

"Thank you, Sarah; you're a good friend," said Olga one last time and disappeared towards her bunk where she would have to climb up two tiers and over at least one person, for there was always someone laying down in sickness and poor health.

By the time Olga had gotten to her bunk she could see that two were asleep at the top. She reached up and grabbed a small piece of cloth that hung upon a nail, her cleaning rag. She took it and moved over towards the washing shed where she'd hoped to be able to get some water. She was in luck.

She took her pyjama trousers off and stood there with nothing on but a worn shirt. Several men could be seen going about their business but she was unashamed, as anyone else was in this camp of filth. She scrubbed hard the thin fabric and tried with all her strength to get the stain from within the pyjamas to wash away. After a few minutes she had attained a reasonable amount of success and so placed the trousers back on and decided on a quick look outside to help them dry upon her legs.

The night was very cold and she shivered there, wondering what it would be like to have something better to eat; somewhere nicer to sleep.

Several towers could be easily seen from where she stood and the guards in these continued their watch, studying their area of responsibility, ensuring that no prisoner went near a fence they weren't supposed to approach, or speak with anyone that it was forbidden to speak with.

Olga had heard that family and friends were prevalent in the camp, that one member from one area within the camp would endeavour to push a potato or turnip through the wire so that another could share in their fortunate lives, for not all in Bergen-Belsen were treated as heavy-handily as another.

As she stood there watching she noticed that there was a child wandering about, a stray child having wandered too far from its hut and seemingly looking for its mother. And as she continued to watch, she saw an adult come out of hiding, walking in a mild rush towards the infant which couldn't have been more than three to four years of age.

"Hey, what are you doing?" yelled Olga, forgetful.

The guard in the nearest tower looked down upon her, thinking her suspicious.

"Who goes there?" yelled the guard and rushed the beam of his searchlight to fall upon her. "What are you doing near the fence?"

"I saw something," yelled Olga in reply. "A child."

"Stay away from the fence," yelled the guard. "Stay where you are and someone will be there shortly, you nosey, Jew-bitch."

Olga looked over and could just barely see that the figure of a woman had reached the child and had picked it up.

"No; there she is," and Olga ran towards the fence.

"Halt!" yelled the guard, and the next moment he fired his rifle and Olga fell down dead.

The other woman halted and looked over her shoulder before returning to her task and carried the child to safety.

She placed the child down out of view from the tower.

"What's your name?" she asked.

The boy was scared, scared to death, but he knew that he was in a camp for unfortunates, kept locked away against his free will, even though he didn't know what 'free will' was.

"Abraham," said the little child in a whisper.

"Well, Abraham; I'm Annie," replied the adult. "Are you alone?" and she knew he was, for she'd seen his mother die.

"My mummy has gone," said Abraham with tears in his eyes.

"Do you know that you shouldn't be near the fence? You'll be shot... dead," she wished to scare the child more than anything else. Her own child had died just that morning and she was without her reason for being tended to like a good little lamb. Whilst she remained with a child she was fed better than the others, and with a child so young she was advantaged by not having to go to work.

"I miss my mother."

"I know you do, Abraham," said Annie. "But we have to help each other now. But you have to listen to me closely; very closely. If you want to stay alive then you have to pretend, Abraham, and we don't have much time."

"Why?" asked Abraham.

"Don't worry about that right now," said Annie. "Just listen to me, and listen carefully. The nasty men that watch us day and night; they will take you away if they find you without a mother, do you understand?"

"Yes," replied Abraham.

"Good; now listen to me... your name isn't Abraham anymore, you hear? Your name is Max."

"I don't like Max," said Abraham.

"You have no choice, Max. You have to be, or they'll take you away and kill you."

"I wasn't naughty, I wasn't bad," said Abraham. "I just want my mother," and he sobbed rather too loudly for Annie's comfort.

She picked him up and scurried away to her hut, the child in her arms. "I'll look after you, Max; you're my son now. We'll look after each other. How does that sound; uh?"

"Will I see my mother again?"

"No, Max; you won't; but together we can live," explained Annie, and both mother and child disappeared into the darkness, one in the arms of the other.

CHAPTER 17

Sarah felt poorly that her friend was dead. One moment she was standing in the line for the ablutions and the next, she had a hole in her head. Those bastard SS were good shots with the rifle, there was no doubt about that. With camp life came much practice for the guards to hone their shooting skills. There was a great injustice about it all, how the SS seemed to think it was all a game, how the mistreatment of the Jews below them would somehow see them be honoured with the presentation of an Iron Cross for a job well done.

Sarah had realised rather quickly, that although she felt for her dead friend, Olga, her own life was more important. It was like having to choose which child was next to be shot: would it be one from her extended family, or the boy in the next barracks? The choice was easy. Life was precious, and no more precious was it than to the person who held it most dearly – the individual.

The following night's meal was the same as the night before, which was the same again for every night that past fortnight: from what she could recall. She was so tired that she rarely knew what was real and what was not; it was all like a dream to her.

She received her ladled water where several green pieces of something could be seen floating on the surface: a little lettuce, perhaps. Her eyes grew wide, just for a small piece of lettuce; she was going crazy with hunger.

Someone looked over to Sarah as she held the bowl to her lips – no one bothered to use spoons any more – and from the corner of her eye, Sarah could see the woman lick her lips. If Sarah was to fall dead that minute her bowl would be emptied faster than she would hit the floor in a spasm of death.

The woman's name was unknown to Sarah but it was obvious she wished to take more than she was welcome to. Sarah would, from this day forth, keep an eye open for the evil looking cow now watching her. Everybody had enemies; everyone wanted extra food to eat.

The kapo of the hut was far too mean to issue a proper portion to those under his care; it was the sex he cared about more than anything else. The kapo was nothing more than a criminal, so why should he be in charge? Then again, the SS were no different, a bunch of criminals who saw it as their duty to torture and kill.

Sarah continued to drink from her bowl and closed her eyes as the watery soup went down her throat. Her throat was a little sore but she wouldn't waste anything that she was given to eat or drink. In her imagination she could swear that she could taste carrots. Maybe the kapo rubbed the inside of the kettle with some carrot juice before it was delivered to her bowl, to tease her imagination, to drive her further into insanity than she had already fallen. It was then that her eyes flew wide open, as she reached the bottom of her bowl, for there was at least a large spoonful of vegetable matter at the bottom. She had struck it rich.

Ah, the delectable taste and texture of real food; it was beyond imagination; it was sheer luxury; and the soup was warm, also. Maybe the kapo was after her body, she thought.

A call suddenly erupted throughout the barracks, the entire camp called to roll call. It was dark outside and freezing, no place for a human being.

The rain was coming down in buckets, no reprieve for those making their way out onto parade, to be lined up in five ranks, covered off from front to rear. It took rather a while before everyone was in position and the guards made their way through the huts, counting all of those with a doctor's order to stay in bed.

The SS corporal came storming out of the hut from behind Sarah.

"There's a body in the hut, you filth-mongers," yelled the guard. "You and you; get your filthy arses inside and drag it out; now!"

Sarah turned around having not seen that she was one of those ordered to duty.

"You better be deaf," said the corporal as he lifted his truncheon and smashed it into her face, knocking out all of her teeth, "you stupid, lazy bitch. Get off your knees and to work; I have no need for my boots to be cleaned. It's raining you stupid cow; move it!"

Sarah had no use for tears; they'd been used up long ago. Here she was on her knees, her teeth knocked out and swallowed up by the mud of the parade as the rain continued to fall without remorse.

Sarah got up and followed the other person into the hut; it was Olga.

"Olga, my dear friend," said Sarah. "You've come back."

"Stop your talking," said the corporal and gave her a shove from behind.

Sarah fell forward, into the mud once more, and into the person in front of her.

"Olga, help me," said Sarah as she looked up from the mud at the foot of the steps into the hut. "Help me, Olga."

The woman looked down upon Sarah and then to the corporal. "I don't know what she's saying. I'm not Olga."

"Shut your mouth," said the guard. "You go and get the body by yourself and deposit it in the gutter... you can take care of it in the morning."

The corporal looked down upon the smiling Sarah, and she looked up with arms held out for Olga, her dearest friend.

The corporal swung his truncheon from high to low, bringing it down hard and upon Sarah's outstretched arms. Both snapped, heard over the roar of the rain.

Sarah sank further into the mud and the corporal beat down upon the woman until she was dead by bashing, or by drowning in the mud, either way the guard couldn't care less. To the guard she was nothing more than a stinking Jew, another number, another animal amongst animals which deserved to be beaten.

Senior Sergeant Weingartner, the blockführer, moved over to where the corporal was standing.

"She'd gone mad," said the corporal, "a lunatic."

"She got what she deserved," said the sergeant. He looked down upon the back of the dead woman and noticed the legs of the one beside her. She'd pissed herself, the steam of the urine erupting from the pyjamas like the vapours from a volcano.

"Trying to keep warm, are you?" asked the sergeant sarcastically. "Look at me when I speak, whore-bag."

The woman looked at the sergeant, shaking from the cold of the night, the rain continuing to fall upon them all.

The sergeant lifted his whip and placed it under her chin. "If you were 40 pounds heavier you might be worth something. Get your scrawny arse over to the fence and stay there until you're relieved of your punishment."

As the woman moved away the sergeant addressed the parade. "Anyone else wishing to defile this ground may do so, but next time I shall not be so lenient. Corporal."

"Yes, sergeant."

"See to it that the woman remains at the fence until first light."

"Yes, sergeant."

CHAPTER 18

It was an underestimate to assume that several thousand bombers had flown overhead during February, overhead the camp during nights which allowed for good visual recognition of targets, the number in all reality being a lot more than an inmate's imagination could commit to. It got the strength of the poor souls up, those relinquished to the cruelty of the SS feeling an emotion of happiness within them, their confidence soaring high on wings-of-a-prayer, for it all meant that the war was nearing its end; there was simply no other explanation. The very thought of the war ending ripped the prisoners from the brink of their despair, even if for a short time only.

The commandant was quick to see that the planes could easily cause quite the headache, and in particular was the threat of a ground assault upon his very camp; but he had considered that the allies wouldn't dare assault a prisoner of war camp, let alone a camp full of pathetic Jews, the source of his aggravation. He hated them all with such great passion that if the same amount of passion was to be consumed writing a sonnet or similar, it would be remembered as the greatest gift to mankind, ever.

Kramer ordered that a work party be organised for the defences of the camp to commence. He ordered that a trench be dug for the protection of the SS and this was to be dug with the prisoner's food bowls – why on earth would he wish to provide them with tools? The task was insane and served no purpose, but it did provide the commandant with feelings of joy, to see that he held much power and influence over those he called 'scum'.

The weather had not improved much over the past few weeks and the ground was back-breaking hard from the cold nights. A little snow could be seen to fall from the sky, through dirty and broken panes, looked upon by wandering eyes as they perused the surroundings for answers.

When would the war end? When would the torture stop? When would the tormentors receive just punishment? They were questions that had no answer for a lot of the people in Bergen-Belsen, for a lot of those in this place of hell would be dead before salvation could be granted.

A mysterious hand rubbed a clear space upon a window pane, to attain a clearer view of what was happening outside. Different parts of the camp could be seen from this single vantage point. There were so many different nationalities here that had it easier than others, and most of it stemmed from whether or not you were a prisoner of war or a Jew whose arse was marked with a big red 'X'.

Most of the 'Exchange Jews' were seen to wear a visible yellow star sewn upon their lapel or breast and although a prisoner uniform (pyjamas) were worn by many, a majority of these favourites wore civilian clothing. The last thing the SS wanted was for poor propaganda to escape to the West, but it was too late to worry about such things, for news travelled quickly; this was why those that were classified as 'exchange Jew' were treated better than all the others. But the condition of the camp was not widely known to the rest of the world in the present moment, and this was a good thing for the SS, and could only help the German cause as opposed to ruin it.

A SS guard moved between two watch towers, moving steadily upon his feet with a leash in his hand. He carried a rifle upon his shoulder, attached by its strap, and the German Sheppard was controlled well by him as they both moved up and down their responsibility. It was their duty to ensure that no conversation between prisoners, from one compound to the next, was shared. 'Exchange Jews' could not be permitted to depart the camp of horror with dirty laundry sewn within their lips.

The entire camp was surrounded by a double fence of barbed wire and not a second went by where there was not a single metre of ground that was not covered by German eyes. Armed guards and dogs; more dogs and their handlers; rifles loaded and ready to use; there was simply no escape.

The hard labour of digging a trench under Kramer's order continued for many days and men were whipped and beaten, punched and kicked, kicked and scolded. Everyone was treated like an animal, but some animals received fairer treatment than others.

Eventually the work was done and the trench was finished. It was now time to inspect the work carried out by the prisoners.

Kramer looked over the work which had been done and was pleased that it had been carried out as per his orders, but he had had a change of mind, and so, two weeks after the trenches had been ordered dug, he ordered them filled.

Only a lunatic could cause such pain to be forced upon many prisoners, day after day, after day, all held against their will, but it takes a highly motivated lunatic to run a concentration camp.

CHAPTER 19

In the early days of camp life it was seldom seen that a person, as an individual, would be confronted with the horrors of death. If death occurred then it was a sad occasion, in particular for family and friends – where such existed. And it was always good to have friends, in particular towards the end of the war, for when the time of Hitler's downfall was upon them all it was good to have someone close to the breast that would die for your cause; and many people in the insanity of camp life wished for heavier clothing to stave off the cold, and clothing could most favourably be obtained from the dead. A dead person had no need for clothing or food and no sooner did someone pass away and their personal belongings were confiscated quick-smart by those who knew the person best. There was no reading of wills necessary, just quick hands and fast minds.

As time passed, so did the occurrences of death. What was rarely seen was now a part of everyday life. Day in and day out, night after night; someone would die, their bodies would be stripped, their belongings dissolved; and where the fortunate were concerned, death showered them with great respect, for the deceased were thrown into the gutter to be picked up later, not to be shoved under the floorboards and forgotten. Such were the advantages of friendship that to be placed in the gutter was a mark of respect, for it meant twice the handling and a possible service when the dead were collected the following morning.

Something of a horrid nature was then brought to air, for someone had stolen a loaf of bread from the kitchen. For this a punishment would be issued to the entire camp, for one mans' crime was for all to share.

Everyone was to stand on parade, to stand there in the snow, and for nine hours be subjected to the freezing wind and white specks of ice that fell from the sky. Kapos were placed in charge, ordered to watch over those on parade, and from high in the towers along the barbed wire fence the ever watchful eyes of the guards looked upon everyone to ensure that nothing and no one fell out of place.

The kapos had little choice but to suffer the weather as did the inmates, but the kapos had something to keep them warm: the beating of those before them.

The exercise of beating old men and women provided the kapos with the opportunity to maintain their warmth throughout the hours that they had to stand there, taking time off now and again for a drink of water or something small to eat.

By the time it was over and the punishment was seen to fit the crime, rations were stopped for two days and everyone was fallen out to move back to their huts and continue with their horrible lives in unsanitary conditions.

A man was laying half frozen on the ground, exposed to the open air, stepped over by hundreds of inmates as they moved into warmer surroundings. It was freezing cold, so cold that it was unimaginable how the man was still alive. He held up his hand for help, hoping for someone to pick him up and carry him inside, but he was heavy and everyone else was tired. Each and every one needed to conserve their energy for the loved ones in their life, not to be tied down by attending to an old man. Give an inch and he would take a mile. Help him now and he would return to be helped again, and again, and again later on. It simply couldn't be permitted to happen.

The old man's feet felt as though they were frozen, frozen solid, and he couldn't move. The pain was too great, the infliction beyond contemplation.

And the horrors of the night were as bad as those by day, where lice and bed bugs had their way upon every person and if an individual was unlucky, an inmate from the bunk above would shit on their head.

Such was life in this place.

Sonja got up and took her place in line for the toilet. She was fortunate this morning because there were not many in the queue. Most were too sick to move, or too tired to get up, which was unfortunate for the sanitary conditions of the hut, for almost everyone had diarrhoea.

Sonja moved into the toilet and there she found a dead body, an elderly lady, dead upon the toilet seat, sitting there having relieved her bowels but dying before given the chance to wipe her own arse. What an unforgiving position this was.

But the pity she felt for the deceased was superseded by her own need to relieve herself and so she sat upon the bare porcelain just in time. Her bowels emptied, like running water from a tap. She had now done her morning duty, but she was still sitting there when an old man then came and sat beside her, and did as he needed to do on another. There was no shame felt, no discomfort in the situation, for they shared a common misery and the last thing on their mind was to show any decency whilst shitting: and all before the dead was removed from her place upon the bar.

Finally it was time to move, time to get ready for the morning's roll call. She got to her feet and was about to remove herself from the stench of her surroundings when a sudden felt urge fell upon her. She felt disgusted in herself for not having helped the dead woman. The least she could do was place her outside so that she could receive a cremation – even if cremation might not be granted, for there were a hell of a lot of bodies mounting up outside.

Sonja heaved and jerked and pulled with all her strength, doing all she could to remove the body of the dead woman. The man on the toilet that sat next to her was still sitting, looking upon her as though thinking how stupid she was to be wasting her time with such a foolish errand.

Inch by inch, the body was dragged along the floor, picking up faeces as she was pulled, literally cleaning the excrement that was evident upon the floorboards of their shitting quarters. She continued to pull and finally came to the door where all that was left of Sonja's energy was enough to push the remains with her foot into the cold morning air. Across from her was a pile of dead, and it grew in height, length and width, and deposited there were those that had been erased from the face of the world, to be lost forever of human contact.

The body fell away from the step and Sonja looked to the side. There she saw an old man, frozen stiff from the night before, unable to extricate himself from his position. Why hadn't someone helped him?

Sonja looked up again, further afield. The cart was coming, the cart with a body upon it, and she could see the small crowd of people as they watched it being pulled along, and she could hear the comments of the SS guard on duty.

This was the parade of the dead, a ceremony so often seen, witnessed more and more as the days went by. A family member had died and was thrown upon a cart to be wheeled away to the pile of stench and decaying corpses: this was the 'death cart'. The recently deceased loved one received a few shed tears and when a young one had passed away the tears and sobs were heavier and the sadness more terrible. There was no decent burial to speak of. And as the cart was wheeled away by several weak men, so crippled with disease that it was hard to stay on two feet, the SS guard puffed on a cigarette and passed an unfavourable comment upon the poor teenager that was alive just the night before.

"You stinking Jews, always wasting your time. If you have strength to cart away the body then you have time to work. Yes; you three; report to me when your job is done. I'll put you to work, licking my boots clean," the sergeant looked to the sobbing few that watched the cart being pulled away. "I have shit all over my boots; it's your shit and you can have it back, you pathetic scum of a race." The sergeant drew on his cigarette and seemed drunk with power, and looked again to the cart being pulled along slowly. "I had my way with that one. Squirm, she did, and all for the price of a slice of bread. You filthy swine make me puke... imagine that; selling your virginity for a slice of bread."

And the mother could only cry for her daughter, a final touch in farewell, her hand touching the arm of the deceased. Her mother could easily forgive her daughter's encounter with the sergeant, for in essence it was of no issue at all, but the sergeant; such hatred for these swine of men she held within her that she would never forget them, never forgive.

CHAPTER 20

American planes zoomed overhead and engaged a target some distance away, plumes of smoke eventually being seen as they encrusted the clear sky. It was amazing that such an event could bring so much joy to a person, and so much fear, too; both at the same time.

The inmates feared that the machine gun fire from the aircraft would indiscriminately target them, bullets sprayed from a barrel finding themselves falling amongst the throng as they watched with their hands on their hearts, praying to be delivered from the hellhole known as Bergen-Belsen.

Every single person felt the uplifting spirit within them, the sheer jubilance that the war could be approaching something of an end, a most favourable outcome for their situation, where weeks or years of being treated like an animal had been suffered, different stints of time being drawn upon each of those held against their will.

If the allies were so close to concern themselves with engaging targets around the camp then the fight must surely have been in the allies favour. And then a little pessimism, too, entered their minds, for they needed to also consider that this might simply be a single engagement where targets behind enemy lines were more readily hit with little retaliation, an incursion deep into hostile territory which amounted to fewer casualties of their own being suffered.

Again the planes flew overhead, and whether or not they were the same ones or not, the onlookers did not know, but they scrambled into the gutter alongside the street when the firing got too close for comfort, where SS guards had also buried their faces. Both prisoner and guard were now alongside the other, and it seemed, somehow, just a dream. So briefly did the inmates feel as though they were one and the same, joined together in misery, and then the feelings of despair and hatred for these devil worshippers hit them hard once more, for no other than a devil worshipper could inflict such heinous acts of criminal injustice upon the weak and meek.

Air raids by day and by night; again the feelings of joy and fear erupt from within. It was all possible that a bomb could fall upon the huts in the dark. But the knowledge that the allies were advancing upon the enemy that imprisoned them all was a savour in the face of the doom that surrounded the innocent, and enlightened everyone to the streaks of yellow grime that were painted upon the backs of those wearing the SS symbol upon their collar, for deep down they were nothing other than cowards, one and all.

It was absurdly amazing, that with all the contempt and punishment that the SS forced upon the inmates, that a single truth, in a majority of the cases, did come of fruition: that a single guard, regardless of the symbol upon his collar, could not beat the weak into submission, for the weak were too strong of heart to give in to those so easily swayed by the devil himself. It was far easier to give in to the Devil than it was to follow a religion; the Jews were strong.

And then a daydream hit Franzi like a fallen brick upon the head. She thought she could see that one of the SS looked familiar, like a husband to a friend she once knew. And then it struck her hard. These SS were fundamentally recruited from those husbands so drunk with power that they felt it their duty to punch and kick and maim their wives as though a common dog, but instead of wives they beat Jews. She; Franzi; was an animal in their eyes, for whatever reason she did not know, treated with no respect whatsoever, maintained like cattle on a farm for the purpose of hard labour and exchange, like currency. She was a commodity. Each and every one of them was a commodity through and through, a bargaining chip, a piece of meat, collateral (though worthless), and like the shit that one wipes from the bottom of his or her shoe they existed in great numbers and were everywhere.

She shook her head and forced the wretched fantasy from within, the thoughts of despair that were starting to strangle them all. They were human beings and deserved as much as any other, to be treated with the respect they deserved. She'd done nothing to deserve this treatment, as had none of them.

The air raids continued well into the week and became second nature, a formality which disturbed the nights and days, the sirens penetrating Franzi's weary bones. Now that she was starting to get used to the sirens and bombs, the episodes of fear that once struck her were beginning to abate, and only the joy she hid within her provided great hope for the future. But the feelings were kept so well hidden, even from conversation, for the last thing she needed was to anger a guard, or one of those under his charge: the stinking kapos.

<h2 style="text-align:center">CHAPTER 21</h2>

It was March and the turnips kept on coming.

There was a call for some work to be done as many bags of turnips had arrived. These dirty vegetables needed to be peeled and cut up before being turned into the kitchen kettles. The work was laborious to say the least but there was consolation at the end of the day, for all of those working on the turnips would receive an extra litre of turnip soup at the end of the day's work.

It was a small savour, this extra soup, for the meals were scanty at best: turnips, soup, and a piece of bread if they were lucky. The meal times were now almost non-existent. The guards didn't care whether the prisoners ate or not, let alone drop dead from hunger: one less mouth to feed.

The fat German whores, SS guards one and all, who feed their hungry mouths like pigs at a trough, stood over the weak like the men, and they looked as hard as nails, but are, in the reality of it all, sluts one and the same. There was no real delicate word for these daughters of bitches – the whole damn German race deserved to be annihilated for what they had done: first World War one, and now this madness.

One of the wives saved a few shreds of turnip for her husband who had been suffering badly in the forest, cutting up wood for the stoves of the kitchen, and no doubt, the fire in which the commandant used to keep warm at night when eating a thick steak – no turnips for him.

Her poor husband found it hard to turn out a full day's work in accordance with the guard's wishes, for this was the 'tree commando', which meant hard labour and hard rules. It was here that he was beaten, along with many others, beaten senseless and without good cause: but then again, there never was a good cause for beating a prisoner. If he could just stay ahead, just a little, the others would receive the beating and he would go unscathed. But he was lucky, lucky because many men and women suffered from something, be it a hernia, angina pectoris, diabetes, tuberculosis, starvation, diarrhoea, spotted fever, typhus, typhoid, influenza, gastro-enteritis, scabies, bronco-pneumonia, pressure sores, suppurating wounds, gangrene, or some other ailment: there was a list that kept on growing by the day.

This was the way the system worked; allow your friend and comrade to take the beating in order for you to survive. It was a sorrowful affair, wishing another to take a beating in place of you, but it was the only way to survive, and so if you see your brother taking a hiding you simply shut your mouth and continue with your work, because you had a duty to fulfil in regards to your younger sister, to ensure she survived this horror camp as best she could, or that your wife or child didn't get called out in front of a parade and whipped for the good of nothing.

Ah; those blessed aircraft overhead. The war would surely be over soon for the aircraft overhead appeared frequently and the front line could be heard as it advanced a little each day, in particular at night when there was a strong wind from the west.

From the hour that they were marched into the forest by the guards, where their dogs endeavoured to take a bite of a prisoner from time to time, the SS guards putting strain on the long chains, until the time the workers were marched back, there was no real relent in sight.

It was said by many of the men that the guards seemed quite content to beat them senseless as it was a means by which to keep them warm, but with the approach of warmer weather the beatings for warmth were replaced by more beatings because Germany was losing the war. The inmate never wins; was always a prisoner, always a slave, always the Jew who didn't deserve to be free; an animal to be penned up for ever and a day.

Suddenly there was a call for some men to come running, for a stump needed to be removed post-haste, and the thoughts that run through a man's mind during such hard labour were suddenly washed away, for now was the time to ensure that extra beatings were held at bay.

"You ten men, there," shouted a corporal. "And you lot... get to task – move it!"

The twenty men moved as fast as they could and the stump came into view. It was reasonably small and couldn't possibly be attended to by so many. Too many men in such a small amount of space would impede the work. Who's to work and who's to watch? To stand back and watch was cause to be beaten, beaten to within an inch of your life, and so the men fight each other for the task, pushing one another out of the way in order to get their hands dirty on a job that they didn't have the energy to do. Damned if you did and damned if you didn't, and with that came the rain of blows as several guards moved in with truncheons and started hitting the men over the head.

Blood covers the truncheons in seconds and then another guard moves in with a short whip, letting loose with the power of his arm, metering out his punishment against those getting in the way of the work, and it takes almost a minute of beatings to disperse the men, two of which have died. Punishment for the others was now dealt out which consisted of solitary work upon some of the hardest to move stumps in the vicinity. They would work until they dropped and when they dropped they were beaten once more for being lazy.

A man was almost strangled to death by his own scarf, held up between two guards who had fun tormenting the inmate for not working fast enough, and Phillipje felt sorry for him, but to feel sorry for another was a lasting mistake; wasn't it enough that he was already covered in blood, from head to toe, simply because the guards turned on him like rabid dogs? He stared in error and the guards pounced on him one last time – and it was, indeed, the last time.

But by nightfall the work was done and the bodies of the two dead men were dumped nearby, left for the insects and scavengers of the night to do with as they saw fit.

Henny awaited the return of her husband but he didn't come back and she learns of his death whilst he was at work in the forest. She now fell out of favour with the kapo, Kasimir Cegielski, and the kapo wasn't pleased at all. He finds reason to have her punished and she is later sent to the bunker where she is savaged by dogs under the guise of Irma Grese who had made a name for herself by early March.

Irma Grese, a new arrival, the most notorious after Kramer and only 22 years old. She was the senior supervisor at Auschwitz until January 1945, and returned to Ravensbrück before being dispatched with her hunger for torture to Bergen-Belsen in March. She had an appetite for cruelty and sexual excesses; she was sadistic in her beatings of women with her plaited whip, whipping them until they were dead, and the arbitrary shooting of prisoners came without good reason, and she loved to see her half-starved dogs savage a prisoner. She wore heavy boots and carried a whip and a pistol, used physical and emotional torture, and enjoyed killing in cold blood. But her piece of resistance was her lampshades, made from the skin of three prisoners which she kept in her hut. If the devil had a wife then she was it.

The kapo cared little and now searched for another victim, another young girl to make him happy, but it was hard to find the right one because to him they were mostly ugly; mostly too thin and diseased.

CHAPTER 22

The crematorium had folded, there was no more trying to cope with the mounting dead. There were up to 500 deaths a day now. The burning of the dead was a pointless task and the effort was as futile as a man pissing in a gale whilst trying to fill a cup at his feet. But smoke continued to pour from its chimney, the insanity of the futile task simply too ridiculous to comprehend. Hour after hour it continued to burn without end, the stench of the burning mingling with the rotting corpses that were piling higher and higher.

By the end of March there had been around 18,000 deaths in the entire camp; almost 200 amongst those whom had special treatment; such a small number in comparison, and a true indication as to how better off some of the inmates had it when compared to others, but the right to exist had to be looked upon as being shared by all, not just those of special interest: and what was it to be 'special' in any case? It didn't take a special person to wish for the end of the war. So many wished to see the war end and enjoy the comforts of life once again.

So many people died during the night and it wasn't until morning that they were dragged outside to be piled alongside the others who had died. The piles were growing at an alarming rate. The bodies were ransacked of all their clothing, their shoes, their possessions, and so mostly decomposed naked, rotting into the soil, to become food for the worms and maggots – there was no honour in death; not here.

If the dead had occupied a bunk the position was soon taken by the living and anything of value that might be there was used to the best of the ability of the one that had absconded with it.

Nothing would be left unattended for long; nothing would be left to fall by the wayside; everything had dozens of eyes holding to it, ready to steal for the sake of bartering for food. Everything in the camp had a use and was worth something, be it a kerchief, a spoon, a bowl, or a piece of cloth to wrap your head in; everything was worth something.

Shoes in particular were always an item of great value for no one in the entire camp, apart from those that sat upon the watchtowers with guns, had seen a good pair of shoes for almost two years. It was survival, and the fittest had the advantage. The weak would be dead soon enough and so why waste one's energy in trying to save the dead? It was everyone for himself and only where family was concerned did matters of survival spread from one person to another... but then, not even family could sway the minds of the few, for life had different values for some when compared to others, and it was easy for the torments of the camp to turn good men into degenerated bastards.

Bread ration was reduced to less than a slice a day and the soup was nothing more than water with a few signs of something floating in it, be it spittle from a SS guard, one of the kapos, or the greatest gift of all, a maggot on which to chew. And this was all that was fed to the multitudes, the 44,000 odd prisoners that made up the stench of the camp. And then the inmates' eyes opened in impossible wonder, as another truck made its way into the camp to offload more prisoners.

The meals were a far cry from what could surely be considered as luxurious, but here in Bergen-Belsen, a piece of rotten fruit was a gift from heaven, and three pints of turnip soup per day along with 200 grams of black bread was better than a poke in the eye with a stick.

A wife hid a small portion of soup under her bed, keeping it safe for her husband. A kapo came in and saw her acting suspiciously. He found the soup and threw it over her face, the bowl he confiscated. There was no justice. She broke down crying after he had left the barracks. Life seemed so pointless. It was too hard to survive. If the war didn't end soon then their lives would be no longer.

Work in the kitchen was looked upon as a great favour now, but individuals weren't picked by guards or even kapos, the individuals, instead, would literally fight over the right to work. For the sake of getting their hands on a mug of soup and the opportunity to bite into the hard core of a turnip, or the skin of a potato, came a mass of women, all screaming for the same job.

They pushed each other and showed no mercy or leniency towards one another. It was here that each and every woman was fighting her way into the kitchen, and each was of equal status, and in a vast majority of cases the women were squabbling for the right to provide something extra, no matter how small, for their husband or child: it mattered little, for everyone was undernourished or put to heavy work cutting wood in the 'tree commando'.

Yes; a wife felt so compelled to work for the extra food that she'd do anything for it, even to go as far as stab her long-time friend in the back by making out that she'd committed some small crime in order for her to be made to stand at the fence or be denied a job. Sometimes it backfires and the accused is dragged away to the bunker or worse – could there possibly be worse?

They shoved and kicked, elbowed and kicked, punched and pulled and pushed; there was no decorum, no restraint. A shot rang out and a body fell to the ground, the pushing and shoving stopped momentarily and then continued. There was no stopping the mayhem, each and every one of these women was desperate to get an extra cup of soup, and the struggle continued along with a few arrests until the doors were shut because the positions were filled and the bodies that lay dead upon the ground were carried away by the order of the guards.

Other work parties were created, more work for over a thousand women, but this work was not heavily sought for there was no just reward in the form of food. The work was ridiculous, the most ridiculous so far, and not a single one of the multitudes that were forced to gather and work could comprehend what the hell was going on, but one woman heard that the source of their hours of labour was to be used in German war planes.

And what was the insanity? These women were to plait cellophane.

The Third Reich was surely on the brink of surrender. The money-saving choirs in the camp of cellophane plaiting, shoe cutting and the building of more barracks by the hands of those imprisoned, buildings which had no windows, leaking roofs and three-tiered bunks to house the thousands of prisoners still arriving, barracks being built that were little better than tents and the only benefit was for the lice and bed bugs which found the accommodation extremely rewarding and in easy reach of the skin that they get their teeth into.

This was a nightmare come true. And over the coming weeks there was seen to be more and more people subjecting themselves to having their hair cut short in order to keep the lice away, but it did no good and the infestations found harbour in armpits and crotches. Some mad inmates prefered to keep the lice for the sake of looking normal with a head of hair. There were mixed emotions. One would say that if sanity could be maintained for resembling something human then that was good. To feel human meant life, to be insane meant death. Only the strength of body and mind would survive. And so the sane and insane keep their hair for different reasons; the insane did not know the difference and the sane for no other purpose than to remain in control of their meagre possession which would grow back eventually if cut in any case.

Life was ridiculous and unfair.

CHAPTER 23

Work in the kitchen wasn't just about peeling spuds or turnips, but other duties would be performed and some of these tasks had to be tackled early.

Woken at 2:30am; at work in the kitchen by 3:15am. Less than one percent of the total in Bergen-Belsen were expected to perform kitchen duties for the masses.

The Poor State of War and Conflict

The kitchen was a mass of kettles; these were what turned out the watery soup, many times in a single day, for there were many barracks and prisoners that needed to be fed an unappetizing mixture of water and water, with water added for flavour.

Rinse the kettles, hose them out, fill them up, stir them well, deliver them to their stations and return the empty kettles back to the kitchen before starting all over again. If there was a break in the day then the prisoners were fortunate, but from the hard work a single consolation was attained: they were permitted to eat as much as they wanted... but how much turnip and water could one person possibly stomach?

It was impossible to imagine the effect that getting dressed so early in the morning could have on a person, in particular where there was human shit all over the floor and the mattresses. The occupants of the barracks try their hardest to use buckets or pails but it was no use. Diarrhoea was rife throughout the camp: no one enjoyed this foul mess falling upon their head from the bunk above where three people shared a common misery. It was hard to get the energy to wash, in particular on a cold morning, let alone stomach the stench which existed throughout the entire camp, but they would continue to do their best in order to stay alive. But harder than getting dressed was shoving food down your throat in order to attain the energy required to work... it was impossible and so many dropped from exhaustion and were then punished for not doing their work.

The kitchen corporal was seldom late and arrived along with the work details, and already there were men inside lighting the fires for the huge kettles in which to make the watery soup; this was done prior to the smaller kettles being filled and distributed. The kettles in many cases were now ported around on revamped prams, babies and young children being evicted, their bed confiscated for the good of the workers. So it was now that even the men were thinking of their energy and didn't give a damn about the comforts of the so-very young. But strife once again had to be dealt with as over time, one after another, the prams became broken and were cast aside upon a scrap heap beside the dead.

Large hoses were pulled around with two or three women to each, struggling with the anacondas of the kitchen in order to clean out and scrub the kettles of the contents from the night before, which smelt foul but they couldn't tell the difference: what was the difference between the smell of shit and that of the kettles? The smell of the kettles was scrubbed out, but the smell of shit lingers in their nostrils for ever and a day. But they were used to it now – how insane was that, to be used to the smell of shit as though it was smeared upon your upper lip on a hot summer's day?

A single SS guard could be seen half asleep, his hand supporting his head as he gains a few more hours of slumber before being relieved later on in the morning. He could wake at any time, to look around the kitchen to ensure that all were working. These SS were like vipers that wake from a dream and spit venom without second thought, easily triggered into using a whip to thrash at the back of a young woman.

The female inmates were so ugly now that the SS guards rarely looked at them as sexual objects and their fantasies go unfulfilled, and in place of the sexual pleasure came a string of violence and hatred, hatred that was always present but not always released, for some men of the SS were as cunning as dogs, even if out-ranked by them. Any number of inmates would kick a dog but not waste the effort on a thick-headed guard, although one would give a guard a glass of water if he were drowning.

The coffee in the kettles was ready and the kettles lined up for distribution amongst the different huts, and the men come and go as they shuffle away with their heavy loads, putting kettles upon their transports.

It was now time for the kitchen hands to have breakfast; and where the authority of the kitchen was in anything but a very bad temper, then sweet porridge and coffee was consumed in a delectable manner.

By 6:30 the kitchen kettle-washers were joined by many others and the task of washing and cutting vegetables began once more. The wooden benches once sat upon by inmates no longer existed, as they have been used in building other barracks for the influx of poor bastards and bitches that continue to march through the front gates of hell, and so the workers would stand all day and do their duty, getting ready the midday meal of crap which could be poured through a sieve, and if an inmate was lucky then they might find a piece of the vegetable which, having been slaved over all morning to procure from the whole, had found its way into one's mouth.

The meal was cooked in large vats, dozens of them lined up in rows, like the SS. Everything reminded the inmates of the SS; they couldn't get those nasty creatures out of their minds, not for a second.

The men appeared again and moved off with the food containers, delivering the meal to the huts, but no sooner had they gone then they seemed to be back again. Once more the task of cleaning the kettles from the morning coffee begins and ends, and afternoon coffee is prepared, and along with this mammoth task they also have to clean the vats; it was endless, the work just kept on coming.

More food was now prepared for the last meal of the day, which amounts to nothing in real terms and the food was getting less and less, the portions smaller and smaller. At the current rate the food would stop completely and then they would all die, and so, even though the work was hard in the kitchen there was a little reward in the food that was consumed, but the hunger was always present and brave women dared to steal what they could in order to provide husbands with a little something to help them with the hard labour they had to endure.

The night was upon them all and it was time to go back to the barracks. Three women were caught trying to smuggle peel from the grounds and they were summarily punished by being thrown into the bunker.

Whether or not the 'dog woman' paid a visit was mostly up to the guard on duty and the severity of the crime which had been committed.

CHAPTER 24

It was almost morning and the camp was stirring. A woman in a bunk opposite Franzi coughed constantly and yet another scratched uncontrollably from the tier above; it's a dreadful noise. There was a dead body lying next to her and from above there lay another with severe diarrhoea, and the shit fell through the thin mattress and onto Franzi's body of skin over bone, it's warm... a small relief. She could hardly move but had to get out of the hut. She had to wash and get rid of the dead body, but she could hardly move.

It was almost time for roll call and she found it in herself to somehow get to her feet and as she did she looked out upon the ever growing mounting of dead men and women; the SS pride and joy, the world's disgrace and shame.

A figure of a man could be seen staggering towards the mountain of dead, at a height of five to six bodies, and then he collapsed momentarily, nothing more than a stick figure which was hard to see, for the bare flesh of the dead acts as a camouflage for the naked body of the man who finds it hard to stagger into place. But finally he arrived and he crawled into position, a hiding place from which the SS would not find him. He looked as though he was one of the dead, indistinguishable from the other remains. Franzi felt pity for the man, a great surge of sadness falling upon her as she watched, as the man intended to hide from the SS and the roll call, for he obviously didn't have the energy to continue with the work that's forced upon him, and to be forced into work would be the death of him. But there was also sadness for the unnecessary waste, for the man would undoubtedly die where he lay if he stayed there too long. Perhaps it was best; perhaps this was the best thing for him. His sunken eyes closed and he remained still, hoping to crawl out of the mountain of

dead later that day, perhaps in time for something to eat and if not...
then that would be the last anyone saw of him. He was just one more
body to be added to the masses of the dead.

And now the man was forgotten because the SS commenced to call
for the parade which was nothing other than a sadistic measure of
abuse to add to the war crimes committed by these heinous scum.

Sleep the night before was almost non-existent because the lice
saw to it that everyone with the energy to do so spent hour upon hour
scratching away at the body until it was so sore that infection sets in
and matters of medical concern grow out of control. There was no
salvation, no way in which to receive relief. Too tired they all are, all
so very tired. But it was not just the lice, but the bedbugs and the
fleas, an impossibility to imagine, the suffering that had to be
contented with on a day to day basis, where the nights drag on and
grow in length: and some think that it is better to suffer the abuse and
work by day, receiving beatings upon the head, shoulders and body.
It was better to suffer humiliation and insults than suffer another
night in the bunks.

The bunks are tiny; barely room enough to sit up on the lower
bunks and only just enough space to crawl in and out of your infested
space on the upper, each level shared by two to three people. The
overcrowding was impossible; and there was no energy to cry, and a
cold breeze would often be felt coming through the bare rafters of the
roof, to be suffered by those on the top bunk. Which was worse: to
suffer a breeze or to be shat upon from the bunk above? It was a
question without an answer for both meant the same thing in the end;
an unpleasant death.

The passage down the centre of the barrack was impossible to
negotiate. There was shit all over the floor from the diarrhoea, and the
stench was growing worse and worse: the Jews knew this as a fact
because they had become so accustomed to the stink of the whole
damn place that for it to smell worse than the day before would surely
mean a further slump in hygiene: such a stupid word to use; hygiene.
It simply didn't exist; nowhere except possibly in the SS quarters,
their clothing store, or the doctor's office – oh, and not to forget that
saint of a man, Joseph Kramer, who was so loving that his
relationship with Irma Grese was more than lust, for although it was
a relatively clandestine arrangement between them, where love
making was as pathetic as their claims to be human, the torture of the
prisoners was talked about over meals, and their intentions, to be
drawn upon the weak on the morrow, were shared with smiles upon
their faces.

Irma Grese passionately stroked Kramer's scar and kissed it. Such
was life to be a whore and the devil. To speak their names seemed a

crime in itself and so often it was heard amongst the Jews that the Criminal did this, or the Dog Woman did that, but Irma Grese was not to be confused with Juana Bormann who was known quite categorically as 'the woman with the dogs'. Such wretched people didn't deserve an ounce of recognition, no more than Hitler, deserving to be denied the opportunity to be recognized as a man of history, for he was nothing more than a murdering bastard.

To Franzi it seemed plain and simple: Kramer was the master, and she was the dog, and the allies were the animal lovers coming to her rescue. Yes; she was falling insane, the torment of time in this place being too hard to overcome.

CHAPTER 25

The men and women of the camp moved around half naked in most cases, in particular when in the washrooms. There was no embarrassment and everyone looked the same, for the women, in general, no longer had breasts, and there was not an ounce of interest in the opposite sex for the sake of recreational or horizontal pleasure. Such luxuries of human existence had disappeared a long time ago. Each sex moved around as though oblivious to the other, where each person was nothing more than a skeleton wrapped up in tight skin.

Franzi no longer bothered to avert her eyes; no one else did; it's not even a contemplation of mind: no one cared anymore.

And the morning's ablutions were finished with, but stomachs still turned over and shit fell freely to the floor.

Roll call was made and there were people missing, either too sick or too exhausted to come out into the open, but the open was better than being cooped up in a hut full of faeces, lice and lingering disease.

Franzi looked up and down the mass of Jews lined up for roll call and noticed that there were already close to a hundred skeletons – known as people – standing up and facing the fence, being punished for some damned unknown and ludicrous reason for which the SS guards had decided to punish. It was beyond foolishness. But the guards made up excuses, be it laziness, late for roll call, late for work, answering back, speaking without permission, not standing up straight, being too ugly, looking a guard in the eye... it didn't matter for a reason could be found and it was easy for the SS to find a reason for they had been doing it for so long that it now came natural. It was second nature for a guard to issue a punishment, giving a reason why such was being placed upon the individual, and all carried out without the guard so much as looking upon the person being punished.

A SS guard entered a barrack building with the kapo, Kasimir Cegielski, and found the culprits, five men and three women. They were accused of being lazy. They were a 'bunch of lazy pigs' according to the SS and extremely unlucky in the eyes of those at roll call. Franzi only wished, with all the strength she had left within her fragile body, that they wouldn't be punished so severely, but the SS made everyone stand for so long at roll call when they could have been sitting down in the kitchen and trying to put peel into their mouths.

The SS were mostly young men; fit and strong, healthy, well fed and muscular; but all they did was abuse, and beat, and beat some more. And so there were beatings to follow and more punishment after that.

They were beaten, all eight of them, beaten excessively and ordered over to the fence; there they were made to stand all day.

A guard offered some advice on how he had to remain standing for hours on end, doing his duty, and the lazy Jews got to sit down and rip apart a few pairs of shoes, or the men of the 'tree commando' got to work in the open, away from the filth. His complaints go on death ears, but the guard believed in what he said and abused those at roll call by making them stand for two hours without a move: move and you get whipped, fall down and you get whipped some more; fail to stand up when whipped and its bunker.

Finally Franzi got her opportunity to attend the kitchen and she managed to do her work and get some peel into her mouth, and by the day's end she fell out of the kitchen along with the others she had endured her day with. Then she saw those at the fence.

The eight men and women sent to the fence remained there until well after the sun had gone down, after which they would be permitted back into the barracks: after being issued the disgruntled whipping from guards to hurry them along.

There was no justice; Franzi couldn't take much more. She walked towards the women on the fence, to give them an encouraging word. A guard saw her stray from the move back to the barracks and Franzi was absconded to the bunker for three days without bread or water.

One of the women had fallen dead and two men and one woman taken for further punishment to the bunker below ground. A further two men, found to have potatoes in their possession the day before, stolen from the SS storehouse, were summarily sentenced to 28 days bunker, where they were secretly taken away and fed to the dogs.

CHAPTER 26

The inmates numbered over 15,000 in late December 1944, and now, in late March, there were in excess of 44,000 of them; it was ridiculous; it was simply beyond all contemplation.

The labourers for the chopping of wood were gathered and marched away and on reaching their destination were fallen out to commence the arduous task they had been so unfairly targeted with, but not before two men were pulled aside for talking out of place. They were summarily punished by being forced to stand bent over with their hands open and palms upon the ground. They remained in this position for an hour.

A man asked whether or not they'd be able to stand upright by themselves after the punishment was over with and the comment didn't go unpunished – he was beaten to death in front of everyone.

That evening the men returned and got their ration, which consisted of what would be barely enough to feed a two-year old child. How the men worked on such small portions, without any measure of nutrition within, was beyond contemplation.

On return a man fell slovenly over his own feet and tripped another two behind him. He was extracted from the commando as it came to a halt and made to stand for four hours in front of the fence as punishment for bringing condemnation upon the parade. He was later returned to his barracks with a flogging to the back of the head to drink his soup of spinach water which his wife had managed to barter for, swapping her diamond wedding ring - extracted from orifice - in order that her husband could have something before retiring to bed. The pity in her eyes was enough to make anyone cry and wince in pain.

But the following morning seemed to bring a little sunshine and a group of thirty-five prisoners were drafted together with an excursion to come. They were to be escorted into the forest where it had been discovered that wild potatoes were growing in abundance. The men were to be put to work with digging up the potable food and to also see how extensive the commodity was.

The men were given their orders and several sacks in which to bring back what they found. They stood as erect as they possibly could and nearly all of them were smiling, for they were going on a walk into the wilderness, away from the camp, to bring something back for them and their families – where families existed.

The gates in front of them opened and then closed again as they passed through, and the sergeant of the work party ordered them left and right and left again until they were ordered to halt.

The walk had been marvellous and the fresh air was beyond belief; it was so different out here away from the camp, away from the stench... away from the security of the wire fence, and it was then that the guards unshoulder their weapons and shot dead all thirty-five of the prisoners.

There were no potatoes there in the forest.

The guards returned to camp and the sergeant reported that there had been an attempted breakout; that the prisoners did try to escape. His duty was done; he will sleep well tonight; he was proud to be a German.

CHAPTER 27

There was a little commotion, something out of the ordinary was occurring. A POW from an adjoining camp was being extricated from his surroundings and brought along the main road towards Josef Kramer's office, though the devil himself was waiting for the arrival of the prisoner from outside one of the barrack huts, where the mounting dead were in easy view.

The gentleman walked with pride, the crisp air on this 28th day of March being felt upon his face, his head held high; he was a soldier of the British Royal Marines.

The marine's guard of two were nothing more than an escort as the British soldier walked along between them, neither offering resistance of any description nor allowing himself to be tormented by the smell and horror of so many dead. He knew what the camp was like; he'd not been far from it for some time now, and the smell always drifted across into his section of the camp.

The marine came to a stop in front of the commandant and looked him in the eye, seeing the devilish mind tick over as it waited for a salute, a salute which was never going to come.

Some time passed before Kramer opened his mouth. "I've heard of your insolence," said Kramer, "and of your failure to help us with questions that we have surrounding a certain... shall I say... conspiracy."

"This is war, Hauptsurmführer," announced the marine, "I fail to see where conspiracy fits into it."

"Ah, at least you've remembered me; a pity you can't remember to salute."

"I know why I'm here, more or less, and you'll find that I shall continue to... disappoint you. I've told all of those that have interrogated me that I know nothing."

"Of course you don't, that's why we're going to... have a quiet word," said Kramer. "This way, please."

The small congregation continued on towards the bunker but stopped just short as the door burst open.

Franzi was being escorted out by the scuff of the neck, battered well from behind as she fell through the open door and into relative freedom. She was happy to see the sky again, happy to have lived through punishment known as the bunker.

Kramer looked stifled by the upset of the composure of the prisoner and of the guards as they did their best to keep within arm's reach of the one under their care and beat her with their truncheons once more.

"You stupid, shit-whore!" shouted one of the guards. It was then that he noticed Kramer and immediately came to attention and paid his compliments.

"Carry on," said Kramer and turned to see one of the marine's escorts being brushed aside by the Brit, by a forceful hand, as the guard endeavoured to usher the British soldier through the open door.

Franzi fell to the ground again and looked around and up to the marine standing there, so peaceful and serene he seemed to be, with marks upon his face where he'd obviously been beaten.

"Ah!" yelled Kramer. "Trying to escape," he accused.

"I don't take kindly to being man-handled," said the marine as he looked one of the guards in the face.

"Do you intend to answer my questions?" forced Kramer.

"I have nothing to say," said the marine.

"Shoot this man," directed Kramer to one of the guards.

"Sir?" stated the stunned guard.

"Shoot this damn man; he's trying to escape... now!"

The guard pulled his revolver from its hiding and pointed it at the head of the marine who did nothing other than smile. The weapon was fired and the body fell to the ground.

"Get his clothes off and hide his body amongst those other vermin; for he's no better than a stinking Jew," directed Kramer and stepped off briskly to his office.

"Get on your feet, you slut!" yelled the guard from the bunker, pulling Franzi up by the roots of her hair. "On your feet bitch before I give you cause to lie down again."

Franzi was stunned beyond belief. The marine had just been killed in cold blood. Wasn't it enough that they, the innocent, should be treated so badly, to be indiscriminately killed for no other reason than to appease the frantic madness of Hitler; but to kill a soldier in such a way, without good cause, was beyond the code of conduct of men at war?

CHAPTER 28

The SS guard, Gertrude Sauer, stood at arm's length from the prisoner to her front and stepped back a little, the smell from the Polish woman's armpit most terrible, a smell which was slapping the guard in the face: the sight of the lice crawling over her skin almost making her sick.

"Get it up; higher!" yelled Gertrude.

Piroska could say nothing, had no option but to do as she was ordered. The strain upon her was enormous. She was being punished for stealing a pumpkin, punished on the first day of April as though she was some joke.

Further noises of strain came from deep within the Polish prisoner, grunting in her effort to keep the pumpkin above her head and at arm's length.

"You stinking, whore-thief. Stoning is too good for you Polish bitches," yelled Gertrude as she walked around Piroska's front, hitting her own palm with the whip she carried, drawing the Jew's eyes to the instrument of her fear. She had been beaten too often these past few days and for no other reason than being a Polish Jew.

"Keep that pumpkin up if you want to live," warned Gertrude. She came around the back of Piroska and lashed out with a hit to the back of her legs, which were by now quite red and burning with pain.

Piroska almost dropped the pumpkin but managed to keep control of it. It's amazing how heavy a pumpkin got, how small it first appeared.

"Did you sleep with many guards in Auschwitz?" demanded Gertrude of her plaything. She struck again the back of the legs, harder than before and the pumpkin came down to Piroska's waist before quickly being lifted again above her head. Again the stinging of Gertrude's whip hits her on the back of the legs.

"Drop it again and its bunker for you," warns Gertrude who was beginning to grow tired of the game she played. She had better things to do, a meal to eat and fresh water to drink; a slice of bread and cheese perhaps: she also knew a woman companion who had some chocolate of which she could share.

Piroska grunted again, her continuing effort to keep the pumpkin above her head drawing every ounce of energy that she had, but her punishment was almost over for Gertrude was hungry.

Piroska wasn't sure how she could continue at this pace, holding the pumpkin up above her head, but she knew it meant her survival so she would do all she could. The pains in her body would have to be forgotten, the pain in her arms and legs brushed aside; she would have to rise above this torture so that she could experience free life once more, to endure a free life filled with bad memories.

Gertrude stopped in front of her prisoner. "Put the pumpkin down." Piroska obeyed with much relief, and then came the final blow. Gertrude lashed out with one almighty whipping to Piroska's face, knocking the Polish woman to the ground.

Several teeth were knocked loose and there was now a small cut above her lip where bruising was quick to form.

"Get up on your feet, you stupid bitch, before I find a red-hot poker to shove up your arse," threatened Gertrude. "Now take that pumpkin to the kitchen, where it belongs, and if I see you thieving again then it will be the death penalty for you."

And so Piroska picked up the pumpkin with her face bleeding and did what she had to do before seeking rest in her hut.

CHAPTER 29

It was a reasonably pleasant Sunday and a small congregation of inmates looked out towards the main gate of their camp. There was a truck and it was destined for the kitchen.

What a relief such a sight was and everyone knew where it was destined for. No other reason existed for a truck to be brought into the confines of their misery unless it was to deliver food of some description – maybe it was something other than turnip.

The truck drove along and the driver, being either ignorant or simply without the skills to drive the vehicle, ran over a body lying upon the ground.

A bag of raw turnips was loosely sealed within the back and several pieces fell from the truck and onto the ground, a half dozen or more; they were rotten and squashed easily as they hit the hard surface of the ground, but some survived the fall.

Corporal Otto Calesson saw the look in the eyes of the prisoners and called to the guard nearby to look at what was about to unfold.

"Anchor, you will see what happens when scum are hungry," said Otto before calling out to those watching for any sign of a guard's presence. "You prisoners; you can help yourself to what lies on the road."

The inmates suddenly burst into a run – a fast walk by normal standards – to try and be the first upon the scattered vegetables. They pushed and shoved and fought their way forward. The SS guards laughed and simply couldn't believe the sight they saw before them.

"Do you know what's so funny?" asked Otto of his companion, a new guard having just arrived from training.
"Other than the fact that they look like hungry dogs after a feast, they resemble skeletons fighting for a fur coat," answered Anchor.

"Yes... yes... that is so true," and Otto laughed some more along with Anchor. "But those turnips; they are destined for Kramer's personal pen of twenty-five pigs. It is rotten turnip, not good for the kitchen... no good for human consumption."

"Then it's good that these scum aren't human," said a sergeant from behind.

Otto turned to see the sergeant smiling.

"I see you have found yourselves something attractive to keep you busy," said the sergeant.

"I was just introducing my friend to the prisoners," said Otto in defence.

"I'm not scolding you, dear Otto," said the sergeant. "But next time you plan a party like this, make sure to let me know. There's nothing more I like than to watch a show where the scum of the earth fight so hard for something destined for the trough of a pig," and commenced laughing himself.

And the inmates continued to squabble as they fought over the rotten turnips, drawing what they could into their mouths, regardless of the taste. Those that were hungry for a mouthful of something... anything... it didn't matter what it tasted like, so long as it filled the emptiness of the stomach; even if temporarily. Even a piece of dried up leather would be better than nothing.

Oscar, one of the inmates, missed out on the turnips. He received a knock in the head and a kick in the thigh, and yet he received nothing. He was too slow, too exhausted, and too damn hungry.

He fell back from the ravenous dogs scrambling on the ground, eating what they could salvage from the rotten turnips, and saw the three guards turn their backs on them before retiring.

Oscar fell to the ground from the sheer exhaustion of it all. He had been mentally scarred by all that had gone on around him. For so long he had been here in this camp of pestilence; so long in fact that he could not remember anything else of the world before Bergen-Belsen. This camp was his entire life; of what he could recall of it.

He finally managed to get onto his hands and knees and with much effort commenced to crawl towards a shiny object on the ground near the mountain of dead. He drew closer to it, bit by bit, and soon realised that it was a small knife used for eating. It's been so long since he's used a knife that he's not sure if he knows how. He's used to drinking soup from a bowl and shoving bread in his mouth, but not eating with a knife.

He finally got within distance and reached out, grabbing it by its handle. It drew it near and looked at it, and from his peripheral he saw a dead body lying on the ground next to the mountain of rotting flesh. The body was reasonably new. The man he saw would have died just that morning, or even later than that. It was even possible that his heart was still warm... lovely and tender... succulent and rewarding.

He moved up to the dead body and fell across it and with great precision he cut into the chest of the dead, cutting as best he could a hole to the heart. He managed, after several minutes, to extricate himself several mouthfuls of heart and he put it into his mouth. He started to chew. Mmmm; so lovely it was; real meat. It's like heaven to him, like nothing before he's tasted these past few years. It's better than a juicy steak, better than sausage, or pie, or ham off the bone. He couldn't believe how good it was, how lucky he was to get to it first. He no longer cared about the damn turnips for he had found something much better and far more rewarding.

He sinks his teeth again and again into the muscle of the heart and was momentarily satisfied for the meal, when, with a sudden surge of normality, his mind cleared way to clear thinking and he realised what had become of him.

He wept silently to himself for what he had done; for what could not be undone, and he could not be forgiven. He had eaten man-flesh, he had sinned a terrible sin. He had molested another human being, defiled what should not be defiled. He could never forgive himself for what he had done.

CHAPTER 30

Ernst Kaltenbrunner was the head of the Reich Security Main Office and it came into his palm, a direct order from Hitler himself, that all of the prisoners of Bergen-Belsen were to be summarily killed as it wasn't fitting that the prisoners should be allowed to fall into the hands of the Allies, not alive in any case. He then passed this order on to Kramer who received it with as little emotion that could possibly be evoked from such an order. To Kramer the death of thousands meant little to him, for if he'd really cared then he would have done something long before now.

But it came to pass that negotiations with the British were about to commence in regards to Bergen-Belsen, negotiations which very well might see to it that war crimes against humanity might be diverted if it could be seen that the fault of the killings was derived from actions compounded by certain figures of the Third Reich, or even individual members of the SS itself. Kramer would do well to receive such a favourable outlook in the circumstances that war had dealt him. Not only this, but a kind word from Felix Kersten, a Swedish chiropractor that had treated Himmler, saw to it that the order was reversed and Kramer handed the opportunity of a lifetime; Himmler had now taken control of the dying situation to try and save a little face, and Kramer, too, saw his opportunity.

Himmler felt the distaste of imprisonment in his mouth. It was the first week of April and he knew, as others did too, that the war would soon be over. Although he had never really changed his tune in regards to the treatment of the prisoners, and naive in regards to the way in which they were treated, needed to now ensure that some form of action was carried out in order to save his own neck. He'd originally ordered the Head of the Gestapo, Heinrich Müller, to keep the prisoners healthy and alive, this ordered back in 1943; and now he faced the implication of being partly responsible for the Jews disposition: and so he was.

Josef Kramer, the Camp's Commandant, was the man with two faces: one of evil and the other a mask that portrayed a kind-hearted individual: but nothing could be further from the truth. The scale of the genocide present within his camp was simply unforgiving and orchestrated well by him and the SS. But now, something had to be done to make it look as though Kramer had made an effort to aid these poor creatures of the community. Along with Dr Fritz Cline, his chief physician, the camp was quarantined and an order for the transport of vegetables and meat was handed out to the appropriate authorities that he had in his reach. But it was to no avail and his struggle to see him placed out of harm's way had no effect upon his disposition, his past lack of human decency overshadowing his meagre attempts.

Himmler, also, needed to act quickly if he was to extricate himself from accusations which he could see were forthcoming and so over the next five days saw to it that an order of his was executed without question. Three transports of prisoners from within the camp of Bergen-Belsen were to be evacuated, more if possible. The order saw to it that Kramer acted with a little jest in his step for the first time in many years and prisoners from the Neutral camp, the Star Camp, and the Hungarian Camp, were evacuated under consideration that they were 'exchange Jews' and held foreign passports.

Surely, Himmler thought, a little justice would go a long way and with such actions of charity would come some forgiveness; and he needed the allies on his side, secretly wishing for the allies to join with Germany in a war against Russia.

CHAPTER 31

The water ration was stopped, no more soup; and no more bread, nothing at all to come the prisoners' way. Everything had stopped on 7th April, as though a cork in a bottle had been rammed tight. There was no water supply whatsoever to speak of. This was a catastrophe beyond all others. The unhealthy and the sick, which comprised everyone within the camp, were absolutely reliant on water and simply couldn't live without it.

The Germans were losing the war, a great loss to their precious

Third Reich and its abilities to perform. If they were to lose then the Jews should lose too.

The amount of spite that the Germans felt for these poorly treated Jews was so insurmountable that it simply could not be registered. The feelings of the SS towards these people were just so understated that it was impossible to contemplate that such hatred could exist. What did the Jew do that was so damaging to the German way of life? Many of them owned businesses of all description and led a clean way of life, never pestering others nor bludging off of the government in any way or form; why should they be dealt such a bad card in life?

And so the SS seldom entered the camps from this day on and roll calls, although continuing, were not as frequent, allowing the sick to die in relative peace: if struggling with insurmountable pain could be considered as being 'peaceful'.

Work parties were seen to drop almost immediately but some work needed to be maintained, such as the forced labour suffered when being handed the duty to unblock the sewerage, returning to the barracks covered in vile filth, shit and piss.

And so the days continued, individuals doing all they could to see that they survived the war, but there was still no end in sight, regardless of the air raids and planes overhead. The misery of the entire situation was growing by the hour, getting worse and worse by the day. There seemed to be no relief to come and many felt that the coming days would see them die, just as their friends had died before them, or family members had been given a farewell as they were carted away to be burnt at the crematorium or thrown upon the mountain of dead like common garbage. It seemed to many of them that that's what they had become; common garbage to be brushed aside, to decay in the gutters of society.

Was there not a single person in the world that cared about them?

CHAPTER 32

On April 8th, around 30,000 more prisoners were injected into the camp of Bergen-Belsen, an unbelievable number to say the least. No food, no water, and more prisoners. Here was a camp built for no more than 10,000 and in the matter of hours it had swelled out of all proportion.

For those of the camp that could get to a window, or even a door, the sight of all the people entering the camp under the whippings of the guards was simply too much to bear and so these wretched thousands, the newcomers to hell, had backs turned upon them.

There was little hope for survival now, little hope to see the war through. Conditions within the camp were bad enough as it was, but now; it was sheer torture of the likes no one had seen since the age of chivalry.

From all over the Neuengamme area they came, all of the camps within that geographic location evacuated and placed in the hands of Kramer and his whip-wielding guards. The camp now numbered over 60,000 prisoners from all sectors of life, from prisoners of war to civilian Jews; there was no quarter of the community at large that was exempt from Hitler's insanity or his call for the continuing murder of innocents, and so the torture and atrocities went on.

So many prisoners and so few places left to house them.

The dilapidated barracks were full with three-tiered bunks and the stables full to the brim, and tents were used to the extreme of insanity. But one call for clemency was heard, one call and one call only, from the pages of the Geneva Convention.

The typhus epidemic, along with the guidelines as laid down by the Geneva Convention, was considered well, and it also suited the Nazis for whom wished to maintain a cruel hold of the Jews of their camps. It was not possible to evacuate diseased prisoners and so the overflow was cramped ever more into accommodation already bursting at the seams: yes indeed, the Nazis made something of this rule.

Down the road, the Army Training Centre was also used for its asset, the barracks adjacent and in close enough proximity to the severity of guards under Kramer, for them to continue with their cruelty. Fifteen thousand prisoners were transferred here.

CHAPTER 33

There were so many bodies lying around that it was an unbelievable sight, even to those closest to the circumstances so rife. Thousands upon thousands were lying in small mountains, some having decayed a lot and others just starting to smell of that sickly odour known as death. And so the SS, under the orders of Kramer, made what was seen as their final effort to hold back the tide of accusations against them by burying bodies in mass graves in remote spots away from the camp, where it was hoped that the allies would not find them. On this day, April 11th, commenced the hiding of the dead.

Another mass grave was being dug nearer the barracks but wasn't as large as the other. It appeared as though the SS were trying to outwit the British by consecrating a few bodies in graves under their noses but concealing the majority far away and out of sight. It was the threat of war crimes which lingered in the air. The work was also continued during the night, aided by the light given off by kerosene lamps. Work parties were now mostly organised to dig and bury, not to peel and cook.

As the SS worked, their white armbands slipped from their upper arms, little flags of truce which showed their concerns for the advancing allies; this was their sign of surrender: but the atrocities continued behind their masquerade. It was a true account of their courage and bravery, where they pretended to display their cooperation and willingness to cease with hostilities but continued with the atrocities which were fixed like pillars of iron within their heads. It was said many times that you should never accept a gift from a Greek; maybe it will now be understood, for all time, that you should never accept the cooperation, leniency, or assurance of a Nazi, regardless of the form in which they showed themselves; past, present, or future; because as with the gift from Greece, the after-affect was always death.

For three days, until the 14th, all available prisoners, regardless of age, who were in condition to be forced to work, were pulled into line and made to bury the dead. It was a struggle against the clock, a means by which to avoid the accusations of war crimes.

Kramer, the 'Beast of Belsen', permitted the use of music to spur the work on and as over 2,000 men and women dragged the remains of human life along the ground, two orchestras played music under the guidance of the guards.

The dead were dragged around with the aid of leashes, straps of leather or cloth attached to wrists and ankles. From the time the sun appeared on the horizon and until it disappeared from view at night the inmates were forced to work their fingers to the bone, shifting thousands upon thousands of bodies from the camp and into mass graves. Whoever said you couldn't move mountains, for several piles of human monstrosity, of deathly carnage, were moved over the dreadful period of four days but still, even after so much work and effort, there were still over 10,000 corpses that remained in place.

The guards were at their least merciful now, for they were seeing to it that they survived the war. The guards wished to see their families again, to see their mothers and fathers; none cared for the Jew. It was nothing to a Nazi that the wretches under their guard should fall by the way and succumb to the calling of their brethren who lay dead and without voice amongst the 10,000 in view.

The whips of the guards rained heaviest now, more than ever before. The use of their bayonets drew more blood in the few days of burial than they'd seen all year. The SS had been given a true gift, for it didn't matter if a prisoner died now as they could simply be thrown into the grave in which was being filled. So a man was clubbed over the head and fell unconscious to the unhallowed ground; so what? He was still breathing and had the taste of life on his tongue, could smell the air around him – and although it stinks of foulness it was still pertinent to life. The guards ordered the Jews close at hand to continue with the filling of the mass grave, the earth covering over the recently fallen. Men and women were buried alive, rubbed from existence as though a bad stain in life.

The SS guards didn't give a damn and the flag of truce upon their sleeves meant nothing to them except that it was a piece of cloth in which to wipe their sweaty brow, sweat from the hard labour of flogging the sick.

CHAPTER 34

As the sun reached its highest point in the sky on April 12th, a Mercedes carrying a white flag upon its bonnet appeared out of nowhere, two German colonels pulling up in front of the British 159th Battalion's forward headquarters.

The entourage stepped out of the vehicle in the style of a true gentleman, but these officers were Nazis too, and couldn't be counted on, for their camouflage of humbleness hid their true maliciousness and their well-spoken sentences of choreographed speech were flawed with their efforts in trying to receive reprieve for those under their command.

Stepping out in front of their hosts the Germans were greeted in the usual fashion that one would expect. This was Colonel Schmidt and Lieutenant Colonel Bohnekamp; with them were a medical officer and a translator.

The two German officers presented themselves in their full regalia, stone-cold and hard faces looking from below the rim of their peaked caps, their uniforms an example of how an officer should be dressed – it was the task of the lackey to perform the daily maintenance upon an officers kit and make coffee on demand: it was usually obvious as to how many slaves a single commander had under his sway by the way in which he dressed and carried himself.

The two German officers were then blindfolded and taken to 8 Corps Headquarters where negotiations were to be drawn up between the two forces; negotiations which the Germans hoped would bring about a toned reception in reflection of their kindness.

There was an exhausting underestimation on behalf of the German pigs who tried to deal the hand they held as best as possible, indicating with a rather cool and collective, very straight face, that there were 9,000 sick in the camp of Bergen-Belsen, when in fact the number was so much higher, and many had typhus. The British officers were alarmed by such a number, and had it been revealed of the true scale and nature of the situation regarding the matter then the

German officers may have been shackled right then and there.

"We have a request which might sound... surprising," said the German to the British officer to his front, "but in the interests of the Geneva Convention, and for the preservation of life, we are indebted to advise you of a problem which has come about from the allied bombings of the rail network and roads in the vicinity of this camp."

"Please continue," said the British officer.

"Supplies to the camp have been cut off around the towns of Bergen and Belsen. In this vicinity is a camp which houses approximately fifty-thousand prisoners, nine thousand of which are sick, some with typhus; there is no available water, no medical supplies and very little food. Each time we try to supply the camp your aircraft destroys the supplies. We currently have over two-thousand Hungarian and German regular soldiers guarding the camp."

"And SS?"

"Yes; of course," admitted the German. "There are SS, too, but most are administrational staff, which is a different matter altogether," and the fake within his voice betrayed the German officer. "I am happy to arrange for them to help you with the transition of the camp."

"I see," answered the British officer.

"We wish you to occupy the camp as soon as possible," said the German, hurriedly, avoiding further talk of the SS, "in order to prevent any outbreak of disease in accordance with international interests of health and safety." It was a remarkable feat in itself that the officer could keep a straight face whilst laying his cards upon the table. "We wish to offer a limited truce."

"That's absurd. We already have a bridgehead over the river Aller and have crossed over this with our tanks, as you well know. You'll have to offer more than a simple truce." said the British officer, General Taylor-Balfour, still startled by the fact that 9,000 inmates were sick; he was disgusted. He could feel his stomach turn over with the thought of so many helpless people: trapped and helpless they were. "The truce is in your favour, not ours. Our advance upon your lines and safe havens give us the overwhelming advantage. Taking care of this camp, Bergen-Belsen, will only impede us more."

The officer was silent for a moment. "We can offer to you and your forces another bridge over the river Aller and we will also propose not to destroy this."

The British thought then: how desperate these Nazis were.

The German officers knew that the death rate in the camp was growing by the day and that, even as they spoke, the dead were being buried in secret locations to hide the atrocities. There was a fine point in allowing the British an early entry to the camp, but it was also a bad decision to allow the situation to worsen by postponing any action against the outbreak of disease; after all, this was still Germany and the lives of civilians were at stake.

"We must have complete control of the area around the camp, for at least six kilometres all around. We must be permitted to keep our lines of communication open at all costs, and your petty offerings don't allow us to continue with the advance as we would like. We can commit to the aid and the taking over of the camp, for the good of the community at large, but must have a clearer understanding as to ownership and control in order to prevent any of the sick from spreading disease."

The German officers were frantic at the thought of 'ownership' but had nowhere else to turn. "We will give you what you have suggested. You can have the bridge and the area immediately around the camp. We would formally request map coordinates in order to see the arrangements met."

"But the typhus is a problem and I can see no alternative but to seal off the area as soon as possible," said the British officer.

"I agree with this," said the German. "It is in all our interests to prevent further tragedy."

"Might I suggest that you mount posts at either end of the area to warn of the typhus epidemic; you can man these with unarmed guards."

"Unarmed?" asked the German.

"We cannot have armed Germans in an area deemed to be under British control; not unless you, an officer, intends to stand at the post yourself, or the intervening commander of our forces permits the carriage of such weapons," and the sparkle in the British officer's eyes saw the German submit to defeat. "I'll require your full cooperation. All Germans in the camp are to wear white armbands in order for us to know that they accept these terms, and they are to perform duties as required."

"White armbands; yes, that has already been done."

"You do work quickly, don't you, Colonel?"

"My interest is in saving lives," said the German.

"A German soldier, saving lives," said the British officer curtly.

"I agree to your request for your requirement to fulfil your duties and our responsibilities, but the regular army must be released so that they can continue with their duties to Germany, bearing arms and their equipment. This I must insist upon."

"As you wish," said the British officer. "I'll have my orderly see to it immediately and then we can sign some papers. I'm sure there will be some finer details that need to be considered, but all-in-all I think we can agree on the manner of the predicament. As for the SS guards; one is no different than another. Any personnel that remain behind will be deemed as guards, regardless of uniform, one and all, and subjected to military law. A soldier is a soldier; is he not?"

The German was silent for a second and then nodded in defeat. "Yes, I suppose they are." Their lives now rested on the quick burial of the dead, but he would warn Kramer of the likely predicament that was awaiting the SS guards, for he knew they wouldn't be received well.

"Good," said the British officer. "I'm glad we could come to some agreement on this matter. It's of the greatest importance to prevent an epidemic as early as possible."

The achievement in organizing the limited truce was beyond imagination to many, but for war crimes convictions to be dropped, Bergen-Belsen was to become a power-pawn for the Germans. Negotiations were fierce; more so from the British side of the argument, and in rather a fast committal of past actions the British accepted what it was that the German authorities had to offer. The agreement was for the avoidance of battle in the area surrounding the camp. The agreement saw to it that a neutral zone was established around the camp and was estimated at around 48 square kilometres, being eight in length and six in width.

There was agreement that the British would take over control of the camp, that the German SS and regular army would be replaced by the allies, the towers to take the form of a cordon to contain the disease and general outbreak of typhus as opposed to forming a ring of iron where rifles lashed out their evil from time to time upon the unsuspecting. The British bombing and shelling of the area ceased almost immediately. It was also clearly made understood that most of the SS guards would be removed and their role as guards taken up by Hungarian soldiers and the German regular army prior to the British arriving, if not already carried out, although the SS administration staff, in general, would remain in situ until the British took control of Bergen-Belsen and allowed the SS to retreat back to their duties elsewhere, be it another camp or fighting somewhere near the front line. The assurance of allowing the SS staff, and regular soldiers, safe passage from the campgrounds within six days was not a watertight agreement and allowed for much interpretation. There were reported to be a battalion of German infantry and a Hungarian regiment in situ at the camp, and the Hungarians, although subjected to work under the British, would need to be set free at some stage in the future.

A cease-fire agreement was therefore reached between the British Chief of Staff, General Taylor-Balfour and the German Military Commander of the area around Bergen-Belsen.

CHAPTER 35

An English officer was escorted by two SS guards, on Friday 13th of April, rifles by their side and bayonets fixed. The officer had a white flag.

His curiosity was too much for him and he looked constantly, left and right, looking over the mountains of dead, and unbelievable they were in his view, for he had never seen so many dead in a single place at the same time. Never before in his entire life had he seen such slaughter.

The look upon the faces of the guards could not be more displeasing, the obvious power they once held now evaporated. Their hands had been washed of all supremacy and now they were about to be dealt the vengeance that the inmates so wished they'd have to suffer. They had never suffered defeat in their lives, but their fathers and mothers had known of a time, when Hitler was nothing more than a corporal and running errands for officers, when twenty-seven years earlier they had their arses whipped by those unwilling to be treated by fists of iron.

The prisoners who looked upon the British officer knew almost immediately that he was an ally, although most considered the idea that he was nothing more than another prisoner, a prisoner of war that was going to be subjected to the free will of Josef Kramer and either sent immediately to the bunker or killed.

A few of the inmates were encouraged to see that the man was in fact rather clean and had obviously arrived from a quarter where there was little fighting, or that his role in the army was not that which involved the day to day slaughter of the enemy, where it was one of a soldiers many duties to try and gather as much of the enemies blood upon his bayonet as was humanly possible. No, this officer was a class above the rest, intelligent, and respected by his peers.

When the British officer disappeared out of view the men and women of the camp commenced to talk, even the sores in their mouths unable to stop them from remarking on the appearance of one so clean and orderly: it was nothing compared to the talk that became a story and retold many times that late afternoon and evening, of the officer that went to see Kramer, and then returned by the same way in which he had entered, and without a single mark upon him.

The talk of liberation once more filled the air of some of the huts but remained relatively quiet amongst the camp as a whole. The days spent burying the dead had seen to it that many were too exhausted and traumatised to even contemplate the appearance of a saviour, too victimised to think that the war would soon be over and that they would all be free.

On his return to the British command post the officers had trouble accepting that such atrocity awaited them. How could it be true that so many dead existed in this camp, that the bodies could simply be exposed to the elements of the weather, for diseases to filter out amongst the prisoners of the camp and subject them to all manner of horror and distaste? Surely the visiting officer had seen but a small part of the camp which constituted the bulk of the 9,000 sick inmates having been herded together for some reason, and not the main camp itself, and that the shock of what he saw was an exaggeration. The obvious shock of seeing so many dead and dying within the camp was too much for the officer to bear. As for the mountains of dead described by him, it could only have been an error in judgement on his behalf and the bodies themselves were surely stacked upon mounds of dirt or high ground, not upon other bodies hidden beneath: surely there must have been a plausible reason as to why it stood so high. It seemed ludicrous that such a report should come back to them, in particular when assurances had been given that the camp held but 9,000 sick and 41,000 in assumed good health, and that there was no mention of so many dead. The camp was large indeed, several quarters to the whole, this Jewish quarter by far the worst.

Why would the Germans be so anxious to hand over a camp in such a dilapidated state?

CHAPTER 36

The situation in the camp was suddenly made worse by an episode of Nazi cruelty that simply could not be explained. The sheer audacity of those in one of the towers overlooking a water supply point came to air.

Water for washing was made so scarce that disease was soaring and hygiene was plummeting to an all-new low, a point needing no clarity by those suffering the ordeals being suffered, nor confirmation from the SS guards who orchestrated the conditions now infesting the camp.

The conditions were rife and although acknowledged were not provided any attention whatsoever by the guards, and clean water for drinking was even scarcer, much worse now than ever before. It was one thing to make water soup from filthy water, but to put the same repugnant water into your mouth in order to quench the thirst that hung there was a deplorable state of affairs: and watery soup was now but a dream of many for it was no longer being served.

Water was a commodity taken for granted so often, a substance of life and great worth; it was relatively easy to obtain – considering the topography and geographic location of Bergen-Belsen – but it was denied the thousands that relied upon it the most as they continued to decay with the rest of the camp, becoming buried under a mountain of human faeces. But the guards drank well and the dogs drank too, for the guards loved their dogs as much as the dogs loved their sport of ripping flesh from faces. But there was a pump not so far away from several of the barracks, a pump that could give them all the water they needed.

The eyes of the imprisoned darted this way and that, sizing up the opposition; sizing up their cruelty and the lengths to which they would go to in order to bring punishment upon them all.

The Jews knew well that the SS were mostly vacant the towers aloft, and that Hungarian guards had taken their places. What had a Jew ever done to a Hungarian? Nothing... so why would they be denied the most meagre of mouthfuls of water, just a little to wet their lips.

Word passed from one mouth to the other, eyes opened up so they could all see the light at the end of the tunnel, where each would receive their dyer need, the substance that would drive their thirst from them.

Their throats burned and itched, and couldn't take any food in a lot of cases, unless it was in the form of soup, but no soup was to be had: so sore they were. But something had to be done in order to receive a little solace, even if for just a few hours where their throats would feel the benefit of their risk-taking.

The masses of Jews so desperate to wet their mouths congregated around several of the entrances to the huts and then rushed for the source of their desire, a water point not so very far away, a little clear ground around it but fairly close to several barracks where shelter could be sought if the guards were to come running with whips in hand and bayonets fixed. It was also true that there was safety in numbers and the likelihood of being targeted was less when there were more people around.

The rush of humanity came upon the ground, so sacred it was, for it held water, the clear essence of every man, woman and child, the liquid gold which couldn't be lived without, the daily requirement for which the body desired and screamed out for.

Guards then swamped the mass of humanity and commenced to hit them with the butts of their rifles, and others still got their sticks and whips and did what they could to cause more misery, but this was nothing to what the Hungarians in the towers around proceeded to do, and from out of one of the lookouts came several voices and these were followed by the cracking and thumping of ammunition being fired from rifles.

The Poor State of War and Conflict

The Hungarians had begun shooting from high above, shooting at the unprotected and the weak, gazing through their sites in order to hone their shooting skills.

Two Hungarians laughed and shared a cigarette as they took turns in the killing, watching their victims fall without mercy, as the soldiers squeezed their triggers and inhaled another mouthful of smoke.

The SS below were a little shocked, too, for they were in the fray which was being caused and so the guards quickly adhered to the threats from above and pulled back, corralling the innocent in order for them to become easier targets for the Hungarians.

Medislaw and Vladislaw, two kapos with similar cast ideas of what it meant to be a man in power, were lined up with the SS guards and released their flurrying blows, bringing their whips down hard upon the head of those thirsty for water and too weak to fight back: but what did it mean to fight back, but bunker.

"Look at me, look at me now," said one guard to another as he drew his eye up against the iron sights of his rifle and with a smile upon his face he shot in the back a young girl who had joined her mother in an effort to get something to drink, to fill a small vase with water so that they could help with the ailing health of their sick grandmother who was too frail to walk or speak.

The victim fell dead, a grimace of horror painted upon her face, and as she fell the kapo Medislaw whipped her over the head for no good reason and she continued to the ground with blood trickling from her entry wound.

"Help me, Vladislaw," pleaded Medislaw, for there were too many to beat with a single whip. He continued whipping as fast as his hand could deliver the blows. "They like the beating so much; they keep coming for more," and he laughed, for he considered it much fun to bring such calamity to bear upon the shoulders of so many. The power he held in his hand was uplifting him, providing him with a false sense of pride.

Another victim fell dead in front of Vladislaw and he yelled back to his friend, "I'm sorry Medislaw," and another was shot before him, an elderly man falling dead. Vladislaw laughed, the smile so thickly set upon his face that he was overcome with frenzy, "but I am up to my armpits with filth."

Clara, the mother of the fallen daughter, turned to urge her child along, but on seeing the space where she was, now vacant, felt a terrible surge of fear penetrate her from head to foot. The startled and shocked look upon her face was not seen by those that whipped or those in the tower as they picked off their victims one by one. Suddenly she saw her daughter laying upon the ground, being trodden on by those in mass hysteria.

"Zelda! Zelda! Oh no... my God; what has happened?" and she fell beside her daughter, bringing her into her lap as a kneecap from someone close by kicked her in the side of the neck, but she was quick to sit back up and cradle her child in her arms. She looked into her face, her eyes closed, her breathing having ceased. The mother knew her daughter was no more and it took all of her energy just to hold her in the lap of love.

Another push and a kick came her way and then an inmate fell upon Clara, pushing her to the ground, face thirst in the mud.

Clara got up again upon her knees and once more the congestion of everyone around forced her back into the ground where a mouthful of mud was choked upon and then spat out. She's suddenly clubbed in the back of the head and the kapo searched for another victim. A woman fell beside Clara, having been shot in the head, her brains stuck to the side of her face, the eyes still open and staring right through Clara's soul.

Clara found it hard to then drag herself out of the fray, where whippings and shootings continued on and on. She clawed her way to the closest hut, crying as she moved, crawling through the mud and then over another body as one of the Hungarians in the tower smiled and slapped his friend on the back, pointing to the dead, boasting on how well he delivered the shot to the neck.

Clara pushed on, the pain of her loss, the pain of the misery, the pain of the exhaustion, hunger, and anger, almost too much to bear, but she continued until she fell safely into the dark shroud created by the open doorway and was delivered safely out of harm's way.

Clara rolled over and looked out upon the group, several hundred people clambering for water, for help, for solace; but none of it came. All that was delivered was more death and further whippings from the kapos that watched on as shots were fired into the corralled inmates.

By the time it was over there were over two-hundred dead littering the ground and over the next few days more were to join them, for the Hungarians were always on the lookout for an easy target.

Clara didn't know what to think or feel. The horrors of what had just happened were beyond all contemplation; it was sheer ludicrous and a mass murder of the likes she would never forget, not for so long as she lived, and she didn't know how long that would be. She considered her thoughts and realised without too much difficulty that her life, too, would be over sooner than she wished.

Clara waited until all was quiet and then she made her way back to her hut where her grandmother was waiting for water.

"Ah, Clara," said the grandmother of Zelda, Engelina. "Did you get some water?"

"No, mother; I'm sorry," answered Clara.

"Oh, dear; I don't think I can last much longer. I need something to drink, just a little," said Engelina. "Please, Clara; for your mother; just a mouthful."

"You'll have to wait for the soup," said Clara but she knew that there would be none. She would have to chance her luck and return to the water point if she was to get anything to drink, and then, of course, she ran the risk of bunker or death.

"Clara," said Engelina. "Where's Zelda?"

"She's gone to another hut, to help a friend. She'll be back in a few days; yes, she will," and Clara looked blankly at the wall, the dark interior, and contemplated death or possibly deliverance, deliverance from this hell hole called Bergen-Belsen. She craved for the day when the war would be over and all of those responsible for her daughter's death were brought to justice, and whether she lived to see that day or not, it mattered little, so long as justice was served.

CHAPTER 37

That night, in the silence that grew in the minds of all, the SS guards in a vast majority of cases were exchanged in place by Hungarian soldiers, continued on from the night before, the towers that sat so prominently around the camp being maintained throughout the night and not deserted for a second.

The shooting of the prisoners by an Hungarian the day before was nothing for a soldier of the SS. To him it was what must be endured, what was deserved, what was to be. In the eyes of German soldiers they were nothing more than stinking Jews, so why should they care that the Hungarians wished to practise their shooting skills. There was so little room in the camp already that the continuing slaughter was seen as a favour to those still alive.

One man had died during the night and he was seen as a pest. Someone had to now shove him outside, to be picked up by those who carted away the dead, but the reality was that there were so many dead that the collection of the bodies no longer continued. It was therefore up to the individuals to see to it that the dead were turned over to the mountain of flesh; but it was so far to walk.

A couple of men, thin and hungry, exhausted and slow, handled the body carelessly but managed to get it stowed beneath the floorboards, floorboards which had been loosened for the very need that engulfed the barracks. One of the two men considered leaving him where he lay until morning, to then shove him out into the cold morning air, but so be it to say that neither of them could give a damn anymore:

wasn't it enough that they slaved to bury him beneath loose floorboards?

It took forever to haul the body into place and then drop it unceremoniously beneath the hut, to then cover it over so as to be unseen by the naked eye, and as the last of the floorboards was placed back into position there was a thunderous noise coming from somewhere outside. Somewhere in the camp was a commotion that couldn't be explained, and screams so terrifying that they could never be repeated did fill the night air, reverberating right throughout the area. It was so loud and heinous that it could be heard all the way down at the panzer school.

Blank faces looked from one to the other. What was it? What was happening? Was it the allies? Have they arrived at the camp?

A fellow inmate fell into the barrack and coughed loudly. He collapsed and tried to get his breath. He was unsettled but fell into the space made vacant by the old man that had just recently died, the bed space still available, for the two men on the same bunk didn't have the energy to roll over.

Jacob finally calmed himself and the coughing was abated, it was then that another from the opposite bunk opened his eyes from where he lay and asked the new-comer a question.

"What has happened?" asked Robert.

Jacob collected his thoughts and although he didn't feel like saying anything, commenced to tell his story, for he didn't want anyone else to fall victim to the malicious Hungarian soldiers who roosted upon the highpoints all around the camp.

"I have just witnessed something so terrible that it should not be spoken of," advised Jacob. "But I'll tell everyone here, whether they have the energy to listen to me or not, that the Hungarians are worse scum than the SS guards; far worse they are."

"Tell me," said Robert. "I'm listening."

"I don't know if I can. I might fall asleep as I tell you."

"It doesn't matter; I'll be asleep before you finish."

"Very well," said Jacob and he commenced with his story. "The Hungarian guards have dealt a vicious hand to hundreds of prisoners. They don't care whether they are old or young, woman or man; it matters not a shred to them," and he coughed some more before returning to the story. "The guards left the main gate open and organised for a kapo to lay a visit to several of the huts. The word was passed around that we were free, free to go about departing the camp. We were told that we were no longer prisoners and that the allies were so close that they were within walking distance. Many of us didn't believe them but others, those that had gone mad, listened and took heed."

"There are so many insane about," agreed Robert. "So many that they can't be counted."

"I can count them, count all of those in my hut that were mad with the desire to be free. More than 400 of them. They took the bait against better advice and strolled as best they could towards the open gate. It was then that a Hungarian officer took charge, and in complete ignorance to the Geneva Convention he ordered that the guards open fire with their machine guns. They are dead now, all of them. They were running in all directions, in the dark, the spotlights from the towers shining upon them and the machine-gunners kept on firing. There was some sniper fire too, men in the towers making the most of the opportunity they'd been given."

"They aren't men," said Robert.

"Yes, you are right. A man would not do what the Hungarians have done. The SS, yes, they would have done it."

"It was probably by order of the SS," said Robert.

"An order from Kramer himself," added Jacob. "I didn't know anyone that had fallen; not well in any case; just a few acquaintances, but the sheer slaughter of it all, it's too much to bear. I was lucky to get out the back of the hut for fear that they might come through and kill everyone."

"Why? Why did they do it?" asked Robert.

"It was a punishment for someone having stolen some bread."

"Who; who would steal from the Hungarians and be so stupid enough to be seen?"

Jacob was silent and the silence of the night told it all.

"So that is why you are here?"

"Don't turf me out," pleaded Jacob.

"I don't have the energy to," said Robert, "and besides, you cannot be blamed for being hungry; it isn't your fault; you're just stupid for being caught."

"Yes, you're right. Thank you," said Jacob. "Thank you for listening. It means a lot to me."

"What will you do tomorrow?" asked Robert.

There was no answer.

"Are you asleep, Jacob?" asked Robert again of the new member of their hut.

The man beside Jacob answered for him. "No, Robert; he is dead; he's been shot. He has blood seeping from his back."

"I see it now," said Robert. "He was one of those who tried to make it out of the gate."

"Why would he be so stupid?"

"Because he is like most of us here; he is insane."

CHAPTER 38

On April 14th, the front lines of the advancing allies could be tasted, and the smell of liberation was in the air; everyone was hearing stories that the British would be upon them soon, and that a man dressed in British uniform had been seen just the day before, walking in the camp as though belonging to it. It would do well to be dressed in something warm and comfortable for when they arrived, for the journey back to one's own county would be a long and a hard one.

A man so close to death was walking beside the mass of bodies when he suddenly collapsed, falling upon the many that had fallen before him, in the heap of dead that skirted the fringe of the mountain. He was dead, life escaped, and there were a pair of eyes that saw him fall, but they were too slow in action for there was further movement. And then another old man came upon the scene, having not noticed the first fall the way he had, and neither did he know of the pair of eyes that were watching his every movement.

The old man was wandering about without concern or a cause and then with such great fortune fell upon the prize which was a gift from God himself. There before him was an overcoat upon a body, having gone seemingly unnoticed by the many. He, as quickly as he could, stripped the clothing from the body, the thick coat which was now his. He looked wearily around to ensure that no SS, Hungarian, or regular soldier, was watching his move. There was no hesitation in his action for he had no idea how long the war would go on for, or even that it would end, but he had to give it a fighting chance. Who was he to lay down his life willingly? Wasn't it God's will that each and every man should fight for his right to live? Wasn't it God who would simply take his life when He wanted it.

He wore the coat back to the hut and climbed upon his bunk before collapsing into a sleep from which he woke in the middle of the evening, for he had been followed by another that was witness to his good fortune and that person was now disturbing him. It was his nephew, a much younger man than himself.

The nephew liked the coat, liked what he saw, and understood that his uncle, the old man, would die before him. It was simple knowledge of the way things worked in Bergen-Belsen: the sick and the frail, in particular the old, mostly died first.

It was a sad case of affairs, but almost everyone was dressed in mere rags which rot on their bodies and were filled with lice. Men did all they could, in the end, to ensure their survival.

The nephew calmed the old man and pulled the coat from his shivering body, looking from left to right to ensure that no one saw him. He knew the British were coming and he needed something warm to wear in order to get away from the camp as quickly as possible, and the red spots on his arms were clear indication that he had typhus.

"Come, uncle," said the young man. "Give me the coat. I need it more than you. What are you going to do with it, ah?"

The old man couldn't fight, for he was too weak, but struggle a little he did, and during the course of being stolen from, said not a single word.

The nephew placed the coat on proudly as the uncle looked up from his spot upon the bunk. He was so very sad to see one of his own steal from him. The look in his face showed the true sadness of it all. He didn't cry, he didn't complain, but struggling a little was all he could do, but even then he had tired quickly and so the nephew took with relative ease, what wasn't his to take.

The nephew had stolen from the uncle and the uncle would now perish in the cold of the night, so close to liberation, but death was closer, and that night he died in the misery of the knowledge that his own family had denied him the right to live. The nephew felt no remorse at all; it was a matter of survival. It was a simple calculation: he had many years of life left to live, and the old man had but few.

This was the scenario seen over and over again, where behaviour was more in tune to that of wolves in the wild than human beings, but weren't human beings animals: and here before them all was the proof. The nephew would have to live with what he had had, would have to forgive himself for his transgressions upon his very own family later on in life. There was no justice in what he had done but in the nephew's eyes he was simply assuring that he survived, knowing that the old man, his uncle, would be dead soon enough, even if liberated he would soon be dead, for the old man's arms had more red spots than he.

The nephew snuck back to his bunk and put the coat on before clambering into his place beside two others. They were happy of his find, happy that he had a coat, for they too, could share in his good fortune by snuggling close to him, and if the nephew was to die then they would see to it that he was disrobed in an instant.

There didn't seem to be blatant murder between the inmates but their actions upon one another were causes that contributed to death all the same. The men and women of the camp weren't murderers, but many of them were guilty of manslaughter in some small way.

CHAPTER 39

On the night of April 14th, the SS guards congregated and discussed their situation.

The allies were coming and it wasn't going to be a friendly encounter. The SS guards would never allow themselves such an easy capture, in particular where there were so many living witnesses to the crimes they had committed over the past few years; even those SS that were relatively new to the camp had committed crimes against humanity, crimes which were against the Geneva Convention.

The guards had gathered together an assortment of clothing and soon found themselves drowned in friendly chatter and conversation as each and every one of them dressed themselves in civilian clothing.

They were talking, laughing, and sharing cigarettes.

Rucksacks were packed full of food, food meant for the prisoners of the camp. What did they care, they were to escape, never to be caught. So a few more Jews would die; it didn't matter to them, not in the least.

Each man helped himself to the platters of bread and cheese, provided for by Kramer himself, a little reward for the devotion that the SS guards had paid him and the camp's higher authority, which included Hitler himself, of course. There was even a framed photograph of Hitler to be seen hanging from the wall: all commandants with brown noses had a picture of Hitler on their wall.

Kramer, the cunning dog he was. The entire exercise of dwindling numbers of SS guards at post was one of his small ideas, an exercise to divert the attention away from the prying eyes of the camp that something was about to happen. It never occurred to him that the inmates of the camp were more concerned for their well-being and safe return home than the disappearance of the SS guards. Either way, be it in bulk or one at a time, the inmates of the camp were simply overjoyed to hear that the allies were on their way, but they kept the joy from being displayed in the open, hence they be shot, or given bunker and fed to the dogs.

The SS had stayed clear of the barracks and let no one see them when they attended the meeting with their commandant, and Kramer gave them all a hearty farewell speech which was applauded by the SS guards in unison; they were pleased to see that their efforts were appreciated.

Some of the prisoners were suspicious of the approaching liberation, which was spoken of but not guaranteed, and so few knew the truth that their word couldn't be counted upon as being true, but because some of the SS had been seen and overhead to be talking amongst themselves several of the inmates drew up plans for their departure and the arrival of the British.

Some of the inmates knew something was up, felt it in their bones, and small groups of them got together to talk on what measures they should take in regards to the running of the camp once the allies arrived. Bergen-Belsen should be run by them, the slaves of the Third Reich. This camp had been their torturous home and the time would come soon enough when they would have to deal with an uncertain future and see to it that their people were cared for. What better way to do this than run the administration of the camp for themselves.

The allies would have done their duty by liberating the camp and the inmates would be truly grateful for that, and each of the elders within the camp knew that the more help that they could provide to the allies in regards to the administration of the camp, a camp they knew inside out, the more it would free the liberators of the most meaningless tasks. It was crucial to all those in Bergen-Belsen that over the days after the British entered their domain that they would be able to get on with their duty and hunt down those murderous antagonist bastards known as the SS.

The SS guards, on the other hand, knew a little about tactics, knew that they were relatively a small group and could be easily found in the few days after the arrival of the British, and with this knowledge they devised a plan. In order to hide their tracks they would endeavour to employ the assistance of others and so the call went out to all of those that had helped with the running of the camp, for the more there were to hunt down, the better their chances of escape. Many kapos rallied to the call and prepared to make good their escape with the SS, alongside their compatriots, seeing this as their last opportunity to escape from the crimes they'd committed against humanity. It was an escape from their convictions of death.

The kapos were too dim-witted to know what was going on in the mind of Kramer and his SS guards, but they could taste the freedom which they also desired; they were happy to give up their daily whipping of the prisoners for this humble opportunity to escape with the SS guards, regardless of their previous torments.

And so, as the darkness of night continued, broken only by sirens of the night and the searchlights of war, the men who thrived on hatred, crawled off like dogs into the country, to try and evade their persecutions.

CHAPTER 40

On the Sunday afternoon of April 15th, 1945, the allies took control of the German Army Training Garrison – the Panzer Training School and barracks – which was situated one and a half kilometres down the road from Bergen-Belsen. A General headquarters was set up in this barracks with its lush surroundings appealing to the high-ranking officers who had not yet witnessed first-hand the squalor which was about to confront them, and chief members of staff met here to commence with organising the relief operation. The prisoners were now to also be referred to as internees; no longer prisoners of the Third Reich.

The Allied 21st Army Group was sufficiently pleased with the cooperation of the Germans thus far and the sight of the 15,000 internees maintained near the garrison, although an unpleasant scene that disgusted the British and Canadian soldiers, was nothing to what was about to be witnessed once the gates of Bergen-Belsen were entered.

The limits of the neutral territory were finalised and so were the basic ground rules for the treatment of the SS and regular soldiers currently guarding the concentration camp, ground rules which were to be awkwardly accepted in the face of what was about to come of age and history.

The 11th Armoured continued on their way and stopped momentarily on reaching the main gate of the camp, Bergen-Belsen, seeing several German officers awaiting the arrival of the British, before they continued on in their tanks, several remaining behind.

Several soldiers stepped from their vehicles and approached the fence, throwing up the contents of their stomachs on seeing what lay before them. They quickly returned to their vehicles and continued on their way, shaking from the horrible scene that had hit them like a mallet.

With their vehicle escort gone the British officers approached the main gate sided by an entourage of British soldiers, 240 in total, who were mostly apprehensive in regards to what they might find, for the state of the camp was deplorable from where they stood and beyond any reasonable explanation.

Josef Kramer smiled as he met Lieutenant Derrick Sington. Kramer was standing there in a fresh uniform at the entrance to the camp, the thoughts of the state of the camp going through his mind as he hoped, beyond all reasonable hope, that he'd be seen as a German who'd tried his utmost to save as many dying people as could be saved.

"I can only hope for an orderly transition," said Kramer as he stood there with 30 armed SS, some of which were female; miserable dogs not worth a penny. "I think what we need is cooperation between us. There is so much I can do to help you, in particular considering how well I know the camp and the prisoners. It is an unpleasant situation that we have here but I'm sure that the advice I have will do us well to overcome all that we are faced with, and I must warn you, that this camp contains professional criminals, political prisoners, and homosexuals."

From within the camp several shots were heard and Kramer was quick to provide further orientation by saying: "The prisoners are rioting and trying to force their way into the food storage facility. We have to open fire, sometimes; they leave us no choice."

The heat under the collar of one of the officers nearby was simply too much and he leant forward and in a vicious manner gave the commandant a warning. "We will shoot one SS man for every damn internee killed," and the look on Kramer's face did not change, and nor did the attempts on the part of the Germans to give aid to the former prisoners. Not a single German did anything more than was forced upon him when it came to helping the sick and wounded. There was no good cause for all of the starvation; the Germans were surrounded by farms of cattle, hens, geese, ducks and crops. There wasn't a German to be seen, for miles around, that went without a single meal.

Lieutenant-Colonel Taylor of the British Army then arrived, and having heard the shooting in the distance gave the order for those before him to be immediately disarmed, which the soldiers about him saw to immediately; at least some of the killing would stop, he thought, but for the time being the guards at their posts would remain armed and able to carry out their duties, but under a heavy, watchful eye.

Shortly after having met Josef Kramer and others at the camp entrance, the camp was entered by a group of officers, including Brigadier Llewelyn Glyn-Hughes, the medical officer in command of the relief operation.

Kramer was surrounded by MPs, showing the allies into the camp, taking his time to enable the destruction of the camp records within the reception area and other offices to continue, so they could be eradicated from existence, forever lost.

Some internees of exception, kept in isolation for so long, were also killed where they lay or dragged outside before the British even entered the camp, to be killed and thrown upon the pile of corpses which was five deep in most cases, if not more. The British, however, saw the plot in Kramer's actions and pressed on with the move of men to key points within the camp, to do what they could to prevent the destruction of documentation and personnel, each appointed man so tasked followed by their entourage of troops, and where applicable, several tanks.

The sights before them indicated the type of man that Kramer was and the scene painted the picture for what evidence was to be found, and if these criminals of war were ever to be brought to justice then the MPs and the others of the units currently present needed to move as quickly as possible.

There wasn't just the evidence, for that was superficial, but the men, women, and children needed to be saved. They were the witnesses and could give real evidence to what had happened within the camp. But death wasn't to be averted simply because of the inconvenience it would cause, of course not. These people deserved life, deserved better than to be treated in this poor fashion, and such a poor state they were all in that words could not convey the horrors of the camp to the fullest.

Alongside Sington, of the 14th Amplifier Unit, came officers of Intelligence Corps and the 63rd Anti-Tank Regiment, Royal Artillery. A van with a loudspeaker and its crew, three of whom were Jewish, commenced immediately to convey their message of liberation, and despite the tears that welled in their eyes they continued to pass on the news that they, the internees, were now saved.

"You are free... you are free," came the voices of the liberators as they cast their message far and wide and in several different languages. The camp was known to comprise of Romanian, Polish, Yugoslav, French, Belgian, Russian, Czech, Greek, Hungarian and German people; Jews, Prisoners of War and criminals; just to name a few. They were from right across the face of Europe. "Food and medical aid will come; be calm."

The commander of the Anti-Tank Regiment, Lieutenant-Colonel Taylor, was flabbergasted as were all else that day, but he continued with the task of touring the camp as Derrick Sington continued reciting in German that the camp had been liberated and that the internees should, for the time being, remain where they were.

The sights and smells were literally too much to bear. The German estimates of sick could only be an outrageous underestimate. There were piles of dead; thousands of them; too many to be counted and each at a different degree of decomposition. Men and women staggered around the compound, some cheered, others collapsed. Some of the internees came wandering up the allies, their liberators, with smiles upon their pathetically thin faces, their outstretched arms nothing more than bone covered with skin of red sores and spots. Lice could be seen upon the heads of some, miniscule pests crawling in their thousands over their victims in great masses, so thick that it was impossible to believe. The further they entered the camp and the more the internees became aware, and a suffocation of humanity crowded in upon the British soldiers, trying in all their might to hiss and hug them.

Men and women pulled young sprigs from the birch trees that grew alongside the road which divided the camp and flung them graciously upon the allies. One sprig fell upon Kramer's shoulder and he flicked it away in disgust.

A German soldier then fired several shots into the air, to give warning to those that clambered around, for the Jews to get out of the way and to restore order. Sington withdrew his pistol and on giving a warning for the soldier to cease his action the kapos that remained behind leapt to action and started beating the internees. It was a frightful sight that sickened every British soldier there, but nothing could be done at the present for the crowd was too thick and large.

But there was a job to be done and the reality of the camp must be pushed aside, and Llewellyn commenced to carry out his bidding.

The bodies were piled everywhere, and in some places it was hard to tell which were dead and which of those might still be alive, and harder still to tell the difference between a man and a woman, and movement could be seen amongst the piles of dead as though being 'nearly dead' was the same as 'being dead' and hence they were treated in the same way by those that were maintained in the camp.

Llewellyn moved closer for more clarity, to see for himself what manner of diseases might be prevalent in the camp, by looking over the dead, and he could clearly see, on closer inspection, that there was mass evidence of cannibalism in the camp. There were literally hundreds of bodies amongst the mountains of dead that had had their liver, kidneys and heart removed. It was such a sickening thought but as he looked around he thought, just for a fleeting moment, how it could be possible. People did all manner of strange things in order to stay alive.

Several of the wondering sick, skeletons of skin on bone, tripped over themselves and lay there upon the ground, unable to get up, and others who were more able, approached the liberators with arms outstretched, to hug the dear men that had come to save them from the Nazi Regime and the cold-blooded manner in which it viewed the rights of others to live freely.

As news spread of the liberation the soldiers became swamped by internees that resembled stick figures, everyone wishing to give thanks to the soldiers that had come to set them free.

CHAPTER 41

Overcrowding within Bergen-Belsen was taking its toll upon those imprisoned there, and the sheer lack of running water, food and medicine, simply added to the uncontrollable outbreak of typhus which had to date been blamed directly for the death of some 37,000 internees. Only now, with the liberators on the porch, was some reprieve to be received from the disease.

One such diseased person now approached a soldier of the British army, staggering with great difficulty towards the soldier who was horror struck by what he saw. It was Franzi, she came to tell the man about the dead marine, how the soldier of the British army had been ordered shot by Kramer himself. The soldier took the news directly to his commander and Franzi was given some special care, an apple to eat and some water. And as Franzi was being taken care of there was further movement in the camp. From elsewhere within, far from the main gate, something was stirring.

Groups of British soldiers were moving around and could just make out the scene quite some distance away as some internees had come together, moving out from their huts. Some of the internees were lining up as best as possible, many dead and dying still occupying the bunks of buildings or upon floors where bunks simply did not exist; but it was more than clear: the internees were dragging themselves from their huts by the thousands. It was the normal procedure for a roll call but so few parades had been held over the past few days; but it was simply instinct that they should line up to be counted?

Throughout the camp so large there was much evidence to show that the internees didn't know they had been liberated. Some were too weak, some were insane, and others refused to believe that they had been saved and felt deep down that it was all another ploy of the SS to have them killed for trying to escape.

But the internees could hear the noise growing around them. There was noise developing from outside the camp, not too far away. A few rifle shots could be heard and vehicles in the distance, tanks and armoured cars approaching from afar. The changing of gears could also be heard so it was evident that there was a truck nearby. Were they being moved to another camp? There were no SS guards to be seen, no one to do the count. And then some SS came to view, staff members, not guards – or so they say – but technicians and clerks, but in the eyes of the former prisoners these scum were as bad as one another; they were all guards, all guilty of punishing them when punishment was not just. Here they were, walking around the camp wearing white armbands as a sign of surrender to British and suddenly, there it was, a military vehicle that was not German, and so it had to have been British or American, possibly Russian even.

Most of the internees were far too weak to give celebration to the sight of the gates being opened and the entrance of the British as they came upon the unforgettable sight before them. These liberators were sickened to the core by what they saw and smelt. These men so hardened by battle were shaken to the bone.

Many battles had been fought, many dead contended with, but nothing like this Hell Camp had ever been encountered before. And as a few cheers went up and smiles appeared on faces for the first time in many years, so too did the feelings of degradation, for some of the soldiers that had come to give aid were bent over near the fence and throwing up whatever food was within them. Both sides of the fence were sickened, in different ways, but at least the internees were free.

Laughter commenced to grow, as too did the weeping, so many different emotions being felt all at the same time. The internees were simply... listless and lost. The sheer joy that was felt within these skeletons of human life was simply... so joyous. But even now as the British entered the camp, the SS that remained, along with the Hungarian guards, were shooting internees in the distance, for whatever reason they could find. Out of sight, out of harm's way, no witnesses to point a bony finger in their direction.

CHAPTER 42

British soldiers couldn't believe their eyes, the piles of dead that were decaying before them. The children's compound next to this main stretch weren't even spared the insanity of it all, where the naked bodies of men and women simply lay there rotting away, the stench filling the air for miles around.

The children had grown accustomed to the sight as had many of the adults, but for the children there was the added anxiety of not knowing if that figure upon the ground was their mother or aunt, and that man with the mark upon his face... was that father?

And the piles of dead were so steep in places that they involuntarily collapsed into the gutter alongside the street of the camp, disease to be carried away with rain when it came. There were even bodies hanging from the electric fences where people had thrown themselves quite deliberately to their death in order to be rid of the suffering which they had to endure. No matter where you looked, death was there and not a single soul, whether capable or not, attempted to remove a dead body in the middle of the road or a corpse that hung from a fence.

And then a man could be seen dragging himself upon the pile of corpses, dragging himself into position, to lay himself to rest. He felt dead already but had just enough energy to displace himself upon those that had passed this world for another filled with merit and salvation. He finally collapsed upon a comrade and the last of his breath escaped him as he died in front of the liberators, as they entered the camp to give relief to the multitudes.

It was indescribable, not in a thousand years could one give a precise description on what was discovered within the wire fences of Bergen-Belsen; not even a photograph could express the sheer horrors that were encountered. The gutters were full of corpses; the huts, too, were littered with dead, some of which were still lying next to the dying and sick. The British could see, quite easily, where the freshly filled mass-graves existed, one of which was still in the process of being filled. In huts where there were no bunks the bodies of men and women were curled up in balls for there was no room to lay out straight, no room to stretch, no space in which to roll over. How was it possible to fit one thousand people into a barracks or other building that was suited for no more than one hundred, and how many huts were there? There were more than a hundred huts altogether.

The world would be shocked to hear of Bergen-Belsen, and as the liberators went about their duties the world around continued as it did. The birds were flying in the sky as normal, here as in any other place upon the face of the earth, and Germans living down the road denied knowing anything of the horror camp, saying that they didn't know anything about it, that they couldn't smell the death of the camp. How was it that thousands upon thousands of German citizens didn't know what was going on near their own town; it was absurd?

CHAPTER 43

Lieutenant-Colonel Taylor returned to the front gate and ordered that all the SS be arrested and placed under guard in their barracks; the killing had to be stopped and someone needed to be answerable for the condition of the camp.

The Military Police had wasted no time at all in positioning themselves at what was unanimously considered as the entrance to the camp, monitoring all those that entered and exit with good cause, although the last thing that the military wished for was for typhus to be spread by those wandering the neutral zone and further afield, and so, although liberated, a vast majority of the internees weren't so confident as to think of themselves as free.

The internees were wondering around as though dazed and confused, some with apparently no good reason, as though their minds were empty of any sane thought, walking blindly here and there, some becoming startled on hearing the banging of pots, and so came the order from the MPs at the gate that adhesive tape should be placed over vehicle horns so as to prevent anyone from pressing them, for some internees were so fragile that the blast from a horn could surely kill them as easily as could the malnutrition and disease.

A few more officers, very late in arrival, then approached the main gate to the horror camp.

As they approached the entrance to Bergen-Belsen they could

smell the rotting flesh, even though it was just momentarily experienced, for the wind had died down to but a whisper of its former April zest.

"I heard that a little blame came our way in regards to the lack of medical supplies and food," said one officer, "our aircraft doing a marvellous job at spoiling the supply lines."

"Yes; I heard similar."

"But did you hear of the latest report?"

"No. What is that?"

"The Germans cut the supply of water themselves, and even sabotaged the electricity to the camp."

"Those bastards will have to answer for that."

CHAPTER 44

An officer in SS uniform could be clearly seen quite some distance off, standing over an internee who had sunk to their knees, seemingly pleading for clemency, asking for a slice of bread and forgiveness in the wake of their graduation from prisoner to internee. The SS officer lifted his arm and within the clenched fist of his hand could be seen a whip, its lashings flying through the air, knots evident along its strips of leather in order for it to cause much pain and misery as it was cast down upon a Jew.

A British soldier sprang to action and ran across the ground littered with bodies of the dead and the walking insane; of those sane enough to search for clothing, food and water, and those simply staggering around looking for relatives or a helping hand.

A few startled stares were cast his way, looking upon him in wonder, unsure of what he was about, and a few internees felt somewhat afraid that they had done something wrong and that the liberator was out to do them harm. But the soldier forged ahead, forgetting his place, forgetting absolutely that the last thing needed was for those of the camp to be startled in any way.

Damned if you did, and damned if you didn't; but from deep within the British soldier escaped a simple command: "Stop acting like a savage."

The soldier with white arm band, a signature that he'd surrendered to the allies, thrust down upon the innocent Jew several more times before looking up at the armed liberator as he closed the gap.

The SS officer had no weapons other than the whip he'd just taken was a shelf within an office and a sidearm which he was permitted to carry. Others, in particular the Hungarians upon the towers surrounding the camp, carried rifles and were well equipped to inflict great damage where needed, and several of these men watched from above as the scene unfolded before them.

The British soldier was taking a chance with destiny and luck but those upon the towers around the camp didn't dare to think twice of bringing fire to bear upon him. Killing a Jew was one thing for the Hungarians to do, but to shoot dead a British soldier when white bands were worn by them all was not worth thinking about. So the prying eyes of the Hungarians in view of the commotion simply turned a blind eye and they continued smoking their cigarettes.

The Geneva Convention was represented in all quarters, treaties and protocols that protected all people from atrocity, but the concentration camps seemed to be free of this encumbrance, but the SS officer in particular should have known better. There could be no denying the facts. This inhuman behaviour was nothing compared to the truth of the years of abuse but was enough for the British soldier to forget himself that minute as he arrived upon the scene and lashed out with a fist upon the face of the officer.

The SS officer fell upon the ground, shocked slightly by what had just occurred, but not because of what the liberator had done to him, but because he realised, just then, that he was powerless to do anything about it.

The internee could not believe what had just happened. One moment he was being whipped by an officer of the SS and the next the officer was drawing his hand from his face, seeing if blood had been spilt. The internee could not believe that the might of the SS had been subdued by the free hand of a British soldier so easily.

And from near the entrance of the gate the commotion that had drawn quite a lot of attention was immediately conveyed from man to man and the situation in regards to the guards in the towers being permitted to bear arms was taken into consideration. The British simply could not take the risk of the Hungarians opening fire upon them, for the internees were telling stories that chilled British blood.

Another British soldier then looked up towards one of the gates to the camp and saw several of the internees staggering out of the campgrounds, in obvious search for food. They might be carrying typhus and here they were, walking freely from the camp. The Hungarian soldiers cared little, smoking their cigarettes and not even attempting to look up or stop the two from walking past them and into freedom.

The disease had to be contained, and so the soldier did all he could and reported to his officer in command.

The soldier and an officer with translator beside them then approached the offending Hungarian at the gate, quick action being called for, and as they approached they saw an old woman wrapped in a blanket. She stood talking with the Hungarian guard but all he did was shrug his shoulders and she kept on walking.

The officer and translator spoke with the guard as the soldier retrieved the old woman. The Hungarian told the translator that the old woman was going home to Poland and he started to laugh before being ordered to put out his cigarette, which he did on realising that he was outnumbered and in the wrong.

CHAPTER 45

That late afternoon, Commandant Josef Kramer was taken by the British Military Police, under arrest and removed, and as he was being escorted out of his office he could see that much fury was being unleashed as British troops took vengeance upon several Germans, who were fallen upon with rifle butts and stabs with bayonets.

The power had clearly shifted from the axis to the allies and there was nothing that he could do to slow it. It was turning into a forceful handover, no nicety about it. A swift hand was better than a swift word and the British would not take lightly to any incursion or mistreatment against a helpless internee. Enough was enough and further atrocity was to be curbed immediately.

The commandant was completely unashamed of what surrounded him, didn't care at all about what he had created, and it seemed that he had no idea of what he had caused. The camp was rife with typhus, but typhus had caused far fewer deaths than starvation. How on earth could the staff of the camp be so fat if there was no food to be had? Kramer was taken straight to the Panzer barracks and locked away, to be interrogated over the coming days; the answers to be extracted from him one way or another.

And so the orders were drawn rather quickly after the British entered the camp, seeing for themselves the state of affairs they had voluntarily accepted, and knowing that Kramer was safely locked away it was now time for action, action, action. There was to be no sitting around and doing nothing. Every man available, regardless of rank, was to be kept busy with his duty. There wasn't a moment to lose.

It was a matter for survival that a massive rescue plan be put into action, the heights of which had never been seen before, to the memory and knowledge of all, and should be carried out immediately and without a second being wasted.

The German barracks down the road at the training facility, where 15,000 internees were currently being cared for and released of their shackles, would be employed well as they were modern buildings of brick and well equipped. Not only could they provide shelter to the internees suffering so badly, but they were clean and free of faeces and lice. Such a commodity as this barracks would be put to great use, more so than could possibly be imagined; no longer a haven for which to store men of war but now a secure location for which to help cure the sick.

As the liberation came into full swing it became all the more clearer to the prisoners that they had been liberated, were now known as internees, and that each and every one of them wished to seek food or contend themselves with having it delivered to them. There were currently no obvious rules in place for the delivery of food or water and so the internees seemed to feel as though they had been left to fend for themselves.

Several British troops were hence faced with a dilemma, and that was that the human wave before them wished to ransack the kitchens for every single ounce of food the internees could get their hands upon. But in order for the entire camp to be fed there was to be an orderly manner about them. The British troops, therefore, had little option but to hold back the mass of people by firing warning shots over their heads in the hope that some form of control could be maintained.

Some of the internees, even before that action to call them to order was carried out by the British, felt as though they were still prisoners, still held against their will. To them the British were just another problem to contend with. Again they were being dealt a vicious hand, shots being fired to see them submit to orders: from one state of depressing affairs to another... it seemed the way of all things.

The British didn't wish to waste any time at all in their efforts to provide everyone with proof of freedom, to show that they were there to help; to feed the internees, water them, provide medical assistance and the means for each and every one of them to get back home, to begin again their lives with any loved ones that had managed to survive this great ordeal... this pestilence of man.

Here in this camp, the shock of its very existence, rocked every man and far excelled all of the experienced horrors combined, from all of the battles over the past 12 months and more, from all the way from Normandy to Bergen-Belsen. This was a place like no other, a camp of appalling squalor where disease was rampant, nothing more than the true symbol of Nazi hatred and the barbarity which simply couldn't be fathomed. sixty-thousand internees, dead or alive; they were still human beings.

CHAPTER 46

Needless to say the liberators needed somewhere to house the men that were to carry out their mission in saving the poor souls of

Bergen-Belsen, and so the lengthy execution of their right to expel residents from the nearby towns was enacted.

The internees in particular would be invited later to come and go as they pleased from the confiscated houses that the liberators took from the Germans, so long as they were free of disease, to take what they wanted from the German civilians, to take from those fighting against the allies; and some of the town was set on fire, to be watched as the houses crumbled and burnt to the ground.

Another soldier came up to relieve one of the officers on duty and indicated that the officer was to report immediately to the next highest in rank. He reports and hears that several houses along the street nearest the camp entrance have been taken from the owners, the owners dispatched with an almighty shove. This was to be his place of residence until such a time that the officer was advised that it was time to move on.

Tables and chairs within this house were beautiful and there was a basket of fruit placed in the centre of a dresser. It is hard to understand how such beauty could be in existence, where fresh fruit was available at arm's length, all in such close proximity to a camp filled with rampant disease and squalor of the likes never seen before in the history of man. How was it possible that German citizens could sit back in leisure, their faces full of food, when such degradation existed not so far away? There was no good reason or excuse. The civilian population were as much to blame for the conditions of Bergen-Belsen as the SS guards themselves.

Whilst the German citizens passed their days in good health, the Jews of Bergen-Belsen were living in hell. As the civilians grew stronger the Jews grew sicker, weaker, thinner. Some of the internees were so deteriorated on the day of liberation that nothing more could be done for them and so they would be overlooked for treatment. Doctors would mark a red cross on the foreheads of those whom they thought had any possibility of surviving, for there was no time to waste on those closest to death when others could be saved.

Repatriation was sought by two, for Holland. The young woman who went by the name of Eta accepted her card on giving her details, and as her elderly father then gave his to the British officer at his post.

Eta tried holding onto the old man for fear he might fall, but as he handed his card over to the British officer, he collapsed without warning.

"No! Father," cried Eta as she fell beside him, holding his head from the ground, where it was foul and stinking. "Don't die, not now. We are saved."

The British officer felt the weight of the pain but there was nothing he could do; there was far too much work to be done and so he ordered a private to move in and help Eta out of the way, so that others could log their details and commence with their repatriation.

The private picked the father up with Eta still clinging to him and the body was carried to the side of the tent where the weeping continued. The old man was easy to lift, didn't weigh much at all, and the private could feel the old man's bones – they were like sticks of wood, branches to be thrown upon a fire; kindling perhaps. He was so thin. The private then thought of himself and wondered whether or not he'd catch some sort of disease; possibly typhus, but he only needed to look around him before he realised that there is more at stake than his health, and besides, there were doctors and nurses to treat him if he required it. There was an entire civilization here that needed help, an entire city at his fingertips that was dying before him. There are so many in need that he didn't care about the few lice that fell upon his sleeve.

And so the father died, then and there, having fallen to the ground, dead.

Eta broke down and cried some more for her father but all the tears in the world would not bring him back. So close to real freedom and his life was stolen from him. But it was his willingness to see freedom and liberation that kept him going in the first place. He saw his daughter receive freedom, witnessed her being saved, and that's all he ever wanted. What more could a parent ask for their child?

A priest from Canada passed by Eta and on seeing her being cared for by a soldier he continued on and went amongst the masses, to help where he could; he was Reverence Ted Aplin.

A soldier with a beret also saw the grief stricken girl, a soldier of the 63rd Anti-Tank regiment. He has come in to seek family, he was a relative of one of the internees, and on seeing the deplorable state of affairs began to help where he could, his relatives forgotten as he continued to give aid to those in need.

Twenty-seven water carts then arrived at the camp and a small portion of those having not seen fresh water for so long got to have a drink; like thirsty cattle they were drawn to the containers of water as though able to smell it. Word travelled fast amongst them and soon the entire area was swarming with people wanting to quench their thirst and to take back what they could for those unable to move from their bunks.

Soldiers were billeted outside the camp so that they were close enough to enter camp each day, close enough to serve, as best they could, those that should be served, for not all soldiers were given quarters to live in: not all soldiers had sufficient rank, and so it was for them that they experience the most of the misery within the fenced off areas of Bergen-Belsen.

That first night was one of tension. It was feared that the internees would try to kill every SS soldier in the camp as well as raid the stores for food, and the fears were well considered. Sherman tanks were brought in to give clear warning to those in the camp, and a cordon was placed around the buildings of concern. Nevertheless, by morning all food stores were gone, the SS stores facility had been ransacked, every single turnip in the camp had vanished, and Kramer's personal pen of 25 pigs had disappeared without a trace, not a single sow's ear to be seen.

CHAPTER 47

How was it that the lost dignity of so many years could be restored? It needed to be built, one brick at a time, but done in such quick fashion that not another person would die after this day, but such a vision was too far from the reality of the situation, and all that could be done, was being done.

This was April 16th, and there was much work to be continued and arranged.

The water supply was turned back on and many of those capable now washed themselves unashamedly as best they could, naked and in full view of other internees and soldiers alike, washing themselves clean for the first time in as long as most could remember. And where did the energy come from to carry out such a task, but from the very dignity that they had already been provided, even if it meant washing butt naked in front of so many strange men of the British army?

A DDT truck entered the compound and via the Amplifier Unit instructions were passed around for those available to gather around. It was time to take care, once and for all, the horror of the dreaded lice infestations which had bred itself out of control. Every single person was covered in sores and itches, lice prevalent no matter where one chose to look.

The delousing program commenced immediately and like snow from heaven the white dust settled upon the bodies of those that had managed to get themselves out of doors and into the breeze of the cold afternoon, those that were not desperately sick. Soon they were all covered in white but the remarkable effect of the cure had its way with all, for the lice dropped like the bodies of men, falling from the heads and armpits of those that carried them. It was a true godsend that, at least, some of the torment of their existence had now been eradicated from their lives; if only the SS could so easily be eradicated.

The British were working as hard and as fast as they possibly could, but even at the rate in which they worked it took two weeks before the entire camp was deloused sufficiently. Fresh clothing, confiscated from nearby German homes, sometimes at gunpoint, was provided to those of the camp and they started to feel as though this really was the end of their misery. Gone were the rags and prisoner uniforms, the striped flannel garments and pyjamas, but again, the transition from one to the other took much time and patience.

CHAPTER 48

The women guards were taken to work, to help bury the dead and the decaying, paraded by the British as they were marched to work past the survivors of the camp, those Jews lucky enough to see liberation being delivered.

Needless to say the cowardly lot protested in the way that they were treated, to be escorted in front of the Jews and made to work by burying the dead. A British sergeant then screamed out to them, in good German, that they had created the mess before them and so they should clean it up.

But it wasn't just the women that saw swift justice fall upon them. The Hungarian guards, too, felt the brunt of hatred being dealt to them from the British liberators. It was the sheer shock and disbelief that confronted the allies that turned them into issuing their own punishments and in some cases this was metered out in large quantities, being as severe as it was deserved.

There was refusal on the part of a Hungarian officer to allow himself or his four men to handle the dead as it was against the Geneva Convention to be forced into such labour, and he seemed to have forgotten the four hundred that he had ordered be shot just several nights before.

The British captain in charge then advised the Hungarian, in short, that he was under martial law and could be charged with mutiny, or dealt swift punishment before it being heard by a court. The officer again refused to do as he was ordered.

The captain, having heard enough, the smell of the dead pressing upon him, the sights and sounds closing in upon him, then drew out his revolver and on cocking it did hold the weapon at the Hungarian officer's head and repeated one last time that he should order his men to work and get busy with helping them bury the dead.

The Hungarian again refused to accept the terms of the order and was summarily shot in the head without a further word being spoken. The other four Hungarian soldiers then rushed the captain who stood his ground and watched as eight British soldiers, four either side, opened fire with their sten guns, killing the former guard's dead.

The captain then ordered the soldiers to throw the bodies in the mass grave, along with the Jews, and reported to his superior what he had done. The colonel then replied to the captain's admittance that he had done the internees a service and saved the hangman the dirty task of taking their lives.

Eta was looking for her father but his body couldn't be found; she'd lost him after collapsing the day before, the emotions of the loss forced upon her being too much. His body was amongst the other dead and she searched continuously, but it was useless. The sadness of the situation was unbearable, unthinkable and unacceptable. It was now that she blamed the liberators for gross incompetence before again breaking down and crying. She wept for so long that she fell asleep amongst the dead.

A Hungarian soldier then came up and started to pull on her leg, to drag her to the mass grave that awaited her body. She opened her eyes and stared up at the soldier who was being watched by a man in British uniform.

"I'm not dead yet," said Eta. "Please, have patience."

CHAPTER 49

Two officers were walking, mid-afternoon, from the Panzer barracks towards the camp, a walk of just over a kilometre in distance, and where the wind came from a direction other than from the camp, it was quite wonderful. There were trees all over and there were also patches of ground where the trees had been taken for use in the kitchens, even the roots having been dug from out of the ground.

As the officers walked along the road and into the camp, having passed many others in pursuit of their work and errands, a priest came to view, who had perched himself upon an altar which had been made from several boxes and a red curtain whose demeanour had seen better days when hung up in the halls of the luxury barracks some distance behind the officers.

The priest was giving a sermon to several members of the internees whose state was so poor that it appeared that many of them were accepting this mass as their last: their last rights.

And as the priest continued with what he knew best the unfortunate pressed ever towards him, hunched forward or on their hands and knees, to take into their mouths the blessing being provided. For some this would be the last day on earth and by sunrise they would be dead.

It was a wonder in itself that these people, regardless of religion, had sought to praise God in all his glory, even as death pressed against them. What did these people owe God for their mistreatment? Where was God when they needed him most? But for the strong the answers were obvious, for the Third Reich was being stripped of its glory and embellishments, and was crumbling to its foundation.

It was true; the good would always prosper over evil, no matter how long it took. It was obvious in all this war upon war, this killing upon killing, that God was indeed their savour. Good had won over evil in the past and would do so again in the future; the good would always prosper, in the end, over the insanity of the fanatic. Evil should never again be given the opportunity to deliver such heinous punishment against the innocent; and one of the two officers looked at the other as the priest continued his sermon, even in the face of the fact that another priest from within the camp itself lay dead upon the ground before him, having done his best in providing healing to those in need; and the officer said to his comrade, "They crawl from so far. They should be preserving their energy. The sermons should be taken to the sick, not the sick coming to the sermon."

And even as they spoke the victims of Hitler's cruelty could be seen dragging themselves towards the makeshift altar.

"Yes, indeed," said the second. "I would never have believed that one human being could cause such depravity to fall upon another. This atrocity had to be shouted to the world, for all to hear; it simply shouldn't be allowed to happen again. Perhaps our efforts here will be the preventative measure needed to safeguard the innocent of the future."

The first officer locked eyes with his companion and said, "Yes, wouldn't it be grand; but I fear you are mistaken."

CHAPTER 50

Water tankers and three-tonne trucks with cooking equipment arrived late in the afternoon, food and more water too, and it was then that the internees were ordered back to their barracks so that the distribution of food could be conducted. Aid was sought from those internees that were able to move around and so commenced the feeding of the camp.

Yet the vast majority of the people en mass was still so weak that they did little to help themselves, and soldiers unaware of the true epidemic in terms of people's abilities left food for those within the huts on doorsteps and entrances. But the food wasn't touched and those inside continued to die as they'd died the day before and the week before that.

The food consisted of such nourishment, and the internees had not seen food or eaten for so long, that the very goodness of it all made them feel sick and was the direct cause why so many fell dead shortly after liberation, to no fault of the liberators themselves.

Army rations were the main source of their initial diet for there simply wasn't anything else immediately available; it was simply too rich for their digestive systems to handle and much diarrhoea was again suffered by almost everyone within the camp, and where diarrhoea was alleviated, vomiting usually took its place. No matter what, the food that went in was coming back out, be it via the front entrance or the rear.

Men and women alike, although the children of the adjoining compound were far better off, simply scooped up what food they could, taking it into their mouths and then finding that it was almost impossible to swallow. The ulcers within their mouths were such a great hindrance that convulsions accompanied the swallowing of food; it simply could not be avoided.

Two thousand perished over the next few days due to being fed the incorrect food. The internees were at different levels of malnutrition; some could stomach food and others could not. You're damned if you ate and damned if you didn't. Much more work was needed in considering the diets of those most in need, but time was not on the allies' side.

And how did the liberators feel, providing good food to the internees to then see them curl up and die in pain over the next few days? British soldiers felt as though they were to blame for some of the deaths; felt as though they had contributed to the Jews combined miseries.

CHAPTER 51

The sun had only just arrived upon the horizon on this, the 17th day of April, and the work in the camp grounds was increased from the slow gravity of night work to the full swing of day. The fresh breeze from across the tops of the trees near the forest did little to douse the stench of the dead but the feeling of the wind on the internees' faces gave further assurance that freedom had been handed over to them.

Some of the cleaner barracks, of which were few in the camp, were hastily transformed into makeshift hospitals for the worst of the cases encountered, and other more durable buildings were turned into areas in which the walking sick could be administered.

A sign was erected by the military police at the front entrance of the camp advising that 'dust spreads typhus, 5 mph', a start in the control and eradication of the disease. It was derived that there were in the vicinity of 1,704 'serious' cases of typhus, typhoid and tuberculosis, and many more, milder cases. Lice in the area were rife and this alone contributed to most, if not all, of the typhus outbreaks.

Truckloads of bodies were being removed, the SS visible upon the vehicles, looking sour faced upon the living and then the dead, the mass of bodies, their hard labour stacked miserably where they could be moved once more, into a mass grave, their final resting place.

Some internees were now poking fun at the SS, laughing at them, insulting them. It's all different now that the shoe was on the other foot and the SS and Hungarian guards didn't like it, not one little bit, up to their armpits in death and being ridiculed the way they were, kicks and shoves coming their way, the British unable to restrain the internees' anger at the way in which those bastard SS did deal with their prisoners, how they had degraded human life.

The SS were humiliated time and time again and worked all day, never given time to rest, never given a single moment's solace.

Mass graves: it offered no dignity to be buried in this way, to be shoved into a hole in the ground with thousands of other dead bodies. This was no way for a person to be treated, and so there were still Jews present that thought they were nothing more than mistreated dogs on a leash, but the insanities of the reality evaporated with time and more and more people came to see the situation as it really was. Sanity, after all, was a frame of mind, and only the victim could understand his or her place in society; it wasn't for another to stand up and voice in one clear reflection that this episode of imprisonment could be pushed aside as though it had never happened.

There was no hiding the fragile scars of the mind, there was no speaking of the torture which would be endured each passing day and night as reflection upon the incidents of misery were relived, over and over again. The end was always the same, tears upon the cheek, or a sinking heart that drowned in sheer sorrow and that could never be explained.

CHAPTER 52

A bulldozer was hard at work digging a mass grave, just another reminder of the number of dead, but the death didn't stop there, it continued on for many weeks after liberation.

And a group of some forty Hungarian soldiers were marched along and halted, more than likely those murderous bastards that opened fire a couple of nights before, killing innocents as they tried to escape to meet their liberators as they made their approach towards the camp of pestilence. The Hungarians were being forced to work.

The British guards now guarded the guards; the British guards now kicked the guards; the British guards now hit the guards with the butts of their weapons. Ah, such a beautiful sight to see the arseholes of the world being dealt their just desserts. And amongst the Hungarians and the SS at work were German civilians, forced into helping bury the dead.

A British soldier glanced over to a former SS staff member; saw him handling a body unfitting for the corps. In his eyes he was a guard, SS scum, a bastard of bastards. The officer dashed over to the German and lashed out with a verbal threat.

"Take care of that body, you piece of filth," his German was good; he conveyed his message well. "Mistreat that man and I'll shove my bayonet so far up your arse that you'll be eating it for breakfast."

All the German soldier could do was look down upon the body and look for some semblance, to search for a comparison between it and a human being. To him it was just another Jew, another turd amongst a cesspool of turds. But he found the strength within him to take more care, for he had seen other soldiers of the Third Reich receive the measure of British hospitality to which he had been directly threatened, and he didn't want any of it.

The graves continued to be filled and in the midst of all the work could be seen many German officers, being forced to endure that work which was considered by them to be only fitting for a Jew.

One officer was then seen standing over by a barracks window, fumbling for a cigarette. What guts he did have, what resilience in the face of defeat. A British soldier charged over to him and knocked the hat from upon his head with the end of his rifle and the cigarette fell ungraciously upon the ground. The hat flew through the air and landed on a window ledge and the German was ordered to get back to work by helping move the piles of dead that he had helped create.

The British soldier then saw an innocent face on the other side of the window where the hat had come to rest and as quick as a flash he knocked the hat to the ground, making sure not to touch it with his hands, for anything German placed a foul taste in his mouth. It was a young boy. He then saluted the face to his front, an apology for the disgrace, an apology for disturbing his view, a salute of honour which went to the deserving for having the courage to live through such hell as Bergen-Belsen. The boy saluted back.

A German soldier of the regular army approached the British soldier. He looked from left to right before speaking.

"I can help you," said the German in rather good English.

"What! You filth monger! Get back to work."

"No, listen to me, I know that officer, know him well," said the German soldier. "He is a criminal. I've seen him beat up many poor women in the days leading up to your arrival."

"You don't say," said the British soldier.

"If you can give me some cigarettes, I can tell you who-is-who. My comrades and I have worked hard. It means a lot to get a good meal; you know?"

"Yes... yes, I know," said the British soldier. "Have a look around you, and you can see for yourself how hard it is to get good food."

"Yes; but this is the SS, not the regular army. We have always treated the prisoners of war with respect. It's the SS, they are the scum," and the soldier spat upon the ground."

"You will come with me," said the British soldier. "I'd like to hear more."

CHAPTER 53

All SS personnel had eben arrested and disarmed, Lieutenant-Colonel Taylor having rewritten the truce in the name of justice. It was about time that a little justice was served back to the SS scum.

The arrests continued as a bulldozer went about its work, but with a mass grave dug it was now turned to the task of burying. Due to the slow progress of burying the dead the bulldozer was now employed in pushing the heaps of dead into the grave, and it wasn't a pretty sight.

Bodies were punctured and ripped about, legs and arms ripped from their sockets, stomachs opened to the air around. It was hard work for the men operating the machinery and rests were awarded frequently, for there wasn't a man amongst them that could handle the torture of bodies being ripped apart for very long, and the stench... it was unbearable.

A bulldozer had to be used, there was no choice in the matter, for the diseased and starved were dying quicker than they could be buried, so work by hand alone was out of the question, at least for a while. If only the British could convince the stubborn internees who failed to trust them that they were there to help.

It wasn't until the first British nurses arrived on the scene that the last of the disbelievers trusted in what was being said: that they were free and liberated.

And it was only then, when a new dish of high-calorie food commenced to be fed to them by the hand of these angels, that they wholly believed that they were free. It was then that the nurses were struck hard by the effects of their tender touch, as the liberators had been affected before them. It was sheer horror for them to see that dozens of men and women were dying from the feeding as they were so unused to good food as opposed to slop.

Giving them food was killing them but they all hoped the new meals would turn the tables and bring good health back to all.

CHAPTER 54

The SS staff of Bergen-Belsen were not provided any leniency. The camp was in its third day of liberation and many of them were being sold out by the German regular army for the price of a meal and a cigarette, which was better than being fed the little they received as murderous prisoners. Justice now began to be metered out as it should; in great quantity.

The SS administration staff, as individuals, were now being pointed out and treated in much respect to the way in which they had treated their prisoners. 'This one was a guard, and so was he'; 'I saw that one on the tower, and that one shooting a prisoner dead'; 'and that one over there, he kicked two poor women to death'. And so the evidence mounted against them.

The SS were already being forced to reside in barracks which had once been lived in by internees, and fed the same rations that the dying were being provided. There was no longer any luxury for these pigs of injustice, where their pride was fed by the misfortune of others a lot weaker than them. This was one reason that many SS contracted typhus, and many died with the passing of time, but no one cared; why should they? The regular soldiers weren't treated nearly as badly, for the average British soldier understood, quite clearly, who lay at fault in this dreadful debacle. But now, after the finger-pointing had started, the SS were dealt a more severe blow.

Two SS staff, having performed duties as guards at one time or another, being accused by the internees, were soon set up and thrown into a barrack with many internees, and the internees dealt out their own justice by kicking and punching. It took some time before the two bodies were thrown out of the barrack, dead and with grimaces of pain and suffering written upon their faces.

It was no surprise to see that many of the SS were either shot or worked to death, or bludgeoned by the heavy hand of a sergeant on duty.

The bunker had been cleared of the few internees that had been deprived of their freedom, and others still that had been deprived of life, but it was a shame to see the bunker going to waste and so it was employed well as a place in which to maintain some control over those SS that had been pointed out to the British as being heinous and criminally unjust.

CHAPTER 55

The British sergeant was furious to say the least, for the interrogation should have been completed already, but he held his tongue and was gentleman enough not to allow the men under his charge see how displeased he was with the young officer's inability to carry out his duty.

These damn SS shouldn't be getting off so easily. Not three days ago there were three women found in the bunker; two of them were dead and another was barely alive – the men detained in the bunker were no better off.

"We carried out an interrogation this morning," advised the captain as the unbolted door was pulled open. "We couldn't get much out of them. They're not very pretty to look at, I'm afraid."

"The slime on one boot looks much the same as the other, sir," replied the sergeant as he entered the cell. "Now get up! Come on! Hurry up!" yelled the sergeant as he hit out with the metal rod in his hand, poking one of the half dozen SS as he got up off the stone floor. "Get on your feet, you dirty bastard!"

"Is there anything else, sergeant?" asked the captain.

"No, thank you, sir," replied the sergeant. "I'll take care of them from here, thank you very much."

"Yes, well I'll leave you to it then," and the captain removed himself from the corridor.

The SS had blood pasted all down their fronts and the looks in their eyes were those displayed by the defeated. One of the guards was trembling and looked the sergeant in the eye as best he could.

"Why don't you just kill us instead of tormenting us like this? We don't deserve this. We are men," said the SS bastard. "I can't take it anymore; the beatings, this stinking punishment. Just kill me and be done with it."

The MP beside the sergeant whispered to him then, "He's been saying that damn same thing, over and over again. He was doing it this morning when we came in to give him his just dessert."

"Well, you've done a good job," said the sergeant as he looked down again upon the SS filth. "Now get up, you filthy dogs; MOVE IT!"

CHAPTER 56

An order was delivered to all of the British. There were to be no more beatings, no more open-handed punishment of the SS; it was against the Geneva Convention; and so if punishment was to be delivered it was to be done behind closed doors. And so, to the dissatisfaction of the internees, the beatings were seen to be discontinued.

The SS that remained, along with the others of the German contingent, had now been awarded freer rein upon the way in which they handled the dead and from that moment on became more careless in every task they performed.

Too hard it was to get a filthy, stinking Nazi, by himself. And the women guards were just as bad; filthy swines, easily mistaken for men as their loud mouths could attest. There wasn't a lady amongst the group of scum thought mistakenly as female; it was a joke amongst some of the British that to have sex with one would be like taking a razor to your own genitals: what pleasure was there in that? How could any man, German or not, seek pleasure with one so outwardly hostile and vicious? Ugly was too good a word to use on them. Their snarls were like that of a rabid dog, and that was when they were smiling. And so to work they were forced, to endure the same as the men, to be forced amongst the dead and told to clean up their mess.

The SS women guards did as they were ordered, but worked as slowly as they dared, and as the bodies were handled, being thrown into the large graves, one of them looked up and smiled. She was happy and content to see so many dead, happy in her heart that she had helped clean out the Jews of her beloved country. She continued on through the hours of the day, one body after the next thrown into the hole, and still she smiled.

CHAPTER 57

German Regular soldiers were escorted from camp on April 20th, as per the truce that had been signed, but instead of becoming Prisoners of War they were to be returned to their own lines.

They marched off from the Panzer barracks with their weapons with them and for this kind gesture, of allowing them freedom, they sabotaged the water supply to the barracks and hence the evacuation programme. Even in defeat, and being found guilty of crimes against humanity, the Germans were still proud to commit further heinous acts of destruction against the Jews. This was the day that the evacuation process was to commence, the sick to be drawn from the horror camp and placed into real hospital beds; but now, thanks to the scum of the earth, another delay was suffered.

Why on earth did the allies have to be so honourable?

CHAPTER 58

April 21st, and the evacuation commenced in earnest from Bergen-Belsen, the operation now equipped with approximately 7,000 beds and 250 tonnes of medical supplies and equipment. The job was so large that much was needed and confiscated from nearby towns and villages. For the operation to be successful they need 14,000 blankets, 7,000 mattresses, and 5,000 stretchers; the scale of the evacuation was so large that it was said by a high-ranking official that the British should get on with the task at Bergen-Belsen, or continue with the war, but it could not do both; but to the credit of the Union Jack they continued with every task that they were issued.

The internees were transferred to the Panzer barracks which had been transferred into a hospital and transit camp, and here they were treated and cared for, their emancipated bodies lying upon beds and stretchers waiting to be provided medical attention. Here the starved received much care, but time wasn't on the side of the allies and the patients had to be taken care of and moved on once able to be moved, for there were literally thousands dying of all manner of disease. There was also the German Military Hospital which was a part of the infrastructure for the Panzer school, and it didn't take too long for the entire complex and surrounding buildings to be turned into one hell of a huge hospital in which to service the sick from Bergen-Belsen.

The German Military Hospital was to be known as the Glyn Hughes Hospital and it sat in serene surroundings, with 250 brick buildings and five wings attached, and the entire area was adorned with a huge lawn and garden area. Wards on the ground floor opened up to the sports ground where the sight of shrubs, trees, and clock tower, helped promote healing, but the swastika and eagle, so much larger than life it was, wiped the grins from faces as one looked upon the symbol of those scum that had murdered so many. There were sterilising and anaesthetic rooms and a modern operating theatre; kitchens, cellars, store rooms and a room for which to carry out post-mortems. It was spared no expense.

The Panzer Training School was also a great commodity which was taken advantage of. Its grounds were well manicured with lawns, trees and shrubs. Over one hundred two-storeyed buildings existed here which normally housed up to two hundred men apiece, but now, instead of training men for war, it was to be used for healing the sick. Administration buildings, canteens, kitchens, halls, quartermaster stores, workshops; there was even a picture theatre. A swimming pool, heated bath, and showers galore were but simple appendages to this monstrosity of exquisite beauty and convenience. There were also conveniences for the German officers: solarium, banquet halls, ball-room and ante-rooms, all topped off with parquet floors and crystal chandeliers. It was enough to make anyone from Bergen-Belsen sick to the stomach.

CHAPTER 59

The very weak; the very sick; the almost dead. They were left to die.

There were so many thousands that needed to be saved and only those with a chance at survival were picked up by the stretcher-bearer parties.

The medical officer was first to enter the building and dozens of hands went up in the air.

"Take me, please, I'm sick," said one.

The doctor looked into her eyes and saw that she was indeed sick and probably would not last long. He saw another and pointed her out to the first stretcher behind him.

"Her; and her as well, quickly now."

"And me, please, I have to see my mother."

"No, not her; that one over there," said the medical officer and on they continued, clearing out those they knew could be saved; many of the others would die.

"My wife," said an elderly man as he was stretchered out. "She's over there, look, you can see for yourself."

The medical officer looked over to see an old woman still upon her bunk and holding dearly to her stomach, and then she wriggled a little and held out her hand.

"I'm sorry, we can't take her."

"But, my wife; please."

"Move along now, come on; next stretcher, quickly please."

This went on for eight hours a day, day in, day out. Move into a hut and take your pick, but pick well, for the weakest would simply drain away the resources.

The stretchers were then carried immediately to the stable where twenty stalls were equipped with hot water and scrubbing brushes. This was the 'human laundry' where each and every one was shaved and cleaned with soap before being dusted down by powder: DDT.

Medical staff would take the soap and brushes and start scrubbing away, the pain of the cleaning being very real. Bed sores and ulcers simply burned with pain. Hair was cut off to the scalp, completely inundated with lice, lice so thick that it was absolutely intolerable and sent internees mad with the pain of scratching their heads till they bled and became infected; where were they when the DDT truck first arrived, but too scared or weak to show themselves, at the back of the barracks and unable to extricate themselves from their bunks: many reasons were evident.

German nurses displayed much displeasure at first in the work that lay ahead of them, laughing and joking about the whole sodden idea of washing the Jews, but as the first batch appeared upon stretchers, and they saw the condition in which the internees were in, they put aside their hatred and acted as good nurses do, working their fingers to the bone and treating the sick as they should be treated. Each worked twelve to fourteen hours a day, every day, and surrendered themselves to the fact that the SS were not as human as they first thought. They won the respect of their British counterparts and of the forty-eight German nurses that worked so hard, thirty-two came down with typhus. The British were advised by the German officer in command of the nurses, that they had already been vaccinated against the disease: he'd openly lied.

From the stable the patients were moved to the hospital and here they underwent the treatments required for their particular situation, which were so very much the same that little difference there was between each.

CHAPTER 60

The process of evacuation had now commenced, on April 24th, at 9:00am precisely. The delay was mainly due to confusion in offering orders, departments unsure as to whose responsibility it was to tend the healthy, for most attended the sick, the needy, those requiring immediate assistance.

Barracks were called out and women lined up. They were loaded onto trucks and taken to the Panzer barracks where they were registered by volunteer clerks, and then to the showers where further dusting was undertaken, hot showers and food for all. It continued all day; every day.

And as the weeks unfolded so the sick and healthy were evacuated back to their homelands, but for many of them, they must remain behind with nowhere to go.

On April 29th, all SS prisoners were escorted to Celle gaol and on May 5th a Russian battalion replaced the Hungarian's on guard duty: so much for the dream of Himmler to have the allies go to war alongside him against the Russians.

On May 15th the Russians at guard duty all departed for repatriation; it had been a long war for them, but even longer for those poor souls, the internees of Bergen-Belsen.

May 18th; 13,834 patients had been admitted to hospital, all having passed through the 'human laundry' in the process, and of deaths that had occurred; only two. By May 19th, the entire camp had been evacuated.

Many thanks must also go to the following for their contribution in helping those of Bergen-Belsen:

14th Amplifier Unit
Intelligence Corps
63rd Anti-Tank Regiment, Royal Artillery
10 Garrison
102 Control Section
113 Anti-Aircraft Regiment Royal Artillery
1575 Artillery Platoon RASC
11 Field Ambulance
9 Brigade General Hospital
107 Mobile Laundry
224 Military Government Detachment
618 Military Government Detachment
904 Military Government Detachment
British Red Cross
96 student volunteers from London

IN CLOSING

Many thanks to my grandfather for having served honourably, like all the others in his midst. His service is but a symbol of the goodness that rested within the hearts of the allies, who were tested beyond their call of duty.

The memories of Bergen-Belsen remained with him all of his life as indicated by some of the last words that parted his lips at the time of his death. Even in the hour of his death he could clearly see the horrors imparted upon the Jews by the Germans.

He was a kind, good and loving man, and will be missed, always.

THE LONG ROAD TO RWANDA

The Role of Infantry

To seek out and close with the enemy;
To kill or capture him;
To seize and hold ground;
To repel attack by day and night;
Regardless of season, weather, or terrain.

Citation

Do you know what death is?
Do you know what it smells like?

Nigel joined the Australian Army in 1980 at age 17yrs and two months, and on completion of training at Kapooka was whisked away to the School of Infantry, Singleton, New South Wales, Australia.

He served in the Infantry until injury forced a medical discharge upon him in 1996, after having served in Southeast Asia, 1982; PNG (with the AATPT), in 1990: during the Bougainville Crisis; and in Rwanda, 1995: known world-wide for the Kibeho Massacre which occurred on April 22nd of that year.

Serving in PNG was the major highlight within his career, more so than the service in Rwanda. He hopes that reading this book will indicate to you why that is.

He was married in 1999 and has two children.

Prologue
December, 1980

I joined the Australian Army on 10th December, 1980, just 9½ weeks after celebrating my 17th birthday; still wet behind the ears, but out of diapers. From the recruitment office in Melbourne around thirty of us 'raw recruits' stepped onto a coach and headed for Kapooka in New South Wales. It was here that three months of basic training was to be endured.

Although the training was a shock to some who'd just signed their name to that dreaded, dotted line, nothing much can be reported upon in regards to our stay. Oh; there was this one guy who bumped his head and couldn't get up in the morning: He was medically discharged after just three day's service, suffering headaches. But Kapooka in general was the same, day in and day out; day after day of lectures and evenings filled with 'homework'.

It doesn't leave much for the imagination to reflect upon, in any real measure, when compared to this story as a whole. Training at Kapooka is 'basic training', not infantry training, and that is the premise of this book.

At the conclusion of training at Kapooka we were all classified as being 'basic-trained', and carried with us, to our new postings, the newly-earned rank of Private: being trained at the basic level for acceptance into the Infantry Corps. It can be truly said that each and every one of us had a 'basic' understanding of Infantry skills [skills which could be easily forgotten if pursuing a career as a cook, storeman, or one of the other, many careers made available to you] where the general 'Role of the Infantry' was heard, but never came into full fruition.

Both, best shot, and 'A' grade shot, were awarded to me for shooting ability at Kapooka, my only real, substantial achievement whilst there.

And so, to cut the long story short, and being of no real importance to me, from a platoon of 35 at Kapooka, 13 of us were assigned a posting to the RAINF; our 'call to duty', if you'd like to call it that. For me it was a matter of not being accepted into the corps of my preference [catering], so what choice did I have? I ended up requesting the transfer to 'grunts' simply so I wouldn't have to go and work out of a Q-store for the next 20 years. Oh; if you're wondering why I initially chose catering then the answer is simple enough; I wanted my 20 year service to end with my being able to enter the civilian workforce with good standing and maybe the option of opening a restaurant of my own.

So grateful I am for the way the future turned out.

The Poor State of War and Conflict

I can still recall our arrival at the School of Infantry, located on the outskirts of Singleton, NSW. The obstacle course was the first thing we saw as we approached the rear gate, and entered into what appeared to be nothing less than hostile territory; we could all feel the dreaded fear of the place creeping up our backs. I think the guy next to me shat his pants when he saw the length of the obstacle course: either that or he forgot to clean his teeth that morning.

I won't give any details as to my stay in Singleton as I was eventually posted there as an instructor in 1990 for a period of three years, and I have plenty to say on that a little later on, so hang in there, you'll not miss out on anything. But you can get a real feel for army life at Singleton, more so than Kapooka; or so was my learned appreciation of the whole. But it's not until you arrive at your first major posting that your career can be truly considered as having 'taken off'. I was also an instructor in PNG for a period of six months, where I go into the training of civilian into 'basic trained' private, and private into a reasonably, well-trained infantryman. There is more here, over the coming pages, to provide sufficient light on this subject matter, in particular for those interested in the basic training itself.

And so, here you have it. This is my story; my 15-year career in the Australian Infantry, after having experienced Kapooka and Singleton.

There is also a full glossary at the end of this book for those who may require it.

First Impressions
August, 1981

The wooden buildings were growing mouldy, the odour of mouse droppings and rot rising to slap men in the face as the heat from the Brisbane sun gave willingly to a rising humidity. Boards and rafters creaked under the glimmering waves of heat that had now formed over the contours of the ground around. Two flies were then seen out of the corner of my eye, seemingly scrambling up the wall, sharing their opinions on the new soldier that was now walking back from the urinal. It was me; sure as sure can be; and even with the feeling of wetness in my pants, from not having performed the appropriate three shakes, I still felt content within. I was young but genuine, a boy of seventeen, many years short of manhood and maturity; and I was simply marvelled by all of these new experiences so far.

There was also a lot of experience around me, men who'd endured many years of military life; and to think that I was just beginning my long road towards professional service to my country.

Enoggera Barracks was always under the hammer of perpetual

change, in particular when it concerned the conditions of accommodation. Accommodation was constantly being updated and changed for the better, and the army was always seen to be trying to maintain a step in the right direction – seemingly concerned with 'keeping in stride' with the growing standards of society. It was also very true that the conditions changed vastly from one barracks to the next; the Bronx of Townsville, to the swag style of living-in-quarters at Campbell Barracks, WA.

Although most living-in members of the company were quite comfortable with their new accommodation, living-out members of the platoon had to be satisfied with what they could be provided in regards to 'private space' whilst on duty: a place to store their gear, somewhere to rest during lunch, an area in which to change after PT, or to prepare for weeklong trips into the bush. In fact, there was little facility available to persons that decided to live out-of-barracks, whether they were single or married. In most cases the latter were situated next door to the platoon and company offices; steel lockers in the shower block, nowhere to run and hide when the platoon sergeant came a-hunting for soldiers, placing individuals caught onto a never-ending list of work parties and other meaningless tasks or duties.

It was here that I, the newest of soldiers, was to meet with my platoon commander for the very first time, the steps creaking beneath me as I commenced the short march to the 'fresh-out-of-Duntroon' officer's office.

Here I waited, outside of the platoon commander's door, standing at attention, waiting patiently for my march into position, to the front of the Boss' desk.

This was to be my first meeting with the officer and my eyes didn't stray for a moment as I was marched into place, just three feet from the edge of his desk.

The platoon sergeant gave the orders: 'Quiiiiick march! Right wheel; left wheel; halt! Leffffft tah!' each of the executive commands given with that crisp, slap of precision, except where they were drawn out – it was all done for good reason, I suppose. When I was at Kapooka I thought that all sergeants had a lisp, and that having a speech impediment was a prerequisite for promotion. I guess the other soldiers at Kapooka felt the same as me, too, because they always looked so defeated and sad with these types of prospects facing us in the future.

The desk must have been a Boer War antique, many years separating the young blood of the platoon commander and the face of the office furniture. Its surface was riddle, the officer's workspace giving off a look of 'I-need-my-retirement-now'. It was a silent cry for retirement that was never heard, not even by the flies that walked the wall.

I now stood face-to-face with my new platoon commander; he was sitting confidently and silently behind his desk, his refuge, his place of work and hiding. I peered down at the reports that had been written on me, the new march-in. There was a mixture of remarks from my instructors at Kapooka and Singleton, a complete repertoire of my training results, training that I had endured during my struggle to become an infantryman.

I looked down, my name being spoken with a slather of bitterness: 'Private Clayton.'

'Yes, sir.' I was nervous, but steady; who wouldn't be nervous. I wasn't yet 18 years of age, being told that I could go and drink myself stupid at the bar on barracks and in town, but still not old enough to be deployed into active service – this was my understanding, and very little effort was placed on trying to steer young men away from drinking: to abstain from alcohol, something the army should be more interested in, but not, to the detriment of many men.

My eyes quickly found a mark on the wall above and behind the officer's head; I concentrated my stare on this, but the pressure to look down was too much. I tempted fate then and looked down into the seated man's eyes, his hands playing hypnotically with a pen.

My career in the infantry had now well and truly commenced, with the jotting down of notes – either that or the officer was simply trying to look as though he knew what he was doing for the sake of gaining respect from his peers and subordinates.

'I've read through your reports and it appears that you've met with all of your test results to an average degree of competence, not excelling in any particular infantry skill; oh, except that you can run reasonably well.' This must have been his way of breaking-the-ice.

'Believe me, skills are extremely important here. We class this platoon as one of the best….' isn't that what they all say? I mean... come on... was this platoon really that good? I wanted to look down at my legs to see if one of them was being pulled.

He paused then, for just a second, seemingly thinking out his strategy with this newest young soldier (an old boy, not quite a man – and I would have put my hand up too, but for the fear that he'd think I was asking permission to go to the toilet). He was thinking of what to say next; his next comment; to save himself the embarrassment of saying the wrong thing, and at the wrong time; or maybe he had some breakfast still stuck in his tooth which he was concentrating on.

It seemed to preoccupy an officer's mind, this saving-of-face, no matter what its form. They always seemed to want to blame someone else for their mistakes, if able to get away with it – soldiers were good for that, if nothing else. But maybe this was also a show of discipline, his wish, and need, to make things clear, as well as precise. An officer wanted all those subordinate to him, to look up to him with respect, and this had to be earned. He was a hero to his mother, but a chimp in the eyes of most of his men; and to his girlfriend… a sex toy with rank. But I must be fair in admitting that 40% of all of the officers encountered during my military career were extremely good soldiers; and in all respects; though the gene difference between man and ape – so I am led to believe – was quite miniscule in real terms. But maybe I was being unjustly harsh, for it was hard, even for an NCO, to give commands to his men, and at the same time be their mate. I would remember this; always savour command over friendship, for lives had been lost at the pittance of familiarity.

And what of the reports; surely they couldn't be that bad. Expectations were always high, and had to be, in order to maintain professionalism. But this was my first day in the battalion, home of all manner of man; the drinker, gambler, profiteer, and lawbreaker; the mechanic, butcher, builder, and miner; professional shooter, rehabilitated drug addict, and many-a-score more. All of society's troubles and aspirations thrown together, each uniting for a common purpose and goal: To train for war, or war-like operations… how naive I was; but such naivety would become reality.

Some of the platoon sergeant's, and a few of the section commanders throughout the battalion, had seen service in Vietnam; and some private soldiers, too. This was the 8/9th Battalion, of the Royal Australian Regiment, Brisbane's burden and pride; but lest we forget our sisters, those in dresses; 6RAR: I was always advised that politics in the military were important, and the name calling was by way of the competitive spirit within us all; I can only hope that such an explanation will satisfy the cronies in the buildings across from us. They thought they were so good, just because they jumped out of aeroplanes. I jumped once, when I saw an old lady outside her house dressed in a nightie, but I didn't think it was worth bragging about.

The platoon commander continued: 'I won't put up with anything but a one-hundred percent effort, one-hundred-percent of the time. I'll get you to fill out some forms later on today, just your personal particulars – for my records. Do you have a will-and-testament lodged?'

'Yes, sir,' short and sweet. I think I saw him smile; he must have been impressed with my answer.

'Good.' The conversation continued for a short time before I was marched out of the office and sent on my merry way to mingle with other members of the platoon. It was here that a story rose out of the ashes in direct answer to a question asked by me. Small holes in the rear wall of the living-out member's quarters, the outside sunlight easily penetrating the thin shell of the wall; what were they; how did they get there?

Private Robert Crisp released a short muffled laugh. 'A few years back... a section commander was giving a lesson on the set-up and firing of the claymore mine. He thought it was inert so set it up for demonstration in firing. When he hit the tit, it blew up. Caused a few injuries, too. It apparently blew his legs off,' and he laughed again.

If you've seen the effects of an M18A1 being detonated then it would be easy to dismiss the claim, but at the time there was no one around to assume that the story was anything else but matter-of-fact, and it was told many times over the years. Was this to mean we were all fools, and easily misled? Nowadays it's simply one of those stories that gets you thinking; something that someone has told someone else in the hope of seeming more important than they actually are, like an officer walking around with a smile on his face, as though he's just received a compliment from the CO, when the truth of the matter is, he's just figured out how to undo the fly in his pants. Nevertheless, their sense of humour was indescribable, but seeing the hundreds of holes in the wall certainly put an eerie truth to the story.

I could only wonder: If I were in such a situation and blown up by a claymore; would I procure a laugh, or a first-aid dressing?

Bully-at-Large
September, 1981

You beauty... work parties and duties week; what more could one ask for from the Australian Army... any army for that matter? Bashing dixies, washing cups, and scrubbing those thick-skinned pots and pans... the ones with inch thick crud burnt on the inside, courtesy of the cook: that was catering for you; cooking meals fit for a king, and then coming into work and burning everything in sight to feed the soldiers' appetites. There's nothing better than early mornings, late nights, and that fresh smell of leftovers from the bins full of trough food; fit for pigs at the local hobby farm and the Officers Mess. But I never met a cook I never liked, until he cooked a meal. So glad I never became one.

A 15-hour shift in the kitchen, cleaning up after two battalions of pig-eating grunts wasn't without its enjoyment and friendly chatter... except where the uninvited came sneaking around.

How was it that a large-framed man (the term used with much restraint) of 25 years, could sneak up behind a boy of 17 and slash – quite heavily, mind you – the blade of a knife across the back of his neck? I considered myself rather fortunate that the knife was blunt, but the fact that the knife had been held under a tap of hot-running water didn't do much for the shock of the incident; it felt as though I had indeed been slashed with a sharp-edged knife – and this incident was repeated three times during the course of the day. I guess he didn't like the food much and was trying for something with more flesh upon it.

Shame on me; shame, shame, shame. Was I to put up with this for the few hours I was in the mess hall, or stick up for myself and then be clobbered and bashed on my way back from the toilet block when the lights were out and the big thug was running loose around the barracks at night? In all truth the guy concerned for the immature behaviour had probably missed out on some casual sex and had decided to take out his aggravations on... me. Could I be summoned to court for saying his name? Pte Mason: If I knew then, what I know now, you'd be crying yourself to sleep with your thumb in your mouth; as it is you're probably bald, divorced, and have a bad case of... actually, you're probably dead already.

It's hard to admit, and even disappointing to say, that I wasn't yet man enough to stand on my own two feet, and that the army had recruited this dim-witted individual. Yes, shameful I know; I was supposedly a professional soldier yet unable to defend myself. But the bully... it's hard to fathom the intellect of such a person, and even harder to accept that he'd managed to pass the army's psychological testing, in particular when his only comment was; 'tell anyone I did this and I'll kill you'. Maybe he'd been in the infantry too long. It wasn't like being at high school where I was known to turn around and clobber a guy back. Here on barracks you never knew what was lurking around the corners at night: At least after school, after returning a bully's anger, you could retreat to the safety of home; here on barracks all you had was a room to share with three other men, and the naked picture of a blonde taped on the ceiling above where you slept.

Yes indeed, there was a strange assortment of men that had signed the dotted line and most of them seemed to be living in the same building as me. Maybe it was time I changed from being a half-decent and respectable student to a rough-n-tough infantry soldier, and if any changes did take place then they weren't going to happen overnight; not unless I started concentrating on my situation and stopped looking at that damn picture on the ceiling above my bed.

Duties week, a fine collection of tasks that needed to be competed for, sold, bought, and auctioned off; and where there was a weekend's worth of duties to be gained from the guy in the room next door, there was money to be made; besides, what was I going to do on weekends.

The Poor State of War and Conflict

A few days in the kitchen, dodging knives, could have been turned into a hobby with me, except for the fact that the incident only occurred once. It's honest to say, and quite understandable too, that individuals would sell their weekend duties in order for them to get away to the Gold Coast for a few days and nights of uninterrupted, horizontal pleasure with the neighbourhood cat; and some of the guys even went out with ladies.

Guard duty was, I considered, one of the best duties to be gained: A few hours of rove-n-picket would be followed by rest and relaxation on the bunk bed, and in front of a small television; or for some, sitting on the dunny with a porno magazine... gee whiz; what about those sick bastards who stuck the pages together. But whoa, what's that I see; the bully walking from the toilet block with a grin on his face and a magazine in his hand, and on seeing me his grin was dislodged for quite some time. It seems that my intuition was correct and he had been missing out on sharing something special with the opposite sex.

Water Discipline
October, 1981

I soon found myself on my first ever exercise, amongst the drying contours of the Shoalwater Bay Training Area. The bush trip was similar to most but with the added privilege of paying homage to the northern battalions; 1RAR and 2/4RAR. We were to act as the infiltrating enemy force, known quite simplistically as the Musorians, a fictitious enemy to the northern regions of Australia, an enemy that was forever invading this great country of ours. And for all of the high-school drop-outs out there, the name Musorian can be more readily translated into any of the following: Indonesians, Asians, Russian, Koreans... you get the picture. An American marine amphibious unit was also present during the four-week long exercise. This unit was withdrawn early on in the tactical exercise of 'engaging the enemy at time of war' for deployment on a much more realistic scale; in order for them to clash in arms with some very real and far away foreign and very hostile enemy. It didn't really matter much to the Yanks where it was in the world; so long as the enemy wore a turban on their head they were happy to shoot them.

The evacuation process certainly gave way to a lot of daydreaming as Australian diggers delved upon the move, feeling a little bit left out of the picture. The natural instinct was for an individual to prove himself in front of a live enemy, rather than employ himself in the shooting of blank ammunition at friendly troops; some of whom wore familiar faces. We had all enlisted by employing our freedom-of-choice; I was here because I wanted to be here, not because mummy told me to get a job. And it might seem like a strange thing to say, but most of us could see how fulfilment might be received by being committed into the arena of conflict.

These northern battalions were known as the ODF, a force to supposedly reckon with, but on closer inspection seemed no different than members of the 8/9th Battalion. I considered the roles of each of the battalions, Townsville compared to Brisbane. 8/9RAR was apparently trained in all aspects of desert warfare, beach assaults, urban warfare, and brandished with the responsibility of 'training battalion'; the ODF were jungle fighters, patrolling through the scrub with their knuckles scraping across the ground, and at the same time scratching at their heads and armpits looking for ticks.

Not a single one of these aspects of warfare ever appeared to be taken into our framework of training to any great degree, but the future would bear some fruit and produce experiences in regards to one of them in particular.

But how true was the role of those in the ODF?

I heard a story once that mentioned that the jungle of Tully was visited no more than once a year by any individual company of soldiers from Townsville. Of course, there were always individuals that escaped its clutches – or was it laziness on part of the soldier's lack in spirit, where an over-zest effort was made, on that individual's part, to keep from exercises within that area of Australia? It was always raining up there. Maybe some guys didn't like taking long showers, and Tully was like one big shower head following you around wherever you went; it just couldn't be turned off.

Training must be conducted in order to maintain discipline and the ever-changing circle of knowledge. Call me crazy if you will, but I rather liked it in Tully, though a few bitches of complaint did escape me on the odd occasion – I even once went out of my way and volunteered myself for a trip in order to get a posting to another rifle company in 1994: A little more on that, much later on.

I compared the operations as they stood, all of the cross training and obvious broad skills that were to be learnt; but I had a different task to undertake at present. The enemy force was approaching our Musorian company position. Here the northern battalions advanced, set out in assault formation, ready to inflict as many casualties as possible upon us, a superimposed firing of shells from artillery and mortar creating a dent in our defences. DS moved around the perimeter throwing grenade simulators on the ground. They made a big BANG, but I wasn't scared; not until one idiot accidentally tossed a grenade in my pit.

The soldiers from 1RAR then came into view.

The Poor State of War and Conflict

We watched in all eagerness, the will to win overspilling all of our senses, so that nothing really mattered, so long as we performed our job to the best of our ability; or was I speaking for the minority? We carried out fire control orders as they were flung in all directions, a verbal assault of commands from section commanders and platoon sergeants alike, whilst platoon commanders sat back in their pits with that crazy smile painted on their faces.

We fired our French-made blank ammunition as indicated, into the closing ranks of the approaching foe. I paid more attention now – what a rabble; but what did I know? This was my first ever exercise – of a real definition – for those exercises conducted in singleton were lucky to be a week in duration; this four-week stint in the bush however, was to be my first of many.

I heard the section commander give another fire control order and as I turned around for confirmation I saw the head of the platoon commander, the whites of his teeth seen through his lips as he smiled. I turned again and commenced firing.

I paid more attention now at what was going on to my front as several soldiers closed in on my position, almost close enough to see the white of their eyes. Closer still, unshaven. And then they were upon me, fighting through on their guts, gasping at the air as they fought from fighting bay to fighting bay. They were crawling forward on their guts, throwing themselves from shell scrape to shell scrape in semblance to what you'd see in any war movie; but this was no game, this was 'training for war'. I saw another soldier and thought that he was doing very well with his 'running-about', and then I realized that he'd landed on an ant nest and had one biting him on the scrotum. They went through all the actions as taught, bayoneting the enemy as they pushed on through to the depth pits of our Musorian defensive position.

Finally it was over, the assault had finally come to an end and now a reorganisation of troops on the ground was taken into hand, and the poor soldier that had been bitten on the scrotum had his pants around his ankles, and the platoon sergeant felt a little awkward as he knelt there before the private's private.

Platoon commanders, and section commanders alike then blast out orders over broken gasps and wind-cracked lips.

The force from the north was soon secure on the ground and were told by the platoon commander to form a harbour (a defensive position of troops set up in a circular pattern), set up similar to that of the face of a clock. Some officers even looked at their watches when they did this, so that they wouldn't get it wrong, looking at their watches and then at the ground, telling section commanders to 'put your machine gun over there, Corporal,' and then smile at him as his order was being carried out.

The centre of the clock was the HQ element, and the hours of the clock were the two man pits, weapons pointing outwards in all round defence. The section commander along with his scout acted as the depth for each individual section. There were three sections to a platoon, three platoons to a company, and so on and so forth: it was fortunate that the highest ranking soldiers in this man's army could count to three, or we'd all be in strife. The harbour position looked vastly like a cordon designed with one simple task in mind, to provide all round defence in respect to the ground you were currently occupying at the time. It was now that I turned my head to look at the soldier beside me. His uniform stank and it was stained beyond belief. His shirt and trousers were torn in some places, fraying here and there. The man from 1RAR turned his head slowly to face me, relieving his observation from possible enemy counter attack for just a moment, the four days of growth upon his face choking under the layers of camouflage cream.

He looked into my eyes as though to ponder something with a half-smile cascading across his face, seemingly content with the job he was doing, capable of continuing on forever and a day. His mouth opened and spittle ran down his chin. He wiped it away with embarrassment, 'G'day mate, how ya gowen?'

'Good, thanks mate, yourself?'

'Ah yeah, not bad. Hey, ya aint got any spare wata on ya, have ya? Just a mouthful, while me CSM aint watchen.'

I pulled my water bottle from its cover, 'Sure.' I could only hope that he wouldn't get any spit in it.

'We aint aloud ta touch ours unless we get told we can. Prob'ly get charged if we did. Bloody wata dis'pline. Sux it does; bloody sux.'

Now, he was more-than-likely telling the truth, and then again, he could have been a compulsive liar and just after my water, but character of body can usually be determined. I'd heard of this so-called 'water discipline,' just hadn't yet experienced it - maybe due to the fact that I always tried to carry plenty. I guess it was simply another way of saying that the resupply situation sucked big-time and due to the inability of the supporting units to provide an adequate water supply, the troops on the ground could not be sufficiently supplied with their daily ration. It was far easier to call it 'water discipline' and be done with it.

It might be interesting to note that within a few years 'water discipline' was scrounged upon by the medical fraternity within the military; it would seem that the army was crumbling under the pressures of society and its standards, much the same as the change in accommodation back in barracks was now becoming fit to live in and quite tolerable. It looked like the resupply of grunts on the ground had to be improved upon, and there was no choice in the matter. There was, of course, only one thing wrong with that. We now had to carry more water in order to maintain a good supply. The overall weight of my back pack now ranged anything from 30 to 40 kilograms in weight – all the bloody time: which was truly amazing considering how small the 1980's Aust pack was.

Orders

October, 1981

Bush; I loved being in the bush.

I was lying down with my rifle extended, the barrel pointing outwards and away from the perimeter. I was maintaining watch from a sentry post which had been positioned by the section commander under direction of the boss – I wanted to call the boss Smiley behind his back but didn't know how the others would take it.

I couldn't see the remainder of the platoon that sat in the perimeter of security just 30 metres to my rear and had no friendly covering fire to speak of – if I was to withdraw from my post due to being in contact with the enemy. What I did have was a short covered route that took me back to the section machine gun and a smoke grenade which I needed to throw in order to help conceal my move from enemy view. I knew, too, that the smoke grenade – by all realistic terms – only offered concealment from view and not from hostile fire, but the smoke grenades did come in a lot of pretty colours. Many other thoughts travelled my mind as I slipped into a daydream.

I was only going to be here 30 minutes, after which I'd be relieved and afforded the time for something to eat, prior to the platoon fighting patrol being resumed. It had been a hard morning so far and we still had a long way to go. This was the part where we had to 'seek out and close with the enemy': That was my favourite bit.

Orders for the patrol the day before, as given by the platoon commander, had been quite precise and covered all aspects for the smooth running of our fighting patrol; although breaking-wind and nose-picking was genuinely considered as a free-for-all and not covered in orders: Unless moving into an ambush site; when that happened you had to do silent farts, just like the Queen of England does in her palace.

Sitting through orders was a constant recurrence in the army, either in barracks or in the field, especially during IET at the School of Infantry. Here in the field we received at least two sets of orders a day, but whilst in camp little more than an update to keep us informed of up and coming events. This however, wasn't the problem, the sheer length of orders was, especially if you were on barracks and it was nearly time for morning tea. It usually came down to what was referred to as 'time and space', and rarely was enough time ever provided for decent orders to be given, especially when the canteen was selling hot pies with sauce.

Now, I didn't realise it, but I was slipping further into a world of my own, thinking of all the things I wanted to do on returning to camp. I commenced to play with the trigger guard of my rifle and watched an ant as it made its way across the barrel and down towards the dust cover of the SLR I held in my hands. I then commenced to do some house cleaning and removed some dust from my nose.

Suddenly a sound caught my ear. I looked up. There to my front were two motorbikes as they made their approach from the T-junction and down to the closed gate just 20 metres to my slight right.

I pulled myself down for better cover but maintained good visual on the pair. Who were they? Were they the enemy? What should I do? I pulled my finger from my nose.

Five metres separated the two men who sat upon revving engines, the visors to their helmets pulled down over their faces. The front man came to a stop, side-on to the gate. He reached out to lift the latch. The man to the rear, what was he doing? Looking around, searching the ground around him and covering his mate. No weapons were visible. Maybe they were special soldiers and carried guns in their pockets.

Another sound was then heard, this time to my rear. I turned to see what it was, and that was all it took. The man on the second bike had seen movement. As though linked by an intercom they both turned in synchronisation, speeding off from whence they came, nothing more than a cloud of dust left to billow out from beneath their tires.

'Shoot! Shoot!' The platoon commander had arrived to see for himself what the noise was, and being obviously too scared to dirty his own rifle by shooting at those on the bikes, wanted me to act on his behalf.

'What, sir?'

'Shoot them, now! Quickly, before they get away!' I could see that he was anxious and excited because he wasn't smiling any more.

I looked up; my weapon finally lifted into my shoulder in readiness to fire. Too late, they'd vanished. Nothing but dust could be seen.

'What the hell do you think you're doing, Private Clayton?' he yelled sarcastically. And what are you doing, sir, trying to see if you can break the record for weapons cleanliness in the field? 'I didn't know they were the enemy, sir,' was all I could say.

'You're a bloody idiot! You were told earlier.'

I felt like saying, 'I wasn't really picking my nose,' but thought the comment would clarify his accusation against me as being a 'bloody idiot'.

'Sentry orders said I should shoot on seeing the enemy, sir, but nothing was said about bikes.'

'You're a bloody fool. They were probably SAS.' Wow; they were special soldiers: I was right. They must have had deep pockets to keep their weapons in.

My Platoon Commander turned to depart. 'I told you this morning, no friendly forces exist within our area of operations.... Blah, blah, blah, blah, blah.'

So he was right and I was wrong. I'd have to learn to pay more attention to orders and not pick dust from my nose during picket, but it was no good crying over spilt milk. What if I'd shot and killed a friendly? But what if the enemy I didn't shoot at, later on, shot another member of the platoon? What if the platoon commander was to vanish in a puff of smoke; not that pretty smoke from the smoke grenades, but any old smoke? Maybe next time I'd have better sense, and better luck.

And as for the officer in question not firing his weapon, I must admit that his experience did out-weigh mine, and I was a private soldier of extremely little experience. Orders were an intricate part of the 'rules of engagement', and always would be, whether they were right or wrong.

Gun Picket
October, 1981

I was growing keener – slowly but surely – and most of that which we carried out during the exercise was more-or-less considered as 'on-the-job-training'. Many of my previous mistakes had paved the way to a fuller understanding on how peacetime operations were carried out – or so I thought.

The older soldiers – meaning those with vaster experience than me; and weren't hard to find – had pointed out that 'you always learnt', and this was regardless of how many years of experience you had gained through bush trips, simple tasks on barracks, and training exercises in general. One soldier once said to me, 'it's not until you've had as many morning teas as me that you realise you've got a few years under your belt.' I'd take that on board; I never knew if it would come in handy, but you never know about these things... and I did like having morning tea, so I guess I was halfway there already.

Sleep in the bush was a wondrous thing to have but it was so often very hard to get, especially when you were sexually aroused and lying there with your eyes wide open. I recall one night in particular.

The night was pleasantly warm due to the vastly overcast skies above. A light breeze was blowing and visibility was none existent. I'd just crawled into my sleeping bag and my sense of being slowly drifted away and I fell asleep, quite content in my sleeping bag and oblivious to the world around me. It was some time later, whilst lost in a blissful dream, where a belly-dancer was performing tricks before me, stroking my leg sexually with a feather duster, that I suddenly found myself rudely woken up. It was time for picket, being brought evident by the invisible man that stood over me, giving out a little kick to my leg, 'Get up, it's your picket.' My eyes opened to nothing but the black of night. All I could manage at the time was a short, 'Huh, what?' My whisper was heard and accompanied by a hungry yawn. 'It's your bloody picket. Get up.'

I fumbled for my watch and found the button for the little light within, a pixie at my beck and call – at least, that was what it was until I woke properly. The time was confirmed. I squinted again at the face of the watch, and then scratched my head as though searching for a clearer understanding as to what was going on. What the hell happened to the belly dancer? My sweet dream had been interrupted precisely at the wrong instant. Damn it! Experiences with feather dusters didn't come along very often.

It was 2330hrs. 'Huh, yeah. Okay. I'm coming.' I got to my feet and searched for my webbing.

It didn't take long before I heard: 'Come on, mate, what the hell you doing? I want to hit the farter.'

'I'm looking for my… ah, found it.' I fondled around, fighting to gain access to the harness of my webbing.

Time passed slowly for the waiting man, each second assuming the role of ten; 'What the hell are you doing?'

'I can't get my webbing on.'

'Shit. Give it here.' It was twisted awkwardly but logically, it always was. 'Here, get up and put the bloody thing on will ya? I want to get some shut-eye.'

I was finally ready. I picked up my rifle and followed the guy towards the machine gun by holding on tight to his harness, following carefully, staggering with a yawn. I still had no idea who this guy was, the cranky son-of-a-bitch. Some bloody mate, waking me up for a stupid picket.

But how much further from the truth could I be. Not one man in existence, within the ranks of the infantry, enjoyed doing picket. Not one man enjoyed doing 10 seconds more picket then he had to, let alone several minutes. Maybe, if luck were with us, an insomniac would be inducted into the section; better still, two.

I was soon at the gun pit; the man – now to my rear – positioned me safely and silently. Then came his whispered brief: 'Sit there. The guns in front of your right knee.'

'Thanks, mate.'

'Yeah; right,' and then he mumbled something to himself and disappeared back to his sleeping bag.

The surrounding blackness was as dark as I ever thought possible. I thrust my hand up in front of my face and waved it spastically. Nope; I couldn't see it. I then turned my head to the right. 'Hey; pssssst. You there?' The other section member on the gun. He was here – somewhere. 'Pssssst, you there?'

'Yeah.'

'Who is it?'

'It's Bob.'

'Where's the gun?' My hand was grabbed by the invisible individual and placed onto the butt of the machine gun. 'Ah, right.'

'The picket list and torch are on the left of the butt.' I was extremely glad that he said 'the butt' and not 'my butt'; I didn't fancy reaching over in his direction and touching his backside.

'Got it.' I placed my hand back into my lap, sitting; thinking. Only two hours and fifty minutes to go. A short picket compared to the night before. I could only wonder if that belly dancer would be waiting for me when I returned to my sleeping bag.

Bob then said to me: 'It's your turn to sleep.' The dead man on the gun, a style of picket used by 'very' few, and only experienced three times by myself during my entire 16- year career. One man slept at the gun whilst the other remained awake, and the following episode illustrates exactly why 'dead man on the gun' should never be used.

I had a smile on my face. The dancer was closer than I thought. 'Thanks, Bob.' How nice of him. He was a true friend; even if I couldn't remember what he looked like.

'I'll wake you when it's time.' I wish he wouldn't, but that's the way the cookie crumbles I suppose.

I slipped into slumber, oblivious to the passing minutes.

I awoke suddenly, a shudder flying through me, pins and needles attacking my arm. I quickly established the time by pressing the light on my watch – yes; the pixie was still there.

I was an hour overdue for the waking of my relief. I searched for the picket list and torch, and after getting low onto my stomach I scoured the paper for the name of the man I was supposed to have woken an hour before. The smallest bead of red light was emitted between my fingers. 'Hey, where's Banks sleep?' I asked Bob. There was no answer. The man to my right, was he awake, or asleep? 'Pssssst. You there?' But it wouldn't have been Bob; would it? Not on a staggered picket.

'What?'

'I'm supposed to wake Banks; an hour ago. How come you didn't wake me up?'

'Don't worry about it,' came the muffled voice.

He must have been asleep, too; 'I don't know where he sleeps.' This was confusion at its best, for this night's picket had been split into two, the platoon manning just two guns as opposed to manning three. There were men in this platoon I simply didn't know; the other 25 were crazy bastards.

'Rifle pit, twenty metres over that way.'

Great help. Not only couldn't I see my hand in front of my face, but I didn't know where 'over that way' was. 'I don't know where his pit is,' I said.

I then realised that the man to my side wasn't Bob at all. He stood up and grabbed me by the harness, lifting me to my feet. I was turned into the general direction. 'Go that way for twenty metres. If you can't find him... come back and I'll fetch him for you.' Now that sounded fair enough. Twenty metres – twenty-four paces. 'If you hit the fence then you've gone too far.'

Hmm; sounded like good advice to me. 'Thanks mate.' I stepped off slowly, counting each step carefully as I maintained my direction. I knew how to count to twenty-four, and it didn't take long. Within less than half a minute I'd gone the distance.

I searched around on my knees. No one was found. I searched and searched again. No; nothing.

Several minutes passed before a thought entered my mind. I'd not gone far enough. A further twenty paces in the dark should compensate me for the short strides I was obviously taking. I counted again, accurate and sure. Coming to a stop I searched again. No relief was found.

I stood there, bewildered. What should I do? Go back to the gun, that's it. The other bloke can go look for the relief. I set off again after pivoting myself 180 degrees, wandering off towards the machine gun.

I counted carefully, but how many paces should I go? 'Pssssst, you there?' No answer. Around 30-odd guys lying in the bush around me, and not only couldn't I find any of them, but none heard my pleas for help – I found that somewhat hard to believe. I bet if I pulled out my penis and had a piss I'd hit someone square on the head. 'Hey mate. You there?' My whispers for aid continued to go unanswered. I'd obviously gone off in the wrong direction. I'd have to go back towards the rifle pit and keep going till I hit the fence, then I'd be right, I'd be safe, I'd know where I was: I'd be at the fence.

I continued searching, and wouldn't you know it; a full two hours had passed and the sun had commenced its climb above the horizon, and still I couldn't find anyone. I sat motionless; defeated. As soon as it was light enough I'd find my way back. It couldn't be far to the platoon position.

Eight hundred metres later and I found the perimeter. The platoon sergeant was going to go ballistic over this. He didn't like losing soldiers, unless they had crabs crawling around inside their crotch or something like that. Never again would I make the same mistake. Next time I'd be right on the ball.

Lost Yanks
October, 1981

During the American soldiers' withdrawal of the Kangaroo exercise a few stories arose to dominate the conversations during lax periods of defensive routine. One such conversation was in the case of our standing patrol which was brought from its stand-down status to 100% stand-to, due to what was initially deemed to have been enemy movement to our front; but in actual fact it wasn't the enemy at all; it was one of those guys who didn't like people that wore turbans on their head.

I was on picket at the machine gun, lying with my ever-watchful eye searching for any possible sign of enemy incursion or movement, ears trying to listen to what lie beyond the range of the songs given off by the owls of the night. In the distance an APC engine could be heard to thunder to life, and experience so far had taught me that any other APC in the vicinity (of the same call sign) would also have turned over their engine; a simultaneous action. This was done to help conceal the true numbers from enemy ears, a practice of tactics that always seemed to be observed.

The night was still young when I caught a glimpse of something to my front, and as I stared I realised that it was a small hand-held torch flickering in the distance. Every soldier of the section was quick to jump into the comfort of his pit when woken, each with his rifle held steadily in his hand. The light at present was advancing slowly, definitely a torch and about 40 metres off down the spur to our direct front. One guy thought it might be the 'min min light', but he was wrong. Everyone watched in bewilderment, and until the voices reached our ears we had no idea who it was.

The accents were unmistakable. Three yanks were to our front and gabbling on to their heart's desire; something about boon-twangs and cod-wallops, high-fives and weeding the garden; or something like that. They were slightly muffled due to the distance, but became ever more distinct as the ground between them and our standing patrol diminished.

Our section commander jumped from his pit and approached the three men once they were just ten metres to the front of the standing patrol position. It scared the shit out of them. 'Hey, man; you scared the shit out of us,' said one of the yanks.

The night wasn't as dark as previous nights and so the basic shape of the Americans were seen reasonably clearly by us all, and I think one of them had dark glasses on, but I couldn't see properly. 'Damn, man; I can't see shit out here.'

All of them had their weapons slung and the commander of the group just stood there, blazing his torch over the contours of the map that he carried, 'Shit man, where'd you come from?' He was definitely more surprised to see our section commander than we were to see them.

'I'm Corporal Roberts. What's up?' asked the section commander of the man with the torch.

'Hell, man. We haven't got a clue where we are. This goddamn map's all stuffed up.'

Roberts went to his aid, eyeing the map and placing a steady finger to the map's surface. 'Just there, mate; right on that spur which slopes down to the North.'

'Ah shit. We're not supposed to be there. Goddamn.' He pondered the map for a brief second. 'We've got to get to this place right here,' he pointed, 'the road junction.'

Roberts held back his laughter. 'Just go back down this way and you can't go wrong.'

'Yeah, right. Thanks, man.' He turned and the group of three proceeded back down the way they'd come, map thrust up to his face every now and again until they disappeared out of sight and sound, the owls once again dominating the night after the fading of the last 'goddamn-this-map-man'.

Maybe he should have taken his dark glasses off.

Some stories were ludicrous, to say the least; like this next one:

The moon could be seen in its first quarter before becoming shrouded in a sheet of black menacing cloud. The soldier had just come from his stint on the machine gun and he was looking forward to a good night's sleep.

The cloud opened up and the rain started to fall, steadily at first. Lightning could be seen in the distance, followed shortly by thunder that out-weighed the option of remaining where he was. He didn't like sitting under trees in a lightning storm, and we were in the bush, surrounded by them.

Another yawn escaped his lips as he crawled from his sleeping bag, rolling it up quickly and placing it under his arm. The armoured personnel carrier to his rear looked so inviting right then. He thrust his pack under the closest tree and headed for the vehicle with his rifle in hand, looking around as he moved, ensuring he wouldn't be seen. He was a sly little bastard. No one was going to wake him up until the sun came up the next morning; he was set on that point; for the cloud was opening to a downpour that he wanted to avoid at all costs.

He crawled under the small clearance between the ground and the metal hulk of the APC, thinking solemnly how smart he was; after all, his hutchie had holes in it and a wet night just wouldn't do.

He was soon sound asleep, and the rain fell faster and harder, no relent in the storms growing fury to be seen over the coming hours. The widening pools grew and the ground drank as fast as it could, the soil around growing wet, becoming softer and softer as the minutes ticked by. The grounds finally gave slowly, the APC sinking with gradual motion.

The soldier woke, feeling the crushing pain, unable to scream out. He tried desperately to thrash and dig his way clear, like he was a windmill, or doing calisthenics. The rain fell and fell, the APC's tracks sank, the bottom of the vehicles monstrous hulk now met with that of the sodden ground; the yank was now entombed in a casket of mud and on the sun rising his body was discovered.

The nights were always dangerous, and this brings to mind another story of an American victim.

Night patrolling was no man's favourite, unless you were a stalker and liked wearing women's clothing.

Moving slowly and cautiously was the key to success in reconnaissance by night, but it was raining. Larry felt that he could afford to lift the pace slightly. It didn't matter any longer how much noise he made because the downpour hid the sound of his movement.

He maintained his vigil, patrolling his arcs as best he could; after all, he was the lead scout and he had the best eyes in the section: I bet he wasn't wearing dark glasses. Raindrops dripped from the brim of his hat, cold liquid ran the length of his back, and his feet began to feel the slosh of his soaked socks. He wasn't a happy-Larry. He continued though, paying little heed to the discomfort he suffered.

Some heavy scrub presented itself to his direct front. He fought with it, pushing through with regret as he tripped over a protruding root and fell to his death, down a 30- metre cliff face. And that's not funny, because it's true and really happened, and you should never poke fun at the dead; that's what my mum says.

And the stories just keep on coming, like a jack-in-the-box.

Stand-down had been passed from pit to pit. It was time for sleep. The rifleman moved towards his erected hutchie, and the sleeping bag which he had laid out before the sun had set. He was a smart man, smarter than the rest.

His webbing was removed and the rifle placed onto this. His bush hat was also placed down, over the body of his weapon; this would help keep moisture from attacking its metal skin. He knew about rust and was a good soldier.

He grinned to himself – no, he wasn't an officer – he was looking forward to a bit of shut-eye before he had to take his turn on picket at the machine gun. He placed the first of his legs deep into the instantly warming sleeping bag, followed shortly by the next, squeezing down deep and grabbing the zip between his finger and thumb.

All of a sudden a shocking pain hit his leg, again and again. He tried to scramble from the confines of his bag, the zipper reached for; the kicking of his legs, bit again and again, the pain, the zipper, the kicking. It was as if he was dancing, but with lots of pain involved.

He managed to get free, 14 snakebites to his legs. He peered down, just making out the scaly menace. He kicked out at it and was bit again. He gave chase after the escaping snake, heading off into the bush, shouts echoing around him: 'What was it? What's going on, man?' Deeper into the unknown he went, into the dying night, the escaping peril. The pain was unbearable now, attacking the heart and bringing a horrific contortion to his face. He was found later, dead, the terrible pain scribed over his facial expression; but you've got to ask yourself: Would dancing lessons have helped?

And the motto is: Mother Nature was neutral; kind one day and murderous the next.

Single Picket
October, 1981

Kangaroo 81 was reaching its final stages when an order for a surveillance operation was passed on to our section 2IC and three other private soldiers of the section – including yours truly. I was looking forward to it because Surveillance usually meant that you had time to rest, and all this walking through the bush was making me tired.

Intelligence reports from previous patrols had been gathered and it was proposed that 2/4RAR were going to take advantage of the road that sat just five kilometres to our north. This was a possible route that could quite easily lead the enemy into a suspected FUP, in final preparation for the decimation of 8/9RAR's Musorian Defensive Position. Regardless of the facts that lead to this highly valued information, the CO at the time felt that all boundaries around the area of operations, especially those cut or paralleled by road, or dirt track surface, should be secured by way of eyes and ears – a combined series of listening and watching posts. He must have been a smart officer to think up all of that.

We set upon our task, clear in mind as to the mission parameters. Patrolling to a secure observation post took a little under two hours, by which time the sun had commenced its decline to a beautiful hue, before the final blackness of night took stage. It was almost like being on holiday.

It had been decided to conduct a single picket, 2.5 hours in duration for each individual. All four of our section lay down beside each other in preparation for the night's duty, in order of relief. I was first on picket.

The 2IC said to me: 'Nigel; when you wake me for picket, make sure I'm sitting up and wide-awake. I talk in my sleep sometimes, so just be sure I'm right before you go to sleep. Ask me a few questions or something, but make sure I'm sitting up; ok?'

'Yeah, sure. No problem.' Night routine had now commenced.

The minutes ticked by, all 150 of them, one by one, boring and solemn, and in particular, repetitious. What thoughts travel a soldier's mind during such periods of solitude? I'll tell you: All thoughts; the more thoughts the better, for the more thoughts you experienced the faster time would pass you by; but also, the more thoughts, the less concentration on the task at hand. But I can't tell you every thought I had because some weren't very clean.

Only repeated sessions of picket could quench the ability for anyone to wander off into a deep sleep, a self-discipline that could never be thought of as being hard by anyone who didn't understand the job of the Infantryman. It was also a good idea to sometimes sit on a sharp rock.

The more pickets you did and the more the mind won into self-control, blocking out that which was unimportant, but remaining weary of any possible threat around. It was like driving a car down the road and suddenly realising that the car to your front was braking fast, so you do the same, saving yourself from smashing into its rear, though you're quite unaware as to the past three kilometres of journey which was now behind you; unless you're a pathetic bastard, and then you just crash. To be aware of all around you without realising it, in particular the sounds which require immediate attention; like a mortar bomb exploding deep in the distance of the night; what was the bearing to the sound? Several bearings, taken from several OPs could determine the approximate position of the possible mortar base plate position, by way of intersection. Was that a vehicle moving along the road six kilometres to the North? Which direction was it travelling? What type of vehicle was it? How many?

Ah... most of the time we didn't give-a-shit. But tonight, all my senses were alert: Only the slack individuals are incapable of paying heed to his personal responsibilities; besides, I was starting to really like my job.

Some would laugh at the last paragraph; those who couldn't understand; those who were slack in discipline, morale and equity; but everyone had a job to do, even the grunt who spent weeks on end in the field. No shower, no compromise, no comforts of life or amenities; just the will power and patience to live like a pig in filth, and to do well at it. This was a personal devotion; to live like crap.

The picket was soon over for me. I leant over and shook the foot of the 2IC, LCPL Smyte. Shaking the foot, a tactic employed so that the waking man wouldn't jerk up, thrashing out with a clenched fist – which occurred on several occasions. 'Hey, your turn for picket,' I whispered.

'Huh. What?'

'Sshhh. Time for picket. Sit up.'

Smyte sat, eyes gradually opening to the night. 'What?'

'It's your picket.' I was somewhat concerned and looked hard at the waking man. He was an ugly bastard but I didn't care. All I wanted to do was go to sleep. 'You awake or what?'

'Yeah, yeah; I'm awake.'

'You sure?' his nose was huge.

'Yeah.' He turned and looked at me with the rubbing of his eyes. 'I'm fine. Go to sleep.' No further words were necessary. I lay down and drifted off to be met by a wonderful dream filled with naked women.

The morning broke; singing birds and the bright rays of the sun bringing all to consciousness. Smyte reached over and shook me by the foot. 'Hey, you fell asleep on picket, didn't you? You're a butt-ugly, idiot; you stupid stinking turd. You're a useless bastard.'

'You what? You're joking, right?' was my defensive response. How dare he say I fell asleep on picket or that I was useless.

'Shit.' Smyte brought his watch up to his face. 'Great, we're late. We've got to be back at the defensive position in less than an hour. You just couldn't stay awake, could you?'

'I woke you up, Corporal; just like you said.' Maybe I should have made him sing a song or recite a poem when I woke him up.

'Yeah, sure.'

I took the brunt of the accusation, and became concerned with the fact that I'd done what was asked, and missed out on 150 minutes of sleep, by doing a picket which had died in the hands of the more senior soldier, a senior soldier with rank on his shoulder and a head full of nothing but a cold word.

The Poor State of War and Conflict

Oh well, what can you do? Everyone, regardless of rank, was exposed to making mistakes.

In New Zealand
March 1982

Robert Studd and I stood shivering in the fighting bay, the plummeting cold of New Zealand affecting us both.

It was the comfort of the two-man tents erected within the perimeter behind us that was present in our minds, not the job of security. Comfort was a luxury beyond belief in the field and those simple pieces of fabric behind us were everything at the moment. The two man tents acted as a windbreak more than anything else, a shield against the petrifying wind chill factor.

It was midnight in a landscape that consisted mostly of rolling plains and little else. If there was a tree in the area then it was marked on the map; and that was fair dinkum, no boasting about it. We were in the Lake Tekapo training area and in the past 24 hours had seen but a single tree. We missed seeing trees out bush. It puts mans' mind to rest knowing that he has a tree to piss against.

I climbed from the confines of the gun pit to fetch my relief for picket, saying nothing to Robert. He was awake and knew the routine well.

I headed off towards the low silhouette of a two-man tent; hard to see even from my present distance of just twenty metres, arms held in tight against my body for warmth, misty vapours of breath escaping the confines of my mouth as I breathed in and out like a choo choo train.

I was soon at the entrance to the tent and kneeling down. I hobbled forward, under the flap and to the foot of my replacement. I grabbed his foot and shook it. 'Pssssst. Get up. Your picket.' The relief woke with a moan and I reversed out to sit and wait, holding my hands across my chest. I knew he was awake because I could hear him cussing and carrying on. He didn't like the army very much, and didn't like taking orders from officers, but what can you do? Officers love giving orders, even if they were stupid ones like, 'sit there, Private,' and you were already sitting; or, 'come here, soldier,' and you were already walking towards him. It made them feel superior. I guess that's why they invented saluting, so that they felt recognised.

Several minutes of waiting had passed when a shot suddenly rang out through the night, a contact on the perimeter had occurred.

The platoon reacted immediately, standing-to, and the section commander could be heard bellowing out for information, an echoing authority for those concerned to break the silence and give a target indication. And then Robert Studd suddenly found himself under verbal reprimand.

I ran over to the gun pit and knelt down beside it.

'But I thought it was Nigel coming back with the relief,' Robert explained to no avail. I think he was lying because he had that dumb-schmuck look on his face: I could see it quite clearly, because I was real close, and from the light given off by the moon; but I didn't want to get too close in case the section commander started swinging punches.

'You've got to be joking, Studd.' Corporal Matthews brought the weapon down from his shoulder and crouched on one knee beside the gun pit, a voice in the darkness giving indication as to the enemy's location. The enemy was indeed nearby. Suddenly a figure could be seen running off into the night. Corporal Matthews engaged the target with several rounds. 'What the bloody hell happened, Studd?'

Robert looked up from within the pit, to the crouched form of his section commander, no machine gun present. 'Well; Nigel went to get Greg for picket when I heard a noise to my front. I thought that Greg had got lost and was on his way back into the perimeter. I asked who it was. All he said was that I should give him the gun. I thought that he'd seen something.'

'So you gave him the machine gun?'

'Yeah.'

'You're an idiot, Studd! What ever happened to the challenging procedure and password?'

'I thought it was Greg.'

'Shut up! Here.' He thrust his weapon out for Robert. 'And watch your bloody front. The platoon commanders going to be real happy with this, I can tell you that for nothing.' He probably would be, too. We didn't have Smiley anymore and this new officer was always laughing, just like when you first lose your virginity.

The incident with the machine gun was never lived down. The section machine gun was returned five days later with the inscription 'First Blood' still scribed on the feed cover, a motto that the machine gunner had placed there four months earlier. It's too bad that the gun never lived up to its name.

Leopard Tanks
August, 1982

Diamond Dollar was an exercise involving direct work with APCs and tanks, most of which was conducted using live ammunition. Numerous lessons were given to the battalion during the first six days of the exercise, lessons to familiarise us with tanks, familiarisation that was essential for the understanding of all fundamentals.

Much was learnt. Harbour drills, clearing defiles, giving target indications by tank telephone and radio, fire control orders, types of ammunition available to the 'beasts of war' and much, much more. We even had a safety brief and were told not to carry our weapons onto the tanks. One of our guys didn't listen properly and must have thought they said that you had to carry your weapons onto the tanks because when the tank commander turned the turret during a demonstration his SLR got crunched up and mangled. Gee, it was so funny. I'd never seen a corporal lose his boot up a soldier's arsehole before, but on that day we were all in for a real treat.

Safety officers made themselves easily recognisable by way of wearing white armbands and remaining 'clean skin' (not wearing any webbing). They were always present during the live fire serials of the exercise, the dawn assaults upon wooden figure-eleven targets being numerous in number and undertaking. They used to walk around with big sticks, white bandages attached to them, as though trying to look more important than the officers. I recall one assault in particular that was endured time and time again, until the CO was happy with its result.

The leopard tanks crept forward with the forward most assaulting troops of the battalion in line with the second road wheel – a purely safety aspect for the conduct of fire and movement with the vehicles. I could see safety officers hitting soldiers with their sticks, telling them to pull back a little. And then, as soon as we closed into 'effective firing' range of enemy bunkers and fighting bays – a position set up by the battalion only days before – a mass of fire was produced, tanks and soldiers letting rip.

The ground vibrated in tune with the thundering engines, the noise was incredible. Lying on the ground was like lying down on top of a vibrating mobile phone – not that I knew what it felt like, I'd just heard stories – and the less said on that, the better. Control of the sections by voice became a real problem. All section commanders then reverted to the use of field-signals for the moving forward of their groups within the sections.

Another deafening blast from a tank sent a shock wave of admiration and perpetual relief through the soldiers as a round of HE ammunition shattered a target to smithereens, an enemy simulated gun pit which was there one minute and gone the next. Two hundred metres from the enemy pits and an arsenal of all calibre of ammunition streaked through the air, air that in turn could be heard cracking into the vacuums created by the path of the projectiles. This was the part of the 'role of infantry' where we were to 'kill or capture him,': I liked that bit, too. Noise upon noise, an adrenalin rush of satisfaction, satisfaction in the belief that no real foe could withstand the devastation that was now being created, filled us with cheer. It felt like Christmas but without the presents. As with normal though an appreciation that this was only a one-way firing range was taken into mind (there was no enemy shooting back at us; no defensive 'live' fire).

Slowly but surely the assaulting troops closed the gap towards the staked targets and machine-prepared pits in which they stood. We received the order to fix bayonets and the man next to me smiled, his eyes bulging out of his head. Some soldiers were real happy in the infantry, I could tell.

It was time again for another fire control order that was to align the massive barrel of the tank up with another enemy bunker.

'Nigel!' The section commander turned towards me, thrusting out with a pointed finger towards the tank to the left flank, 'Give a Fire Control Order!'

'WHAT?'

The tank fired another shot, with an inherent explosion, followed by the expulsion of gases from the muzzle break, which made it impossible to hear a thing. And out to its flank an APC with its .30 and .50 calibre guns was blazing a trail of dust that lead from the front of the vehicle to the sandbag wall of its target, the APC lying down its barrage of covering fire. All gave its accumulative gift of deafness freely.

Again the section commander gave the pointing finger, an over exaggerated thrust to counteract his frustration; frustration built up by the difficulties now showing on his face. 'Fire! Control! Order!' He was starting to look agitated; I could see he was getting red around the collar: Maybe the platoon commander was watching him.

I turned to the tank and back again. The commander held his left hand up towards his ear to signal the use of a telephone. I understood that signal. I nodded in acknowledgment, picked myself up, and raced to the rear of the tank, keeping low as I moved, maintaining a reasonable distance from the rear of the tank so as not to be inadvertently crushed if it should be put into reverse – an unlikely but scary thought.

Three metres behind the covering metal hulk of the tank, and with handset in hand, I looked out for confirmation of a target. There was still a lot of dust flying around. Little was seen as the tank crawled forward a little more and I followed up the rear until a target presented itself.

The commander at the turret waited patiently, loaded and ready to fire. I then saw an opportunity. 'One hundred and fifty metres, reference barrel, right, one O'clock, enemy bunker at base of large ghost gum!' There were about a hundred or more ghost gums in the area but the tank commander pretended to know what I was talking about.

'Seen!' The commander pushed the tank forward as I secured the phone back into its metal pillbox. The barrel exploded with deafening noise and the target was obliterated from existence. My section commander looked relieved. I guess this meant that the platoon commander was going to be happy with the results. The platoon sergeant and corporal were good mates; the sergeant was always patting the corporal on the shoulder and saying things like, 'well done, Corporal; good job,' just loud enough for the platoon commander to hear. It was times like that that we all wanted to be corporals.

The assault continued until we were within effective small arms firing range but without tank fire support due to safety restrictions and closeness of targets. The DS continued to move around and hitting soldiers on the backs with their sticks, saying, 'you're dead, you little shit,' and then moving on to find someone else to pester.

As Infantry we now had to fight through on our guts, crawling and fighting the whole distance that remained between us and the objective. Then, after quite some time, we were finally done and the objective was won. We could now go into our harbour drill and sit there, watching the DS standing around with their arms folded in front of them, as though they were God; but playing God was the RSM's job.

Much was learnt during the morning's activities with the monstrous metal coffins, and a bond of knowledge was tied to the mind forever and a day, an unforgettable experience for sure.

Rum Courage
August, 1982

We found ourselves sitting silently, faces full of muck, clothing smelling like that of a sewer - To anyone except those that had been wearing them for the past sixteen days. We were watching the living beauty, the transformation of day into night, hatches to all APCs gaping to the cooling air that surrounded us as the sun made its journey to the far side of the world, to be seen by the world's populace, from all of the planet's trouble spots. It was really relaxing to be able to sit there with your hand in your pants and watch nature at its best.

As we sat waiting our turn to play out our roles in the mock assault ahead many of the other countries of the world were carrying out morning routine and preparing themselves for a real conflict, [or maybe night routine] to cause nothing but devastation, carnage and casualties upon their own species. Man; a creature of the world bent upon killing for the sake of killing, to leave decaying corpses to litter the surface of their land; quite unlike other animals of the world who killed for food, to sustain the essence of life itself – was that a fair comparison?

The platoon sergeant visited each of the sections as they rest in the metal hulls of the APCs, taking with him a bottle of rum, to be shared equally amongst the section commanders and then these portions amongst the men – but he always slipped our corporal more than the others. Suddenly I didn't care anymore about the stupid bastards on the other side of the world, for the sergeant was now my friend, too.

Section commanders took their quota and began the equal distribution, not a drop wasted to the dry and dusty grounds of Shoalwater Bay.

Each soldier held his cup canteen out patiently for his share of the rum, and those that didn't drink gave their portion readily to the man beside them. Morsels were swallowed, followed by widening grins that were brought on by the pleasurable warming of the rum.

Cups were folded away and placed back into the water bottle covers. It wouldn't be long now and the assault would commence.

Orders for the night attack finally came over the speakers, breaking the silence in the rear of all APCs in the area. All listened intently, or so it seemed. Some soldiers simply sat there with their bush hats tipped forward, hiding their eyes, trying to catch up on a little sleep.

Solid compressed-aluminium doors were then closed and secured on the raised ramps, machine gunners and section commanders stood in the open hatches of the APCs and the vehicle engines were turned over simultaneously. The guys that were sleeping now woke up and could only wonder as to where the smell of rum was coming from, but I didn't tell them; I just told them to 'go back to sleep'.

The APCs pressed on towards the line of departure, bodies vibrating heavily inside, with some men being thrown around like rag dolls in the confines of the personnel carriers. All section members, of all sections, would break from the safety of their vehicles in two minutes and the assault into the night would commence – by foot and without the comfort of fire support from our APC .30 and .50 calibre friends.

All faces appeared serious now, serious and tired, some with eyes closed and others looking precariously over their weapons in final preparation for the coming assault, and one man learned back and stole some of the rations that belonged to the APC driver, shoving a tin of corned beef into his basic pouch.

We were all so very tired. Another night move, another enemy position, more human shaped targets; and yet another night move was to follow this assault. If we kept on going like this then the driver wasn't going to have many rations left.

One man looked over to another, 'I hate this shit.' Eight years on and he was still saying the same, and a few years after that he was in Somalia. And when in Africa he found himself amongst the same type of characteristically built individuals that were doing exactly the same thing some ten years before, when they were all drinking rum, thinking of a warm and comfortable bed, and stealing rations from the driver of the APC.

Lost Cause
August, 1982

Thirteen APCs raced out of the creek-line some fourteen hundred metres short of the objective, a huge objective which now stood to our direct front; three monstrous features; the enemy position. Three distinct knolls of interest existed here and each was heavily defended.

Our 'friendly' company assault was aided by a superimposed small arms fire, and simulated artillery and mortar fire support. Sustain fire machine guns sat at right angles to the main axis of assault, and DS threw whiz-bangs around the objective to portray the friendly onset of bombs and shells striking the ground. They always did a good job. Throwing whiz-bangs upon the ground was like chicken-feed to them.

Foliage in the area offered little concealment but the soft waves of undulating ground gave to periodic sanctuary of cover from fire; a rock here, an indent in the ground there; wherever it was possible to gain an advantage it was sought. If it had been raining it would have been a different kettle of fish, because none of the soldiers like sticking his head in the mud.

Although the assaulting vehicles were outside of Musorian small arms fire, they weren't out of reach of the enemy company 60mm mortars. Commanders and drivers alike were soon forced to secure the hatches to the main cavity of APC's, drivers and commander's cupolas also being secured, a protection from shrapnel hence gained. This gave the soldiers in the back greater opportunity to have a quick rest and to steal more rations.

Visibility was now drastically reduced and ground was slowly gained on the enemy objective, for drivers were forced to peer out of glass ports which were literally inches thick, each a rectangle the size of two fists placed side by side. This had forced the reduction in speed. This adjustment in speed however was given praise by many of the soldiers as they were now receiving less bumps and bruises from being tossed around within the confines of the death traps, and those with light fingers continued to concentrate more on their task at hand.

DS in the backs of HQ vehicles assured the degree of protection to each of the vehicles was carried out. A death penalty would more than likely be the outcome to any vehicle load of troops whom disobeyed the command and the DS were always happy to award wounded.

A minefield was haphazardly entered, unmarked and unknown until the DS gave a command for one of the vehicles of the platoon to halt and for its occupants to debus. I guess he would have been disappointed because he wasn't able to use his big stick to whack the soldiers, instead he just waved his hand over them, as though he was Moses, and told them to stay where they were: 'Stay where you are, you're all dead.' They were now out of the exercise, just for the duration of the assault. They had supposedly run over an anti-tank mine and were, for all intents and purposes, considered dead.

The platoon commander would now have to take his particular objective with no depth section, which was a reliable source of reserve during any assault, and so we pushed on with two sections and entered into enemy small arms firing range. And then the word was passed around; the platoon was going to exit the vehicles shortly.

APC .30 and .50 calibre weapons opened up to help with the covering of infantry on the ground as they left the confines of the APCs behind them. Ramps folded down to reveal the outside world and we sprang into action, leaping from the vehicles, taking a sharp left hand turn, to hit the dirt and push out into assault formation.

Our platoon was now linked with the neighbouring platoon. Private Kurtts was to the far right of the flank and used as the linkman for our joining. He wasn't a very good soldier. He was looking in the wrong direction until his corporal threw a big rock at his head. It was pretty funny too, the way in which it bounced off his skull and Kurtts then turned around to face the enemy.

The sloping ground to the front was so ominous; it was enough to put the fear of God into an atheist. But we had little choice but to go up it: It wasn't like working as a QANTAS baggage handler and going on strike because you felt like taking a day off due to the work being too hard.

A fight through method of assault was adopted immediately and the enemy-held ground taken inch by precious inch, men working in pairs as they moved forward, providing each other with covering fire, but maintaining the line of assault throughout. Every time I hit the ground, after taking a bound forward, the radio I carried hit me in the back of the head. I had to keep looking around to make sure it wasn't a DS with his stick in his hand, but it wasn't.

The Poor State of War and Conflict

As we ascended the hill the two platoons arrived at the base of their objective as laid down in orders, two distinct knolls rising from the rocky hill that we were now fighting up. The saddle between each of the platoon's objectives played with the minds of the soldiers and as per normal each individual began to converge upon the targets on the knolls to his front. Everyone wanted a piece of the action, to be the one to jump into an enemy pit and be seen to clear it of enemy. These first two features had to be won and secured quickly, before the flanking third platoon, to our left, swung around to the remaining objective to the rear. Although this segregated platoon was in close small arms fire with the enemy, they couldn't begin their assault until friendly fire was in a position to pin down their particular objective [friendly covering fire]. Every round mattered in real life, each square inch of ground was as sacred as the next, and the only secure piece of turf was the stuff on which you were standing.

A DS strode up behind the man with the machine gun, a stick held tight in his hand. He stretched out and tagged the man on the shoulder. The gunner turned, sweat pouring from his face.

'You're dead,' the DS ordered.

'No I'm not.'

'You're dead. Stay put, and no more firing.'

'Bullshit, I'm not dead.' He got up and took another bound forward, two more metres. An enemy pit sat to his front and the enemy opened fire. If only he'd remained crawling along on his guts like everyone else and he wouldn't have endangered his life – or that of his mates.

'You're bloody dead!'

'Bullshit.'

'Another word from you, sunshine, and you're on a charge. You're dead, now stay put.' The DS pushed on past the cursing soldier and towards another – they loved their job. 'You're dead, get down and stay down.' The DS continued on and on.

By the time the objective was secured only five men of our platoon remained alive; the remainder of the company wasn't much better off. A good 80% of the company now lie dead and spread out along the extended trail, from the low ground to the peak of the three objectives.

Not a good result by anyone's terms. But how realistic was the assault? No one really ever wanted to die for his or her country; it was far better to make the other guy die for his – after all, we weren't fanatics: That's left to the terrorists who think they have 72 virgins waiting for them in heaven.

Bunghole
August, 1982

We were well into the exercise and the time had arrived to lose all of the APC support; the remainder of the exercise was to be conducted on foot, an advance to contact, prior to a further three days spent conducting activities revolving around that of a battalion in defence. Even at this point in time all of the soldiers had their minds focussed on the city lights and nightclubs of Brisbane.

I looked over towards the section commander for confirmation, 'What?'

'Go over and get some spare food. Just tell the commander that we've got no stuff left and are starving to death:' hmmmm, ransack the APCs of everything we can before they depart; good idea.

'What do you want?'

The 2IC spoke up: 'Get some bunghole.' He then received a cold stare from some within the section.

'No way. I'm not eating that shit,' another voice from somewhere behind. The platoon was harboured up in a non-tactical environment prior to the advance to contact; H hour – after that there would be little time to rest.

The section commander: 'Good idea; bunghole it is. Go get it, Nigel. And quickly, before they take off.'

I picked myself up and raced over towards the crew member atop the APC. The NCO was checking his two weapons and cupola; playing with his headset and eyeballing the map that he held in his left hand. He was chewing on a ration pack biscuit and looking down upon me as I made my approach, his mind awash with tasks.

'Hey mate; you haven't got any bunghole to spare have you; or maybe something else?'

'Bunghole? sure. I hate the shit myself.' He peered down into the APC interior, his driver handing him two cans of the finest vintage, a Christmas style cake rich with fruit, and as dry as… 'Here, catch.'

'Thanks mate.' I returned to the section commander and handed it over. The can was soon opened and the smell simply wafted out.... mmm; delicious.

It was somewhat of an advantage in advance to contact exercises, preventing the need to go to the shitter each day as part of a normal daily routine – or so it seemed. It was said by many to be better than the diarrhoea powder in the army med-kits, which each section 2IC carried, and it wasn't uncommon to see guys taking this in aid to induce constipation for a week, a benefit that secured peace of mind in some individuals. No one enjoyed going to the crapper during a tactical exercise, wiping your arse with a piece of flimsy paper, with the possibility of getting shit over your finger and under your nails. Section members advanced like a swarm of flies around the cans as they were opened with a metallic click, each and every one looking on as though a naked woman was about to be revealed.

The fruity rolls were cut into equal portions and all stuffed their faces on returning to their packs, sitting there, chewing, swallowing, fingernails full of dirt and uniforms stinking, crumbs being picked from trouser legs as they were dropped and quickly placed into mouths.

Smile upon smile burnt at the muscles of faces, a burp here and there giving that indication of gratification. Another was heard, a pig type burp with corners of the mouth pulled back willingly to extenuate the sound. All were trying effortlessly to achieve the loudest call of satisfaction, a burp that would have received a hit around the back of the head from any wife or girlfriend with the words 'you pig' accompanying the slap.

I lay back on my pack, sighing with pleasure and closed my eyelids, trying for another 30 minutes of shut-eye before the deadline for the battalion to move was finally upon us all.

It would be a long time between trips to the dunny from this day forth.

Smell This
August, 1982

On return to the barracks the mind was awash with thoughts; beers, sex, food, and for some sleep. From the time that the final words 'Company dismissed' reaches your ears only two things stand between you and the pub; the clothes you have had on your back for the past four weeks, and the jam between your toes.

March in step as fast as you can back to the barracks, for there are only four showers on each floor of our accommodation, and approximately 16 soldiers to each floor waiting to use them – the others of the platoon of 30 having headed for home, wife, and warmth of bed.

You wrestle with the key around your neck and get it into the door; you push it open and commence to strip the clothes away; first the boots, then the socks, and the uniform in general. Grab your towel, soup and shaving kit, get hold of the shampoo and step into the shower block as quick as can be.

The camouflage cream was literally caked upon your face; shaving will fix the worst of the gunk. Into the shower and start scrubbing away, and 15 minutes later you are still covered in filth; cam in the ears, on backs of hand, and in every wrinkle of your weary face.

After some considerable time, and much anxiety stressed from other members of the platoon waiting for a shower, you finally emerge from the shower cubicle and head back to your room to get dressed. You get hold of the doorknob, turn it quickly and step through the doorway (the one you share with four other men). You step into the room, your first beer in a month not that far away, and you suddenly find yourself choking on the fumes, for its only now that you realise how badly you needed a shower; you wouldn't touch your clothes with a ten-foot pole, let alone attempt to pick up your crystallized socks. The stench was always wicked.

Orchid, Orchid; Where Art Thou
August, 1982

Robert Crisp and I – along with the remainder of the platoon – ventured down to Holsworthy in the latter part of the month, for a short three-day exercise with a logistic support group. A scenario had been painted for the platoon to indicate that we were operating out of the north, near Darwin. It was too bad that the same scenario couldn't govern the weather conditions; it was atrocious.

For the logistics exercise to be a success, the campsite required that poles be made for the erection of camouflage nets over vehicles. It was quite usual for the poles to be made from lightweight material, similar to bamboo, but the 'system' was not always effective and initiative was often required.

The platoon sergeant attended a briefing from those appointed to the security group (the infantry element on the ground), so even before the exercise had commenced we were well swamped with work parties of wide variety.

It came to pass that a short trip, by truck, was required into the field in order to obtain, via fowl means or fair, wooden poles for the purpose mentioned above. It was cold and wet, but to hell with that, we were infantry soldiers and a part of our motto was 'regardless of season, weather, or terrain'.

We arrived in the forest ready to do our deed upon this haven for trees; protected by law... No wonder the platoon sergeant was looking over his shoulder every few minutes, lifting his head at the slightest sound that was NOT vibration from the chainsaws as they were throttled into action.

The platoon sergeant pointed here and pointed there; this tree will do, and so will that one too... but the trees in question; weren't they too thick... too large to be employed as they were supposed to be employed. And a cold stare was met by the man in authority, for the platoon sergeant himself had other ideas on his mind, not the exercise in general.

'There; over there, Private Andrews."

'Okay, Sarge, I see it.'

And what was it, you ask; why, another orchid high up in a tree, for his collection back home, broad leaves which would one day spring beautiful colour to adorn his home; the entire forest was at the sergeants beck-and-call, to do with as he pleased; and the soldiers, we were but another tool for him to unleash upon the State Forest.

What a despicable character, and although he held a soft spot for the beautiful orchid, he clearly held no regard for nature itself.

Exercise LSG
August, 1982

Enemies on this exercise were also a figment of the imagination, and this 'lack of enemy' only tempted to lower the platoon's morale further than what it was, all brought on by the stresses of the current situation. To maintain a security picket on any of the platoon gun positions was seemingly foolhardy, but carried out regardless. After all, what was the point in conducting a picket, when no enemy incursion was possible? This was another time when 'dead man on the gun' was employed by me.

Work parties were a common thing, and a heavy burden to the platoon from the start, so not only were pickets and sentry positions manned as per normal, but a heavy workload and burden of additional duties was now set upon us all. We had to suffer this humiliation because we were 'dumb grunts' and being such meant that we'd be happy doing work parties. Maybe the 'support group' thought we'd go jumping for joy about the whole set up, smiles on our faces as though we were puppies trying to hump the leg of our masters.

Setting up tents took up a majority of the work parties and then of course came the laying of the electrical cable, which had to be laid throughout the campsite, from the strategically placed generators, to – and through – all of the tents in the area.

Light bulbs were then attached to specific points along this cable so that when the generators were turned over and running, the tents would become illuminated – work in the dead of night could now be pursued. Most of the pogo bastards probably needed the light to see what they were doing when blowing up their blow-up dolls prior to bedtime, so they had something to lie upon at night, in the same way that grunts laid on top of women: And all grunts know that it's more fun to lie on top of a woman than a pneumatic: so who's the more stupid?

It wasn't until the day after the cable had been erected that it was passed down to the platoon members that the cable now had to be painted a different colour. They probably needed something nicer to look upon. It must have been horrible for them to see that white cable stretched out above them whilst wrestling with their blow-up dolls.

Everyone appreciated this pogo-officer's brilliant scheme. All we had to do now was to go around and paint the white cable, olive drab. Wonderful initiative from another officer of a depreciating and somewhat, estranged corps. I didn't like those officers very much; they always had a small sparkle in their eyes and lips pursed, as though they wanted to bend you over the nearest fallen log. It was enough to make you shudder, unless you liked being stuffed like a turkey.

The reason of course was explained to all. To manufacture the cable in the colour that the army required cost too much, so it was marvellously cheaper to purchase white cable and then add a splash of 'logistical support group' initiative. Yeah, right; I think they just did it on purpose so as to make themselves feel more superior than us; to make themselves feel special. Well, that's okay, because we might not have been special soldiers with deep pockets but we were smart enough to conduct 'dead man on the gun'. But why paint it whilst it was up? 'Because the tents had to have light as soon as possible,' said one of their officers with a grin on his mouth, 'the cables receive priority', the same as everything else in the bloody army. One thing you had to learn in the army was to prioritise your priorities. Light was far more important than green cable and tents had to be erected in case it rained. Wouldn't want a pogo to get wet now, would we?

The idea behind the entire scheme was so that any low flying aircraft – so was the logic – wouldn't be able to see the white cable showing through the foliage provided by the trees. What aircraft? But what about the tents and their silhouettes?

Crisp and I were soon given orders and we in turn gathered our resources. Six-foot broom handles were issued and to the end of these a paintbrush was attached. A formidable plan was then formulated and executed with pride.

Dip the brush into the can of paint and paint the cable whilst it was still erected. A sound conclusion to the most idiotic of ideas, but we all realised from the start that we were there for this very reason, to do work parties, to carry out tasks that the pogo fools themselves couldn't be bothered with. Once again we were to be used as a resource instead of as a platoon of infantry. No wonder there wasn't any enemy around; that would have taken us from the precious tasks offered by the pogo officer.

The Poor State of War and Conflict

Thirty-six hours of painting saw to the end of the task and the exercise. All members of the platoon were more than overwhelmed to see an end to the biggest ever 'rock show' on earth.

PS: It wasn't mentioned, but whilst being painted, some tents were moved. Yes; about 20% of all tents erected were moved no more than ten metres, picked up by groups of men and moved with cable in place... like that of a cable car. Three metre lengths of white cable now dominated the area.

But who was the bigger fool; really? The officer who couldn't correctly position his tents on the ground in some form of proper organisation, or the poor old grunt on the ground who had to go around with more olive drab paint?

Commonwealth Games
September-October, 1982

The Commonwealth Games of Brisbane was something special to look forward to for a majority of the 8/9th battalion. Some were used as drivers for the different teams of the commonwealth, and others like me took pride in distinguishing themselves as a member of the Guard of Honour, and some just stayed on barracks with their fingers in their butt and being employed on work parties as required. The guard was used primarily for the opening and closing ceremonies of the commonwealth games and took part in honouring the Queen at the time of her arrival in Australia. I was honoured too, because I liked being a guard. Once, a long time ago, I wondered what it would be like to be a guard, guarding another guard, but I never found out.

In the four weeks leading up to the 105-man guard for the opening ceremony, well in excess of 117 hours of drill was performed in rehearsals; all of which was taken out on the parade ground at 8/9RAR, Enoggera Barracks. The RSM liked marching us up and down the parade ground – I guess he was bored and didn't have anything else to do, and I was always happy to help him out. Several full dress rehearsals were also encountered during the lead up training, but less the low flying aircraft. But nothing could prepare us for the noise as we marched into the arena of the games themselves, it was unbelievable; the crowd, the low flying aircraft, and the commentator's voice as it echoed throughout the auditorium, but it was exciting too, because the girl in the front row of seats was performing like Sharon Stone from Basic Instinct.

The commands that had been rehearsed in the build-up of anticipation were barely heard over the combined decibels; even the wind seemed to be against us as it lashed out a sudden gush that blew off five slouch hats in front of 350 million viewers. It was nice to see someone from the crowd pick up one of the hats which was in direct danger of being driven over by a vehicle as it came passing the front of the guard.

Without boast there was a story printed in a London paper which stated that the first gold medal should have been given to the Guard of Honour for their efforts. It gave a nice feeling to receive public recognition, even if it was from across the sea.

But the misfortunes were not over with by a long shot, for the next step was to greet the Queen at the airport with a hearty welcome of precision drill. This was unfortunately let down, for as the Queen stepped out from the door of the plane, an order for present arms was given, at exactly the same time that the artillery commenced with its twenty-one gun salute. Nothing could be heard over this.

Half the guard paid compliment by thrusting their rifles out central to their bodies, and the others remained steady with rifles tucked in close under their armpits, steady as a rock. But seeing the Queen's head bobbing up and down as she walked past during her inspection of the guard must have been some consolation for all of the drill rehearsals endured; surely. I wanted to ask her if she really did silent farts, or if it was just a furphy, but I didn't think she'd know what furphy meant, so didn't bother asking.

The closing ceremony was of little concern, nothing more could possibly go wrong, and didn't. It went like clockwork and all were glad to see the end of the drill rehearsals, but the RSM seemed disappointed that he had to go back to being bored: It must have been a horrible job, baby-sitting officers in BHQ.

A surprise did come through the mail though, for all of those who performed as part of the Guard of Honour. All 105 men received a commemorative medallion, but it wasn't made of gold, so I guess the article in the London paper didn't have the effect that we'd all hoped for.

The only downfall of the guard was the fact that most of the guys on that parade never got to see the fruits of their labour on TV or video. Such was life I suppose.

Close Call
November, 1982

Exercise Aries Pride was the final exercise for the year.

On the morning of a starlit night, A Coy was formed up in an FUP awaiting the order to move forward in an extended line – to close with the enemy. I was smiling because I was thinking of Brisbane, and then I turned around and saw the pearly whites of the platoon commander, which quickly tore my smile away; I didn't want him getting the wrong impression. There was sufficient cover from view in the re-entrant, and it was our firm belief that the trees that were in the vicinity had been planted by the hand of God – why?

Illumination from 81mm mortars came in thick and fast over the objective so that fire support could be brought to bear on the enemy position. With the illumination the commanders could adjust the friendly fire to better break up the enemy defences and to hopefully force the enemy to cower in the bottom of their pits during the A Coy advance – saving on friendly casualties.

The line of fire for the mortars placed a high trajectory over the heads of troops on the ground and as each round burst into illumination, hundreds of metres above these contours, the canister in which each was originally contained would drop to Earth, its task of delivery having been met. The approach of these canisters could quite easily be identified as they whistled through the air and thumped into the ground. In some cases they sounded like that of the tempo created by a drummer, each spinning out of control through the cold night air, tumbling to earth faster than a speeding locomotive. One might daydream and consider that the drumming was actually the drummer of a band and that he might have fallen out of an aeroplane from overhead on his way to the Tamworth music festival; but I waved the stupid dream from my head; but a drummer, drumming away, is exactly how it sounded. Anyway; a good dozen or so of these fast-falling objects literally crashed through the canopy of the trees to the depression – re-entrant – in which the friendly Coy waited; into the very midst of our confines.

One hit a branch and was deflected to miss a man by no more than two centimetres. Many were blessed with lucky escapes that night, and within a year a ban was placed on all firing of illumination over the heads of troops. I was surprised it took a year to have the ban put into place, but the army was always surprising me with its slow reaction to circumstance in getting things done. Our Platoon Sergeant said it was the stupid officers fault and when I asked him which one he said, 'all of them', and I was surprised that it took so many officers to make such a slow decision because I'd heard that 'two heads were better than one'. Then the Platoon Sergeant said that 'too many cooks spoilt the broth' and I suddenly realised why the food in the mess hall always tasted like shit.

The second close call came two days later during a battalion advance to contact along three separate ridges. Each Coy of the Battalion had its own ridge, which consisted of numerous live-fire target positions; Numerous, figure-eleven targets, being deployed as Coy, PL and SECT stands – a live fire contact lane. As each objective was taken, the information was passed back to BHQ; a coordinated

BN – Coy by Coy – advance to contact. I was reassured by the exercise because there were only three ridges and I knew that this was in the capabilities of the officers in charge, because they were all good counters when the number was no more than three.

One of these companies came upon an enemy position, and one of the platoon commanders, not fond of taking advice offered by subordinates (in particular section commanders), decided that he knew where he was on the ground, and that all others were geographically embarrassed – that was to say, they were hopelessly lost. He then proceeded with his call to bring sustained machine gun fire support to bear upon the objective – remembering that this was a live fire exercise.

The gun line quickly prepared the ammunition and was about to bring fire to bear upon the enemy position some 1,200 metres away when one of the commanders of that group lifted a pair of binoculars to his eyes. That was strange. One of the figure-eleven targets was moving, and he'd not been smoking a joint because drugs weren't allowed in the army, so the movement was not part of his imagination.

He gave the command to check fire and the men on the firing line moved back from their firing positions.

Incorrect grid coordinates had been sent to the SFMG firing line. What was thought to be an enemy position was in fact the position to which A Coy was holding. I then realised why there were always so many officers, because a six-figure grid reference was in fact 'two sets of three numbers'. It was no wonder the RSM had grey hair; it was from working in BHQ.

This type of mistake was seen more than once during my career in the army, due to incompetent individuals who didn't care to ride on advice as given by others. Maybe the officers should have been made to work in pairs all the time. There happens to be a few around whose promotion has become directly affected by such mistakes. Let's hope that a lesson was learnt in each of the circumstances. The accidental calling in of mortars, adjacent to a friendly position, was to be the worst I heard of that year, but hearsay was nowhere near as reliable as being there on the ground, at the time of the incident. Some of the officers were good for saluting, and... well... that's about it, really.

Tully
March, 1983

The Field Force Battle School was to be the first treat for A Coy, and Tully in March was a place you didn't want to be in if you didn't like the rain, but then again, nearly every month in Tully was the same, wet and miserable. It was one of the heaviest rainfall areas in Australia, and the monsoon season was in full swing.

The big adventure started like many, with an innocent flight in a C130. This took the clan to Townsville where we stayed the night prior to being loaded onto trucks for the two hour trip into the mouth of the jungle, the last night of innocence for several weeks. Something had to be done and fun had to be sought.

Orders were passed down to stay away from town, namely a disco christened Scums, a favourite hide for many of the Infantry soldiers of Townsville. But rules were made to be broken and so Scums was visited by many.

It came as quite a surprise to wake in the morning and find that the Coy had spent an entire night in Townsville without causing any trouble, and none being marked as AWOL during the morning parade, which was held at O-dark-hundred. There were however a lot of sore heads that morning and it was obvious that some had finished drinking just moments before loading themselves onto trucks.

The boys from Brisbane clambered aboard the trucks and pulled the tarps down tight before arranging their gear in such a manner that some shut-eye could be attained during the short trip to Tully. It wasn't until we reached the halfway point in the journey that the rain started to fall, the end to any sobering thought of 'an easy trip' fleeing from mind.

Very few of the soldiers had been to Tully before now, but those that had gave us all a wake-up call as we approached the small township of Tully. Sleeping equipment was quickly stowed into packs as we passed through the town.

Although it was only 0630hrs, it was still fairly dark outside the confines of the trucks. The cloud cover was ominous and the rain kept coming down, faster and faster. The trucks pulled over, 600 metres short of the Battle School, and drivers were quick to drop the tailgates. There the DS commenced with their torment: 'Where's you OC?' He was easy to find; he had the biggest smile on his face. 'Ah, there you are. Sir, if you wouldn't mind, I want you off of these trucks as quickly as possible. We have a lot to do and little time to do it in.' I realised that these DS knew what they were talking about because they all had big sticks, just like I'd seen in the past, and I was beginning to wonder whether or not a big stick was a part of their 'complete equipment schedule' and actually issued to them.

The trucks disappeared out of view, out of the rainstorm that was to maintain its ferocity; a sorry sight to some of the sore heads that only now had started to clear of their alcohol induced trances. This wasn't any dream; this was the twilight zone.

Section commanders were seen coming back from their orders

group and information was passed on down the line to soldiers. 2IC's were then taken from the sections by platoon sergeants. Work details were now issued. Ammunition, rations, radio batteries, M30 grenades, trip flares, and an assortment of other equipment was passed around, most of which was shoved into packs: 'Hurry up you people. You have two minutes.' The DS were ever helpful.

'Hey, Nigel.'

'What?'

'You know where the camp is from here don't ya?'

'No.'

'You see that dirt road over there. Well, you follow that up and over that small rise. It's 600 metres away.'

'I don't understand.'

'You're damn right you don't. We're walking in the long way.'

'The long way.'

'Yeah.'

I continued to pack my newly issued equipment and stores, and looked Andrew in the face. 'But it's only a six kilometre walk in.'

'You didn't look at the map did you? It's as steep as you've ever seen,' and with that he started laughing.

The first thirty minutes or so was relatively easy but the ground soon took to a gradual rise, steeper and steeper it grew. It really wasn't the steepest I'd ever seen, or even that hard for that matter, but those that had had a hard night before, or who had taken care to avoid extra physical activities in their own time, found the going somewhat difficult. There was one guy in particular to my front that just couldn't keep up with the pace. He must have been at least thirty kilograms overweight and not used to such activity. He was the company clerk. What did they do, give him a typewriter to carry in his pack? He looked like he was going to drop dead at any minute, gasping for air the way he was. Guys were ordered to push from the rear, holding him up by the pack he wore, to literally take turns in assisting him up the rise. I just prayed that he didn't fart when it was my time to push him from the rear, and when it was my turn I made sure I kept my mouth closed so I wouldn't get any fart fumes in it.

The Australian issue pack that we carried on our backs was as small as a carton of beer; big enough for a sleeping bag, two days' worth of rations, shaving kit, spare sock, a spare set of work clothes and something warm to wear at night. But now with the additional assortment of equipment issued via the DS they weighed a tonne, much of it strapped on the outside of the pack in sandbags.

The DS certainly knew how to weigh soldiers down. I could remember my first ever exercise with the BN in 1981. Back then our packs were so full of gear and busting at the seams that each man had to strap a sandbag full of equipment to the outside of his pack in order to carry the additional seven ration packs issued, simply because of 'because'. It was somewhat quite pathetic. Back then it was because of the resupply, but now it was because the DS were sadistic bastards.

Another twenty odd minutes of climbing saw an end to the steep gradient and a great relief as I could now open my mouth, and the ground levelled slightly before reaching a spur line, which led down and around to the rear of the camp, where we were to be based for the next two weeks.

And now for the commencement of training.

The accommodation for the course was five-star – compared to living in the field. Open windows, no doors, no heating or seats of any description. Like you'd imagine the waiting room for execution of a cow at an abattoir. There were two floors, several rooms to each. Some of these rooms were used for lessons, so sleeping in them was forbidden. All 30 of our platoon fit into the first room, taking up every possible centimetre of space. At least we were receiving field allowance for the two-week duration, that in itself should be enough for the purchase of another dozen beers in our favourite nightclub.

On a visit to the latrines – which consisted of four porcelain bowls, a urinal, and next door to that about half a dozen (bare essential) shower cubicles – I noticed a piece of graffiti on the back of one of the doors. It read: '22 days and no rain'. Some pogo transport driver, doing hell knows what in Tully, had gotten away without a drop of rain falling from the now covered sky. It was enough to make anyone sick. All I could do as I sat on the porcelain was listen to the rain hitting the tin roof above, no immediate relief in sight.

A voice was then suddenly heard in the background, yelling out for all to hear: 'Get your webbing and rifles, form up outside; two minutes!'

So the jungle training had definitely commenced, no less than two nights a week of which were to be spent in ambush, for anything up to five hours duration – and that bloody rain.

Ambush – the DS loved them

The Dalmatian came sniffing around again just on last light. Every time we lay in ambush the dog was there. I didn't know which of the DS owned him, but we all hated him. There we lie in the pouring rain. A rustle was heard. That damn dog was sniffing around. He would go up quite casually to a soldier lying silently in wait for the enemy, cock its leg, and urinate over him, steam rising through the jungle vines. Every ambush was the same, with at least one soldier being pissed on. Of course, if you moved or said anything then the DS was there to leap down your throat in an attempt to pull out your damn larynx. The dog knew this and so always went about his business with a smile, his tail held high in dominance; he knew what he was doing.

The nights here were the worst. You could never see a thing, ever. Even when the stars were out you couldn't see anything – so we were told – due to the thickness of the canopy above. But I didn't recall seeing any stars that trip, I couldn't even see the rain cloud. And the rain was never accompanied by wind; it just fell, hour after hour after hour.

Night harbour

Whenever a night harbour was set up, perimeter cord would be placed around the position from pit to pit. All you had to do when finding a relief for a gun picket was to follow the cord around the perimeter. Remembering what the terrain had looked like by day and picturing this in your mind, or by tying knots in the perimeter cord, you could almost always find where you were going. The only problem being was the soldier you were going to wake up.

'Pssssst. I know you're there somewhere, Wayne. It's your picket.' The soldier would usually be awake but praying that you'd move on your way to leave him alone. 'Wayne.' A light whisper. 'Pssssst.'

'Shut up down there!'

Bloody DS.

A good trick to employ when getting back at someone was to walk past his hutchie spot just before nightfall with a tube of condensed milk or jam from the ration pack, and squirt this around his sleeping area; it would bring rats in from everywhere. But even without this tempt of ingenuity the rats would search you out eventually. Many soldiers would wake in the morning to find that a hole had been gnawed through their canvas pack, the shortbread biscuits stolen from the rations within.

We were half way through the trip when I was confronted by one of these ever-hungry rodents of the bush.

I searched for the button of my watch and from within my sleeping bag sought the time. 0130hrs. I was on picket from 0230hrs till 0550hrs (reveille).

What was it that had woken me? Why, the rain. It had stopped, just the occasional splatter of a few drops from the branches above falling onto my hutchie. I turned onto my back and closed my eyes once again.

Shit! I woke with a jolt. What was that? Something was near my pack.

I slowly removed my hand from within my sleeping bag and

waited.

My pack was at my head, half of which was lying in the jungle, exposed to the elements. Better it got wet than me: I didn't like sleeping with mud in my ear. The noise came again. I could only imagine what it was, a tiny rodent trying to gnaw its way through my pack. Well, the bastard wasn't going to get my rations. I waited in ambush, and as the next sound of scratching came to my ears I lashed back with a clenched fist, hitting something hard and fury. Jesus Christ! It was huge. I decided then and there that I no longer wanted my biscuits, and that if the rodent wanted them so badly then he was welcome to them.

Then it started to rain as before.

And with the rain came the leeches; and as it was always raining... say no more. The next day, during the normal running of morning routine, Peter Sheer decided he needed to visit the centre of the platoon position in order to see the platoon sergeant. 'What's up, Private Sheer?'

'I got a problem Sarge. I need to see the doc.'

'Can't it wait? The trucks are picking us up at midday.'

'Not really, Sarge, no,' and with that he pulled his trousers down. A leech had crawled up his urinary tract. He received all the sympathy in the world from platoon headquarters after that, and the remainder of the platoon received a good hearty laugh at his misfortune.

NO. We truly loved Tully. No digging you see. But what time was saved through not digging holes in the ground was quickly used up trying to keep the weapons free of rust. The damn SLR was always a problem to look after in the field.

Three cleans a day whilst in a field environment, and the occasional maintenance during a five-minute break in a patrol, would still not prevent the build-up of rust. The SLR must have been the worst weapon in the world for this; a genuine rust-magnet. Thank God we didn't all have to carry the M60. But section scouts had it best, for the M16 (an automatic armalite) very rarely rusted.

It didn't happen very often, but occasionally a soldier would approach the platoon sergeant with his weapon in hand, pull-through dangling from the flash suppressor (the open end of the rifle barrel). Another barrel jammed by some fool trying to force a too large-a piece of cleaning flannelette through his weapon.

Magazines were another important issue to contend with, in particular when returning back to the five-star accommodation of Tully.

The 2IC (a captain) of Tully sprang another surprise inspection on all of the soldiers' equipment, to ensure that everything was serviceable. Without fail he would always find something wrong with just about everyone in the platoon.

We were formed up in three ranks when the 2IC approached.

The 2IC picked up one of my magazines and peered inside. 'What's this?'

I had to maintain a positive upper hand, but had none. 'I don't know sir.'

'It's shit; what is it?'

I looked him in the eye. 'Shit sir.'

He picked up another. 'And what about this one?'

What could I say: 'Errrrr— that's shit too, sir.'

He snapped abruptly. 'No it's not. It's bloody dirt and rust.' He then proceeded with the inspection, to find someone else to chew out. Even to this day I have trouble distinguishing the difference between shit, and dirt and rust.

The obstacle course was another experience. It had to be completed in ten minutes, and if it wasn't, then you had to do it again and again until you achieved the time required. The section I was in had one downfall in the form of one rotund. For an infantry soldier he was fat, and lazy, fattest man in the company, apart from the company clerk. There simply was no excuse for someone, anyone, whether in the infantry or not, to be overweight – unless for medical reasons. More than 90 percent of cases concerning obesity can easily be put down as sheer laziness; after all, no one forces people to put food in their mouth, unless you're trying to eat your biscuits before the sun goes down at night to prevent the rats from making a visit upon your pack.

Due to his being overweight the section had the pleasure of attempting the obstacle course three times in the same afternoon before we could complete the task within the time frame laid down. We always seemed to be 30 seconds over time.

On the third attempt we dragged him, pushed him, and literally carried him over the obstacles to finish in time.

He ran up towards the ten foot wall and fell upon it, his arms stretched upwards. He was too tired to stand on his toes so he needed some friendly persuasion – I think I saw someone accidently smack in the face. Two men then bent down and lifted him by the feet. His fingers reached for the top but he again fell short of helping us out by trying to pull himself up, and he decided, then and there, that he was completely exhausted, and he needed to allow the two men atop the wall to reach down before lifting him up and over – I think I saw an elbow accidently slip and knock him in the mouth, but I might have had some of that Tully, 2IC shit-in-my-eye.

We were always helpful and tried our best to persuade him to try harder. We were always thinking of our mates.

We were given a tick in the box, but I still believe that we had failed to complete it in the time required, but because of the combined section effort we had been given a pass by the DS.

The fat guy was kicked out of the army two years later with a friend, for harbouring more than 40 stolen M26 grenades and 1,200 rounds of M60 link; he was never seen again after that.

One of the obstacles on the course at Tully was a set of horizontal monkey bars that had to be crossed by the challenging soldier in one of two ways, either going underneath, swinging from rung to rung, or crawling over the top. Now due to the fact that it was wet, and everyone was drenched to the bone, the bars were found to be quite slippery. Due to this reason, most went over the top. Mick Wakelin was one of these soldiers.

During rehearsals all were met with one of the funniest things seen all trip. As Mick came crawling over the top of the obstacle, his 'manhood' fell from its quarters within his unbuttoned fly, and as he proceeded across the bars, his 'manhood' hit every single rung. He was well gifted in that region of the anatomy.

The last night in the field before our return to Brisbane was one of my most sleepless. During stand-to that particular day, and as the sun was disappearing once again, the man who shared a pit with me whispered: 'Don't move.'

'What… what is it?'

A second later and he let out a quick sigh of relief. 'Ah; it's okay now.'

'What is?'

'Ah, nothing. Just a sort of fist-sized spider sitting on your back.'

'Where'd it go?'

He pointed: 'Just over there somewhere.'

I had a good look around at the base of the tree next to which we were lying behind, near where the spider had supposedly vanished. It was full of large holes, all of which disappeared into depths of darkness, and each was covered in cobwebs.

'I don't fancy sleeping here the night.' There was never any hint to his bending-of the-truth, so I took it all as gospel. In Shoalwater Bay blokes used to dig up bird spiders from time to time, but we were a long way from there at present.

But time flies when you're having fun, and having fist-sized spiders running freely across your back is almost as fun as wearing a spider on your face.

But it wasn't long before the two-week trip was over with and all were exuberant about seeing the coaches turn up. No time was wasted in stowing gear below the coaches and then clambering aboard for a window seat. This was by far better than travelling in trucks.

As we hit the main road and passed what had been our drop-off point some fourteen days earlier, we could see B Coy. They were packing their packs full of rations, ammunition and other equipment. Section commanders were receiving orders and DS were yelling out commands, each and every person preparing himself for the six-kilometre walk into Tully. All A Coy could do was point and laugh.

And as we drove off I think someone flashed a browneye.

Tobruk
June, 1983

Although the exercises of 1982 were repeated again this year, Diamond Dollar did come about a small change. Movement to SWBTA was by way of the Tobruk, Australia's troop carrying vessel. Many hated the trip but others absolutely loved it.

Seasickness seemed to be a very small problem, with most going unscathed and free of sickness. It could also be said that the battalion was lucky that no individual suffered from claustrophobia. I couldn't recall the exact amount of equipment, or numbers to personnel that this seafaring vessel was capable of carrying, but two battalions housed in dog boxes was something of a sound estimate. There were also ten tanks below deck, and sixty odd vehicles, of all descriptions, above. If there was a human equivalent to the RSPCA then the army would have been under fire from all quarters.

It was a ship filled with sleeping quarters [berths] and little else. The chow area only seated a small portion of those on board, but had a system of rotation and displayed all timings for all to see, eg; lunch was rostered for up to five or six sessions, taken between 1100hrs and 1400hrs.

The bunks were just large enough to sleep upon, with legs pulled up slightly, every cubicle, to every room/wall, housing soldiers in areas not much bigger than coffins. When taking into consideration our packs, webbing and weapons, it meant that no room whatsoever was available to move around in. If there were ever a case where we needed to abandon ship, well... most men would have to try and tuck their heads between their legs and kiss their arse goodbye... but for lack of room wouldn't be able to bend over: It would have been easier to kiss somebody else's arse goodbye, a true haven for any homosexual, and I suspected we had a few of those in our midst, but nothing could be proven.

A small canteen did exist on board and was open for business for an hour at lunch, and for several more after dinner. Here you could buy cigarettes, chocolates and soft drinks, all tax-free; and for the homosexuals, lollipops to curl their tongues around.

Beer was 25 cents a can and the distribution of such worked out to a plan. At 1800hrs, if you wanted your ration of two beers per man, then you reported below deck to one of the storage areas. 'Come on fellahs. Keep the bloody noise down. Form a single file. That's it.'

'I didn't think you were a drinker, Scott,' said one man.

'I'm not. Andy saw me earlier on. I'm getting my share for him. What about you?'

'Bloody platoon sergeant nabbed me. He said I was too sick to drink on account that I missed out on working in the heads this morning. Had to report to sick bay with a crook gut.'

'You seasick?'

'No. I just didn't want to work in the heads. I don't swab shit for no man. I've estimated that the platoon sergeant got six non-drinkers earlier on today. That's twelve bloody beers.'

'Andy got seven of the bastards.'

The platoon sergeant gave two raffle tickets to each man as he approached. 'Sign here. Here are your two tickets, Private Smith.'

'Thanks, Sarge.' And once Smith had signed for them, handed them back to the platoon sergeant. 'Enjoy.'

And Scott was next. 'Didn't think you drank, Private Wheelan.'

'Thought I'd have a couple, Sarge. Didn't want to let the team down,' and the cans would be ceremoniously handed over to one of the other hands.

Who ever said you couldn't get pissed whilst on the Tobruk, was absurdly incorrect. Cards were a favourite pastime for some. With four packets of tax-free cigarettes in hand, a game of pontoon would commence. For six hours or more they would play, and when one player was finished, another quickly took his place. Malcolm Peters departed with a smile on his face; five packets up.

'That pays double.'

'No it don't.'

'Where I come from it does.'

'It pays triple in Melbourne.'

'Who asked you, idiot? I said at the start we weren't playing that bloody rule.'

'You're just making the rules up as you go along,' and suddenly the alarm bell went off. 'Shit!' Time for battle stations drill. What were the chances, the one and only drill for the entire trip, and it had to happen when I was trying for a five-card trick. So three days was more than enough experience for all. Roller coasting waves wasn't everybody's forte. But with the lack of water arrived the expedient digging of shellscrapes. APC doctrine was maintained, and as each stop was only a short one – but longer than that required for a five-minute durry (Cigarette) – shellscrapes were a desired and called for principal of nature, a real necessity if life was to be maintained – due to the fact that the enemy carried 60mm mortars. The area of operations was praised however, for one thing, if not another, for digging a shellscrape took as little as 15 minutes in the sandy soil; venturing inland a few days later proved to be much harder on our hands. A count of seven shell scrapes in one day was our best. One of the niceties of working with APC support was that you certainly got around.

I had been promoted to section scout for the trip and absolutely adored the opportunity to carry out all tasks assigned to the job; early morning clearing patrols, reconnaissance duties, and other short excursions into the bush when accompanying the platoon commander on his appraisals for firm base and ambush position. Due to my present duties I also had to be paired off with the section commander whilst in a harbour position, whether it be night or day, during any type of defensive activity; except the old you-beaut contact drill, when contact with the enemy turned fruitful, and the scouts first job was to return fire into the enemy and/or the enemies likely firing position.

The section commander in my case was a big thug, and when a digger himself was reported to have started fights for the promise of a schooner. 'How come you Poms are always marrying blacks?' he asked.

'I say what?'

A burst of 'live' machine gun fire cracked over our heads.

'You Poms are always marrying blacks aren't ya? Your countries full of the bastards. The Indians and all of them Arabs, and such.'

A burst of fire again ripped through the air.

I gave him a strong look of protest and then changed my look to a sarcastic grin. The section commander had just been married to a Thai, although I certainly wouldn't classify them as black. And by all standards, I was nowhere near as racist as some of the others in the platoon.

'Don't say it, Nigel. I'll drop ya like a bag of shit.'

Machine gun fire.

'I wasn't dreaming of it,' I replied, and before I knew it a message had arrived for the section commanders to report to the platoon commander, and 2ICs to the platoon sergeant. Another opportunity for the elements of PHQ to share in a brew.

Machine gun fire.

A warning order accompanied the runner's news. The section commander gave this to me. 'Go read this out to each of the pits.' Machine gun fire. 'I shouldn't be more than twenty minutes,' or when the brews have been drunk.

He was back sooner than expected, along with the section 2IC, who started without haste to give each soldier his work details for the coming assault. Looks like the corporals didn't get to wet-their-whistle after all. By the time the 2IC had finished with his tasking all were seated on the ground, looking out periodically towards the platoons' killing ground, awaiting orders. This 'glancing out' was a force of habit more than anything else, and wasn't really necessary during this exercise, for the assault to come was of the live fire variety – no 'flesh and blood' enemy existed.

Machine gun fire continued throughout – unopposed friendly fire.

'Listen up, men, someone's stuffed up again and forgot the digger at the bottom – as usual.' The normal practice or teaching was for the hierarchy to ensure that time was allowed for all members of the assaulting force to receive proper orders. This allowed ample exposure to administration time for allocation and carrying out of tasks, for the preparation of ammunition and other essential stores. This very rarely happened. The apparent reason in this case was due to the fact that safety staff had to be fully briefed and pioneer platoon fully rehearsed – in respect to bangalore torpedoes that had to be positioned. The section now had ladders to make, to which we would climb over enemy wire obstacles, and later put them to good use as litters for the carrying of the dead and wounded. The Battalion live fire attack did go well however. Two rifle companies up and one in depth.

We all approached the enemy position with the invaluable Vickers machine guns continuing with their fire support. They'd been firing for ten solid hours now, straight over our heads, through the night and into the day. The CO at the time wanted this exercise to portray all in its most realistic quality. It was then that I saw something quite remarkable. A DS was putting his stick to good use, brushing aside a man's rifle as his live ammunition was being fired, the rifle pointing dangerously close to another man in the distance. What would they think of next? This was initiative at its best. And here I was, thinking that DS really stood for 'Dip-Shit' or 'Dopey Sergeant'.

The pioneers moved forward and laid their bangalore torpedoes, blowing gaps in the wire in the hope of gaining quicker penetration of the enemy fortification, as opposed to climbing the ladders we'd made. Once again we'd wasted time and resources to manufacture something for no good reason. Those bastards! They knew we weren't going to be using the ladders; not for climbing, nor for carrying wounded.

The bangalores would prevent us from being drawn into enemy firing lanes, or becoming bogged down, and would help us maintain a little conformity to the coming assault. And there was at least one thing that could be said about these figure-eleven targets; as enemy, they certainly knew how to stand their ground.

The assault itself went as many others, and that was that for the exercise; the following day would see an evacuation back to Brisbane; oh, but one thing remained. The battalion had to form up in an extended line and go back over the ground we had just crossed, to pick up every piece of brass from expended ammunition as was humanly possible. A minimum of 75% had to be returned to the manufacturer for recycling. It's too bad that 75% of the trees we'd chopped down for the ladders couldn't be replaced.

Malaysia
December, 1983

All members of the company clambered aboard the aircraft with great anticipation for that which lay ahead, arriving at the RAAF air base in Butterworth Malaysia a little before 2000hrs on the 29th NOV with pockets filled to the brim with condoms. Tasks met during this trip seemed to be somewhat belittling to most of the members of the rifle company, from the hierarchy, right down to the administrational staff. Mind you, if anything was to go astray, be blown up, or someone was killed, then look out; somebody's arse was going to end up in a sling for a long, bloody time.

So the task ahead was that of security, a job that had been maintained by the infantry since Australia's arrival some time back when Humphrey Bogart's Great, Great Grandfather was still in diapers and had a snotty nose.

An early rise on the first morning saw the company move into its accommodation, our home for the next three months. The day was surprisingly short with all of the tasks and speeches being met by the troops, those in front nodding their heads periodically and those towards the rear shaking off yawn after yawn. The Malay way of life, customs, and 101 rules and regulations, were spilled out at a hundred miles an hour for the soldier's complete absorption of what life was like in this country. Most ignored this ritual. 'Young men' brought up in a white man's environment normally did shun anything which was alien to them, but an understanding would slowly come about – with the passing of time. But even politicians of years' experience sometimes found a bad word for immigrants (please explain); it all stems from what we are taught at a younger age, regardless of whether we were intelligent or simply sold fish and chips, or what we might have been exposed to at times of hardship: was selling fish and chips hard? Australia itself was a great nation that understands the fundamentals of a multinational society, and a rifleman coming out of his years of adolescence needs a bit of breathing space in order to grasp that same understanding.

Protection of the Australian air base was the obvious priority, but there was no way in which any of us was going to miss out on this opportunity for a free holiday and a little cuddle. But with this opportunity at hand also came abundant time to train, for without the battalion breathing down our backs, every minute of the day seemed to be stolen by the platoon and company headquarters elements in order for them to train their soldiers as they believed best suited the current situation. So training did start in earnest, but at times infantry training seemed to be nothing more than glorified. We all felt a bit like a train driver, each of us training to do a job, but never getting to fulfil; and the older soldiers were even worse off, for rust was being to show on the old-horses of the Coy. So even at this early stage of my career, I was thinking of whether or not I was ever going to get the opportunity to serve overseas; other than what was currently being experienced.

The system for duty in Malaysia was quite simple. The company consisted of three platoons and each platoon had three rifle sections. Each platoon would take on full responsibilities for the task of security for three days [again that number three] whilst the other platoons conducted training, and took time to visit other areas of this wonderful country when time was permitted. For example; a visit to Pulada, a live firing range: Whilst we were here we were going to take full advantage of the ammunition allocation to which the company was receiving, and Pulada was one of the greatest chances we had to blow-away live ammo. We were in the infantry, firing weapons was our bread-n-butter, and to a man of experience cleaning weapons no harder than cleaning a toaster.

The three tasks assigned to a platoon on roster were very straightforward. One section maintained a rove-and-picket, which was a 'foot' mobile patrol around the living quarters and rifle company armoury; another section on QRF, designed for immediate call out to any part of the air base from the QRF guard room; and finally, a section on stand-by, responsible for replacing the QRF within minutes, if the QRF was called out to respond to insurgence. The third section (replacing the QRF) would then prepare for possible reinforced call-out, or call out of their own to a secondary location. On call out the rove-and-picket would continue with their task whilst the original QRF were carrying out their task, speeding around the airfield, in an open-air truck, in order to cordon off the supposed infiltrated area.

Each section task also had numerous pages of Standing Orders that had to be read and understood by the persons conducting any of the duties above. No matter how many times we'd been read the orders before, all were to be read again next time we mounted duty, and our signatures had to be put to paper indicating that we understood those orders. Live ammunition was carried by us; we weren't on Active Service but at any time of day or night we could be called upon to load live ammunition into weapons and deal with any situation which presented itself to us.

The members of the QRF carried live ammunition in magazines; the tops of these were secured with black tape for identification purposes and as prevention against accidental feeding of ammunition into the chamber of the weapons we were assigned, at a time when such hostility wasn't required. Magazines were then placed into basic pouches, to be carried on our person during call out. Call outs 'rehearsals' were conducted twice a night, one before midnight and one after.

On call out – which was initiated by the battalion orderly sergeant – the QRF would leap like startled Gazelles onto the back of the truck with webbing and rife. (Webbing during the trip consisted of a bum pack, ammunition pouches, water bottles and other varying necessities that each individual saw fit to carry, or by which had been laid down by platoon/section SOPs. Needless to say, if you were sitting on the toilet and halfway through your business, you would have to grab whatever you were 'doing' and snap it off, finishing the task at hand at a later date. The allocated driver would then speed off to the area of concern. If you didn't have time to clamber aboard, then you held on for dear life as your mates tried to pull you over the tailgate, another bend in one of the many roads being attacked with savage screeching of tires and griping of gears. All of this was conducted to the aggressive tone of the section commander – sitting next to the driver – whose only words of comradeship were: 'Step on it, arsehole, or I'll drop ya like a bag of shit!'

Once at the destination all would de-bus the truck and race off to secure – for example – each corner to the building of concern (to cordon off the premises of all entry or exit as indicated by the section commander). The section's entry into any of the buildings was not permitted – unless ordered by a higher authority.

Once the area was secure, the section would await the arrival of the local Malaysia Military Police – MP. This was followed by a routine of nationality-meets-nationality, heads being nodded in friendly gesture, and the call out being given the all clear for immediate stand-down of the section on the ground. The section would then return at a leisurely pace back to the QRF room where the toilet was once again employed and your business continued.

Only one other duty was maintained 24hrs a day, seven days a week. There was a small holding pen – concrete shed/bunker – that had been transformed into an armoury, in which all of the company's weapons were stored, some 50 metres from the QRF room. It was fitted with a bed, shower and toilet. A member of the company would be locked up inside this small dwelling to watch over the weapons during the course of his duty. All meals were brought to him by the QRF and this was also the only time in which the cell doors were opened – apart from when relieved of duty each morning. Other occasions for which the doors were opened were in the case of a medical emergency, fire, or when weapons were required by any member/s of the company for training purposes. When this occurred, the weapons register was filled out and the said article/s signed for.

The cell wasn't much more than a cement block with vertical bars set at the front – which also formed the door to the armoury. It wasn't uncommon to have drunken mates return home in the early hours of the morning, waking this guy up, and then dropping stink bombs into the cell. There was no escape from this as opening the cell door was against orders, and such a breach of orders wasn't to be contemplated. You might imagine a tired and weary man with his head pushed up against the inside of the bars, his hands clutching hard his encumbrance, snarling at his mates as they laughed in their drunken stupor. But that was okay, because there was always a way to get back at the bastards; like waiting for them to get drunk when you were free of the cell and then shaving off one of their eyebrows, as shaving one was twice as wicked as shaving two. Some mornings you'd wake to see a man wearing a single bandaid above one of his eyes, on other occasions you'd see a man leant over a sink in the ablutions as he attempted to shave the other eyebrow so that the pathetic look was more evenly spread across his face. Vengeance was so sweet.

For a meal on the base it was best to catch the trucks shuttle-run which the company provided, as the distance to the mess was not a favourable one for walking, in particular when you were suffering from a hangover with a bandaid hanging over your eyebrow.

If you missed the trucks shuttle-run then a visit to the Chow Wallah was essential. Situated in the same building as the boozer, but with a wall separating the two, a short walk of 40 metres would be carried out for the purpose of purchasing cigarettes, soft drink, and a variety of other essentials – which included vegemite sandwiches.

An Indian fellow who'd worked on the air base for a good many years, ran the 'Chow Wallah's' store. Prices in his tiny shop were considerably cheap but money easily spent. His shop – for the use of a better word – was also christened by stink bombs whilst his family was inside. As the stink bombs were crushed under-foot, the door was pulled closed and held from the outside to prevent any escape. The stunt didn't go down too well with the CSM and others, and such activities ceased under the weighty threats of 30 days in the armoury given by the key figureheads from within the company; 'you are here as 'Ambassadors' of Australia'.

The Public
January, 1984

One of our favourite drinking establishments was the BC bar, the Butterworth Cafe, usually referred to as the Bat Cave – very cool in mid-December due to the ceiling fans and coolness of sweet beverage. It was situated not much more than a few hundred metres down the road from the front gate to the air base, but then again we were usually inebriated when attending this abode, so we lost two steps in three through staggering.

One of the young ladies here had some problem of sorts, whether it be that she didn't have a tongue or simply suffered a traumatic incident at some time in her life, she just couldn't use speech as a means of communication. The platoon's favourite of all section commanders soon arrived at a firm decision. 'I'll make her talk. Watch this,' and of course, meant no harm.

The ceiling fans were now to be employed as a crucial element to the man's plan of attack. The section commander came in from behind her and placed his hands around her thin waist, allowing support enough to lift her to the wrath of the spinning blades. Without haste her friendly neighbourhood pourer-of-beer came in from behind and started to punch the man in the back. He then let down the silent mute with nothing more than a chuckle escaping his lips. All the young lady could do was convey her thanks for his use of psychology against her infliction, expressing her thoughts by means of rapid hand movements, known in simple terms as obscene sign language, to which even the dumbest of grunts could understand.

Other fun activities could be found further afield.

It was just after 0200hrs when Stallone and I were making our way back towards the ferry, for the thirty-odd minute return trip across the bay, not a soul in sight. Now Stallone was branded the ex-heavy weight champion of an island not so far away, big and placid looking, and full of kindness.

Suddenly two females approached from a side street with smiles across their faces and offerings of sexual pleasure for only ten Ringgit.

Stallone took control and commenced negotiations.

He soon had the sexual pleasures down to two Ringgit each. With this he was more than pleased.

On accomplishing this my dark comrade pulled me aside and said: 'Hey, Nigel, watch this,' and thrust his hand under the skirt of one of the wenches before retracting it, himself stepping back a good two metres. For a fleeting moment I thought that he'd discovered a string hanging from the woman, but what he'd discovered hanging there instead was a penis. 'Bloody shims, Nigel!' A man with tits usually recognised by the Adam's apple, and at other times harder to spot: But I guess a penis in the hand isn't as easily mistaken as an Adam's apple to the eye. For a moment there I also saw the shim's eyes light up and a smile fall upon its face; 'it' must have thought that all its birthdays had come at once.

We were on our way in no time at all, being showered in threats of violence as we took off down the road, several trishaw drivers looked up and over towards us briefly before continuing on their way – what did they care for the antics of two Australians. Stallone could do nothing but laugh.

Not all soldiers in the platoon learnt from their lessons early on in the trip, and several of the much-much-older members of the company found themselves in quite a bit of embarrassment when in Singapore. But even now, the truth behind these stories will forever remain top secret.

Close Encounter
January, 1984

It was always suggested that no man proceed outside of the barracks area by himself for reasons of safety. But that was like telling a little boy that he couldn't have any candy until after dinner and then placing the candy jar in front of his face with the lid removed. Anyway, the Malaysians on the front gate certainly didn't regulate these rules and were more often than not seen to give us a hearty wave with a smile as we came and went as we desired.

So I weighed up the odds, Yep. Stuff it, I'd go.

So within no time at all I was on the ferry and approaching the docks of Penang, one hand in my pocket having a good scratch and the other on my wallet. The ramps were secured and off I stepped, straight into the throngs of trishaw drivers who all insisted that they were the cheapest for only two Ringgit.

I was suddenly grabbed on the arm and as I swung around a short guy wearing a scar across his face said: 'You come, me cheap. Two Ringgit anywhere you like go.' He wasn't intimidating at all, but I wouldn't want to have met the fellow who'd given him the scar.

'Why not,' I said. 'Just take me to the Hong Kong bar thanks.'

So I followed, and as we approached his trishaw, another man, but slightly older in appearance, tugged at my sleeve. 'Hong Kong bar, one Ringgit, very cheap; you come.'

'Bloody oath I will.'

As I clambered aboard his trishaw, a smile cascaded over my face in recognition of the windfall of luck I was having. Today was going to be a lucky day. I turned to look out towards my left as I sat upon the wooden seat, for no apparent reason, and as the driver of my urban convertible peddled off a silver blade could be seen to glint by way of the sun's rays. It was the other trishaw driver, obviously displeased with the loss of a potential customer, trying to stab me. I was fortunate to escape from serious injury, just in the nick of time. Yep. Today was my lucky day.

The trip was slow, the peddler of this contraption breathing in heavy gasps as though preparing to take his last. I could have walked faster. I don't know who was more inconvenienced; myself for the slow ride, or the trishaw driver for having to pull me along for a single Ringgit.

A doorway then caught my eye. People inside were sitting around seemingly waiting for something or someone. A mouse was then seen scurrying around the walls of the small room in which the people waited, and then another.

'Hey, what's that over there?'

'Is Doctor Lim's clinic. Not far now. Hong Kong bar come soon.' I had to presume the worst from the scene, that the doctor wasn't a veterinarian and that those seated in the waiting room weren't there for an animal show.

Later that same night I met up with some friends on the ferry back to the mainland. I soon departed company with them however and found myself someone more interesting to converse with. I don't know which was more interesting; the smile on her lovely face or the breasts popping out of her blouse.

Time travelled quickly and my Malay company departed. Once again I found myself alone and ready to disembark. The ferry was docking. Now, I was so drunk that I had somehow found myself below the main deck where vehicles normally made their way onto the ferry, but that didn't pose a problem, for I knew my way around.

'You. Hey!' I turned to see a stranger approach. 'You have cigarettes?' I was as drunk as a skunk, so I should have some somewhere. I padded my pockets and looked the stranger in the eye, rocking slightly upon my feet. He seemed armless enough and wore ragged clothes. Why not. 'Take the pack mate. Here. And the matches too.'

'You Aussie?'

'Yeah.'

'You go air base?'

'That's right.'

'My Brother is taxi driver. I tell him to take you for cheap.'

So I followed in earnest.

On reaching the taxi I found five men dressed in below standard dress. Normal enough. 'I need a taxi to the RAAF base,' I explained to all.

My newfound friend looked at me. 'No, you wait. I fix.'

He went to the side of one of the waiting men, and commenced his explanation, not quite audible enough for me to hear, and not spoken in English.

The man came back with the response, standing between our two parties, the now official interpreter. 'My Brother, he say ten Ringgit.'

'Bloody what? That's more than normal.'

'No. is cheap.'

'Piss off. I want me cigarettes back,' and with my hand held open I stepped closer, 'and my bloody matches.'

I was handed two cigarettes nervously and the taxi drivers shuffled in their places. 'I want more. I gave you a whole pack.'

'No. You go now. You walk.'

I stepped closer still, and as I looked out to the side a further twenty odd taxi drivers were seen to come out from nowhere.

'Nigel!' I stopped and turned about. 'Get your arse over here now. And don't bloody run.' My mates from the top deck. 'Time to go home.'

'But that bastards got my durries.'

'You can have some of mine.'

Two close calls in one day. It 'was' my lucky day.

On reflection I think that if the shoe was on the other foot, and places and countries were traded, in this given situation, that the group of Australians would have kicked the hell out of the Malay. So I never really did have a bad thought against the man and his taxi-driver friends. They were far less racist than most of us.

The Bunny Bar
January, 1984

One of the more highly classed bars of town in which we sometimes frequented, and found ourselves admiring, was an upstairs palace known exclusively as the Bunny Bar. Ladies of the night – and day – could be found here, more pricey than normal, but rather gorgeous – or so we were led to believe. Only two entrances existed to the Bunny

Bar, one was a small elevator, the other was a narrow staircase.

The whole platoon had managed to find its way here; all except the boss, platoon sergeant, five non-drinkers, and the boxer Stallone.

I turned to one of the older guys, Smithy. 'Where are all the whores, mate? Doesn't seem to be any around.'

He turned on his stool. 'See that door over there with those two big bloody gorilla type bouncers?'

'Biggest guys I've seen in this country.'

'Well, behind that snot-blowing door are the whores. All ready and waiting. All you have to do is buy them a drink and the negotiating starts. You have to be pretty nifty with your mouth to get a good price in there, I tell you that for nothing.'

'You want to go in then, Smithy, Just you and me? I'd go myself only I'm a bit pissed.'

'Why not.' And with that we entered the insalubrious hindquarters.

We soon found ourselves a seat and had no sooner ordered our drinks when two females came along and sat down beside us – by-far more beautiful, characteristically cheerful, and open minded, then any Australian-born counterpart, but then again, I guess they had to be, for this country was so full of whores that you couldn't walk into a bar without knocking one over.

My smile soon dissipated however when I received my change from the first round of drinks, looking up at the waitress with a gleam of murderous intent. Jesus Christ. No wonder all of the boys only came to the Bunny Bar to drink in the other lounge. This backroom business was a rip off – though still cheap by Australian standards.

'I think you might have been right, Smithy. If this place was anything to go by the price of these two piss-ant drinks of ours, then we're in trouble.' I turned my head to the young female that sat beside me and tried a smile. 'How much, sweetie?'

Her lips parted sexually with a starting price, when a commotion was heard to rise from the main area of the bar.

Smithy was already at the door. 'Hey, Nigel. The boys are leaving for the next bar. Let's get the hell out of here.'

'Right with you mate,' I said and turned to the others at our table. 'See you ladies later.'

We joined our comrades in arms at the elevator that was designed for 14 persons, the 22nd man pushing from the rear as he too, stepped into the box. 'Get in boys.' A bouncer grabbed the last man by his arm. Big mistake. The section commander turned on his heels and bang, punched him hard; smack in the centre of the head. 'Piss off.'

The door closed, the platoon descended in the elevator, and the doors opened. We had missed the ground level by three feet – too much weight. One by one we now climbed out as the manager of the hotel pulled at his hair, screaming obscenities in a language none understood, and then more in broken English, looking much like the Malay answer to Basil Fawlty.

The following morning, and for some strange reason, we found that we'd been banned from going to the Bunny Bar again during our stay in the country. From that day on, all visits were cut to just a few, and on entry we would inform the management that we were RAAF, and that we hated the AJs to death – ID was rarely asked for. They too had to enforce their rules and regulations by standing behind their ban, but on the same token they needed customers for the lovely ladies in the adjoining room. It would seem that our wallets were able to negotiate practically anything.

New Year's Eve - Pulada
1983 – 1984

Just a few days after our return from Thailand, we were packing our field gear in preparation for Pulada. It wasn't what you'd call a bush trip; just 'a part thereof'.

Most of the nights were to be spent in the comforts of a featureless building that was large enough to take all 30 members of the platoon. The only comforts of home were what each individual carried in his pack. Not even cots were issued, an item used extensively during non-tactical deployments into the field, usually seen in most BHQ and rear echelon areas during large scale exercises, where the distance between those elements, and the minor infantry call signs, was anything from ten kilometres to one hundred. Kangaroo exercises in the late eighties were a prime example of this. Never let it be said that a pogo had it hard.

And as promised, there was a shower block with sinks, and discoloured walls where the mirrors had been smashed years before and removed, no doubt, by the few residents who lived in these parts. It was a fine thing to have if you didn't mind putting up with cold water and scorpions. You could almost guarantee that death would be around the corner if bit by one of those little bastards, not like the Australian cousin which just made you a little queasy.

Early mornings and nights were repetitious, brought on by the fact that there was no lighting available for late night card games or the reading of novels and stick books. New Year's Eve here was one for the memory, something never to be forgotten. On this occasion the coming of the New Year would be seen from the comfort of an all-night ambush.

We'd returned from the ranges early for preparation of the ambush to come; cleaning weapons, last nap, last feed, camouflage those faces, check magazines and get ready your warm weather gear. Mossy repellent on, stretcher tops packed in case of casavac, orders groups and rehearsal sessions. Carry out preparation of claymores, trip flares, early warning devices; test fire machine guns, M16s, SLRs and pack signal flares. Prepare gun stakes, night sight devices, and comms-cord; have your last cigarette, last piss and shit and prepare to move. That was the icing on the cake, for a reconnaissance was needed as well as a safety DS brief, a necessity for all live fire activities, and that's exactly what this was. Nothing we'd never carried out before.

After the ambush was initiated all went through the procedures – tactically mind you – of reinitiating, searching for the enemy, taking of POWs and medical treatment to wounds sustained. Then came the withdrawal to the firm base and the move from the firm base back to the barracks with the cold water and scorpions. Time for a quick shave and onto the trucks; we were going to the anti tank range for the firing of the 84mm Carl Gustaf. It was here that one of the biggest flukes ever was performed. A guy named Pugsy achieved a headshot with the weapon from over 550 metres. Definitely more arse than class.

The best thing of all however, was what lay ahead of the platoon; for at the fortnights end was a three-day trip to Singapore. Good byyyye ambush.

Singapore
January, 1984

The three days in Singapore was hectic to say the least. Every man seemed to do nothing more than race around in an effort to see as much as humanly possible. This certainly didn't interfere with our heavy consumption of the amber nectar. You may imagine a taxi being driven down the main road of the city, a few heads sticking out of the windows, and with can in hand all you can hear is, 'come on, driver; hurry up, hurry up; next bar, next bar. I've seen this bloody road before – ah look. Looks like a museum or something – step on the bloody thing, driver; I'm nearly empty'.

Shopping in Singapore took care of most wages, with many of the soldiers being caught surprised that none had come across a Mickey Mouse Rolex. Bugis Street saw to what cash remained. All the good looking females were her, and all were shims as well – what a waste and a shame – most with distinguishing voices which were deeper than any of those in the platoon, Adams' apples bobbing up and down as they spoke. You should have seen the look on the CSM's face as a shim sat down either side of him – he didn't know which way to look;

left, right, or down at the two hands that were making a move towards his fly.

During the first two nights in Singapore the precedent was set. All would congregate in Bugis Street as though to the call of nature and led by the star that brought the three wise men to Bethlehem. A hangout was formed at the crossroad, smack in the centre of the two streets that formed a huge café-type area with seating and tables, where all would eat and drink like it was going out of fashion. Even late at night the kitchens could be seen smoking away, cooking rice dishes to fulfil our needs, and those of any tourists, each of the chefs seemingly cowering under the onslaught of flies.

Beer and spirits were downed one after the other, everyone was laughing and having a great time. It made for a late night and even later rise.

I thankfully never made the third night to this congregation. The mate I was shacked up with had made a reverse charge call back to Australia from his hotel room against all advice. I'd informed him to check with reception as to cost, but no. The extent of damage ended up costing me all I had. Someone had to bail the guy out.

Anyway; that night down on the legend hangout came screams of blistering pain and mayhem. For whatever reason unbeknown to the Australians, but caused by mischievous goings on, the stall holders and residents from around commenced a reign of terror with iron bars, wooden bats, and buckets of boiling water. A few of the platoon were taken to hospital, but nothing too serious. Bugis Street was closed down and we holidaymakers were moved by C130 back to Butterworth with hangovers as big as our ego's.

It stands to mention that American and British sailors were also present on Bugis Street during the clash of the titans. During this battle it was the yanks that turned tail and fled, leaving the Poms and Aussies to conduct a fighting withdrawal with honour. Damn Yanks; always late to enter a fight and always eager to leave one, and anyone claiming them to be the best soldiers in the world should be ashamed for the lie: if anything they are one of the worst.

Rogue
February, 1984

Of the three months in Malaysia, all the platoon could muster in respect to days in the field – in a tactical environment – was three (although the trip was initially planned for seven). The OC at the time explained why. Simply put, the first exercise area to which they were looking at was under the constant harassment of guerrilla activities, and the second was flooded by way of natural disaster. The third choice was accepted, although deferred for several days. You can imagine the images going through my mind when he said 'guerrilla'. I thought that there were silverbacks thrashing through the scrub and beating their chests; it took me a while to realise he was referring to rebels.

Finally however we headed off.

The platoon was tactical from the moment we set foot on the soil, pushing out into a defendable position, whilst a work-party of five grabbed packs from the trucks, the trucks in turn took off down the road and vanished from sight at the same instant that the rain commenced to fall. The enemy (a small group of three soldiers from the company) had been given map coordinates. The platoon was now to search them out and attack their position. To move without being seen – to aid in our approach – a nearby creek-line was used to our advantage. The foliage was thick for a good fifty metres either side of the approach. The map also showed the entire area of operations as a low depression, which was why the weather had almost claimed this area as a victim of flood. So here we were, up to our waists in stagnant water, and being showered upon from the thickening clouds above. The move forward came to a stop. Had the scout seen the enemy? No; just a deadly snake taking a swim across the front of the scout's path. 'Okay, keep moving. It's okay, if it bites you'll be taken to hospital; don't worry,' said one of the officers. That bastard; who did he think he was, my mother?

The third day in semi-jungle had drawn to a close and the platoon was preparing for night routine when the platoon sig came down to my pit. 'Your 2IC wants me to tell you that you're on picket first. You and me.'

'How come you're with us?'

'I'm not really tired and your section's got the least number of blokes.' An extremely light whistle was heard. The signaller turned to receive the stand-down signal from the scout. We both picked ourselves up and headed over to the machine gun, to find mud upon mud around our ankles. We sat down, the rain continuing to fall. I could feel the mud in the crack of my arse so quickly moved over a foot and found a sharp rock to sit on instead.

'Anyway, Nigel,' he continued as the look of discomfort faded from my face, 'there's a rogue elephant loose.'

We watched our arcs continuously, although very little could be seen in the dark of the jungle. Ears and other senses played an important role here. I quite honestly thought that after many years of experience that there was truth behind the sixth sense, although I would only experience it a dozen times or so during my 16 year career. Decisions had been made on such instincts, and usually for the better. But here is the reality: ie; six billion people in the world, each one experiences four dreams per night, that's 24 billion dreams each day, and even if only 0.01 percent of those dreams were to come true then that would be… ah…. Come on grunt… quite a lot. Coincidences are no different. Is there truth behind the sixth sense, behind the saying 'I knew that was going to happen, I had a dream last night'. Sorry, no; just a dream; just chance, simple luck.

'A bloody what?' I whispered. Did he say road or vogue? I'd heard of Vogue Magazine, but never a vogue elephant, but I could see how it would be on the 'road'.

'A rogue elephant. It broke loose from its chains earlier on today. It was being used in a chain gang just up the road a bit.'

'Bullshit,' I said. Why would it be in a chain gang, come on! Did it commit a crime or something?

'No; fair dinkum.'

'I don't believe you.'

'It's the bloody truth, Nigel; I'm telling ya straight. The enemy group were brought in through another section's gun fifteen minutes ago because of the danger.'

'How come no one's said anything to me about it?'

'I'm telling you now. I was told to pass it on as I was coming down to see you.' So I turned my head to face the front once again, the beauty of the night taking control, although the rain still fell, insects giving eternal resonance to the surroundings as they always did, no matter what jungle we happen to be in – even in the openness of the training area of Shoalwater Bay. Then in the distance a groaning was heard. Was it distant thunder, or a pissed off elephant?

The following morning, after all tactical routine had been completed, the exercise was pulled to a halt. The platoon headed off for the nearest road in single file. The trucks would be there to meet us. It wasn't until we were heading out of the area that I really believed the story of the rogue elephant, and the piles of shit we saw along the road on the way out of the jungle simply added testimony to the fact.

Disease
February, 1984

We returned back to Australia on the 22nd, and for those that were married it wasn't too soon. About two thirds of these had been unfaithful to their wives, and those that had been faithful had well-trained hands.

One particular guy, a day before returning, had reported to the medic that he'd been pissing razor blades. He was given a few shots for it and told to abstain from sex for a few days. 'But I'm married. My wife was going to expect it. I can't tell her, no, I'm sorry, I have a headache.' So he devised a plan that could easily have backfired.

On the first night with his wife, they made passionate love. The following afternoon he confronted her. 'You bitch. You've been with someone else; haven't you?'

'No. No, it's not true!' she said.

'Then why am I pissing razor-blades?'

'Okay. I only did it the once. I promise. Just a one night stand.'

It would seem that the women back home were having just as much fun as the men.

Duke of Gloucester Cup Squad
May, 1984

The Duke of Gloucester Cup competition team was known as the DOG squad by members of the 8/9th Battalion, a competition that was brought back into existence in 1983 after many years of absence. Apparently the yearly venue used to compare shooting results between Infantry units and the team with the highest average took the line honours that came in the form of a large cup/trophy. The cup would then be proudly displayed in a cabinet case of the winning battalion, in BHQ, where only a small percentage of the BN members would actually get to see it; namely the hierarchy. Soldiers do the work, rank gets the trophy. There was a little conjecture that the cup should have been displayed in the OR's boozer; after all, it was a section competition and had nothing to do with officers. It was in prime position near the entrance to BHQ where an officer could stand beside his wife and proudly state, 'look, darling; we won this last year,' to be met by her puppy-dog eyes, and she thinking how hard he must have worked, and how deserving he was to get some extra special sex that night.

The competition had now been given a face-lift and each battalion's representation had to compete over a five-day period. Each team consisted of a section of ten men – along with several reserves in the case of injury.

Infantry style events were the key to the new précis that saw a specific activity being completed for each day of the five-day period. The competition was conducted in Singleton NSW, the home of the infantry soldier, a home where mummies and daddies weren't allowed and boys had to learn to become men.

Monday

A Test of Elementary Training (TOET) was to be conducted on the M16, M60, SLR and M203, along with a short rifle shoot with the SLR down at the 25m range. During this type of shoot/test, the DS would place drill rounds amongst the live ammunition. Two ten-round magazines with two and three drill rounds respectively in each would force the shooter to carry out his 'Immediate Action' (IA) and 'Stoppage' drills to see how proficient he was with the weapon. Time and time again was spent rehearsing the IA and stoppages until they became second nature: Weapon fires, weapon stops, tilt right, cock the weapon, lock the working parts to the rear, tilt left and look in. Rounds in the magazine, no round in the chamber, release the working parts forward and continue firing. Weapon stops again, tilt right, cock and lock, tilt left and look in. Rounds in the magazine, no round in the chamber, gas stoppage. Release working parts forward, apply safety catch, pull weapon back, re-adjust the gas setting, weapon into the shoulder, safety to fire, and continue firing.

That mind you was just one example of many. All weapons have specific rules which govern its operation and these have to be applied in specific order, to force habit upon the soldier, to hopefully enable each individual to remedy IA and stoppages without the need to think about what he's doing – like I said, second nature. Like approaching a busy road, you don't say to yourself that you have to check left and right before crossing, you just do it; or you see a beautiful girl across the road and your tongue suddenly flops out upon the footpath and you have to spend the next few minutes trying to tuck it back in. Nobody likes to look like a fool or to spend free-time scraping gravel from their tongue, but it's natural that these things take place when seeing a good-looking chick. I always say that it is better to be pestered by your tongue on the footpath when seeing a pretty girl, than it is to choke on it from seeing an ugly one.

Tuesday

A half-yearly 'Battle Fitness Test' (BFT) was conducted, 15km's of running in boots with ten kilograms of webbing plus an individual weapon – be it M203, SLR, M16 or M60, an additional 3-10 kilo's.

The new health and safety act doesn't allow for a soldier to run more than two kilometres of the 15, but back then there was no such explicit directive, and as for everything else this had to be trained for. Most of our fitness training involved several hours of physical training per day.

1 hour 17 minutes was the best the others and I could muster in

training for the 15km run, and on the day of competition this proved to be inadequate.

At the completion of the run, the second phase of assessment came into effect. This came in the form of a shoot, after all, the idea of conducting a battle fitness test was to be able to run 15km and conduct a battle of some description at its conclusion. If this was the case, why was it that during my entire 16-year career, I never once got to conduct a platoon or company attack at the end of a 15km run, organised as a battalion test of fitness? Wasn't I always being told to 'train hard, fight easy'? The army was sometimes so contradicting in its ways. I personally had never heard of so much bull. No matter how hard you train, during battle conditions you were going to be pushing yourself to the max. If your personal fitness was going to have a direct effect on your mates' lives, then you would take care to maintain your fitness, if not, then you were unreliable and inadequate as a soldier. But how can you take care of your fitness if you were stuck in the depths of the jungles of Vietnam for 12 months. Most rely on guts. Fitness – to a certain degree – was a statement of mind.

Anyway, today's shooting test was a modified falling plate. Balloons had replaced metal plates. The scoring system had something to be desired.

By the end of the day's activities our section didn't feel the best. We wouldn't know the results until Friday, but it wasn't looking great at present.

Wednesday

A marksmanship shoot was usually offered to soldiers who had passed the previous elementary practice; if you don't pass the elementary, you don't do the marksman. A minimum of 200 was required from a total score of 275. Doesn't really sound like much, until you do the shoot.

The lead up training for the boys of 8/9RAR went well and all were expecting to achieve the 200 required, with myself anticipating a score of 210. The 210 soon ended up being 178 as a funny thing happened whilst at the manufacturer. The scoring targets were normally cut from a single piece of ply, three targets being obtainable from the wood in question. Today we found – after the shoot – that by way of 'someone's' ultimate wisdom, 'someone' wanted to get four targets per piece to save on funds. I guess this must have been the first of the defence cuts, and all the while I thought there was something horribly wrong with my eyes. So out of the six battalions – a possible 60 marksmanship passes – only three passed due simply to the width of all targets being drastically reduced.

According to statistics of the representation down here there should have been a good 35 to 45 passes. Stuff the cut backs, and that's all I have to say about that, because I knew as Gump does; that life was meant to be a carton of squirrels, or something like that.

Thursday

Drill day. The test today was the pro-forma still being performed throughout the battalions in 1996, except the battalions in '96 performed this with the steyr, and slight modification on its march-past and march-off. It was a guard mount format of 30 minutes duration dressed in polyester uniform, embellishments, grade one slouch hat, black belt and spit polished boots – back in the good old days 'high shine' boots were never used, just spit, water, parade gloss and elbow grease attacking an everyday normal boot. It usually took many days to get a good shine, if not weeks.

Black belts also had to be lacquered and polished – not just a piece of car seat belt cut to suit the wearer as was the case today. It was no wonder that discipline fell through the roof in later years. Too many easy options were coming into play.

A dress inspection was followed by a weapons inspection. One DS looked us over whilst the other deducted points for faults, all one million and one of them; then came the drill, more than 50 verbal orders, some requiring three to six separate movements.

Discipline seemed to be the key factor here, simple concentration on the job without infringement. Keep the eyes looking directly to your front, if you didn't, and the eyes wondered, then you lost points for it. Quite simple really. And as for the women watching the parade from the front row, as a friend of mine from the rear rank would say, keep your damn legs together.

Friday

The big finale. Obstacle course day.

The weapons which we took so much care in refining for the perfect shot to be fired, and hours to clean with toothbrush and toothpick in readiness for the inspection during the drill on Thursday, was now going through the mud, water, knocks and basic abuse; all of which was part and parcel of any obstacle course. This would be the biggest buster and lung burner of them all, because today we had to push ourselves beyond that which we'd trained. Every second counted here. Can you imagine coming second place to a battalion who had beaten you by a matter of one second? This was all-possible and could never be lived down; better to lose by several minutes or not at all, so there was no choice, we had to go for broke.

A little under 20 minutes was the estimate for a section to complete the 17 to 20 obstacles ranging from vertical ropes, horizontal ropes, and swinging ropes; four, six and ten foot walls; 20 foot ladder wall, monkey bars, height reducing jumps, tunnel, bear pit, wire obstacles and others. Teamwork was the only road to success.

An equipment check was to be carried out prior to the obstacle course being conducted and on completion was to be conducted again to ensure that nothing was missing. All was to go with us; webbing and individual weapons, spare gun barrel, all remaining CES to all weapons, med kit, full water bottles, two grenades (M30) per person and other field equipment such as toggle ropes, and stretcher tops/ground sheets.

On conclusion of the second equipment check, after the course had been run, came the throwing of the M30 practice grenades. An infantry soldier was supposed to be able to throw one 35 metres, a big ask in itself.

So two grenades per man were thrown at a small fighting bay some 25 metres away. What do you do; a straight throw for accuracy but a smaller opening due to trajectory, or do you lob the grenade up for higher trajectory giving less accuracy but larger target opening. It all averaged out to be the same, each to his own, but throw both the same way in order that the second throw can be adjusted to suit. Most BNs only received an average 25 percent achievement in hits.

This brought the comp to its conclusion, all apart from the announcement of the overall cup winners and grinners. It wasn't the 8/9th battalion. Maybe next year.

Reconnaissance Course
November, 1984

The course this year was not much more different than the previous; it was still out in the field. During the course there was one incident to which I could recall as though it occurred yesterday; it was the only thing that differentiated it from the previous, apart from the new faces.

It was during the final week of the course and all had been given orders for the close reconnaissance and surveillance of a suspected enemy camp sight. The squad's orders were the same as always, to obtain as much information in its broadest of terms on SALUTE HIM; strength, arms, logistics, unit, tactics, equipment, habits, intentions and morale. A field sketch was also required, which included details such as the distance between enemy pits, gathered by way of counting the amount of paces the enemy took from one to the other and then converting this into metres (depending on the enemies average height). We were also required to record things such as weapons arcs of fire, attained by way of compass bearings.

At present we had one pack, this contained the radio, one sleeping bag, a hutchie and a one-man ration pack between the five members of the squad, as two days earlier the DS had purposely informed the enemy of our recon patrol's position. On encountering the enemy – under specific circumstances – our recon force of five was to tactically withdraw in the opposite direction. Due to this the enemy now had nearly all of our equipment.

A message was received over the radio; it was 1400hrs. We were to move to a pick up point designated by the DS via a 'safe route' as indicated by him. He would accompany us for ease of navigation. Any blind man, without a seeing-eye dog, could see from ten miles that it was a set up; unless of course you were a dumb-smuck or a drop-out-uni-student.

So here we were, strung out in single file and moving alongside an animal track, when all of a sudden a vehicle could be heard just out of eyesight some 50 metres to our front. The lead scout turned to signal this information back down the line when the brush to the right woke up all the dead by way of several hundred blank rounds and several grenade simulators being consumed in a matter of seconds. We hit the deck, laid down covering fire, and withdrew as taught.

Realistically we'd all be dead, but so long as we carried out our procedures as taught, and to the letter, then the DS was quite content to let us live on under his ever watchful eye – how kind of him.

Within a minute we had broken contact with the enemy. The DS appeared at the acting patrol commander's side. 'You've got a wounded soldier, Pete. Your scout's been hit in the arm and is suffering from shell shock.'

The wounded soldier was shuffled onto a shoulder.

Pete deployed a man to either flank, and we all raced off up the hill towards the road and the waiting rover; our method of exfiltration. Twenty metres remained until safe evacuation... ten. The men on the flanks dropped to counter any likely enemy movement from the rear as the vehicle was approached with the fireman's carried scout.

Another surprise was confronted. The driver, another DS, eyeballed our group as we approached from just three metres. 'It's too hot! It's too hot!' he hollered, and sped off into the distance leaving behind nothing more than a cloud of dust with a few words like 'you bastard' escaping our lips.

No time to reflect on what could have been. A quick whistle and heads turned. We headed off into the creek-line on the reverse side of the spur for protection. 'What you going to do, Pete?' asked the DS.

'Give first aid and get the hell out of here.'

'Where?' probed the DS.

'Out the creek and up this re-entrant. It's a covered route. A hundred metres and we'll take off on a bearing towards the AO boundary.'

'Go to it then.'

'Nigel; fix the scout up,' allocated Pete, 'we're leaving in one minute,' and with that Pete briefly assessed the situation whilst I went about the business of applying a field dressing to the scouts proposed wound.

The DS was at my side. 'What you going to do?'

'Just apply this to stop the bleeding.'

'Is that it?'

'He's conscious so I don't need to worry about nothing else.'

'Well he won't be for long unless you treat him for shell shock as well. I want to see you reassure him.'

That's the last thing I would have thought of in this tactical situation. What the hell. I'll reassure him; couldn't hurt.

The DS said: 'What the hell you doing?'

'Reassuring the patient and fixing his wound.'

'You're talking too loud, the enemy will hear you.' Five seconds later. 'You're still talking too loud.' I lowered my voice to a fine whisper. 'It's still too loud.'

'If I whisper any more the bastard won't hear me.'

'Right, that's it.' The DS stood. 'You're lucky I don't put you on a bloody charge for insubordination.' He looked around at the others, as though he'd been a naughty boy. 'End of exercise, fellahs. Move yourselves up this spur till you hit the road and head back in. Clayton, you make sure you stay a good one hundred metres behind us all. You hear me?'

'Yeah, sure.'

He took off up the slope that led towards a road and then the course administration tent.

When I reached the road the other four were waiting, the DS not in sight. 'What's going on?' I asked of the other members of the squad.

'He said that you stuffed things up and that we should beat your head in before taking you with us back to the admin tent,' replied Pete.

'So what's going to happen?' I was inquisitive for obvious reasons.

'Nothing.' And with that we ventured into the admin area to prepare the patrol report; we were also given our packs back.

Four days later I was informed that I'd failed the course for the second time. It seemed to me that the chief instructor didn't like having anyone that was smarter than him on the course, which I guess is why he didn't have many friends.

3/4 Cav
March, 1985

Due to commitments with the DOG squad some members had inadvertently missed their opportunity to partake of the Subject One for Corporal Course with the 8/9th battalion. The CO, however, managed to arrange something for us; or was it the RSM with his god-like influence.

Four of the team – including myself – now found ourselves on the doorsteps of 3/4CAV, ready to tackle the subject course for corporal along with 30 or so members of that unit – it was interesting to note that the unit ended up moving north some years later, the 2/14 Queensland Mounted Rifles taking its place in Brisbane, only a few hands of regular remaining stationed in situ.

We were divided up into the three different sections and during the three day field phase at the back of Enoggera Barracks were given positions as section commanders within the sections due to the cav private soldiers lack with experience in employing minor infantry tactics (not dissimilar to the infantry jumping into an APC as crew commander; we'd be more than lost). The fourth Infantryman acted as platoon sergeant, and we each rotated through the task over the days spent in the field.

At the completion of the six week course we all found that we had all come within the top five places of the course, a very reasonable effort considering our understanding of infantry minor tactics. As we departed their hospitality many things came back to mind, one of these was a cav soldier's method of arousal during the introduction phase of his weapon lesson. He was being tested on his instructional technique, primarily; giving a structured lesson to a section group on the pistol 9mm L9A1.

A friend of his had met with an unfortunate accidental, whereby suicide was endeavoured, and did prove fatal. So what was wrong with his lesson? Well; it doesn't go down too well when you point a pistol to your head, indicating that a good use for it was in committing suicide; it wasn't as though he had a feather duster in his hand. It was at times like this that people needed the utmost support possible, and the gentleman in question was removed from the course, less the smile on his face which might have been present if he had in fact held a feather duster. A lot of stories commenced to float around at about this time, in regards to the incident, but we can't very well adhere to hearsay, for it was sometimes incorrect, and in this circumstance, rumours quite troubling. No one person was safe from ridicule, but at least with the army you had a family in which to brace your fall; or so we all thought and were led to believe.

Exercise Close Country
June, 1985

Glenn Innes was about 300 kilometres South of Brisbane, and down there, somewhere, was a wonderful little place which could be classified as nothing less than rain forest – the rain never ceased during the course of our stay. Thank God that was only two weeks. It never really surprised me that the army could find the worst training areas with the highest rain fall; it's as though they organised the rain, the CQ having placed an order for 'dark skies and thunder'.

It wasn't uncommon to have guys come down with heat illness, even in weather conditions as those experienced here. The Coy CSM was more concerned about this than anyone else. His only comment however, used to be something along the lines of, 'come on, fellahs; get him squared away and fixed up. I don't want him dying on me, there's too much paperwork involved'.

Many a man came down with something. Never on Civilian Street would you see guys like this, doing what they were doing, and in the condition that they were in. I for one hadn't eaten in three days, had a heavy cold, was coughing up phlegm, had a runny nose, diarrhoea, and just literally felt like dying. The section commander had me share a pit with another to watch over me, to report on my eating habits. I'd been told to eat but found it extremely difficult. I missed out on three nights of gun picket due to the illness but found that I couldn't sleep anyway. It was suggested that I be removed back to barracks due to ill health but I stubbornly refused and desperately tried forcing the food down my throat. The section and platoon attacks had to be conducted though, and as the section was down to six men I still availed myself to the assaults, in order that the work could be spread more evenly around.

Time and time again the same hill was taken in grotesque similarity to the movie Hamburger Hill. Fire and moving up the slope was accompanied with a quick dry reach and then coughing up of all sorts of shit, then move again, another bound towards the dug in enemy defensive position.

And then one day we pushed the enemy off. Look out for counter attack; rehearse the procedures tactfully over and over again. Then we withdraw from the position, and I have no idea why; so let's take that bloody hill again tomorrow morning, and without a sigh, for we were to start all over again, all from scratch; and that's no lie.

A section patrol was required; an aggressive search for the small groups of enemy that still existed was required. The section's departure from the platoon position followed brief orders.

Only 500 metres of the patrol route had been covered when I made my first pit stop. Three more soon followed, each stop accompanied by the pulling down of my trousers, dropping a load of diarrhoea, and then taking a few seconds for the luxury of a wipe with wet paper in the never relenting rain. Up with the trousers and continue with the patrol. The section was now down to five men so I had little choice but to continue with the tasks handed down from above. I felt sorry for those behind; you could see them screwing up their face as they closed the gap, seeing me dump a load of diarrhoea and continue on with the patrol. It was the only time the section commander didn't insist the men behind me patrol their arcs professionally as he was aware of the problems associated with stepping in runny shit. You can imagine a man returning home after work, his girlfriend or wife traipsing behind him and looking for shit stains on the carpet as though he was a naughty puppy.

The following day I was feeling much better and approached the section commander about being put back on the gun picket, and he was happy that I was back to normal. He was hesitant at first but needed the manpower for the 12-hour shift – no one enjoyed four and more hours of picket. (No dead man on the gun was heard of these days, not in this platoon in any case).

Hutchies were permitted at night due to the downpour from the heavens above, until contact by the enemy had been made.

Then the enemy arrived with an aggressive initiation of fire from several weapons. Stand-to was passed around, each man scrambling from his sleeping bag, feeling around for his webbing in the dark still nine tenths asleep, eyes only a quarter open. Hutchies were quickly pulled down to prevent any possible silhouette, for the enemy may use this as a reference for our likely pit position. Then with webbing on and the rifle in hand each individual would get down in the mud, usually next to a large tree, behind a log, in a depression in the ground, anything to give protection from enemy small arms fire and shrapnel from grenades and other foreign matter. No digging was permitted in the forest so we didn't have pits to get into – which would have been filled with rain in any case, a situation I had faced in the past: we were not stranger's to the brutal nature of working tactically in the bush.

Suddenly all went quiet. Ten seconds later and the creatures of the night commenced again with their serenades, a rustle in the foliage from all around being heard; bush roaches, rats and all other manner of night-life poking their heads up once more. I thought it was marvellous. Here we were, young men lying in the dirt and the rain, and the only things with an ounce of brains seemed to be the tiny creatures of the night.

Then an exclamation of horror was heard as our platoon arachnophobic stepped into another palm sized spider similar to the St.Andrews Cross, then more silence – you should have seen him a year later when he dug up a bird spider in Shoalwater bay; it was quite a time before he returned to his fighting bay. I didn't know what was better; the rats and spiders of Tully, stealing your rations and clambering over your back, or the spiders in-your face at Shoalwater Bay [and other places like Glenn Innes]. I loved the bush, but sometimes it simply didn't love you back, no matter how many days you accumulated in the field. It was like having a girlfriend who always complained of having a headache, and no matter how many painkillers they took, they simply wouldn't submit to letting you enjoy the full reward of sexual pleasure unless you went out and brought her something special, like a dildo with a smiley-face painted upon it. You always had to take the good with the bad, which is why many guys were happy to take to the bush and leave the girls back at home: it was easier to live like shit in the bush than it was to put up with the shit dribbling from a woman's mouth, or so I'd been told, because I had nothing but the utmost respect for woman – never before have I seen a female with her mouth shut for more than five minutes, even when asleep... that's what my mate says.

The rain hadn't changed, it still fell at a constant drizzle, more a worry in regards to weapon maintenance than anything else. A five-minute break in a patrol constituted time for cleaning of your weapon. Never in my four years within this battalion had I seen so much rust; clean the weapon last thing at night and the following morning your rifle looked like it'd been covered in red dust; those with the M16 usually slept with them in their sleeping bags. But you could always draw from the 'signs' indicated by the platoon sergeant; if he went bush with steel wool in his weapon cleaning kit then you knew you were in for a very uncomfortable trip - this place was worse than Tully but would have been heaps better if the bloody rain would simply STOP!

The enemy soon bumped our position again to ensure all were alert, section members returning SLR and M16 small arms fire, maintaining a silence with the machine guns in perfect defiance to the enemies search for their whereabouts. They were circling the position, trying to single out the platoon's gun positions in the hope of neutralising these for a dawn assault, either before everyone was awake and at stand-to or during the platoon's morning routine when 30 percent of all weapons would be field stripped for cleaning.

Twenty minutes had elapsed and stand-down would be passed

around soon. Then out of nowhere a combination of shots was fired from deep within the scrub. The enemy was still in situ. Maybe the guys in the platoon would be better off at home with girlfriends, at least they'd get some sleep.

The platoon returned fire as indicated by the fire control orders issued by platoon commander and section commander alike.

A further twenty-five minutes had passed and a guy approached unseen from the rear. 'Stand-down.' And the bush was lit up with another bout of exchanged fire. 'Shit,' and the messenger disappeared back to the Boss.

Another thirty minutes of silence brought the platoon sig back to my pit. 'The Boss wants 50 percent stand-to all night; 100 percent on contact.' Well, there goes all hope for sleep. There was still six hours of night remaining, so if the enemy didn't fire another shot all night then each of us would receive about three hours' worth of… shit. Another shot fired in our direction. Would this harassment never end?

Junior NCO Training
July, 1985

A seemingly new concept had been brought into the battalion known as JNCO training. The 'course' duration was two weeks, and was conducted in similarity – so all students had been led to believe – to that of a SASR patrol course, though in comparison, extremely easy. Whether or not that stood to be the truth was beyond most of us and farthest from concern, as very few would ever get to find out, and a majority simply were not interested in attempting that arena of infantry skill.

All we really knew was that the officer in control of the training had just returned from the West after doing the course previously mentioned, whether he passed or not was another question; going by his attitude I would say 'not'. He certainly mused to put Adolf Hitler to shame with his antics and mannerisms, seemingly big-noting himself at every opportunity, but then again, it was more than likely that he was simply making the most of his training, and endeavouring to pass onto us what he had so far learnt, which must have included putting his foot in his mouth. Maybe that particular SAS course never did 50 push-ups as punishment/amusement, but foot-in-mouth exercises instead.

There were 40 of us on the course and all were bedded down on cots in a hut within the administrational area of Shoalwater Bay Training Area. We were soon to learn that the cots would be lucky to see use as we were to average only five hours sleep a night during the two week period, and then not usually on the canvas stretchers.

Many push-ups with pack on backs were forced upon us all. It seemed pure luck that no back injuries were caused through such needless feats of physical abuse, but I'm sure that wear-n-tear upon our bodies would have taken place to some degree.

The following is just a minor example of a day's routine.

We'd just returned from a patrol at 1600hrs. The members of the section were then rotated through all jobs within the section formation of 12 men. The new section commander now reported for an orders group and the section 2IC for administrational details, the remainder of the group took to the cleaning of weapons, preparation of mud models for orders, and conducted a general equipment check on all that the section carried.

Orders were then received.

We were on the truck by 1900hrs and taken to an insertion point. Quite ironically, after de-bus from the vehicles, the rain commenced to fall very heavily. Drenched in seconds we pushed off on patrol through the scrub, to a destination where a standing patrol task had to be met.

2000hrs; we were in position on a small knoll that was found at the end of a spur, itself belonging to an even larger knoll. After a short five minute stand-to period in the downpour we prepared for the digging of our fighting bays – the dimensions of which allowed two standing men room to fight from, using the ground to the front edge of his pit as an elbow rest, being chest height in depth.

A picket on the machine gun was maintained as well as a 50 percent stand-to in the other pits around; therefore, if you didn't dig, you watched your arcs for enemy movement and changed over tasks with the man in the pit with you, every twenty minutes or so.

0100hrs; the pits were down to fighting bay depth. The rain had not stopped and a command to stand-down was given to the section as indicated by the accompanying DS. 0220hrs; stand-to, enemy movement to the front of the position was evident. 0400hrs; still standing-to. A message was then received over the radio informing the section to marry up with the other minor call signs of the platoon. Fill in those pits first, packs on backs, and let's go.

0530hrs; we were in position watching a road. One of the other minor call signs had already joined us and we were now waiting for the other. Ten minutes later and the last of the students arrived. 100 percent stand-to was maintained.

The truck was then called for over the radio. 0615hrs and no truck. It was bogged two kilometres up the road. It was still raining.

The platoon made an administrational move up the dirt road, as we were all required back in the administrational area no later than 0715hrs. The truck took 20 minutes to reach, and after a further 20 minutes of failure to budge the vehicle, the truck finally gave way to our persistent pushing and digging.

All students quickly clambered aboard and headed back to camp in readiness for another re-shuffle, more orders and another patrol to God knows where, and duration unknown.

The rain stopped as we entered the barracks area.

There just had to be a job better than this – not.

Rappelling
November, 1985

The DOG squad came and went once more, every minute of which was enjoyed by all, myself being awarded with an engraved knife as reward for being 'best soldier'; and it would seem that fortune was to follow this competition, for I had missed out this year from being bored to death by sitting on an unknown course full of theory instruction and no action. Instead I received a spot on an airborne rappelling course that was to be run over a period of just three days – short and sweet.

The 18 students were to be taught all they needed to know about the rope, knots, carabiner and aircraft. Safety was the prerequisite to their first descent from UH1H (chopper). 15 jumps had to be made for qualification; two practice jumps were made clean skin (no webbing, rifles or packs) followed by several in patrol order (webbing and rifle) and finally marching order (the pack and everything in it as though going to the bush on exercise).

Five guys approached the aircraft, two from the starboard and three from the port. The loop of the figure-eight was offered to the aircrew. This was the secure end of the rappelling rope. A floor mounted metal pin was to be placed through the loop, hence rendering it secure to the centre of the chopper, so that when it finally came time for jumping out, you wouldn't fall to your death.

They now faced each other, and on indication that all was secure, placed the rope filled sandbags from their left hand, into the right, prior to turning on their butts and facing outwards. The chopper now lifted from the ground to make for a quick trip around the airfield prior to the jump.

The two-minute safety check signal was given by the loadmaster. Ensure the rope was secure in position, and by logical sequence follow the rope down from the figure-eight knot to the figure-eight descender (carabiner), check that the gate to the carabiner was closed securely. From here the rope should flow unobstructed into the sandbag that was held securely in the right hand.

As you approached the jump zone, the signal to move out onto the skids was given. Now you stood on the skids facing in, holding onto the rappel rope as each waited for the chopper to make its final manoeuvre into position some 25 metres above the insertion point. Another signal and all threw the bags containing the rope down to earth, the Bluewater revealing itself from the sandbag so that each had a secure line from the helicopter all the way down to the ground in which to travel.

All would now lean backwards with toes on skids so as to achieve an 'L' shape position with their bodies – unlike that of the Blackhawk. The final chopping signal from the arm of a member of the chopper crew arrived and all twisted their ankles, relinquishing their foothold on the skids, making for a controlled descent to the ground below.

Once on the ground, take several steps back so that the load-master can see you, if everything was okay, give the thumbs up and the rappel rope falls to earth on being released by the air crew withdrawing the metal pin. Feed this rope back into the sandbag as taught and then await your next jump.

Quite a thrill.

Mortar Platoon
1986

It was a decision of the hierarchy that as I had been in the battalion for several years and hadn't yet been posted to support company, that it was prime time I extended my experiences and received a posting to mortars. 'But,' I had pointed out, 'I haven't even done a mortar course.' 'No need to worry,' was the reply, 'you can do one next year.'

Fine.

Being sent to a platoon to do a job that you didn't want to do was quite terrible, my entire year was spent in miserable temperament.

How could I get out of this? I soon decided on a rather simple solution. I would use this year to do whatever I could to stay away from the platoon. Volunteering for bush trips was one way, another was to stay busy with the SASR Cadre Course, and if that failed I had the DOG squad and Reconnaissance course. That would do for starters. But anything to prevent from receiving a mortar course.

As I hadn't done a mortar course I wasn't permitted by law to act as a number one on the mortar tube during live fire practices. I wasn't even supposed to be on the mortar line, but they couldn't exactly employ me in the command post; that was an even bigger no-no. I was absolutely forbidden from having any involvement with that. The CP was where charge settings for bombs, and calculations of bearing and altitudes were derived, as well as basic receipt of fire missions, and registration of targets from soldiers in the field.

So working on the line it was, as number three, although there were several occasions to which arose where I was involved in throwing bombs down the 81mm tubes and getting experience with assisting in misfire drills.

Each tube – to which the battalion had six, but during war entitled to eight – consisted of three men. A number 1, number 2, and you guessed it, a number 3. The No 1 was primarily responsible for setting the direction and altitude onto the C2 sight system as indicated by the section commander via the CP – two tubes per section. In most cases a red and white post, similar to the look of a barbershop pole, was positioned around ten metres from the tube, but not always to the front. This was the aiming post and used specifically to get the tube in alignment with grid North so that all bearings set on the sights were in correspondence with those on the ground. A good No1 could have sights set and a mortar tube laid on target ready for the first round within 90 seconds of deployment.

The No1 would receive commands from the section commanders to fire; he would then relay this to the No2. After each round was fired (dependent on orders) the No1 would confirm by looking through the sights that the tube was in fact aligned with the aiming post, being both vertically and horizontally correct in reference to the plotted target.

The No2's prime task was the placing of bombs down the tube after being handed it from the No3. He also swabbed out the tube after every five rounds to prevent obstruction on the interior wall of the mortar as the charge bags on the bombs were disintegrated on detonation, but did leave some debris on occasion. He would also assist the No1 in the carrying out of any misfire drill – in most cases this was where a bomb was prevented from striking the firing pin due to debris becoming lodged between the tube and the bomb.

The No3 prepared ammunition as indicated by the CP by removing the appropriate number of charge bags and arming the round by pulling the safety pin from the bomb. He would prepare the number of rounds as indicated by the CP or section commander.

It was quite a remarkable little unit when firing a mission. It was a great support weapon capable of giving indirect fire up to a distance of five kilometres, but I was still happy to see the end of the platoon however. At the end of the year I was posted to C Coy on promotion to LCPL. I think the platoon was also sad to see me go because I was quite often employed as a pack-horse, and on one occasion carried two radios with spare batteries, with my own equipment on top of that.

It was time for the DOG squad again and volunteers dribbled in from the different companies.

This year it had been given quite a face-lift. An offer for an Australian rifle section to compete in the Cambrian March in the UK was given. Their yearly competition involved more than 40 teams from across Europe. It took the shape of a section being put through its paces, as a real section should; in the field doing it hard. AMerican soldiers didn't attend this, I guess it was deemed as being too hard for them to do.

The Australian-epic area of operations was chosen wisely. As the Barrington Tops (near Singleton) was climatically similar to the area in which the English competition was to be held, it was decided to have the Australian teams compete it out here. This year the team was literally competing for a trip overseas, for a ticket on a plane to take them to the Mother Country, to compete against a rival of mind, for a prize which could only ever be seen by the heart and never with the eyes. The 8/9RAR team members were just sorry to say that one of their main figureheads, from within the section that year, didn't have the same aspirations and drive as others for the winning of the competition. This became ever evident over the three days and nights of competition. The Corporal did an extremely poor job that year and received a lot of criticism from the section. The A-hole was from pioneers, if I recall, and we mostly held little respect for him.

The army took advantage of this activity and made a 29 minute documentary on the competition. Since then I've never heard of or seen the army display the piece as a publicity stunt. Here was a prime tool for the recruitment of soldiers into the forces and yet it wasn't being employed. Was there going to be another cut back of funds and numbers within the Defence Force, or didn't public relations and good clean advertisement come to mind? Maybe I watched too little TV and drank too much beer.

Before the competition kicked off we all spent the afternoon relaxing and carrying out battle procedure. Several hours later we were 100 metres down from the School of Infantry HQ, waiting for the first of the choppers, to take the first of the teams to the freezing heights of Barrington.

The 30min chopper ride concluded with the section being purposely dropped off at a position some distance from the insertion point as decree by the competition program, quite a shock surprise to us all. The only information we received from the chopper pilot was that we were within two kilometres of our supposed drop-off point. A position was finally determined after 15 to 20 minutes of trying to decipher what we couldn't see, which included farm houses several kilometres away, and the car headlights off in the distance.

Even from this early stage in the competition most realised that no matter how hard we tried, that a win would not be within our grasp. This was evident when the section commander wanted to stop at 0200hrs for the purpose of giving all a short break. A few others, along with myself, commented on how we could rest at the stands we were to encounter enroot, and that even if we didn't get much sleep over the next three days, that it didn't really amount to anything because it was only a few nights. What was the loss of a few hours gonk? 'No. We'll stop for a few hours.' Sometime in the morning, just before sunrise, our 'team' – the word being used lightly – continued on our 'not so' merry way. The morale had now been given the kick in the guts it didn't need. We were out here to do a job, not to sleep; damn it!

The next decision shattered all even more. That afternoon at 1400hrs it was noted by the section commander that one of the navigation legs on the 40km trek was off by itself. A plan was soon arrived at to send himself and one other – less their packs – to retrieve this check point whilst the remainder under command of the 2IC – very competent in his ways – would continue to other checkpoints and then wait for the section commanders return at a specific location. In other words, going against the rules of the competition, but using initiative to try and make up for the time he'd already lost the group: what a dumb arse!

By 1600hrs the 2IC's group had arrived at the marry-up point, but no section commander. 1800hrs and still no contact with the section commander. 0800hrs the following morning and he finally made an appearance. How the hell did they keep warm – they built themselves a fire of course. So instead of making up two hours in time, the section commander had lost a further 15 odd hours. We were now a good 18 hours behind our best possible time. We could only hope that the other sections were having the same problem with their commander.

Two days later scores were read out and 8/9RAR were informed that they had lost with flying colours, but hadn't come last, that honour was given to a team with obviously less ambition than can be found in a pile of shit – well done 5/7RAR.

1RAR took the line-honours that year and went over to compete in the competition overseas. The Australian team came first, winning the competition with ease. Just goes to prove which army was the best in real terms, just as the Australian competition proved which sections had pride in their jobs as Infantry soldiers, and which NCOs cared not for their rank and position within the battalion. My mate reckoned that our section commander would have done better as an officer.

Some NCOs certainly didn't deserve their rank, but the thing is, bad NCOs were so far and few between. The competence and professionalism of the Australian Army was simply beyond reproach.

It would also be fair to say, however, in defence of my accusations against the individual above, that the platoon in which he was posted (in SPT Coy) had different aspirations than those of a rifle section. It was therefore possible that his attitude towards the task at hand, wasn't entirely his fault; he may well have been against the temporary posting from the start, but as an NCO should have continued without complaint to do the best that he could.

SASR Cadre Course
March, 1986

I knew during BRL in Melbourne that my application to try for the SAS had been given the thumbs up, and that the initial course of 24 days was to begin on the 6th March. I thought it might be fun being a special soldier, and I loved the idea of having extra pockets in which to hide things.

I had decided not to commence with my preparation for the course until my return to work in late January, allowing for a good six weeks of physical build up. As it turned out, this was more than ample, as I'd already had a good foothold on my fitness. I even surprised myself one day by completing a 15km run in patrol order, with M60 machine gun, in 91 minutes. It was no wonder my heart rate was down to less than 40 beats a minute.

The day of concern however was soon upon me and the course of 100 odd students, and as I sat in the belly of the C130 in Townsville, awaiting the final leg of our journey to Perth, I couldn't help but to look around at the others who had decided to try out for the course. This was their preference for career progression, and as I looked around I tried to evaluate them by expression; some showing nervousness and uncertainty; what were their motives for putting themselves on such a course as this?

There was a guy of 25, spoke very posh and snobbish, a bloody good hand; another who read women's magazines, fantastic guy; both passed the course. And there were several – just a few – who boasted how tough they were, what they had done, how good they were as a soldier, how they picked up women by the dozens – they were some of the biggest losers it was my displeasure to meet; extremely self-centred. These 'tough guys' were some of the first to go back to their units after just five days on the course, a course that had been designed so specifically. Here they ran, running with tails between their legs, and with excuses as big as their now deflated egos and looks of embarrassment. It seemed to me that a majority of those that passed the course were 'mind' wise, with the attitude, mentality, and temperament, to go along with it – no need for a personal trainer here. Of course, not all of those removed from the course were big-headed; most were genuine and friendly.

Food was plentiful on the course, which was a good thing. I'd lost five kilograms in six weeks of training and was about to lose a further seven kilograms over the next 14 days – no bull.

During the course we were to be assessed during two physical training periods a day, an hour in the morning and another in the afternoon, not to mention punishment activities and other sprints around the area surrounding Northam Camp. All of this was carried out in order to get from one activity to the next. That was certainly one thing that could be said about the 'selection' course, it was a hell of a lot more physically demanding than anyone had said. I'd tried to imagine what the PT during the course would be like when I was conducting my own training periods, but never visualised it as being so hard. Only the extremely exceptional of the hundred that were here found it easy, most found it difficult, though refused to say so – a good mental attitude, so long as it worked for the individual.

A 3.2km run was the first of the major tests. It had to be completed within 16 minutes – one kilometre every 5 minutes; 200 metres in 60 seconds; shouldn't be a problem. All students waited for the starting whistle to be blown, dressed in uniform, boots, 10kg webbing and carrying 4.3kgs of weapon. The run was conducted around an airfield so you could see the start/finish line. Several laps of the airfield were required, quite a psychological hit to the head; but then again, any track would have been. And another thing, the DS weren't afraid to point out, just before the whistle being blown, that 70% of all those in the past had failed this activity the first time around. At least this meant you got to try again if you failed.

The course this year managed a good 40% pass, myself only scraping in with 13-odd seconds to spare. The second major test on the course, however, was the 20km route march. The students on the course reported, forming up into three ranks with their marching order placed at their feet, all ready for inspection by DS. Ten guys were to be hand-picked by the DS so as to have their equipment weighed. If any of these were caught underweight then two things would occur. Firstly everyone would undergo a weight check and secondly, the culprit would end up with an additional five kilograms overweight in the form of rocks being placed into the top of his pack;

oh, and if he managed to finish the 24 day course, his chances of being denied a pass were huge – for he would have been found guilty of an attempt to cheat. For these reasons most on the course ensured that they carried a few kilos more than that required; just in case.

The forced march was soon under way and men slowly spread out as the distance covered, grew. A funny thing happened here. A DS passed me by and put mention to the fact that I was leaving some members of my group behind as others had done before me. The DS said that the test should be completed as a team. Now if I was to fail to finish the march in the 3hrs 15min allotted, would my remaining 'as a team' become a defence against my being removed from the course; was it worth the risk in finding out? I decided not and continued, for my chances of survival were better if I went it alone (and this was the way in which I'd trained, by himself, pushing myself along by use of personal pressure and self-motivation, not having to rely on others for support.

After only eight kilometres I felt that I wasn't going to pass the march. I just wasn't stepping out enough, each stride seemed to fall short of that achieved by the previous, and what about those guys behind me, were they mentally calculating the distance travelled? I had done this enough times in my career to know how far I'd gone – not to mention the checkpoint at the five kilometre mark. My feet were also starting to tenderise in the heat of the day. I'd have to do as some others were doing, I would now have no choice but to run a light shuffle, and as I commenced to double time down the road a thought came to mind. I'd read a book years before, some guy on the British selection course had failed to pass a navigation test because he was several minutes late to finish, and he had a fractured ankle. I decided to go a little faster.

The 15 kilometre mark came into visual and I slowed the pace slightly, I had enough time remaining, surely – watches had been banned from all other activities on the course, except this one; but I couldn't recall being informed of that. A guy passed me by and told me how much time remained. Good, ample enough.

Two minutes later and the DS informed him differently, and as I was determined not to take a chance on the DS having been wrong I continued with the pace – or was he trying to psych me out? Five more clicks and fifty minutes to do it in.

I finally approached the finish line and crossed with 15 minutes to spare, 20km in 3hrs – not too bad. I was soon informed that the first to cross the line had done so in 2hr 40min. That soldier was apparently pulled aside by the DS who were unimpressed with his effort. He'd completed the march with ease but had refrained from giving any boost of morale to his mates and only strove to please himself – just like most of the others had done, whether they finished under time or over. It seemed that in some cases mateship was the key to success, but then again that could have been a hidden front to aid in the study of each individual's reaction to suggestions of a varying sort as given by the DS.

On our return to the rooms the following morning – after an hour of PT – we found that a member of our group had been removed from the course. This was obvious as his chair, bedside table, and bed, were gone. Nothing remained except an empty space. No messing around here, when they take you off of the course, they take everything except the bloody floorboards. It was said that they did this so as not to affect the morale of other students, but the thought of this scared some guys shit-less – the DS, were again, messing with our minds.

The 24hr navigation test was upon us. We stepped off individually mid-morning and had a specific amount of checkpoints to achieve by day, and three checkpoints (minimum) by night. The day phase wasn't the problem.

It had just turned 2200hrs and I had left my first compulsory night checkpoint and was beginning my manoeuvres for the second. To go across country and numerous creeks was asking for trouble, so I decided on the alternative. I would head on a bearing for 1200 metres, turn right and take off on a different bearing for a further 1600 metres; both were along spurs with only one re-entrant to be crossed on the first leg, and several others on the second. Shouldn't be a problem.

I came upon a small bush, and as I pushed through, tripped on a loose stone, my leg falling out from under me, forcing me to overstep my mark, to meet with a six foot drop to a dry re-entrant floor full of boulders. I sat still for several seconds, thinking. Does any part of me hurt? Have I damaged anything? No, all was fine. I climbed the six-foot escarpment on the other side and continued on my way until I reached my pivot point. I pulled out the map. With the torch held close to the ground I searched for confirmation of my next bearing. The next portion of my trip involved two more re-entrants similar to the one I'd just fallen into. It just wasn't worth the risk of injury.

I bedded down for the night. Maybe if I completed the navigation test within the 24hrs without all three-night checkpoints up my sleeve, and did well in other aspects of the course, they would forego getting rid of me.

I continued with my journey the following morning after breakfast, a can of corn beef and a quick coffee.

Reaching the last of my checkpoints was no relief as I now had to get myself back to the start point, the final leg of my journey. The distance was just over seven kilometres and I had 1hr 45min remaining. I would have no choice but to take the distance in one hit, there was no time to break the distance up into more easily to manage navigational bounds. I placed my bearing to the compass and just as I was about to step off the DS called me over.

The picture was painted. A guy from the Navy [yeah, sure] whose job didn't involve navigation as such – but the individual had skills required by the SAS – had but one leg remaining as I – or was he a spy planted within the course? [of course]. It was requested that I take the man with me. No problem.

I'm sure I was being tested: It was soon evident to me that the guy liked conversation as during the fast pace through the scrub he continued to chatter on about numerous subjects, and here I was trying emphatically to navigate and count paces for accurate measure of the metres covered. Something had to be done, even at the expense of seeming unnecessarily rude. 'Listen mate. We've got more than another six clicks to travel, less than an hour and half to do it in, and I'm trying to count my paces. The last thing I need right now is conversation. Would you mind not talking?' Quite a simple solution.

Time passed us by quickly and when next I looked at my watch I discovered that we had three minutes remaining, and according to my calculations about 200 metres to travel. I stopped and looked around.

'What do you think?' I asked of my 'Navy' acquaintance.

'I'm not sure,' was his reply.

The ground around was flat but a creek junction was marked on the map. 'This foliage around us here; does it look strange to you?'

We assessed the ground alike. 'It's certainly different.'

'Look at the way it lays on the ground,' I pointed out, 'like a 'Y'. What do you think? Could this be the junction?'

It was a near impossible decision, and I was receiving no aid. If it were a junction then our angle of approach would have to be altered slightly, if not, we should go straight ahead. The time ticked by. We now had two minutes remaining.

'It certainly looks like the foliage here was lower in comparison to the stuff around. Could be….' And there in the distance. A generator had just been turned over. An army generator by no mistake, just through the scrub a bit. This was a creek junction. 'That's it. Quick, let's go!'

We walked into the camp two minutes late. Would they fail me for this, only completing one night checkpoint and being two minutes late? To tell of my fall in the creek line would be futile. I should have continued regardless.

It was day 12 on the course and I was standing outside the office of decision, myself and three others (two of whom passed the course, and several months later finally marched into the regiment). I was called into the office – being told basically the same as the others before me.

The officer looked up. 'It's been brought to my attention that you've been taking it easy and haven't been putting the effort in. I require a one hundred percent effort, one hundred percent of the time. I find your report disturbing to say the least. If you don't pull your socks up sunshine, you'll find yourself being marched off of this course. Do you have any questions?'

'No sir.'

'Get out.'

Oh well. What could one say?

That night I phoned home and was informed that an Aunt was coming out from England for a short stay, that she would be dead from cancer before the year was out, her trip coinciding with the SAS patrol course – as far as I could determine. I put the phone down and crawled off to bed.

The following day the students who still remained on the course loaded themselves onto the coaches for the trip to the Stirling Ranges. We were to find ourselves here for the next five days, climbing mountains, by ourselves, navigating over five peaks in the process. This was supposedly the test of all tests. The mountains were just that, mountains of shale and rock that were near on impossible to walk upon. It wasn't uncommon to find yourself falling time and time again, many times in an hour, and with an extremely heavy pack on your back, injury was very possible.

The first of my checkpoints was Mt.Hassel. A close look at the map showed two possible routes to the top. The first would take me around to the far side and an extra two or three kilometres in march. The short leg was up the wind shattered portion facing me, very steep, but very short in distance. For some strange reason I chose the steepness. The steepness soon became a cliff face and as I climbed I realised my mistake. It was too late now to turn back, as to do so would make it near impossible to complete all checkpoints in the five-day period, or so I thought.

I occasionally looked back behind me, ensuring my backpack didn't throw me off balance. The drop behind was a good 150 metres. This was definitely no slope. The wrong placement of a foot would see me fall to my death upon the rocky outcrop below, and that wasn't even the bottom, there was another hundred metre drop beyond that [or so it seemed] - I was hoping that my 'perspective' had created an illusion. Never again would I be so quick to try and take the shortest leg. I should have known better, experience should have told me that I had made the wrong decision in my approach.

Two and half-hours later and I finally made the checkpoint. It was worth the climb just for the view, but I wasn't here on a sightseeing venture.

I met with the DS and reported my location to the centre administration area via the 77 set radio: Each of the students carried one. The DS then made a comment. 'I wouldn't spend too much time here if I was you.'

'How come?' I asked.

'You were one of the first of your group to leave, but the last to achieve his checkpoint.' The individuals of the group he was referring to were sent on their merry way at 30-minute intervals.

I took this new information on board and was soon on my way to the next destination.

At 1100hrs the following morning I could clearly see the monstrous feature to my front. That was my next checkpoint, Mt.Magog. I calculated that I'd be lucky to get to the checkpoint by 1700hrs; then I weighed up my options and all that had occurred over the past week.

I'd been warned that my effort wasn't good enough, probably due to the navex. Then there was the fiasco with Mt.Hassel and the coming death of a relation. Should I quit now, because it certainly looked as though I was heading for failure? Should I take the opportunity to visit my Aunt when she arrived in Australia, to see her before she died? Was family more important than a career with the SASR? Was I going to receive a tick in the box – doubtful?

I chose the hard option and pulled myself off from the course, and to this day still don't really understand why I chose to quit, whether for my Aunt or for my inability to complete the navex under the time restraints. But I do believe, after contemplating it all, deep down, beneath the surface, that if I'd not made that phone call home that I would have completed the course. I don't say this to make myself look bigger and better than I am, but because being in the SAS had been a dream of mine. I had what it took but I also had a conscience which allowed for my aunt to see me one final time.

I would leave the course till another day.

Five years earlier, in 1981, during my posting in Singleton, I did request a chance to conduct the SASR course. I was provided an interview, possibly out of sheer courtesy – which I appreciated immensely, for it showed that they understood how genuine I was. I was however turned down – I was only 17 at the time.

In 1988 I again withdrew from the course even before getting on the plane, this time due to a back injury incurred two weeks before the commencement of the course, and though it was only minor, chances were I'd really have a problem if I attempted the course – this I knew from experience.

The Poor State of War and Conflict

In 1992 I was denied the opportunity to make another attempt. It was probably for the better, as my injuries were playing up extensively. My body was becoming broken. The more I did, the more broken I became, and the more serious matters appeared.

Was this maturity or did I just need a swift kick in the arse to put a smile back upon my face, because I wasn't smiling much these days?

Cooktown
1987

Exercise Diamond Dollar was an exercise with a difference for the battalion this year as an emphasis was to be placed on aid to the civil power. One of C Coy's first tasks in the exercise was to give protection to the local police station as well as some other buildings of particular importance. Concealment from the enemy wasn't of great concern for the company over the first week of exercise, for as all well knew, security arrives in its best form with the actual presence of an authoritative figure. In this case authority had been given to the 7.62 ammunition that most carried, although the M60 machine guns were absolutely forbidden to be fired, unless specifically given the order to do so by higher elements. Showing just cause for firing an automatic weapon, or weapon on automatic, in the case of the M16, couldn't be justified if a civilian was killed, unless the enemy had launched a large scale assault against any of the key establishment to which the company was protecting.

The enemy had blended into their atmosphere rather easily, made up by individuals, and small bands of soldiers from a variety of battalions and the SASR. They grew beards, had boats, maintained jobs, and had become one with the population – in some cases but not all – and had reportedly established themselves a routine. The locals became a great source of information here. The police as well could easily point the finger at those who were new to the town.

Routine on the ground was quite slow and tedious. It involved basic security work; maintaining pickets around the key installations, conducting ID checks with suspicious persons; and eating the mangoes that were given freely by the trees that grew around us.

It was during the first phase of the exercise that a DS approached me and two others.

He informed us that a bomb had been placed into the letterbox, that stood on a post at the gate to the police station, just five metres from where we sat – no one actually carried this action out mind you, but the DS had been informed that casualties were required. We three had supposedly received cuts to the faces and were suffering haemorrhage from the ears.

The rules governing this exercise, in respect of exercise casualties, were very simple.

The medivac system had to be tested and exercised, the same as everything and everyone else. We were further advised by this DS that we were to be taken by rover to the battalion RAP and from there wait to be picked up by military ambulance, to be taken to the field hospital where we were to be treated for the wounds sustained. We would then stay out of exercise for a period of 24hrs before being returned to C Coy as a replacement to the lost numbers.

Very interesting; I wonder if it were officers that had thought that one up? 1. To RAP; 2. To Field hospital; 3. Return. Huh; three, the magic number. Yes, it was an officer initiative.

The rover evacuation to the RAP took no more than 30 minutes to organise and execute, then three hours was endured before a decision was made that the ambulance wasn't coming. We would therefore have to be taken by rover the short trip to one of the rear echelons, namely the 8/9th Battalion's location of field kitchen. Other elements were also to be found here, those required by the battalion for the administrational purposes of running the exercise.

We were off loaded with our packs and approached by an officer. 'Look men. I haven't got time to talk to you now. We've got our arses hanging out doing security patrols and manning sentry points around the echelon at the moment. You boys shouldn't be here too long, maybe 24 hours. As soon as the first available vehicle heads back to the front, I'll give you a ticket. We're a bit understaffed though in the field kitchen. Hope you don't mind helping out?'

'No sir,' and with that we commenced peeling the potatoes required to feed six hundred men. Mmmmm... You've got to love the army.

Two days later I approached the officer in reference to being taken back to the company in Cooktown. 'Sorry son. Haven't got any vehicles. I told you that the other day.' Thanks, arsehole. 'Now, I'll get back to you soon,' (Meaning next week some time).

With that being said we commenced to peel more potatoes and some carrots, just like we'd been doing for the past two days. I did suggest that we help out with the security patrols [as they were supposedly short in manpower], but no; spuds were more important than security, which directly contradicted what the officer had said a few days before in regards to security patrols. Officers were sometimes so full of themselves.

On the afternoon of the second day a CPL cook came up to me. 'Listen mate. We're a bit stretched at the moment. Would you mind doing some sentry work?'

'So long as it doesn't involve peeling spuds.'

'No, but the shift is about three and a half hours.'

Whoopee bloody do. 'That's okay.' Bloody oath it was. 'What about the other two guys with me?'

'You'll all get a turn.' I was shown the sentry position.

Now, to the rear of the field kitchen was a stretch of thick bush, and forty metres beyond that was a small creek-line. That's where the sentry position had been placed. I couldn't believe my eyes when I saw it.

There was a canvas stool that you sat on and under this was a pile of stick books ready for the reading. It was in the shade and perfectly cool. On relieving the cook that was there – and had been for the past five hours – I asked for the orders on the sentry position.

'What orders?' replied the cook.

'The 18-odd points which need to be covered when relieving a sentry; arcs of fire and actions on contact; everything.'

'I haven't got any orders,' he said. 'Just watch the road.'

'What road?'

'It's beyond the bushes over there, somewhere. It's just two metres past those.'

'I can't see anything.'

'No. But you can hear vehicles going up and down. If you hear one, just go and look. But I wouldn't bother if I were you.'

So this was what they needed the man power for, to peel spuds whilst the cooks sat back reading stick books, doing sentry work on a road that was never going to be seen. A plan of attack was decided upon. I wrote a quick note and took this to the cooks. This was to be delivered to C Coy's CSM along with the fresh ration dinner that night; no room on the vehicle for anything (or anyone) else mind you.

The following morning I was pleasantly surprised to find that all three of us were to be sent back to the section, reinforcing it back to its original strength of seven men. It was then that the CSM made a firm decision not to send any further casualties back to the RAP unless told to do so directly by a DS – but under protest of course. All worked out fine for the next few days and by then it was time for the company to change roles with another company, and we headed for the wilderness. We were going bush housed snugly in the back of APCs.

It's stories like these that really make you feel sorry for the poor officers back in the echelons. It's no wonder the padre was always there; they needed him to help relieve their stress.

As for the officer, whose mouth did the work of his arsehole, the less said about him the better.

Exercise OTBO was once again being held in the wastelands of SWBTA. All of the fieldwork during this exercise was of a live fire nature. The DOG squad however was exempt from this due to meeting the training criteria and basic bulk of training requirements that included the dreaded 20km march with packs every single day.

The logistical support of the battalion during the exercise was bountiful. Here the team could conduct ambush drills, section attacks and basic field techniques, until they were coming out of our ears. This was certainly the most training we'd received as compared with any other DOG squad of previous years. Once again the team consisted of a ten-man section, with two reserves and an allotted driver.

The Ambush (training)

We lay in ambush with blank ammunition exchanged for the live that we'd been used to carrying. Simply put, several members of the battalion were being employed as enemy for the night.

The scope of the DOG competition was completely known but not solid. It was a logical and realistic assumption that a live fire ambush conducted for assessment by the DS in Singleton would be sprung within 30 minutes of being set up due to restrictions in timings. Besides that, the RSM had been informed of some competition stands for ease of

section preparation, and he was standing in silence just behind our team alongside the training SGT, both of whom were watching with a keen eye and obviously full of interest.

It was a comfort to know that the night was fairly well lit. Not a cloud existed and the moon was a quarter full. This would certainly aid in all aspects of the sections standard operational procedures and conduct of the withdrawal from the ambush site.

Movement was detected within the half-hour. Three bodies were walking along the track to our front. The section commander would now wait for them to move into the centre of the killing ground prior to initiating the ambush with his M16, and on this failing to fire, for any particular reason, the alternate method of initiation would be used; the scout would fire his M16. All weary heads were turned to face the front with fingers on triggers as the enemy moved past. Suddenly, a tenth of a second after the section commander's initial application of pressure upon the trigger and firing of the first round of ammunition, then the bush commenced to echo with five seconds of automatic and rapid firing from all section weapons, into the killing ground.

Then silence. Time for a quick assessment; was there more enemy approaching; should those caught in the ambush be fired upon with a second initiation? All seemed fine and only seconds after silence befell the surrounding dark the command for searchers out was given.

As the order was being carried out the DOG squad training SGT came in behind the section commander. 'Scott; you're wounded.' So as section 2IC, the show now belonged to me.

Quick orders were all that were required. All were experienced men with common sense to suit.

Two riflemen grabbed Scott by the harness and dragged him away from the ambush sight to the rear some 25 metres where they had prepared several stretchers as per ambush SOP requirements. One was dismantled as Scott was placed onto the other.

The section was quickly deployed on the ground as medical aid was carried out on the supposed sucking chest wound that the section commander had received. I then called in a fire mission by using the direct fire support we had in the form of a section of mortars.

This was used to cut off any likely approaching enemy at a road junction some five hundred metres away, and having spent eleven months in mortars, the target registration numbers were somewhat easier for me to remember.

By the time the fire mission had been called in and a quick but short adjustment had been made to counteract another likely enemy approach, the section commander was wrapped and ready for the 500-metre move to the administration area where packs had been left.

All the while this was being conducted the training sergeant and RSM were watching in silence, assessing any faults, to be used as debrief points after the short exercise had met with its conclusion.

I quickly deployed a scout either side of myself and followed the compass bearing in the direction of the admin area, with the stretcher party close in tail, and the gun group split either side of these as rear and flank protection.

Visibility was good for about fifty metres but none of the ground we were covering looked familiar as yet, but I was also to remember that the light was different at 1800hrs, for it was still dusk back then.

We'd soon covered the distance required. I signalled for the scouts and asked for a confirmation on the distance so far travelled. The group average was slightly over the distance required, so the two scouts were sent off to the flank for a quick reconnaissance.

This was the likely solution to our problem, the only solution. They reported back within two minutes that they had indeed found the packs.

On arrival at the administrational area all threw their packs onto backs, rotated two of the guys on the stretcher, and were informed by the training SGT that the ambush scenario was now complete. We now had to stretcher the wounded section commander down the road a short five kilometres.

As for the ambush – the RSM was quite content with the test results and seeing first hand that all SOPs were being employed to the satisfaction of the section commander and training SGT. A month later we were down at Singleton awaiting our chopper insertion to the Barrington Tops.

The team this year was the best I'd worked with. We all felt that a 'win' was on the cards. Our section commander was more than competent and looked up to by all in the section.

The First Night (competition)

The competition was off to a blazing start and it was all good news to see that the section commander this year was more than interested in giving his best to the competition and the soldiers.

The first day's competition came to an end and as it turned dark a DS approached Scott with the requirements for the night's activities. We were to move to the top of a large feature and set ourselves up a night harbour position in a location indicated by another DS, who was to meet us there. A distance of no less than thirty metres would segregate each of the six battalions. Once in position, sections were to conduct night routine, and this would be assessed by several DS during the night; they would venture around to visit each of the sections at undisclosed times.

This was the most disappointing of the stands for one reason, and one very good reason. It was disappointing to note that some of the other battalions had decided not to run a proper gun picket that night because of the rain and cold. The weather was that bad that they probably figured that the DS wouldn't be around. As it turned out, they did. They saw firsthand that the section representing the 8/9th battalion, and several others, were filling all requirements as laid down, but 1RAR were not – just to mention one. It was then the DS's prime decision to declare that this portion of the competition not be assessed. They would instead assess the night harbour another night when – hopefully – the rain had ceased; it never eventuated.

So here we were, doing all the right things, spending a miserable night in the scrub, conducting night routine from within a section harbour position. We sat and watched the rain drop off of our hats, periodically looking out drearily over the sloping ground to our front, to some house a good twenty kilometres away that had its porch lights turned on. All of this whilst other battalions – one in particular – slept without concern or worry.

According to the competition criteria, each assessed stand was marked out of a score of 100 points. It was therefore logical that if 8/9RAR had conducted the test to the best of their ability and someone else did not, then they would surely out score them by as much as one hundred points. It stood to test patience when at the conclusion of the competition we had lost by 65 points to 1RAR who didn't do their night routine as laid down in orders. 1RAR… scumbags. 8/9RAR, having completed it correctly, received no points whatsoever as it was decided the morning after the test that it wouldn't be fair to these 'other' battalions. Well let's all have a nice little cry. I was led to believe that 1RAR enjoyed their trip to England again that year – thanks to the DS and their unscrupulous ways. Did the DS take a bribe? And to think that I had always thought that honesty was the best policy. It was quite obvious to me that 1RAR had more NCO's and soldiers, that cringed and made a fuss, at every opportunity, than what could be found elsewhere. 8/9RAR was more disciplined than the battalions to our north, and we had just proved it.

The DS obviously held a different point of view when it came to moral equity, they being tainted with the love of their former battalion.

As for the overall results, the 8/9th battalion came second in the Duke of Gloucester and first in the McDonalds cup (a new aspect which looked specifically at ambushing, navigation, and shooting).

This was prejudice beyond belief, but it wasn't until I met with someone of 4RAR that I knew something was mighty wrong with the people whom made the decisions as to those that received promotion to the next highest rank; but my posting to 4RAR was still a long way off yet, and a story which should remain shrouded in darkness… in other words, the less said about the men of the 4RAR BHQ element, the better.

From Fighting Bay to Hospital Bed
1988

I soon found myself in Reconnaissance Platoon after being awarded a plaque as student of merit (best soldier) for my efforts in late 1986, and digging a fighting bay whilst posted to the platoon was one of the last things on my mind.

The BN's major exercise for the year was EX Silk Purse and Recon's first task was the conduct of a reconnaissance of a beachfront vehicle track due to the heavy rain the area had received that month.

We were checking it for its ability in taking the weight of rovers, APCs
and trucks.

Information needed to be recorded on all aspects so that a decision could be made as to whether particular types of vehicles could use the road. What detours – if any – were needed, establish whether any changes to the map were required, and mark these changes as appropriate to our map, recording the widths of the track, inclines/depth of creek lines, etc, etc; and the list goes on. During the three-day task we only once encountered hostile activity and that was a small enemy group boarded up in an old shearing shed. We took them out via unrealistic fashion – vehicle assault. It had all been prearranged with compliments of the PL SGT to help keep everyone on their toes and to aid with the writing of SOPs for vehicle mounted patrols, to which this was the platoon's first. I still recall spending many, many hours writing the SOPs which never seemed to be employed by the platoon due to changes in policy a little later on. Again, I had wasted many, many hours of work.

At the task's conclusion the patrol married up with the remainder of the battalion not long after dark. The position was under construction on our entry to the position and we could hear the digging going on around us. We were now shown our area of responsibility.

The platoon was to remain here in the Battalion Firm Base for the night and commence tasking the following morning, meanwhile fighting bays had to be dug as quickly as possible as the enemy had the capability of directing mortar fire upon our current position.

It didn't take long to pair off, and with entrenching tool in hand, each man commenced pounding at the ground. Shovels and picks would be brought up from the stores area as soon as possible but meanwhile we had to use our entrenching tools.

The job took a good five hours as the ground was fairly hard, and on completion I reached down to pick up my 45kg pack.

Quite suddenly I found myself in excruciating agony and in a position on my elbows and knees, the most comfortable posture possible - back pain. After I was lifted to a stretcher I was taken down to the RAP in the centre of the BN position. The RMO soon had drugs injected into the cheek of my arse. I now had 15 minutes to roll over onto my back before I fell asleep; it took a minimum of ten just to roll onto my side.

The following morning I was evacuated by road to another medical centre and after five hours here transferred to a hospital bed in Rockhampton.

Whilst I was there I saw two nurses. The first on my being admitted

– who also took time to ask if I wanted any pain killers – and the second was three hours after I'd been lying there in more pain than I care to remember.

'Are you still here, Mr.Clayton?'

'Yeah, that's right.'

'Well you can't stay here I'm afraid. We need the bed.'

'What exactly would you like me to do? I can hardly move.'

'If you give me a phone number I'll get someone to come and pick you up.'

Unbelievable. Here I was, unable to do anything, still dressed in the stinking fatigues I'd been wearing and sweating in over the past four days, and they wanted me to 'phone home'. Who did they think I was, E.T. or some local. 'I don't come from here,' she must have thought I was from the Army Reserve, they had a unit stationed close by.

'What about the barracks phone number?'

'I don't know that. I don't come from here.'

A look of scorn fell upon her face, 'that stupid fat cow'. 'I suppose I'll have to do it myself,' she said in the most sarcastic of manners and departed, with a waddle.

An army ambulance picked me up several hours later. It was around 1800hrs and I hadn't had anything to eat all day. I was taken directly to the barracks where I was helped very slowly to a bed in a spare room and told that I should get someone to get me a meal, as he, the driver of the ambulance, had other things to do. With that my help departed. I was once again by myself.

Two hours later I finally saw someone. It was a transport driver from my battalion.

'What are you doing here, Nigel?'

'Not much, Brett. Done my back in. Apparently I have to stay here until the next available aircraft South.'

'That's not for almost a week. You'd be better coming back with us in the truck.'

'I can't travel in no truck. My backs stuffed.'

My friend thought it over for a few seconds. 'I think I can help you there. We've got a load of parachutes in the back, picked up from an airfield after 3RAR's drop. They're all loosely thrown in. I reckon if you take enough pain killers, and we avoid the potholes,' which was doubtful, 'between here and Brisbane, you'll not have a problem.'

'I guess you're right. No one knows I'm here. If I don't go with you guys I'll be dead in a week.' So I took the option open to me and returned to Brisbane – which turned out to be ten times more comfortable than the ambulance drive – and on arrival was informed that no one had heard, or seen, a report of my injury, nor knew of my returning. They found it all very strange that I should have been dumped the way I was and forgotten about. I was asked if I needed to be put in hospital, or whether I had a home to go to.

'No thanks. I have a home to go to,' and spent the next few days in my room on the barracks, whilst another guy brought back from the exercise due to a sprained ankle, fetched meals for me from the mess hall.

After all, one hospital experience was enough.

As for the fat rotund at Rockhampton Hospital, I have a message for you… but do I really need to spell it out?

Interrogation
April 1989

During the running of the reconnaissance course this year, platoon headquarters extended an invitation to 1 DIV INT to come along and carry out their forte of interrogation techniques upon all of our students. All of the instructors from the platoon had been through it before at some stage or another during their military career, and it was an experience never to be forgotten.

The students were gathered together one afternoon and told that they were being taken down the road two kilometres so that they could all watch a movie called 'The Iron Cross', to be watched on a bed sheet that had been set up against the wall of a toilet block on Greenbank Range. This camp was used exclusively to house soldiers during live firing exercises/practices through the course of a normal training year. The movie was to give them a deserved break in training.

They were soon on the back of the truck and some started to become suspicious when the rear flap to the vehicle was pulled down and secured to the tailgate: 'Don't worry fellahs, it's just to keep the dust out.' The welcome they received on arrival at the toilet block was well orchestrated.

1800hrs. All 20 students on the course now had their hands tied, were blindfolded, and wore not a stitch of clothing on their bodies. The interrogation was about to commence.

For 12 hours they remained in a mosquito filled shower block listening to a Thai music tape that was played none stop for the duration of their supposed capture. An interrogator sat in one corner, and every now and again, CLANG! He would hit a bucket once with a wooden spoon. The soldiers sat in a squatting position. CLANG-CLANG! They stood. CLANG-CLANG-CLANG! They spun around 360 degrees.

One by one they were taken by a different interrogator who set upon to use his skills of interrogation upon his victim, first a soft and mellow approach, and then later the harsh and threatening approach; and again the physical wear-him-down approach.

This was all an introduction to interrogation for the benefit of the soldiers' learning.

Years before on previous reconnaissance courses however, where I had been the student, a particular SGT (who in the early 90s was posted to Range Control and 'is not' permitted to be in command of troops any longer) ran things his way. He had been seen tying a guy to a tree and punching him, and forcing another underwater in a creek bed, almost drowning the poor guy (who was saved from death by the hand of another instructor). He had forced another to put his hand into a box and made him keep it there, though the snake was dead (and if you didn't know, a dead snake is still quite capable of killing even 24hrs after death) but the student didn't know this; and last but most certainly not least, he was seen to have thrown something out of a fast moving army rover he was driving – and the less said on this, the better. He was known to have done numerous other things that could only be expected by someone the likes of… 'Censored'; and if the RSPCA were to hear the stories of him, would have him put away for the rest of his natural life.

In regards to the interrogation being conducted, a few things had to be remembered.

All students had received a lecture on the Geneva Convention 48hrs prior to the interrogation as required, asked if they had any medical ailments such as a bad back ten minutes prior to the interrogation being undertaken, and were entitled to a night free of interrogation if they'd gone through the process before. All students went through the process without complaint however, as all wanted to march into Reconnaissance Platoon at the conclusion of the course with the knowledge that they had persevered all that we threw at them.

The 12 hours of interrogation passed without incident. Activities such as this had specific and strict guidelines; quite far-fetched compared to what would really happen. All had to remember also that a private soldier – when speaking of the infantry in general – only has limited knowledge on up and coming events with concern to friendly forces. All he needed to do was refrain from talking to the enemy for six to twelve hours; after that the soldier may as well spill his guts, especially if it meant getting a decent meal. Chances are he didn't know anything important.

The SAS – for example – were another kettle of fish. Here it's said that they undergo a minimum of three days interrogation and forego most of the niceties that had been given to the students on the 8/9RAR reconnaissance course. One more thing of importance should be remembered; civilised countries such as Australia are 'supposed' to be bound by guidelines as laid down in the big book of rules governing interrogation, where as other countries not abiding by such rules give themselves an open slather – so what was taught in practise isn't what you'd normally experience in real life.

At the conclusion of the course five new guys were welcomed into the platoon, along with a further half of the course having received a pass on the course as a whole.

Unfortunately, a platoon of our size couldn't take them all.

Suspended Extraction
Mid 1989

It was with luck that a proposed, combined course to qualify students in the art of repelling and suspended extraction, as well as others already with the qualification of repelling, to become qualified instructors of the same, was to fall the platoon's – Recon's – way.

The first two days of the course was conducted in Brisbane, with the student instructors learning all they needed to know about the ropes, accessories and teaching of techniques. This was followed by the student instructors teaching the students the art of repelling, all under the watchful eye and scrutiny of their instructor, a SGT from commandos who had apparently spent some time with the SASR. His technique of teaching, the general structure, and his mellow temperament, allowed for an enjoyable and easy flowing course.

After two days of basics and dry repelling from the mock tower positioned to the rear of the Enoggera Barracks fire station, the student instructors were ready to teach the same again, but from Blackhawks. The only two real differences between Blackhawk and UH1H was that when you jumped there was no need to move out onto the skids, as Blackhawks

didn't have them; and secondly, the ropes were secured to the ceiling of the Blackhawk aircraft, not the floor as was the case with the UH1H. Students were not, however, going to teach the forward exit style of exiting an aircraft, which involved the taking up of a metre of rope in slack and simply stepping from the chopper – as we'd done on numerous occasions on the mock tower.

For the final stages of the course, a trip to Townsville was voyaged, as this was the area to which the Blackhawks had been primarily stationed. It was like thrusting a tool into a babies hand, where 1RAR and 2/4RAR would have enjoyed themselves immensely; after all, we were quite aware as to how they cried their eyes out when on the

Barrington Tops, and none of us wanted to see them upset further, in particular the politicians who were bent upon military cutbacks.

The course was soon underway with one of the soldiers continuing even with a badly sprained ankle, making sure he kept his mouth shut as he well knew that loose lips sink ships and in this case, no more jumps if the injury was known about by the hierarchy present.

After the initial phase of the hands-on it was time for the suspended extraction phase of the course. Here the chopper would land to allow groups of four to hook up, before the chopper lifted to a height of 25 metres above the students. The throttle was then gently engaged, and the students would be lifted from the ground, arms linked, and taken for a quick joy ride around a five-kilometre circuit. It stands to reason that in the real situation that the chopper wouldn't take to landing for hook up, but would simply throw the ropes down to the ground for the troops there to secure themselves to the rope in seconds flat. Flying around beneath the chopper was quite exhilarating to say the least.

The course was a definite must and all felt as though they could quite honestly say that they could see why so many people loved hang-gliding.

It must be the most fantastic sport.

Exercise Kangaroo 89 - Movements
Day 1
Sunday, 6th August
1600hrs

Parade timings for roll call had been set on the Friday dismissal parade and became a disappointing reality, which fell into step with other exercises, to the point where they always seemed to commence and conclude on weekends. It was supposed by many that the Generals wanted to get their money's worth, considering that we were paid on a theoretical basis of 24 hours a day. Very convenient indeed was this rule, calling upon us to work 24/7 whenever they felt like it. Most married members found themselves struggling to keep their heads above water as it was, and it was said on numerous occasions that most infantry soldiers were below the average wage – according to statistics. As for me, I didn't really care; so long as I could afford to put a stubby in my hand it really didn't bother me.

Every soldier had all of his equipment placed into three ranks to the rear of A Coy, the pre-pre-embarkation assembly area which catered for recon platoons specific flight number, a flight which was to take us via the comfort of a QANTAS flight to the airport in Darwin. Once there we were to wait for transport to take us to another airfield before a final flight by C130, across the border into WA, was carried out.

The CQ was one of the first HQ element persons to arrive. He soon had the Q-store opened and armoury unlocked. Soldiers of A Coy lined up and one by one signed for their particular weapon – Reconnaissance platoon had been directed to move their platoon's worth of weapons to A Coy on the Friday for ease of final administration. All of the controlled stores that the patrol required for operation in the field were also issued on the Friday and marching order secured in Support Coy, to be picked up prior to weapons issue; this alleviated the problem of mass panic that was the usual outcome to pre-bush admin – we were ready for bush within minutes.

The gear that reconnaissance platoon carried looked quite cumbersome and could well have been given to them to savagely add weight to that which they already carried.

Within my patrol of five we carried an F1 radio and accessories, four claymores, claymore multi-firing device, patrol ambush light, night scope, binoculars, scout regiment telescope, helicopter landing panels, strobe light, all equipment as required for living in the field and a minimum equivalent of eight water bottles per man – more if you knew your appetite for drinking brews was significantly more than the average. This didn't include simple necessities such as smoke grenade or to the basics normally carried on patrol. In some cases we carried two radios, an F1 and a 77. This all came to quite a weight, and we were still yet to receive rations and ammunition. A good book was also a must and was usually rotated through the platoon, and sometimes these had dirty words in them, like vagina and arsehole, but we didn't really mind that much because we were real men – not like those plastic ones from the reserve.

1800hrs

The patrol had been moved to the Enoggera area theatre for the 'dangerous cargo' brief. The entire battalion was here, apart from a few odds and ends that included the road party that had departed a week earlier. They were charged with taking a whole heap of stores into the training area, along with several eskies for the road trip... but I don't know what they needed the eskies for. One guy said it was to help keep him cool because he hated to get hot and fidgety, and he couldn't sleep properly at night without a XXXX – I guess he said it like that because he didn't like swear words much so I wasn't going to offer him a read of our platoon book. If it was up to me I would have put a few good-old Queensland beers in the esky and had a few on the way, but I guess not everyone was as smart as me.

The brief went for at least five minutes and could have been significantly cut shorter with the following: 'No lighters, matches, ammo, hexamine tablets, pressure cans or batteries in cameras are permitted on this flight. If you have any on you, declare it now'. It was no wonder guys were getting out of the army in droves, fools taking five minutes to deliver a five second spiel. With talks of this nature, and petty rules to accompany them, who of a sane and stable mind could prevent themselves from yelling out obscenities at the top of their lungs? I thought that we must all be mad in one way or another.

Then came the inspection. One by one our gear was inspected for the prohibited articles mentioned above, and just for safe measure, so that it was all above board and legal, the MPs were there to watch over the procedure.

Tags were placed onto webbing and packs after inspection, and once equipment had been repacked, another transport corps wallah came forth: I could tell he wasn't from the infantry because he had a really big gut which hung over his belt and his teeth were shitbrown from drinking too much coffee from behind a desk. He cleared his throat, just like my

friend did once when flying over Townsville beneath a chopper, having swallowed a fly, whilst performing an extraction, and said something really stupid. He now wanted all breechblocks taken out from weapons and placed into packs. I wondered how high an IQ you had to have to think up these ideas, that individual would then know the theory behind the metaphysical structure of black holes and warp time factors of equimolecular proportion.

Soon after the movements brief and assignment to buses, the patrol was on its way to the airport. At 2210hrs we were finally in the air and heading for Darwin.

Exercise K89 - Drugs
Day 2
Monday, 7th August
0100hrs

We arrived in Darwin to find the temperature sitting on a sticky 26 degrees. If this was the temperature here, and now, what was it going to be in Kununurra by day?

All of our equipment was soon moved onto awaiting trucks and on this task being met we moved ourselves into the foyer where a short wait for buses was to be endured. The short wait turned into a two-hour thumb wrestle fight with boredom. What the hell was going on? One of the guys had reported seeing the coaches; they were just out of reach behind one of the airport complex buildings. The drivers were also present and sitting behind steering wheels. At first I thought that maybe the drivers were too stupid to know where to drive too, even though they could clearly see us, but that wasn't the case at all.

The battalion soon learnt of the reasons behind the delay when a vehicle carrying members of the SIB rolled in and the battalion was formed up into six ranks. An announcement was then made by the CO who indicated his displeasure on a specific article that had been found on the aircraft after the unit's departure from it. A syringe with illegal substance had been found in one of the toilets: For a moment I thought it might have been our book. Then I thought; 'maybe one of the soldiers from the 'hygiene section' had been scrubbing the toilets out'; I mean to say, you'd have to be high to have your head stuck in a toilet all day, scrubbing everyone else's shit from a porcelain bowl.

The entire battalion now found itself being sniffed by dogs (who had already been through our packs) and we were asked to roll up our sleeves. I was glad that the dogs didn't sniff too hard because I think I forgot to put clean underwear on. The battalion medical officer then went around to inspect arms for puncture marks – assisted by some officers of the battalion – and gazed deep into each and everyone's eyes for signs of drug use. I could see him as he walked past each of the men. He would look into their eyes and smile. Now I don't know why he did this, but two things crossed my mind. Either he was happy that the soldier was 'clean' or he was a homosexual trying to get-it-on; and then I suddenly remembered, he was an officer, and smiling was a part of his duty.

They found nothing wrong with anyone and finally arrived at the conclusion that the syringe must have been discarded in the toilet before we had even boarded the aircraft.

The last guy kicked out of the battalion for drug use was an officer. I dare say that the CO would have had the officers checked behind closed doors, because they weren't checked then and there with the remainder of the battalion. How would it have been for morale to see an officer break down into tears in front of the entire battalion, confessing to a sinful life of drug use and prostitution? It reminded many of an incident some six years before when a thief was actually drummed out of the unit, being stripped of his embellishments by the CO in front of the entire battalion. Great stuff for morale to see that justice was being done. That was one thing that never used to go without a bruised face or harsh word, thieves and bludgers – thank God they were a dying breed; or were they?

At 0530hrs all were on board the coaches and on their way to Larrakeyah Barracks where we received one more brief and placed into further groups for the flight by C130 into Kununurra some

The Poor State of War and Conflict

350km's South West South, 27kms West of the WA/NT border.

Once in Kununurra our Recon patrol was placed into an administrational area where we received our ammunition and hexamine tablets, those brought up by road convoy.

Tomorrow the main body of the battalion would be placed into their tactical environment at the FSB Stan, a flat dust bowl of searing heat.

Exercise K89 - Late Infiltration
Day 4
Wednesday, 9th August
2000hrs

Our patrol (63B) made for its insertion point; we were loaded onto UH1H. 63A (another 5-man call-sign) was also along for the ride in another chopper just behind ours.

We were in the lead chopper and as we approached the insertion point dropped abruptly into the safe hands of a small clearing, where we commenced to debus.

Within seconds my patrol had dispersed and was secure on the ground, packs on backs. Seconds later the chopper carrying 63A could be clearly heard to fly overhead. Once the chopper with 63A aboard passed us by our chopper commenced to build on its accumulation of revolutions, lifting from the ground to follow behind. The charade, a method of leap-frog movement, was conducted to aid in the concealing of the chopper's change in pitch, to deny the enemy information by sound as to our being inserted.

We soon picked ourselves up from the ground to be met by a small band of pioneers of the battalion. They had arrived here earlier in the morning, along with a boat and small outboard motor, a motor that according to orders wasn't supposed to be employed.

Visibility across the river to our front was very poor, but the landing point was known. It lay almost three kilometres downstream.

We clambered aboard and found the small paddles anything but helpful. The river was more like a lake, rather motionless. A snail doing breaststroke could have moved down stream with more speed.

The first task was to cross the 200 metre gap and then move stealthily down the river to the point over a kilometre away where boats would be left behind to be taken away by pioneers.

Time passed slowly, and with the passing of the first 60 minutes came the chalking up of only 500 metres. At this rate we'd be worn out before mission parameters could be met. A decision to make land was made then and there, take a short breather for assimilation by sound of what may lay in the immediate vicinity, confirm navigation details, and move off on our merry way with packs on backs.

The move wasn't too difficult, although many homes were encountered. Luck seemed to have changed slightly in favour of our patrol. Each house we passed seemed to have some kind of interior light on, or even a small porch or other outside light. Now I wasn't Einstein, but it wasn't hard to figure that it would be near on impossible for anyone to see us from within their homes, even though the distance between the homesteads and ourselves was as little as 40 metres, as we were in the open but shrouded by the dark of the night.

By 0100hrs we had arrived at a water pump and a ten metre wide canal that stretched out some 600 metres to the West. A white ute also had itself parked near the water pump, seemingly facing the river in such a position that the occupant would be able to see the entire waterway pass him by. If it was the enemy then we were lucky to have left the boats where we had, to then continue by foot, or we would have been seen sure enough.

I pulled the patrol back into the natural depression that had the best tree and bush cover around.

This act brought about a warning we had received the day before, about crocodiles.

Any time we found ourselves closer than 20 metres to a river, we had permission – as laid down in the safety guidelines for the exercise – for the commander of that group to load up with live ammunition. The commander was also the only man in each group not to have been issued with a BFA, for to be issued with such could have been rather dangerous if called upon to fire live ammo.

We were now ten metres from the riverbank and in such a depression of mangroves that my 20 round magazine of live ammo was secured immediately.

The sun commenced its climb at 0500hrs and the single picket during the night to maintain a watch on the ute overlooking the river turned up nothing of consequence.

Information was more easily available now however; the vehicle occupant's age, description, vehicles make, registration, etc. All was collected, encoded, and sent via the radio we carried. It seemed quite suspicious that someone should be watching the river like this, but due to the slope of the ground and shading of the interior, it was hard to say whether he was asleep or awake.

By 0530hrs the guy in the Ute was off on his way, and so were we, across the small canal and into a LUP, a location just as attractive to crocodiles than earlier on.

Day patrols were sent out; two two-man groups, with the fifth member given the live ammo, and informed to remain behind and hidden with the packs, codes and radio.

The Poor State of War and Conflict

The groups remained out all day, five buildings coming under the watch of several hours' worth of surveillance each, all in the aid to determine whether or not they were safe houses used for the harbouring of enemy forces or individuals. One such building was a banana shed, where several workers were found packing the yellow fruit into crates. This area must have been literally swarming with snakes, and here I was, me and my mate, crawling around in the long grass, but none were encountered.

Shortly after midday all had returned to the LUP. Several hours sleep would now be taken advantage of prior to a more formidable reconnaissance and surveillance being conducted on buildings (at night) that seemed to be more suspicious during the passing of the daylight hours.

It was 2300hrs. I approached a suspect house with another man, a building that was hidden well amongst the palms of a banana plantation. It would have been virtually impossible to get in here during the day – an effort was made, but penetration was limited to just fifty metres due to the throngs of workers. Our skilled two-man patrol had been fortunate not to have been compromised earlier on in the day, and lucky we were to have withdrawn from our task when we did, for more workers were brought into the area soon after lunch.

Twenty metres now separated us from the building thought to be suspect. We stood and listened. Fifteen minutes later and all remained quiet. The lights were off and not a move made from within the wooden walls of the old Queenslander style homestead.

We turned to retreat, and as we did so a dog commenced barking.

We stepped off slowly, hoping the dog was barking at something else, but no. The distance between it and us was quickly halved – it was coming towards us.

The outside lights of the house were turned on and the owner stepped out. We were thirty metres off from the porch; the distance between the dog and us commenced to decrease. The dog was now backed up by his master, courage instilled. It was now ten metres to our flank, and joined by another four-legged friend. 'Get 'em boys!' was the master's command. And the dogs were upon us. A torch beam followed the dogs who were now at our side. We stood our ground with steadfast will – in any realistic situation, I would have offered my left forearm to the menacing jaws, before thrusting a knife into the throat of the attacking dog, drowning him in his own blood; but this was an exercise, and such methods of defence discarded quickly.

'You guys,' he immediately recognised us as the army, 'you enemy or friendly?' He soon calmed the dogs down.

'Friendly, mate. Definitely friendly.' We introduced ourselves.

'I'd ask ya in for a beer but I don't suppose you'd be allowed.' He smiled, several teeth missing from his upper jaw. 'This here be my oldest dog. He's a bit deaf though. A damn snake bit him yesterday as well.'

'Poor dog,' I said.

'Yeah, but he's a good dog.'

'I don't suppose you've seen anyone acting suspicious around these parts?'

'Only you two. There's been no new people around here for years. Just the owners and plantation workers. All the locals have dogs too, ya know; all around these parts.'

'Is that right?'

'Yeah,' and the discussion continued for a short time.

'Well thank you for your time.' What else could be said? 'Hope you have a nice night, and see you around.'

'No worries, mate.'

And with that we parted company.

We decided to give several other houses a going over, but as each of these was approached, dogs would start to bark: 'Locals.' So an early retirement of the mission was encountered.

63B were extracted at 0430hrs and returned to Fire Support Base Stan some three hours later. It was here that we found out from a reliable resource that the enemy, those that we were searching for, had been extracted from the area some 18 hours before our insertion.

So much for military intelligence.

Ex K89 - 15km Close Reconnaissance
Day 7
Saturday, 12th August
1330hrs

Once again, we of 63B, found ourselves bound for the wilderness by courtesy of the newbeaut army chopper pilots; destination; some rise in the ground known as Bluff Mountain.

To be flown directly to its peak would have compromised our position, so a landing zone 1.6km away was considered to be the appropriate measure of security required in hiding our true destination to any nearby enemy – we would have to climb.

During orders – given by the reconnaissance platoon commander – an order to carry out water resupply was given. The patrol was to descend the mountain every time water replenishment was required. After several minutes of discussion it was decided to carry a jerry can to the top of the mountain instead. This turned out to be hectic to our health, by way of its weight, and by the time we'd reached the top of the feature one third of the water had been consumed.

Once at the top of the mountain, the major objective could be seen. It was a road that ran parallel to the line of sight with objective 'two; the road's extent couldn't be seen. The second objective was a farmhouse near a three-way road junction; it was fifteen kilometres away. The patrol's task in regards to this was to watch and record all vehicle movement, in and out of the farm, and to which direction they approached or departed. The occupant number, registration, colour and make of the vehicle were also required. With the SRT set up, the best we could manage was the obtaining of the type of vehicle and its colour.

One of the more unusual orders was also met with this trip and directed that there was no need to encode any information prior to broadcasting it over the radio. This was apparently so that the CO back in FSB Stan had the option of acting immediately to any incident as quickly as possible – which didn't mean much to us any more due to past experiences.

That afternoon, and the following morning, our patrol reported seeing an SAS patrol using the road; once to the farm, and once from it. This information was apparently acted upon some 24 hours later by way of B Coy on trucks, paralleling the road from just short of the farm, and up to and past Bluff Mountain. On initially sighting this platoon, a confirmation was made with the remainder of the patrol. Was it not stated in orders that 'no' friendlies were operating in our area of operations? Correct.

If I found it difficult to distinguish a vehicle's make which sat in the open at 15 kilometres, how on earth was I to establish whether this was friendly or enemy, as the trucks in question were hidden well by the surrounding countryside as they traversed the road towards us.

The call was made and I describing the movement as enemy. Some minutes later we were informed to disregard the sighting – meaning it was friendly.

It sort of contradicted what had happened to me during my first ever-bush trip; back then I'd gotten myself in the shit for not considering those on the motorbikes as enemy; now I was in the shit for considering two trucks as enemy when in fact they weren't. No matter which way you looked at it, no matter what the rank, all persons tried with great effort to hide their inadequacies by blaming others for things that went wrong; and then again, no one was safe from making a simple mistake, and all should be forgiven. Consider for example a reverse to the decisions that had been made by me, that was to say, not reporting the trucks, but shooting at those on the motorbikes. Everything would have worked out fine and nothing further said, for luck would have taken a ride on the back of a 'stab-in-the-dark' guess.

It seemed to me that all things needed to be taken on merit, and decisions had to be made by the man behind the trigger at the time of the confrontation; if that decision should be wrong, then so be it. Contradictions like the above occurred all of the time in the army, but regardless of its outcome, or regardless of who was in the wrong, it always seemed to be that 'you' were the one with 'your' name in the dreaded black book. As before, it was as simple as forgive and forget.

That afternoon the call we were waiting for finally arrived. We were to be airlifted back to FSB Stan. A question was asked as to the pick-up point, it was to be 1km to the West. Why not to the top of Bluff Mountain? The answer; the enemy may see us being picked up and the position compromised. But we weren't coming back here. But then again, what did it matter? The soldier at the bottom of the ladder couldn't do much for any particular circumstance or situation, when someone above him was unwilling to stick his own neck out for that particular individual, and officers rarely stuck their necks out. This was apparent to me, and probably why I was always upsetting someone, for I always liked the ability to voice my opinion, whether it be right or wrong, and many of the officers above me didn't readily accept that type of behaviour; in a strange way I could tell, because there seemed to be fewer smiling officers when I was around – or was the army changing.

The move to the exfiltration point took two hours, numerous cliff faces of no more than ten metres in drop, revealing themselves as every step was taken, and not a single one of them seemingly marked on the map; they were like giant thumbs sticking out of the ground, joined by buttresses of solid rock.

Once at our destination we were required to cut back the foliage for the chopper.

But weren't we trained for suspended extraction?

No, best not interfere this time around; let the officers have their wicked way with us.

One thing was for sure; the army in general was growing more pathetic with each year that passed. Here we were, trained with the ability for suspended extraction, but unable to perform it; and as for not being picked up from atop the mountain, that in itself could just not be explained. I personally felt that even in these fairly early years that it would be hard to recommend the army to anyone. It was a shame that good times were forgotten in times of bad.

Ex K89 - Wasted Effort
Day 13
Friday, 18th August
0430hrs

Orders revealed that a reconnaissance of some low ground, namely a basin, needed to be cleared visually of all enemy presence. The area of concern was the buffer between two areas of operation, that is to say, it was the responsibility of no single unit in particular and required specific permission from Brigade for any such move into it to be undertaken.

Permission was granted and all of 63B's equipment was readied for the three-day task.

The insertion point was to be on some of the higher ground near the basin as it was strongly suggested that this would once again deceive the enemy as to the true objective, and also permit the insertion to be conducted out of view of the basin in question.

The tactic of using two choppers in the aid of concealing the change in chopper pitch was once again employed. A small force of three men was also being inserted for the three day long reconnaissance, to aid in communication. The men from signals platoon were to set up a re-trans station and remain with this on some of the higher ground in the vicinity. Many problems were being encountered with comms, due primarily to the ionosphere.

1200hrs

The UH1H came into a hover some eight feet from the rocky terrain below and over the headphones to which I wore came the voice of the army pilot suggesting that we get out 'now'. He handed over a piece of paper with the grid reference location and I looked at this as he spoke into his headset.

'Aren't you going to land?' I asked.

'No. It's too risky. Now get out. I haven't got all day, mate.'

I removed the headset and signalled the others to climb out onto the skids. I was then met by several horror stricken stares. 'Get out. Hang from the skids and drop,' I yelled.

One member being only five feet tall shook his head.

'We aren't landing so you better jump,' was all I could say.

I climbed out, followed by the others. Hanging from the skid with 40 to 45 kilograms in pack on your back proved arduous (not to mention the weight of weapon and webbing) and we were still half a metre short of the rocky surface below – if you happen to be six foot tall. It wasn't like dropping onto a football field with nothing on your back; this was a landscape of hardened steel, and of the five men in 63B, three of us had a history of bad ankles and back problems due to conditions of employment.

Each dropped with packs on backs and weapons in hand. The chopper took off. A quick survey proved that all ankles had survived the fall. Now for the first of the navigation and radio checks, both of which proved unconvincing and inoperable; so much for re-trans.

We commenced to move towards the known basin area and by 1300hrs had confirmed our exact location on the map.

The lay of the ground compared with the 1:100,000 map proved mind provoking at times, many of the cliffs being unmarked as per the previous mission; boulders sized between that of a golf ball to a basketball also made the move slow and dangerous.

We continued down what at first appearance, and according to the map, was a good line of approach towards the basin. We were in a creek line where the banks rose a good fifty metres on either side. The journey was short lived however as we soon came to another cliff face; this one being of an eighty metre drop and once again, not marked on the map.

It was late afternoon and coming up to scheds. It was decided to stay there the night, 20 metres from the cliff face, protected by that and the 50 metre high – 70 degree – sides.

There was to be no moon tonight and movement in this country in the dark was asking for trouble. Tonight would also be a bad time to find out that you were a sleepwalker for the cliff was ever on my mind.

The following morning at 0600hrs we commenced to climb from our predicament, down the 50 metres in 30 minutes. The trek to the basin was remarkably easy from here, travelling the 800 metres down the spur in two hours; less than half-a-click per hour – not bad for this country.

By midday we (63B) had established ourselves a LUP and tried emphatically to reestablish comms. Even with the re-trans station this proved to be an impossible task. It was about then that a boat was heard travelling the river some two kilometres to our front.

It didn't take much common sense to realise that it was meant for us. Who else knew that we were here? Why was it apparently moving up the river, making ten-minute stops along route, and firing the odd shot from a rifle? We headed off towards the source of the noise.

We finally emerged from the brush to find a small group of 8/9RAR pioneers. BHQ were apparently worried over the lack of communications that they had received from us.

The re-trans had been airlifted out, we were required back at Stan, and the BN was closing a cordon on a large group of enemy somewhere to the north. The recon PL COMD was also becoming disgruntled with our efforts; but then again, who really cared. It was obvious to me that the only reason he was spitting venom was due to the kicks in the arse he was receiving from higher, which was by no way 63B's fault. More encouragement was needed from higher, not kicks in the pants for something that was not directly our fault. There were always two sides to a story.

63B received two missions after this, but both proved to be of little interest. The enemy never came to view during the exercise, although we were fired upon once from a distance of two hundred metres during a reconnaissance of an area which was already being patrolled by a friendly force; a waste of time and effort on our part.

All were returned to Brisbane on Monday 28th after 23 days bush; less than anyone would have liked, but more than ample for an exercise which gave little interest; most of the large exercises were like this. But then again, what was our job in the infantry? More than 95 percent of an Infantryman's time was supposedly spent searching and waiting for the enemy, less than a few percent being spent in engagement or under fire.

This exercise was not common. Although displeasure has to be voiced, it was not uniform throughout the army. All-in-all the army was an adventure that will last in my memory for eternity. We also need to keep in mind the military argument of 'the big picture', which, as it suggests, means that there was more to 'it' than met the eye.

In short; although I am peeved, I did understand.

Papua New Guinea
July 1990

The Australian Army has more than a few instructors/advisers in PNG at any given time. Most of these are of the rank of Warrant Officer and are quite obstinate in their ways. There were however, Sergeants doing the same job back in the 80s, but not any longer (to my knowledge). These sergeants were of no less merit to themselves or their country.

On the 7th February 1990 the 8/9th Battalion was given the news that a 65-man contingent was to head for the sunny shores of PNG on 12th July and establish themselves at the training establishment known as Goldie River.

They were to be known exclusively as the Australian Army Training Project Team, the first training team since Vietnam. Compared with the backdrop of Vietnam, our task was substantially less fragile in terms of its diplomatic importance, but not by terms of merit. We weren't going to be shot at or killed by the hand of a well-organized unit, but in comparison with the growth of social standards within Australia, faced a formidable task that was just as exciting to mind, and as impressively important to the growth of individual pride.

Why were they sent here? Simply to increase the strength of the PNGDF to a sizable force for the protection of its borders – this was the political statement shared by most. PNG only had the strength of three regular infantry battalions and the Indonesian/PNG border was a large undefined area where clashes between forces of Indonesia nationality occurred quite often. But of course, others would say that the instructors were there to train soldiers purposely for Bougainville.

On the 12th day of July the contingent boarded a QANTAS aircraft with great anticipation for what lay in wait for them during their six-month deployment. The contingent arrived in Port Moresby at 1320hrs that same day.

Goldie River
12th July

The road to Goldie River Barracks was for the most part unsealed, as were many of the roads out from Port Moresby's industrial, commercial, and residential centres. It certainly appeared to most, that the 'welcome dollars' that the Australian government was sending over in aid, was going to waste. It was originally felt and confirmed that the money was being spent on roads and schools etc. Many of the 65-man contingent believed, however, that the corruption of the government was brought out into the open that year, but unsure as to the measures that the Australian government took against actions such as high officials accepting bribes for votes of confidence. But I guess this was a better option than allowing PNG to have tried to pursue aid from the communists [Russians] back in 1973.

The surrounding countryside was in tune to that of Townsville, the major difference being the basic living standards; the way in which they led their lives, the poverty and way of society, and its wave of crime that put Australia's to shame; thank God.

It took about 30 minutes to reach the gates of Goldie. It was a pleasant change from what had been seen so far. But the scene around was a masquerade that hid Goldie's problems so easily on that first day in country.

The barracks themselves were very similar to Lavarack Barracks; a blueprint had apparently been brought up from the North of Queensland and used to build some of the camp. Even the OR's kitchen was a mirror image to those in Australia.

The camp boozer must have been a local initiative. No walls, two pool tables, several picnic tables, and a wooden box that normally housed a TV, were all the commodities of the dwelling. The TV itself had been confiscated by the PNG CO of the area, due to horseplay amongst his soldiers one night, and was probably still stashed at his home for his own personal convenience.

Here the soldiers of Goldie would come, every payday, cash in hand, and blow nearly the lot in one hit. Fight after fight was normally the outcome, but we of the contingent would just have to wait and find out for ourselves.

I had seen very little of this place which was to be my home for the next six months, but a tour of the area would be conducted on the morrow. Were we to be impressed by anything here? I strongly doubted it.

The ration store was in a shambles. Snakes and rats had to be beaten back with sticks and clubs. On showing the medic the standards of the store, he confessed that all had a big job ahead of them. Even before the clean-up had commenced he realised how lucky all were that none had come down with any serious illness.

The transport yard needed attention. The PNGDF TPT PL had quite an ill effect upon all of the vehicles in the vicinity. If a vehicle didn't start for whatever reason, then it was towed to the yard and left to rust, and fall apart.

Maintenance on vehicles was pretty much non-existent. Tools were minimal; usually borrowed by the soldiers working there, who in turn failed to bring them back to the workplace. Light fingers were a major problem in Goldie.

Most of the vehicles were found to have small deficiencies of some description, such as having no oil in the engine, no petrol in the tanks, or air in tyres; all of which could easily have been fixed.

A $40,000 cooling system had been purchased for the RAP some years ago and just two months before the contingent's arrival it had broken down. Instead of getting it fixed for a price of $5,000 it was decided by someone in authority that it required replacing. So they brought another one of inferior quality for the low price of $25,000.

They had already proved that they had little common sense and a poor attitude towards their equipment. The logistic and administrational system certainly failed to operate effectively, or was it the men who worked (couldn't work) the system?

125, brand new, military compasses, were supposed to be in a safe, in the Q-store, that the instructors were to be operating out of. On approaching the PNG SGT, our SSGT was advised: 'No. We don't have any compasses here.'

Our SSGT decided to push the issue further and inspected the safe himself, shazam, 125 compasses.

The PNG SGT would still deny their existence however, as he had no paperwork on them, although he did admit seeing someone writing something, somewhere, some years before.

The RAP had a hell of a job ahead of them too. Not only did it take them all week to scrub back the filth from the walls in this 'operational' RAP, but also mass bribery was to meet them at every corner they turned.

To the rear of some of the rifle ranges – which were required for the training of the 300 PNG soldiers – were large chicken coops. The local tribe of the area owned these. They would be willing to move the chickens to a different location so long as they received free medical treatment. So once a week the RAP had to pick up sticks and visit the local tribe.

Most of the locals that worked in the area, or who were related to someone of the military in some way – living on the barracks – visited the RAP frequently. Most came due to children that had been affected by mosquito bite, and many were infected with malaria/polio.

The RAP witnessed many deaths and was always confronted by long lines of patients each morning. Two children in particular couldn't be helped. They were so sick from infection that they were half brain-dead due to lack of preventative measures being taken against the dreaded mosquito.

The RAP organised a dousing of the area, fumigating the entire camp, and killing off the uninvited mozzie. Once a week seemed to do the trick.

It took a considerable amount of trouble to sort out all of these problems, and we hadn't even started to climb the ladder as yet.

Atrocities
16th July

The contingent soon found themselves with the opportunity to converse with the regular soldiers of the PNG Army. I was more than surprised to find that some were very keen and knowledgeable, others deserve nothing less than a firing squad.

UH1H aircraft, of which were given to PNG as a token gesture of goodwill by the Australians, to be used for medical evacuation of ground troops in Bougainville, and for the ferrying of medical supplies, weren't.

I had found myself a veteran who had a mouth most humble. He couldn't help but to spill his guts, to tell of his stories, to tell of his heroics.

A member of the BRA was taken aboard one of these choppers and was questioned, or more specifically, interrogated. Whether or not he gave into the wishes of the PNG soldier was never told, but I was informed how they threw him out of the chopper to his death, into the Solomon Sea. This certainly coincided with a story I'd heard of a body being washed onto the silky shores of the Solomon Islands earlier that year.

And another: A Company of 32 soldiers, carrying out operations in Bougainville, soon became fatigued; they had been there for three months – quite a stint (without rest) by anyone's terms. They were informed that they were to be relieved in place by another company of regulars.

A lot of the men were unhappy with this arrangement, as they had not yet killed anyone, unlike some their wantoks before them. How could they possibly return home without first doing the job for which they had come, to inflict death? They were on the verge of a mutiny.

The company commander finally gave his orders. They would attack at dawn, an unsuspecting village which could quite easily have hostiles in their midst. The village was taken out and the soldier's egos satisfied – many innocents died.

And yet again: A sniper fired upon a PNGDF section on patrol, the very section that was under command of the guy I was speaking with. The sniper had killed his lead scout.

One of the sniper pair escaped unharmed, but the other had been wounded in the shoulder – the man responsible for the kill.

The section commander approached the scout and looked into his eyes. The sniper had done his job, nothing more and nothing less. The commander of the section lifted his SLR and placed the butt firmly into his shoulder; and holding the barrel against the sniper's head, pulled the trigger. No prisoners would be taken.

Miscellaneous Affairs
25th July

Diarrhoea had spread throughout the camp overnight. Our bodies just weren't used to the bacteria and other constituents found within the water.

A test on the water source proved it to be unhealthy for human consumption, so it had to be purified by the individual prior to drinking. Two purification tablets, to every water bottle of water, was the order of the day, and some of the guys who weren't affected applied a smaller dose of purification, administering less and less as each day passed.

Was so much purification in the water bad for our bodies, our inner organs; it certainly couldn't be doing us any good.

Sometime later a report proved that the problem did lie in the water tank situated upon the hill overlooking Goldie. It was the direct responsibility of the local caretaker to purify the water on a daily basis, the water itself being pumped directly from the river, the same river that flowed down from that which was used by local tribes. It was enough to make your stomach turn over backwards and do cartwheels: faeces in the water.

The caretaker had decided not to purify the water, as the climb up the hill was too much for him to be bothered with, which was the same way in which he looked at the hot water system for the barracks. The reason no one had any hot water, wasn't because the system didn't work, but because the caretaker had failed to keep the gas-pilot lights, lit. The medic soon had words with him about matters of health and safety. This must have had some effect upon him, for the problem with the purification of water soon ceased to exist.

One bed and a single locker, per man for the six months in the country. During the six months we were permitted in town on less than eight separate occasions [give or take].

26th July

Tuarama Barracks, just on the fringes to Port Moresby, had been placed on alert. There was expected to be a riot in direct response to the K4,000,000 (kina) given as bribes to officials for their votes of confidence. The riot never eventuated.

27th July

One of the contingent found himself in a situation which could have been rather messy, not because he was faced with possible injury or death, but because he was the only married member of the contingent who was seen or heard to try and play around, with the opposite sex. PNG was much different than Malaysia; in particular from when I was there last, for this place was dangerously overflowing with disease.

He had found himself a young lady and took her for a walk down to the pier. Here they sat and talked – amongst other things.

Sometime after their arrival at the secluded spot – around 2200hrs – a group of no less than six rascals arrived.

They held him at knife-point, told him to hand his clothes over, and went through the pockets. They then took the young lady with them, threatening the soldier; that he'd be killed if they returned in five minutes and found him still there. Screams and murmurs could then be heard coming from where the woman had disappeared, and as the soldier ran for help, the gang of rascals proceeding to bash and rape their victim. Maybe if he'd done what he was told and remained in place at the club, which had security guards present, none of that would have happened. I thought he was stupid and very self-centred.

The young lass spent five days in hospital before returning to the Aussie for more affection. Some people just didn't learn.

4th August

Twenty tonnes of ammunition for the course arrived aboard three Hercules aircraft. Not all was used for the Recruit/IET course: I'll let you use your imagination…

The Kokoda Trail
11th August

The course in Goldie was to commence soon. To date, all that the contingent had done was to carry out administration for the course to come. So much lay ahead of us, from erecting gallery ranges to sneaker ranges (varying types of rifle range), to moving in 300 beds, preparing lesson plans for the sixteen week course, and bringing in stores which were to be issued and used by the soldiers in question. Now it was time to take a short few days break, to either rest back in barracks and do nothing, or to see a bit of the country.

19 decided upon the Kokoda trail as a means of amusement, taking along with them two members of the PNGDF, who themselves were sergeants and instructing on the course alongside the Australians.

After being flown into Popendetto, a two-hour wait for transport was suffered. The transport had been arranged by one of the PNG soldiers, his sole reason for taking the journey was due to his wanting to see his family, to which he hadn't seen for quite some time. A cousin of his had arranged for the neighbourhood police to pick our group up by truck.

By the time we reached Kokoda village, we were ready for the big trek – the museum there was nothing more than a small open shed, but very much worth the visit.

We walked for several hours that first day, coming to a stop on reaching the first of the many hills to be encountered. As we weren't to commence until the following day anyway, we saw nothing wrong with taking an early break, to take in the surrounding atmosphere, the solitude of the jungle.

The final hours of light were put to good use, spent rearranging the packs we carried, our house for the next few days. Here we carried our food which was to last us the short trip.

It just wasn't good enough that we should rely on food from the villages – even though we would pay for it. It may have saved some the locals a trip however, as it wasn't uncommon to see men and women travelling for two to three days from the highlands down to the areas near Moresby, to sell their crop at the markets.

A minimum of one-day worth of water was also carried by each trekker, along with a group radio and other equipment for communication with Goldie. Essential warm weather gear, sleeping bag, and hutchies were other necessities.

The first day of walking was quite breathtaking, but certainly not the best; much more was to come. The jungle was a most peaceful place, by day and night.

We spent our first scheduled night in a place called Alolo Village. Here we found a Kokoda Trail sign that had been ripped from the post and thrown to the ground to rot. It was in fairly good condition, so was picked up and carried the remainder of the walk, to eventually find its way into the Rams Retreat – the 8/9RAR boozer.

We passed all of the places seen by any adventurer willing enough to make this most worthwhile of walks; Mt.Bellamy, Lora Creek, Templeton's Crossing, and of course Owen's Corner.

All the sights were seen; the foot bridges, mountain streams, foxholes and shellscrapes. Ammunition was easy to come across as well, old 303 ammo and mortar bombs.

At one stage during the adventure, it took almost four hours to travel a distance of 400 metres – due to the lay of the ground. It was quite harsh in some places. Another thing that was a wonder to see was the aircraft landing strips. These rolled with the contours of the ground and suddenly stopped, the edge of the strip dropping away to a valley hundreds of metres below. Not much different to an aircraft carrier really, which rolled with the waves, creating its own rolling curves and cliff, so I wouldn't classify it as unique.

The 15th was our final day, a short four hours of walking bringing us out to Owen's Corner, another extremely steep climb; but at least this had fewer false crests, something which was encountered too often during the climbing of some peaks, and quite demoralising.

This was one experience that would live forever in the hearts of those that trekked the trek; it was made all the easier too; for a battle wasn't being waged as we walked it.

I noted with great inspiration that an Australian man, who didn't have the use of his own legs (wheelchair bound), literally walked the entire trail on his hands in ten days: it made our effort of just a few days seem rather insignificant.

New Recruits
23rd August

The first of the recruits arrived from outside Moresby today. They were met as one would like to have been met, speaking to them firmly but not belittling them – quite dissimilar to the Australian Army recruit/IET system which only forced an opinion upon the soldier that, yes, the instructors were immature fools with no real hold on reality. So much for the system of fools. But the opinions of men and women not open to ridicule or military training, would naturally find it hard to cope with harsh words and a cold stare. Kapooka and Singleton were not holiday camps, but training establishments of the hardest kind.

43 heads were counted, as they were loaded onto the trucks, 45 had been expected.

One of the older guys from Mt.Hagen pointed out that four of the recruits had run off down the road when the buses had turned up to bring them into Goldie. All they were after was a free air flight to their capital in the hope of finding other employment. But if four had made a run for it, there should be 41 heads, not 43.

A check was conducted by name. Two of the men here weren't recorded on the list we'd prepared earlier. Unfortunately they couldn't be taken. They were informed to go through the correct channels of enlistment and advised on how to go about it, being told that they had exactly one week before the course actually commenced. They would miss out on most of the preliminaries but could catch up on these later – dependent on how long they took to join us in Goldie. They immediately made their way to the recruitment office as advised.

29th August

They arrived in large numbers, most by foot, few by bus. Once through the gates of Goldie, their names were taken down, and after cross-reference, they were placed into a platoon in order for administration to commence.

Most of the platoons had been arranged in such a way that those members marching into a platoon would find themselves amongst others from their place of birth, or near as possible to it. But after the preliminaries week and introduction to the course, they would be split up once more into a more logical pattern for training, along with a large diversity of age groups combined within a single section. Here a mixture of experiences and knowledge would be sought, separating certain recruits from any high authority that was found to be present from their highland's tribe or birthplace. There was a situation encountered on Goldie where a regular private soldier was of a higher order of rank within his province than that of a warrant officer he now worked under. Whilst in camp everything was fine, but once outside of the front gate, and no longer on military soil, the private was in charge and in complete authority over that of the Warrant Officer.

There was also a situation in Moresby where a truck driver had run over a little girl. Being from a different province, the little girl's wantoks claimed compensation; k1,000,000 and several thousand pigs was the going rate. All you could hear over the radio for the next three days were announcements trying to persuade the two groups not to clash in bloodshed.

An arrangement was met and compensation paid, but not for the amounts requested – several hundred pigs was the outcome; that's what her life was worth in the end.

Age was also a factor in recruitment. One of the recruits looked extremely young, and on further investigation was found to be only 14 years of age. No real proof could be gained and the PNGDF seemed not to care about his age. The contingent had no alternative but to allow him on the course. He passed all objectives on the sixteen-week course and with better results than some of the older soldiers; so on completion of the course he was 14 years of age and ready to kill.

One of the recruits enlisting did so under a false name. The only reason he was caught out was due to the fact that the real owner of the name was already in Goldie – most didn't have birth certificates as they were born in the highlands, in places like that found along the Kokoda Trail and sometimes even more remote than that.

31st August

All of the recruits were brought together today and arranged into ten platoons of thirty men.

This was the big adjustment to separate the provinces as best as possible and equally between the platoons. There were now two companies, each comprising 150 men.

Of the 30 men in the platoon I was operating from, we received only two of our original soldiers back. The other twenty-eight were new faces. Now came the first of the crunches to time and space for the first week of training, for we had no idea if these soldiers had been inducted correctly, or even if they had all of their administration details taken care of. This could bring about a lot of late nights – but it was only for one week.

Problems
1st September

The course was under way, but not without its headaches, all of which were brought on by the recruits.

'Corporal, I don't have a knife and fork.'

'Corporal, I lost my towel.'

'My shorts don't fit.' It wouldn't help to explain to these soldiers that they had a variety of nine different sizes to choose from, whereas the last course which had just marched out, under the guidance of the PNG instructors, had a choice of just two – a choice of only four when it came to boots. Boots were something else, for most of these guys had never worn them before. 'Corporal, my shoes don't fit and they hurt my feet, do I have to wear them?'

'I think I'm twenty one years old, Corporal; but I'm not sure.'

'No, Corporal. My Father's first name is my last name, and my first name belongs to someone else; I liked the sound of it so took it for myself.'

'No, Corporal. He's name is Namor.P, mine is P.Namor.'

One of the questions asked was why they had decided to join the army.

'To protect the borders of PNG.'

'To serve the people.'

'To get away from my province. I hate the people there.'

'I have nothing better to do.'

'My crocodile farm will need three more years to mature. I'll join the army and get out later.'

What could you say: 'Well done men; you all passed the questions with flying colours.'

A quick explanation on 'flying colours' was then conducted.

Another recruit was found emptying the contents of the bag he was carrying into his locker. Instead of containing clothes, it contained 200 buai nuts, a drug similar to that of the coca leaf of Peru (as far as I understand it).

A search was conducted, each of the instructors searching his own section. No buai was found in our platoon, but the 25 odd knives were confiscated until march-out.

2nd September

The instructors were informed to conduct their own medical parades in the mornings due to the influx of soldiers reporting for sick parade each day.

'Oh, Corporal. I have pains under my chest and around my armpit area. I need to see the doctor.'

'How do you think you got them Recruit Siaoa?' (see-'ow-'a)

'I think it was doing push-ups.'

'Then I suggest you get back into the ranks and cover off, before you get another 20 push-ups for wasting my time.'

Three recruits approached me, asking to see the doctor. They were complaining of constipation. When asked how long they had it for they said since they'd arrived at Goldie some six days before. After one owned up to the problem, more and more started to come out of the woodwork. Half of the platoon was infected.

I gave each a pill and told them to see me in the morning.

The following morning saw the same guys complaining that they now had diarrhoea.

4th September

Four recruits were taken to the medic. They were each diagnosed as having Malaria. The CO of the Australian contingent was soon informed as all platoons had started to show signs of having the same problem.

A course of malaria pills was strongly suggested.

PNG officials immediately denounced the idea and forbade the contingent to treat the problem.

Each instructor was also teaching as per the Australian method of instruction. This was soon discarded. The recruits seemed to look at the instructors as a mirror image, and no matter what was done, the same mistakes arose time and time again. Lessons were then changed to suit the drill being taught, some as I stood beside them, and others as I stood with my back turned on them. The change in the methods of instruction worked and an overall faster progression made thereafter.

Platoon Commander
11th September

I found that the platoon was rather lucky, when taking into account its structure of instructors. We had the good fortune of having an Australian SGT, our only demise was the platoon commander who happened to be a PNG regular, the most hated man in the company.

He couldn't help but to show off and boast on how he was trained in Australia, always remarking on how good he was.

A few of the Australian officers were questioned reference this, and it was announced as a fact that this particular officer was indeed trained overseas, but PNG students on an officer course in Australia were subjected to a shorter course as compared to others – and, from what I understood, usually involved receiving a pass, regardless of how good or bad the student fared. Of course, there was the exception to the rule, and some PNG students made rather good officers. Our platoon commander was not one of these.

On occasion he would find a seat to the rear of the lecture room, in most cases that being a large tent with the sides rolled up due to the heat and lesson structure.

Up would shoot his hand, every time a question was posed to the soldiers. He was never asked to give an answer, and he certainly had nothing to gain, or prove, by doing such.

He couldn't help himself during some of the lessons, putting his nose in where it wasn't welcome. 'No, Corporal Clayton. Not like that. We always used to do it like this in Duntroon,' and would then go on to explain things to the recruits. One day he was pulled aside quite politely, so as not to damage his reputation with the soldiers, not that any more damage could have been done. 'Listen sir. If you want to give the lesson then go ahead and give it. If not, go away and pester someone else.'

20th September

According to PNGDF law, a soldier wasn't permitted to smoke cigarettes during working hours. The Australian instructors turned a blind eye to this fact, allowing the students their indulgence during breaks between lessons.

At one stage I could see a few of the soldiers talking amongst themselves. They didn't appear to be in the best of spirits. On questioning them I found out that their beloved PL COMD had caught one of the recruits smoking during work hours and had ordered him to put it out in his mouth, which of course the soldier did.

The soldiers were then pooled together and tactics drawn. If any wished to smoke he could, but to do so he would have to walk the short distance of thirty metres from the tent and down into a large drain that ran the length of the sports oval adjacent to them. In this way they would be less likely to be seen by their PL COMD. He seldom showed his face nowadays, having become a little bashful. He was probably tired of the NCOs' sarcastic remarks. 'And always maintain a sentry to watch for the Boss,' was our warning to them all.

10th October

The PL COMD tried pushing his luck one day. He had pulled aside two Australian NCOs from a neighbouring platoon and was chewing them out over something that at this stage was unclear to me. They were also in earshot of the recruits, which just wasn't on. If an NCO was to be disciplined, then it should be conducted out-of-sight: unlike what I did behind his back, so I guess I was no better.

I approached.

He was apparently trying to find evidence of a recruit's effort, in blaming a NCO, for something that remained the fault of the recruit. The officer took the side of the recruit, apparently a relation.

It was decided to interject with a change of subject as the officer had now threatened to charge the NCOs. 'Excuse me sir.'

'Yes?'

'I hear that you made a few of the soldiers put out their cigarettes in their mouths the other day; is that correct?'

'Why is that, Corporal?'

'Well, I'll tell you, sir. If I see or hear of your doing that type of thing again, I'll be taking the information to the OC and have you placed on a charge.'

'You are going to charge me?'

'Yes, sir. That's right. What do you have to say to that?'

'Well.' The subject, once again, changed rather rapidly. 'I just wanted to say that there will be a conference later on today; reference tomorrow's activities. That's all.'

'Fine, sir. See you later.'

That seemed to be the last time that he pursued anything reference NCOs and their right to train soldiers as they saw fit.

10th November

Today was the day of the gas tent.

A tent had been erected near the river where the breeze was strongest, so that on a soldier's exit from the tent in question, the gas crystals could be more effectively washed away with the helping hand of a splash of water on face.

Numerous lessons were the normal lead-up to this activity before gas masks were issued. Each soldier was talked through the checking of his mask, checking it for size and the refitting of gas filters when required.

The PL COMD took this opportunity to show up, announcing to everyone that he'd done this ten times before and that there was nothing to it. He looked down at one of the soldiers who was sitting crossed-legged and checking his mask, when the officer snatched it from his person. His plan was to show off as usual, and he wanted nothing more than to be one of the first to go through the gas chamber.

Now, once inside the tent, a few tests were to be conducted by the soldier. Firstly you ran in with the gas mask strapped to your leg. You have to very quickly place the mask on, clear the trapped gas from the fitted mask, and check the seal; all part of the drill taught.

Secondly you were required to break the seal, and then reseal and clear the mask before coming under the effect of the gas. If affected however, you then had to proceed with the actions of clearing the mask over and over again until such a time that you could breathe normally. Last of all, you were required to remove the mask completely and give answers to questions posed by the instructor in the tent at the time.

'What's your name?'

'It's... it's... I... Joseph... no Bob.'

'What's your girlfriends name?'

'It's ah... No it's... I don't have one,' and out he would come to receive the splash of water on his face in the loving cool breeze, wiping away the snot pouring from his nose as he stood there half bent over and gasping for breath.

It was quite a sight to see the PL COMD go into the tent and then come running out because the mask didn't have a correct seal due to it being a size too large.

The tent of concentrated tear gas had done its job.

Individuals
11th September

Early one afternoon a soldier from within the platoon approached with what he believed was a major problem.

His act was genuine and had him removed from the course and sent home.

He was complaining of severe pains that were shooting through his body, 'like a fever,' he said. And he knew how he came about getting the pains.

Back in his village he had lost his parents and some close friends; they had died because a sorcerer from another province had placed a spell on them; the same spell that now affected him. He had to get back to his village so that he could render the situation harmless.

He received his discharge papers within two weeks.

M79 weapon range.

From day one on the course, all had to be on their toes for even the slightest problem that might crop up within the section, platoon, company, and course as a whole; such things as personal hygiene, for some of the soldiers, had never:

Used a toilet before; didn't know how to use a shower (and one man tried to defecate in one); didn't know how to brush their teeth with toothpaste and brush, or; had never seen, used, or heard of a razor blade before.

Regardless of whether the individual needed to shave or not, he was required, as laid down in standing orders, to shave every single morning before 0615hrs.

I walked into the latrines at 0800hrs to find one of the soldiers shaving. 'What are you doing, Recruit Pew? Didn't you shave earlier on?'

'Yes, Corporal. But I was a bit prickly, so I thought I'd shave again.'

He was given several days 'extra regimental training', as it was a hell of a lot easier than charging the soldiers, but only after a confession on his part had been received, that he had in fact lied, and did not shave earlier on.

Time in training was a major factor here. The section commanders could hand out punishments of up to five days 'extra regimental training', and none ever went over-board.

Discipline had to be taught as soon as possible during this sixteen-week course; the only discipline they'd probably ever encounter during their time in the PNGDF.

That night Pew informed the NCO in charge of the ERT parade that he couldn't do the punishment drill as he had a bad headache and his arms were sore. The drill was given regardless, and 30 minutes later he collapsed. His pack was removed from his person and he was sat down to rest – for the others, the drill continued. Even NCOs made bad calls of judgement from time to time.

Recruit Siaoa used the privilege of approaching the NCOs 'after hours' quite frequently. He was keen to learn. He knocked on the door.

'Who is it?'

'Recruit Siaoa, Corporal.'

'What do you want?'

'I would like….'

'Get in here.'

'Yes, Corporal, thank you, Corporal.'

'Listen, Recruit Siaoa, you don't have to say 'thank you, Corporal' after every sentence. I want it to stop. Use a bit more aggression, especially when you knock on the door. The army will look after you if you break your knuckles.'

'Yes, Corporal; thank you.'

'Where's your hat? You know you're supposed to have it on when you come to see us. You know that, don't you, Recruit Siaoa?'

'Yes, Corporal.'

'You can give me twenty push-ups later on.'

'Yes, Corporal, thank you.'

'Now what is it you want?'

'You wanted to see me about my written medical test.'

'That's right. Tell me, Recruit Siaoa; how do you treat a snakebite wound? Let's say… to the leg.'

'First I would cut open the infected area and suck out all of the bad blood. I would then elevate his feet so that the blood could rush to his heart.'

'No, Recruit Siaoa. That's what you're 'not' supposed to do. You just killed a man; and probably yourself too.'

'I think I might have got it wrong.'

'Yeah. So do I.'

Unfortunate Events
14th September

Another of the Australian soldiers received a Dear John letter today. We'd been in the country not much more than a few months and the women were dropping their boyfriends, and fiancés, like flies.

What exactly did they think they were getting themselves into when they started going out with a member of the infantry was beyond any sane person. Here they were, sitting back in the lap of luxury known as Australia, and all they could seem to do was worry about where their next cuddle was going to come from. It was all very sad. It was no wonder that many of the guys remained happily single, playing at nothing more than to use the women they came into contact with instead of being used themselves – at least there was a little honesty in not leading a female on to think she was something... more permanent.

2nd October

One of the contingents few luxuries disappeared today. Someone had stolen the video player from our makeshift boozer, so now the boys couldn't even watch their loved ones on the videos sent from home.

Evidence in reference to the theft was easy to come by. There were large bare footprints of the culprit on the floor of the single room building, a building that had been transformed into the only means of group socialisation for us. Not only that, but his fingerprints were also everywhere we cared to look.

The PNGDF MP's were called, but all efforts to conduct a search were dropped.

Another example of the wantok system.

11th October

A crocodile was reported to have been spotted just a few hundred metres from the barracks.

This put slight worry in everyone's minds as quite frequently there was the requirement, for training purposes, to cross Goldie River by foot.

Although this water was only knee deep at its shallowest point, it still forced a decision of safety to be made.

When crossing the river, as a section was required, I always made sure that there were others around me. There just had to be safety in numbers, so the open file method of movement was employed; a standard box shape formation with scouts to the front. I figured that the croc-farmer of the platoon had a better chance of survival than me, so why not employ him?

Final Week in Papua New Guinea
End of Days

The combined Recruit/Initial Employment Training course had commenced on the 3rd September; all of the soldiers marched out on the 21st December in front of family and friends. From here they would march into their battalions.

It was only hearsay, but very prominent in its outspoken voice, that from here a reported 100 were to venture over the Solomon Sea, to Bougainville on 3rd march, 1991.

Three of the recruits – who were now classed as Private – from my section, were more than happy to hear that they would be a part of that 100.

Short speeches were given by individual instructors behind closed doors on behaviour; what not to do, to be wary of their officers and NCOs, not to fall victim to the whims of others by doing for the sake of doing, but to maintain the code of conduct as taught by the Geneva Convention.

As for the equipment that was issued to them on behalf of the Australian government, well, that would more than likely be taken from them by the other soldiers of their battalion in Tuarama Barracks; that was the way in PNG. They, too, would commence to brainwash the new soldiers' minds, to fill their heads full of unnecessary garbage, to reteach what they had been taught. Only the strong willed would overcome this bombardment of untruths.

It was a shame to say that a good 20% of the soldiers should never have been given a tick in the box, but this was a numbers game – as it was with the PNGDF officers in Duntroon – and selection of all descriptions outside of the instructor's control.

Their overall standards were less than that of an Australian soldier, but then again some of these recruits had no education, didn't know how to use a toilet, and had never seen a pair of shoes before, and yes; one guy in my section couldn't even speak English. The course was also a combined course and several months shorter than what the Australians would have received. These few did have one thing over the Australian recruit and IET; a few had more personal guts and drive, in particular when compared to those of the Ready Reserve – the university student (and I'm sorry that the truth is now out-there).

They were now to find out how luxurious they had their training and food, and see first-hand how well the Australian administration and logistic system worked in comparison to the PNGDF. From here their overall efforts would decline with the new teaching of laziness creeping into their newly found ranks at Tuarama. They were going to be shat upon from a great height on their march into their battalion.

I was personally more than happy with my section's results; the 2nd and 3rd best at physical training; the overall 2nd best soldier of 300 recruits; and a team which proved time and time again that they had the best section drills, and fire and movement techniques, than all of the others pooled together – as mentioned by the CSM and other high rankers of the contingent.

All of this would hopefully do them some good when in conflict with their Brothers from across the Solomon.

We returned to Australia on Christmas Eve, having made a little ground in respect to understanding the ways and mannerisms of the PNGDF, but we did feel as though we had accomplished, quite well, the task for which we had really been sent: to train them for conflict in Bougainville.

The first six months of 1991 would see another 300 trained, all in aid to strengthening the PNGDF.

Service in PNG with the AATPT is worth more to me than the service in Rwanda.

Initial Emplyment Training
February, 1991 to December, 1993

IET training for the Infantry was conducted at the School of Infantry, Singleton, NSW. Each course consisted of eleven training weeks, with all but two of the weekends being given to the soldiers for the purpose of recuperation and personal administration. Although it was sometimes boasted to be a physically demanding course, it was nothing that couldn't be achieved by anyone marching out of Kapooka.

I couldn't recall seeing any more than nine platoons of IET being trained at any one time, each in a different week of training; this also depended on the time of year. The school could only train what came from Kapooka, and they in turn could only train the numbers enlisted in accordance with the yearly quota.

The town of Singleton depended quite heavily on the School of Infantry for its survival, no less than they depended on the miners from down the road. At one point, when rumours were spread about the infantry centre being relocated, the locals were said to have screamed blue murder and began to protest via petition. I never saw this petition, nor was I too concerned about the matter, as I had found that many truths on barracks were exaggerated. But look out if you did something against the grain, either in town, on barracks, or even down the road at Newcastle; for most of the barracks would know of it the following morning – and that was the only truth I was really concerned about.

Locals were soon settled however, when they realised that 90 million dollars was being spent on the Infantry wing of the barracks. The infantry were to remain after all.

Temperatures during winter dropped to below freezing and by summer it was as hot as Townsville. Flies were by far worse than the heat, arriving with the waves of scorching temperatures, laying their eggs in the flesh of dead kangaroos, the larvae soon coming of maturity. One season was as bad as the next.

If you were keen to be in the infantry, then this place was going to be one of the highlights of your career, each day bringing about something exciting and new. If your request at Kapooka was to be posted into a non-field force corps, then you were going to have one of the most miserable times possible, knowing in your own mind that living in hell would be a whole lot better.

All-in-all, I personally enjoyed the posting, in particular my second year there. The first year saw me receive, on behalf of my section, the Chief Instructors Trophy for having the champion section; and the third year was simply pitiful, where working under most officers was a pain in the arse, pure and simple.

School of Infantry
Teaching the Basic of Basics
1991-1993

Platoons would vary in size from 30 to 75 men – between 3 and 4 sections per platoon.

Sections normally averaged 14 men at 'week one' of training, but dwindled slightly as the weeks progressed, sometimes to as few as eight, eight being more in tune in regards to that of the size of a section in the rifle battalion.

The first few days of 'week one' always seemed to be the slowest, with an opening address being given by the OC, and a variety of talks by others being met: The PL COMD, PL SGT, MPs, Pay, Movements, Orderly room personnel, Coy CSM, Padre and platoon administration corporal.

Kit checks on equipment issued since the soldiers joining the army took almost an entire afternoon, followed by an introduction to the PTIs at the gymnasium, along with a quick 35-minute circuit of physical training.

This week also saw a trial run of the CFT being undertaken, the real test being conducted sometime in the near future. The PTIs conducted this trial run so that the overall fitness level of the platoon could be engaged, some of the PT lessons conducted during the running of the course then changed to meet the requirements as indicated by the trial. This also gave indication to the PTI as to individual weaknesses, thereafter he would indicate to the instructors the type of punishments which should be issued and when, benefiting the soldier concerned, so that each individual had a better chance of passing the course and marching into a rifle battalion on the conclusion of his training.

The CFT was a simple test and didn't require any brain matter to be employed in its performance. Climb a rope twice, which was between 3 and 4 body lengths in height, with webbing and rifle. Two; run through a small obstacle course in less than 40 seconds, consisted of a small 6 foot wall, negotiating a dodge through 3 fence-like adaptations, jumping a ditch, side step through half a dozen horizontal logs, turning around at a post, and then conduct the same in reverse. Three; fireman's carry a man 100 metres in 60 seconds, and four; complete the 15 kilometre run under the time limit imposed, a time which has changed several times during the course of its history.

Lessons during the first few days were very basic, (remembering that these soldiers were only trained to the level in which all soldiers must endure as a basic recruit, in order for them to be further trained as a private in (hopefully) the corps of their choice (or that to which best suited their individuality and demeanour)): Lessons such as the organisation of an infantry BN, PL, SECT, and battalion histories.

Wednesday would see them venture to the field for three days and two nights. Here they would be taught the most rudimentary of infantry skills: Living in the field, how to conduct a double staggered picket, how to bed down for the night, night routine, day routine, gun pickets, sentry duty, sounds by day and night, erecting hutchies, establishing a section post, track plans, target indications, fire control orders, judging distance, personal hygiene, target detection, range cards, and the list goes on and on; just the basics.

Along with this short bush phase, a dramatized night move was conducted after enemy mortar simulation was directed onto each 'section post' position. The move from the area was to be quick and swift, to teach discipline in regards to moving by night, having minimum gear out at any one time, and the keeping of noise down to a minimum; all in the pitch of darkness. The following morning they would be returned to the section post and see exactly what had been left behind in the rush to scramble to safety. All were shocked at the amount of equipment left by them to be employed by the enemy as he saw fit.

The final morning brought about a short walk to coaches and then their return to barracks. Here they would clean their weapons under the watchful eye of the instructors, themselves giving advice as necessary.

All of the soldiers were looking forward to a restful weekend, after this, their first week in training.

First Week in the Field
1991-1993

A soldier confronted me, just hours after he'd been placed on the ground and issued his arcs of fire, his position within the 'gun pit': This was to be his position within the platoon harbour and would eventually be turned into a fighting bay with OHP. The soldier insisted I 'come-see'.

I approached the gun position to see three faces staring at me, and all appeared rather concerned. It was soon pointed out to me the reason for their dismay; there was a huge bull ant nest just two metres from where they sat… inch long, red ants, with nippers as large as anyone would care to imagine.

The issue was this; the soldiers felt that they should be provided with another position, as their current one was simply not suited to them. Fair enough, too; after all, what would the platoon commander know about 'defence' and 'lines of fire'? Now how was I to approach the platoon commander and advise him that the gun position 'stank' and that it just wasn't good enough to have the soldiers sleeping so close to such a menace? Wasn't it enough that they had to spend four days in the field without a shower?

So with a gentle touch and a soft approach I explained to the three soldiers, and in a manner – to be accepted by the fraternity – that I didn't give a rats bleeping bleep about the bleep, bleep bleeping with such a bleeping bleeps bleeper bleeps and furthermore, you bleepers bleeping can all go and get bleeped.

The soldiers well understood the position I was faced with and saw fit to drop the subject; but still one thing concerned them; what if the ants came sniffing around looking for food.

I turned around with eyeballs clicking and smiled at all three, explaining further, and quite calmly, that they should try feeding the ants a small portion of food from their ration packs, preferably the luncheon meat, last thing at night; this would sooth the ants so that they would sleep blissfully throughout the night.

Two months later, before filling in pits and marching back to the barracks in full kit, I questioned one of the soldiers about the ants and as to whether or not anyone had been bitten.

'No, Corporal; we fed them just like you said and they never came near us.'

Shooting Skills
1991-1993

There was one course of action a corporal could take with his soldiers, which would endeavour to teach the soldier in question what he had failed to assimilate during the practical phases of the course. This course of action was a removal of the individual from the platoon he was in, and then placing him into another that was further behind in training, therefore, re-teaching and re emphasising to the student what was required. Of course, these measures weren't implemented straight away, although most instructors could usually predict who was going to be a prime candidate for such a move.

I now stood behind such a soldier, but due to the perseverance of that individual, he got to remain with the platoon through the entire running of the course. The following explains why.

One of the main aspects of an infantry soldier was his ability to kill the enemy. How could one do this if he was unable to hit a target with the very basic of weapons such as the SLR or Steyr? Allowing him to march into a battalion would be like allowing a blind man to become a taxi driver, which I guess has been known to occur from time to time.

The soldier wore a patch over his left eye. The reason for it, he says, was that his eye was lazy and that a pogo instructor from Kapooka had told him to wear the thing, telling him that there wouldn't be a problem when he marched into the School of Infantry. That instructor definitely made the matter worse.

How were infantry instructors expected to train a soldier to kill, if when confronted by the enemy his first requirement was to cease all actions until he had a patch placed over his eye? Quite ridiculous from anyone's point of view. You certainly couldn't expect him to patrol through the bush with the eye patch on his face.

The soldier had the weapon pulled into his right shoulder. He was asked, 'are you left or right handed?' 'Right handed.' 'Which is your master eye?' 'My left.'

Further examination; on requesting him to; first close his left eye and then his right, proved that his right eye was incapable of remaining steady or fully open. Basically, he was incapable of taking a sight picture when trying to close his left eye; but on closing his right, his left would remain perfectly steady and fully open.

He was then informed that he was no longer to operate the weapon right handed, for he was now a left-hander. Within six weeks he was shooting as well as any of the others in the platoon and was never required to be put back in training.

Very few of the instructors' problems at Singleton arose from minor incompetence displayed by individuals at Kapooka, namely those instructors from a non-field force environment; for most of those at Kapooka did an overwhelmingly exceptional job.

Allowing non-field force personnel to instruct also allowed for a fuller understanding of how the military functioned, but, let's face it... some instructors just required a good kick in the arse.

Weapons Training
1991-1993

A bulk of the weapons and navigation training was to be taught early on in the course, but revision upon revision was an on-going occurrence, never enough being seen.

A soldier was always taught in the most logical of sequences, and when this came to the teaching of weapons, then the foremost aspect must surely be description, characteristics, tabulated data, and then the carrying out of the safety precautions; taught to be carried out as an individual, and as a group.

Once the basics were taught the men could then get on the ground and get dirty, working the weapon, with their hands and minds, simultaneously, being shown first hand all of the drills to be taught during any one lesson prior to the said lesson being talked through and rehearsed. The soldiers would slowly build their knowledge on the weapon taught until each was capable of carrying out each action when given the appropriate word/s of command.

The SFMG MAG58 was only one of the many weapons to be taught. The IAs and stoppages of this weapon seemed to be the most demanding and hardest to learn.

Weapon fires, weapon stops. Cock the working parts to the rear, lower the butt, lift up the feed cover and clear the feed plate. Lower the feed cover, fire the action, lower the butt and open the feed cover. Place on some link, close the feed cover, cock the weapon, push the cocking handle forward and continue firing.

Then the operation becomes slightly more controlled by the soldiers, emphasis being played out on all commands. IAs and stoppages were then pieced together, to create the logical sequence that was required to remedy the weapons stoppages.

Time and time again the actions were rehearsed until all soldiers had carried all actions out to a satisfactory standard. In a few weeks' time they would be tested on the fundamentals of all weapons. The SLR or Steyr (dependent on the year of training), the M16, the MAG58, the Minimi, the M203, M79, 66mm SRAAW, grenades, claymores and trip flare. Besides these came other pieces of equipment. Patrol ambush light, radio, night sight and compass. Then knowledge; weapon pit construction, ambush drills, fire and movement, searching POWs, range card construction, standard operational procedures, types of patrols, section formations, field signals and cook a meal whilst in the field. The list goes on forever, and even after sixteen years, one still learnt and continually revised, the built up of knowledge never ceasing for a moment during a soldier's career.

The above was a minute speck compared to what the instructors taught during the conduct of the training course at Singleton – a grain of sand upon a vast beach of many grains.

A Week at the Range
1991-1993

An entire week was spent at the range qualifying students in all of the small arms weapons.

Weapons that created shrapnel were fired and thrown on other purpose built ranges.

Although a soldier was not actually tested on his operational skills of the weapons during this week – which apparently changed in 1994 – he did risk being thrown off of the range, and put back in training, if he proved himself to be unsafe whilst on the range and/or behind a weapon under his control. There was no room for unsafe persons, or those incapable of conducting themselves in a safe manner. The soldiers were, however, required to qualify in some aspects of the shoots that they were about to encounter.

A grouping and zeroing practice took the bulk of a day to complete. This was a crucial part of the week for the soldiers, for without a weapon being zeroed to the individual, how was he to hit the target. Most were too inexperienced to 'aim off'. All the soldier had to do was to create a line of sight from the eye, through the aperture, to the tip of the foresight (or through optic sights) and then, of course, the target. To some it seemed an impossible task.

Shooting was conducted from the 100m mound, the 200 and 300. The instructors were there too, coaching the firers through each of the shots where required, even where the shoot conducted was a terminal test. Re-shoots were a 25% occurrence.

Most of the problems arose from soldiers not listening to simple suggestions; suggestions that if not carried out, would do nothing but impede the final shooting result.

How many times do you tell a soldier to squeeze the trigger and not to pull it? How many times do you tell him not to jerk the weapon? And advise on how to hold the weapon off of the ground to aid in breathing (for the SLR and M16) and support. It was no wonder instructors were all stressed and growing grey hairs.

By the end of the week, all had passed, usually by way of threats of kicks to the groin.

Field Punishment
1991-1993

Time for the field again, the infantryman's bread-and-butter. Before now the soldier had learnt just the basics of skills that would get him through the process of a day and a night; building blocks of knowledge were still to be placed however, an endless placement, one upon the other.

Their skills with the weapons they used in the field were in some cases atrocious and hard to maintain a watch on. With anywhere up to 14 guys to report on in a week it wasn't easy to catch guys out when one made an error; and it 'was' a matter of catching them out.

If ever they made a mistake, or were unsure of what to do, they would always go to their mates first. There they would be given advice, but not advice that was always stable. If he made a big blunder, he was more apt to think to himself, 'you-beauty, I got away with it.'

They failed to see that if the same mistake was to occur during the final testing phase, that they could very well end up being back-squat, to be taken from the platoon they were in and placed into the one which, in most cases, was 2 to 5 weeks behind in training. Here he would be retaught everything he'd already learnt, so that the instructors could be happy in the fact that when the student marched into the battalion they would be of a standard acceptable to the unit.

It came to pass during one of my earlier platoons that a particular soldier I was training was far below the acceptable standard. I tried emphatically to have him placed back in training on three different occasions, my final attempt being accompanied by written statements, and have the soldier confront, a face-to-face interview, with the platoon commander, who's most emphasised words during his first meeting with the instructors were: 'I want to pass all of the soldiers that we train.' It turns out that this officer had a brother in the army, and that brother had been my platoon commander for around twelve months back in 1983 – but at least his brother of years past was competent in his ways. Good officers were always hard to come by in Singleton; don't ask me why. When I found myself in 2/4RAR in 1994, I was approached by a section commander who asked if I was the same instructor that had sent him a soldier some years before. I tried to explain to him what the situation was at the time, but I don't think it was accepted. Thanks to a platoon commander whose only thought was for himself, I was now suffering sly remarks unfitting to be worn; but then again, some of the discipline encountered in Townsville was woeful.

During the first night of this bush week I had spent several hours in the administration tent some five hundred metres from where the soldiers conducted their night routine. Here I wrote notes on soldiers, good and bad; this was done daily. On completion I took off into the night and headed for the section post. On coming up to the gun I saw a dull glow, and there in the bottom of the gun-pit were three soldiers smoking cigarettes. In most cases it's hard not to lose one's temper at times like this, but boys will be boys, and solutions to problems had to be thought out the best as possible. For simple problem solving the cigarettes were confiscated for a minimum of 24 hours.

The following morning I awoke to see another soldier urinating on the spoil of his pit just two feet from where he slept, ate, and basically lived. From here on, anytime he felt like urinating, he was to inform me directly. He would then be issued a tree some four hundred metres away, and told to run over and dig a hole in the ground so that he could do his deed.

If he were caught to be urinating in an illogical place again, I would do my best to place him back in training.

All in all the week was going well. This was another learning week, not a testing week. The new platoon commander failed to see it as such. His only comment was 'stuff 'em. They're only IETs.' He was my hero. Unfortunately, as an NCO, I believed that soldiers came first and dickheads last.

Fun at the Grenade Range
1991-1993

Emphasis was placed on the M26, M18A1, 66mm SRAAW and M203 at the beginning of 'week six'.

Tuesday would see the platoon move out to the grenade range where they would spend the following three days and two nights.

This was one of the objectives of the course, but very simple. If you couldn't throw a grenade on a range, you couldn't do so in war. I never saw anyone fail this phase of the course, but a few close calls were met. It was the cause of another handful of grey hairs on head.

M30 grenades were a practice grenade, and two of these were to be thrown in exact similarity to that of the M26 fragmentation grenade. The short exercise with the M30 had to be conducted within 72 hours or less of actually throwing the real McCoy.

M26

A man stands opposite you as required, ready to throw a grenade at a target represented as a bunker. He has sweaty palms and you can see the uneasiness in his eyes and upon his face.

He holds the grenade to his chest and identifies his target; then, placing his finger into the safety pin he pulls. It comes from the grenade and slight force is felt upon the grenade safety lever in the man's palm, the striker pin trying to push its way free so as to strike the primer.

The man holds the grenade at arm's length to ensure that the whole of the safety pin has been extracted, that the hole is free of any obstruction, then back into the chest. Confirm your target and throw the grenade.

The man stands and watches its flight through the air to the target. He knows that the striker has hit the primer, igniting the delay element that gives 4 to 5 seconds of delay. He wants to get down below cover but has to wait for the command.

The grenade hits the ground and commences to roll towards the target, then suddenly swings to the right, coming to rest several metres to the targets right side, and then the command comes. You both duck for cover behind the wall to your front and the grenade explodes. 'Next!'

Each man receives between 2 and 5 grenades, and you have – let's say – 45 in the platoon. After the grenades came the 66mm and the M203 (in the years before end 1992, the grenade on L1A2 launcher used to be fired from the end of the SLR by way of grenade cartridge F2). It all made for a long week. Although injuries were extremely rare, close scrapes were seen on the odd occasion. One such incident saw a guy freeze when the grenade safety lever was flung from the grenade whilst attached to the SLR by way of the L1A2. He now had a maximum of four seconds to fire the weapon so that cover behind the wall could be sought – slightly different to taking time out to aim the weapon at a target and grasping the SLR correctly with butt held against the hip (which would have been the case if the safety lever had remained in place). He fired the SLR on being told, 'Fire the weapon NOW!' No problem, but his hip never forgave him. Two days later he was still bruised from the kick of the weapon. He was lucky not to have had his thumb behind the grip of the weapon when it was fired, otherwise he would have discovered a broken thumb also. Another consideration has to be thought of here. If the soldier failed to comply with what was ordered, then the rifle, along with the attached grenade, would have to have been thrown over the wall of the pit, by the instructor. The weapon would have been destroyed.

Thank God for discipline and soldiers who obeyed orders. Another lucky scrape, and another grey hair.

Unauthorised Discharge of Weapon
1991-1993

A further five days in the field towards the latter portion of the course started to see skills come together with less and less occurrences of stupidity arising from thoughtless minds acting irrationally.

Patrolling was the essence of the week's training; fighting patrols, patrolling techniques, minefield incident drills, immediate ambush, ambush drill, counter ambush drill, reconnaissance patrol, standing patrol, clearing patrol, clearing defiles, and obstacle crossings – both major and minor, both as a section and as a platoon. All made up a small

part of the job.

When the above wasn't being pursued then day routine would be in full swing.

Digging to stage three was required to be completed as soon as possible so that during 'week nine' more patrols and defensive routine could take full effect. Stage three for the soldiers didn't entail riveting the fighting bays, but did include the digging of sleeping bays, and erection of overhead protection. The sleeping bays were dug as an extension to the existing 'fighting bay'. Sleeping in such a hole in the ground with a roof was quite cool by summer and warm by winter. Not good for the claustrophobic of mind.

Digging usually finished at 0100hrs each morning, four hours sleep a night being the norm.

Operating the radio was also important. During the running of the course the soldiers had heard of the Artillery's Initiation Program, where a few of the Arty Corps members had problems facing up to expectations, and were obviously troubled with sexual fantasies. It was here that sick individuals gave the army a bad name and reputation. Due to these stories of pathetic proportion, the infantry soldiers, whilst on course, came up with some rather strange code words and passwords – but all in the name of good fun, poked in the direction of the Artillery. Some of the more profound were 'sausage sizzler', 'humming lips', and 'tight ring'. According to what all had heard, or had been told, the artillery initiator of this ritual was imprisoned for six months; sorry, no room for sick bastards in the military. To 'say' something was one thing, but to 'act it out' was simply sick.

Another occasion for laughter during the week was when the platoon commander had an unauthorised discharge (firing his weapon without authority or reason to do so).... A soldier had reported to the administration tent in readiness for removal from the platoon, as he was not meeting with the standards required – but neither was the PL COMD. The soldier was quite distraught, and when told to unload his SLR, was not quite quick enough for the PL COMD. The PL COMD in turn grabbed the soldier's weapon, commenced to clear it, failing to cock the weapon fully to the rear, and fired the action. A shot rang out for all to hear – lucky the weapon wasn't pointed at anyone, because even firing blank ammunition can have dangerous ramifications.

The PL COMD never said a word about this on return to the barracks and kept it from the OC's ears, even though it was an officer's duty to 'charge' himself when required.

This poor excuse for an officer obviously didn't have the nerve to admit when he was wrong or made a mistake.

Many soldiers during the conduct of teaching a platoon had UDs, and after the incident in Somalia, the punishment for such rose to 14 days confined to barracks, and a fine of $400.

A few weeks after this saw the 14 days dropped. Further into the

year still and it came to reign that a soldier should not be charged with a UD if he wasn't qualified to use the weapon in question. Now, none of the instructors were qualified in the weapon, so how were they to teach it. This was remedied by placing all instructors on a Steyr Conversion
Course.

After this, qualifying a soldier still did not occur until he had passed his test. The test was then quite rapidly brought forward from 'week four' to 'week three', remembering that it'd already been brought forward from 'week eight' to 'week four' earlier on in the year (a few days before moving to the range for a week at Stockton). So according to the law of qualifications, if a soldier failed his weapon handling at the range, he should be retested or put back in training. It was one headache after the next, all brought on by a few high-ranking officers of that year, who liked nothing more than to ignore any idea an instructor had in respect to training.

Now, if a soldier hadn't been qualified in the weapon he was using, or similarly, was taught by an instructor who wasn't qualified, how on earth could he be fined $400 for such a thing as a UD? It came to play that not a single soldier received the money back as an error on behalf of the School of Infantry; prejudice beyond the standards befitting for a so-called society where all were treated fairly and the same.

The army was quite pathetic at times, and as for the officer with the UD, the less said about him the better. Thank God they weren't all like him, and thank God that being in the army, in its majority, was a fantastic place to be.

Close Terrain
1991-1993

Training in close terrain was always give-and-take. Most enjoyed operating in close country, but as an instructor, it was a shambles.

The soldiers to date had only learnt how to move through open country, and although movement through thick brush and vines, across creeks and around boulders, was no challenge for the IET, it came a fact of nature that the instructor could not evaluate the students correctly, because in most cases a single file method of movement had to be conducted. This saw the section spread out over more than sixty metres, and in an area that had a visual distance of just twenty – larger sections were spread even further afield.

Attacks on small groups of enemy were sometimes a cluster, with individuals disappearing from view, due to the extended line of assault being far too long to control, yelling time and time again, 'I can't hear you, Corporal'. No instructor could bring himself to believe that.

Injuries of a varied description were also numerous, and the time taken to travel to such a field environment took far too long. This denied the soldiers the time needed to practise the skills taught, and in the case where injuries were sustained, the taking of that individual from the 'field' environment and into the 'hospital' environment.

Re-org was called and the soldiers commenced to move as indicated by the section commander, into a position of all round defence.

The No2 on the gun came scrambling out of the bush with his rifle in one hand and his shirt in the other.

'What the hell are you doing?'

'I landed in a nest of inch ants,' and was indeed covered in bites.

'Well I didn't think you were sun-baking. You allergic? You want anything from the med kit?'

'No, Corporal.'

'Then put your shirt on and go help man the gun.' If you were in the field with the battalion for four weeks, you weren't going to get any sympathy, so why start here. He had to learn to treat his own wounds. He would be checked again later in any case, and the section medical kit was always available.

In most cases, the close country environment required that each individual cleaned his weapon three times a day. If this didn't occur, in particular with concern to the SLR, then rust soon started to appear.

One morning, after morning routine had been conducted – in this particular case 'it' being cut short due to orders for a patrol the evening before – the soldiers were called into the section commander's pit for a brief on performances and debriefing of the nights activities, a quick five minute pet-talk – if you'd like to call it that.

'Okay, men. Put your hand up if you had a brew this morning.'

Six of the nine placed their hand in the air, each not sure why they were asked such a stupid question, but others believing that the NCO was trying to find out who'd organised themselves in such a way that it was possible for them to grab a quick morning coffee, 'hot or cold'. Those that had a brew then had their weapons inspected for cleanliness and compared to those who 'hadn't' had a brew. A lesson was learnt, some punishments issued, and similar mistakes made the following morning. The lesson was this: Meals always came second to weapons: you would have had trouble killing the enemy with an empty tin can, but a weapon that functioned well performed much better.

Constant fault checking was the key to success.

Officers, Not Men
1991-1993

Some stories now, of officers, not men, at the School of Infantry.

As mentioned previously, a BFT was one of the benchmarks for an infantry soldier; so too should it be for the instructors... fair enough.

I recall quite adamantly how an officer in 1993 took it upon himself to order his NCOs up-and-down a vertical rope, in order that each of the men – myself included – could pass the BFT, along with the soldiers of the company. I see nothing wrong in this; I believe in fair treatment and that none should be given favouritism over another.

Over the Run, Jump, Dodge course we went, one after the other, the fireman's carry, and then the ropes:

'Are you not joining us, sir?'

'No... I hurt my finger.'

And yet another, believe it or not, down at the ropes... hanging there, soldiers waiting, innocent to the goings-on around them. The company had just completed the BFT and were forming up in three files, ready for the march back to the barracks. Our Platoon Commander, of Army-Reserve status, saw the local – unauthorised – mascot walking over; Deputy the Dog.

The officer bent over and picked up a few stones, pelting them with vicious demeanour at the innocent animal. On the third stone I just couldn't help myself; and being right or wrong, said the following:

'Hey, sir; that's pretty manly of you; throwing stones at an innocent dog.'

'What was that, Corporal Clayton?'

He must have assumed I hadn't the guts to repeat myself, in particular in front of the soldiers... damn him. 'I said, it's not nice, a man throwing stones at a dog.'

The officer in question called me over, out of earshot. 'Just because you've done 13 years' service, Corporal Clayton, doesn't mean anything to me.' Didn't mean much to me either... 'I'll put you on a charge if you're not careful.'

But do you think it would stand; Dickhead?

Period of Transition
1993-1994

It soon came to pass that my posting at the School of Infantry was over and the time to move on had arrived, I unfortunately had no say in my destination, although this was one particular aspect of my life which didn't affect my personal outlook on career progression. My only aspiration now was to complete my 20 years of service in order to receive a lump sum payment and small pension on retirement from the forces.

When the posting order finally arrived it was accompanied with a little relief. I was being posted to 2/4RAR; a by far better predicament than that of any of the Sydney based battalions – or so I thought (personal preference).

The first twelve months experienced in the battalion were similar in respect to training and teachings as those of other battalions, but the professional standard and attitudes of all soldiers were very slightly below that anticipated. My thoughts on this also happen to coincide with the views of 13 sergeants in which I'd had something to do with, during my posting at both Singleton and Brisbane. They, too, agreed that the 8/9th battalion was better in all respects and that the soldiers of Townsville were somewhat like a Neanderthal with concern to brains, temperament, and attitude. How hard it is, not to exaggerate; because when all is considered they are mostly genuine, friendly, and easy to get along with… humph, did I just say that?

This became more than evident when I received a posting to B Coy for a trip to New Zealand for a period of five weeks. It was here that I received strong suggestions from particular elements of the company (being of higher rank than me) that I not change my attitude, or my personality, as most members to whom I was going to become familiar were undisciplined and insubordinate. Never in my fourteen years had I met with such insolent soldiers who claimed to be men of great stature.

We were several weeks into the trip when one of the other NCOs of the company confronted the platoon sergeant with complaints from the soldiers that I was being somewhat unfair in my treatment of them. The NCO was then informed to leave the subject be, and that I was doing okay. At least now some of the more aggressive and argumentative members of the platoon started to get the message that they needed to grow up a little and stop being somewhat, fool-hardy.

How was it that men like these could think themselves as the best in the regiment when they hadn't even seen how other battalions operated. The 8/9th battalion, back in 1990, was by far better than this unit. So it came to pass that I didn't change my ways, and kept myself and my hierarchy under the terms of agreement as to the 'way I was'. Some of the soldiers started to show signs of change in some form of discipline. It was certainly nothing less than disgraceful to see one individual in particular, stand to the rear of a group of men that were all receiving a brief by the platoon sergeant, merrily talking away to a friend. I'm sure that if the shoe was on the other foot that the individual would have been more than displeased to have been rudely interrupted – I heard, many years later, that he'd received a promotion to sergeant himself: Pte Casuallybad. The soldier in question was also known – on quite a few occasions – to say, 'I'm one of the best soldiers in this unit', and when he said it, he meant it.

I'll never understand where he got the idea that he should have been promoted. The man was always complaining about not getting to do real infantry tasks, but anytime he went bush, or was seen to be taking part in other aspects of infantry training, would be one of the first to say, 'why do we have to do this shit for?'. Never did a day go by where he wouldn't complain about something. But then again he didn't have red hair, as some of the soldiers I had experiences with, who had, just had to prove how ill-disciplined and insubordinate they really were. There was even another known to have cursed the platoon commander behind his back during his handling of the massacre at Kibeho, and the comments made were entirely undeserved; but of course, I can't give you his name, such a 'worm-of-a-man' he was. But I'm pleased to say that not all soldiers encountered were as bad as these examples; these few guys were nothing less than rotten apples that deserved nothing less than to be thrown away by a group of starving kids residing in Ethiopia, whether such soldiers had white hair or red; whether feeling 'well' of themselves or 'worn numb' in the head.

Ideology was a bad thing, in particular when things didn't prove themselves to be, as they should. The only reason, as far as I could understand, as to why discipline was the way it was, may have been the idea that this was a 'Deployment Force' available for deployment, at a moment's notice. Such labelling made big heads bigger and loud mouths 'dribblers'.

A small percent of the NCOs were no different, disobeying orders and blatantly disregarding New Zealand's standing orders (when posted there for four weeks in 1994 with B Coy, 2/4RAR), by walking between boozer and lines with a can of beer in hand, abusing other NCOs who tried effortlessly to remind them that they shouldn't be doing such; and all in front of soldiers who wore the rank of private. There was even a period where groups of Private soldiers had plans to gang up on individual NCOs, to purposely beat them senseless, simply because they were doing what they were asked, doing nothing less than their job in most cases.

I could only give praise to soldiers of the platoon to which I was attached, that although they were displeased with the change in their routine of being ill-mannered and continuously disobedient, that they stood up for their NCOs by threatening to beat up on any other soldier within the company, if they as much as put a finger on their section commanders. Was discipline changing for the better, was it all a fluke, and were the threats to corporals going to cease?

This act turned all of the tables around, and as such brought to light some of the more outstanding qualities of the men in this group of thirty odd soldiers, in particular when the platoon were informed – along with the remainder of the company – that they were to be deployed to Rwanda. Guys like myself felt as though we could be very comfortable in carrying out such a task with those that we now worked with. The soldiers that worked below me were definitely reliable.

They weren't that bad after all, although I did escape a midnight bashing by a tattooed freak one night, in Queenstown, on the southern island of NZ, for as soon as he saw I was awake, awaiting him to make the first move, his attitude changed and he cowardly crawled off to bed.

It seemed to me that I had been much mistaken, and that my displeasure in individuals ability to disrupt the workings of a 'finely tuned machine', had grown out of control for a few simple reasons: I was stagnating, and basically tired of training for something which didn't appear to be forth-coming. It would seem that my piss-poor attitude towards others was due, not only for their lack in discipline, but my festering itch to get something done in the 'real world' – something we were training for, but never carried out.

It seemed obvious to me that others were simply showing the same attitude that I had locked away inside of me for years and years and years – or was I mistaken?

I do now apologise to those individuals and groups for what I have written, but it must be recorded; after all, why should I hide behind a shield and a lie.

Rwanda

Rwandan history, for a vast majority of the world, started on 6 April 1994, when anti-aircraft fire brought down a passenger plane in Kigali. Two presidents died on that flight, they were Rwanda's, President Juvenal Habyarimana, and Burundi's, President Cyprien Ntaryarima. It triggered an explosion from the air; and from the ground… a massacre that had never been seen before in the history of African affairs; it was sheer genocide.

It seems too much of a coincidence to think that the plane was shot down by accident, or even that those responsible didn't know who was on board at the time… ludicrous. The following day, several murders took stage; the Prime Minister of Rwanda, Agathe Uwilingiyimana and family; peacekeepers also came under this hammer of murderous content, for ten Belgians were killed, soldiers doing their duty in trying maintain order in a city on the verge of crisis; petty crisis no more, for there was no turning back the heinous tide which had now been unleashed.

The Tutsi population were of the country's minority, and the elimination of this race was the answer to the Hutu's forage for victory; for class and status.

Rwanda boasted the highest population density of human beings in one single African country, where eucalyptus trees were as common as people. It was a framework of fertile hills surrounded by land, locked in, no access to the ocean: Other than Lake Kivu to the West. In fact, four other countries bordered Rwanda: Zaire to the West, Uganda to the North, to the Tanzania East, and Burundi to the South.

It was a country administered by other powers, the Germans for quite some time – and we know what happened to that power-hungry nation of Jew-haters. Power switched to the Belgians who, for fear of the struggles and shifts in power between Tutsi and Hutu, turned favouritism from one to the other within the space of a few years.

Civil war came to the country in 1959, where the Hutu majority took swift action and reprisal against their brothers of colour and kin. Many Tutsi extremists, power brokers, and innocents alike, fled the country they had loved for so long, their seat of power and status changed for the worst. Hutu men and women, children too, enjoyed their newfound existence of majority rule, which they had always been in possession of, but never employed. Independence in 1962 brought about the end of the change that had started just 3 years before.

But like the IRA of Ireland, and terrorists of Iraq and Afghanistan, the Tutsi saw to it that revenge attacks into their once-homeland were attended to. The Tutsi weren't welcome in any land, and so say all they encountered, 'return to your land, for we have no space for you here'. So in 1990 an invasion was attempted by the exiles in Uganda, 7,000 strong and after a return to their original status. The Rwandan Patriotic Front (RPF) was hence born and forced a peace agreement to take form in 1993, whereby the UN was asked for aid… UNAMIR was formed (United Nations Assistance Mission in Rwanda – assistance in the implementation of a peace agreement where both parties, the Hutu and Tutsi, could live in peace).

Fingers started pointing, the Hutu displeased with the way in which things in general were proceeding. The UN was favouring the Tutsi: This was the claim and accusation. Hutu death squads walked the streets at night, cowering in corners as they did their deeds, killing innocents, the Tutsi, who for a better word, had forced the UN to take the side of the enemy – but I am no history-buff and limited in my education.

The shooting down of the aircraft on the 6th April was blamed squarely on the Belgians, and I guess they would try to insist that the radio broadcast, condemning the Tutsi and labelling them all as enemies of the state, was the fault of the Belgians as well. The RPF couldn't resist the opportunity provided to them and invaded Rwanda, developing a rapid advance onto the capital, Kigali. The Hutu majority shook in their boots and the murders of hundreds of individuals took a turn for the worst, and the Hutu unleashed their hatred for the Tutsi, upon women and children, the young and the old, and they fled like the cowards that they had shown themselves to be. In the villages from all around, thousands of Tutsi were massacred. The Tutsi (RPF) soldiers advanced upon the withdrawing Hutu, advancing upon empty lands filled with displaced persons, the Hutu withdrawing, leaving a carpet of blood to fill the void between the two factions.

France entered the picture and placed a Humanitarian Protection Zone, dividing the country into three main areas; one controlled by the RPF, one by the Hutu, and the other, France. But life was short-lived and the HPZ was soon lost, and UN soldiers deployed to the country were forced, for Rules of Engagement reasons, to sit back and watch as the murders and humanitarian crisis continued, and the RPF took control of Rwanda.

Australia now enters the scene and the first deployment of Australian troops to enter the country step from a plane in Kigali, once a city of 300,000 souls, now and a city of 5,000 men, women, and children (these are documented figures I heard about and more-than-likely not representative of the actual number).

The peace process for the Australians had commenced.

Point of View

During the deployment of Australian Infantry troops to Rwanda, many a variety of task was met: Carrying stretchers through the AUSMED hospital; escorting dental technicians, medics and other specialised personnel through the winding hills of this land-locked country; and conducting security pickets on key installations to which were our sole responsibility – namely the hospital and our barracks in Rwanda's capital of Kigali.

And although any inspiring infantryman was prepared more for a situation as likely to be found during the war in Vietnam or the Falkland Islands not all criteria to his forte were to be encountered during his deployment to Rwanda. Although many would argue the sanity of such prose, I could possibly substantiate such by saying that we

were all regulars, and only the keen were to be given a ticket for the task ahead, and that the task given to the Infantry soldiers during this deployment could only be expressed as static and mobile security.

Many disciplinary upsets were met by the keen eye of the infantry soldier in this segment of his life which was far different to that for which he had trained so hard. He wasn't fighting a war, but war was evident; he didn't get to fire his steyr or pistol, but weapons from all around lashed out their evil; and he never killed, but bodies were all around. All he could do was report an incident, only permitted to deploy preventative measures if human rights were being violated and only under specific situations (our Rules Of Engagement), but basically, not permitted to fire any weapon unless under dire circumstances (literally, self-defence); you might imagine the disgust felt by us all. But initiative and common sense were to be the main weapons of this deployment.

Departure and Arrival
19-20th February 1995

The departure from Townsville was originally set for 2145hrs on the 18th, though due to problems with the aircraft in which was to take the contingent to Rwanda, the timings were changed. The Boeing 747 of Tower Air had been grounded and parts now had to be flown in from Singapore, in order for repairs to take place.

Much apprehension was met over the next fourteen hours, as all could only wonder as to whether the aircraft was going to make it to the small African country, for stories started to flow in from all sources. All odds stood in favour of the aircraft plummeting into the ocean, killing us all instantly. It reminded me of an incident some nine years before when a company exercise saw us airlifted out by Chinook. We'd just passed over some ranges when there was some engine trouble. We made a hard landing on a pasture, the approach being at an almost completely devastating angle, and after being asked to step from the aircraft were asked for our service flannelette, the same we used when cleaning our rifles.

The aircrew took these simple pieces of cloth and then went about cleaning the engine and after 90 minutes of laying around, playing cards, we were ushered back on board and once again took to the air.

By 1200hrs on 19th all had commenced to move onto the aircraft, this was followed by an uncomfortable airborne time of sixteen hours, with two stops being met – Singapore and Nairobi.

Touch down in Kigali was much to the relief of the 300 odd

members of the contingent, a contingent that was to primarily provide medical support to the forces of the United Nations. The company of infantry soldiers provided for the security of the Australian contingent as a whole.

As we moved into the main building of Kigali airport, the first effects of the civil war were seen. Glass shattered windows, bullet holes and even evidence of RPG rounds having been fired; the scars of war were everywhere. Craters created by 60mm mortars or grenades also covered the floor of what once must have been a very handsome building. RPA soldiers also made themselves present in what must have been their effort to show some type of authority by force, a stand that only brought an unkind stare of an aggressive nature from some of the Australian infantry soldiers.

The move through customs was surprisingly quick, and as members of UNAMIR II, soon found ourselves loaded onto transport and ready for the short half hour trip to the barracks in which we were to spend a majority of our six month stay, a period of time that passed with the blink of an eye.

The barracks came to view at 0430hrs and were moved into, UNAMIR I members moving out, the rotation being completed by 1100hrs. The first contingent was more than happy to see the end of their six-month tour.

The accommodation was divided according to numbers, task, rank and gender. The rifle company building was cramped to say the least, with 18 persons per room. This was sorted within several weeks, allowing for a section of ten men to have a room to themselves.

Although privacy was a problem, there was no other better way of getting to know each other. I was quite sure that we would be sick of the sight of each other by the time we returned home.

The routine of the Rifle Company took a while to get off of the ground, but once each of the rifle sections had rotated once through each of the main tasks, all was 'sweet potato'. There were three tasks; barracks security, hospital security, and rest. Rest week was not what it implied. It wasn't spent on backs reading books, but gave the sections responsibilities of providing security to varying groups venturing outside of the barracks, conducting a variety of tasks.

The contingent was in full swing by the end of the first month, and most aspects of the stay soon became second nature.

The Hospital
Late February

As each section took on the responsibilities of security for the hospital, a tour was met with in order to introduce all to their new surroundings. The main complex of the hospital was a well-organised structure. All of the basic necessities for which it required to run were to be found in the one wing. A laundry was also established next door and there was a morgue no more than 100 metres from the hospital's back door.

One platoon would spend a week here, rotating its sections through the three main tasks that were to be maintained during the six-month period. Security for the front and rear gate was priority. On several occasions members of the RPA found themselves disarmed and escorted into the grounds of the hospital when visiting friends of theirs, patients of the UN; it was one of the many needs of the trip, the Australians being required to treat soldiers and civilians alike, where there was the 'order' and 'moral obligation' for such to take place.

The UN was trying to establish a relationship that would be beneficial to UNAMIR II during the duration of its stay and a worldwide friendship that could help to ease the suffering of the people.

Some civilian patients were in the direct threat of being executed by the RPA, so whilst any RPA soldier was being escorted through the main complex, to the ward which housed the RPA patient, the RPA soldier – or suspect spy – would be prevented from venturing into rooms to which he had no business. Hence, he was being restricted to the floor space in accordance to the looming threats, refusing the RPA from freely gaining information that could disclose to him whether or not the hospital held the man or woman that they were after. In one such case a little boy was given aid by the hospital, and then finally a job within its walls, as the RPA would have executed him if he so much as stepped outside of its walls; and when I say 'little boy', I mean just that.

Here too, was a couple of Rwandans who worked as interpreters for the Australians (being given the position via the UN). Each spoke between three and five languages, most of which were on the verge of fluency. I was at one stage advised that they were also at risk if they chose to walk freely outside of the protection offered by the walls of the hospital. On more than one occasion these two were offered threats of death by the RPA. Towards the end of the tour it was announced via different means that certain persons were making arrangements for these two, to be allowed into Australia, under legislation of status as a permanent residence, for to stay in Rwanda would have meant certain death. This was the type of reception one got for working with the UN.

The front gate security also required members of the section on this post to escort medics, and other persons between the hospital and front gate of the barracks. The distance between the two was a good 300 metres, a right angle bend in the road making it impossible to see one complex from the other. On some occasions medics went against the imposed standing orders, and travelled the road without escort, literally taking their safety into their own hands.

Due to the system used, those travelling from the barracks to the hospital would be provided escorts from the guardroom, on the front gate of the main compound. Due to other tasks, and vehicle escort requirements between UN headquarters and UNAMIR's location, it was an inconvenience for the medics to wait for an available escort on some occasions. I never heard of anyone waiting more than 15 minutes for an escort. Emergencies were provided for immediately, even if it meant calling the hospital up via landline and requesting an escort from them, due primarily to numbers depletion and other tasks having to be met by

the section in the guardroom.

The third task to be provided for within the hospital was the 'rest section'. This section provided men for stretcher parties and assisted the medics when patients were dropped off for treatment: Car accidents, landmine blasts, burns victims, broken bones etc.

The rifleman's simple task was to cut the patient's clothes with scissors, removing them from the body in preparation for medical aid to be administered. The only bright side to the task – if such a word could be used – was the experience of seeing first hand a medical team going to work on patients, and the effects of injuries such as a missing foot caused by antipersonnel landmines.

On many occasions soldiers were able to witness the complete operation, as there was always the space available for soldiers to stand in the back of the operating theatre and watch the surgical team go to work; scrubbing open wounds, scraping tissue from bone, or simply cutting legs off from above or below the knee.

The NGO wards were to the rear of the hospital. This was where Rwandans were treated on a large scale. Australian nurses aided by giving first hand instruction, assistance and advice, to the workers and nurses here – those of Rwandan heritage. The entire place stunk like nothing I'd smelt before, patients lying in their own excrements; the simple overcrowding of such a place. It was disgusting. It was filthy. It was unbelievably unhygienic.

Minor Incidents
Bodies

The atrocities created by the hand of this civil war were clear from the very start, and just down from the hospital was a large depression in the ground. This particular depression was an excavation of sorts said to have housed some 4,000 victims of the war (though 10,000 may have been a more correct figure), a mass grave of discarded flesh.

For days on end a mass of black smoke could be seen to rise over the tops of trees as bodies were burnt. Bodies were also evident along the roads; rows and rows of them, all covered in plastic sheeting; hundreds upon hundreds. These stunk even more so than the NGO wards at the hospital. Now we knew what the smell of death smelt like.

Guys from the Infantry Company would point to black birds that flew around the masses, saying how the food it carried in its beak wasn't a worm, but more than likely the flesh from a corpse. One man reported how he saw a dump truck drive past the front of the hospital, stockpiled with bodies, arms and legs visible around the lip of the dumpster. The morgue was another experience, where a body was seen to have no face, its eyes literally hanging from the sockets. Living shells of life also came in the form of children, dozens upon dozens visiting the soldiers at the rear gate of the hospital, all with limbs missing. And then another blast was heard in the distance, another landmine putting claim to a few more limbs of children; and that was another thing playing on the minds of some individuals, the actual threat of mines being trodden on.

Going for a run around the immediate area, as a section, brought light to bear upon more reality as hundreds upon hundreds of bodies would be run past, all lined out in rows and decaying, most (if not all) beneath some form of covering and out of view.

A man was herding his small band of 20 odd sheep along the roadside, himself at the rear of the sheep. He was the one to step on a hidden mine; no more leg. A six-year-old boy was playing with some friends when he saw a grenade. He kicked it and lost his foot, his face was also buried under fragments caused by the weapon – just 100 metres from our barracks.

It was reported that the Interahamwe (Hutu militiamen) were coming into Kigali by night, burying mines for more victims. It was also reported that they might try and plant some near the contingent's barracks, to force some type of action between the UN and RPA.

It was nice to know that the Australian presence was acknowledged.

The Padlock

One night whilst on the front gate at the hospital, I sat with another. It had just turned 2100hrs and all was quiet. Not even the RPA were out tonight. Normally they patrolled Kigali from dawn till dusk in section and platoon lots, establishing ambushes or simply forcing their way into homes. Three out of every seven days you could see tracer ammunition flickering through the night sky, two to three round bursts being fired as another human life was put to waste by the RPA. It all took a week or more to get used to.

An RPA ute with six persons in the rear passed between me, and the RPA opposite the hospital – the reciprocate guard box which had been placed shortly after the Australians had erected theirs. He looked up briefly and then stared out down the road. An RPA officer was approaching. His rank was confirmed as he approached the gate… he didn't hug and kiss the guard; he must have been an officer.

A minute later and the medic came running up from behind: 'Who's this?'

'Corporal Clayton, sir. Why, what's up?'

'Someone's just fired a weapon at us.'

'I don't think so, sir. If someone had fired a weapon, we would have heard it.'

'I'm telling you, someone has fired a shot at us. If you were with us when the round came through the glass window, you wouldn't be saying that.'

The officer wasn't convinced, but had taken to panic, as did the others in his midst.

They were all quick to hit the floor.

The infantry platoon commander was called up and the story explained to him. The medical officer was still unconvinced however; no matter how much I and the other guard on duty swore that we'd heard no rifle being fired.

An inspection of the said window revealed a large hole. A search for the bullet by the half dozen officers present turned up nothing. I soon found the article responsible for the hole. A tiny padlock. Obviously thrown by either the occupants of the vehicle that had passed earlier, or the officer who was seen to approach the RPA compound front gate.

All things soon settled down again, and normal routine was once more adjusted to.

The padlock that obviously had a muzzle velocity as that of a round of ammunition was discarded.

This put an end to the medic's mad minute of panic, although justly so. It could quite easily have been a hand grenade. All were vulnerable and no chicken wire was available for the screening of windows or guard box. Wire was however put on order; just never issued. Ground floor hospital rooms were blacked out though, screening the occupants from view, in particular protecting those who were wanted by the RPA.

More than once the RPA did make the threat to attack the hospital and barracks.

Luckily for them it didn't result, or there would have been a hell of a lot of dead RPA. No foe was going to take out the Infantry Company, not alive in any case, not after what had happened to the Belgiums prior to our being committed.

15th April

It was said that the padlock affair was the RPA's method of payback for an incident that should never have occurred. One of the Australian soldiers had fired a sling shot at the RPA guard box opposite the hospital. This act of stupidity could have quite easily have caused a major incident and triggered an eventual clash of forces.

The said soldier remained in the country however, against the option of shipping him back to Australia, and he was posted to the SASR the following year.

If the SAS were allowing such soldiers into their midst, then there was room for any fool with a body which acted before the brain. The SAS must have been desperate and without the knowledge that I possessed. It was also another understanding that at any time the SASR numbers saw depletion in their ranks, due to aircraft accident, etc; that the following years course was somewhat 'less picky' in the soldiers they passed and welcomed into their ranks.

In fact, I can honestly say that I know of several SAS soldiers of whom should not be there, due to incompetence, and hope I never have to see them again.

RPA Lust

A nurse was running towards the rear bunker of the hospital, quite shaky from an experience that she wasn't going to forget for quite a while. There was also a lesson to be learnt here.

Whilst assisting a patient outside of the hospital grounds – within the designated NGO ward area – the nurse was approached by four members of the RPA, grabbed and pushed backwards towards one of the beds. Whatever happened next was very vague, but she escaped unharmed – the RPA lust for rape was very evident.

From that day forth she would always insist on having someone with her; and who could blame her.

In situations like this the rules and regulations of the area were somewhat of a contradiction by terms; one for us, and one for them.

Not far up from the bunker and hidden by the shade of several trees almost a hundred metres away, was an RPA sentry post that was seldom seen. These soldiers, as for all of the RPA seen (the NGO ward area being their responsibility), moved around with their weapons slung or held in hand. The Australians were restricted in the fact that no weapon on their part was permitted past the rear bunker and into the NGO ward boundaries. The best the Australian could do in respect to this was to restrict all personnel of movement into this area during times considered to be unnecessarily violent.

And as for the bunker; it wasn't uncommon to have rocks thrown at us during the night from within the dark of the shadows. This was just one of the small evils that the rear security element had to put up with.

Hygiene

Some of the sights seen from the rear gate were funny but filthy. Women from within the ward closest to the security here would squat just 20 metres from the boys and urinate. Each night was the same.

It came as a surprise to see that the grass in that area wasn't affected in any way and grew just as green as in other areas.

Theft

Our relationship with those in this country was practically none existent. The RPA were getting, and we weren't receiving; our tokens of good gesture were seemingly taken but never returned.

It was at one stage during the second half of the tour, and passed down from headquarters itself, that the relationship with the RPA was in some cases quite good. The only advantage to this may have been that the contingent wouldn't be wiped out by the thousands of AK47 and machete-wielding murderers. Their aggression for such was known, and there were more than several instances where somewhat of a Mexican stand-off was met, except that the Australians didn't return the RPA's verbal threats of death.

As the relationship was supposedly improved (through the eyes of those on high horses), RPA officers with motorolas were given a fair go, for they found that they had no means for which to recharge their batteries, but were now provided an open door. The batteries were now brought to the front bunker of the hospital where the RPA soldier waited whilst an Australian digger ventured into the hospital orderly room, exchanging it for a fresh one.

After several days of this, minor vengeance was sought by soldiers returning from the orderly room with either; a battery which had been reported as being faulty, or an explanation expressing deep regret that no recharged battery was available, and that they should 'come back later, mate'.

Where the RPA came into contact with motorolas in the first place was a concern in itself, let alone the fact that they now wanted us to supply them with recharged batteries for their stolen merchandise.

It was during this same period that some drivers for the UN had been given permission to park their minibuses out in front of the hospital for security reasons, parking it in front of the bunker. The drivers simply handed their keys over to the guys on duty in exchange for a receipt. The guard on duty maintained a half portion of this receipt. As all drivers were Rwandan, it was hard to extinguish one from the other – not meaning any prejudice, but they mostly looked the same, as I'm sure we mostly looked the same to them, which was good for some of us as it meant that when we accidently gave the 'finger' as opposed to scratching our faces that they would have no idea who was responsible when confronting us the following morning.

Due to complications met by one of the infantry minor call signs of another section, keys to one of the vehicles were handed over quite willingly to an RPA thief in civilian clothing. From that day on all drivers were required to sign in and out, as well as to be wearing their personal UN ID card. If on picking up a vehicle the following morning, the driver failed to fulfil these requirements, then the member of the contingent to which saw the driver sign in, was sought and asked for confirmation as to whether or not he was the 'right guy'. This act had its effect on the RPA trying their hand at theft, and enforced the rule for the need of drivers to bring in UN ID, for most disliked being kept waiting when they had a timed schedule to maintain. It also brought confusion to bear upon the shoulders of diggers who would look at the driver and mutter something along the lines of, 'yeah, that's looks like the guy who gave me the keys', when in fact he had no idea, because even if the driver had flashed us a 'brown eye' he would have still had a familiar look about him.

The theft of vehicles from the Australian side of the fence was from that day maintained at one, far from the numbers reported by other UN forces and NGOs in the country. It was a disappointing reality to see first-hand that some of the UN's funding was being flushed down the toilet through such losses. Numerous UN utes were stolen by the RPA. These vehicles were given a facelift by way of camouflage paint, and the only way of knowing that they were stolen from the UN was the fact that they were running very well and didn't have any dents in them for the first few days of their stolen existence.

Nothing, however, could be done in terms of requisition.

Kibeho I

Even before the massacre on 22nd April, 1995, Kibeho was not a very nice place; that description being very placid indeed. Hardliners of the former government were swaying judgement upon the innocents, employing every strategy to keep them in place, within the cordon of the IDP camp. The RPA (Rwandan Patriotic Army, renamed shorter after the

French evacuated the country) were ever concerned with the goings-on for it was their accusation that the camp was being used as a base from which the hardliners could conduct their raids in and around Butare. The RPA commenced to filter the IDPs out of Kibeho and back to their home communes, something that the IDPs would feel comfort in, however, with the pressing accusations and search for evidence, that individuals had any connection, whatsoever, with the former government, or somehow related to raids in the area (related to an Hutu, or having committed crimes against the former RPF in general, or a Tutsi) forced the IDPs to destroy their identification cards, and anything else that might associate them with the Hutu… and who could blame them?

On the 18th of April the RPA made a move and two battalions were sent into Kibeho, surrounding the camp so that there was no way in, and no way out. Some of the soldiers were between 7 and 12 years of age. Firing shots from rifles to force the throngs together, to be more easily controlled, burning their small adobes as they marched the IDPs to their fate.

Every single individual would be interrogated in some way in order to evaluate whether they were Hutu or Tutsi. The 120,000 or so IDPs were now congregated on the high ground of Kibeho, forced to live in conditions that were constantly stirring for the worst. For those that passed scrutiny, they were given the go ahead to find their way back to their home communes, for those that wore accusation of being associated, in any way, with Hutu hardliners; they were executed or thrown into jail, jails which were 'standing room' only:

The prisons were atrocious.

The UN pressed an ultimatum on the 19th and the RPA seemed to settle, a team of 32 Australians were prepared and deployed to Kibeho, setting up a site whereby the injured could start to receive medical aid and 'hopefully', by our advertised presence, prevent further atrocity. IDPs were cleared from the camp, Zambian forces, and Australian, helping people onto UN trucks so that they could be ferried away from hell.

On the 20th the RPA were seen quite clearly, beating men women and children with sticks and clubs, forcing them into imaginary corals, and some time after this IDPs commenced to grow more weary, deciding to take action, by picking up stones and pelting them at the RPA.

Machine gun and rifle fire was the answer, the RPA letting loose with retribution, refusing to submit to the stone-throwing innocents – although we must remember that there were hardliners here too, and it was quite realistically them that had started the commotion, and why not, for they had the protection of 120,000 IDPs.

In the night there was the constant firing of weapons, just as we had witnessed in Kigali, from the safety of our barracks, but the vicious assaults of Kibeho were much worse and would soon escalate out of control.

On the 21st the wounded were cared for, under the watchful eye of the RPA, who insisted that no person receive more than 5 minutes of care, moving the wounded through as quickly as they could, those with gunshots, broken bones, and machete wounds.

Kibeho II
18th-21st April 1995

On the 18th, the legal officer for the contingent was to make a personal visit to Butare, a population of 29,000 – 45 minutes from Kibeho. His prime task was to visit the prison there.

Permission was also sought for entrance into Kibeho whilst in Butare, for this was on the agenda for the legal officer's 'finding of facts'.

As the truck entered the camp, all could see the direct effect of the RPA's call to force between 70,000 and 120,000 refugees onto a prominent spur to the centre of the camp, this being encircled by a small valley. Blue and green plastic sheeting could be seen everywhere, this was the roofing for the IDPs' stick and mud huts – it was no wonder that the refugees had to walk a minimum of two kilometres to get firewood for the much needed fuel for fires and cooking.

Everywhere one looked was dead of activity, except the spur-line that sounded like a million geese chattering away to their heart's content.

The RPA had said that the herding of the IDPs was required if they were to be shuttled off back to their communes. The RPA were sick to death of the crowd, and knew full well that there was a hell of a lot of Hutu extremists amongst these people. It was these Hutu militia of old which had supposedly caused the problems of the 22nd April 1995.

There were many ramifications behind the legal officer's visit, not all of which were disclosed to the infantry soldiers. Although my section and I were to spend several days with him, he was conversed with only when he handed out his directions for the smooth running of his task at hand. One such task was to gather information on the overcrowding of prisoners, and their standards of living in such over-cramped places, that there wasn't even room to lay down or sleep; and even if the prisoners did, it would have been in their own excrements. None of those imprisoned saw any legal process prior to conviction, and many were innocent.

Very few IDPs were leaving via the erected boom gate entrance, to depart the swamped crowd of 100,000 in Kibeho. A vast majority were forced to leave, their water containers punctured with knives by the RPA, and personal belongings thrown to the ground and kicked; many were brutally pushed under the temporary gate, forced to be on their way

to Butare. Some were fortunate enough to be allowed their possessions. Another man was being escorted by three RPA. He had his hands held high and didn't want to go. No shots were heard, but he was taken away and executed by machete.

The truck loaded with the security section was just twenty metres from the boom gate, the sights and smells hitting our nostrils. One of the guys pointed out a running figure in the distance. He was being chased and shot at by two RPA. The man ran into a mud hut on the hillside opposite. The RPA followed and two shots were heard. The RPA exited and walked off. This act was followed 30 minutes later by another RPA firing a burst of 20 rounds into a smaller group of some 70 odd IDPs 50 metres down the slope from the main crowd. Closer inspection proved that no one had been hit – either that or any dead/wounded had been carried away before a group of medics could push their way through the crowd and to the area of concern.

During the next two hours the legal officer was off with his interpreter and two security, talking with different members of representation from CARE Australia, other NGOs, and members of the Zambian security force posted there, whilst around us, from time to time, individuals were manhandled and 'taken-care-of' RPA style.

At the conclusion of a day's negotiation, the section of security under my command, along with the legal officer, would withdraw before dark to the safety of a Zambian compound in Butare.

By late afternoon on the 21st we were on our way back to Butare, taking time out to visit one of the prisons and another refugee camp on return. We were stopped by two RPA who stood their ground at the entrance of the small commune, and reported that the refugees there had been removed and sent on their way back to their own communes. The RPA soldier laughed whilst conversing with the interpreter who knew full well that the IDPs were still in place just beyond view, hidden by a few trees, rising ground, and the large centre commune building of the province which sat at our side. The truth was found on reaching Butare. The IDPs of that particular camp were still in place, so it stood to reason that the RPA didn't want IDPs returned as gravely as they made out. Each camp was being systematically sifted through for members of the former government, be they of a political or military importance mattered little, for they would all meet with imprisonment or death.

Whilst at this commune a report was heard as it was sent from Kibeho to Kigali, via another group of soldiers who had arrived in Kibeho on our mission being granted a minor victory by a higher authority, a direct response to the information gathered by the legal officer. A group of 17 odd IDPs had just been massacred by AK47 and machete. Later still and a further 200 had been said to have met their death, by which time the legal officers group of 12 had returned to the barracks in Kigali.

We were to hear later of two reports. The first explained 11 dead children aged between two and thirteen, the second was of 20 dead, 16 shot, two trampled (one of which was six months old) and two killed by machete attack. Both reports were the result of incidents caused on the afternoon/evening of 21st April 1995. The worst was yet to come.

Massacre
22nd April 1995

On that fatal day of 1995, at 0650hrs, a small group of 32 of the Australian contingent, along with a few members of the Zambian security force, became involved in what would never be forgotten. They became a part of the mix and threatened all alike by the Interahamwe, a crowd of over 100,000 IDPs and 2,500 RPA – some of whom were as young as 7 years old.

There have been two books written on the massacre. One is titled 'Combat Medic', by Terry Pickard, and the other 'Pure Massacre', by Kevin O'Halloran; both are invaluable and provide much detail in regards to incidents and timings. These two books should be read for a larger, overall understanding of the events, and for an insight into the thoughts of soldiers on the ground at the time. Another called 'The Kibeho Massacre: As it Happened' was written by me some years later; it is also worth reading, but I suggest the previous two as mentioned above. However, if you like poetry then I suggest 'Kibeho: An Epic Poem'.

From within the crowd the hardliners emerged, thrashing out with their machete, killing all they came across: Babies, women, and the old and frail.

The Zambian compound, upon the spur and high ground, received pot shots, being fired upon from somewhere within the crowd; a hardliner perhaps, or a RPA soldier hoping to force the UN to retaliate, or trying to kill a member of the Interahamwe; and another storm was also brewing, a tropical upheaval of torrential rain, and the crowd commenced to move.

The RPA considered their position, and deemed the wavering crowd as an attempt to break the human cordon around them.

The RPA opened fire with their automatic weapons, rocket propelled grenades and other arms of destruction; sniper fire and fire from Ak47s and machine guns; machete attacks continued unrelenting in their ferocity, even 60mm mortars were seen to have been used, but it was hard to see or hear amongst the mayhem and cries of horror. Interahamwe within the crowd were taking to refugees with machete and the RPA were applying force from the cordon. The IDPs couldn't win. They stampeded, many children and babies being trampled to death during the torment.

There were continuous attempts to force the UN to offer some form of protection to the IDPs by opening fire themselves – the Zambians, however, stood strong. It was quite evident, in all respects, that the RPA wished for some reason to kill every UN peacekeeper and NGO in the area. But how can we be so sure? RPA soldiers were executing men and women in front of the Australian and Zambian soldiers, teasing them to take action, but the only action implemented was to stretcher the wounded to the medical station for aid, and as the wounded were carried, weapons slung over shoulders, the RPA continued with their atrocities by chasing IDPs and shooting them in the back as they made a run for it.

The Australians did as ordered and stood fast, witnessing first-hand the atrocities of that day; RPA continuing unabated, murdering innocent IDPs in front of them, seemingly hoping, praying to God, that the Australians would intervene in some way so that they could then dispose of us as well.

The Australian medics and ground troops sealed a bond, working together like no other. One by one the injured IDPs were brought on stretchers by the infantry to be given medical assistance by medical staff, and on the 23rd April, the true nature of all came to be seen as more of the contingent was deployed to the area.

We [and let's make this clear: myself not included] now numbered 14 doctors and nurses, 30 infantry and six logistics personnel.

Then a Casualty clearing Post [or 'Point' as some might prefer] was established, and further horrendous work continued over the coming days of offering aid to these poor people, the worst situation, for all it was worth, since the most evil days imaginable from both World Wars.

More than 4,050 IDPs had met with death that fatal day. The number was higher but the RPA had taken to evacuating the bodies on trucks to lighten the threat against them regards accusations of genocide; as the sun went down the RPA task had changed, from mass murder, to the clearing away of evidence.

During the body count, one man came across more than 20 dead babies, all hidden from view under the heaps of rubbish that was caused by the massacre. Much of the devastation was hidden from view. Was it possible that individuals thought that if they were hidden that they might forego execution by the hand of the RPA? Many an execution was seen by the Australian contingent, some carried out as the RPA laughed, watching the Australian troops as they carried out their cold blooded murder; shooting another individual in the head, the body falling heavily to the ground. It didn't give you a nice feeling to see a helpless victim being run down and murdered, and I can speak from experience.

650 IDPs were found wounded, piles of dead being stepped over as the infantry stretcher-carried wounded to the Australian Casualty Clearing Post.

It was reported later that the RPA came very near to firing their antitank weapon on buildings that supposedly hid 1,700 hardliners. This action – if carried out – would have been catastrophic. The only deterrent was the very presence of Australian and Zambian forces, but not deterrent enough; and it was to the Australians and Zambians that the very blame for atrocities went.

But where did the blame really lie? I heard, quite convincingly, that a report put some of the blame upon the soldiers of UNAMIR II for not preventing the massacre: 32 Australian soldiers against two battalions in open warfare.

And yes, propaganda was also in full swing. According to the inhabitants of Rwanda and neighbouring countries, the RPA were the lifesavers, aiding the IDPs against the Interahamwe and Former Rwandan Government Forces, whilst the Australians did nothing to assist. This was brought to light on the 30th April when the RPA drove around on the backs of utes denouncing UNAMIR, claiming themselves as stoppers of the genocide, saying how they shed their own blood to save the lives of the Rwandan people and troops of UNAMIR. The people quite believed the RPA, but to what degree and by what numbers, no one really knew.

But this day was soon to pass and the memories left to live on.

From 23rd April 1995, to 9th May 1995, 1,500 IDPs had to be

evacuated from the confines of the few buildings of Kibeho. These few had found sanction in a cordon of walls and would budge for no man. This was the compound next door to where the Zambian peacekeepers maintained their headquarters.

Many poor souls lived a life of hell during that 16 day period, bringing corn to the boil which had just moments before been picked from their faeces, deposited on the ground by all of the people combined. All excretion was sifted through for the undigested kernels.

Water was also rare. The RPA wanted these people out of Kibeho as soon as possible, and had punctured the IDPs' water containers. Most of the IDPs were forced to drink their own urine: but one thing baffled me. The urine they were drinking was, for the most part, yellowish in colour. I had always assumed that the yellow tinge seen in urine was an indicator of excess vitamins and minerals – but I could quite easily have been wrong. But if I was correct, then where was the nourishment coming from. Were these few, members of the Interahamwe, and somehow being provided aid; or was there more nourishment in maggots and recycled corn than I knew?

Another woman was approached, to be convinced by me that she would be evacuated to a place where she'd be given food and shelter, but only if she left with me then and there.

She looked sick and moved slightly from where she sat, maggots and blood dribbling from her anus as she moved. I'd heard that maggots cleaned the flesh, helping persons to heal, and how true this was I had no way of knowing, but you could see in this woman's face that there was no chance of survival, there was absolutely no way in which she could live through this ordeal that she was suffering so badly, yet so heroically. She would be dead soon, and someone else would pick up the maggots to be eaten later, to have them put in with the corn, and other scraps, such as cut up portions of animal skin from leather shoes.

This place was beyond explanation, beyond sordid, the most disgusting place on earth that I could possibly imagine.

There was one thing for sure, all of the soldiers here, who had been protected by a technologically sound society all of their life, had never seen things like this before.

There are mothers back home who want Australians to remember their sons who served in Afghanistan and Iraq, and deservedly so, but I wonder how many remember all of the above.

We all remember ANZAC day, and so we should, but who of us remembers the massacre at Kibeho, which occurred just three days before the commemorated date?

The clearance of IDPs from Kibeho, continued. We had departed Butare in a truck with rover support, medics, infantry, and communications. We knew well that the IDPs had to be evacuated from Kibeho, and as soon as possible.

None of the Australian contingent were permitted to remain in Kibeho overnight, due to the seriousness of the problems that had unfolded over the past few days, so a camp at be set up not far from that hell hole, where bodies had been picked up and thrown into mass graves, the wounded and sick given medical aid. To prevent further death the IDPs simply had to be moved back to their communes.

It was during one of these trips (by road) that the movement of the truck commenced to aggravate my back injury... it had been a nun that had set the pain in motion. No blame will ever go to her, but she was a little overweight; with only two men to stretcher-carry her, myself and one other, and the effects of the continued work that we had been performing in the country, were taking its toll. The nun on the stretcher was the straw that broke the camel's back – literally.

Shortly after initially receiving the injury, the savage beatings-of-pain had been administered first aid, all seemed to go well... and then weeks later, this; the damn trucks and poor conditions of the road system within this country were seeing the end of my career draw closer; and the pain mounted as we continued, with this, another visit to Kibeho.

By the time the truck had been parked next to the old Zambian compound, all on board had accepted another eye-full of desertion; the entire landscape around was void of people; not even the RPA could be seen, but I knew there must be some around here somewhere. It was like a giant tip had centred itself on a lone spur between two valleys.

Sticks and branches made up the skeleton city of broken down adobes, where blue plastic sheeting, given by CARE, flapped in the little breeze that blew from the valleys below.

The truck had been parked; I was seated in the front seat. I sat motionless, the pain unbearable – and few of you, reading this, will understand how I could possibly continue how I did, in respect to the amount of pain I am telling you I was in? I can only defend myself by offering my military record as an itinerary of the things I had attempted over the years, and those that I had passed. The things I had achieved during the past 15 years cannot be attributed to a bludger and that when I say I was in pain, that is exactly what I mean. I always pushed myself beyond the pain, always doing more than what I knew others would do in the same situation. This was not a civilian job, you don't just phone in and say you're not showing, simply because you feel under the weather; this was the infantry.

The platoon sergeant came to the door after the driver had made his exit, and opened it as though a chauffeur. 'You coming, Nigel?' and on giving my reply was provided with a few painkillers… although these had little effect.

It took me ten minutes to get into the Zambian compound, an area of ground surrounded by buildings, a giant open area where thousands of Rwandan IDPs had congregated. I could only remain for 30 minutes, for the pain was getting too much. I returned to the truck. A medic arrived later on in the day, just prior to our trip back to our campsite, and prescribed a pill which – for its size – had powers that I cannot explain… damn, I was hoping for a cuddle and a kiss. Within ten minutes I was feeling light headed and the road trip out-of-there was like a dream.

Aftermath
9th May 1995

I returned again to Kibeho, even with my injury, but after it had settled down a bit, and continued to do what I could to help with the evacuation process.

The CCP remained in situ until all remaining IDPs had been evacuated back to Butare and from there back to their home communes. It was another sad thing to see that a lot of these people were shunned by their own kind because of the weight of propaganda that was floating on every breath of wind. No one in Butare wanted to be seen conversing with, or harbouring someone from Kibeho.

The final days saw two men from my section in particular giving their helping hand to the contingent's commitments. Against the wishes of Non-Government Organisations (similar to CARE and World Vision), these two soldiers lead the path to success by learning some of the local language Kinyarwanda. Applying this to logic they commenced to collect the hundreds upon hundreds of machetes in the area, confiscated them. This prevented the IDPs from cutting wood for fires from banisters, railings and other wooden objects; preventing them from cooking; from cutting up their leather goods for food; taking from them their only means of support. This was accompanied with harsh words and forcefulness. The IDPs had no choice but to leave. Was this what the RPA had initially tried to do? The Australians, in a strange way, had reverted to the tactics of the RPA.

All of the NGOs in the area appeared to be sour at this apparent act of cruelty, for the taking of the IDPs' means of creating fire and food.

But at least they now stood a better chance of survival. Anything was better than eating corn from faeces and drinking urine. On more than one occasion were Australians asked for saviour, IDPs coming up to them and saying, 'kill me. Kill me. Shoot me please', not all spoken in English, but some by means of sign language, pointing to the weapons we carried and then to their heads, nodding 'yes, do it'. I could see the anguish in their faces as they did this.

Rubbish was moved around with applied aggression by several Australian Infantry, and when a grenade was found hidden under an old and worn mattress, their voices rose a little more. Windows were smashed (but I can't substantiate by whom), and belongings of the IDPs were grabbed and then carried to the main entrance of the IDP sanctuary. Some would follow, some would not.

Then, as though by a miracle granted us all, the last few hundred got up and departed.

No one was sorry to see this place emptied or disappear behind them, and the Australians loaded themselves onto the trucks and departed for Kigali.

On return to the barracks all equipment was deloused and a few months further into the trip, all equipment of a canvas and cloth type, which had seen wear and tear in Kibeho, was purified by flame.

So now the worst of the tour was behind us all.

Many thoughts linger on a person's mind after such things as Kibeho.

This entire country had a share in this war of machete against flesh and bone, against degradation of the body, mind and soul.

When you've seen such things, nothing else matters, nothing can really be more important. Therefore, to go on, would be a waste. Nothing can compare to that already said.

What else can I tell you, the reader?

But I shall continue with my story.

PTSD

After the massacre, the job continued; after all, we were to be here for a further four months.

It was upsetting to see that not all persons involved with Kibeho received some form of counselling; sure, some were offered the service and either accepted or declined, others were 'advised' that they needed to attend; those who were supposedly 'more of a concern' than others, for they had been on-the-ground at Kibeho, at the time of the massacre, had no choice but to attend.

A story reached my ear of how one of the counsellors had entered a congregation of soldiers, where, after introduction, advised all that he understood what the soldiers were feeling, for he too had witnessed some horrible scenes, where bodies lay dead and mangled due to a coach having crashed – back in Australia. Many soldiers – if not all – were insulted by this, and if you have taken stock of what has previously been written then you might understand why; but no true appreciation can be attained without having been there at the time of the massacre, or for those more fortunate, to have simply aided with the IDPs return to their communes (but different things, affect different people, and in different ways).

I recall two incidents in particular – not being able to mention others, due to legal reasons – after having received my discharge from the military:

I was on a train, heading for the city. A 13-year yells out to his mates: 'There it is!'

They pointed and laughed; carrying on like fools, receiving silent stares from all around… all I could do was turn my head, disgusted at their attempts to humour one another. And what was it they had been pointing at? That morning trains had been delayed, for an elderly person had been hit by a train, the body still on the 'out-going' track, covered in a blanket and surrounded by police – no, I didn't look; it was on the news that night. Their parents must have been proud – but what did they know about death?

There was another incident, which matters little; really. I was working 'casual' at the Rye RSL, a customer came to the counter, arm in a sling, metal pins visible. He was one of the survivors of the Port Arthur Massacre – and without sounding rude: A picnic compared to Kibeho. He had a few family members along, all with smiles. Pats on the back came in thick and fast, drinks here and there; yes indeed, sympathy was flowing well; and I continued with my work in silence, thinking to myself; how many lives had he saved to deserve such congratulations? Was he congratulated for being a survivor? Was he congratulated for escaping death? Or was he being congratulated for the pain he had suffered, a minute speck of suffering when compared to some of the injuries inflicted upon the IDPs of Kibeho, as illustrated without restraint in 'Combat Medic' and 'Pure Massacre'?

I felt as though the contingent was being insulted.

I had read somewhere, that within ten years of the massacre at Kibeho, around 50% of those men and women of Australia, sent to do their duty, had received treatment for PTSD at some time between 1995 and 2005. I guess they call it 'post traumatic' because it's triggered by an event/occurrence after the actual event, something that the memory regards as being similar. But truly, what treatment was there? You can't exactly get a scalpel and cut someone's memory from his or her brain, and I am no damn psychologist. We must all presume, therefore, that PTSD cannot be cured. I guess those affected by PTSD need to be considered, and above all, remembered; I for one won't forget them.

Recovery

Around 4 weeks (give or take) after I suffered the inconvenience of an injury to my back, I was confronted with the fact that it was now time to take nine days leave.

Leave was taken by a small percentage of soldiers at a time, spread out over the tour; everyone received this gift of gifts, and the world was at our fingertips. We had soldiers going to the UK, South Africa, Thailand, and you guessed it, back to OZ; just to name a few. What was I to do? My injury was still in its infancy, it needed rest prior to returning to duty, or I would be sent back to Australia before having served my time in this country. I decided to spend my leave in Kenya, most of my time flat on my back, going for short walks, sitting around and hoping for my injury to heal enough for me to continue with my work.

Nine days was a long time, even longer when you are bored out of your brain, and when it comes down to it, this entire idea was conjured up simply for me to get well enough to continue in Rwanda, to witness more pain and killing. My injury had improved but the pain would never go away again, not like it had all of those times over the past 7-8 years of my infantry career where pain had been experienced.

Effort, in some cases, gets you nowhere; it provides you with nothing more than self satisfaction, that you did your best to achieve your goal… even if you fail.

The Flag

What was discipline and when was it prone to being employed? Does discipline take on more emphasis at one time over another, or was it equally distributed? It was always hard to answer when taking into consideration the diggers. It seems to me that it was always an essential part of discipline to stand fast for the flag: Flag-goes-up, stand at attention; flag comes- down, stand at attention. It's not that damn hard to misinterpret or easy to make a mistake; it happens at the same time every day and there was a whistle blast that lets everyone in hearing distance know that the flag was about to be hoisted or lowered. I would say that the blood spilt for the flag and country was enough in itself to give good reason for 'standing fast', so why was it so hard for the soldiers to carry out the simple task? You'd see the soldiers marching around or doing some physical activity, then just before the whistle blast was due the area around would be vacated... soon after, of course, the soldiers would come out of their hide-holes.

We were entering Ruhengeri at one time, escorting a few medics into the town; in order for them to get a tour into the hills to see the gorillas in their natural surrounds; when all of a sudden the local populace, thousands of them, stopped what they were doing and stood fast: I was acting as security for the truck drive into the mountains, not partaking in the intrusion of the gorilla's natural habitat.

The Rwandan flag; it was being hoisted. It then suddenly appeared to me that these people had more national spirit than we did, but I soon realised too, that anyone who didn't stand fast would be proving allegiance to the former government and would be tempting the very fury of a machete-wielding RPA soldier.

Life certainly stank in this land-locked country; for danger lurked around every corner.

Convoy RTU

My section had been called to duty. We had to provide infantry support to a medical team visiting another medical facility-come-orphanage; they were gravely in need of medical assistance due to there always being a long line of patients: The amount of children present at the centre, and the influx of returning IDPs since UNAMIR's presence in the country, coming in from all quarters of Rwanda.

Several rovers and our infantry truck where winding through the hills of this – sometimes – beautiful country, and when you've seen some of the horrors of this country you can't help but to look out for something more appealing to the eye, even if momentarily, but you also need to watch the road....

We came to a halt. The rovers have pulled over to an accident on the side of the road.

A UN rover had driven over the edge of the winding road and plummeted about 40 metres down a steep embankment. Trees in the hills side prevented the rover from travelling too far down the slope and it would seem that no deaths had occurred. Some members of our infantry element hopped off the truck to provide assistance where required, others maintained vigil on the area surrounding us. Several medics clambered down the 45-degree slope, our doctor – a Major – insisting on having a closer look. She stumbled... snap.

She had fractured her wrist and needed medical attention herself – lucky we were UNAMIR. A few other medical personnel seemed overly concerned, and obviously knew more than me. I failed to see the problem when I received further pieces of information to be added to the puzzle. She had a fracture, was in pain, and had to be attended to back at Kigali.

I continued to look the Captain in the eye. She said to me: 'You're in command of the convoy, Corporal.'

It wasn't a passing-of-command, it was reminding me of my status. Certainly, this was a medical mission, and for all intents and purposes we – the infantry – were here to provide aid to the medical team. All of this said, due to the situation in the country, section commands were the overall commanders of a convoy when one departed Kigali due to the importance of applying 'Infantry Minor Tactics,' to any number of probable scenarios, amidst this civil war.

This was a medical mission with a need to provide the much-needed assistance to the Rwandan community. I was not a medic and failed to acknowledge the amount of pain the Major was in, and considered briefly that we had the medical supplies with us to treat her for her pain; but take into consideration the roads surface, the amount of time to simply turn around and go back, or to continue with the task and then return to Kigali later, was too much for me to consider when an observer of someone hurt so badly... hadn't we all seen enough pain to last us. I asked the Major a simple and straightforward question: 'I have no idea how much pain you're in, or if you're even able to continue on this road. If you can't do your job then to continue with the task would be a waste. Would you like to turn back?

The mission was cancelled, we returned to barracks; the children would have to wait until another day; after all, it's no good going on safari to kill a rhino, armed with a peashooter.

Snake Bite

It was around 2130hrs and my shift on the front security post of the hospital was to commence in 30 minutes. Even now my attention was easily drawn to the sights and sounds around: The machine gun fire, the Ak47s, and the tracer flying through the night air as RPA set upon more unsuspecting hardliners. The RPA barracks entrance was also opposite the hospital, our sentry post opposite the RPA; only 20 metres separated the two. Another two RPA soldiers were entering, escorting an elderly man, he being supported between them. They continued on into the fading light, towards one of the barracks buildings in the distance. Ten minutes later, BANG! Another dead civilian. The death was never-ending.

The 2IC of another section then saw me moving in the security bunker and asked me over, which I happy did. As I approached I could see two locals, a mother and a father; the mother held a child.

I looked into her arms and saw what was thought to be a boy of three, and looked Lance Corporal Lane in the eye.

'They don't speak English but I think they're saying that the child's been bitten by a snake. What do you think we should do?' he asked of me.

The child seemed to stare at me with fear, and I could understand why – or so I thought. We had been advised that parents in this country told their children that they should never go too far when playing, and always beware of white men, because white men liked to eat small children.

'Let's take them into the RAP; we might be able to get someone to have a look,' which was a dangerous call, for the hospital was there for the UN. The Rwandan people had their own medical facilities, and if we started to help one or two then the following day might see hundreds queuing up for treatment. The medics helped individuals where possible,

and I was certainly aware of this; they were forever providing medical aid to car crash victims, mine victims, to people with gunshot wounds, amputations, broken bones....

The couple with the child followed as we led them into the RAP where one of the SAS guys was seen maintaining some of the stock upon the shelves; the child probably thought we were looking for the salt and pepper, knife and fork....

'Jock.'

'Yeah.'

'We got this child here; think it's a snake bite, didn't know if you could help-out or not.'

The SAS soldier walked towards the patient, had a quick look, and gave indication that he was happy to assist.

The 2IC and myself departed the RAP; the 2IC back to his post and me to mine.

The next morning we heard that the child had survived his snake bite; it was little mercies like this that made the trip to Africa worthwhile: I'm sorry I couldn't say the same for the old man who'd been escorted into the RPA barracks.

Pain

My injury was getting worse. I took the opportunity to attend the RAP as often as I could, which usually amounted to at least three times a week, and if stationed at the hospital, whenever I could; other times it simply wasn't available to me... I still had a job to do. I couldn't understand the situation. Here I was, in terrible pain, getting assistance from the RAP – sometimes on a daily basis – and I was still in Rwanda. Sure I wanted to be here, but that wasn't the question… should I be here?

What aid did I receive? Painkillers were provided to me, eight a day from the medics, as this was all 'anyone' was supposed to have; I was known on occasion to slip into the section medical kit on barracks and help myself to pills. I also received stretching exercises and time on an exercise bike.

At one stage we had to conduct the military fitness test and sit-ups, push-ups, and a 5km run. One of the soldiers in my section was sent to retrieve painkillers from the medical kit… I would have to take double ration to get myself through this test. Unfortunately I never achieved a pass and from that day forth was given a permanent 'chit' from conducting physical activity, but I was still in Rwanda doing my duty. Anytime we conducted patrols, escorts, or rove-n-picket, section webbing had to be worn; however, I made a few changes. I emptied my water bottles, all but a few mouthfuls; and I only ever carried a single magazine of live ammunition, as opposed to a full quota. Rove-n-picket duty for me now involved taking a rest every 20 minutes, whereby I would sit down for 5-10, and this was permitted – several officers knew I was doing this.

Road Block
July

RPA roadblocks were something that was seen every day. Most of these were permanent, in particular at the major arterials that flowed in and out of towns.

The roadblocks weren't something that you'd expect to find in a normal society.

Here in Rwanda a roadblock was distinguished by a piece of string that was pulled taunt across any road. In some cases this was accompanied by a witch's hat, a box, or even large rock, placed to the middle (possibly to symbolise the segregation of the two way traffic; who knows). Needless to say that the roadblocks were always monitored by a section to platoon strength RPA unit, depending on its importance, the threat, and locality.

One such permanent roadblock was erected at the South East entrance into Ruhengeri, a population of a said 30,000 people. In late June this roadblock was the scene of some concern as a Zambian working with the UN had shot an RPA soldier. Before this incident occurred, all UN traffic was permitted immediate passage through such a roadblock.

Some changes were now going to take place.

During the contingents stay in Rwanda, most took the advantage of invading the natural habitat of the gorillas to the North West of the country, in the region where volcanoes were numerous and according to all statistics, ready to blow at any time in the near future.

Each visit to see the gorillas by a group of Australians required a section of infantry for security, and a rover with radio mounted for communications with Kigali and any military observers, who were situated in any of the towns of this small land-locked country.

The rifle section was in the lead truck and approached the roadblock, and via an RPA soldier's uncertainty, the vehicle was permitted to pass through the roadblock; but he quite quickly stopped the two vehicles following behind us.

The guys on the rear of this vehicle soon informed the driver and me that those behind had been stopped. The convoy now found itself separated by fifty metres of road, the RPA between both parties. Our section of security was now separated from its main task, the protection of the rear two vehicles and their occupants.

I set about to reverse back but was prevented from doing so by an RPA officer. He wanted all Australians off vehicles, to use this opportunity to search the cabins etc. But contingent orders didn't allow for this to happen. So the officer was denied his request.

Ten minutes of harassment and apprehension dominated our two groups; the RPA officer was seemingly nervous as to the aggressive nature of those on board, and then myself worried over the fact that the RPA officer's weapon had a round up the spout and his finger was on the trigger, ready to fire. Any second now and all could turn to mayhem, and I could be the owner of a large gaping hole in my gut.

I approached the sig to try and establish communications with the military observers in Ruhengeri. If anyone could get us out of this predicament, they could.

The RPA officer deployed his men and all manner of things weren't looking good, when luck suddenly fell our way; MIL OBS hadn't received our call, but just as I peered up I saw their rover driving past. The RPA officer also saw this and within seconds the convoy was permitted to proceed.

A lesson was learnt. A finer distance between each vehicle was going to be required, and speed reduced, when approaching roadblocks. I couldn't tell whether the members of the section were relieved or disappointed, as during the entire exchange of differences, they had hands on weapons, ready to go into action, to take out as many RPA as they could before they in turn met with death…. More than luck was with us that day.

When working in the hospital, it was an everyday occurrence, for someone to be expected to work in the emergency ward. The 'rest' section of the platoon normally filled this duty, although, due to the restriction of 'space and time', and the number of doctors required to be

working on the injured person, it was normal for only one, or possibly two, to be asked to assist.

Two soldiers were carrying the stretcher and I followed. We were being led into the emergency ward where several doctors were waiting for their patient.

We turned into a corridor and could see a few figures dressed in gowns entering an open door to the ward. We followed the lead of our escort and turned into the room, the stretcher being placed upon the table, the unconscious form of a Rwandan national lying there, his clothing not having seen a washing tub for what appeared to be a month. All of the buttons were done up, his belt was tight around his middle to hold up his jeans and the jeans themselves, filthy; then his shoes came into view… one was attached, the other was half missing. It was hard to see at this stage what was 'shoe' and what was 'flesh', for the land mine he had trodden on had done its job well.

Everyone went about their task; I took up a pair of scissors and cut away the jeans, from the wound itself and up to the groin, across, and down the other leg; his shoes were removed with care, in particular where the foot wound existed.

Once the offending footwear was removed it was a little easier to see the damage that the mine's blast had caused. Half of his foot was missing… draw an imaginary line from the fourth toe (in from the left) and down to the beginning of the outside of his heel; that was the damage inflicted, half his foot cut away by an explosion.

The wound was cleaned and they prepared him for surgery… there was a hell of a lot of dirt in amongst the flesh.

I looked over my shoulder and another 5 doctors and nurses could be seen hard at work, a nurse half on top of another patient, half straddled as though trying to mount a horse, forcing pressure down upon his chest in the hope of getting him breathing… you could see from where I stood that the chest bones were displaced a good 8-10 centimetres every time she attempted to revive him; but he died.

The man with the missing foot was treated accordingly and would live to see another day, and what was experienced in the emergency ward during that 20-minute period was part-n-parcel of an everyday occurrence, but in all reality this sequence of two short events were NOTHING when compared to the horrors of Kibeho: it was like comparing a grain of sand to a basketball.

The populace of this country were operated upon, where the contingent had the ability to act, but priority always went to the UN… it just happened to turn out that very few UN personnel needed the services that we provided, so our attention and assistance could be redirected elsewhere.

To Kigali Airport

The six-month tour went by very quickly, and for me personally, the four few months were spent in constant pain. Why had I endured? Why didn't I opt to return home? Why were those with a rank higher than mine willing to keep me in the country?

All of those directly responsible for me knew of my injuries, but still I remained. I can only draw a single conclusion from this; my overall performance was of a standard accepted as appropriate or higher – why else? I could therefore go home, knowing that I had achieved a little, but the idea that we had 'not' been entrusted with better Rules Of Engagement, was disappointing to say the least; but then again, if we carried out actions in accordance with less stringent Rules Of Engagement… we could all be dead right now. It might be that death – for some of those that had toured in Rwanda – would have been preferred.

The sites drifted past us now, as the final leg to the airport was made on the back of trucks, no weapon in hand, dressed in uniform only. This country was still a mess, and would be for a long bloody time. The orphans in the orphanages might get to grow to adulthood, but squaller was their life, now and forever into the future. If the RPA didn't get
them, then the volcanoes that loomed in the distance would.

I couldn't help but feel I was doing a disservice to this country. I would have loved to stay for another twelve months or more, regardless of the pain in my lower back; but then there were so many others who just wanted to get home… so few of them wanted to remain behind.

And even as the plane took off from the ground I peered out of the window and hoped that I could one day forgive myself for not doing more. I had nothing to go home to, no wife and kids… just a room on the barracks. Being in Rwanda was as comfortable for me as being back in Townsville.

Home

It was fairly easy to get back into the swing of things back on barracks, but the memories of the stay overseas haunted most of us at night – some more than others. I could understand why it was that we had it so good in Australia, whilst in Rwanda they had it so hard. Politics, resources, and the neighbours that surrounded your part of the world: that was the answer; not guts, pride, spirit, or the colour of your skin.

Back in Australia there were a few promotions to be seen, postings to be requested, accepted, and turned down. For me, I had the RAP to attend on a regular basis, even though the easy-going life back on barracks provided me with a better opportunity to rest my injury. It was, however, too late for recovery and I was soon provided with a medical downgrade to P3L7, which basically made me unfit for the infantry. I was to be posted to 1RAR, Mortar Platoon – of all the platoons to send me, they wished me there; those bastards. But none of it eventuated. The posting was cancelled, my promotion to sergeant revoked, and a new position was provided me… down to Holsworthy barracks, sitting on my ass for the remainder of my career, being screwed around by the RSM of a battalion – and others like him – who had 'little' idea or understanding of my career as a whole.

I was swung like a pendulum from task to task… I had no real job. I requested a corps transfer; to Clerical, to MPs, to the Q-stream, the bloody post office. Nothing was accepted. It was then that it hit me; after 16 years' service I was no longer viable. If they truly wished, so much, to keep me in an office environment, why the hell wasn't I being provided with a corps transfer to Clerical? Simple; they wanted to abuse me, not use me.

I was downgraded and the new rules underlining employment within the army were changing, in particular, for the infantry.

My time was up.

Final Curtain

I was medically discharged from the army on 24th September 1996, after 16 years' service, my back finally giving way to constant pain during the final months of my stay in Rwanda, a stay supported by the overdose of pain-killers that I took from day by day. I accepted the discharge, as this meant no more physical activity accompanied with pain, and although I had problems since 1987, the injury had always come good after several weeks of treatment and rest; but not this time around. My knees were also no better off as I had good reason to report these to the RAP on two separate occasions when posted to Singleton in the early 90's, and both ankles were showing severe signs of wear-n-tear, only one of which received recognition from the

RAP, as it was always hard to report on injuries when in the field. But in the past, as read by you, the reader, I continued with my job and tried to look after myself as best I could, weathering the storm, suffering the pain, and getting on with the job I loved so dearly.

The army was developing a new rule of thumb; by the end of 1997, all those that were below medical standard for their specific corps, were to be discharged. A clipping found in the newspaper of November 1997, and various news reports, put testimony to this.

I never would get to receive my lump sum and pension after 20 years' service, but I did get to do a few worthwhile things whilst in the army.

These things will never be forgotten and the memories will live with me forever.

As for personal achievements:

I was the only 'A' grade shot in my platoon at Kapooka.

I was the best shot at Kapooka.

I qualified as 'marksman' many years running, and proudly wore my 'crossed rifles'.

I was a member of the guard during the Commonwealth Games in Brisbane.

I conducted 3 recon courses.

I was an instructor on 4 recon courses.

I am qualified as an airborne rappel instructor and in suspended extraction.

I was on the Duke of Gloucester 5 times running and reserve for another.

I received 'student of merit' for my efforts on a recon course.

I received a 'best soldier' award in 8/9RAR.

I received recognition for having the best section in Singleton.

I instructed at the School of Infantry for three years.

I was given the opportunity to train for the SASR.

I served in Malaysia.

I served in PNG as a member of the AATPT.

I served in Rwanda.

I am a trained signaller: *blah*.

I am trained with mortars, both basic and officer/NCO: *blah*.

I served with Mortar Platoon: double *blah*.

I am fully qualified as Sergeant.

Maybe it is clear, and maybe it is not, but I do honestly value my service in PNG higher than that in Rwanda, though Rwanda is more memorable. I value it more… maybe because we achieved a goal. In Rwanda we had our hands tied and failed to help those most in need.

Does this make sense?

Upgrade

In late 2005 I received information that the service in Rwanda had been upgraded to warlike.

It seems that everyone, especially the politicians and the UN, had underestimated 'everything'. It also helped bring to light what I read in 'Pure Massacre', how several soldiers compared the tour of Rwanda with that of East Timor. East Timor was nothing more than a holiday compared to Rwanda, they agreed; and yet it took so long for the authorities to realise this. And although I can't speak for what service in Rwanda was like when compared to Iraq or Afghanistan, I'm guessing there was a visual gap of difference; just compare Kibeho with Bergen-Belsen; peacetime service with war; and there you might find an answer; but it's not for me to draw any conclusion, but maybe I would like people to understand the truth and reality behind service in Rwanda, and that it was not 'a-piece-of-cake' as everyone back home assumed it to be.

In 2019 we received the Meritorious Unit Citation

Maybe less stringent Rules Of Engagement should have been put in place.

And a last word regards the Returned from Active Service Badge [RASB]. Most guys in the infantry will receive an 'Infantry Combat Badge' [ICB] just for being in a war zone, whether having come under fire or not. I hear someone say, 'so what', and another comment, 'he's only jealous'. This is all beside the point. The point is that I am in the infantry and being so, with a record I consider rather accomplished, it's embarrassing to be considered as non-field force, or anything other than infantry, even for a second. Everyone has a job to fill and all are proud of their corps, as I am of mine. There are guys out there wearing an ICB for being in a war zone but were never fired upon, or never fired a shot in anger; just like me and the others of UNAMIR II. I read a book recently about a Vietnam Veteran suffering PTSD. He has an ICB but never fired a shot, he was never fired upon. But did we experience combat? But even then, some of the guys did have shots falling all around them as in the book 'The Kibeho Massacre' proves. Believe it or not we are not looked upon as having accomplished anything substantial as it is, and having nothing whatsoever against Vietnam Veterans I hate to say that there are a few there that have even turned their noses up at us for wearing a blue beret and having received a RASB. Who are they to point the finger and scold? It's as though they don't know the reality of the tour; it's as though we are inferior. I've even heard others comment on veterans of Rwanda as bludgers due to individuals going PTSD, but can you see now why PTSD is so rampant with those of UNAMIR II.

Maybe they should do away with a badge completely and award something extra for those that have actually come under fire and did their duty in the face of evil; but as we have seen, evil comes in many different forms.

I have nothing more to say on Rwanda per se, but one thing regards some disturbing slander on You Tube. A soldier I knew, who served in Rwanda, stated on his channel that the Infantry Combat Badge [ICB] is 'what it is all about'. You are wrong. You were insubordinate then and a loud mouth now, as per you stinking mate, with poor attitudes towards your NCOs and officers. The Police, Nurses, State Emergency Service volunteers, Fireman, etc, etc, etc; all are more deserving than you are. The ICB is NOT 'what it is all about', and if you cannot see that then I feel sorrow for you.

A Final Word

Cooks always turned out a good meal, and any fun poked in their direction is just that, fun.

I have as much appreciation for the American soldiers as I do any other, but those who have served in a 'combat' zone are the most looked-up-to.

Grunts are not stupid but very smart; otherwise we'd all be led by fools and end up dying for the wrong cause; and rank, in the long-and-short of it all, has little to do with intelligence or common sense.

Women of all calibre are to be looked up to and for the most part, those associated with infantry soldiers in particular are the pillars of men's dreams.

I was extremely fortunate not to have been in Kibeho on 22nd April, as to have been there would have been a great injustice to what I had been taught over the years, and I don't know anyone who was thankful for being there on the 22nd: to have 'wanted' to be there on the day would illustrate just how little you really cared for the people of Rwanda; needless to say that it would have been better if it had never eventuated. I can't imagine what it would feel like to witness so many being massacred before my eyes and then turn my back upon it all, being able to do absolutely nothing about it. It was bad enough witnessing just a few executions, let alone thousands, so I considered myself rather fortunate in regards to that; as for my other experiences... they were to be expected, I suppose. No wonder those poor bastards who witnessed the massacre of over 4,000 IDPs suffer PTSD.

I salute you all; but who am I really to give you such a well-earned compliment, but a broken down machine of little worth.

But something more should be taken away here. If I was on the ground at the time of the main massacre, would I have refrained from opening fire upon the RPA? I don't know if I could have restrained myself, and thankful, I am, not to have been tested in such a way: but would the RPA deserve such bad treatment. There is also one last thing to say. Do I blame the RPA for the massacre at Kibeho? Look at it this way, for just a second; the Hutu killed over a million Tutsi, is it not fair that revenge be performed? If a murderer comes into your home and kills your wife and two kids, will you see him arrested to spend the rest of his life in prison, or would you tie the bastard up and torture him to death? Maybe you believe in 'turning the other cheek' and would allow him to flee, in order to commit such a crime again.

Glossary

WEAPONS:

Claymore – Anti-personnel mine
M16 – Semi-automatic rifle
M18A1 – see Claymore
M203 – M40 style grenade launcher attached to the undercarriage of
  the M16
M26 – HE fragmentation grenade
M30 – practise grenade
M60 – GPMG: General Purpose Machine Gun
M79 – grenade launcher (ammo as per M203)
MAG58 – Machine gun
SFMG – Sustain Fire Machine Gun
SLR – Self-Loading Rifle
SRAAW – Short Range Anti Armour Weapon
Minimi – 5.56mm machine gun

RANK:

Boss – Platoon Commander
CO – Commanding Officer
CPL – Corporal
CQ – Company Quartermaster
CSM – Company Sergeant Major
LCPL – Lance Corporal
NCO – Non Commissioned Officer
OC – Officer Commanding
PL COMD – Platoon Commander
RSM – Regimental Sergeant Major
SGT – Sergeant
SSGT – Staff Sergeant
2IC – Second in command

OTHER:

Admin COY – TPT, Medical, Cooks, Q-store…
AJ – Army Jerk
AO – Area of Operations
APC – Armoured Personnel Carrier
AWOL – Absent Without Leave
BFA – Blank Firing Attachment
BFT – Battle Fitness Test

BHQ – Battalion Headquarters
BN – Battalion (consists of 3-4 rifle companies, HQ element,
    Administration Coy, Spt Coy)
BRA – Bougainville Republican Army
BRL – Battalion Recreational Leave
CCP – Casualty Clearing Post
CES – Complete Equipment Schedule
CFT – Combat Fitness Test – the old BFT
Coy – Company (3 platoons + HQ element)
CP – Command Post
DIV – Division
DS – Directing Staff
ERT – Extra Regimental training
FSB – Fire Support Base
FUP – Forming up place
HE – High explosive
HQ – Headquarters
IA – Immediate Action
ID – Identification
IDP – Internally Displaced Persons
IET – Initial Employment Training
INT – Intelligence
JNCO – Junior Non Commissioned Officer Training
LUP – Lying Up Place (for admin/sleep)
MIL OBS – Military Observer
MP – Military Police
NGO – Non-Government Organisations
ODF – Operational Deployment Force
OP – Observation Post
OR – Other ranks (PTE, CPL and below)
PL – Platoon (3 sections and HQ element)
Pogo – Non field-force
POW – Prisoner of War
PT – Physical training
PTI – Physical Training Instructor
QRF – Quick Reaction Force
RAAF – Royal Australian Air Force
RAP – Regimental Aid Post (medical)
RAR – Royal Australian Regiment
Rascals – Group of criminals
RMO – Regimental Medical Officer
RPA – Rwandan Patriotic Army
SASR – Special Air Service Regiment
Scheds – Scheduled communications via radio

SECT – (approx 9-10 men)
SIB – Special Investigation Branch
SOP – Standard Operational Procedure
SPT Coy – supports the battalion to which it is attached (consists of
    Hvy Wpns Pl, Recon Pl, Pioneer Pl, Mortar Pl, Signals Pl)
SRT – Scout Regiment Telescope
SWBTA – Shoalwater Bay Training Area
TOET – Test of Elementary Training
TPT PL – Transport Platoon providing direct assistance to the
    Battalion attached to
UD – Unauthorised Discharge – of weapon
UH1H – Helicopter
Wantok – Friend/Comrade